Confessional
A Prayer for the Dying
Day of Judgement
The Thousand Faces of Night

Jack Higgins

Diamond Books
an imprint of HarperCollins*Publishers*,
77–85 Fulham Palace Road,
Hammersmith, London W6 8JB

This Diamond Books Omnibus edition first published 1993
9 8 7 6 5 4 3 2 1

ISBN 1 85813 268 1 (UK)
ISBN Diamond Books 0 261 66163 9 (international edition)

Photoset in Linotron Times by Rowland Phototypesetting Ltd,
Bury St Edmunds, Suffolk

Printed in France by Maury-Eurolivres

Contents

Confessional 9
A Prayer for the Dying 223
Day of Judgement 387
The Thousand Faces of Night 577

By the same author

The Eagle has Landed
Touch the Devil
The Testament of Caspar Schultz
Passage by Night
The Savage Day
The Iron Tiger
In the Hour Before Midnight
Wrath of the Lion
Solo
The Last Place God Made
The Dark Side of the Island
Dark Side of the Street
Luciano's Luck
Storm Warning
The Violent Enemy
Exocet
Night of the Fox
The Eagle Has Flown

Writing as James Graham

A Game For Heroes
The Wrath of God
Bloody Passage
The Khufra Run

Writing as Harry Patterson

Cry of the Hunter
Come the Dark Stranger
Brought in Dead
The Graveyard Shift
Dillinger
To Catch a King

Confessional

FOR MY CHILDREN

Sarah, Ruth, Seán and Hannah

PROLOGUE
1959

When the Land Rover turned the corner at the end of the street, Kelly was passing the church of the Holy Name. He moved into the porch quickly, opened the heavy door and stepped inside, keeping it partially open so that he could see what was happening.

The Land Rover had been stripped down to the bare essentials so that the driver and the two policemen who crouched in the rear were completely exposed. They wore the distinctive dark green uniforms of the Royal Ulster Constabulary, Sterling submachine guns held ready for instant action. They disappeared down the narrow street towards the centre of Drumore and he stayed there for a moment, in the safety of the half-darkness, conscious of the familiar odour.

'Incense, candles and the holy water,' he said softly and his finger reached to dip in the granite bowl beside the door.

'Is there anything I can do for you, my son?'

The voice was little more than a whisper and, as Kelly turned, a priest moved out of the darkness, an old man, in shabby cassock, his hair very white, gleaming in the candlelight. He carried an umbrella in one hand.

'Just sheltering from the rain is all, Father,' Kelly told him.

He stood there, shoulders hunched easily, hands thrust deep in the pockets of the old tan raincoat. He was small, five feet five at the most, not much more than a boy, and yet the white devil's face on him beneath the brim of the old felt hat, the dark brooding eyes that seemed to stare through and beyond, hinted at something more.

All this the old priest saw and understood. He smiled gently, 'You don't live in Drumore, I think?'

'No, Father, just passing through. I arranged to meet a friend of mine here at a pub called Murphy's.'

His voice lacked the distinctive hard accent of the Ulsterman. The priest said, 'You're from the Republic?'

'Dublin, Father. Would you know this Murphy's place? It's important. My friend's promised me a lift into Belfast. I've the chance of work there.'

The priest nodded. 'I'll show you. It's on my way.'

Kelly opened the door, the old man went outside. It was raining heavily now and he put up his umbrella. Kelly fell in beside him and they walked along the pavement. There was the sound of a brass band playing an old hymn, *Abide with Me*, and voices lifted, melancholy in the rain. The old priest and Kelly paused, looking down on to the town square. There was a granite war memorial, wreaths placed at its foot. A small crowd was ranged around it, the band on one side. A Church of Ireland minister was conducting the service. Four old men held flags proudly in the rain, although the Union Jack was the only one with which Kelly was familiar.

'What is this?' he demanded.

'Armistice Day to commemorate the dead of two World Wars. That's the local branch of the British Legion down there. Our Protestant friends like to hang on tight to what they call their heritage.'

'Is that so?' Kelly said.

They carried on down the street. On the corner, a small girl stood, no more than seven or eight. She wore an old beret, a couple of sizes too large, as was her coat. There were holes in her socks and her shoes were in poor condition. Her face was pale, skin stretched tightly over prominent cheekbones, yet the brown eyes were alert, intelligent and she managed a smile in spite of the fact that her hands, holding the cardboard tray in front of her, were blue with cold.

'Hello, Father,' she said. 'Will you buy a poppy?'

'My poor child, you should be indoors on a day like this.' He found a coin in his pocket and slipped it into her collecting tin, helping himself to a scarlet poppy. 'To the memory of our glorious dead,' he told Kelly.

'Is that a fact?' Kelly turned to find the little girl holding a poppy timidly out to him. 'Buy a poppy, sir.'

'And why not?'

She pinned the poppy to his raincoat. Kelly gazed down into the strained little face for a moment, eyes dark, then swore softly under his breath. He took a leather wallet from his inside pocket, opened it, extracted two pound notes. She gazed at them, astonished, and he rolled them up and poked them into her collecting tin. Then he gently took the tray of poppies from her hands.

'Go home,' he said softly. 'Stay warm. You'll find the world cold enough soon enough, little one.'

There was puzzlement in her eyes. She didn't understand and, turning, ran away.

The old priest said, 'I was on the Somme myself, but that lot over here,' he nodded to the crowd at the Cenotaph, 'would rather forget about that.' He shook his head as they carried on along the pavement. 'So many dead. I never had the time to ask whether a man was Catholic or Protestant.'

He paused and glanced across the road. A faded sign said *Murphy's Select Bar*. 'Here we are, then. What are you going to do with those?'

Kelly glanced down at the tray of poppies. 'God knows.'

'I usually find that He does.' The old man took a silver case from his pocket and selected a cigarette without offering one to Kelly. He puffed out smoke, coughing, 'When I was a young priest I visited an old Catholic church in Norfolk at Studley Constable. There was a remarkable medieval fresco there by some unknown genius or other. Death in a black hood and cloak, come to claim his harvest. I saw him again today in my own church. The only difference was that he was wearing a felt hat and an old raincoat.' He shivered suddenly.

'Go home, Father,' Kelly said, gently. 'Too cold for you out here.'

'Yes,' the old man said. 'Far too cold.'

He hurried away as the band struck up another hymn and Kelly turned, went up the steps of the pub and pushed open the door. He found himself in a long, narrow room, a coal fire burning at one end. There were several cast-iron tables and chairs, a bench along the wall. The bar itself was dark mahogany and marble-topped, a brass rail at foot level. There was the usual array of bottles ranged against a large mirror, gold leaf flaking to reveal cheap plaster. There were no customers, only the barman leaning against the beer pumps, a heavily built man, almost bald, his face seamed with fat, his collarless shirt soiled at the neck.

He glanced up at Kelly and took in the tray of poppies. 'I've got one.'

'Haven't we all?' Kelly put the tray on the table and leant on the bar. 'Where is everyone?'

'In the square at the ceremony. This is a Prod town, son.'

'How do you know I'm not one?'

'And me a publican for twenty-five years? Come off it. What's your fancy?'

'Bushmills.'

The fat man nodded approvingly and reached for a bottle. 'A man of taste.'

'Are you Murphy?'

'So they tell me.' He lit a cigarette. 'You're not from these parts.'

'No, I was supposed to meet a friend here. Perhaps you know him?'

'What's his name?'

'Cuchulain.'

The smile wiped clean from Murphy's face. 'Cuchulain,' he whispered.

'Last of the dark heroes.'

Murphy said, 'Christ, but you like your melodrama, you boys. Like a bad play on television on a Saturday night. You were told not to carry a weapon.'

'So?' Kelly said.

'There's been a lot of police activity. Body searches. They'd lift you for sure.'

'I'm not carrying.'

'Good.' Murphy took a large brown carrier bag from under the bar. 'Straight across the square is the police barracks. Local provision firm's truck is allowed through the gates at exactly twelve o'clock each day. Sling that in the back. Enough there to take out half the barracks.' He reached inside the bag. There was an audible click. 'There, you've got five minutes.'

Kelly picked up the bag and started for the door. As he reached it, Murphy called, 'Hey, Cuchulain, dark hero?' Kelly turned and the fat man raised a glass toasting him. 'You know what they say. May you die in Ireland.'

There was something in the eyes, a mockery that sharpened Kelly like a razor's edge as he went outside and started across the square. The band were on another hymn, the crowd sang, showing no disposition to move in spite of the rain. He glanced over his shoulder and saw that Murphy was standing at the top of the steps outside the pub. Strange, that, and then he waved several times, as if signalling someone and with a sudden roar, the stripped Land Rover came out of a side street into the square and skidded broadside on.

Kelly started to run, slipped on the damp cobbles and went down on one knee. The butt of a Sterling drove painfully into his kidneys. As he cried out, the driver, who he now saw was a sergeant, put a foot hard on Kelly's outstretched hand and picked up the carrier bag. He turned it upside down and a cheap wooden kitchen clock fell out. He kicked it, like a football, across the square into the crowd which scattered.

'No need for that!' he shouted. 'It's a dud!' He leaned down, grabbing Kelly by the long hair at the back of the neck. 'You never learn, do you, your bloody lot? You can't trust anybody, my son. They should have taught you that.'

Kelly gazed beyond him, at Murphy, standing on the steps outside the bar. So – an informer. Still Ireland's curse, not that he was angry. Only cold now – ice cold and the breath slow, in and out of his lungs.

The sergeant had him by the scruff of the neck, up on his knees, crouched like an animal. He leaned, running his hands under the armpits and over the body, searching for a weapon, then rammed Kelly against the Land Rover, still on his knees.

'All right, hands behind you. You should have stayed back home in the bogs.'

Kelly started to get up, his two hands on the butt of the Browning handgun he had taped so carefully to the inside of the leg above the left ankle. He tore it free and shot the sergeant through the heart. The force of the shot lifted the sergeant off his feet and he slammed into the constable standing nearest to him. The man spun round, trying to keep his balance and Kelly shot him in the back, the Browning already arc-ing towards the third policeman, turning in alarm on the other side of the Land Rover, raising his submachine gun, too late as Kelly's third bullet caught him in the throat, driving him back against the wall.

The crowd were scattering, women screaming, some of the band dropping their instruments. Kelly stood perfectly still, very calm amidst the carnage and looked across the square at Murphy, who still stood at the top of the steps outside the bar as if frozen.

The Browning swept up as Kelly took aim and a voice shouted over a loudspeaker in Russian, booming in the rain, 'No more, Kelly! Enough!'

Kelly turned, lowering his gun. The man with the loudhailer advancing down the street wore the uniform of a colonel in the KGB, a military greatcoat slung from his shoulders against the rain. The man at his side was in his early thirties, tall and thin with stooped shoulders and fair hair. He wore a leather trenchcoat and steel-rimmed spectacles. Behind them, several squads of Russian soldiers, rifles at the ready, emerged from the side streets and doubled down towards the square. They were in combat fatigues and wore the flashes of the Iron Hammer Brigade of the élite special forces command.

'That's a good boy! Just put the gun down!' the colonel called. Kelly turned, his arm swung up and he fired once, an amazing shot considering the distance. Most of Murphy's left ear disintegrated. The fat man screamed, his hand going to the side of his head, blood pumping through his fingers.

'No, Mikhail! Enough!' the man in the leather overcoat cried. Kelly turned towards him and smiled. He said, in Russian, 'Sure, Professor, anything you say,' and placed the Browning carefully down on the bonnet of the Land Rover.

'I thought you said he was trained to do as he was told,' the colonel demanded.

An army lieutenant moved forward and saluted. 'One of them is still alive, two dead, Colonel Maslovsky. What are your orders?'

Maslovsky ignored him and said to Kelly, 'You weren't supposed to carry a gun.'

'I know,' Kelly said. 'On the other hand, according to the rules of the game, Murphy was not supposed to be an informer. I was told he was IRA.'

'So, you always believe what you're told?'

'The Party tells me I should, Comrade Colonel. Maybe you've got a new rule book for me?' Maslovsky was angry and it showed for he was not used to such attitudes – not from anyone. He opened his mouth to retort angrily and there was a sudden scream. The little girl who had sold Kelly the poppies pushed her way through the crowd and dropped on her knees beside the body of the police sergeant.

'Papa,' she wailed in Russian. 'Papa.' She looked up at Kelly, her face pale. 'You've killed him! You've murdered my father!'

She was on him like a young tiger, nails reaching for his face, crying hysterically. He held her wrists tight and suddenly, all strength went out of her and she slumped against him. His arms went around her, he held her, stroking her hair, whispering in her ear.

The old priest moved out of the crowd. 'I'll take her,' he said, his hands gentle on her shoulders.

They moved away, the crowd opening to let them through. Maslovsky called to the lieutenant, 'Right, let's have the square cleared.' He turned to the man in the leather coat. 'I'm tired of this eternal Ukrainian rain. Let's get back inside and bring your protégé with you. We need to talk.'

The KGB is the largest and most complex intelligence service in the world, totally controlling the lives of millions in the Soviet Union itself, its tentacles reaching out to every country. The heart of it, its most secret area of all, concerns the work of Department 13, that section responsible for murder, assassination and sabotage in foreign countries.

Colonel Ivan Maslovsky had commanded Department 13 for five

years. He was a thickset, rather brutal-looking man, whose appearance was at odds with his background. Born in 1919 in Leningrad, the son of a doctor, he had gone to law school in that city, completing his studies only a few months before the German invasion of Russia. He had spent the early part of the war fighting with partisan groups behind the lines. His education and flair for languages had earned him a transfer to the wartime counter-intelligence unit known as SMERSH. Such was his success that he had remained in intelligence work after the war and had never returned to the practice of law.

He had been mainly responsible for the setting up of highly original schools for spies at such places as Gaczyna, where agents were trained to work in English-speaking countries in a replica of an English or American town, living exactly as they would in the West. The extraordinarily successful penetration by the KGB of the French intelligence service at every level had been, in the main, the product of the school he had set up at Grosnia, where the emphasis was on everything French, environment, culture, cooking and dress being faithfully replicated.

His superiors had every faith in him, and had given him *carte blanche* to extend the system, which explained the existence of a small Ulster market town called Drumore in the depths of the Ukraine.

The room he used as an office when visiting from Moscow was conventional enough, with a desk and filing cabinets, a large map of Drumore on the wall. A log fire burned brightly on an open hearth and he stood in front of it enjoying the heat, nursing a mug of strong black coffee laced with vodka. The door opened behind him as the man in the leather coat entered and approached the fire, shivering.

'God, but it's cold out there.'

He helped himself to coffee and vodka from the tray on the desk and moved to the fire. Paul Cherny was thirty-four years of age, a handsome good-humoured man who already had an international reputation in the field of experimental psychology; a considerable achievement for someone born the son of a blacksmith in a village in the Ukraine. As a boy of sixteen, he had fought with a partisan group in the war. His group leader had been a lecturer in English at the University of Moscow and recognized talent when he saw it.

Cherny was enrolled at the University in 1945. He majored in psychology, then spent two years in a unit concerned with experimental psychiatry at the University of Dresden, receiving a doctorate in 1951.

His interest in behaviourist psychology took him to the University of Peking to work with the famous Chinese psychologist, Pin Chow, whose speciality was the use of behaviourist techniques in the interrogation and conditioning of British and American prisoners of war in Korea.

By the time Cherny was ready to return to Moscow, his work in the conditioning of human behaviour by the use of Pavlovian techniques had brought him to the attention of the KGB and Maslovsky in particular, who had been instrumental in getting him appointed Professor of Experimental Psychology at Moscow University.

'He's a maverick,' Maslovsky said. 'Has no respect for authority. Totally fails to obey orders. He was told not to carry a gun, wasn't he?'

'Yes, Comrade Colonel.'

'So, he disobeys his orders and turns a routine exercise into a bloodbath. Not that I'm worried about these damned dissidents we use here. One way of forcing them to serve their country. Who were the policemen, by the way?'

'I'm not sure. Give me a moment.' Cherny picked up the telephone. 'Levin, get in here.'

'Who's Levin?' Maslovsky asked.

'He's been here about three months. A Jewish dissident, sentenced to five years for secretly corresponding with relatives in Israel. He runs the office with extreme efficiency.'

'What was his profession?'

'Physicist – structural engineer. He was, I think, involved with aircraft design. I've every reason to believe he's already seen the error of his ways.'

'That's what they all say,' Maslovsky told him.

There was a knock on the door and the man in question entered. Viktor Levin was a small man who looked larger only because of the quilted jacket and pants he wore. He was forty-five years of age, with iron-grey hair, and his steel spectacles had been repaired with tape. He had a hunted look about him, as if he expected the KGB to kick open the door at any moment, which, in his situation, was a not unreasonable assumption.

'Who were the three policemen?' Cherny asked.

'The sergeant was a man called Voronin, Comrade,' Levin told him. 'Formerly an actor with the Moscow Arts Theatre. He tried to defect to the West last year, after the death of his wife. Sentence – ten years.'

'And the child?'

'Tanya Voroninova, his daughter. I'd have to check on the other two.'

'Never mind now. You can go.'

Levin went out and Maslovsky said, 'Back to Kelly. I can't get over the fact that he shot that man outside the bar. A direct defiance of my order. Mind you,' he added grudgingly, 'an amazing shot.'

'Yes, he's good.'

'Go over his background for me again.'

Maslovsky poured more coffee and vodka and sat down by the fire and Cherny took a file from the desk and opened it. 'Mikhail Kelly, born in a village called Ballygar in Kerry. That's in the Irish Republic. 1938. Father, Sean Kelly, an IRA activist in the Spanish Civil War where he met the boy's mother in Madrid. Martha Vronsky, Soviet citizen.'

'And as I recall, the father was hanged by the British?'

'That's right. He took part in an IRA bombing campaign in the London area during the early months of the Second World War. Was caught, tried and executed.'

'Another Irish martyr. They seem to thrive on them, those people.'

'Martha Vronsky was entitled to Irish citizenship and continued to live in Dublin, supporting herself as a journalist. The boy went to a Jesuit school there.'

'Raised as a Catholic?'

'Of course. Those rather peculiar circumstances came to the attention of our man in Dublin who reported to Moscow. The boy's potential was obvious and the mother was persuaded to return with him to Russia in 1953. She died two years later. Stomach cancer.'

'So, he's now twenty and intelligent, I understand?'

'Very much so. Has a flair for languages. Simply soaks them up.' Cherny glanced at the file again. 'But his special talent is for acting. I'd go so far as to say he has a genius for it.'

'Highly appropriate in the circumstances.'

'If things had been different he might well have achieved greatness in that field.'

'Yes, well he can forget about that,' Maslovsky commented sourly. 'His killing instincts seem well developed.'

'Thuggery is no problem in this sort of affair,' Cherny told him. 'As the Comrade Colonel well knows, anyone can be trained to kill, which is why we place the emphasis on brains when recruiting. Kelly does have a very rare aptitude when using a handgun, however. Quite unique.'

'So I observed,' Maslovsky said. 'To kill like that, so ruthlessly. He must have a strong strain of the psychopath in him.'

'Not in his case, Comrade Colonel. It's perhaps a little difficult to understand, but as I told you, Kelly is a brilliant actor. Today, he played the role of IRA gunman and he carried it through, just as if he had been playing the part in a film.'

'Except that there was no director to call *cut*,' Maslovsky observed, 'and the dead man didn't get up and walk away when the camera stopped rolling.'

'I know,' Cherny said. 'But it explains psychologically why he *had* to shoot three men and why he fired at Murphy in spite of orders. Murphy was an informer. He had to be seen to be punished. In the role he was playing, it was impossible for Kelly to act in any other way. That is the purpose of the training.'

'All right, I take the point. And you think he's ready to go out into the cold now?'

'I believe so, Comrade Colonel.'

'All right, let's have him in.'

Without the hat and the raincoat Mikhail Kelly seemed younger than ever. He wore a dark polo-neck sweater, a jacket of Donegal tweed and corduroy slacks. He seemed totally composed, almost withdrawn, and Maslovsky was conscious of that vague feeling of irritation again.

'You're pleased with yourself, I suppose, with what happened out there? I told you not to shoot the man Murphy. Why did you disobey my orders?'

'He was an informer, Comrade Colonel. Such people need to be taught a lesson if men like me are to survive.' He shrugged. 'The purpose of terrorism is to terrorize. Lenin said that. In the days of the Irish revolution, it was Michael Collins' favourite quotation.'

'It was a game, damn you!' Maslovsky exploded. 'Not the real thing.'

'If we play the game long enough, Comrade Colonel, it can sometimes end up playing us,' Kelly told him calmly.

'Dear God!' Maslovsky said and it had been many years since he had expressed such a sentiment. 'All right, let's get on with it.' He sat down at the desk, facing Kelly. 'Professor Cherny feels you are ready to go to work. You agree?'

'Yes, Comrade Colonel.'

'Your task is easily stated. Our chief antagonists are America and Britain. Britain is the weaker of the two and its capitalist edifice is being eroded. The biggest thorn in Britain's side is the IRA. You are about to become an additional thorn.'

The colonel leaned forward and stared into Kelly's eyes. 'You are from now on a maker of disorder.'

'In Ireland?'

'Eventually, but you must undergo more training in the outside world first. Let me explain your task further.' He stood up and walked to the fire. 'In nineteen fifty-six, the IRA Army Council voted to start another campaign in Ulster. Three years later, and it has been singularly unsuccessful. There is little doubt that this campaign will be called off and sooner rather than later. It has achieved nothing.'

'So?' Kelly said.

Maslovsky returned to the desk. 'However, our own intelligence sources indicate that eventually a conflict will break out in Ireland of a far more serious nature than anything that has gone before. When that day comes, you must be ready for it, in deep and waiting.'

'I understand, Comrade.'

'I hope you do. However, enough for now. Professor Cherny will fill you in on your more immediate plans when I've gone. For the moment, you're dismissed.'

Kelly went out without a word. Cherny said, 'He can do it. I'm certain of it.'

'I hope so. He could be as good as any of the native sleepers and he drinks less.'

Maslovsky walked to the window and peered out at the driving rain, suddenly tired, not thinking of Kelly at all, conscious, for no particular reason, of the look on the child's face when she had attacked the Irishman back there in the square.

'That child,' he said. 'What was her name?'

'Tanya – Tanya Voroninova.'

'She's an orphan now? No one to take care of her?'

'Not as far as I know.'

'She was really quite appealing and intelligent, wouldn't you say?'

'She certainly seemed so. I haven't had any dealings with her personally. Has the Comrade Colonel a special interest?'

'Possibly. We lost our only daughter last year at the age of six in the influenza epidemic. My wife can't have any more. She's taken a job in some welfare department or other, but she frets, Cherny. She just isn't the same woman. Looking at that child back there in the square made me wonder. She might just fit the bill.'

'An excellent idea, Comrade, for everyone concerned, if I may say so.'

'Good,' Maslovsky said, suddenly brightening. 'I'll take her back to Moscow with me and give my Susha a surprise.'

He moved to the desk, pulled the cork from the vodka bottle with his teeth and filled two glasses. 'A toast,' he said. 'To the Irish enterprise and to . . .' He paused, frowning, 'What was his code name again?'

'Cuchulain,' Cherny told him.

'Right,' Maslovsky said. 'To Cuchulain.' He swallowed the vodka and hurled his glass into the fire.

1982

1

When Major Tony Villiers entered the officers' mess of the Grenadier Guards at Chelsea Barracks, there was no one there. It was a place of shadows, the only illumination coming from the candles flickering in the candelabra on the long, polished dining-table, the light reflected from the mess silver.

Only one place was set for dinner at the end of the table, which surprised him, but a bottle of champagne waited in a silver ice bucket, Krug 1972, his favourite. He paused, looking down at it, then lifted it out and eased the cork, reaching for one of the tall crystal glasses that stood on the table, pouring slowly and carefully. He moved to the fire and stood there, looking at his reflection in the mirror above it.

The scarlet tunic suited him rather well and the medals made a brave show, particularly the purple and white stripes of his Military Cross with the silver rosette that meant a second award. He was of medium height with good shoulders, the black hair longer than one would have expected in a serving soldier. In spite of the fact that his nose had been broken at some time or other, he was handsome enough in a dangerous kind of way.

It was very quiet now, only the great men of the past gazing solemnly down at him from the portraits, obscured by the shadows. There was an air of unreality to everything and for some reason, his image seemed to be reflected many times in the mirror, backwards into infinity. He was so damned thirsty. He raised the glass and his voice was very hoarse – seemed to belong to someone else entirely.

'Here's to you, Tony, old son,' he said, 'and a Happy New Year.'

He lifted the crystal glass to his lips and the champagne was colder than anything he had ever known. He drank it avidly and it seemed to turn to liquid fire in his mouth, burning its way down and he cried out in agony as the mirror shattered and then the ground seemed to open between his feet and he was falling.

A dream, of course, where thirst did not exist. He came awake then and found himself in exactly the same place as he had been for a week, leaning against the wall in the corner of the little room, unable to lie down because of the wooden halter padlocked around his neck, holding his wrists at shoulder level.

He wore a green headcloth wound around his head in the manner of the Balushi tribesmen he had been commanding in the Dhofar high country until his capture ten days previously. His khaki bush shirt and trousers were filthy now, torn in many places, and his feet were bare because one of the Rashid had stolen his suede desert boots. And then there was the beard, prickly and uncomfortable, and he didn't like that. Had never been able to get out of the old Guards' habit of a good close shave every day, no matter what the situation. Even the SAS had not been able to change that particular quirk.

There was the rattle of a bolt, the door creaked open and flies rose in a great curtain. Two Rashid entered, small, wiry men in soiled white robes, bandoliers criss-crossed from the shoulders. They eased him up between them without a word and took him outside, put him down roughly against the wall and walked away.

It was a few moments before his eyes became adjusted to the bright glare of the morning sun. Bir el Gafani was a poor place, no more than a dozen flat-roofed houses with the oasis trimmed by palm trees below. A boy herded half a dozen camels down towards the water trough where women in dark robes and black masks were washing clothes.

In the distance, to the right, the mountains of Dhofar, the most southern province of Oman, lifted into the blue sky. Little more than a week before Villiers had been leading Balushi tribesmen on a hunt for Marxist guerrillas. Bir el Gafani, on the other hand, was enemy territory, the People's Democratic Republic of the South Yemen stretching north to the Empty Quarter.

There was a large earthenware pot of water on his left with a ladle in it, but he knew better than to try to drink and waited patiently. In the distance, over a rise, a camel appeared, moving briskly towards the oasis, slightly unreal in the shimmering heat.

He closed his eyes for a moment, dropping his head on his chest to ease the strain on his neck, and was aware of footsteps. He looked up to find Salim bin al Kaman approaching. He wore a black headcloth, black robes, a holstered Browning automatic on his right hip, a curved dagger pushed into the belt and carried a Chinese AK assault rifle, the pride of his life. He stood peering down at Villiers, an amiable-looking man with a fringe of greying beard and a skin the colour of Spanish leather.

'*Salaam alaikum*, Salim bin al Kaman,' Villiers said formally in Arabic.

'*Alaikum salaam*. Good morning, Villiers Sahib.' It was his only English phrase. They continued in Arabic.

Salim propped the AK against the wall, filled the ladle with water and carefully held it to Villiers' mouth. The Englishman drank greedily. It was a morning ritual between them. Salim filled the ladle again and Villiers raised his face to receive the cooling stream.

'Better?' Salim asked.

'You could say that.'

The camel was close now, no more than a hundred yards away. Its rider had a line wound around the pommel of his saddle. A man shambled along on the other end.

'Who have we got here?' Villiers asked.

'Hamid,' Salim said.

'And a friend?'

Salim smiled. 'This is our country, Major Villiers, Rashid land. People should only come here when invited.'

'But in Hauf, the Commissars of the People's Republic don't recognize the rights of the Rashid. They don't even recognize Allah. Only Marx.'

'In their own place, they can talk as loudly as they please, but in the land of Rashid . . .' Salim shrugged and produced a flat tin. 'But enough. You will have a cigarette, my friend?'

The Arab expertly nipped the cardboard tube on the end of the cigarette, placed it in Villiers' mouth and gave him a light.

'Russian?' Villiers observed.

'Fifty miles from here at Fasari there is an airbase in the desert. Many Russian planes, trucks, Russian soldiers – everything!'

'Yes, I know,' Villiers told him.

'You know, and yet your famous SAS does nothing about it?'

'My country is not at war with the Yemen,' Villiers said. 'I am on loan from the British Army to help train and lead the Sultan of Oman's troops against Marxist guerrillas of the D.L.F.'

'We are not Marxists, Villiers Sahib. We of the Rashid go where we please and a major of the British SAS is a great prize. Worth many camels, many guns.'

'To whom?' Villiers asked.

Salim waved the cigarette at him. 'I have sent word to Fasari. The

Russians are coming, some time today. They will pay a great deal for you. They have agreed to meet my price.'

'Whatever they offer, my people will pay more,' Villiers assured him. 'Deliver me safely in Dhofar and you may have anything you want. English sovereigns of gold, Maria Theresa silver thalers.'

'But Villiers Sahib, I have given my word,' Salim smiled mockingly.

'I know,' Villiers said. 'Don't tell me. To the Rashid, their word is everything.'

'Exactly!'

Salim got to his feet as the camel approached. It dropped to its knees and Hamid, a young Rashid warrior in robes of ochre, a rifle slung across his back, came forward. He pulled on the line and the man at the other end fell on his hands and knees.

'What have we here?' Salim demanded.

'I found him in the night, walking across the desert.' Hamid went back to the camel and returned with a military-style water bottle and knapsack. 'He carried these.'

There was some bread in the knapsack and slabs of army rations. The labels were in Russian.

Salim held one down for Villiers to see, then said to the man in Arabic, 'You are Russian?'

The man was old with white hair, obviously exhausted, his khaki shirt soaked with sweat. He shook his head and his lips were swollen to twice their size. Salim held out the ladle filled with water. The man drank.

Villiers spoke fair Russian. He said, 'He wants to know who you are. Are you from Fasari?'

'Who are you?' the old man croaked.

'I'm a British officer. I was working for the Sultan's forces in Dhofar. Their people ambushed my patrol, killed my men and took me prisoner.'

'Does he speak English?'

'About three words. Presumably you have no Arabic?'

'No, but I think my English is probably better than your Russian. My name is Viktor Levin. I'm from Fasari. I was trying to get to Dhofar.'

'To defect?' Villiers asked.

'Something like that.'

Salim said in Arabic. 'So, he speaks English to you. Is he not Russian, then?'

Villiers said quietly to Levin, 'No point in lying about you. Your people are turning up here today to pick me up.' He turned to Salim. 'Yes, Russian, from Fasari.'

'And what was he doing in Rashid country?'

'He was trying to reach Dhofar.'

Salim stared at him, eyes narrow. 'To escape from his own people?' He laughed out loud and slapped his thigh. 'Excellent. They should pay well for him, also. A bonus, my friend. Allah is good to me.' He nodded to Hamid. 'Put them inside and see that they are fed, then come to me,' and he walked away.

Levin was placed in a similar wooden halter to Villiers. They sat side-by-side against the wall in the cell. After a while, a woman in a black mask entered, squatted, and fed them in turn from a large wooden bowl containing goatmeat stew. It was impossible to see whether she was young or old. She wiped their mouths carefully, then left, closing the door.

Levin said, 'Why the masks? I don't understand that?'

'A symbol of the fact that they belong to their husbands. No other man may look.'

'A strange country,' Levin closed his eyes. 'Too hot.'

'How old are you?' Villiers asked.

'Sixty-eight.'

'Isn't that a little old for the defecting business? I should have thought you'd left it rather late.'

Levin opened his eyes and smiled gently. 'It's quite simple. My wife died last week in Leningrad. I've no children, so no one they can blackmail me with when I reach freedom.'

'What do you do?'

'I'm Professor of Structural Engineering at the University of Leningrad. I've a particular interest in aircraft design. The Soviet Airforce has five MIG 23s at Fasari, ostensibly in a training role, so it's the training version of the plane they are using.'

'With modifications?' Villiers suggested.

'Exactly, so that it can be used in a ground attack role in mountainous country. The changes were made in Russia, but there have been problems which I was brought in to solve.'

'So, you've finally had enough? What were you hoping to do, go to Israel?'

'Not particularly. I'm not a convinced Zionist for one thing. No, England would be a much more attractive proposition. I was over there with a trade delegation in nineteen thirty-nine, just before the war started. The best two months of my life.'

'I see.'

'I was hoping to get out in nineteen fifty-nine. Corresponded secretly with relatives in Israel who were going to help, then I was betrayed by someone I had thought a true friend. An old story, I was sentenced to five years.'

'In the Gulag.'

'No, somewhere much more interesting. Would you believe, a little Ulster town called Drumore?'

Villiers turned, surprise on his face. 'I don't understand?'

'A little Ulster town called Drumore in the middle of the Ukraine.' The old man smiled at the look of astonishment on Villiers' face. 'I think I'd better explain.'

When he was finished, Villiers sat there thinking about it. Subversion techniques and counter-terrorism had been very much his business for several years now, particularly in Ireland, so Levin's story was fascinating to say the least. 'I knew about Gaczyna, where the KGB train operatives to work in English and so on, but this other stuff is new to me.'

'And probably to your intelligence people, I think!'

'In Rome in the old days,' Villiers said, 'slaves and prisoners of war were trained as gladiators, to fight in the arena.'

'To the death,' Levin said.

'With a chance to survive if you were better than the other man. Just like those dissidents at Drumore playing policemen.'

'They didn't stand much chance against Kelly,' Levin said.

'No, he sounds as if he was a very special item.'

The old man closed his eyes. His breathing was hoarse and troubled but he was obviously asleep within a few moments. Villiers leaned back in the corner, wretchedly uncomfortable. He kept thinking about Levin's strange story. He'd known a lot of Ulster market towns himself, Crossmaglen for example. A bad place to be. So dangerous that troops had to be taken in and out by helicopter. But Drumore in the Ukraine – that was something else. After a while, his chin dropped on to his chest and he too drifted into sleep.

He came awake to find himself being shaken vigorously by one of the Rashid tribesmen. Another was waking Levin. The man pulled Villiers to his feet and sent him stumbling through the door. It was afternoon now, he knew that from the position of the sun. Much more interesting was the half-track armoured personnel carrier. A converted BTR. What the Russians called a Sandcruiser, painted in desert camouflage. Half a dozen soldiers stood beside it wearing khaki drill uniforms, each man holding an AK assault rifle at the ready. Two more stood inside the Sandcruiser, manning a 12.7mm heavy machine gun with which they covered the dozen or so Rashid who stood watching, rifles cradled in their arms.

Salim turned as Levin was brought out behind Villiers. 'So, Villiers Sahib, we must part. What a pity. I've enjoyed our conversations.'

The Russian officer who approached, a sergeant at his shoulder, wore drill uniform like his men and a peaked cap and desert goggles that gave him an uncanny resemblance to one of Rommel's Afrika Corps officers. He stood looking at them for a while, then pushed up the goggles. He was younger than Villiers would have thought, with a smooth unlined face and very blue eyes. 'Professor Levin,' he said in Russian, 'I'd like to think you lost your way while out walking, but I'm afraid our friends of the KGB will take a rather different point of view.'

'They usually do,' Levin told him.

The officer turned to Villiers and said calmly, 'Yuri Kirov, Captain, 21st Specialist Parachute Brigade.' His English was excellent. 'And you are Major Anthony Villiers, Grenadier Guards, but rather more importantly, of the 22nd Special Air Service Regiment.'

'You're very well informed,' Villiers said. 'And allow me to compliment you on your English.'

'Thank you,' Kirov said. 'We're using exactly the same language laboratory techniques as those pioneered by the SAS at Bradbury Line Barracks in Hereford. You, also, the KGB will take a special interest in.'

'I'm sure they will,' Villiers said amiably.

'So.' Kirov turned to Salim. 'To business.' His Arabic was not as good as his English, but serviceable enough.

He snapped a finger and the sergeant stepped forward and handed the Arab a canvas pouch. Salim opened it, took out a handful of coins and gold flinted in the sun. He smiled and handed the pouch to Hamid who stood behind him.

'And now,' Kirov said, 'if you will be good enough to unpadlock these two, we'll get moving.'

'Ah, but Kirov Sahib is forgetting,' Salim smiled. 'I was also promised a machine gun and twenty thousand rounds of ammunition.'

'Yes, well my superiors feel that would be putting far too much temptation in the way of the Rashid,' Kirov said.

Salim stopped smiling. 'This was a firm promise.'

Most of his men, sensing trouble, raised their rifles. Kirov snapped fingers and thumb on his right hand, there was a sudden burst of fire from the heavy machine gun, raking the wall above Salim's head. As the echoes died away, Kirov said patiently, 'Take the gold, I would earnestly advise it.'

Salim smiled and flung his arms wide. 'But of course. Friendship is everything. Certainly not worth losing for the sake of a trifling misunderstanding.'

He produced a key from a pouch at his belt and unlocked the padlock, first on the wooden halter which held Levin. Then he moved to Villiers. 'Sometimes Allah looks down through the clouds and punishes the deceiver,' he murmured.

'Is that in the Koran?' Villiers asked, as Hamid removed the halter and he stretched his aching arms.

Salim shrugged and there was something in his eyes. 'If not, then it should be.'

Two soldiers doubled forward on the sergeant's command and ranged themselves on either side of Levin and Villiers. They walked to the Sandcruiser. Villiers and Levin climbed inside. The soldiers followed, Kirov bringing up the rear. Villiers and Levin sat down, flanked by armed guards, and Kirov turned and saluted as the engine rumbled into life.

'Nice to do business with you,' he called to Salim.

'And you, Kirov Sahib!'

The Sandcruiser moved away in a cloud of dust. As they went up over the edge of the first sand dune, Villiers looked back and saw that the old Rashid was still standing there, watching them go, only now his men had moved in behind him. There was a curious stillness about them, a kind of threat, and then the Sandcruiser went over the ridge and Bir al Gafani disappeared from view.

The concrete cell on the end of the administrative block at Fasari was a distinct improvement on their previous quarters, with whitewashed walls and chemical toilet and two narrow iron cots, each supplied with a mattress and blankets. It was one of half a dozen such cells, Villiers had noticed that on the way in, each with a heavy steel door complete with spyhole, and there seemed to be three armed guards constantly on duty.

Through the bars of the window, Villiers looked out at the airstrip. It was not as large as he had expected: three prefabricated hangars with a single tarmacadam runway. The five MIG 23s stood wingtip to wingtip in a line in front of the hangars, looking, in the evening light just before dark, like strange primeval creatures, still, brooding. There were two Mi-8 troop-carrying helicopters on the far side of them and trucks and motor vehicles of various kinds.

'Security seems virtually non-existent,' he murmured.

Beside him, Levin nodded. 'Little need for it. They are, after all, in friendly territory entirely surrounded by open desert. Even your SAS people would have difficulty with such a target, I suppose.'

Behind them, the bolts rattled in the door. It opened and a young corporal stepped in, followed by an Arab carrying a pail and two enamel bowls. 'Coffee,' the corporal said.

'When do we eat?' Villiers demanded.

'Nine o'clock.'

He ushered the Arab out and closed the door. The coffee was surprisingly good and very hot. Villiers said, 'So they use some Arab personnel?'

'In the kitchens and for sanitary duties and that sort of thing. Not from the desert tribes. They bring them from Hauf, I believe.'

'What do you think will happen now?'

'Well, tomorrow is Thursday and there's a supply plane in. It will probably take us back with it to Aden.'

'Moscow next stop?'

There was no answer to that, of course, just as there was no answer to concrete walls, steel doors and bars. Villiers lay on one bed, Levin on the other.

The old Russian said, 'Life is a constant disappointment to me. When I visited England, they took me to Oxford. So beautiful.' He sighed. 'It was a fantasy of mine to return one day.'

'Dreaming spires,' Villiers observed. 'Yes, it's quite a place.'

'You know it then?'

'My wife was at university there. St Hugh's College. She went there after the Sorbonne. She's half-French.'

Levin raised himself on one elbow. 'You surprise me. If you'll forgive me saying so, you don't have the look of a married man.'

'I'm not,' Villiers told him. 'We got divorced a few months ago.'

'I'm sorry.'

'Don't be. As you said, life is a constant disappointment. We all want something different, that's the trouble with human beings, particularly men and women. In spite of what the feminists say, they are different.'

'You still love her, I think?'

'Oh, yes,' Villiers said. 'Loving is easy. It's the living together that's so damned hard.'

'So what was the problem?'

'To put it simply, my work. Borneo, the Oman, Ireland. I was even in Vietnam when we very definitely weren't supposed to be. As she once told me, I'm truly good at only one thing, killing people, and there came a time when she couldn't take that any more.'

Levin lay back without a word and Tony Villiers stared up at the ceiling, head pillowed in his hands, thinking of things that would not go away as darkness fell.

He came awake with a start, aware of footsteps in the passageway outside, the murmur of voices. The light in the ceiling must have been turned on whilst he slept. They hadn't taken his Rolex from him and he glanced at it quickly, aware of Levin stirring on the other bed.

'What is it?' the old Russian asked.

'Nine-fifteen. Must be supper.'

Villiers got up and moved to the window. There was a half-moon in a sky alive with stars and the desert was luminous, starkly beautiful, the MIG 23s like black cutouts. *God,* he thought. *There must be a way.* He turned, his stomach tightening.

'What is it?' Levin whispered as the first bolt was drawn.

'I was just thinking,' Villiers said, 'that to make a run for it at some point, even if it means a bullet in the back, would be infinitely preferable to Moscow and the Lubianka.'

The door was flung open and the corporal stepped in, followed by an Arab holding a large wooden tray containing two bowls of stew, black bread and coffee. His head was down and yet there was something familiar about him.

'Come on, hurry up!' the corporal said in bad Arabic.

The Arab placed the tray on the small wooden table at the foot of Levin's bed and glanced up, and in the moment that Villiers and Levin realized that he was Salim bin al Kaman, the corporal turned to the door. Salim took a knife from his left sleeve, his hand went around the man's mouth, a knee up pulling him off balance, the knife slipped under his ribs. He eased the corporal down on the bed and wiped the knife on his uniform.

He smiled. 'I kept thinking about what you said, Villiers Sahib. That your people in the Dhofar would pay a great deal to have you back.'

'So, you get paid twice – once by both sides. Sound business sense,' Villiers told him.

'Of course, but in any case, the Russians were not honest with me. I have my honour to think of.'

'What about the other guards?'

'Gone to supper. All this I discovered from friends in the kitchens. The one whose place I took has suffered a severe bump on the head on the way here, by arrangement, of course. But come, Hamid awaits on the edge of the base with camels.'

They went out. He bolted the door and they followed him along the passageway quickly and moved outside. The Fasari airbase was very quiet, everything still in the moonlight.

'Look at it,' Salim said. 'No one cares. Even the sentries are at supper. Peasants in uniform.' He reached behind a steel drum which stood against the wall and produced a bundle. 'Put these on and follow me.'

They were two woollen cloaks of the kind worn by the Bedouin at nights in the intense cold of the desert, each with a pointed hood to pull up. They put them on and followed him across to the hangars.

'No fence around this place, no wall,' Villiers whispered.

'The desert is the only wall they need,' Levin said.

Beyond the hangars, the sand dunes lifted on either side of what looked like the mouth of a ravine. Salim said, 'The Wadi al Hara. It empties into the plain a quarter of a mile from here where Hamid waits.'

Villiers said, 'Had it occurred to you that Kirov may well put two and two together and come up with Salim bin al Kaman?'

'But of course. My people are already half-way to the Dhofar border by now.'

'Good,' Villiers said. 'That's all I wanted to know. I'm going to show you something very interesting.'

He turned towards the Sandcruiser standing nearby and pulled himself over the side while Salim protested in a hoarse whisper. 'Villiers Sahib, this is madness.'

As Villiers dropped behind the driving wheel, the Rashid clambered up into the vehicle, followed by Levin. 'I've a dreadful feeling that all this is somehow my fault,' the old Russian said. 'We are, I presume, to see the SAS in action?'

'During the Second World War, the SAS under David Stirling destroyed more Luftwaffe planes on the ground in North Africa than the RAF and Yanks managed in aerial combat. I'll show you the technique,' Villiers told him.

'Possibly another version of that bullet in the back you were talking about.'

Villiers switched on and as the engine rumbled into life, said to Salim in Arabic, 'Can you manage the machine gun?'

Salim grabbed the handles of the Degtyarev. 'Allah, be merciful. There is fire in his brain. He is not as other men.'

'Is that in the Koran, too?' Villiers demanded, and the roaring of the 110 horsepower engine as he put his foot down hard drowned the Arab's reply.

The Sandcruiser thundered across the tarmac. Villiers swung hard and it spun round on its half tracks and smashed the tailplane of the first MIG, continuing right down the line as he increased speed. The tailplanes of the two helicopters were too high, so he concentrated on the cockpit areas at the front, the Sandcruiser's eight tons of armoured steel crumpling the perspex with ease.

He swung round in a wide loop and called to Salim. 'The helicopters. Try for the fuel tanks.'

There was the sound of an alarm klaxon from the main administration block now, voices crying in the night and shooting started. Salim raked the two helicopters with a continuous burst and the fuel tank on the one on the left exploded, a ball of fire mushrooming into the night, burning debris cascading everywhere. A moment later, the second helicopter exploded against the MIG next to it and that also started to burn.

'That's it!' Villiers said. 'They'll all go now. Let's get out of here.'

As he spun the wheel, Salim swung the machine gun, driving back the soldiers running towards them. Villiers was aware of Kirov standing as the men went down on the other side of the tarmac, firing his pistol deliberately in a gallant, but futile gesture. And then they were climbing up the slope of the dunes, tracks churning sand and entering the mouth of the *wadi.* The dried bed of the old stream was rough with boulders here and there, but visibility in the moonlight was good. Villiers kept his foot down and drove fast.

He called to Levin. 'You okay?'

'I think so,' the old Russian told him. 'I'll keep checking.'

Salim patted the Degtyarev machine gun. 'What a darling. Better than any woman. This, I keep, Villiers Sahib.'

'You've earned it,' Villiers told him. 'Now all we have to do is pick up Hamid and drive like hell for the border.'

'No helicopters to chase us,' Levin shouted.

'Exactly.'

Salim said, 'You deserve to be Rashid, Villiers Sahib. I have not enjoyed myself so much in many years.' He raised an arm. 'I have held them in the hollow of my hand and they are as dust.'

'The Koran again?' Villiers asked.

'No, my friend,' Salim bin al Kaman told him. 'It is from your own Bible this time. The Old Testament,' and he laughed out loud exultantly as they emerged from the *wadi* and started down to the plain below where Hamid waited.

2

D15, that branch of the British Secret Intelligence Service which concerns itself with counter-espionage and the activities of secret agents and subversion within the United Kingdom, does not officially exist, although its offices are to be found in a large white and red brick building not far from the Hilton Hotel in London. D15 can only carry out an investigation and has no powers of arrest. It is the officers of the Special Branch at Scotland Yard who handle that end of things.

But the growth of international terrorism and its effects in Britain, particularly because of the Irish problem, were more than even Scotland Yard could handle and in 1972, the Director General of D15, with the support of 10 Downing Street, created a section known as Group Four with powers held directly from the Prime Minister of the day to co-ordinate the handling of all cases of terrorism and subversion.

After ten years, Brigadier Charles Ferguson was still in charge. A large, deceptively kindly-looking man, the Guards tie was the only hint of a military background. The crumpled grey suits he favoured, and half-moon reading glasses, combined with untidy grey hair to give him the look of some minor academic in a provincial university.

Although he had an office at the Directorate General, he preferred to work from his flat in Cavendish Square. His second daughter, Ellie, who was in interior design, had done the place over for him. The Adam fireplace was real and so was the fire. Ferguson was a fire person. The rest of the room was also Georgian and everything matched to perfection, including the heavy curtains.

The door opened and his manservant, an ex-Gurkha *naik* named Kim, came in with a silver tray which he placed by the fire. 'Ah, tea,' Ferguson said. 'Tell Captain Fox to join me.'

He poured tea into one of the china cups and picked up *The Times*. The news from the Falklands was not bad. British forces had landed on Pebble Island and destroyed eleven Argentine aircraft plus an ammo dump. Two Sea Harriers had bombed merchant shipping in Falkland Sound.

The green baize door leading to the study opened and Fox came in.

He was an elegant man in a blue flannel suit by Huntsman of Savile Row. He also wore a Guards tie, for he had once been an acting captain in the Blues and Royals until an unfortunate incident with a bomb in Belfast during his third tour of duty had deprived him of his left hand. He now wore a rather clever replica which, thanks to the miracle of the microchip, served him almost as well as the original. The neat leather glove made it difficult to tell the difference.

'Tea, Harry?'

'Thank you, sir. I see they've got the Pebble Island story.'

'Yes, all very colourful and dashing,' Ferguson said as he filled a cup for him. 'But frankly, as no one knows better than you, we've got enough on our plate without the Falklands. I mean, Ireland's not going to go away and then there's the Pope's visit. Due on the twenty-eighth. That only gives us eleven days. And he makes such a target of himself. You'd think he'd be more careful after the Rome attempt on his life.'

'Not that kind of man, is he, sir?' Fox sipped some of his tea. 'On the other hand, the way things are going, perhaps he won't come at all. The South American connection is of primary importance to the Catholic Church and they see us as the villain of the piece in this Falklands business. They don't want him to come and the speech he made in Rome yesterday seemed to hint that he wouldn't.'

'I'll be perfectly happy with that,' Ferguson said. 'It would relieve me of the responsibility of making sure some madman or other doesn't try to shoot him while he's in England. On the other hand, several million British Catholics would be bitterly disappointed.'

'I understand the Archbishops of Liverpool and Glasgow have flown off to the Vatican today to try to persuade him to change his mind,' Fox said.

'Yes, well let's hope they fail miserably.'

The bleeper sounded on the red telephone on Ferguson's desk, the phone reserved for top security rated traffic only.

'See what that is, Harry.'

Fox lifted the receiver. 'Fox here.' He listened for a moment then turned, face grave and held out the phone. 'Ulster, sir. Army headquarters Lisburn and it isn't good!'

It had started that morning just before seven o'clock outside the village of Kilgannon some ten miles from Londonderry. Patrick Leary had delivered the post in the area for fifteen years now and his Royal Mail van was a familiar sight.

His routine was always the same. He reported for work at headquarters in Londonderry at five-thirty promptly, picked up the mail for the first delivery of the day, already sorted by the night staff, filled up his petrol tank at the transport pumps then set off for Kilgannon. And always at half past six he would pull into the track in the trees beside Kilgannon Bridge to read the morning paper, eat his breakfast sandwiches and have a cup of coffee from his thermos flask. It was a routine which, unfortunately for Leary, had not gone unnoticed.

Cuchulain watched him for ten minutes, waiting patiently for Leary to finish his sandwiches. Then the man got out, as he always did, and walked a little way into the wood. There was a slight sound behind him of a twig cracking under a foot. As he turned in alarm, Cuchulain slipped out of the trees.

He presented a formidable figure and Leary was immediately terrified. Cuchulain wore a dark anorak and a black balaclava helmet which left only his eyes, nose and mouth exposed. He carried a PPK semi-automatic pistol in his left hand with a Carswell silencer screwed to the end of the barrel.

'Do as you're told and you'll live,' Cuchulain said. His voice was soft with a Southern Irish accent.

'Anything,' Leary croaked. 'I've got a family – please.'

'Take off your cap and the raincoat and lay them down.' Leary did as he was told and Cuchulain held out his right hand so that Leary saw the large white capsule nestling in the centre of the glove. 'Now, swallow that like a good boy.'

'Would you poison me?' Leary was sweating now.

'You'll be out for approximately four hours, that's all,' Cuchulain reassured him. 'Better that way.' He raised the gun. 'Better than this.'

Leary took the capsule, hand shaking, and swallowed it down. His legs seemed to turn to rubber, there was an air of unreality to everything, then a hand was on his shoulder pushing him down. The grass was cool against his face, then there was only the darkness.

Dr Hans Wolfgang Baum was a remarkable man. Born in Berlin in 1950, the son of a prominent industrialist, on his father's death in 1970 he had inherited a fortune equivalent to ten million dollars and wide business interests. Many people in his position would have been content to live a life of pleasure, which Baum did, with the important distinction that he derived his pleasure from work.

He had a doctorate in engineering science from the University of Berlin, a law degree from the London School of Economics, and a master's degree in business administration from Harvard. And he had put them all to good use, expanding and developing his various factories in West Germany, France and the United States, so that his personal fortune was now estimated to be in excess of one hundred million dollars.

And yet the project closest to his heart was the development of the plant to manufacture tractors and general agricultural machinery outside Londonderry near Kilgannon. Baum Industries could have gone elsewhere, indeed the members of the board of management had wanted to. Unfortunately for them and the demands of sound business sense, Baum was a truly good man, a rare commodity in this world, and a committed Christian. A member of the German Lutheran Church, he had done everything possible to make the factory a genuine partnership between Catholic and Protestant. He and his wife were totally committed to the local community and all his three children attended local schools.

It was an open secret that he had met the Provisional IRA, some said the legendary Martin McGuiness himself. Whether true or not, the PIRA had left the Kilgannon factory alone to prosper, as it had done, and to provide work for more than a thousand Protestants and Catholics previously unemployed.

Baum liked to keep in shape. Each morning, he awakened at exactly the same time, six o'clock, slid out of bed without disturbing his wife, and pulled on track suit and running shoes. Eileen Docherty, the young maid, was already up and making tea in the kitchen although still in her dressing gown.

'Breakfast at seven, Eileen,' he called. 'My usual. Must get an early start this morning. I've a meeting in Derry at eight-thirty with the Works Committee.'

He let himself out of the kitchen door, ran across the parkland, vaulted a low fence and turned into the woods. He ran rather than jogged at a fast, almost professional pace, following a series of paths, his mind full of the day's planned events.

By six forty-five he had completed his schedule, turned out of the trees and hammered along the grass verge of the main road towards the house. As usual, he met Pat Leary's mail van coming along the road towards him. It pulled in and waited and he could see Leary through the windscreen in uniform cap and coat sorting a bundle of mail.

Baum leaned down to the open window. 'What have you got for me this morning, Patrick?'

The face was the face of a stranger, dark, calm eyes, strong bones, nothing to fear there at all, and yet it was Death come to claim him.

'I'm truly sorry,' Cuchulain said. 'You're a good man,' and the Walther in his left hand extended to touch Baum between the eyes. It coughed once, the German was hurled back to fall on the verge, blood and brains scattering across the grass.

Cuchulain drove away instantly, was back in the track by the bridge where he had left Leary within five minutes. He tore off the cap and coat, dropped them beside the unconscious postman and ran through the trees, clambering over a wooden fence a few minutes later beside a narrow farm track, heavily overgrown with grass. A motorcycle waited there, an old 350cc BSA, stripped down as if for hill climbing with special ribbed tyres. It was a machine much used by hill farmers on both sides of the border to herd sheep. He pulled on a battered old crash helmet with a scratched visor, climbed on and kick-started expertly. The engine roared into life and he rode away, passing one vehicle, the local milk cart just outside the village.

Back there on the main road it started to rain and it was still falling on the upturned face of Hans Wolfgang Baum thirty minutes later when the local milk cart pulled up beside him. And at that precise moment, fifteen miles away, Cuchulain turned the BSA along a farm track south of Clady and rode across the border into the safety of the Irish Republic.

Ten minutes later, he stopped beside a phone box, dialled the number of the *Belfast Telegraph*, asked for the news desk and claimed responsibility for the shooting of Hans Wolfgang Baum on behalf of the Provisional IRA.

'So,' Ferguson said. 'The Motorcyclist the driver of that milk cart saw would seem to be our man.'

'No description, of course,' Fox told him. 'He was wearing a crash helmet.'

'It doesn't make sense,' Ferguson said. 'Baum was well liked by everyone and the local Catholic community was totally behind him. He fought his own board every inch of the way to locate that factory in Kilgannon. They'll probably pull out now, which leaves over a thousand unemployed and Catholics and Protestants at each others' throats again.'

'But isn't that exactly what the Provisionals want, sir?'

'I wouldn't have thought so, Harry. Not this time. This was a dirty one. The callous murder of a thoroughly good man, well respected by the Catholic community. It can do the Provisionals nothing but harm with their own people. That's what I don't understand. It was such a stupid thing to do.' He tapped the file on Baum which Fox had brought in. 'Baum met Martin McGuiness in secret and McGuiness assured him of the Provisionals' good will, and whatever else you may think of him, McGuiness is a clever man. Too damned clever, actually, but that isn't the point.' He shook his head. 'No, it doesn't add up.'

The red phone bleeped. He picked it up. 'Ferguson here.' He listened for a moment. 'Very well, Minister.' He put the phone down and stood up. 'The Secretary of State for Northern Ireland, Harry. Wants me right away. Get on to Lisburn again. Army Intelligence – anything you can think of. Find out all you can.'

He was back just over an hour later. As he was taking off his coat, Fox came in.

'That didn't take long, sir.'

'Short and sweet. He's not pleased, Harry, and neither is the Prime Minister. She's good and mad and you know what that means.'

'She wants results, sir?'

'Only she wants them yesterday, Harry. All hell's broken loose over there in Ulster. Protestant politicians having a field day. Paisley saying I told you so, as usual. Oh, the West German Chancellor's been on to Downing Street. To be frank, things couldn't be worse.'

'I wouldn't be too sure, sir. According to Army Intelligence at Lisburn the PIRA are more than a little annoyed about this one themselves. They insist they had nothing to do with it.'

'But they claimed responsibility.'

'They run a very tight ship these days, sir, as you know, since the re-organization of their command structure. McGuiness, amongst other things, is still Chief of Northern Command and the word from Dublin is that he categorically denies involvement of any of his people. In fact, he's as angry as anybody else at the news. It seems he thought a great deal of Baum.'

'Do you think it's INLA?'

The Irish National Liberation Front had shown themselves willing to strike in the past more ruthlessly than the Provisionals when they felt the situation warranted it.

'Intelligence says not, sir. They have a good source close to the top where INLA is concerned.'

Ferguson warmed himself at the fire. 'Are you suggesting the other side were responsible? The UVF or the Red Hand of Ulster?'

'Again, Lisburn has good sources in both organizations and the word is definitely no. No Protestant organization was involved.'

'Not officially.'

'It doesn't look as if anyone was involved officially, sir. There are always the cowboys, of course. The madmen who watch too many midnight movies on television and end up willing to kill anybody rather than nobody.'

Ferguson lit a cheroot and sat behind his desk. 'Do you really believe that, Harry?'

'No, sir,' Fox said calmly. 'I was just throwing out all the obvious questions the media crackpots will come up with.'

Ferguson sat there staring at him, frowning. 'You know something, don't you?'

'Not exactly, sir. There could be an answer to this, a totally preposterous one which you aren't going to like one little bit.'

'Tell me.'

'All right, sir. The fact that the *Belfast Telegraph* had a phone call claiming responsibility for the Provisionals is going to make the Provos look very bad indeed.'

'So.'

'Let's assume that was the purpose of the exercise.'

'Which means a Protestant organization did it with that end in view.'

'Not necessarily, as I think you'll see if you let me explain. I got the full report on the affair from Lisburn just after you left. The killer is a professional, no doubt about that. Cold, ruthless and highly organized and yet he doesn't just kill everyone in sight.'

'Yes, that had occurred to me too. He gave the postman, Leary, a capsule. Some sort of knock-out drop.'

'And that stirred my mind, so I put it through the computer.' Fox had a file tucked under his arm and now he opened it. 'The first five killings on the list all involved a witness being forced at gunpoint to take that sort of capsule. First time it occurs is nineteen seventy-five in Omagh.'

Ferguson examined the list and looked up. 'But on two occasions, the victims were Catholics. I accept your argument that the same killer was involved, but it makes a nonsense of your theory that the purpose in killing Baum was to make the PIRA look bad.'

'Stay with it a little longer, sir, please. Description of the killer in each case is identical. Black balaclava and dark anorak. Always used a Walther PPK. On three occasions was known to escape by motor cycle from the scene of the crime.'

'So?'

'I fed all those details into the computer separately, sir. Any killings where motor cycles were involved. Cross-referencing with use of a Walther, not necessarily the same gun, of course. Also cross-referencing with the description of the individual.'

'And you got a result?'

'I got a result all right, sir.' Fox produced not one sheet, but two. 'At least thirty probable killings since nineteen seventy-five, all linked to the factors I've mentioned. There are another ten possibles.'

Ferguson scanned the lists quickly. 'Dear God!' he whispered. 'Catholic and Protestant alike. I don't understand.'

'You might if you consider the victims, sir. In all cases where the Provisionals claimed responsibility, the target was counter-productive, leaving them looking very bad indeed.'

'And the same where Protestant extremist organizations were involved?'

'True, sir, although the PIRA are more involved than anyone else. Another thing, if you consider the dates when the killings took place, it's usually when things were either quiet or getting better or when some political initiative was taking place. One of the possible cases when our man might have been involved goes back as far as July 1972, when, as you know, a delegation from the IRA met William Whitelaw secretly here in London.'

'That's right,' Ferguson said. 'There was a ceasefire. A genuine chance for peace.'

'Broken because someone started shooting on the Lenadoon estate in Belfast and that's all it took to start the pot boiling again.'

Ferguson sat there, staring down at the lists, his face expressionless. After a while, he said, 'So what you're saying is that somewhere over there is one mad individual dedicated to keeping the whole rotten mess turning over.'

'Exactly, except that I don't think he's mad. It seems to me he's simply following sound Marxist-Leninist principles where urban revolution is concerned. Chaos, disorder, fear. All those factors essential to the breakdown of any kind of orderly government.'

'With the IRA taking the brunt of the smear campaign?'

'Which makes it less and less likely that the Protestants will ever come to a political agreement with them, or our own government, for that matter.'

'And ensures that the struggle continues year after year and a solution always recedes before us.' Ferguson nodded slowly. 'An interesting theory, Harry, and you believe it?'

He looked up enquiringly. Fox shrugged. 'The facts were all there in the computer. We never asked the right questions, that's all. If we had, the pattern would have emerged earlier. It's been there a long time, sir.'

'Yes, I think you could very well be right.' Ferguson sat brooding for a little while longer.

Fox said gently, 'He exists, sir. He is a fact, I'm sure of it. And there's something else. Something that could go a long way to explaining the whole thing.'

'All right, tell me the worst.'

Fox took a further sheet from the file. 'When you were in Washington the other week, Tony Villiers came back from the Oman.'

'Yes, I heard something of his adventures there.'

'In his debriefing, Tony tells an interesting story concerning a Russian Jewish dissident named Viktor Levin whom he brought out with him. A fascinating vignette about a rather unusual KGB training centre in the Ukraine.'

He moved to the fire and lit a cigarette, waiting for Ferguson to finish reading the file. After a while, Ferguson said, 'Tony Villiers is in the Falklands now, did you know that?'

'Yes, sir, serving with the SAS behind enemy lines.'

'And this man, Levin?'

'A highly gifted engineer. We've arranged for one of the Oxford colleges to give him a job. He's at a safe house in Hampstead at the moment. I've taken the liberty of sending for him, sir.'

'Have you indeed, Harry? What would I do without you?'

'Manage very well, I should say, sir. Ah, and another thing. The psychologist, Paul Cherny, mentioned in that story. He defected in nineteen seventy-five.'

'What, to England?' Ferguson demanded.

'No, sir – Ireland. Went there for an international conference in July of that year and asked for political asylum. He's now Professor of Experimental Psychology at Trinity College, Dublin.'

Viktor Levin looked fit and well, still deeply tanned from his time in the Yemen. He wore a grey tweed suit, soft white shirt and blue tie, and black library spectacles that quite changed his appearance. He talked for some time, answering Ferguson's questions patiently.

During a brief pause he said, 'Do I presume that you gentlemen believe that the man Kelly, or Cuchulain to give him his codename, is actually active in Ireland? I mean, it's been twenty-three years.'

'But that was the whole idea, wasn't it?' Fox said. 'A sleeper to go in deep. To be ready when Ireland exploded. Perhaps he even helped it happen.'

'And you would appear to be the only person outside his own people who has any idea what he looks like, so we'll be asking you to look at some pictures. Lots of pictures,' Ferguson told him.

'As I say, it's been a long time,' Levin said.

'But he did have a distinctive look to him,' Fox suggested.

'That's true enough, God knows. A face like the Devil himself, when he killed, but of course, you're not quite right when you say I'm the only one who remembers him. There's Tanya. Tanya Voroninova.'

'The young girl whose father played the police sergeant who Kelly shot, sir,' Fox explained.

'Not so young now. Thirty years old. A lovely girl and you should hear her play the piano,' Levin told them.

'You've seen her since?' Ferguson asked.

'All the time. Let me explain. I made sure they thought I'd seen the error of my ways so I was rehabilitated and sent to work at the University of Moscow. Tanya was adopted by the KGB Colonel, Maslovsky, and his wife who really took to the child.'

'He's a general now, sir,' Fox put in.

'She turned out to have great talent for piano. When she was twenty, she won the Tchaikovsky competition in Moscow.'

'Just a minute,' Ferguson said, for classical music was his special joy.

'Tanya Voroninova, the concert pianist. She did rather well at the Leeds Piano Festival two years ago.'

'That's right. Mrs Maslovsky died a month ago. Tanya tours abroad all the time now. With her foster-father a KGB general, she's looked upon as a good risk.'

'And you've seen her recently?'

'Six months ago.'

'And she spoke of the events you've described as taking place at Drumore?'

'Oh, yes. Let me explain. She's highly intelligent and well balanced, but she's always had a thing about what happened. It's as if she has to keep turning it over in her mind. I asked her why once.'

'And what did she say?'

'That it was Kelly. She could never forget him because he was so kind to her, and in view of what happened, she couldn't understand that. She said she often dreamt of him.'

'Yes, well as she's in Russia, that isn't really much help.' Ferguson got to his feet. 'Would you mind waiting in the next room a moment, Mr Levin?'

Fox opened the green baize door and the Russian passed through. Ferguson said, 'A nice man, I like him.' He walked to the window and looked down into the square below. After a while, he said, 'We've got to root him out, Harry. I don't think anything we've handled has ever been so vital.'

'I agree.'

'A strange thing. It would seem to be just as important to the IRA that Cuchulain is exposed as it is to us.'

'Yes, sir, the thought had occurred to me.'

'Do you think they'd see it that way?'

'Perhaps, sir.' Fox's stomach was hollow with excitement as if he knew what was coming.

'All right,' Ferguson said. 'God knows, you've given enough to Ireland, Harry. Are you willing to risk the other hand?'

'If you say so, sir.'

'Good. Let's see if they're willing to show some sense for once. I want you to go to Dublin to see the PIRA Army Council or anyone they're willing to delegate to see you. I'll make the right phone calls to set it up. Stay at the Westbourne as usual. And I mean today, Harry. I'll see to Levin.'

‘Right, sir,’ Fox said calmly. ‘Then if you’ll excuse me, I’ll get started,’ and he went out.

Ferguson went back to the window and looked out at the rain. Crazy, of course, the idea that British Intelligence and the IRA could work together and yet it made sense this time. The question was, would the wild men in Dublin see it that way?

Behind him, the study door opened and Levin appeared. He coughed apologetically, ‘Brigadier, do you still need me?’

‘But of course, my dear chap,’ Charles Ferguson said. ‘I’ll take you along to my headquarters now. Pictures – lots of pictures, I’m afraid.’ He picked up his coat and hat and opened the door to usher Levin out. ‘But who knows? You might just recognize our man.’

In his heart, he did not believe it for a moment, but he didn’t tell Levin that as they went down in the lift.

3

In Dublin, it was raining, driving across the Liffey in a soft grey curtain as the cab from the airport turned into a side street just off George's Quay and deposited Fox at his hotel.

The Westbourne was a small old-fashioned place with only one bar-restaurant. It was a Georgian building and therefore listed against redevelopment. Inside however, it had been refurbished to a quiet elegance exactly in period. The clientele, when one saw them at all, were middle-class and distinctly ageing, the sort who'd been using it for years when up from the country for a few days. Fox had stayed there on numerous occasions, always under the name of Charles Hunt, profession, wine wholesaler, a subject he was sufficiently expert on to make an eminently suitable cover.

The receptionist, a plain young woman in a black suit, greeted him warmly. 'Nice to see you again, Mr Hunt. I've managed you number three on the first floor. You've stayed there before.'

'Fine,' Fox said. 'Messages?'

'None, sir. How long will you be staying?'

'One night, maybe two. I'll let you know.'

The porter was an old man with the sad, wrinkled face of the truly disillusioned and very white hair. His green uniform was a little too large and Fox, as usual, felt slightly embarrassed when he took the bags.

'How are you, Mr Ryan?' he enquired as they went up in the small lift.

'Fine, sir. Never better. I'm retiring next month. They're putting me out to pasture.'

He led the way along the small corridor and Fox said, 'That's a pity. You'll miss the Westbourne.'

'I will so, sir. Thirty-eight years.' He unlocked the bedroom door and led the way in. 'Still, it comes to us all.'

It was a pleasant room with green damask walls, twin beds, a fake Adam fireplace and Georgian mahogany furniture. Ryan put the bag down on the bed and adjusted the curtains.

'The bathroom's been done since you were last here, sir. Very nice. Would you like some tea?'

'Not right now, Mr Ryan.' Fox took a five pound note from his wallet and passed it over. 'If there's a message, let me know straight away. If I'm not here, I'll be in the bar.'

There was something in the old man's eyes, just for a moment; then he smiled faintly. 'I'll find you, sir, never fear.'

That was the thing about Dublin these days, Fox told himself as he dropped his coat on the bed and went to the window. You could never be sure of anyone and there were sympathizers everywhere, of course. Not necessarily IRA, but thousands of ordinary, decent people who hated the violence and the bombing, but approved of the political ideal behind it all.

The phone rang and when he answered it, Ferguson was at the other end.

'It's all set. McGuiness is going to see you.'

'When?'

'They'll let you know.'

The line went dead and Fox replaced the receiver. Martin McGuiness, Chief of Northern Command for the PIRA, amongst other things; at least he would be dealing with one of the more intelligent members of the Army Council.

He could see the Liffey at the far end of the street, and rain rattled against the window. He felt unaccountably depressed. Ireland, of course. For a moment, he felt a distinct ache in the left hand again, the hand that was no longer there. All in the mind, he told himself, and went downstairs to the bar.

It was deserted except for a young Italian barman. Fox ordered a Scotch and water and sat in a corner by the window. There was a choice of newspapers on the table and he was working his way through *The Times* when Ryan appeared like a shadow at his shoulder.

'Your cab's here, sir.'

Fox glanced up. 'My cab? Oh, yes, of course.' He frowned, noticing the blue raincoat across Ryan's arm. 'Isn't that mine?'

'I took the liberty of getting it for you from your room, sir. You'll be needing it. This rain's with us for a while yet, I think.'

Again, there was something in the eyes, almost amusement. Fox allowed him to help him on with the coat and followed him outside and down the steps to where a black taxicab waited.

Ryan opened the door for him and said, as Fox got in, 'Have a nice afternoon, sir.'

The cab moved away quickly. The driver was a young man with dark, curly hair. He wore a brown leather jacket and white scarf. He didn't say a word, simply turned into the traffic stream at the end of the street and drove along George's Quay. A man in a cloth cap and reefer coat stood beside a green telephone box. The cab slid into the kerb, the man in the reefer coat opened the rear door and got in beside Fox smoothly.

'On your way, Billy,' he said to the driver and turned to Fox genially. 'Jesus and Mary, but I thought I'd drown out there. Arms up, if you please, Captain. Not too much. Just enough.' He searched Fox thoroughly and professionally and found nothing. He leaned back and lit a cigarette, then he took a pistol from his pocket and held it on his knee. 'Know what this is, Captain?'

'A Ceska, from the look of it,' Fox said. 'Silenced version the Czechs made a few years back.'

'Full marks. Just remember I've got it when you're talking to Mr McGuiness. As they say in the movies, one false move and you're dead.'

They continued to follow the line of the river, the traffic heavy in the rain and finally pulled in at the kerb half-way along Victoria Quay.

'Out!' the man in the reefer coat said and Fox followed him. Rain drove across the river on the wind and he pulled up his collar against it. The man in the reefer coat passed under a tree and nodded towards a small public shelter beside the quay wall. 'He doesn't like to be kept waiting. He's a busy man.'

He lit another cigarette and leaned against the tree and Fox moved among the pavement and went up the steps into the shelter. There was a man sitting on the bench in the corner reading a newspaper. He was well dressed, a fawn raincoat open revealing a well-cut suit of dark blue, white shirt and a blue and red striped tie. He was handsome enough with a mobile, intelligent mouth and blue eyes. Hard to believe that this rather pleasant-looking man had featured on the British Army's most wanted list for almost thirteen years.

'Ah, Captain Fox,' Martin McGuiness said affably. 'Nice to see you again.'

'But we've never met,' Fox said.

'Derry, 1972,' McGuiness told him. 'You were a cornet, isn't that what you call second lieutenants in the Blues and Royals? There was a bomb in a pub in Prior Street. You were on detachment with the Military Police at the time.'

'Good God!' Fox said. 'I remember now.'

'The whole street was ablaze. You ran into a house next to the grocer's shop and brought out a woman and two kids. I was on the flat roof opposite with a man with an Armalite rifle who wanted to put a hole in your head. I wouldn't let him. It didn't seem right in the circumstances.'

For a moment, Fox felt rather cold. 'You were in command in Derry for the IRA at that time.'

McGuiness grinned. 'A funny old life, isn't it? You shouldn't really be here. Now then, what is it that old snake, Ferguson, wants you to discuss with me?'

So Fox told him.

When he was finished McGuiness sat there brooding, hands in the pockets of his raincoat, staring across the Liffey. After a while, he said, 'That's Wolfe Tone Quay over there, did you know that?'

'Wasn't he a Protestant?' Fox asked.

'He was so. Also one of the greatest Irish patriots there ever was.'

He whistled tunelessly between his teeth. Fox said, 'Do you believe me?'

'Oh, yes,' McGuiness said softly. 'A devious bloody lot, the English, but I believe you all right and for one very simple reason. It fits, Captain, dear. All those hits over the years, the shit that's come our way because of it and sometimes internationally. I know the times we've not been responsible and so does the Army Council. The thing is, one always thought it was the idiots, the cowboys, the wild men.' He grinned crookedly. 'Or British Intelligence, of course. It never occurred to any of us that it could have been the work of one man. A deliberate plan.'

'You've got a few Marxists in your own organization, haven't you?' Fox suggested. 'The kind who might see the Soviets as Saviour.'

'You can forget that one.' Anger showed in McGuiness's blue eyes for a moment. 'Ireland free and Ireland for the Irish. We don't want any Marxist pap here.'

'So, what happens now? Will you go to the Army Council?'

'No, I don't think so. I'll talk to the Chief of Staff. See what he thinks. After all, he's the one that sent me. Frankly, the fewer people in on this, the better.'

'True.' Fox stood up. 'Cuchulain could be anyone. Maybe somebody close to the Army Council itself.'

'The thought had occurred to me.' McGuiness waved and the man in the reefer coat moved out from under the tree. 'Murphy will take you back to the Westbourne now. Don't go out. I'll be in touch.'

Fox walked a few paces away, paused and turned. 'By the way, that's a Guards tie you're wearing.'

Martin McGuiness smiled beautifully. 'And didn't I know it? Just trying to make you feel at home, Captain Fox.'

Fox dialled Ferguson from a phone booth in the foyer of the Westbourne so that he didn't have to go through the hotel switchboard. The Brigadier wasn't at the flat, so he tried the private line to his office at the Directorate-General and got through to him at once.

'I've had my preliminary meeting, sir.'

'That was quick. Did they send McGuiness?'

'Yes, sir.'

'Did he buy it?'

'Very much so, sir. He'll be back in touch, maybe later tonight.'

'Good. I'll be at the flat within the hour. No plans to go out. Phone me the moment you have more news.'

Fox showered, then changed and went downstairs to the bar again. He had another small Scotch and water and sat there, thinking about things for a while and of McGuiness in particular. A clever and dangerous man, no doubt about that. Not just a gunman, although he'd done his share of killing, but one of the most important leaders thrown up by the Troubles. The annoying thing was that Fox realized, with a certain sense of irritation, that he had really rather liked the man. That wouldn't do at all, so he went into the restaurant and had an early dinner, sitting in solitary splendour, a copy of the *Irish Press* propped up in front of him.

Afterwards, he had to pass through the bar on the way to the lounge. There were a couple of dozen people in there now, obviously other guests from the look of them, except for the driver of the cab who'd taken him to meet McGuiness earlier. He was seated on a stool at the end of the bar, a glass of lager in front of him, the main difference being that he now wore a rather smart grey suit. He showed no sign of recognition and Fox carried on into the lounge where Ryan approached him.

'If I remember correctly, sir, it's tea you prefer after your dinner and not coffee?'

Fox, who had sat down, said, 'That's right.'

'I've taken the liberty of putting a tray in your room, sir. I thought you might prefer a bit of peace and quiet.'

He turned without a word and led the way to the lift. Fox played along, following him, expecting perhaps a further message, but the old man said nothing and when they reached the first floor, led the way along the corridor and opened the bedroom door for him.

Martin McGuiness was watching the news on television. Murphy stood by the window. Like the man in the bar, he now wore a rather conservative suit, in his case, of navy-blue worsted material.

McGuiness switched off the television. 'Ah, there you are. Did you try the Duck à l'Orange? It's not bad here.'

The tray on the table with the tea things on it carried two cups. 'Shall I pour, Mr McGuiness?' Ryan asked.

'No, we can manage.' McGuiness reached for the teapot and said to Fox as Ryan withdrew, 'Old Patrick, as you can see, is one of our own. You can wait outside, Michael,' he added.

Murphy went out without a word. 'They tell me no gentleman would pour his milk in first, but then I suppose no real gentleman would bother about rubbish like that. Isn't that what they teach you at Eton?'

'Something like that.' Fox took the proffered cup. 'I didn't expect to see you quite so soon.'

'A lot to do and not much time to do it in.' McGuiness drank some tea and sighed with pleasure. 'That's good. Right, I've seen the Chief of Staff and he believes, with me, that you and your computer have stumbled on something that might very well be worth pursuing.'

'Together?'

'That depends. In the first place, he's decided not to discuss it with the Army Council, certainly not at this stage, so it stays with just me and himself.'

'That seems sensible.'

'Another thing, we don't want the Dublin police in on this, so keep Special Branch out of it and no military intelligence involvement either.'

'I'm sure Brigadier Ferguson will agree.'

'He'll bloody well have to, just as he'll have to accept that there's no way we're going to pass across general information about IRA members, past or present. The kind of stuff you could use in other ways.'

'All right,' Fox said, 'I can see that, but it could be a tricky one. How do we co-operate if we don't pool resources?'

'There is a way.' McGuiness poured himself another cup of tea. 'I've discussed it with the Chief of Staff and he's agreeable if you are. We use a middle-man.'

'A middle-man?' Fox frowned. 'I don't understand?'

'Someone acceptable to both sides. Equally trusted, if you know what I mean.'

Fox laughed. 'There's no such animal.'

'Oh, yes there is,' McGuiness said. 'Liam Devlin, and don't tell me you don't know who *he* is.'

Harry Fox said slowly, 'I know Liam Devlin very well.'

'And why wouldn't you. Didn't you and Faulkner have him kidnapped by the SAS back in seventy-nine to help you break Martin Brosnan out of that French prison to hunt down that mad dog, Frank Barry.'

'You're extremely well informed.'

'Yes, well Liam's here in Dublin now, a professor at Trinity College. He has a cottage in a village called Kilrea, about an hour's drive out of town. You go and see him. If he agrees to help, then we'll discuss it further.'

'When?'

'I'll let you know, or maybe I'll just turn up unexpected, like. The one way I kept ahead of the British Army all those years up north.' He stood up. 'There's a lad at the bar downstairs. Maybe you noticed?'

'The cab driver.'

'Billy White. Left or right hand, he can still shoot a fly off the wall. He's yours while you're here.'

'Not necessary.'

'Oh, but it is.' McGuiness got up and pulled on his coat. 'Number one, I wouldn't like anything to happen to you, and number two, it's a convenience to know where you are.' He opened the door, and beyond him, Fox saw Murphy waiting. 'I'll be in touch, Captain.' McGuiness saluted mockingly, the door closed behind him.

Ferguson said, 'It makes sense, I suppose, but I'm not sure Devlin will work for us again, not after that Frank Barry affair. He felt we'd used him and Brosnan rather badly.'

'As I recall, we did, sir,' Fox said. 'Very badly indeed.'

'All right, Harry, no need to make a meal of it. Phone and see if he's at home. If he is, go and see him.'

'Now, sir?'

'Why not? It's only nine-thirty. If he is in, let me know and I'll speak to him myself. Here's his phone number, by the way. Take it down.'

Fox went along to the bar and changed a five pound note for 50p coins. Billy White was still sitting there, reading the evening paper. The glass of lager looked untouched.

'Can I buy you a drink, Mr White?' Fox asked.

'Never touch the stuff, Captain.' White smiled cheerfully and emptied the glass in one long swallow. 'A Bushmills would chase that down fine.'

Fox ordered him one. 'I may want to go out to a village called Kilrea. Do you know it?'

'No problem,' White told him. 'I know it well.'

Fox went back to the phone booth and closed the door. He sat there for a while thinking about it, then dialled the number Ferguson had given him. The voice, when it answered, was instantly recognizable. The voice of perhaps the most remarkable man he had ever met.

'Devlin here.'

'Liam? This is Harry Fox.'

'Mother of God!' Liam Devlin said. 'Where are you?'

'Dublin – the Westbourne Hotel. I'd like to come and see you.'

'You mean right now?'

'Sorry if it's inconvenient.'

Devlin laughed. 'As a matter of fact, at this precise moment in time I'm losing at chess, son, which is something I don't like to do. Your intervention could be looked upon as timely. Is this what you might term a business call?'

'Yes, I'm to ring Ferguson and tell him you're in. He wants to talk to you himself.'

'So the old bastard is still going strong? Ah, well, you know where to come?'

'Yes.'

'I'll see you in an hour then. Kilrea Cottage, Kilrea. You can't miss it. Next to the convent.'

When Fox came out of the booth after phoning Ferguson, White was waiting for him. 'Are we going out then, Captain?'

'Yes,' Fox said. 'Kilrea Cottage, Kilrea. Next to a convent apparently. I'll just get my coat.'

White waited until he'd entered the lift, then ducked into the booth and dialled a number. The receiver at the other end was lifted instantly.

He said, 'We're leaving for Kilrea now. Looks like he's seeing Devlin tonight.'

As they drove through the rain-swept streets, White said casually, 'Just so we know where we stand, Captain, I was a lieutenant in the North Tyrone Brigade of the Provisional IRA the year you lost that hand.'

'You must have been young.'

'Born old, that's me, thanks to the B Specials when I was a wee boy and the sodding RUC.' He lit a cigarette with one hand. 'You know Liam Devlin well, do you?'

'Why do you ask?' Fox demanded warily.

'That's who we're going to see, isn't it? Jesus, Captain, and who wouldn't be knowing Liam Devlin's address?'

'Something of a legend to you, I suppose?'

'A legend, is it? That man wrote the book. Mind you, he won't have any truck with the movement these days. He's what you might call a moralist. Can't stand the bombing and that kind of stuff.'

'And can you?'

'We're at war, aren't we? You bombed the hell out of the Third Reich. We'll bomb the hell out of you if that's what it takes.'

Logical but depressing, Fox thought, for where did it end? A charnel-house with only corpses to walk on. He shivered, face bleak.

'About Devlin,' White said as they started to leave the city. 'There's a tale I heard about him once. Would you know if it's true, I wonder?'

'Ask me.'

'The word is, he went to Spain in the thirties, served against Franco and was taken prisoner. Then the Germans got hold of him and used him as an agent here during the big war.'

'That's right.'

'The way I heard it, after that, they sent him to England. Something to do with an attempt by German paratroopers to kidnap Churchill in nineteen forty-three. Is there any truth in that?'

'Sounds straight out of a paperback novel to me,' Fox said.

White sighed and there was regret in his voice. 'That's what I thought. Still, one hell of a man for all that,' and he sat back and concentrated on his driving.

An understatement as a description of Liam Devlin, Fox thought, sitting there in the darkness: a brilliant student who had entered Trinity College, Dublin, at the age of sixteen and had taken a first class honours degree at nineteen, scholar, writer, poet and highly dangerous gunman for the IRA in the thirties, even when still a student.

Most of what White had said was true. He had gone to Spain to fight for the anti-fascists, he had worked for the Abwehr in Ireland. As to the Churchill affair? A story whispered around often enough, but as to the truth of it? Well, it would be years before those classified files were opened.

During the post-war period, Devlin had been a Professor at a Catholic seminary called All Souls just outside Boston. He'd been involved with the abortive IRA campaign of the late fifties and had returned to Ulster in 1969 as the present troubles had begun. One of the original architects of the Provisional IRA, he had become increasingly disillusioned by the bombing campaign and had withdrawn active support to the movement. Since 1976, he had held a position in the English Faculty at Trinity.

Fox had not seen him since 1979 when he had been coerced, indeed, blackmailed, by Ferguson into giving his active assistance in the hunting down of Frank Barry, ex-IRA activist turned international terrorist for hire. There had been various reasons why Devlin had gone along with that business, mostly because he had believed Ferguson's lies. So, how would he react now?

They had entered a long village street. Fox pulled himself together with a start as White said, 'Here we are – Kilrea, and there's the convent and that's Devlin's cottage, set back from the road behind the wall.'

He turned the car into a gravel driveway and cut the engine. 'I'll wait for you, Captain, shall I?'

Fox got out and walked up a stone flagged path between rose bushes to the green painted porch. The cottage was pleasantly Victorian with most of the original woodwork and gable ends. A light glowed behind drawn curtains at a bow window. He pressed the bellpush. There were voices inside, footsteps and then the door opened and Liam Devlin stood looking at him.

4

Devlin wore a dark blue flannel shirt open at the neck, grey slacks and a pair of highly expensive-looking Italian brogues in brown leather. He was a small man, no more than five foot five or six, and at sixty-four his dark, wavy hair showed only a light silvering. There was a faded scar on the right side of his forehead, an old bullet wound, the face pale, the eyes extraordinarily vivid blue. A slight ironic smile seemed permanently to lift the corner of his mouth – the look of a man who had found life a bad joke and had decided that the only thing to do was laugh about it.

The smile was charming and totally sincere. 'Good to see you, Harry.' His arms went around Fox in a light embrace.

'And you, Liam.'

Devlin looked beyond him at the car and Billy White behind the wheel. 'You've got someone with you?'

'Just my driver.'

Devlin moved past him, went along the path and leaned down to the window.

'Mr Devlin,' Billy said.

Devlin turned without a word and came back to Fox. 'Driver, is it, Harry? The only place that one will drive you to is straight to Hell.'

'Have you heard from Ferguson?'

'Yes, but leave it for the moment. Come along in.'

The interior of the house was a time capsule of Victoriana: mahogany panelling and William Morris wallpaper in the hall with several night scenes by the Victorian painter, Atkinson Grimshaw, on the walls. Fox examined them with admiration as he took off his coat and gave it to Devlin. 'Strange to see these here, Liam. Grimshaw was a very Yorkshire Englishman.'

'Not his fault, Harry, and he painted like an angel.'

'Worth a bob or two,' Fox said, well aware that ten thousand pounds at auction was not at all out of the way for even quite a small Grimshaw.

'Do you tell me?' Devlin said lightly. He opened one half of a double mahogany door and led the way into the sitting room. Like the hall, it was period Victorian: green flock wallpaper stamped with gold, more Grimshaws on the walls, mahogany furniture and a fire burning brightly in a fireplace that looked as if it was a William Langley original.

The man who stood before it was a priest in dark cassock and he turned from the fire to greet them. He was about Devlin's height with iron-grey hair swept back over his ears. A handsome man, particularly at this moment as he smiled a welcome; there was an eagerness to him, an energy that touched something in Fox. It was not often that one liked another human being so completely and instinctively.

'With apologies to Shakespeare, two little touches of Harry in the night,' Devlin said. 'Captain Harry Fox, meet Father Harry Cussane.'

Cussane shook hands warmly. 'A great pleasure, Captain Fox. Liam was telling me something about you after you rang earlier.'

Devlin indicated the chess table beside the sofa. 'Any excuse to get away from that. He was beating the pants off me.'

'A gross exaggeration as usual,' Cussane said. 'But I must get going. Leave you two to your business.' His voice was pleasant and rather deep. Irish, yet more than a hint of American there.

'Would you listen to the man?' Devlin had brought three glasses and a bottle of Bushmills from the cabinet in the corner. 'Sit down, Harry. Another little snifter before bed won't kill you.' He said to Fox, 'I've never known anyone so much on the go as this one.'

'All right, Liam, I surrender,' Cussane said. 'Fifteen minutes, that's all, then I must go. I like to make a late round at the hospice as you know and then there's Danny Malone. Living is a day-to-day business with him right now.'

Devlin said, 'I'll drink to him. It comes to us all.'

'You said hospice?' Fox enquired.

'There's a convent next door, the Sacred Heart, run by the Little Sisters of Pity. They started a hospice for terminal patients some years ago.'

'Do you work there?'

'Yes, as a sort of administrator cum priest. Nuns aren't supposed to be worldly enough to do the accounts. Absolute rubbish. Sister Anne Marie, who's in charge over there, knows to every last penny. And this is a small parish so the local priest doesn't have a curate. I give him a hand.'

'In between spending three days a week in charge of the press office at the Catholic Secretariat in Dublin,' Devlin said. 'Not to mention flogging the local youth club through a very average five performances of *South Pacific*, complete with a star cast of ninety-three local school kids.'

Cussane smiled. 'Guess who was stage manager? We're trying *West Side Story* next. Liam thinks it too ambitious, but I believe it better to rise to a challenge than go for the easy choise.'

He swallowed a little of his Bushmills. Fox said, 'Forgive me for asking, Father, but are you American or Irish? I can't quite tell.'

'Most days, neither can he,' Devlin laughed.

'My mother was an Irish-American who came back to Connacht in 1938 after her parents died, to seek her roots. All she found was me.'

'And your father?'

'I never knew him. Cussane was her name. She was a Protestant, by the way. There are still a few in Connacht, descendants of Cromwell's butchers. Cussane is often called Patterson in that part of the country by pseudo-translation from Casan, which in Irish means path.'

'Which means he's not quite certain who he is,' Devlin put in.

'Only some of the time.' Cussane smiled. 'My mother returned to America in 1946 after the war. She died of influenza a year later and I was taken in by her only relative, an old great-uncle who ran a farm in the Ontario wheat belt. He was a fine man and a good Catholic. It was under his influence that I decided to enter the Church.'

'Enter the Devil, stage left.' Devlin raised his glass.

Fox looked puzzled and Cussane explained. 'The seminary that accepted me was All Souls at Vine Landing outside Boston. Liam was English professor there.'

'He was a great trial to me,' Devlin said. 'Mind like a steel trap. Constantly catching me out misquoting Eliot in class.'

'I served in a couple of Boston parishes and another in New York,' Cussane said, 'but I always hoped to get back to Ireland. Finally, I got a move to Belfast in 1968. A church on the Falls Road.'

'Where he promptly got burned out by an Orange mob the following year.'

'I tried to keep the parish together using a school hall,' Cussane said.

Fox glanced at Devlin, 'While you ran around Belfast adding fuel to the flames?'

'God might forgive you for that,' Devlin said piously, 'for I cannot.'

Cussane emptied his glass. 'I'll be off then. Nice to meet you, Harry Fox.'

He held out his hand. Fox shook it and Cussane moved to the French windows and opened them. Fox saw the convent looming up into the night on the other side of the garden wall. Cussane walked across the lawn, opened a gate and passed through.

'Quite a man,' he said, as Devlin closed the windows.

'And then some.' Devlin turned, no longer smiling. 'All right, Harry. Ferguson being his usual mysterious self, it looks as if it's up to you to tell me what this is about.'

In the hospice, all was quiet. It was as unlike the conventional idea of a hospital as it was possible to be and the architect had designed the ward area in a way that gave each occupant of a bed a choice of privacy or intimacy with other patients. The night sister sat at her desk, the only light a shaded lamp. She didn't hear Cussane approach, yet suddenly he was there, looming out of the darkness.

'How's Malone?'

'The same, Father. Very little pain. We have the drug in-put just about in balance.'

'Is he lucid?'

'Some of the time.'

'I'll go and see him.'

Danny Malone's bed, divided from the others by bookshelves and cupboards, was angled towards a glass window that gave a view of grounds and the night sky. The night light beside the bed brought his face into relief. He was not old, no more than forty, his hair prematurely white, the face like a skull under taut skin, etched in pain caused by the cancer that was slowly and relentlessly taking him from this life to the next.

As Cussane sat down, Malone opened his eyes. He gazed blankly at Cussane, then recognition dawned. 'Father, I thought you weren't coming.'

'I promised, didn't I? I was having a nightcap with Liam Devlin, is all.'

'Jesus, Father, you're lucky you got away with just the one with him, but big for the cause, Liam, I'll give him that. There's no man living done more for Ireland.'

'What about yourself?' Cussane sat down beside the bed. 'No stronger fighter for the movement than you, Danny.'

'But how many did I kill, Father, there's the rub, and for what?' Malone asked him. 'Daniel O'Connel once said in a speech that, although the ideal of Irish freedom was just, it was not worth a single human life. When I was young, I disputed that. Now I'm dying, I think I know what he meant.' He winced in pain and turned to look at Cussane. 'Can we talk some more, Father? It helps get it straight in my own mind.'

'Just for a while, then you must get some sleep,' Cussane smiled. 'One thing a priest is good at is listening, Danny.'

Malone smiled contentedly. 'Right, where were we? I was telling you about the preparation for the bombing campaign on the English Midlands and London in seventy-two.'

'You were saying the papers nick-named you the Fox,' Cussane said, 'because you seemed to go backwards and forwards between England and Ireland at will. All your friends were caught, Danny, but not you. How was that?'

'Simple, Father. The greatest curse on this country of ours is the informer and the second greatest curse is the inefficiency of the IRA. People full of ideology and revolution blow a lot of wind and are often singularly lacking in good sense. That's why I preferred to go to the professionals.'

'Professionals?'

'What you would call the criminal element. For example, there wasn't an IRA safe house in England during the seventies that wasn't on the Special Branch's list at Scotland Yard sooner or later. That's how so many got caught.'

'And you?'

'Criminals on the run or needing a rest when things get too hot have places they can go, Father. Expensive places, I admit, but safe and that's what I used. There was one in Scotland south from Glasgow in Galloway run by a couple of brothers called Mungo. What you might call a country retreat. Absolute bastards, mind you.'

The pain was suddenly so bad that he had to fight for breath. 'I'll get sister,' Cussane told him in alarm.

Malone grabbed him by the front of his cassock. 'No, you damn well won't. No more painkillers, Father. They mean well, the sisters, but enough is enough. Let's just keep talking.'

'All right,' Harry Cussane said. Malone lay back, closed his eyes for a moment, then opened them again. 'Anyway, as I was saying, these Mungo brothers, Hector and Angus, were the great original bastards.'

Devlin paced up and down the room restlessly. 'Do you believe it?' Fox asked.

'It makes sense and it would explain a great deal,' Devlin said. 'So let's just say I accept it in principle.'

'So, what do we do about it?'

'What do *we* do about it?' Devlin glared at him. 'The effrontery of the man. Let me remind you, Harry, that the last time I did a job for Ferguson, the bastard conned me. Lied in his teeth. Used me.'

'That was then, this is now, Liam.'

'And what is that pearl of wisdom supposed to mean?'

There was a soft tapping at the French window. Devlin opened the desk drawer, took out an old-fashioned Mauser pistol, with an SS bulbous silencer on the end and cocked it. He nodded to Fox, then Devlin pulled the curtain. Martin McGuiness peered in at them, Murphy at his shoulder.

'Dear God!' Devlin groaned.

He opened the French window and McGuiness smiled as he stepped in. 'God bless all here!' he said mockingly and added to Murphy, 'Watch the window, Michael.' He closed it and walked over to the fire, holding his hands to the warmth. 'Colder as the nights draw in.'

'What do you want?' Devlin demanded.

'Has the Captain here explained the situation to you yet?'

'He has.'

'And what do you think?'

'I don't think at all,' Devlin told him. 'Especially where you lot are concerned.'

'The purpose of terrorism is to terrorize, that's what Mick Collins used to say,' McGuiness told him. 'I fight for my country, Liam, with anything that comes to hand. We're at war.' He was angry now. 'I've got nothing to apologize for.'

'If I could say something,' Fox put in. 'Let's accept that Cuchulain exists, then it isn't a question of taking sides. It's accepting that what he's doing has needlessly protracted the tragic events of the past thirteen years.'

McGuiness helped himself to a whiskey. 'He has a point. When I was O.C. Derry in nineteen seventy-two, I was flown to London with Daithi O'Connell, Seamus Twomey, Ivor Bell and others to meet Willie Whitelaw to discuss peace.'

'And the Lenadoon shooting broke the cease-fire,' Fox said and turned to Devlin. 'It doesn't seem to me to be a question of taking sides any more. Cuchulain has worked deliberately to keep the whole rotten mess going. I would have thought anything that might have helped stop that would be worth it.'

'Morality is it?' Devlin raised a hand and smiled wickedly.

'Good then, let's get down to brass tacks. This fella, Levin, who actually saw Kelly or Cuchulain or whatever his name is, all those years ago. I presume Ferguson is showing him pictures of every known KGB operative.'

'And all known adherents of the IRA, UDA, UVF. Anything and everything,' Fox said. 'That will include looking at what Special Branch in Dublin have because we swop information.'

'The bastards would,' McGuiness said bitterly. 'Still, I think we've got a few that neither the police in Dublin nor your people in London have ever seen.'

'And how do we handle that?' Fox demanded.

'You get Levin over here and he and Devlin look at what we've got – no one else. Is it agreed?'

Fox glanced at Devlin who nodded. 'Okay,' Fox said. 'I'll ring the Brigadier tonight.'

'Fine.' McGuiness turned to Devlin. 'You're sure your phone's not tapped or anything like that. I'm thinking of those Special Branch bastards.'

Devlin opened a drawer in the desk and produced a black metal box which he switched on so that a red light appeared. He approached the telephone and held the box over it. There was no reaction.

'Oh, the wonders of the electronic age,' he said and put the box away.

'Fine,' McGuiness said. 'The only people who know about this are Ferguson, you, Captain, Liam, the Chief of Staff and myself.'

'And Professor Paul Cherny,' Fox said.

McGuiness nodded. 'That's right. We've got to do something about him.' He turned to Devlin. 'Do you know him?'

'I've seen him at drinks parties at the university. Exchanged a civil word, no more than that. He's well liked. A widower. His wife died before he defected. There's a chance he isn't involved in this, of course.'

'And pigs might fly,' McGuiness said crisply. 'The fact that it was Ireland he defected to is too much of a coincidence for me. A pound to a penny he knows our man, so why don't we pull him in and squeeze it out of him?'

'Simple,' Fox told him. 'Some men don't squeeze.'

'He's right,' Devlin said. 'Better to try the softly-softly approach first.'

'All right,' McGuiness said. 'I'll have him watched twenty-four hours a day. Put Michael Murphy in charge. He won't be able to go to the bathroom without we know it.'

Devlin glanced at Fox. 'Okay by you?'

'Fine,' Fox told him.

'Good.' McGuiness buttoned his raincoat. 'I'll get off then. I'll leave Billy to look after you, Captain.' He opened the French window. 'Mind your back, Liam.' And then he was gone.

Ferguson was in bed when Fox phoned, sitting up against the pillows, working his way through a mass of papers, preparing himself for a Defence committee meeting the following day. He listened patiently to everything Fox had to say. 'So far, so good, Harry, as far as I can see. Levin spent the entire day working through everything we had at the Directorate. Didn't come up with a thing.'

'It's been a long time, sir. Cuchulain could have changed a lot and not just because he's older. I mean, he could have a beard, for example.'

'Negative thinking, Harry. I'll put Levin on the morning flight to Dublin, but Devlin will have to handle him. I need you back here.'

'Any particular reason, sir?'

'Lots to do with the Vatican. It really is beginning to look as if the Pope won't come. However, he's invited the cardinals of Argentina and Britain to confer with him.'

'So the visit could still be on?'

'Perhaps, but more important from our point of view, the war is still on and there's talk of the Argentinians trying to get hold of this damned Exocet missile on the European black market. I need you, Harry. Catch the first flight out. By the way, an interesting development. Tanya Voroninova, remember her?'

'Of course, sir.'

'She's in Paris to give a series of concerts. Fascinating that she should surface at this particular moment.'

'What Jung would call synchronicity, sir?'

'Young, Harry? What on earth are you babbling about?'

'Carl Jung, sir. Famous psychologist. Synchronicity is a word he coined for events having a coincidence in time and, because of this, the feeling that some deeper motivation is involved.'

'The fact that you're in Ireland is no excuse for acting as if you've gone soft in the head, Harry,' Ferguson said testily.

He put down the phone, sat there thinking, then got up, pulled on his robe and went out. He knocked on the door of the guest room and went in. Levin was sitting up in bed wearing a pair of Ferguson's pyjamas and reading a book.

Ferguson sat on the edge of the bed. 'I thought you'd be tired after going through so many photos.'

Levin smiled. 'When you reach my age, Brigadier, sleep eludes you, memory crowds in. You wonder what it has all been about.'

Ferguson warmed to the man. 'Don't we all, my dear chap? Anyway, how would you feel about running over to Dublin on the morning plane?'

'To see Captain Fox?'

'No, he'll be returning here, but a friend of mine, Professor Liam Devlin of Trinity College, will take care of you. He'll probably be showing you a few more photos, courtesy of our friends in the IRA. They'd never let me have them for obvious reasons.'

The old Russian shook his head. 'Tell me, Brigadier, did the war to end all wars finish in nineteen forty-five or am I mistaken?'

'You and a great many other people, my friend.' Ferguson got up and went to the door. 'I'd get some sleep if I were you. You'll need to be up at six to catch the early morning flight from Heathrow. I'll have Kim serve you breakfast in bed.'

He closed the door. Levin sat there for a while, an expression of sadness on his face, then he sighed, closed the book, turned out the light and went to sleep.

At Kilrea Cottage, Fox put down the phone and turned to Devlin. 'All fixed. He'll come in on the breakfast plane. Unfortunately, my flight leaves just before. He'll report to the information desk in the main concourse. You can pick him up there.'

'No need,' Devlin said. 'This minder of yours, young White. He'll be dropping you so he can pick Levin up at the same time and bring him straight here. It's best we do it that way. McGuiness might be in touch early about where I'm supposed to take him.'

'Fine,' Fox said. 'I'd better get moving.'

'Good lad.'

Devlin got his coat for him and took him out to the car where Billy White waited patiently.

'Back to the Westbourne, Billy,' Fox said.

Devlin leaned down at the window. 'Book yourself in there for the night, son, and in the morning, do exactly what the Captain tells you to. Let him down by a single inch and I'll have your balls and Martin McGuiness will probably walk all over the rest of you.'

Billy White grinned affably. 'Sure and on a good day, they tell me I can almost shoot as well as you, Mr Devlin.'

'Go on, be off with you.'

The car moved away. Devlin watched it go, then turned and went inside. There was a stirring in the shrubbery, a footfall, the faintest of sounds only as someone moved away.

The eavesdropping equipment which the KGB had supplied to Cuchulain was the most advanced in the world, developed originally by a Japanese company, the details, as a result of industrial espionage, having reached Moscow four years previously. The directional microphone trained on Kilrea Cottage could pick up every word uttered inside at several hundred yards. Its ultra-frequency secondary function was to catch even the faintest telephone conversation. All this was allied to a sophisticated recording apparatus.

The whole was situated in a small attic concealed behind the loft watertanks just beneath the pantile roof of the house. Cuchulain had listened in on Liam Devlin in this way for a long time now, although it had been some time since anything so interesting had come up. He sat in the attic, smoking a cigarette, running the tape at top speed through the blank spots and the unimportant bits, paying careful attention to the phone conversation with Ferguson.

Afterwards, he sat there thinking about it for a while, then he reset the tape, went downstairs and let himself out. He went into the phone box at the end of the village street by the pub and dialled a Dublin number. The phone was picked up almost immediately. He could hear voices, a sudden laugh, Mozart playing softly.

'Cherny here.'

'It's me. You're not alone?'

Cherny laughed lightly. 'Dinner party for a few faculty friends.'

'I must see you.'

'All right,' Cherny said. 'Usual time and place tomorrow afternoon.'

Cuchulain replaced the receiver, left the booth and went back up the village street, whistling softly, an old Connemara folk song that had all the despair, all the sadness of life in it.

5

Fox had a thoroughly bad night and slept little so that he was restless and ill-at-ease as Billy White took the car expertly through the early morning traffic towards the airport. The young Irishman was cheerful enough as he tapped his fingers on the steering wheel in time to the music from the radio.

'Will you be back, Captain?'

'I don't know. Perhaps.'

'Ah, well, I don't expect you to be over fond of the ould country.' White nodded towards Fox's gloved hand. 'Not after what it's cost you.'

'Is that so?' Fox said.

Billy lit a cigarette. 'The trouble with you Brits is that you never face up to the fact that Ireland's a foreign country. Just because we speak English . . .'

'As a matter of interest, my mother's name was Fitzgerald and she came from County Mayo,' Fox told him. 'She worked for the Gaelic League, was a lifelong friend of de Valera and spoke excellent Irish, a rather difficult language I found when she insisted on teaching it to me when I was a boy. Do you speak Irish, Billy?'

'God save us, but I don't, Captain,' White said in astonishment.

'Well, then I suggest you kindly stop prattling on about the English being unable to understand the Irish.'

He glanced out at the traffic morosely. A police motorcyclist took up station on the left of them, a sinister figure in goggles and crash helmet with a heavy caped raincoat against the early morning downpour. He glanced sideways at Fox once, anonymous in the dark goggles, and dropped back as they turned into the slip road leading to the airport.

Billy left the car in the short stay park. As they entered the concourse, they were already calling Fox's plane. Cuchulain, who had been with them all the way from the hotel, stood at the door by which they had entered and watched Fox book in.

Fox and Billy walked towards the departure gate and Fox said, 'An hour till the British Airways flight lands.'

'Time for a big breakfast,' Billy grinned. 'The fine time we had, Captain.'

'I'll be seeing you, Billy.'

Fox put out his good hand and Billy White took it with a certain reluctance. 'Try to make sure it isn't at the wrong end of some street in Belfast. I'd hate to have you in my sights, Captain.'

Fox went through the gate and Billy made his way across the concourse to stairs leading up to the café terrace. Cuchulain watched him go, then went out, back across the road to the carpark and waited.

An hour later, he was back inside, consulting the nearest arrival screen. The British Airways shuttle from London was just landing and he saw White approach the central information desk and speak to one of the attendants. There was a pause and then an announcement over the tannoy system.

'Will Mr Viktor Levin, a passenger on the London shuttle, please report to the information desk.'

A few moments later, the squat figure of the Russian appeared from the crowd. He carried a small case and wore a rather large brown raincoat and black trilby hat. Cuchulain sensed that it was his quarry even before he spoke to one of the attendants who indicated White. They shook hands. Cuchulain watched them for a moment longer as White started to speak, then turned and left.

'So this is Ireland?' Levin said as they drove down towards the city.

'Your first visit?' White asked.

'Oh, yes. I am from Russia. I have not travelled abroad very much.'

'Russia?' Billy said. 'Jesus, but you'll find it different here.'

'And this is Dublin?' Levin enquired as they followed the traffic down into the city.

'Yes. Kilrea, where we're going, is on the other side.'

'A city of significant history, I think,' Levin observed.

'And that's the understatement of the age,' White told him. 'I'll take you through Parnell Square, it's on our way. A great patriot in spite of being a bloody Prod. And then O'Connell Street and the General Post Office where the boys held out against the whole bloody British Army back in 1916.'

'Good. This I would like very much.' Levin leaned back in his seat and looked out on the passing scene with interest.

At Kilrea, Liam Devlin walked across the back lawn of his cottage, let himself through the gate in the wall and ran for the rear entrance of the hospice as the rain increased into a sudden downpour. Sister Anne-Marie was crossing the hall, accompanied by two young white-coated interns on loan from University College, Dublin.

She was a small, sparse little woman, very fit for her seventy years, and wore a white smock over her nun's robe. She had a doctorate in medicine from the University of London and was a Fellow of the Royal College of Physicians. A lady to be reckoned with. She and Devlin were old adversaries. She had once been French, but that was a long time ago as he was fond of reminding her.

'And what can we do for you, Professor?' she demanded.

'You say that as if to the Devil coming through the door,' Devlin told her.

'An observation of stunning accuracy.'

They started up the stairs and Devlin said, 'Danny Malone – how is he?'

'Dying,' she said calmly. 'Peacefully, I hope. He is one of those patients who responds well to our drug programme which means that pain is only intermittent.'

They reached the first of the open plan wards. Devlin said, 'When?'

'This afternoon, tomorrow – next week.' She shrugged. 'He is a fighter, that one.'

'That's true,' Devlin said. 'Big for the cause all his life, Danny.'

'Father Cussane comes in every night,' she said, 'and sits and lets him talk through this violent past of his. I think it troubles him now that he nears his end. The IRA, the killing.'

'Is it all right if I sit with him for a while?'

'Half-an-hour,' she said firmly and moved away followed by the interns.

Malone seemed to sleep, eyes closed, the skin tight on the facial bones, yellow as parchment. His fingers gripped the edge of a sheet tightly.

Devlin sat down. 'Are you there, Danny?'

'Ah, there you are, Father.' Malone opened his eyes, focused weakly and frowned. 'Liam, is that you?'

'None other.'

'I thought it was Father Cussane. We were just talking.'

'Last night, Danny. You must have fallen asleep. Sure and you know he works in Dublin at the Secretariat during the day.'

Malone licked dry lips. 'God, but I could do with a cup of tea.'
'Let's see if I can get you one,' Devlin got up.

As he did so, there was a sudden commotion on the lower level, voices shouting, drifting up. He frowned and hurried forward to the head of the stairs.

Billy White turned off the main highway on to the narrow road, flanked by fir plantations on either side, that led to Kilrea. 'Not long now.' He half-turned to speak to Levin behind him and noticed, through the rear window, a *Gardai* motorcyclist turn off the main road behind them.

He started to slow and Levin said, 'What is it?'

'Gardai,' Billy told him. 'Police to you. One mile over the limit and they'll book you, those sods.'

The police motorcyclist pulled up alongside and waved them down. With his dark goggles and helmet, White could see nothing of him at all. He pulled in at the side of the road angrily. 'And what in hell does this fella want? I wasn't doing an inch over thirty miles an hour.'

The animal instinct which had protected his life for many years of violence made him wary enough to have his hand on the butt of the revolver in the left pocket of his raincoat as he got out of the car. The policeman pushed the motorcycle up on to its stand. He took off his gloves and turned, his raincoat very wet.

'And what can we do you for, officer, on this fine morning?' Billy asked insolently.

The policeman's hand came out of the right pocket of his raincoat holding a Walther, a Carswell silencer screwed on the end of the barrel. White recognized all this in the last moment of his violent life as he frantically attempted to draw his revolver. The bullet ripped into his heart, knocking him back against the car. He bounced off and fell on his face in the road.

In the rear seat, Levin was paralysed with horror, yet he was not afraid for there was an inevitability to all this as if it was somehow ordained. The policeman opened the door and looked in. He paused, then pushed up the goggles.

Levin gazed at him in astonishment. 'Dear God in heaven,' he whispered in Russian. 'It's you.'

'Yes,' Cuchulain answered in the same language. 'I'm afraid it is,' and he shot him in the head, the Walther making no more than an angry cough.

He pocketed the weapon, walked back to the bike, pulled it off its stand and rode away. It was no more than five minutes later that a van making morning deliveries of bread to the village came across the carnage. The driver and his assistant got out of their van and approached the scene with trepidation. The driver leaned down to look at White. There was a slight groan from the rear of the car and he glanced inside quickly.

'My God!' he cried. 'There's another in here and he's still alive. Take the van and get down to the village quick as you like and fetch the ambulance from the hospice.'

When Devlin reached the foyer, they were pushing Viktor Levin on a trolley into the receiving room.

'Sister Anne-Marie's on Ward Three. She'll be right down,' he heard one of the ambulancemen tell the young sister in charge. The driver of the bread van stood there helplessly, blood on one sleeve of his overall coat. He was shaking badly. Devlin lit a cigarette and handed it to him. 'What happened?'

'God knows. We found this car a couple of miles up the road. One was dead beside it and him in the back. They're bringing the other in now.'

As Devlin, filled with a terrible premonition, turned towards the door, the ambulancemen hurried in with Billy White's body, his face plain to see. The young sister came out of the receiving room and went next door to check White. Devlin stepped in quickly and approached the trolley on which Levin still lay, moaning softly, blood congealing in a terrible head wound.

Devlin leaned down. 'Professor Levin, can you hear me?' Levin opened his eyes. 'I am Liam Devlin. What happened?'

Levin tried to speak, reached out one hand and got hold of the lapel of Devlin's jacket. 'I recognized him. He's here.'

His eyes rolled, there was a rattle in his throat and as his grip slackened, Sister Anne-Marie hurried in. She pushed Devlin to one side and leaned over Levin, searching for a pulse. After a while, she stepped back. 'You know this man?'

'No,' Devlin told her, which was true in a sense.

'Not that it would matter if you did,' she said. 'He's dead. A miracle he didn't die instantly with a head wound like that.'

She brushed past him and went next door where they had taken

White. Devlin stood looking down at Levin, thinking of what Fox had told him of the old man, of the years of waiting to get out. And this was how it had ended. He felt angry, then, at the brutal black humour of life that could allow such a thing to happen.

Harry Fox had only just arrived back at Cavendish Square, had hardly got his coat off, when the phone rang. Ferguson listened, face grave, then placed a hand over the mouthpiece. 'Liam Devlin. It seems the car with your man, Billy White, and Levin was ambushed just outside Kilrea. White was killed instantly, Levin died later in the hospice at Kilrea.'

Fox said, 'Did Liam get to see him?'

'Yes. Levin told him it was Cuchulain. That he recognized him.'

Fox threw his coat on the nearest chair. 'But I don't understand, sir.'

'Neither do I, Harry.' Ferguson spoke into the mouthpiece, 'I'll get back to you, Devlin.'

He put the receiver down and turned, hands out to the fire. Fox said, 'It doesn't make sense. How would he have known?'

'Some sort of leak, Harry, at the IRA end of things. They never keep their mouths shut.'

'The thing is, sir, what do we do about it?'

'More important, what do we do about Cuchulain?' Ferguson said. 'That gentleman is really beginning to annoy me.'

'But there isn't much we can do now, not with Levin gone. After all, he was the only person who had any idea what the bastard looked like.'

'Actually, that isn't quite true.' Ferguson said. 'You're forgetting Tanya Voraninova, who at this precise moment is in Paris. Ten days, four concerts, and that opens up a very interesting possibility.'

About the same time, Harry Cussane was at his desk in the press office of the Catholic Secretariat in Dublin talking to Monsignor Halloran who was responsible for public relations.

From his comfortable chair, Halloran said, 'It's a terrible thing that such a significantly historical event as the Holy Father's visit to England should be put in such jeopardy. Just think of it, Harry, His Holiness at Canterbury Cathedral. The first Pope in history to visit it. And now . . .'

'You think it won't come off?' Cussane asked.

'Well, they're still talking away in Rome, but that's how it looks to me. Why, do you know something I don't?'

'No,' Cussane told him. He picked up a typed sheet. 'I've had this from London. His planned itinerary, so they are still acting as if he's coming.' He ran an eye over it. 'Arrives on the morning of 28th May at Gatwick Airport. Mass at Westminster Cathedral in London. Meets the Queen at Buckingham Palace in the afternoon.'

'And Canterbury?'

'That's the following day – Saturday. He starts early with a meeting with religious at a London college. Mainly monks and nuns from enclosed orders. Then by helicopter to Canterbury, stopping at Stokely Hall on the way. That's unofficial, by the way.'

'For what reason?'

'The Stokelys were one of the great Catholic families that managed to survive Henry VIII and hung on to their faith over the centuries. The National Trust own the house now, but it contains a unique feature: the family's private chapel. The oldest Catholic church of any description in England. His Holiness wishes to pray there. Afterwards, Canterbury.'

'All of which, at the moment, is on paper only,' Halloran said.

The phone rang. Cussane picked it up. 'Press office. Cussane here.' His face grew grave. He said, 'Is there anything I can do?' A pause. 'I'll see you later then.'

Halloran said, 'Problems?'

Cussane replaced the receiver. 'A friend from Kilrea. Liam Devlin of Trinity College. It seems there's been a shooting incident outside the village. Two men taken to the hospice. Both dead.'

Halloran crossed himself. 'Political, is it?'

'One of them was a known member of the IRA.'

'Will you be needed? Go if you must.'

'Not necessary.' Cussane smiled bleakly. 'They need a coroner now, Monsignor, not a priest. I've plenty to do here anyway.'

'Yes, of course. Well, I'll leave you to it.'

Halloran went out and Cussane lit a cigarette and went and stood at the window looking down into the street. Finally, he turned, sat at his desk and got on with some work.

Paul Cherny had rooms at Trinity College which being, as so many people considered, at the centre of Dublin, suited him very well indeed.

But then, everything about that extraordinary city commended itself to him.

His defection had been at Maslovsky's express orders. A KGB general was not to be argued with. He was to defect in Ireland, that had been the plan. One of the universities was certain to offer him a post, his international reputation would assure that. He would then be in a perfect position to act as Cuchulain's control. Difficult in the early days with no Soviet Embassy in Dublin and the necessity always to work through London, but now that had been taken care of and his KGB contacts at the Dublin embassy gave him a direct link with Moscow.

Yes, the years had been good and Dublin was the kind of paradise he'd always dreamed of. Intellectual freedom, stimulating company and the city – the city he had grown to love. He was thinking these things as he left Trinity that afternoon, walked through College Green, and made towards the river.

Michael Murphy followed at a discreet distance and Cherny, unaware that he was being tailed, walked briskly along beside the Liffey until he reached Usher's Quay. There was a rather ugly Victorian church in red brick and he moved up the steps and went inside. Murphy paused to examine the board with the peeling gold paint. It said Our Lady, Queen of the Universe. Underneath were the times of Mass. Confessions were heard at one o'clock and five on weekdays. Murphy pushed open the door and entered.

It was the sort of place that merchant money had been poured into back in the prosperous days of the Quays during the nineteenth century. There was lots of Victorian stained glass and fake gargoyles and the usual smell of candles and incense. Half-a-dozen people waited by a couple of confessional boxes and Paul Cherny joined them, seating himself on the end of the bench.

'Jesus!' Murphy muttered in surprise. 'The bugger must have seen the light.' He positioned himself behind a pillar and waited.

It was fifteen or twenty minutes before Cherny's turn came. He slipped into the oaken confessional box, closed the door and sat down, his head close to the grill.

'Bless me, Father, for I have sinned,' he said in Russian.

'Very funny, Paul,' the reply came from the other side of the grill in the same language. 'Now let's see if you can still smile when you've heard what I've got to say.'

When Cuchulain was finished, Cherny said, 'What are we going to do?'

'No need to panic. They don't know who I am and they aren't likely to find out now that I've disposed of Levin.'

'But me?' Cherny said. 'If Levin told them about Drumore all those years ago, he must have told them of my part in it.'

'Of course. You're under surveillance now. IRA variety, not British Intelligence, so I wouldn't worry just yet. Get in touch with Moscow. Maslovsky should know about this. He might want to pull us out. I'll phone you again tonight. And don't start worrying about your tail. I'll take care of it.'

Cherny went out and Cuchulain watched through a crack in the door as Michael Murphy slipped from behind the pillar and followed him. There was a bang as the sacristy door opened and shut and an old cleaning woman came down the aisle as the priest in alb and black cassock, a violet stole around his shoulders, came out of the confessional box.

'Are you finished, Father?'

'I am so, Ellie.' Harry Cussane turned, a smile of great charm on his face as he slipped off the stole and started folding it.

Murphy, with no reason to think that Cherny was doing anything other than return to college, stayed some distance behind him. Cherny stopped and entered a telephone box. He wasn't in it for long and Murphy, who had paused under a tree as if sheltering from the rain, went after him again.

A car drew into the kerb in front of him and the driver, a priest, got out, went round and looked at the nearside front tyre. He turned and catching sight of Murphy, said, 'Have you got a minute?'

Murphy slowed, protesting, 'I'm sorry, Father, but I've an appointment.'

And then the priest's hand was on his arm and Murphy felt the muzzle of the Walther dig painfully into his side. 'Easy does it, there's a lad. Just keep walking.'

Cussane pushed him to the top of stone steps that went down to a decaying wooden jetty below. They moved along its broken planks, footsteps echoing hollowly. There was a boathouse with a broken roof, holes in the floor. Murphy wasn't afraid, but ready for action, waiting his chance.

'That'll do,' Cussane said.

Murphy stayed, his back towards him, one hand on the butt of the automatic in his raincoat pocket. 'Are you a real priest?' he asked.

'Oh, yes,' Cussane told him. 'Not a very good one, I'm afraid, but real enough.'

Murphy turned slowly. His hand came up out of the raincoat, already too late. The Walther coughed twice, and the bullet caught Murphy in the shoulder spinning him around. The second bullet drove him headfirst into a ragged hole in the floor and he plunged down into the dark water below.

Dimitri Lubov, who was supposedly a commercial attaché at the Soviet Embassy, was, in fact, a captain in the KGB. On receiving Cherny's carefully worded message, he left his office and went to a cinema in the city centre. It was not only relatively dark in there, but reasonably private, for few people went to the cinema in the afternoon. He sat in the back row and waited and Cherny joined him twenty minutes later.

'Is it urgent, Paul?' Lubov said. 'Not often we meet between fixed days.'

'Urgent enough,' Cherny said. 'Cuchulain is blown. Maslovsky must be informed as soon as possible. He may want to pull us out.'

'Of course,' Lubov said, alarmed. 'I'll see to it as soon as I get back, but hadn't you better fill me in on the details?'

Devlin was working in his study at the cottage, marking a thesis on T. S. Eliot submitted by one of his students, when the phone rang.

Ferguson said, 'It's a fine bloody mess. Someone must have coughed at your end. Your IRA cronies are not exactly the most reliable people in the world.'

'Sticks and stones will get you nowhere,' Devlin told him. 'What do you want?'

'Tanya Voroninova,' Ferguson said. 'Harry told you about her?'

'The little girl from Drumore who was adopted by this Maslovsky character. What about her?'

'She's in Paris at the moment to give a series of piano concerts. The thing is, being foster-daughter to a KGB general gives her a lot of leeway. I mean, she's considered an excellent risk. I thought you might go and see her. There's an evening flight from Dublin direct to Paris. Only two and a half hours, Air France.'

'And what in the hell am I supposed to do? Get her to defect?'

'You never know. When she hears the whole story, she might want to. See her anyway, Liam. It can't do any harm.'

'All right,' Devlin said. 'A little breath of French air might do me good.'

'I knew you'd see it my way,' Ferguson said. 'Report to the Air France desk at Dublin Airport. They've got a reservation. When you arrive at Charles de Gaulle, you'll be met by one of my chaps based in Paris. Fella called Hunter – Tony Hunter. He'll see to everything.'

'I'm sure he will,' Devlin said and rang off.

He packed a bag quickly, feeling unaccountably cheerful and was just pulling on his trenchcoat when the phone went again. It was Martin McGuiness. 'A bad business, Liam. What exactly happened?'

Devlin told him and when he was finished, McGuiness exploded. 'So, he exists, this bastard?'

'It would appear so, but more worrying from your point of view is, how did he know Levin was due in? The one man who might be able to identify him.'

'Why ask me?'

'Because Ferguson thinks there's been a leak at your end.'

'Well, screw Ferguson.'

'I wouldn't advise it, Martin. Listen, I've got to go. I've a flight to Paris to catch.'

'Paris? What's there, for Christ's sake?'

'A girl called Tanya Voroninova who might be able to identify Cuchulain. I'll be in touch.'

He put down the receiver. As he picked up his bag, there was a tap on the French windows. They opened and Harry Cussane entered.

Devlin said, 'Sorry, Harry, I must fly or I'll miss my plane.'

'Where on earth are you going?' Cussane demanded.

'Paris.' Devlin grinned and opened the front door. 'Champagne, loose women, incredible food. Don't you think it's just possible you joined the wrong club, Harry?'

The door banged. Cussane listened to the engine of the car start up, turned and ran out through the French windows, round to his cottage at the back of the hospice. He hurried upstairs to the secret room behind the water tanks in the roof where he had the eavesdropping equipment. Quickly, he ran back the tape and listened to the various conversations

Devlin had had that day until he came, in the end, to the important one.

By then, of course, it was too late. He cursed softly, went down to use the phone and rang Paul Cherny's number.

6

In the sacristy of the village church as he robed for evening Mass, Cussane examined himself in the mirror. Like an actor getting ready for a performance. Next thing, he'd be reaching for the make-up. Who am I, he thought? Who am I, really? Cuchulain, mass murderer, or Harry Cussane, priest? Mikhail Kelly didn't seem to enter into it any more. Only an echo of him now like a half-forgotten dream.

For more than twenty years he had lived multiple lives and yet the separate personae had never inhabited his body. They were roles to be played out as the script dictated, then discarded.

He slipped the stole around his neck and whispered to his *alter ego* in the mirror, 'In God's House I am God's priest,' and he turned and went out.

Later, standing at the altar with the candles flickering and the organ playing, there was genuine passion in his voice as he cried, 'I confess to Almighty God and to you, my brothers and sisters, that I have sinned through my own fault.'

And when he struck his breast, asking blessed Mary ever Virgin to pray for him to the Lord our God, there were sudden hot tears in his eyes.

At Charles de Gaulle Airport, Tony Hunter waited beside the exit from customs and immigration. He was a tall man in his mid-thirties with stooped shoulders. The soft brown hair was too long, the tan linen suit creased, and he smoked a Gitane cigarette without once taking it from his mouth as he read *Paris Soir* and kept an eye on the exit. After a while, Devlin appeared. He wore a black Burberry trenchcoat, an old black felt hat slanted over one ear, and carried one bag.

Hunter, who had pulled Devlin's photo and description off the wire, went to meet him. 'Professor Devlin? Tony Hunter. I've got a car waiting.' They walked towards the exit. 'Was it a good flight?'

'There's no such thing,' Devlin told him. 'About a thousand years ago, I flew from Germany to Ireland in a Dornier bomber on behalf of

England's enemies and jumped by parachute from six thousand feet. I've never got over it.'

They reached Hunter's Peugeot in the car park and as they drove away, Hunter said, 'You can stay the night with me. I've got an apartment on the Avenue Foch.'

'Doing well for yourself, son, if you're living there. I didn't know Ferguson handed out bags of gold.'

'You know Paris well?'

'You could say that.'

'The apartment's my own, not the Department's. My father died last year. Left me rather well off.'

'What about the girl? Is she staying at the Soviet Embassy?'

'Good God, no. They've got her at the Ritz. She's something of a star, you see. Plays rather well. I heard her do a Mozart concerto the other night. Forgotten which one, but she was excellent.'

'They tell me she's free to come and go?'

'Oh, yes, absolutely. The fact that her foster father is General Maslovsky takes care of that. I followed her all over the place this morning. Luxembourg Gardens, then lunch on one of those boat trips down the Seine. From what I hear, her only commitment tomorrow is a rehearsal at the Conservatoire during the afternoon.'

'Which means the morning is the time to make contact?'

'I should have thought so.' They were well into Paris by now, just passing the Gare du Nord. Hunter added, 'There's a bagman due in from London on the breakfast shuttle with documentation Ferguson's having rushed through. Forged passport. Stuff like that.'

Devlin laughed out loud. 'Does he think all I have to do is ask and she'll come?' He shook his head. 'Mad, that one.'

'All in how it's put to her,' Hunter suggested.

'True,' Devlin told him. 'On the other hand, it would probably be a damned sight easier to slip something in her tea.'

It was Hunter's turn to laugh now. 'You know, I like you, Professor, and I'd started off by not wanting to.'

'And why could that be?' Devlin wondered, interested.

'I was a captain in the Rifle Brigade. Belfast, Derry, South Armagh.'

'Ah, I see what you mean.'

'Four tours between nineteen seventy-two and seventy-eight.'

'And that was four tours too many.'

'Exactly. Frankly, as far as I'm concerned, they can give Ulster back to the Indians.'

'The best idea I've heard tonight,' Liam Devlin told him cheerfully and he lit a cigarette and sprawled back in the passenger seat, felt hat tilted over his eyes.

At that moment in his office at KGB Headquarters in Dzerhinsky Square, Lieutenant-General Ivan Maslovsky was seated at his desk, thinking about the Cuchulain affair. Cherny's message passed on by Lubov, had reached Moscow only a couple of hours earlier. For some reason it made him think back all those years to Drumore in the Ukraine and Kelly in the rain with a gun in his hand, the man who wouldn't do as he was told.

The door opened and his aide, Captain Igor Kurbsky, came in with a cup of coffee for him. Maslovsky drank it slowly. 'Well, Igor, what do you think?'

'I think Cuchulain has done a magnificent job, Comrade General, for so very many years. But now . . .'

'I know what you mean,' Maslovsky said. 'Now that British Intelligence knows he exists it's only a matter of time until they run him down.'

'And Cherny they could pull in at any time.'

There was a knock at the door and an orderly appeared with a signal message. Kurbsky took it and dismissed him. 'It's for you, sir. From Lubov in Dublin.'

'Read it!' Maslovsky ordered.

The gist of the message was that Devlin was proceeding to Paris with the intention of meeting with Tanya Voroninova. At the mention of his foster-daughter's name, Maslovsky stood up and snatched the signal from Kurbsky's hands. It was no secret, the enormous affection the General felt for his foster-daughter, especially since the death of his wife. In some quarters he was known as a butcher, but Tanya Voroninova he truly loved.

'Right,' he said to Kurbsky. 'Who's our best man at the Paris Embassy? Belov, isn't it?'

'Yes, Comrade.'

'Send a message tonight. Tanya's concert tour is cancelled. No arguments. Full security as regards her person until she can be returned safely to Moscow.'

'And Cuchulain?'

'Has served his purpose. A great pity.'

'Do we pull him in?'

'No, not enough time. This one needs instant action. Signal Lubov at once in Dublin. I want Cuchulain eliminated. Cherny also, and the sooner the better.'

'If I might point out, I don't think Lubov has had much experience on the wet side of things.'

'He's had the usual training, hasn't he? In any case, they won't be expecting it which should make the whole thing rather easier.'

In Paris, the coding machine in the intelligence section of the Soviet Embassy started whirring. The operator waited until the message had passed line-by-line across the screen. She carefully unloaded the magnetic tape which had recorded the message and took it to the night supervisor.

'This is an Eyes Only signal from KGB, Moscow, for Colonel Belov.'

'He's out of town,' the supervisor said. 'Lyons, I think. Due back tomorrow afternoon. You'll have to hold it anyway. It requires his personal key to decode it.'

The operator logged the tape, placed it in her data drawer and went back to work.

In Dublin, Dimitri Lubov had been enjoying an evening at the Abbey Theatre, an excellent performance of Brendan Behan's *The Hostage*. Supper afterwards at a well known fish restaurant on the Quays meant that it was past midnight when he returned to the Embassy and found the signal from Moscow.

Even when he'd read it for the third time, he still couldn't believe it. He was to dispose not only of Cherny, but Cussane, and within the next twenty-four hours. His hands were sweating, trembling slightly, which was hardly surprising for in spite of his years in the KGB and all that dedicated training, the plain fact was that Dimitri Lubov had never killed anyone in his life.

Tanya Voroninova came out of the bathroom of her suite at the Ritz as the room waiter brought her breakfast tray in; tea, toast and honey, which was exactly what she'd asked for. She wore a khaki-green jumpsuit and brown boots of soft leather and the combination gave her a vaguely military appearance. She was a small, dark, intense girl with untidy black hair which she constantly had to push back from her eyes. She regarded it with disfavour in the gilt mirror above the fireplace and twisted it into a bun at the nape of her neck, then she sat down and started on breakfast.

There was a knock on the door and her tour secretary, Natasha Rubenova came in. She was a pleasant, grey-haired woman in her mid-forties. 'How are you feeling this morning?'

'Fine. I slept very well.'

'Good. You're wanted at the Conservatoire at two-thirty. Complete run-through.'

'No problem,' Tanya said.

'Are you going out this morning?'

'Yes, I'd like to spend some time at the Louvre. We've been so busy during this visit that it might be my last opportunity.'

'Do you want me to come with you?'

'No thanks. I'll be fine. I'll see you back here for lunch at one o'clock.'

It was a fine soft morning when she left the hotel and went down the steps at the front entrance. Devlin and Hunter were waiting in the Peugeot on the far side of the boulevard.

'Looks as if she's walking,' Hunter said.

Devlin nodded. 'Follow her for a while then we'll see.'

Tanya carried a canvas bag slung from her left shoulder and she walked at quite a fast pace, enjoying the exercise. She was playing Rachmaninov's Fourth Piano Concerto that night. The piece was a particular favourite so that she had none of the usual nervous tension that she sometimes experienced, like most artists, before a big concert.

But then, she was something of an old hand at the game now. Since her successes in both the Leeds and Tchaikovsky festivals she had steadily established an international reputation. There had been little time for anything else. On the one occasion she had fallen in love, she'd been foolish enough to choose a young military doctor on attachment to an airborne brigade. He'd been killed in action in Afghanistan the year before.

The experience, though harrowing, had not broken her. She had given one of her greatest performances on the night that she had received the news, but she had withdrawn from men, there was no doubt about that. There was too much hurt involved and it would not have needed a particularly bright psychiatrist to find out why. In spite of success and fame and the privileged life her position brought her; in spite of having constantly at her shoulder the powerful presence of Maslovsky, she was still, in many ways, the little girl on her knees in the rain beside the father so cruelly torn away from her.

Along the Champs Elysées and into the Place de la Concorde she went, walking steadily.

'Jesus, but she likes her exercise,' Devlin observed.

She turned into the cool peace of the Jardin des Tuileries and Hunter nodded. 'I thought she would. My hunch is that she's making for the Louvre. You go after her on foot from here. I'll drive round, park the car and wait for you at the main entrance.'

There was a Henry Moore exhibit in the Tuileries Gardens. She browsed around it for a little while and Devlin stayed back, but it was obvious that nothing there had much appeal for her and she moved on through the gardens to the great Palais du Louvre itself.

Tanya Voroninova was certainly selective. She moved from gallery to gallery, choosing only works of acknowledged genius and Devlin followed at a discreet distance. From the Victory of Samothrace at the top of the Daru staircase by the main entrance, she moved on to the Venus de Milo. She spent some time in the Rembrandt Gallery on the first floor, then stopped to look at what is possibly the most famous picture in the world – Leonardo da Vinci's 'Mona Lisa'.

Devlin moved in close. 'Is she smiling, would you say?' he tried in English.

'What do you mean?' she asked in the same language.

'Oh, it's an old superstition in the Louvre that some mornings she doesn't smile.'

She turned to look at him. 'That's absurd.'

'But you're not smiling either,' Devlin said. 'Sweet Jesus, are you worried you'd crack the plate?'

'This is total nonsense,' she said, but smiled all the same.

'When you're on your dignity, your mouth turns down at the corners,' he said. 'It doesn't help.'

'My looks, you mean? A matter of indifference to me.'

He stood there, hands in the pockets of the Burberry trenchcoat, the black felt hat slanted over one ear and the eyes were the most vivid blue she had ever seen. There was an air of insolent good humour to him and a kind of self-mockery that was rather attractive in spite of the fact that he must have been twice her age at least. There was a sudden aching excitement that was difficult to control and she took a deep breath to steady herself.

'Excuse me,' she said and walked away.

Devlin gave her some room and then followed. A darling girl and frightened, for some reason. Interesting to know why that should be.

She made her way to the Grande Galerie, finally stopped before El Greco's 'Christ on the Cross' and stood there for quite some time gazing up at the gaunt mystical figure, showing no acknowledgement of Devlin's presence when he moved beside her.

'And what does it say to you?' he asked gently. 'Is there love there?'

'No,' she said. 'A rage against dying, I think. Why are you following me?'

'Am I?'

'Since the Tuileries Gardens.'

'Really? Well, if I was, I can't be very good at it.'

'Not necessarily. You are someone to look at twice,' she said simply.

Strange how suddenly she felt like crying. Wanted to reach out to the incredible warmth of that voice. He took her arm and said gently, 'All the time in the world, girl dear. You still haven't told me what El Greco says to you.'

'I was not raised a Christian,' she said. 'I see no Saviour on the Cross, but a great human being in torment, destroyed by little people. And you?'

'I love your accent,' Devlin said. 'Reminds me of Garbo in the movies when I was a wee boy, but that was a century or so before your time.'

'Garbo is not unknown to me,' she said, 'and I'm duly flattered. However, you still have not told me what it says for you?'

'A profound question when one considers the day,' Devlin told her. 'At seven o'clock this morning, they celebrated a rather special Mass in St Peter's Basilica in Rome. The Pope together with cardinals from Britain and the Argentine.'

'And will this achieve anything?'

'It hasn't stopped the British Navy proceeding on its merry way or Argentine Skyhawks from attacking it.'

'Which means?'

'That the Almighty, if he exists at all, is having one hell of a joke at our expense.'

Tanya frowned. 'Your accent intrigues me. You are not English, I think?'

'Irish, my love.'

'But I thought the Irish were supposed to be extremely religious?'

'And that's a fact. My old Aunt Hannah had callouses on her knees from praying. She used to take me to Mass three times a week when I was a boy in Drumore.'

Tanya Voroninova went very still. 'Where did you say?'

'Drumore. That's a little market town in Ulster. The church there was Holy Name. The thing I remember most was my uncle and his cronies, straight out from Mass and down the road to Murphy's Select Bar.'

She turned, her face very pale now. 'Who are you?'

'Well, one thing's for sure, girl dear.' He ran a hand lightly over her dark hair. 'I'm not Cuchulain, last of the dark heroes.'

Her eyes widened and there was a kind of anger as she plucked at his coat. 'Who are you?'

'In a manner of speaking, Viktor Levin.'

'Viktor?' She looked bewildered. 'But Viktor is dead. Died somewhere in Arabia a month or so ago. My father told me.'

'General Maslovsky? Well, he would, wouldn't he? No, Viktor escaped. Defected, you might say. Ended up in London and then Dublin.'

'He's well?'

'Dead,' Devlin said brutally. 'Murdered by Mikhail Kelly or Cuchulain or the dark bloody hero or whoever you want to call him. The same man who shot your father dead twenty-three years ago in the Ukraine.'

She sagged against him. His arm went round her in support, strong and confident. 'Lean on me, just put one foot in front of the other and I'll take you outside and get you some air.'

They sat on a bench in the Tuileries Gardens and Devlin took out his old silver case and offered her a cigarette. 'Do you use these things?'

'No.'

'Good for you, they'd stunt your growth and you with your green years ahead of you.'

Somewhere, he'd said those self-same words before, a long, long time ago. Another girl very much like this one. Not beautiful, not in any conventional sense, and yet always there would be the compulsion to turn and take a second look. There was pain in the memory that even time had not managed to erase.

'You're a strange man,' she said, 'for a secret agent. That's what you are, I presume?'

He laughed out loud, the sound so clear that Tony Hunter, seated on a bench on the other side of the Henry Moore exhibit reading a newspaper, glanced up sharply.

'God save the day.' Devlin took out his wallet and extracted a scrap of pasteboard. 'My card. Strictly for formal occasions I assure you.'

She read it out loud. 'Professor Liam Devlin, Trinity College, Dublin.' She looked up. 'Professor of what?'

'English literature. I use the term loosely, as academics do, so it would include Oscar Wilde, Shaw, O'Casey, Brendan Behan, James Joyce, Yeats. A mixed bag there. Catholics and Prods, but all Irish. Could I have the card back, by the way? I'm running short . . .'

He replaced it in his wallet. She said, 'But how would a professor of an ancient and famous university come to be involved in an affair like this?'

'You've heard of the Irish Republican Army?'

'Of course.'

'I've been a member of that organization since I was sixteen years of age. No longer active, as we call it. I've some heavy reservations about the way the Provisionals have been handling some aspects of the present campaign.'

'Don't tell me, let me guess.' She smiled. 'You are a romantic at heart, I think, Professor Devlin?'

'Is that a fact?'

'Only a romantic could wear anything so absurdly wonderful as that black felt hat. But there is more, of course. No bombs in restaurants to blow up women and children. You would shoot a man without hesitation. Welcome the hopeless odds of meeting highly trained soldiers face-to-face.'

Devlin was beginning to feel distinctly uneasy. 'Do you tell me?'

'Oh, I do, Professor Devlin. You see, I think I recognize you now. The true revolutionary, the failed romantic who didn't really want it to stop.'

'And what would *it* be, exactly?'

'Why, the game, Professor. The mad, dangerous, wonderful game that alone makes life worth living for a man like you. Oh, you may like the cloistered life of the lecture room or tell yourself that you do, but at the first chance to sniff powder . . .'

'Can I take time to catch my breath?' Devlin asked.

'And worst of all,' she carried on relentlessly, 'is your need to have it both ways. To have all the fun, but also to have a nice clean revolution where no innocent bystanders get hurt.'

She sat there, arms folded in front of her in an inimitable gesture as if she would hold herself in, and Devlin said, 'Have you missed anything out, would you say?'

She smiled tightly. 'Sometimes I get very wound up like a clock spring and I hold it until the spring goes.'

'And it all bursts out and you're into your imitation of Freud,' he told her. 'I bet that goes down big over the vodka and strawberries after dinner at old Maslovsky's summer *dasha*.'

Her face tightened. 'You will not make jokes about him. He has been very good to me. The only father I have known.'

'Perhaps,' Devlin said. 'But it wasn't always so.'

She gazed at him angrily. 'All right, Professor Devlin, we have fenced enough. Perhaps it is time you told me why you are here.'

He omitted nothing, starting with Viktor Levin and Tony Villiers in the Yemen and ending with the murder of Billy White and Levin outside Kilrea. When he was finished, she sat there for a long moment without saying anything.

'Levin said you remembered Drumore and the events surrounding your father's death,' Devlin said gently.

'Like a nightmare, it drifts to the surface of consciousness now and then. Strange, but it is as if it's happening to someone else and I'm looking down at the little girl on her knees in the rain beside her father's body.'

'And Mikhail Kelly or Cuchulain as they call him? You remember him?'

'Till my dying day,' she said flatly. 'It was such a strange face, the face of a ravaged young saint and he was so kind to me, so gentle, that was the strangest thing of all.'

Devlin took her arm. 'Let's walk for a while.' They started along the path and he asked, 'Has Maslovsky ever discussed those events with you?'

'No.'

Her arm under his hand was going rigid. 'Easy, girl dear,' he said softly. 'And tell me the most important thing of all. Have you ever tried to discuss it with him?'

'No, damn you!' She pulled away, turning, her face full of passion.

'But then, you wouldn't want to do that, would you?' he said. 'That would be opening a can of worms with a vengeance.'

She stood there looking at him, holding herself in again. 'What do you want of me, Professor Devlin? You want me to defect like Viktor? Wade through all those thousands of photos in the hope that I might recognize him?'

'That's a reasonable facsimile of the original mad idea. The IRA people in Dublin would never let the material they're holding out of their own hands, you see.'

'Why should I?' She sat on a nearby bench and pulled him down. 'Let me tell you something. You make a big mistake, you people in the West, when you assume that all Russians are straining at the leash, anxious only for a chance to get out. I love my country. I like it there. It suits me. I'm a respected artist. I can travel wherever I like, even in Paris. No KGB – no men in black overcoats watching my every move. I go where I please.'

'With a foster-father, a lieutenant-general in the KGB in command of Department V amongst other things, I'd be surprised if you didn't. It used to be called Department 13, by the way. Distinctly unlucky for some, and then Maslovsky reorganized it in nineteen sixty-eight. It could best be described as an assassination bureau, but then, no well-run organization should be without one.'

'Just like your IRA?' She leaned forward. 'How many men have you killed for a cause you believed in, Professor?'

He smiled gently and touched her cheek in a strangely intimate gesture. 'Point taken, but I can see I'm wasting your time. You might as well have this, though.'

He took a largish buff envelope from his pocket, the one that had been delivered by Ferguson's bagman that morning and placed it in her lap.

'What is it?' she demanded.

'The people in London, being ever hopeful, have made you a present of a British passport with a brand new identity. Your photo looks smashing. There's cash in there – French francs – and details of alternative ways of getting to London.'

'I don't need it.'

'Well, you've got it now. And this.' He took his card from his wallet and gave it to her. 'I'll fly back to Dublin this afternoon. No point in hanging around.'

Which wasn't strictly true, for the bagman from London had flown in with more than the package containing the false passport. There had also been a message from Ferguson for Devlin personally. McGuiness and the Chief of Staff were hopping mad. As far as they were concerned, the leak was none of their doing. They wanted out and Devlin was to mend fences.

She put the packet and the card into her shoulder bag with some reluctance. 'I'm sorry. You came a long way for nothing.'

'You've got my number,' he said. 'Call any time.' He stood up. 'Who knows, you just might start asking questions.'

'I think not, Professor Devlin.' She held out her hand. 'Goodbye.'

Devlin held it for a moment, then turned and walked back along the gardens to where Hunter was sitting. 'Come on!' he said. 'Let's get moving!'

Hunter scrambled to his feet and trailed after him. 'What happened?'

'Nothing,' Devlin told him as they reached the car. 'Not a bloody thing. She didn't want to know. Now let's go back to your place so that I can get my bag, then you can take me up to Charles de Gaulle. With luck, I might make the afternoon flight to Dublin.'

'You're going back?'

'Yes, I'm going back,' Liam Devlin said, and he sank down in his seat and tipped the rim of his black felt hat over his eyes.

Behind them, Tanya Voroninova watched them go, turning out into the traffic of the Rue de Rivoli. She stood there, thinking about things for a moment, then moved out of the gardens and started to walk along the pavement, considering the extraordinary events of the morning. Liam Devlin was a dangerously attractive man, no doubt about it, but more than that, his story had been terribly disturbing for her and events from a past perhaps best forgotten were trying to call her, as if from a great distance.

She was aware of a car pulling into the kerb ahead of her, a black Mercedes saloon. As she approached, the rear door opened and Natasha Rubenova looked out. She seemed agitated. No, more than that – afraid.

'Tanya!'

Tanya turned towards her. 'Natasha – what on earth are you doing here? What's happened?'

'Please, Tanya. Get in!'

There was a man sitting beside her, young and with a hard, implacable face. He wore a blue suit, dark blue tie and white shirt. He also wore black leather gloves. The man in the passenger seat next to the chauffeur could have been his twin. They looked as if they might be employed by a high class funeral firm and Tanya felt slightly uneasy.

'What on earth is going on?'

In a second, the young man beside Natasha was out of the car, a hand taking Tanya above the left elbow in a grip, light, but strong. 'My name is Turkin – Peter Turkin, Comrade. My colleague is Lieutenant Ivan Shepilov. We are officers of GRU and you will come with us.'

Soviet Military Intelligence. She was more than uneasy now. She was frightened and tried to pull away.

'Please, Comrade.' His grip tightened. 'You'll only hurt yourself by struggling and you have a concert tonight. We don't want to disappoint your fans.'

There was something in his eyes, a hint of cruelty, of perversity, that was very disturbing. 'Leave me alone!' She tried to strike him and he blocked her blow with ease. 'You'll answer for this. Don't you know who my father is?'

'Lieutenant-General Ivan Maslovsky of the KGB, under whose direct orders I am acting now, so be a good girl and do as you are told.'

She had no will to resist, so great was the shock, and found herself sitting next to Natasha who was close to tears. Turkin got in on the other side.

'Back to the Embassy!' he told the chauffeur.

As the Mercedes pulled away, Tanya held on to Natasha's hand tightly. For the first time since she was a little girl, she felt really and truly afraid.

7

Nikolai Belov was in his fifties, a handsome enough man with the slightly fleshy face of someone who enjoyed the good things of life more than was healthy for him, the kind of good Marxist whose dark suit and overcoat had been tailored in London's Savile Row. The silver hair and decadent good looks gave him the air of an ageing and rather distinguished actor instead of a colonel in the KGB.

This trip to Lyons could hardly have been classified as essential business, but it had been possible to take his secretary, Irana Vronsky, with him. As she had been his mistress for some years now, it meant that they had enjoyed an extremely pleasurable couple of days, the memory of which had faded rather rapidly when he discovered the situation waiting for him on his return to the Soviet Embassy.

He had hardly settled into his office when Irana came in. 'There's an urgent communication from KGB Moscow for your eyes only.'

'Who's it from?'

'General Maslovsky.'

The name alone was enough to bring Belov to his feet. He went out and she followed him down to the coding office where the operator got the relevant tape. Belov keyed in his personal code, the machine whirred, the operator tore off the print-out sheet and handed it to him. Belov read it and swore softly. He took Irana by the elbow and hurried her out. 'Get me Lieutenant Shepilov and Captain Turkin. Whatever else they're on, they drop.'

Belov was seated at his desk, working his way through papers when the door opened and Irana Vronsky ushered in Tanya, Natasha Rubenova and Shepilov and Turkin. Belov knew Tanya well. His official position at the Embassy for some years had been senior cultural attaché. As part of that cover role he had escorted her to parties on a number of occasions.

He stood up. 'It's good to see you.'

'I demand to know what's going on here,' she told him passionately. 'I'm pulled off the pavement by these bully boys here and . . .'

'I'm sure Captain Turkin was only acting as he saw fit.' Belov nodded to Irana. 'Get the Moscow call now.' He turned to Tanya. 'Calm yourself and sit down.' She stood there, mutinous, then glanced at Shepilov and Turkin standing against the wall, gloved hands folded in front of them. 'Please,' Belov said.

She sat and he offered her a cigarette. Such was her agitation that she took it and Turkin moved in smoothly and lit it for her. His lighter was not only by Cartier, but gold. She coughed as the smoke caught at the back of her throat.

Belov said, 'Now tell me what you did this morning.'

'I walked to the Tuileries Gardens.' The cigarette was helping, calming her down. She had control now and that meant she could fight.

'And then?'

'I went into the Louvre.'

'And who did you talk to?'

The question was direct and meant to entrap by causing an automatic response. To her own surprise, she found herself replying calmly, 'I was on my own. I didn't go with anyone. Perhaps I didn't make that clear?'

'Yes, I know that,' he said patiently. 'But did you speak to anyone when you got there? Did anyone approach you?'

She managed a smile. 'You mean, did anyone try to pick me up? No such luck. Considering its reputation, Paris can be very disappointing.' She stubbed out the cigarette. 'Look, what's going on, Nikolai? Can't you tell me?'

Belov had no reason to disbelieve her. In fact he very much wanted to. He had, in effect, been absent from duty the night before. If he had not been, he would have received Maslovsky's directive then and Tanya Voroninova would not have been allowed to stir from her suite at the Ritz that morning. Certainly not unaccompanied.

The door opened and Irana entered. 'General Maslovsky on line one.'

Belov picked up the phone and Tanya tried to snatch it. 'Let me speak to him.'

Belov pulled away from her. 'Belov here, General.'

'Ah, Nikolai, she is with you now?'

'Yes, General.' It was a meausure of the length of their friendship that Belov missed out the Comrade.

'And she is under guard? She has spoken to no one?'

'Yes to both questions, General.'

'And the man Devlin has not attempted to get in touch with her?'

'It would seem not. We've had the computer pull him out of the files for us. Pictures, everything. If he tries to get close, we'll know.'

'Fine. Now give me Tanya.'

Belov handed her the phone and she almost snatched it from him. 'Papa?'

She had called him so for years and his voice was warm and kindly as always. 'You are well?'

'Bewildered,' she said. 'No one will tell me what is happening.'

'It is sufficient for you to know that for reasons which are unimportant now, you have become involved in a matter of state security. A very serious business indeed. You must be returned to Moscow as soon as may be.'

'But my tour?'

The voice of the man at the other end of the line was suddenly cold, implacable and detached. 'Will be cancelled. You will appear at the Conservatoire tonight and fulfil that obligation. The first direct flight to Moscow is not until tomorrow morning anyway. There will be a suitable press release. The old wrist injury giving problems again. A need for further treatment. That should do nicely.'

All her life, or so it seemed, she had done his bidding, allowed him to shape her career, aware of his genuine concern and love, but this was new territory.

She tried again, 'But Papa!'

'Enough of argument. You will do as you are told and you will obey Colonel Belov in everything. Put him back on.'

She handed the phone to Belov mutely, hand shaking. Never had he spoken to her like this. Was she no longer his daughter? Simply another Soviet citizen to be ordered about at will?

'Belov, General.' He listened for a moment or two then nodded. 'No problem. You can rely on me.'

He put the phone down and opened a file on his desk. The photo he took from it and held up to her was of Liam Devlin, a few years younger perhaps, but Devlin unmistakably.

'This man is Irish. His name is Liam Devlin. He is a university professor from Dublin with a reputation for a certain Irish charm. It would be a mistake for anyone to take him lightly. He has been a member of the Irish Republican Army for all his adult life. An important leader at one stage. He is also a ruthless and capable gunman who has killed many times. As a young man, he was an official executioner for his people.'

Tanya took a deep breath. 'And what has he to do with me?'

'That need not concern you. It is sufficient for you to know that he would very much like to talk to you and *that* we simply can't allow, can we Captain?'

Turkin showed no emotion. 'No, Colonel.'

'So,' Belov told her, 'you will return to the Ritz now, you and Comrade Rubenova with Lieutenant Shepilov and Captain Turkin in attendance. You will not go out again until tonight's performance when they will escort you to the Conservatoire. I will be there myself because of the reception afterwards. The Ambassador will be there and the President of the Republic Monsieur Mitterand, himself. His presence is the only reason we are not cancelling tonight's concert. Is there anything you don't understand in all this?'

'No,' she said coldly, her face white and strained. 'I understand only too well.'

'Good,' he said. 'Then go back to the hotel now and get some rest.'

She turned, Turkin opened the door for her, a slight, twisted smile on his mouth. She brushed past him, followed by a thoroughly frightened Natasha Rubenova and Shepilov and Turkin moved in behind.

In Kilrea, Devlin had not been long back at the cottage. He didn't have a regular housekeeper, just an old lady who came in twice a week, knocked the place into shape and did the laundry, but he preferred it that way. He put the kettle on in the kitchen, went into the living room and quickly made the fire. He had just put a match to it when there was a rap on the French window and he turned to find McGuiness there.

Devlin unlocked it quickly. 'That was quick. I'm only just back.'

'So I was told within five minutes of you landing at the airport.' McGuiness was angry. 'What's the score, Liam? What's going on?'

'What do you mean?'

'Levin and Billy, and now Mike Murphy's been pulled out of the Liffey with two bullets in him. It must have been Cuchulain. You know it and I know it. The thing is, how did he know?'

'I don't have any fast answer on that one.' Devlin found two glasses and the Bushmills and poured. 'Try this for size and calm down.'

McGuiness swallowed a little. 'A leak is what I think, at the London end. It's a well-known fact that the British security service has been heavily infiltrated by the Soviets for years.'

'A slight exaggeration, but some truth to it,' Devlin said. 'As mentioned earlier, I know that Ferguson thinks the leak is from your people.'

'To hell with that. I say we pull in Cherny and squeeze him dry.'

'Maybe,' Devlin said. 'I'd have to check on that with Ferguson. Let's give it another day.'

'All right,' McGuiness said with obvious reluctance. 'I'll be in touch, Liam. Close touch.' And he went out through the French windows.

Devlin poured another whiskey and sat there savouring it and thinking, then he picked up the phone. He was about to dial, then hesitated. He replaced the receiver, got the black plastic box from the desk and switched it on. There was no positive response from the telephone, nor indeed from anywhere in the room.

'So,' he said softly, 'Ferguson or McGuiness. It's one or other of the buggers that it's down to.'

He dialled the Cavendish Square number and the receiver was picked up at once. 'Fox here.'

'Is he there, Harry?'

'Not at the moment. How was Paris?'

'A nice girl. I liked her. Pretty confused. Nothing more I could do than present the facts. I gave her the material your bagman brought over. She took it, but I wouldn't be too sanguine.'

'I never was,' Fox said. 'Will you be able to smooth things down in Dublin?'

'McGuiness has already been to see me. He wants to move on Cherny. Try some old-fashioned pressure.'

'That might be the best solution.'

'Jesus, Harry, but Belfast left its mark on you. Still, you could be right. I've stalled him for a day. If you want me, I'll be here. I gave the girl my card, by the way. She thought I was a failed romantic, Harry. Have you ever heard the like?'

'You give a convincing imitation, but I've never bought it.'

Fox laughed and rang off. Devlin sat there for a while, a frown on his face, then there was another tap on the French window. It opened and Cussane entered.

'Harry,' Devlin said, 'you're sent from heaven. As I've often told you, you make the best scrambled eggs in the world.'

'Flattery will get you anywhere.' Cussane poured himself a drink. 'How was Paris?'

'Paris?' Devlin said. 'Sure and I was only joking. I've been to Cork. Some university business to do with the film festival. Had to stay over. Just driven back. I'm the original starving man.'

'Right,' Harry Cussane told him. 'You lay the table and I'll scramble the eggs.'

'You're a good friend, Harry,' Devlin said.

Cussane paused in the door. 'And why not, Liam. It's been a long time,' and he smiled and went into the kitchen.

Tanya had a hot bath, hoping it would relax her. There was a knock at the door and Natasha Rubenova entered. 'Coffee?'

'Thank you.' Tanya lay back in the warm, foamy water and sipped the coffee gratefully.

Natasha pulled a small stool forward and sat down. 'You must be very careful, my love. You understand me?'

'Strange,' Tanya said. 'No one has ever told me to be careful before.'

It occurred to her then that she had always been sheltered from the cold, ever since the nightmare of Drumore that surfaced only in her dreams. Maslovsky and his wife had been good parents. She had wanted for nothing. In a Marxist society that had been envisaged in the great days of Lenin and the revolution as giving power to the people, power had quickly become the prerogative of the few.

Soviet Russia had become an élitist society in which who you were was more important than what you were and she, to all intents and purposes, was Ivan Maslovsky's daughter. The best housing, the superior schools, her talent carefully nurtured. When she drove through Moscow to their country house, it was in a chauffeured limousine, travelling in the traffic-free lane kept open for the use of the important people in the hierarchy. The delicacies that graced their table, the clothes she wore, all bought on a special card at GUM.

All this she had ignored, just as she had ignored the realities of the state trials of the Gulag. Just as she had turned from the even harsher reality of Drumore, her father dead on the street and Maslovsky in charge.

Natasha said, 'You are all right?'

'Of course. Pass me a towel,' Tanya wrapped it around herself. 'Did you notice the lighter that Turkin used when he lit my cigarette?'

'Not particularly.'

'It was by Cartier. Solid gold. What was it Orwell said in that book of his? All animals are equal, but some are more equal than others?'

'Please, darling,' Natasha Rubenova was obviously agitated. 'You mustn't say things like that.'

'You're right.' Tanya smiled. 'I'm angry, that's all. Now I think I would like to sleep. I must be fresh for tonight's concert.' They went into the other room and she got into the bed, the towel around her. 'They're still out there?'

'Yes.'

'I'll sleep now.'

Natasha closed the curtains and went out. Tanya lay there in the darkness thinking about things. The events of the past few hours had been a shock in themselves, but strangely enough, the most significant thing had been the way in which she had been treated. Tanya Voroninova, internationally acclaimed artist, who had received the Medal of Culture from Brezhnev himself, had felt the full weight of the State's hand. The truth was that for most of her life she had been somebody, thanks to Maslovsky. Now it had been made plain that, when the chips were down, she was just another cypher.

It was enough. She switched on the bedside lamp, reached for her handbag and took out the packet which Devlin had given her. The British passport was excellent; issued, according to the date, three years before. There was an American visa. She had entered that country twice, also Germany, Italy, Spain and France one week previously. A nice touch. Her name was Joanna Frank, born in London, professional journalist. The photo, as Devlin had said, was an excellent likeness. There were even one or two personal letters with her London address in Chelsea, an American Express credit card and a British driver's licence. They'd thought of everything.

The alternative routes were clearly outlined. There was the direct plane flight from Paris to London, but that wasn't on. Surprising how cool and calculating she was now. She would have only the slimmest of chances of getting away, if an opportunity presented itself at all, and she would be missed almost at once. They would have the airports covered instantly.

It seemed obvious that the same would be true of the ferry terminals at Calais and Boulogne. But the people in London had indicated another way, one which might possibly be overlooked. There was a train service from Paris to Rennes, changing there for St Malo on the Brittany coast.

From there, a hydrofoil service to Jersey in the Channel Islands. And from Jersey, there were several planes a day to London.

She got up quietly, tiptoed into the bathroom and closed the door. Then she lifted the receiver on the wall telephone and called Reception. They were extremely efficient. Yes, there was a night train to Rennes, leaving the Gare du Nord at eleven. In Rennes, there would be a delay, but she could be in St Malo for breakfast. Ample time to catch the hydrofoil.

She flushed the toilet and went back in the bedroom, rather pleased with herself for she hadn't quoted a room number or given her name. The enquiry could have come from any one of hundreds of guests.

'They're turning you into a jungle animal, Tanya,' she told herself softly.

She got her holdall bag from the wardrobe, the one she used to take all her bits and pieces to the concerts. She couldn't secrete much in there. It would show. She thought about it for a while, then took out a pair of soft suede boots and rolled them up so they fitted neatly in the bottom of the bag. She next took a black cotton jumpsuit from its hanger, folded it and laid it in the case. She placed the concerto score and the orchestra parts she had been studying on top.

So, nothing more to be done. She went to the window and peered out. It was raining again and she shivered, suddenly lonely, and remembered Devlin and his strength. For a moment she thought of phoning him, but that was no good. Not from here. They would trace the call in minutes the moment they started checking. She went back to bed and switched off the lamp. If only she could sleep for an hour or two. The face surfaced in her consciousness: Cuchulain's bone-white face and dark eyes made sleep impossible.

She wore a gown in black velvet for the concert. It was by Balmain and very striking with a matching jacket. The pearls at her neck and the earrings were supposed to be lucky, a gift by the Maslovskys before the finals of the Tchaikovsky competition, her greatest triumph.

Natasha came in and stood behind her at the dressing table. 'Are you ready? Time's getting short.' She put her hands on Tanya's shoulders. 'You look lovely.'

'Thank you. I've packed my case.'

Natasha picked it up. 'Have you put a towel in? You always forget.'

She zipped it open before Tanya could protest, then froze. She looked at the girl, eyes wide.

'Please?' Tanya said softly. 'If I ever meant anything to you.'

The older woman took a deep breath, went into the bathroom and returned with a towel. She folded it and placed it in the case and zipped it up. 'So,' she said. 'We are ready.'

'Is it still raining?'

'Yes.'

'Then I shan't wear the velvet cape. The trenchcoat, I think.'

Natasha took it from the wardrobe and draped it over her shoulders. Tanya felt her hands tighten for a moment. 'Now we must go.'

Tanya picked up the case and opened the door and went into the other room where Shepilov and Turkin waited. They both wore dinner jackets because of the reception after the performance.

'If I may be permitted the observation, you look superb, Comrade,' Turkin told her. 'A credit to our country.'

'Spare me the compliments, Captain,' she said frostily. 'If you wish to be of use, you can carry my case,' and she handed it to him and walked out.

The Conservatoire concert hall was packed for this occasion and when she walked on stage, the orchestra stood to greet her and there was a storm of applause, the audience standing also, following President Mitterand's example.

She sat down, all noise faded. There was complete silence as the conductor waited, baton ready and then it descended and as the orchestra started to play, Tanya Voroninova's hands rippled over the keyboard.

She was filled with a joy, an ecstasy almost, played as she had never played in her life before with a new, vibrant energy as if something which had been locked up in her for years was now released. The orchestra responded as if trying to match her so that at the end, in the dramatic finale to Rachmaninov's superb concerto, they fused into a whole that created an experience to be forgotten by few people who were there that night.

The cry from the audience was different from anything she had experienced in her life before. She stood facing them, the orchestra standing behind her, all clapping and someone threw a flower on the stage, and more followed as women unpinned their corsages.

She went off to the side and Natasha, waiting, tears streaming down her cheeks, flung her arms around her. 'Babushka, you were wonderful. The best I ever heard.'

Tanya hugged her fiercely. 'I know. My night, Natasha, the one night I can take on the whole world if need be and come out ahead of the game,' and she turned and went back on stage to an audience that refused to stop applauding.

François Mitterand, President of the Republic of France, took both her hands and kissed them warmly. 'Mademoiselle, I salute you. An extraordinary performance.'

'You are more than kind, *Monsieur le Président*,' she answered in his own language.

The crowd pressed close as champagne was offered and cameras flashed as the President toasted her and then introduced her to the Minister of Culture and others. She was aware of Shepilov and Turkin by the door, Nikolai Belov talking to them, handsome in velvet evening jacket and ruffled shirt. He raised his glass in a toast and moved towards her. She glanced at her watch. It was just after ten. If she was to go, it must be soon.

Belov reached for her right hand and kissed it. 'Tremendous stuff. You should get angry more often.'

'A point of view.' She took another glass of champagne from a waiter. 'Everyone who is anyone in the diplomatic corps seems to be here. You must be pleased. Quite a triumph.'

'Yes, but then, we Russians have always had a soul for music lacking in certain other peoples.'

She glanced around. 'Where's Natasha?'

'Over there with the Press. Shall I get her?'

'Not necessary. I need to go to the dressing room for a moment, but I can manage perfectly well on my own.'

'Of course.' He nodded to Turkin who came across. 'See Comrade Voroninova to her dressing room, Turkin. Wait for her and escort her back.' He smiled at Tanya. 'We don't want you to get hurt in the crush.'

The crowd opened for her, people smiling, raising their glasses, and Turkin followed her along the narrow corridor until they came to the dressing room.

She opened the door. 'I presume I'm permitted to go to the toilet?'

He smiled mockingly. 'If you insist, Comrade.'

He took out a cigarette and was lighting it as she closed the door. She didn't lock it, simply kicked off her shoes, pulled off the jacket and unzipped that lovely dress, allowing it to fall to the floor. She had the jumpsuit out of her case in a moment, was into it within seconds, zipping it up and pulling on the suede boots. She picked up the trenchcoat and handbag, moved into the toilet, closed the door and locked it.

She had checked the window earlier. It was large enough to get out of and opened into a small yard on the ground floor of the Conservatoire. She climbed up on the seat and wriggled through. It was raining hard now. She pulled on her trenchcoat, picked up her shoulderbag and ran to the gate. It was bolted on the inside and opened easily. A moment later, she was hurrying along the Rue de Madrid looking for a taxi.

8

Devlin was watching a late night movie on television when the phone rang. The line was surprisingly clear, so much so that at first he thought it must be local.

'Professor Devlin?'

'Yes.'

'It's Tanya – Tanya Voroninova.'

'Where are you?' Devlin demanded.

'The Gare du Nord. Paris. I've only got a couple of minutes. I'm catching the night train to Rennes.'

'To Rennes?' Devlin was bewildered. 'What in the world would you be going there for?'

'I change trains there for St Malo. I'll be there at breakfast time. There's a hydrofoil to Jersey. That's as good as being in England. Once there, I'm safe. I'll catch a plane for London. I only had minutes to give them the slip, so it seemed likely the other routes your people supplied would be blocked.'

'So, you changed your mind. Why?'

'Let's just say I've realized I like you and I don't like them. It doesn't mean I hate my country. Only some of the people in it. I must go.'

'I'll contact London,' Devlin said. 'Phone me from Rennes, and good luck.'

The line went dead. He stood there, holding the receiver, a slight ironic smile on his face, a kind of wonderment. 'Would you look at that now?' he said softly. 'A girl to take home to your mother and that's a fact.'

He dialled the Cavendish Square number and it was answered almost at once. 'Ferguson here.' He sounded cross.

'Would you by any chance be sitting in bed watching the old Bogart movie on the television?' Devlin enquired.

'Dear God, are you going into the clairvoyance business now?'

'Well, you can switch it off and get out of bed, you old bastard. The game's afoot with a vengeance.'

Ferguson's voice changed. 'What are you saying?'

‘That Tanya Voroninova’s done a bunk. She’s just phoned me from the Gare du Nord. Catching the night train to Rennes. Change for St Malo. Hydrofoil to Jersey in the morning. She thought the other routes might be blocked.’

‘Smart girl,’ Ferguson said. ‘They’ll pull every trick in the book to get her back.’

‘She’s going to phone me when she gets to Rennes. I presume, at a guess, that would be about three-thirty or maybe four o’clock.’

‘Good man,’ Ferguson told him. ‘Stay by the phone. I’ll get back to you.’

In his flat, Harry Fox was just about to get into the shower before going to bed when the phone rang. He answered it, cursing. It had been a long day. He needed some sleep.

‘Harry?’

He came alert at once at the sound of Ferguson’s voice. ‘Yes, sir?’

‘Get yourself over here. We’ve got work to do.’

Cussane was working in his study on Sunday’s sermon when the sensor device linked to the apparatus in the attic was activated. By the time he was up there, Devlin was off the phone. He played the tape back, listening intently. When it was finished, he sat there, thinking about the implications which were all bad.

He went down to the study and phoned Cherny direct. When the Professor answered, he said, ‘It’s me. Are you alone?’

‘Yes. Just about to go to bed. Where are you ringing from?’

‘My place. We’ve got bad trouble. Now listen carefully.’

When he was finished, Cherny said, ‘It gets worse. What do you want me to do?’

‘Speak to Lubov now. Tell him to make contact with Belov in Paris at once. They may be able to stop her.’

‘And if not?’

‘Then I’ll have to handle it myself when she gets here. I’ll keep in touch, so stay by the phone.’

He poured himself a whiskey and stood in front of the fire. Strange, but he still saw her as that scrawny little girl in the rain all those years ago.

He raised his glass and said softly, ‘Here’s to you, Tanya Voroninova. Now, let’s see if you can give those bastards a run for their money.’

Within five minutes, Turkin had realized something was badly wrong, had entered the dressing room and discovered the locked toilet door. The silence which was the only answer to his urgent knocking made him break down the door. The empty toilet, the window, told all. He clambered through, dropped into the yard and went into the Rue de Madrid. There was not a sign of her and he went round to the front of the Conservatoire and in through the main entrance, black rage in his heart. His career ruined, his very life on the line now because of that damned woman.

Belov was on another glass of champagne, deep in conversation with the Minister of Culture, when Turkin tapped him on the shoulder. 'Sorry to interrupt, Colonel, but could I have a word?' and he took him into the nearest corner and broke the bad news.

Nikolai Belov had always found that adversity brought out the best in him. He had never been one to cry over spilt milk. At his office at the Embassy, he sat behind the desk and faced Natasha Rubenova. Shepilov and Turkin stood by the door.

'I ask you again, Comrade,' he said to her. 'Did she say anything to you? Surely you of all people would have had some idea of her intentions?'

She was distressed and tearful, all quite genuine, and it helped her to lie easily. 'I'm as much at a loss as you are, Comrade Colonel.'

He sighed and nodded to Turkin who moved up behind her, shoving her down into a chair. He pulled off his right glove and squeezed her neck, pinching a nerve and sending a wave of appalling pain through her.

'I ask you again,' Nikolai Belov said gently. 'Please be sensible, I hate this kind of thing.'

Natasha, filled with pain, rage and humiliation, did the bravest thing of her life. 'Please! Comrade, I swear she told me nothing! Nothing!'

She screamed again as Turkin's finger found the nerve and Belov waved a hand. 'Enough. I'm satisfied she's telling the truth. What would her purpose be in lying?'

She sat there, huddled, weeping and Turkin said, 'What now, Comrade?'

'We have the airports fully covered. No possible flight she could have taken yet.'

'And Calais and Boulogne?'

'Our people are already on their way by road. The soonest she could leave from both places would be on one of the morning ferries and they will be there before those leave.'

Shepilov, who seldom spoke, said quietly, 'Excuse me, Comrade Colonel, but have you considered the fact that she may have sought asylum at the British Embassy?'

'Of course,' Belov told him. 'As it happens, since June of last year, we have a surveillance system operating at the entrance during the hours of darkness for rather obvious reasons. She has certainly not appeared there yet and if she does so . . .' he shrugged.

The door opened and Irana Vronsky hurried in. 'Lubov direct from Dublin for you, Comrade. Most urgent. The radio room have patched it through. Line one.'

Belov picked up the phone and listened. When he finally put it down, he was smiling. 'So far so good. She's on the night train to Rennes. Let's have a look at the map.' He nodded to Natasha. 'Take her out, Irana.'

Turkin said, 'But why Rennes?'

Belov found it on the map on the wall. 'To change trains for St Malo. From there she will catch the hydrofoil to Jersey in the Channel Islands.'

'British soil?'

'Exactly. Jersey, my dear Turkin, may be small, but it is very possibly the most important off-shore finance base in the world. They have an excellent airport, several flights a day to London and many other places.'

'All right,' Turkin said. 'We must drive to St Malo. Get there ahead of her.'

'Just a moment. Let's have a look in Michelin.' Belov found the red guide in the top left hand drawer of his desk and leafed through.

'Here we are – St Malo. Three hundred and seventy-two miles from Paris and a great deal of that through the Brittany countryside. Impossible to get there by car now, not in time. Go along to Bureau Five, Turkin. Let's see if they've got anyone we can use in St Malo. And you, Shepilov. Tell Irana I want all the information she has on Jersey. Airport, harbour, plane and boat schedules and so on – and hurry.'

At Cavendish Square, Kim was making up the fire in the sitting room while Ferguson, in an old towelling robe, sat at the desk working his way through a mass of papers.

The Gurkha stood up. 'Coffee, Sahib?'

'God, no, Kim. Tea, nice and fresh and keep it coming and some sort of sandwiches. Leave it to you.'

Kim went out and Harry Fox hurried in from the study. 'Right, sir, here's the score. She'll have a stopover at Rennes for almost two hours. From there to St Malo is seventy miles. She'll arrive at seven-thirty.'

'And the hydrofoil?'

'Leaves at eight-fifteen. Takes about an hour and a quarter. There's a time change, of course, so it arrives in Jersey at eight-thirty our time. There's a flight from Jersey to London, Heathrow, at ten minutes past ten. She'll have plenty of time to catch that. It's a small island, sir. Only fifteen minutes by cab from the harbour to the airport.'

'No, she can't be alone, Harry. I want her met. You'll have to go over first thing. There must be a breakfast plane.'

'Unfortunately it doesn't get into Jersey until nine-twenty.'

Ferguson said, 'Damnation!' and banged his fist on the desk as Kim entered carrying a tray containing tea things and a plate of newly cut sandwiches that gave off the unmistakable odour of grilled bacon.

'There is a possibility, sir.'

'What's that?'

'My cousin, Alex, sir. Alexander Martin. My second cousin actually. He lives in Jersey. Something in the finance industry. Married a local girl.'

'Martin?' Ferguson frowned. 'The name's familiar.'

'It would be, sir. We've used him before. When he was working for a merchant banker here in the city, he did a lot of travelling. Geneva, Zurich, Berlin, Rome.'

'He isn't on the active list?'

'No, sir. We used him as a bagman mainly, though there was an incident in East Berlin three years ago when things got out of hand and he behaved rather well.'

'I remember now,' Ferguson said. 'Supposed to pick up documents from a woman contact and when he found she was blown, he brought her out through Checkpoint Charlie in the boot of his car.'

'That's Alex, sir. Short service commission in the Welsh Guards, three tours in Ireland. Quite an accomplished musician. Plays the piano rather well. Mad as a hatter on a good day. Typically Welsh.'

'Get him!' Ferguson said. 'Now, Harry.' He had a hunch about Martin and suddenly felt much more cheerful. He helped himself to one of the bacon sandwiches. 'I say, these are really rather good.'

Alexander Martin was thirty-seven, a tall, rather handsome man with a deceptively lazy look to him. He was much given to smiling tolerantly, which he needed to do in the profession of investment broker which he had taken up on moving to Jersey eighteen months previously. As he had told his wife, Joan, on more than one occasion, the trouble with being in the investment business was that it threw you into the company of the rich and, as a class, he disliked them heartily.

Still, life had its compensations. He was an accomplished pianist if not a great one. If he had been, life might have been rather different. He was seated at the piano in the living room of his pleasant house in St Aubin overlooking the sea, playing a little Bach, ice-cold, brilliant stuff that required total concentration. He was wearing a dinner jacket, black tie undone at the neck. The phone rang for several moments before it penetrated his consciousness. He frowned, realizing the lateness of the hour and picked it up.

'Martin here.'

'Alex? This is Harry. Harry Fox.'

'Dear God!' Alex Martin said.

'How are Joan and the kids?'

'In Germany for a week, staying with her sister. Her husband's a major with your old mob. Detmold.'

'So, you're on your own? I thought you'd be in bed.'

'Just in from a late function.' Martin was very much awake now, all past experience telling him this was not a social call. 'Okay, Harry. What is this?'

'We need you, Alex, rather badly, but not like the other times. Right there in Jersey.'

Alex Martin laughed in astonishment. 'In Jersey? You've got to be joking.'

'Girl called Tanya Voroninova. Have you heard of her?'

'Of course I damn well have,' Martin told him. 'One of the best concert pianists to come along for years. I saw her perform at the Albert Hall in last season's promenade concerts. My office gets the Paris papers each day. She's there on a concert tour at the moment.'

'No she isn't,' Fox said. 'By now, she'll be half-way to Rennes on the night train. She's defecting, Alex.'

'She's what?'

'With luck, she'll be on the hydrofoil from St Malo, arriving Jersey at eight-twenty. She has a British passport in the name of Joanna Frank.'

Martin saw it all now. 'And you want me to meet her?'

'Exactly. Straight to the airport and bundle her on to the ten-ten to Heathrow and that's it. We'll meet her this end. Will that give you any problem?'

'Certainly not. I know what she looks like. In fact, I think I've still got the programme from her concert at the Proms. There's a photo of her on that.'

'Fine,' Fox told him. 'She's phoning a contact of ours when she gets into Rennes. We'll warn her to expect you.'

Ferguson said, 'Give me the phone. Ferguson here.'

'Hello, sir,' Martin said.

'We're very grateful.'

'Nothing to it, sir. Just one thing. What about the opposition?'

'Shouldn't be any. KGB will be waiting at all the obvious bolt holes. Charles de Gaulle, Calais, Boulogne. Highly unlikely they'll be on to this one. I'll hand you back to Harry now.'

Fox said, 'We'll stay close, Alex. I'll give you this number in case of any problems.'

Martin wrote it down. 'Should be a piece of cake. Make a nice change from the investment business. I'll be in touch.'

He was totally awake now and decidedly cheerful. No hope of sleep. Things were looking up. He poured himself a vodka and tonic, and went back to his Bach at the piano.

Bureau Five was that section of the Soviet Embassy in Paris that dealt with the French Communist Party, infiltration of trade unions and so on. Turkin spent half an hour with their file on St Malo and the immediate area, but came up with nothing.

'The trouble is, Comrade,' he told Belov when he returned to the office, 'that the French Communist Party is extremely unreliable. The French tend to put country before party when the chips are down.'

'I know,' Belov said. 'It comes of an inborn belief in their own superiority.' He indicated the papers spread out on his desk. 'I've looked Jersey over pretty thoroughly. The solution is simple enough. You know that little airfield outside Paris we've used before?'

'Croix?' Turkin said. 'Lebel Air Taxis?'

'That's right. Jersey Airport opens early. You could land there at seven. Ample time to be down at the harbour to meet her. You have the usual selection of passports available. You could go as French businessmen.'

'But how do we bring her back?' Turkin asked. 'We'd have to pass through customs and immigration for the return flight from Jersey Airport. It would be an impossibility. Too easy for her to create a fuss.'

'Excuse me, Comrade Colonel,' Shepilov put in, 'but is it really necessary for us to bring her back at all since all that is needed in this affair is her silence, or have I got the wrong impression?'

'You certainly have,' Belov told him coldly. 'Whatever the circumstances, however difficult, General Maslovsky wants her back. I'd hate to be in your shoes if you reported that you had had to shoot her, Shepilov. I think there is an easy solution. According to the brochures, there is a yachting marina in St Helier Harbour. Boats for hire. Wasn't sailing something of a hobby of yours back home, Turkin?'

'Yes, Comrade.'

'Good, then I'm sure it's hardly beyond your abilities to sail a motor launch from Jersey to St Malo. You can hire a car there and bring her back by road.'

'Very well, Colonel.'

Irana came in with coffee on a tray. He said, 'Excellent. Now all that's needed is for someone to haul Lebel out of bed. The timing should just work nicely.'

Surprising herself, Tanya managed to sleep for most of the train journey and had to be prodded into wakefulness by two young students who had travelled next to her all the way from Paris. It was three-thirty and very cold on the station platform at Rennes although it had stopped raining. The students knew of an all-night café outside the station in the Boulevard Beaumont and showed her the way. It was warm and inviting in there, not too many people. She ordered coffee and an omelette and went to call Devlin on the public telephone.

Devlin, who had been waiting anxiously, said, 'Are you all right?'

'Fine,' she said. 'I even slept on the train. Don't worry. They can't have any idea where I am. When will I see you again?'

'Soon,' Devlin told her. 'We've got to get you to London safely first. Now listen to me. When the hydrofoil gets into Jersey, you'll be met by a man called Martin. Alexander Martin. Apparently he's a bit of a fan of yours so he knows what you look like.'

'I see. Anything else?'

'Not really.'

'Good, then I'll get back to my omelette, Professor.'

She rang off and Devlin replaced the receiver. A girl and a half, he told himself as he went into the kitchen. In the cottage, Harry Cussane was already phoning Paul Cherny.

Croix was a small airfield with a control tower, two hangars and three nissen huts, headquarters of an aero club but also used by Pierre Lebel to operate his air taxi service. Lebel was a dark, taciturn man who never asked questions if the price was right. He had flown for Belov on a number of occasions and knew Turkin and Shepilov well. He hadn't the slightest idea that they were Russian. Something illegal about them, he'd always thought, but as long as it didn't involve drugs and the price was right, he didn't mind. He was waiting for the two men when they arrived, opened the door of the main hangar so that they could drive inside.

'Which plane?' Turkin asked.

'We'll use the Chieftain. Faster than the Cessna and there's a headwind all the way to Golfe St Malo.'

'When do we leave?'

'As soon as you like.'

'But I thought the airport at Jersey wasn't open until seven?'

'Whoever told you that got it wrong. It's officially seven-thirty for air taxis. However, the airport is open for the paper plane from five-thirty.'

'Paper plane?'

'Newspapers from England. Post and so on. They're usually sympathetic to a request for an early landing, especially if they know you. I did get the impression there was some urgency on this one?'

'There certainly is,' Turkin told him.

'Good, let's go up to the office and settle the business end of things.'

The office was up a flight of rickety stairs, small and cluttered, the desk untidy, the whole lit by a single bulb. Turkin handed Lebel an envelope. 'Better count it.'

'Oh, I will,' the Frenchman said, and then the phone rang. He answered it at once, then passed it to Turkin. 'For you.'

Belov said, 'She's made contact with Devlin from Rennes. There's a new complication. She's being met off the hydrofoil in Jersey by an Alexander Martin.'

'Is he a pro?' Turkin asked.

'No information on him at all. One wouldn't have thought they'd have any of their people in a place like Jersey. Still . . .'

'No problem,' Turkin said. 'We'll handle it.'

'Good luck.'

The line went dead and Turkin turned to Lebel. 'All right, my friend. Ready when you are.'

It was just six o'clock when they landed at Jersey Airport, a fine, blustery morning, the sky already lightening in the east, an orange glow on the horizon as the sun came up. The officer on duty at customs and immigration was pleasant and courteous. No reason not to be, for their papers were in order and Jersey was well used to handling thousands of French visitors each year.

'Stopping over?' he asked Lebel.

'No, straight back to Paris,' the Frenchman told him.

'And you, gentlemen?'

'Three or four days. Business and pleasure,' Turkin said.

'And nothing to declare? You've read the notice?'

'Not a thing.' Turkin offered his holdall.

The officer shook his head. 'All right, gentlemen. Have a nice stay.'

They shook hands formally with Lebel and passed out into the arrival hall, which at that time of the morning was deserted. There were one or two cars parked outside, but the taxi rank was empty. There was a telephone on the wall, but just as Turkin was moving to use it, Shepilov touched his arm and pointed. A cab was drawing up at the entrance to the airport. Two air hostesses got out and went in. The Russians waited and the cab drew up beside them.

'Early start, gentlemen,' the driver said.

'Yes, we're just in from Paris,' Turkin told him. 'Private flight.'

'Oh, I see. Where can I take you?'

Turkin, who had spent much of the flight examining the Jersey guide book Irana had provided, particularly the town map of St Helier, said, 'The Weighbridge, isn't that right? By the harbour.'

The taxi drew away. 'You don't need an hotel, then?'

'We're meeting friends later. They're taking care of that sort of thing. We thought we'd get some breakfast.'

'You'll be all right there. There's a café close to the Weighbridge that opens early. I'll show you.'

The roads, at that time in the morning, were far from busy and the run down to Bel Royal and along the dual carriageway of Victoria Avenue took little more than ten minutes. The sun was coming up now and the view across St Aubin's Bay was spectacular, the tide in so that Elizabeth Castle on its rock was surrounded by water. Ahead of them was the town, the harbour breakwater, cranes lifting into the sky in the distance.

The driver turned in by the car park at the end of the esplanade. 'Here we are, gentlemen. The Weighbridge. There's the tourist office. Open later if you need information. The café is just across the road over there around the corner. We'll call that three pounds.'

Turkin, who had been supplied with several hundred pounds in English banknotes by Irana, took a fiver from his wallet. 'Keep it. You've been very kind. Where's the marina from here?'

The driver pointed. 'Far end of the harbour. You can walk round.'

Turkin nodded to the breakwater stretching out into the bay. 'And the boats come in there?'

'That's right. Albert Quay. You can see the car ferry ramp from here. Hydrofoils berth further along.'

'Good,' Turkin said. 'Many thanks.'

They got out and the cab moved away. There was a public toilet a few yards away; without a word, Turkin led the way in and Shepilov followed. Turkin opened his holdall and burrowed under the clothing it contained, prising up the false bottom to reveal two handguns. He slipped one in his pocket and gave Shepilov the other. The weapons were automatics, each gun fitted with a silencer.

Turkin zipped up his holdall. 'So far so good. Let's take a look at the marina.'

There were several hundred boats moored there of every shape and size: yachts, motor cruisers, speedboats. They found the office of a boat hire firm easily enough, but it was not open yet.

'Too early,' Turkin said. 'Let's go down and have a look round.'

They walked along one of the swaying pontoons, boats moored on either side, paused, then turned into another. Things had always worked for Turkin. He was a great believer in his destiny. The nonsense over Tanya Voroninova had been an unfortunate hiccup in his career, but soon to be put right, he was confident of that. And now, fate took a hand in the game.

There was a motor cruiser moored at the end of the pontoon, dazzlingly white with a blue band above the watermark. The name on the stern was *L'Alouette*, registered Granville, which he knew was a port along the coast from St Malo. A couple came out on deck talking in French, the man tall and bearded with glasses. He wore a dark reefer coat. The woman wore jeans and a similar coat, a scarf around her head.

As the man helped her over the rail, Turkin heard him say, 'We'll walk round to the bus station. Get a taxi from there to the airport. The flight to Guernsey leaves at eight.'

'What time are we booked back?' she asked.

'Four o'clock. We'll have time for breakfast at the airport.'

They walked away. Shepilov said, 'What is Guernsey?'

'The next island,' Turkin told him. 'I read about it in the guide book. There's an inter-island flying service several times a day. It only takes fifteen minutes. A day out for tourists.'

'Are you thinking what I am?' Shepilov enquired.

'It's a nice boat,' Turkin said. 'We could be in St Malo and on our way hours before those two get back this afternoon.' He took out a pack of French cigarettes and offered one to his companion. 'Give them time to move away, then we'll check.'

They took a walk around the pontoons, returning in ten minutes and going on board. The door to the companionway which led below was locked. Shepilov produced a spring blade knife and forced it expertly. There were two cabins neatly furnished, a saloon and a galley. They went back on deck and tried the wheelhouse. The door to that was open.

'No ignition key,' Shepilov said.

'No problem. Give me your knife.' Turkin worked his way up behind the control panel and pulled down several wires. It took only a moment to make the right connection and when he pressed the starter button, the engine turned over at once. He checked the fuel gauge. 'Tank's three quarters full.' He unfastened the wires again. 'You know, I think this is our day, Ivan,' he said to Shepilov.

They walked back round to the other side of the harbour and turned along the top of the Albert Quay, pausing at the end to look down at the hydrofoil berth.

'Excellent.' Turkin looked at his watch. 'Now all we have to do is wait. Let's find that café and try some breakfast.'

At St Malo, the Condor hydrofoil moved out of the harbour past the Mole des Noires. It was almost full, mainly French tourists visiting Jersey for the day to judge from the conversations Tanya overheard. Once out of harbour, the hydrofoil started to lift, increasing speed, and she gazed out into the morning feeling exhilarated. She'd done it. Beaten all of them. Once in Jersey, she was as good as in London. She leaned back in the comfortable seat and closed her eyes.

Alex Martin turned his big Peugeot estate car on to the Albert Quay and drove along until he found a convenient parking place, which wasn't easy for the car ferry was in from Weymouth and things were rather busy. He had not slept at all and was beginning to feel the effects, although a good breakfast had helped and a cold shower. He wore navy-blue slacks, a polo neck sweater in the same colour and a sports jacket in pale blue tweed by Yves St Laurent. Partly this was a desire to make an impression on Tanya Voroninova. His music meant an enormous amount to him and the chance to meet a performer he admired so much was of more importance to him than either Ferguson or Fox could have imagined.

His hair was still a little damp and he ran his fingers through it, suddenly uneasy. He opened the glove compartment of the Peugeot and took out the handgun he found there. It was a .38 Smith and Wesson Special, the Airweight model with the two inch barrel, a weapon much favoured by the CIA. Six years before, he'd taken it from the body of a Protestant terrorist in Belfast, a member of the outlawed UVF. The man had tried to kill Martin, had almost succeeded. Martin had killed him instead. It had never worried him, that was the strange thing. No regrets, no nightmares.

'Come off it, Alex,' he said softly. 'This is Jersey.'

But the feeling wouldn't go away, Belfast all over again, that touch of unease. Remembering an old trick from undercover days, he slipped the gun into the waistband at the small of his back. Frequently even a body search missed a weapon secreted there.

He sat smoking a cigarette, listening to Radio Jersey on the car radio, until the hydrofoil moved in through the harbour entrance. Even then, he didn't get out. There were the usual formalities to be passed through, customs and so on. He waited until the first passengers emerged from the exit of the passenger terminal then got out and moved forward. He recognized Tanya at once in her black jumpsuit, the trenchcoat over her shoulders like a cloak.

He moved forward to meet her. 'Miss Voroninova?' She examined him warily. 'Or should I say Miss Frank?'

'Who are you?'

'Alexander Martin. I'm here to see you get on your plane safely. You're booked on the ten-past-ten to London. Plenty of time.'

She put a hand on his arm, relaxing completely, unaware of Turkin and Shepilov on the other side of the road against the wall, backs partially turned. 'You've no idea how good it is to see a friendly face.'

'This way.' He guided her to the Peugeot. 'I saw you play the Emperor at the Proms at the Albert Hall last year. You were amazing.'

He put her into the passenger seat, went round to the other side and got behind the wheel.

'Do you play yourself?' she asked, as if by instinct.

'Oh, yes.' He turned the ignition key. 'But not like you.'

Behind them, the rear doors opened on each side and the two Russians got in, Turkin behind Tanya. 'Don't argue, there's a silenced pistol against your spine and hers. These seats aren't exactly body armour. We can kill you both without a sound and walk away.'

Tanya went rigid and gasped. Alex Martin said calmly, 'You know these men?'

'GRU. Military Intelligence.'

'I see. What happens now?' he asked Turkin.

'She goes back if we can take her. If not, she dies. The only important thing is that she doesn't talk to the wrong people. Any nonsense from you and she'll be the first to go. We know our duty.'

'I'm sure you do.'

'Because we are strong and you are weak, pretty boy,' Turkin told him. 'That's why we'll win in the end. Walk right up to Buckingham Palace.'

'Wrong time of the year, old son,' Alex said. 'The Queen's at Sandringham.'

Turkin scowled. 'Very amusing. Now get this thing moving round to the Marina.'

They walked along the pontoon towards *L'Alouette*, Martin with a hand on the girl's elbow, the two Russians walking behind. Martin helped Tanya over the rail. She was trembling, he could feel it.

Turkin opened the companionway door. 'Down below, both of you.' He followed close behind, his gun in his hand now. 'Stop!' he said to Martin when they reached the saloon. 'Lean on the table, legs spread. You sit down,' he told Tanya.

Shepilov stood on one side, gun in hand. Tanya was close to tears. Alex said gently, 'Keep smiling. Always pays.'

'You English really take the biscuit,' Turkin said as he searched him expertly. 'You're nothing any more. Yesterday's news. Just wait till the Argentinians blow you out of the water down there in the South Atlantic.' He lifted Martin's jacket at the rear and found the Airweight. 'Would you look at that?' he said to Shepilov. 'Amateur. I noticed some cord in the galley. Get it.'

Shepilov was soon back. 'And once at sea, it's the deep six?' Martin enquired.

'Something like that.' Turkin turned to Shepilov. 'Tie him up. We'd better get out of here fast. I'll get the engine started.'

He went up the companionway. Tanya had stopped trembling, her face pale, rage in her eyes and desperation. Martin shook his head a fraction and Shepilov kneed him painfully in the rear. 'Up you come, hands behind you.' Martin could feel the muzzle of the silencer against his back. The Russian said to Tanya, 'Tie his wrists.'

Martin said, 'Don't they ever teach you chaps anything? You never stand that close to anyone.'

He swung, pivoting to the left, away from the barrel of the gun. It coughed once, drilling a hole in the bulkhead. His right hand caught the Russian's wrist, twisting it up and round, taut as a steel bar. Shepilov grunted and dropped the weapon and Martin's clenched left fist descended in a hammer blow, snapping the arm.

Shepilov cried out, dropping to one knee. Martin bent down and picked up the gun and miraculously, the Russian's other hand swung up, the blade of the spring knife flashing. Martin blocked it, aware of the sudden pain as the blade sliced through his sleeve, drawing blood. He punched Shepilov on the jaw, knuckles extended and kicked the knife under the seat.

Tanya was on her feet, but already there were hurried steps on deck. 'Ivan?' Turkin called.

Martin put a finger to his lips to the girl, brushed past her and went into the galley. A small ladder led to the forward hatch. He opened it and went out on deck as he heard Turkin start down.

It had begun to rain, a fine mist drifting in from the sea as he stepped lightly across the deck to the entrance of the companionway. Turkin had reached the bottom and stood there, gun in his right hand as he peered cautiously into the saloon. Martin didn't make a sound, gave him no chance at all. He simply extended his pistol and shot him neatly through the right arm. Turkin cried out, dropped his weapon and staggered into the saloon and Martin went down the companionway.

Tanya moved to join him. Martin picked up Turkin's gun and put it in his pocket. Turkin leaned against the table, clutching his arm, glaring at him. Shepilov was just pulling himself up and sank on to the bench with a groan. Martin swung Turkin round and searched his pockets until he found his gun. He turned to Turkin again.

'I was careful with the arm. You aren't going to die – yet. I don't know who owns this boat, but you obviously meant to leave in it, you and chummy here. I'd get on with it if I were you. You'd only be an embarrassment to our people and I'm sure they'd like you back in Moscow. You ought to be able to manage between you.'

'Bastard!' Peter Turkin said in despair.

'Not in front of the lady,' Alex Martin told him. He pushed Tanya Voroninova up the companionway and turned. 'As a matter of interest, you two wouldn't last one bad Saturday night in Belfast,' then he followed the girl up to the deck.

When they reached the Peugeot, he took off his jacket gingerly. There was blood on his shirt sleeve and he fished out his handkerchief. 'Would you mind doing what you can with that?'

She bound it around the slash tightly. 'What kind of a man are you?'

'Well, I prefer Mozart myself,' Alex Martin said as he pulled on his jacket. 'I say, would you look at that?'

Beyond, on the outer edge of the marina, *L'Alouette* was moving out of the harbour. 'They're leaving,' Tanya said.

'Poor sods,' Martin told her. 'Their next posting will probably be the Gulag after this.' He handed her into the Peugeot and smiled cheerfully as he got behind the wheel. 'Now let's get you up to the airport, shall we?'

At Heathrow Airport's Terminal One, Harry Fox sat in the security office, drank a cup of tea and enjoyed a cigarette with the duty sergeant. The phone rang, the sergeant answered, then passed it across.

'Harry?' Ferguson said.

'Sir.'

'She made it. She's on the plane. Just left Jersey.'

'No problems, sir?'

'Not if you exclude a couple of GRU bogeymen snatching her and Martin off the Albert Quay.'

Fox said, 'What happened?'

'He managed, that's what happened. We'll have to use that young man again. You did say he was Guards?'

'Yes, sir. Welsh.'

'Thought so. One can always tell,' Ferguson said cheerfully and rang off.

'No, Madame, nothing to pay,' the steward said to Tanya as the one-eleven climbed into the sky away from Jersey. 'The bar is free. What would you like? Vodka and tonic, gin and orange? Or we have champagne.'

Free champagne. Tanya nodded and took the frosted glass he offered her. To a new life, she thought and then she said softly, 'To you, Alexander Martin,' and emptied the glass in a long swallow.

Luckily, the housekeeper had the day off. Alex Martin disposed of his shirt, pushing it to the bottom of the garbage in one of the bins, then went to the bathroom and cleaned his arm. It really needed stitching, but to go to the hospital would have meant questions and that would never do. He pulled the edges of the cut together with neat butterflies of tape, an old soldier's trick, and bandaged it. He put on a bathrobe, poured himself a large Scotch and went into the sitting room. As he sat down, the phone rang.

His wife said, 'Darling, I phoned the office and they said you were taking the day off. Is anything wrong? You haven't been overdoing it again, have you?'

She knew nothing of the work he'd done for Ferguson in the past. No need to alarm her now. He smiled ruefully, noting the slash in the sleeve of the Yves St Laurent jacket on the chair next to him.

'Certainly not,' he said. 'You know me? Anything for a quiet life. I'm working at home today, that's all. Now tell me – how are the children?'

9

At Cavendish Square, Ferguson was seated at the desk holding the telephone, face grave when Harry Fox came in from the study with a telex message. Ferguson made a quick gesture with one hand, then said, 'Thank you, Minister,' and replaced the receiver.

'Trouble, sir?' Fox asked.

'As far as I'm concerned it is. The Foreign Office have just informed me that the Pope's visit is definitely on. The Vatican will make an announcement within the next few hours. What have you got?'

'Telex, sir. Information on the Task Force's progress. The bad news is that HMS *Antelope* has finally sunk. She was bombed by Skyhawks yesterday. The good news is that seven Argentinian jets have been brought down.'

'I'd be happier about that if I saw the wreckage, Harry. Probably half that figure in actuality. Battle of Britain all over again.'

'Perhaps, sir. Everybody claims a hit in the heat of the moment. It can be confusing.'

Ferguson stood up and lit one of his cheroots. 'I don't know, sometimes the bloody roof just seems to fall in. I've got the Pope coming, which we could well have done without. Cuchulain still on the loose over there, and now this nonsense about the Argentinians trying to buy Exocet missiles on the black market in Paris. Orders have gone through to pull Tony Villiers from behind enemy lines in the Falklands?'

'No problem, sir. He's being off-loaded by submarine in Uruguay. Flying from Montevideo by Air France direct to Paris. Should be there tomorrow.'

'Good. You'll have to go over on the shuttle. Brief him thoroughly, then get straight back here.'

'Will that be enough, sir?'

'Good God, yes. You know what Tony's like when he gets moving. Hell on wheels. He'll sort the opposition out over there, no problem. I need you here, Harry. What about the Voroninova girl?'

'As I told you, sir, we stopped off at Harrods on the way from Heathrow to get her a few things. Only had what she stood up in.'

'She'll be broke, of course,' Ferguson said. 'We'll have to tap the contingency fund.'

'As a matter of fact that won't be necessary, sir. It seems she has a very substantial bank account here. Record royalties and so on. She certainly won't have any difficulty in earning her living. They'll be clamouring for her, all the impresarios, when they know she's available.'

'That will have to wait. She's very definitely to stay under wraps until I say so. What's she like?'

'Very nice indeed, sir. I settled her into the spare room and she was having a bath.'

'Yes, well don't let's make her too comfortable, Harry. We want to get on with this thing. I've heard from Devlin and it seems another of McGuiness's hatchet men, the one who was supposed to be keeping an eye on Cherny, has turned up in the Liffey. He doesn't waste time, our friend.'

'I see, sir,' Fox said. 'So what are you suggesting?'

'We'll get her over to Dublin now – this afternoon. You can escort her, Harry. Hand her over to Devlin at the airport, then get back here. You can go to Paris on the morning shuttle.'

Fox said mildly, 'She might just feel like sitting down for a moment. Taking a deep breath. That sort of thing.'

'So would we all, Harry, and if that's a subtle way of telling me how you feel, then all I can say is you should have taken that job they offered you at your uncle's merchant bank. Start at ten, finish at four.'

'And terribly, terribly boring, sir.'

Kim opened the door at that moment and ushered in Tanya Voroninova. Her eyes were slightly hollowed, but she looked surprisingly well, the general effect enhanced by the blue cashmere sweater and neat tweed skirt she had purchased at Harrods. Fox made the introductions.

'Miss Voroninova. A great pleasure,' Ferguson said. 'You've certainly had an active time of it. Please sit down.'

She sat on the couch by the fire. 'Have you any idea what's happening in Paris?' she asked.

'Not yet,' Fox said. 'We'll find out in the end, but if you want an educated guess, the KGB never care for failure at the best of times and if we consider your foster-father's special interest in this case . . .' He shrugged. 'I wouldn't care to be in Turkin or Shepilov's shoes.'

'Even such a shrewd old campaigner as Nikolai Belov will have difficulty surviving this one,' Ferguson put in.

'So, what happens now?' she asked. 'Do I see Professor Devlin again?'

'Yes, but that means flying over to Dublin. I know your feet have hardly touched the ground, but time is of the essence. I'd like you to go later on this afternoon if that's all right. Captain Fox will escort you and we'll arrange for Devlin to meet you at Dublin Airport.'

She was still on a high, and somehow it seemed a part of what had already happened. 'When do we leave?'

'The early evening plane,' Devlin said. 'Sure, I'll be there. No problem.'

'You'll make your own arrangements about the necessary meeting with McGuiness so that she can look at whatever photos or other material they want to show her?'

'I'll take care of it,' Devlin said.

'Sooner rather than later,' Ferguson told him firmly.

'I hear and obey, O Genie of the lamp,' Devlin said. 'Now let me talk to her.'

Ferguson handed her the phone. Tanya said, 'Professor Devlin? What is it?'

'I've just heard from Paris. The Mona Lisa is smiling all over her face. See you soon.'

And in Moscow important things had been happening that morning. Events that were to affect the whole of Russia and world politics generally, for Yuri Andropov, head of the KGB since 1967, was named Secretary of the Communist Party Central Committee. He still inhabited his old office at KGB headquarters at Dzerhinsky Square and it was there that he summoned Maslovsky just after noon. The General stood in front of the desk, filled with foreboding, for Andropov was possibly the only man he had ever known of whom he was genuinely afraid. Andropov was writing, his pen scratching the paper. He ignored Maslovsky for a while, then spoke without looking up.

'There is little point in referring to the gross inefficiency shown by your department in the matter of the Cuchulain affair.'

'Comrade.' Maslovsky didn't attempt to defend himself.

'You have given orders that he is to be eliminated together with Cherny?'

'Yes, Comrade.'

'The sooner the better.' Andropov paused, removed his glasses and ran a hand over his forehead. 'Then there is the matter of your foster-daughter. She is now safely in London due to the bungling of your people.'

'Yes, Comrade.'

'From which city Brigadier Ferguson is having her flown to Dublin, where the IRA intend to give her any help she needs to identify Cuchulain?'

'That would appear to be the case,' Maslovsky said weakly.

'The Provisional IRA is a fascist organization as far as I am concerned, hopelessly tainted by its links with the Catholic Church, and Tanya Voroninova is a traitor to her country, her party and her class. You will send an immediate signal to the man Lubov in Dublin. He will eliminate her as well as Cherny and Cuchulain.'

He replaced his glasses, picked up his pen and started to write again. Maslovsky said in a hoarse voice, 'Please, Comrade, perhaps . . .'

Andropov glanced up in surprise. 'Does my order give you some sort of problem, Comrade General?'

Maslovsky, wilting under those cold eyes, shook his head hurriedly. 'No, of course not, Comrade,' and he turned and went out, feeling just the slightest tremor in his limbs.

At the Soviet Embassy in Dublin, Lubov had already received a signal from Paris informing him that Tanya Voroninova had slipped the net. He was still in the radio room digesting this startling piece of news when the second signal came through, the one from Maslovsky in Moscow. The operator recorded it, placed the tape in the machine and Lubov keyed in his personal code. When he read the message he felt physically sick. He went to his office, locked the door and got a bottle of Scotch from the cupboard. He had one and then another. Finally he phoned Cherny.

'Costello, here.' It was the code name he used on such occasions. 'Are you busy?'

'Not particularly,' Cherny told him.

'We must meet.'

'The usual place?'

'Yes, I must talk to you first. Very important. However, we must also arrange to see our mutual friend this evening. Dun Street, I think. Can you arrange that?'

'It's very unusual.'

'As I said, matters of importance. Ring me back to confirm this evening's meeting.'

Cherny was definitely worried. Dun Street was a code name for a disused warehouse on City Quay which he had leased under a company name some years previously, but that wasn't the point. What was really important was the fact that he, Cussane and Lubov had never all met together in the same place before. He phoned Cussane at the cottage without success, so he tried the Catholic Secretariat offices in Dublin. Cussane answered at once.

'Thank God,' said Cherny. 'I tried the cottage.'

'Yes, I've just got in,' Cussane told him. 'Is there a problem?'

'I'm not sure. I feel uneasy. Can I speak freely?'

'You usually do on this line.'

'Our friend Costello has been in touch. Asked me to meet him at three-thirty.'

'Usual place?'

'Yes, but he's also asked me to arrange for the three of us to meet at Dun Street tonight.'

'That *is* unusual.'

'I know. I don't like it.'

'Perhaps he has instructions for us to pull out,' Cussane said. 'Did he say anything about the girl?'

'No. Should he have done?'

'I just wondered what was happening there, that's all. Tell him I'll see you at Dun Street at six-thirty. Don't worry, Paul. I'll handle things.'

He rang off and Cherny got straight back to Lubov. 'Six-thirty, is that all right?'

'Fine,' Lubov told him.

'He asked me if you'd heard anything about the girl in Paris.'

'No, not a word,' Lubov lied. 'I'll see you at three-thirty.' He rang off, poured himself a drink, then unlocked the top drawer of his desk, took out a case and opened it. It contained a Stechkin automatic pistol and a silencer. Gingerly, he started fitting them together.

In his office at the Secretariat, Harry Cussane stood at the window, looking down into the street. He had listened in to Devlin's conversations with Ferguson before leaving the cottage and knew that Tanya Voroninova was due that evening. It was inconceivable that Lubov would not have heard, either from Moscow or Paris, so why hadn't he mentioned it?

The meeting at Dun Street was unusual enough in itself, but in view of that meeting, why meet Cherny in the usual back row at the cinema first? What could possibly be the need? It didn't fit, any of it, and every instinct that Cussane possessed, honed by his years in the trenches, told him so. Whatever Lubov wanted to see them for, it was not conversation.

Paul Cherny was reaching for his raincoat when there was a knock at the door of his rooms. When he opened it, Harry Cussane was standing outside. He wore a dark trilby hat and raincoat of the kind affected by priests and looked agitated.

'Paul, thank God I caught you.'

'Why, what is it?' Cherny demanded.

'The IRA man who followed you, the one I disposed of the other day. They've set another one on. This way.'

Cherny's rooms were on the first floor of the old greystone college building. Cussane went up the stairs quickly to the next floor and turned at once up another flight of stairs.

'Where are we going?' Cherny called.

'I'll show you.'

On the top landing, the tall Georgian window at the end had its bottom half pushed up. Cussane peered out. 'Over there,' he said. 'On the other side of the quad.'

Cherny looked down to the stone flags and the green grass of the quadrangle. 'Where?' he asked.

There was the hand in the small of his back, a sudden violent push. He managed to cry out, but only just as he overbalanced across the low windowsill and plunged head first towards the stone flags eighty-feet below.

Cussane ran along the corridor and descended the back stairs hurriedly. In a sense, he had been telling the truth. McGuiness had indeed replaced Murphy with a new watchdog, in fact two of them this time, sitting in a green Ford Escort near the main entrance, not that it was going to do them much good now.

Lubov had the back row to himself. In fact, there were only five or six people in the cinema at all as far as he could see in the dim light. He was early, but that was by intention, and he fingered the silenced Stechkin in his pocket, his palms damp with sweat. He'd brought a flask with him and took it out now and swallowed deep. More Scotch to give him the courage he needed. First Cherny and then Cussane, but that should be easier if he was at the warehouse first and waiting in ambush. He took another swig at the flask, had just replaced it in his pocket when there was a movement in the darkness and someone sat down beside him.

'Paul?' he turned his head.

An arm slid round his neck, a hand clamped over his mouth. In the second that he recognized Cussane's pale face under the brim of the black hat, the needle point of the stiletto the other held in his right hand probed in under his ribs, thrusting up into the heart. There was not even time to struggle. A kind of blinding light, no pain, then only darkness.

Cussane wiped the blade carefully on Lubov's jacket, eased him back in the seat as if asleep. He found the Stechkin in the dead man's pocket, took it out and slipped it into his own. He had been right, as usual. The final proof. He got up, went down the aisle, a shadow only in his black coat, and left through one of the exit doors.

He was back at the office in the Secretariat within half an hour, had hardly sat down when Monsignor Halloran came in. Halloran was very cheerful and obviously excited.

'Have you heard? Just had the confirmation from the Vatican. The Pope's visit is on.'

'So they've decided. You'll be going across?'

'Yes indeed. Seat booked in Canterbury Cathedral. An historic occasion, Harry. Something for people to tell their grandchildren about.'

'For those who have any,' Cussane smiled.

Halloran laughed. 'Exactly, which hardly applies to us. I must be off. I've got a dozen things to organize.'

Cussane sat there thinking about it, then reached for his raincoat where he'd thrown it on a chair and took the poniard out in its leather sheath. He put it in one of the desk drawers then took out the Stechkin. What a bungling amateur Lubov had been to use a weapon of Russian manufacture. But it was the proof that he had needed. It meant that to his masters he was not only expendable. He was now a liability.

'So what now, Harry Cussane?' he asked himself softly. 'Where do you go?'

Strange that habit, when speaking to himself, of addressing Cussane by his full name. It was as if he were another person which, in a way, he was. The phone rang and when he answered, Devlin spoke to him.

'There you are.'

'Where are you?'

'Dublin airport. I'm picking up a house-guest. A very pretty girl, actually. I think you'll like her. I thought we all might have supper tonight.'

'That sounds nice,' Cussane said calmly. 'I've agreed to take evening Mass, though, at the village church. I'll be finished at eight. Is that all right?'

'Fine. We'll look forward to seeing you.'

Cussane put the phone down. He could run, of course, but where and to what purpose? In any event, the play had at least one more act to go, all his instincts told him that.

'No place to hide, Harry Cussane,' he said softly.

When Harry Fox and Tanya came through the gate into the arrival hall, Devlin was waiting, leaning against a pillar, smoking a cigarette, wearing the black felt hat and trenchcoat. He came forward, smiling.

'*Cead mile failte*,' he said and took the young woman's hands. 'That's Irish for a hundred thousand welcomes.'

'*Go raibh maith agat.*' Fox gave him the ritual thanks.

'Stop showing off.' Devlin took her bag. 'His mother was a decent Irishwoman, thank the Lord.'

Her face was shining. 'I'm so excited. All this is so – so unbelievable.'

Fox said, 'Right, you're in safe hands now. I'm off. There's a return flight in an hour. I'd better book in. We'll be in touch, Liam.'

He went off through the crowd and Devlin took her elbow and led her to the main entrance. 'A nice man,' she said. 'His hand? What happened?'

'He picked up a bag with a bomb in it in Belfast one bad night and didn't throw it fast enough. He gets by very well with the electronic marvel they've given him.'

'You say that so calmly,' she said as they crossed to the carpark.

'He wouldn't thank you for the wrong kind of sympathy. Comes of his particular kind of upbringing. Eton, the Guards. They teach you to get on with it, not cry in your beer.' He handed her into his old Alfa Romeo sports car. 'Harry's a special breed, just like that ould bastard Ferguson. What's known as a gentleman.'

'Which you are not?'

'God save us, my ould mother would turn in her grave to hear you even suggest it,' he said as he drove away. 'So, you decided to give things some more thought after I left Paris? What happened?'

She told him everything. Belov, the phone conversation with Maslovsky, Shepilov and Turkin, and finally, Alex Martin in Jersey.

Devlin was frowning thoughtfully as she finished. 'So they were on to you? Actually waiting in Jersey? How in the hell would they know that?'

'I asked about the train times at hotel reception,' she told him. 'I didn't give my name or room number. I thought that covered it. Perhaps Belov and his people were able to make the right sort of enquiries.'

'Maybe. Still, you're here now. You'll be staying with me at my cottage in Kilrea. It isn't far. I've got a call to make when we get in. With luck, we'll be able to set up the right kind of meeting for you tomorrow. Lots of photos for you to plough through.'

'I hope something comes of it,' she said.

'Don't we all? Anyway, a quiet night. I'll make the supper and a good friend of mine is joining us.'

'Anyone interesting?'

'The kind of man you'd find rather thin on the ground where you come from. A Catholic priest. Father Harry Cussane. I think you'll like him.'

He phoned McGuiness from his study. 'The girl is here. Staying with me at my place. How soon can you set up the right meeting?'

'Never mind that,' McGuiness told him. 'Have you heard about Cherny?'

Devlin was immediately alert. 'No.'

'Took a very long fall from a very high window at Trinity College this afternoon. The thing is, did he fall or was he pushed?'

'I suppose one could say his end was fortuitous,' Devlin said.

'For one person only,' McGuiness told him. 'Jesus, I'd like to get my hands on that sod.'

'Set up the meeting with the girl then,' Devlin said. 'Maybe she'll recognize him.'

'I'd go to confession again if I thought that could be guaranteed. Okay, leave it with me. I'll get back to you.'

Cussane robed for Mass in the sacristy, very calm, very cold. It wasn't like a play any longer. More like an improvisation in which the actors created a story for themselves. He had no idea what was going to happen.

The four acolytes who waited for him were village boys, clean and neat and angelic in their scarlet cassocks and white cottas. He settled the stole around his neck, picked up his prayer book and turned to them.

'Let's make it special tonight, shall we?'

He pressed the bellpush at the door. A moment later, the organ started to play. One of the boys opened the door and they moved through into the small church in procession.

Devlin was working in the kitchen preparing steaks. Tanya opened the French windows and was immediately aware of the organ music drifting across the garden from the other side of the wall. She went in to Devlin. 'What's that?'

'There's a convent over there and a hospice. Their chapel is the village church. That'll be Harry Cussane celebrating Mass. He won't be long.'

She went back into the living room and stood listening at the French windows. It was nice and not only peaceful. The organ playing was really rather good. She crossed the lawn and opened the door in the wall. The chapel, on the end of the convent, looked picturesque and inviting, soft light flooding from the windows. She went up the path and opened the oaken door.

There were only a handful of villagers, two people in wheelchairs who were obviously patients from the hospice and several nuns. Sister Anne-Marie played the organ. It was not much of an instrument and the damp atmosphere had a bad effect on the reeds, but she was good, had spent a year at the Conservatoire in Paris as a young girl before heeding God's call and turning to the religious life.

The lights were very dim, mainly candles, and the church was a place of shadows and calm peace, the nuns' voices sweet as they sang the offertory: '*Domine Jesu Christ, Rex Floriae . . .*' At the altar, Harry Cussane prayed for all sinners everywhere whose actions only cut them off from the fact of God's infinite mercy and love. Tanya took a seat to one side on her own, moved by the atmosphere. The truth was that she had never attended a church service like this in her life. She couldn't see much of Cussane's face. He was simply the chief figure down there at the altar in the dim light, fascinating to her in his robes as was the whole business.

The Mass continued, most of those in the congregation went forward to the rail to receive the body and blood of Christ. She watched, as he moved from one person to the other, the head bending to murmur the ritual words and she was filled with a strange unease. It was as if she knew this man, some trick of physical movement that seemed familiar.

When the Mass was over, the final absolution given, he paused on the steps to address the congregation. 'And in your prayers during the coming days, I would ask each one of you to pray for the Holy Father, soon to visit England at a most difficult time.' He moved forward a little, the candlelight falling on his face. 'Pray for him that your prayers, added to his own, grant him the strength to accomplish his mission.'

His gaze passed over the entire congregation and for a moment it was as if he was looking at her directly, then he moved on. Tanya froze in horror, the shock, the most terrible she had ever known in her life. When he spoke the words of the benediction, it was as if his lips moved with no sound. The face – the face which had haunted her dreams for years. Older, of course, kinder even, and yet unmistakeably the face of Mikhail Kelly, the man they had named Cuchulain.

What happened then was strange, yet perhaps not so strange if one considered the circumstances. The shock was so profound that it seemed to drain all strength from her and she remained in the half-darkness at the back of the church while people moved out and Cussane and the acolytes disappeared into the sacristy. It was very quiet in the church and she sat there, trying to make sense of things. Cuchulain was Father Harry Cussane, Devlin's friend, and it explained so many things. Oh, my God, she thought, what am I going to do? And then the sacristy door opened and Cussane stepped out.

Things were almost ready in the kitchen. Devlin checked the oven, whistling softly to himself and called, 'Have you laid the table in there?'

There was no reply. He went into the living room. Not only was the table not laid but there was no sign of Tanya. Then he noticed the French window ajar, took off his apron and moved forward.

'Tanya?' he called into the garden, and in the same moment saw that the door in the garden wall stood open.

Cussane wore a black suit and clerical collar. He paused for a moment, aware of her presence although he made no sign. He'd noticed her almost at once during the Mass. The fact that she was a stranger would have made her stand out, but in the circumstances it had been obvious who she must be. Knowing that, there was the ghost of the child there in the face, the child who had struggled as he held her that day in Drumore, all those years ago. Eyes never changed, and the eyes he had always remembered.

He turned at the altar rail, dropping to one knee to genuflect, and Tanya, in a panic now and terribly afraid, forced herself to her feet and moved along the aisle. The door to one of the confessional boxes stood partially open and she slipped inside. When she pulled it close, there was a slight creaking. She heard him walk down the aisle, the steps slow, distinct on the stone flags. They came closer. Stopped.

He said softly in Russian, 'I know you are there, Tanya Voroninova. You can come out now.'

She stood there, shivering, very cold. He was quite calm, his face grave. Still in Russian, he said, 'It's been a long time.'

She said, 'So, do you kill me like you killed my father? As you have killed so many others?'

'I hoped that wouldn't be necessary.' He stood there looking at her, his hands in the pockets of his jacket, and then he smiled gently and there was a kind of sadness there. 'I've heard you on records. You have a remarkable talent.'

'So have you.' She felt stronger now. 'For death and destruction. They chose you well. My foster-father knew what he was doing.'

'Not really,' he said. 'Nothing is ever that simple. I happened to be available. The right tool at the right time.'

She took a deep breath. 'What happens now?'

'I thought we were supposed to be having dinner together, you, I and Liam,' he said.

The porch door banged open and Devlin walked in. 'Tanya?' he called and then paused. 'Oh, there you are. So you two have met?'

'Yes, Liam, a long, long time ago,' Harry Cussane told him, and his hand came out of the right pocket of his jacket holding the Stechkin he had taken from Lubov.

At the cottage, he found cord in the kitchen drawer. 'The steaks smell good, Liam. Better turn the oven off.'

'Would you look at that?' Devlin said to the girl. 'He thinks of everything.'

'The only reason I've got this far,' Cussane said calmly.

They went into the living room. He didn't tie them up, but motioned them to sit on the sofa by the fire. He stepped on to the hearth, reached up inside the chimney and found the Walther hanging on its nail that Devlin always kept there for emergencies.

'Keeping you out of temptation, Liam.'

'He knows all my little secrets,' Devlin said to Tanya. 'But then he would. I mean, we've been friends for twenty years now.' The bitterness was there in the voice, the shake of raw anger, and he helped himself to a cigarette box on the side table without asking permission and lit it.

Cussane sat some distance away at the dining table and held up the Stechkin. 'These things make very little sound, old friend. No one knows that better than you. No tricks. No foolish Devlin gallantry. I'd hate to have to kill you.'

He laid the Stechkin on the table and lit a cigarette himself.

'Friend, is it?' Devlin said. 'About as true a friend as you are priest.'

'Friend,' Cussane insisted, 'and I've been a good priest. Ask anyone who knew me on the Falls Road in Belfast in sixty-nine.'

'Fine,' Devlin said. 'Only even an idiot like me can make two and two make four occasionally. Your masters put you in deep. To become a priest was your cover. Would I be right in thinking that you chose that seminary outside Boston for your training because I was English Professor there?'

'Of course. You were an important man in the IRA in those days, Liam. The advantages that the relationship offered for the future were obvious, but friends we became and friends we stayed. You cannot avoid that fact.'

'Sweet Jesus!' Devlin shook his head. 'Who are you, Harry? Who are you really?'

'My father was Sean Kelly.'

Devlin stared at him in astonishment. 'But I knew him well. We served in the Lincoln Washington Brigade in the Spanish Civil War. Just a minute. He married a Russian girl he met in Madrid.'

'My mother. My parents returned to Ireland where I was born. My father was hanged in England in nineteen-forty for his part in the IRA bombing campaign of that time. My mother and I lived in Dublin till nineteen-fifty-three, then she took me to Russia.'

Devlin said, 'The KGB must have fastened on you like leeches.'

'Something like that.'

'They discovered his special talents,' Tanya put in. 'Murder, for example.'

'No,' Cussane answered mildly. 'When I was first processed by the psychologists, Paul Cherny indicated that my special talent was for the stage.'

'An actor, is it?' Devlin said. 'Well, you're in the right job for it.'

'Not really. No audience, you see.' Cussane concentrated on Tanya. 'I doubt whether I've killed more than Liam. In what way are we different?'

'He fought for a cause,' she told him passionately.

'Exactly. I am a soldier, Tanya. I fight for my country – our country. As a matter of interest, I'm not an officer of the KGB. I am a lieutenant-colonel in Military Intelligence.' He smiled deprecatingly at Devlin. 'They kept promoting me.'

'But the things you've done. The killing,' she said. 'Innocent people.'

'There cannot be innocence in this world, not with Man in it. The Church teaches us that. There is always iniquity in this life – life is unfair. We must deal with the world as it is, not as it might have been.'

'Jesus!' Devlin said. 'One minute you're Cuchulain, the next you're a priest again. Have you any idea who you really are?'

'When I am priest, then priest I am,' Cussane told him. 'There is no avoiding that. The Church would be the first to say it in spite of what I have been. But the other me fights for his country. I have nothing to apologize for. I'm at war.'

'Very convenient,' Devlin said. 'So, the Church gives you your answer or is it the KGB – or is there a difference?'

'Does it matter?'

'Damn you, Harry, tell me one thing? How did you know we were on to you? How did you know about Tanya? Was it me?' he exploded. 'But how could it have been me?'

'You mean you checked your telephone as usual?' Cussane was at the drinks cabinet now, the Stechkin in his hand. He poured Bushmills into three glasses, carried them on a tray to the table in front of the sofa, took one and stepped back. 'I was using special equipment up there in the attic of my place. Directional microphone and other stuff. There wasn't much that went on here that I missed.'

Devlin took a deep breath, but when he lifted his glass, his hand was steady. 'So much for friendship.' He swallowed the whiskey. 'So, what happens now?'

'To you?'

'No, to you, you fool. Where do you go, Harry? Back home to dear old Mother Russia?' He shook his head and turned to Tanya. 'Come to think of it, Russia isn't his home.'

Cussane didn't feel anger then. There was no despair in his heart. All his life, he had played each part that was required of him, cultivated the kind of professional coolness necessary for a well-judged performance. There had been little room for real emotion in his life. Any action, even the good ones, had been simply a reaction to the given situation, an essential part of the performance. Or so he told himself. And yet he truly liked Devlin, always had. And the girl? He looked at Tanya now. He did not want to harm the girl.

Devlin, as if sensing a great deal of this, said softly, 'Where do you run, Harry? Is there anywhere?'

'No,' Harry Cussane said calmly. 'Nowhere to go. No place to hide. For what I have done, your IRA friends would dispose of me without hesitation. Ferguson certainly would not want me alive. Nothing to be gained from that. I would only be a liability.'

'And your own people? Once back in Moscow, it would be the Gulag for sure. At the end of the day, you're a failure and they don't like that.'

'True,' Cussane nodded. 'Except in one respect. They don't even want me back, Liam. They just want me dead. They've already tried. To them also I would only be an embarrassment.'

There was silence at his words, then Tanya said, 'But what happens? What do you do?'

'God knows,' he said. 'I am a dead man walking, my dear. Liam understands that. He's right. There is no place for me to run. Today, tomorrow, next week. If I stay in Ireland McGuiness and his men will have my head, wouldn't you agree, Liam?'

'True enough.'

Cussane stood up and paced up and down, holding the Stechkin against his knee. He turned to Tanya. 'You think life was cruel to a little girl back there in Drumore in the rain? You know how old I was? Twenty years of age. Life was cruel when they hanged my father. When my mother agreed to take me back to Russia. When Paul Cherny picked me out at the age of fifteen as a specimen with interesting possibilities for the KGB.' He sat down again. 'If my mother and I had been left alone in Dublin, who knows what might have happened to that one great talent I possessed. The Abbey Theatre, London, the Old Vic, Stratford?' He shrugged. 'Instead . . .'

Devlin was conscious of a great sadness, forgot for the moment everything else except that, for years, he had liked this man more than most.

'That's life,' he said. 'Always some bugger telling you what to do.'

'Living our lives for us, you mean?' Cussane said. 'Schoolteachers, the police, union leaders, politicians, parents?'

'Even priests,' Devlin said gently.

'Yes, I think I see now what the anarchists mean when they say "Shoot an authority figure today".' The evening paper was on a chair with a headline referring to the Pope's visit to England. Cussane picked it up. 'The Pope, for instance.'

Devlin said, 'A bad joke, that.'

'But why should I be joking?' Cussane asked him. 'You know what my brief was all those years ago, Liam? You know what Maslovsky told me my task was? To create chaos, disorder, fear and uncertainty in the West. I've helped keep the Irish conflict going, by hitting counter-productive targets, causing great harm on occasion to both Catholic and Protestant causes; IRA, UVF, I've pulled everyone in. But here.' He held up the newspaper with the photo of Pope John Paul on the front page. 'How about this for the most counter-productive target of all time? Would they like that in Moscow?' He nodded to Tanya. 'You must know Maslovsky well enough by now. Would it please him, do you think?'

'You're mad,' she whispered.

'Perhaps.' He tossed a length of cord across to her. 'Tie his wrists behind his back. No tricks, Liam.'

He stood well back, covering them with the Stechkin. There was little for Devlin to do except submit. The girl tied his hands awkwardly. Cussane pushed him down on his face beside the fire.

'Lie down beside him,' he told Tanya.

He pulled her arms behind her and tied her hands securely, then her ankles. Then he checked Devlin's wrists and tied his ankles also.

'So, you're not going to kill us?' Devlin said.

'Why should I?'

Cussane stood up, walked across the room, and with one swift jerk, pulled the telephone wire out of the wall.

'Where are you going?'

'Canterbury,' Cussane said. 'Eventually, that is.'

'Canterbury?'

'That's where the Pope will be on Saturday. They'll all be there. The cardinals, the Archbishop of Canterbury, Prince Charles. I know these things, Liam. I run the press office at the Secretariat, remember.'

'All right, let's be sensible,' Devlin said. 'You'll never get near him. The last thing the Brits want is the Pope dead on their hands. They'll have security at Canterbury that would make even the Kremlin sit up and take notice.'

'A real challenge,' Cussane said calmly.

'For God's sake, Harry, shoot the Pope. To what end?'

'Why not?' Cussane shrugged. 'Because he's there. Because I've nowhere else to go. If I've got to die, I might as well go down doing something spectacular.' He smiled down. 'And you can alway try and stop me, Liam, you and McGuiness and Ferguson and his people in London. Even the KGB would move heaven and earth to stop me if they could. It would certainly leave them with a lot of explaining to do.'

Devlin exploded. 'Is that all it is to you, Harry? A game?'

'The only one in town,' Cussane said. 'For years, I've been manipulated by other people. A regular puppet on a string. This time, I'm in charge. It should be an interesting change.'

He moved away and Devlin heard the French window open and close. There was silence. Tanya said, 'He's gone.'

Devlin nodded and struggled into a sitting position. He forced his wrists against the cord, but was wasting his time and knew it.

Tanya said, 'Liam, do you think he means it? About the Pope?'

'Yes,' Devlin said grimly. 'I believe he does.'

Once at his cottage, Cussane worked quickly and methodically. From a small safe hidden behind books in his study he took his Irish passport in his usual identity. There were also two British ones in different names. In one he was still a priest, in another a journalist. There was also two thousand pounds in notes of varying sizes, English not Irish.

He got a canvas holdall from his wardrobe of a type favoured by army officers and opened it. There was a board panel in the bottom which he pressed open. Inside he placed most of the money, the false passports, a Walther PPK with a Carswell silencer and several additional clips of ammunition, a block of plastic explosive, and two timing pencils. As an afterthought, he got a couple of Army field dressing packs from the bathroom cupboard and some morphine ampoules and put them in also. Like the soldier he thought himself to be, he had to be ready for anything. He replaced the panel, rolled up one of his black cassocks and placed it in the bottom of the bag. A couple of shirts and what he thought of as civilian ties, socks, toilet articles. His prayer book went in as a reflex habit as did the other things. The Host in the silver pyx, the holy oils. As a priest it had been second nature to travel with them for years now.

He went downstairs to the hall and pulled on his black raincoat, then took one of the two black felt hats from the hall cupboard and went into the study. Inside the crown of the hat he had sewn two plastic clips. He opened a drawer in his desk and took out a .38 Smith and Wesson revolver with a two inch barrel. It fitted snugly into the clips and he put the hat into his holdall. The Stechkin he put in the pocket of his raincoat.

So, he was ready. He glanced once around the study of the cottage which had been his home for so long, then turned and went out. He crossed the yard to the garage, opened the door and switched on the light. His motorcycle stood beside the car, an old 350cc BSA in superb condition. He strapped his holdall on the rear, took the crash helmet from the peg on the wall and put it on.

When he kicked the starter, the engine roared into life at once. He sat there for a moment adjusting things, then he crossed himself and rode away. The sound of the engine faded into the distance and after a while there was only silence.

At that moment in Dublin, Martin McGuiness was watching one of his men put the receiver back on the phone rest.

'The line's dead, that's certain.'

'That seems more than a little strange to me, son,' McGuiness said. 'Let's pay Liam a visit, and let's drive fast.'

It took McGuiness and a couple of his men forty minutes to get there. He stood watching while his men released Devlin and the girl and shook his head.

'Christ, Liam, it would be funny seeing the great Liam Devlin trussed up like a chicken if it wasn't so bloody tragic. Tell me again? Tell me what it's about, then.'

He and Devlin went into the kitchen and Devlin filled him in on what had happened. When he was finished, McGuiness exploded. 'The cunning bastard. On the Falls Road in Belfast City they remember him as a saint, and him a sodding Russian agent pretending to be a priest.'

'I shouldn't think the Vatican will be exactly overjoyed,' Devlin told him.

'And you know what's worse? What really sticks in my throat? He's no fucking Russian at all. Jesus, Liam, his father died on an English gallows for the cause.' McGuiness was shaking with rage now. 'I'm going to have his balls.'

'And how do you propose to do that?'

'You leave that to me. The Pope at Canterbury, is it? I'll close Ireland up so tight that not even a rat could find a hole to sneak out.'

He bustled out, calling to his men and was gone. Tanya came into the kitchen. She looked pale and tired. 'Now what happens?'

'You put on the kettle and we'll have a nice cup of tea. You know, they say that in the old days a messenger bearing bad news was usually executed. Thank God for the telephone. You'll excuse me for a few minutes while I go across the road and ring Ferguson.'

10

Ballywalter on the coast just south of Dundalk Bay near Clogher Head could hardly be described as a port. A pub, a few houses, half-a-dozen fishing boats and the tiniest of harbours. It was a good hour and a half after Devlin's phone call to Ferguson that Cussane turned his BSA motorcycle into a wood on a hill overlooking the place. He pushed his machine up on its stand and went and looked down at Ballywalter, clear in the moonlight below, then he went back to the bike and unstrapped his holdall and took out the black trilby which he put on his head instead of the crash helmet.

He started down the road, bag in hand. What he intended now was tricky, but clever if it worked. It was like chess really; trying to think not just one move, but three moves ahead. Certainly now was the time to see if all that information so carefully extracted from the dying Danny Malone would prove worthwhile.

Sean Deegan had been publican in Ballywalter for eleven years. It was hardly a full-time occupation in a village that boasted only forty-one men of the legal age to drink, which explained why he was also skipper of a forty-foot motor fishing boat *Mary Murphy*. Added to this, on the illegal side of things, he was not only a member of the IRA, but very much on the active list, having only been released from Long Kesh prison in Ulster in February after serving three years' imprisonment for possession of illegal weapons. The fact that Deegan had personally killed two British soldiers in Derry had never been traced to him by the authorities.

His wife and two children were away visiting her mother in Galway and he had closed the bar at eleven, intending fishing early. He was still awake when Cussane came down the street. He had been awakened from his bed by a phone call from one of McGuiness's men. Deegan offered an illegal way out of the country to the Isle of Man, a useful staging post for England. The description of Cussane which he had been given was brief and to the point.

Deegan had hardly put the phone down when there was a knock at the door. He opened it and found Cussane standing there. He knew at once who his nocturnal caller was, although the clerical collar and black hat and raincoat would have been enough in themselves.

'What can I do for you, Father?' Deegan asked, stepping back so that Cussane might come in.

They went into the small bar and Deegan stirred the fire. 'I got your name from a parishioner, Danny Malone,' Cussane said. 'My name is Daly, by the way.'

'Danny, is it?' Deegan said. 'I heard he was in a bad way.'

'Dying, poor soul. He told me you could do a run to the Isle of Man if the price was right or the cause.'

Deegan went behind the bar and poured a whiskey. 'Will you join me, Father?'

'No thanks.'

'You're in trouble? Political or police?'

'A little of both.' Cussane took ten English fifty pound notes from his pocket and laid them on the bar. 'Would this handle it?'

Deegan picked the notes up and weighed them thoughtfully. 'And why not, Father? Look, you sit by the fire and keep yourself warm and I'll make a phone call.'

'A phone call?'

'Sure and I can't manage the boat on my own. I need at least one crew and two is better.'

He went out, closing the door. Cussane went round the bar to the phone there and waited. There was a slight tinkle from the bell and he lifted the receiver gently.

The man was talking urgently. 'Deegan here at Ballywalter. Have you Mr McGuiness?'

'He's gone to bed.'

'Jesus, man, will you get him? He's here at my place now. That fella Cussane your people phoned about.'

'Hold right there.' There was a delay, then another voice said, 'McGuiness. Is it yourself, Sean?'

'And none other. Cussane's here at my pub. Calls himself Daly. He's just given me five hundred quid to take him to the Isle of Man. What do I do, hold him?'

McGuiness said, 'I'd like nothing better than to see to him myself, but that's childish. You've got some good men there?'

'Phil Egan and Tadgh McAteer.'

'So – he dies, this one, Sean. If I told you what he'd done in the past, the harm he's done the movement, you'd never believe it. Take him in that boat of yours, nice and easy, no fuss, then a bullet in the back of the head three miles out and over the side with him.'

'Consider it done,' Deegan told him.

He put down the phone, left the living room, went upstairs and dressed fully. He went into the bar, pulling on an old pilot coat. 'I'll leave you for a while, Father, while I go and get my lads. Help yourself to anything you need.'

'That's kind of you,' Cussane told him.

He lit a cigarette and read the evening paper for something to do. Deegan was back in half an hour, two men with him. 'Phil Egan, Father, Tadgh McAteer.'

They all shook hands. Egan was small and wiry, perhaps twenty-five. McAteer was a large man in an old reefer coat with a beer belly heavy over his belt. He was older than Deegan. Fifty-five at least, Cussane would have thought.

'We'll get going then, Father.' Cussane picked up his bag and Deegan said, 'Not so fast, Father. I like to know what I'm handling.'

He put Cussane's bag on the bar, opened it and quickly sifted through the contents. He zipped it up, turned and nodded to McAteer, who ran his hands roughly over the priest and found the Stechkin. He took it out and placed it on the bar without a word.

Deegan said, 'What you need that for is your business. You get it back when we land you in the Isle of Man.' He put it in his pocket.

'I understand,' Cussane said.

'Good, then let's get going,' and Deegan led the way out.

Devlin was in bed when McGuiness rang him. 'They've got him,' he said.

'Where?'

'Ballywalter. One of our own, a man called Sean Deegan. Cussane turned up there saying he was a friend of Danny Malone and needed an undercover run to the Isle of Man. Presumably Danny had told him a thing or two he shouldn't.'

'Danny's a dying man. He wouldn't know what he was saying half the time,' Devlin said.

'Anyway, Cussane, or Father Daly as he's now calling himself, is in for a very unpleasant shock. Three miles out, Deegan and his boys nail the coffin lid on him and over he goes. I told you we'd get the sod.'

'So you did.'

'I'll be in touch, Liam.'

Devlin sat there thinking about it. Too good to be true. Cussane had obviously discovered from Danny Malone that Deegan offered the kind of service he did. Fair enough, but to turn up as he had done, no attempt at disguise beyond a change of name . . . He might have assumed that it would be morning before Devlin and Tanya would be found, but even so . . . It didn't make any kind of sense – or did it?

There was a light mist rolling in from the sea as they moved out, but the sky was clear and the moon touched things with a luminosity that was vaguely unreal. McAteer busied himself on deck, Egan had the hatch to the small engine room off and was down the ladder and Deegan was at the wheel. Cussane stood beside him, peering out through the window.

'A fine night,' Deegan observed.

'Indeed it is. How long will it take?'

'Four hours and that's taking it easy. It means we can time it to catch the local fishing boats going back to the Isle of Man with their night catches. We'll land you on the west coast. Little place I know near Peel. You can get a bus across to Douglas, the capital. There's an airport, Ronaldsway. You can get a plane to London from there or just across the water to Blackpool on the English coast.'

'Yes, I know,' Cussane told him.

'Might as well go below. Get your head down for a while,' Deegan suggested.

The cabin had four bunks and a fixed table in the centre, a small galley at one end. It was very untidy, but warm and snug in spite of the smell of diesel oil. Cussane made himself tea in a mug and sat at the table drinking it and smoking a cigarette. He lay on one of the bottom bunks, his hat beside him, eyes closed. After a while, McAteer and Egan came down the companionway.

'Are you all right, Father?' McAteer enquired. 'Cup of tea or anything?'

'I've had one, thank you,' Cussane said. 'I think I'll get some sleep.'

He lay there, eyes almost closed, one hand negligently reaching under the hat. McAteer smiled at Egan and winked and the other man spooned instant coffee into three mugs and added boiling water and condensed milk. They went out. Cussane could hear their steps on deck, the murmur of conversation, a burst of laughter. He lay there, waiting for what was to come.

It was perhaps half an hour later that the engine stopped and they started to drift. Cussane got up and put his feet to the floor.

Deegan called down the companionway, 'Would you come up on deck, Father?'

Cussane settled his hat on his head at a neat angle and went up the ladder. Egan sat on the engine hatch, McAteer leaned out of the open wheelhouse window and Deegan stood at the stern rail, smoking a cigarette and looking back towards the Irish coast two or three miles away.

Cussane said, 'What is it? What's happening?'

'The jig's up!' Deegan turned, holding the Stechkin in his right hand. 'You see, we know who you are, old son. All about you.'

'And your wicked ways,' McAteer called.

Egan rattled a length of heavy chain. Cussane glanced towards him, then turned to Deegan, taking off his hat and holding it across his chest. 'There's no way we can discuss this, I suppose?'

'Not a chance,' Deegan told him.

Cussane shot him in the chest through the hat and Deegan was punched back against the rail. He dropped the Stechkin on the deck, overbalanced, grabbed for the rail unsuccessfully and went into the sea. Cussane was already turning, firing up at McAteer in the wheelhouse as he tried to draw back, the bullet catching the big man just above the right eye. Egan lashed out at him with the length of chain. Cussane avoided the awkward blow with ease.

'Bastard!' Egan cried, and Cussane took careful aim and shot him in the heart.

He moved fast now. Pocketing the Stechkin Deegan had dropped he launched the inflatable with its outboard motor which was stowed amidships. He tied it to the rail and went into the wheelhouse where he had left his bag, stepping over McAteer's body to get it. He opened the false bottom, took out the plastic explosive and sliced a piece off with his pocket knife. He stuck one of the pencil timers in it, primed to explode in fifteen minutes and dropped it down the engine hatch, then got into the inflatable, started the motor and moved back to shore at speed. Behind him, Sean Deegan, still alive in spite of the bullet in his chest, watched him go and kicked slowly to keep afloat.

Cussane was well on his way when the explosion rent the night, yellow and orange flames flowering like petals. He glanced back only briefly. Things couldn't have worked out better. Now he was dead and McGuiness and Ferguson would call off the hounds. He wondered how Devlin would feel when he finally realized the truth.

He landed on a small beach close to Ballywalter and dragged the inflatable up into the shelter of a clump of gorse bushes. Then he retraced his steps up to the wood where he had left the motorcycle. He strapped his bag on the rear, put on his crash helmet and rode away.

It was another fishing boat from Ballywalter, the *Dublin Town*, out night-fishing, which was first on the scene. The crew, on deck handling their nets about a mile away, had seen the explosion as it occurred. By the time they reached the position where the *Mary Murphy* had gone down, about half an hour had elapsed. There was a considerable amount of wreckage on the surface and a life-jacket with the boat's name stencilled on it told them the worst. The skipper notified the coastguard of the tragedy on his radio and continued the search for survivors or at least the bodies of the crew; but he had no success and a thickening sea mist made things even more difficult. By five o'clock, a coastguard cutter was there from Dundalk, also several other small fishing craft, and they continued the search as dawn broke.

The news of the tragedy was passed on to McGuiness at four o'clock in the morning and he, in turn, phoned Devlin.

'Christ knows what happened,' McGuiness said. 'She blew up and went down like a stone.'

'And no bodies, you say?'

'Probably inside her, or what's left of her on the bottom. And it seems there's a bad rip tide in that area. It would carry a body a fair distance. I'd like to know what happened. A good man, Sean Deegan.'

'So would I,' Devlin said.

'Still, no more Cussane. At least that bastard has met his end. You'll tell Ferguson?'

'Leave it with me.'

Devlin put on a dressing gown, went downstairs and made some tea.

Cussane was dead and yet he felt no pain for the man who, whatever else, had been his friend for more than twenty years. No sense of mourning. Instead a feeling of unease like a lump in the gut that refused to go away.

He rang the Cavendish Square number in London. It was picked up after a slight delay and Ferguson's voice answered, still half asleep. Devlin gave him the news and the Brigadier came fully awake with some rapidity.

'Are you sure about this?'

'That's how it looks. God knows what went wrong on the boat.'

'Ah well,' Ferguson said. 'At least Cussane's out of our hair for good and all. The last thing I needed was that madman on the rampage.' He snorted. 'Kill the Pope indeed.'

'What about Tanya?'

'She can come back tomorrow. Put her on the plane and I'll meet her myself. Harry will be in Paris to brief Tony Villiers on this Exocet job.'

'Right,' Devlin said. 'That's it then.'

'You don't sound happy, Liam. What is it?'

'Let's put it this way. With this one, I'd like to see the body,' Devlin said and rang off.

The Ulster border with the Irish Republic, in spite of road blocks, a considerable police presence and the British Army, has always been wide open to anyone who knows it. In many cases, farms on both sides have land breached by the border's imaginary line and the area is criss-crossed by hundreds of narrow country lanes, field paths and tracks.

Cussane was safely in Ulster by four o'clock. Any kind of a vehicle on the road at that time in the morning was rare enough to make it essential that he drop out of sight for a while, which he did on the other side of Newry, holing up in a disused barn in a wood just off the main road.

He didn't sleep, but sat comfortably against a wall and smoked, the Stechkin ready to hand just in case. He left just after six, a time when there would be enough early workers on the road to make him inconspicuous, taking the A1 through Banbridge to Lisburn.

It was seven-fifteen when he rode into the carpark at Aldergrove Airport and parked the motorcycle. The Stechkin joined the Walther in the false bottom of the bag. The holiday season having started, there was a flight to the Isle of Man leaving at eight-fifteen, with flights to Glasgow, Edinburgh and Newcastle as possible alternatives if there was difficulty in obtaining a seat, all leaving within a period of one hour. The Isle of Man was his preference because it was a soft route, used mainly by holiday makers. In the event, there was space available and he had no difficulty in obtaining a ticket.

All hand baggage would be x-rayed, but that was true at most international airports these days. At Belfast, most baggage destined for the hold was x-rayed also, but this did not always apply to the softer routes during the holiday season. In any case, the false bottom of his bag, which was only three inches deep, was lined with lead. The contents would not show. Any difficulty he might have would present itself at Customs in the Isle of Man.

It was approximately eight-thirty and Cussane had been airborne for a good ten minutes when the *Dublin Town*, running low on fuel, gave up the fruitless search for survivors from the *Mary Murphy* and turned towards Ballywalter. It was the youngest member of the crew, a fifteen-year old boy coiling rope in the prow, who noticed the wreckage to starboard and called to the skipper, who altered course at once. A few minutes later, he cut the engines and coasted in beside one of the *Mary Murphy*'s hatches.

Sean Deegan was sprawled across it on his back. His head turned slowly and he managed a ghastly smile. 'Took your sweet time about it, didn't you?' he called in a hoarse voice.

At Ronaldsway Airport, Cussane had no difficulty with the Customs. He retrieved his bag and joined the large number of people passing through. No one made any attempt to stop him. As with all holiday resorts, the accent was on making things as painless for the tourist as possible. Islander aircraft made the short flight to Blackpool on the English coast numerous times during the day, but they were busy that morning and the earliest flight he could get was at noon. It could have been worse, so he purchased a ticket and went along to the cafeteria to have something to eat.

It was eleven-thirty when Ferguson answered the phone and found Devlin on the line. He listened, frowning in horror. 'Are you certain?'

'Absolutely. This man Deegan survived the explosion only because Cussane shot him into the water beforehand. It was Cussane who caused the explosion, then took off back to the shore in the fishing boat's inflatable. Almost ran Deegan down.'

'But why?' Ferguson demanded.

'The clever bastard has been beating me at chess for years. I know his style. Always three moves ahead of the game. By staging his apparent death last night, he pulled off the hounds. There was no one looking for him. No need.'

Ferguson was filled with a dreadful foreboding. 'Are you trying to say what I think you are?'

'What do you think? He's on your side of the water now, not ours, Brigadier.'

Ferguson swore softly. 'Right, I'll get some official help from Special Branch in Dublin. They can turn over that cottage of his for us. Photos, fingerprints. Anything useful.'

'You'll need to inform the Catholic Secretariat,' Devlin told him. 'They're going to love this one at the Vatican.'

'The lady at number ten isn't likely to be too ecstatic about it either. What plane had you booked the Voroninova girl on?'

'Two o'clock.'

'Come with her. I need you.'

'There is just one item of minor importance, but worth mentioning,' Devlin told him. 'On your side of the water, I'm still a wanted man from way back. A member of an illegal organization is the least of it.'

'I'll take care of that, for God's sake,' Ferguson said. 'Just get your backside on that plane,' and he hung up.

Tanya Voroninova brought tea in from the kitchen. 'What happens now?'

'I'm going with you to London,' he said, 'and we'll take it from there.'

'And Cussane? Where is he, would you say?'

'Anywhere and everywhere.' He sipped some of his tea. 'He has one problem however. The Pope arrives Friday according to the morning paper. Visits Canterbury the next day.'

'Saturday the twenty-ninth?'

'Exactly. So Cussane has some time to fill. The question is, where does he intend to go and what does he intend to do?'

The phone rang. McGuiness was on the other end. 'You've spoken to Ferguson?'

'I have.'

'What does he intend to do?'

'God knows. He's asked me to go over.'

'And will you?'

'Yes.'

'Jesus, Liam, did you hear about this Russian, Lubov, turning up dead in the cinema? He preaches a hell of a sermon this priest of yours.'

'He's developed a slightly different attitude to the job since he discovered his own people were trying to knock him off,' Devlin said. 'Interesting to see where it takes him.'

'To Canterbury is where it's taking the mad bastard,' McGuiness said. 'And we can't help with that. It's up to British Intelligence to handle this one. Nothing more the IRA can do for them. Watch your back, Liam.'

He rang off and Devlin sat there, frowning thoughtfully. He stood up. 'I'm going out for a little while,' he said to Tanya. 'Shan't be long,' and he went out through the French windows.

The Customs at Blackpool were just as courteous as they had been at Ronaldsway. Cussane actually paused, smiling, and offered his bag as the stream of passengers moved through.

'Anything to declare, Father?' the Customs officer asked.

Cussane unzipped his bag. 'A bottle of Scotch and two hundred cigarettes.'

The Customs officer grinned. 'You could have had a litre of wine as well. It isn't your day, Father.'

'Obviously not.' Cussane zipped up his bag and moved on.

He hesitated outside the entrance of the small airport. There were several taxi cabs waiting, but he decided to walk down to the main road instead. He had, after all, all the time in the world. There was a newsagents across the road and he crossed over and bought a paper. As he came out, a bus pulled in at the stop a few paces away. Its indicator said Morecambe, which he knew was another seaside resort some miles up the coast. On impulse, he ran forward and scrambled on board as it drew away.

He purchased a ticket and went up on the top deck. It was really very pleasant and he felt calm and yet full of energy at the same time.

He opened the newspaper and saw that the news from the South Atlantic was not good. HMS *Coventry* had been bombed and a Cunard container ship, the *Atlantic Conveyor*, had been hit by an Exocet missile. He lit a cigarette and settled down to read about it.

When Devlin went into the ward at the hospice, Sister Anne Marie was at Danny Malone's bed. Devlin waited and she finally whispered something to the nurse, then turned and noticed him. 'And what do you want?'

'To talk to Danny.'

'He isn't really up to conversation this morning.'

'It's very important.'

She frowned in exasperation. 'It always is with you. All right. Ten minutes.' She started to walk away, then turned. 'Father Cussane didn't come in last night. Do you know why?'

'No,' Devlin lied. 'I haven't seen him.'

She walked away and he pulled a chair forward. 'Danny, how are you?'

Malone opened his eyes and said hoarsely, 'Is it you, Liam? Father Cussane didn't come.'

'Tell me, Danny, you talked to him of Sean Deegan of Ballywalter who handles the Isle of Man run, I understand.'

Malone frowned. 'Sure, I talked to him about a lot of things.'

'But mainly of IRA matters.'

'Sure, and he was interested in me telling him how I managed things in the old days.'

'Particularly across the water?' Devlin asked.

'Yes. You know how long I lasted without getting caught, Liam. He wanted to know how I did it.' He frowned. 'What's the problem?'

'You were always the strong one, Danny. Be strong now. He wasn't one of our own.'

Malone's eyes widened. 'You're having me on, Liam.'

'And Sean Deegan in hospital with a bullet in him and two good men dead?'

Danny sat there, staring at him. 'Tell me.' So Devlin did. When he was finished, Danny Malone said softly, 'Bastard!'

'Tell me what you can remember, Danny. Anything that particularly interested him.'

Malone frowned, trying to think. 'Yes, the business of how I stayed ahead of Special Branch and those Intelligence boys for so long. I explained to him that I never used the IRA network when I was over there. Totally unreliable, you know that, Liam.'

'True.'

'I always used the underworld myself. Give me an honest crook any day of the week or a dishonest one if the price is right. I knew a lot of people like that.'

'Tell me about them,' Devlin said.

Cussane liked seaside towns, especially the ones that catered for the masses. Honest, working class people out for a good time. Lots of cafés, amusement arcades and fairgrounds and plenty of bracing air. Morecambe certainly had that. The dark waters of the bay were being whipped into whitecaps and on the far side he could see the mountains of the Lake District.

He walked across the road. It was not the height of the season yet, but there were plenty of tourists about and he threaded his way through the narrow streets until he found his way to the bus station.

It was possible to travel to most of the major provincial cities by high speed bus, mainly on the motorways. He consulted the timetables and found what he was looking for, a bus to Glasgow via Carlisle and Dumfries. It left in one hour. He booked a ticket and went in search of something to eat.

11

Georgi Romanov was senior attaché in charge of public relations at the Russian Embassy in London. He was a tall, amiable-looking man of fifty, secretly rather proud of his aristocratic name. He had worked for KGB in London for eleven years now, and had been promoted to lieutenant-colonel the previous year. Ferguson liked him and he liked Ferguson. When Ferguson phoned him just after his final telephone conversation with Devlin and suggested a meeting, Romanov agreed at once.

They met in Kensington Gardens by the Round Pond, a rendezvous so convenient to the Embassy that Romanov was able to walk. Ferguson sat on a bench reading *The Times*. Romanov joined him.

'Hello, Georgi,' Ferguson said.

'Charles. To what do I owe the honour?'

'Straight talking, Georgi. This one is about as bad as it could be. What do you know about a KGB agent, code name Cuchulain, put in deep in Ireland a good twenty years ago?'

'For once I can answer you with complete honesty,' Romanov said. 'Not a thing.'

'Then listen and learn,' Ferguson told him.

When he was finished, Romanov's face was grave. 'This really is bad.'

'You're telling me. The important thing is this. This madman is somewhere in the country having boasted of his intention of shooting the Pope at Canterbury on Saturday and frankly, with his track record, we have to take him seriously. He isn't just another nutter.'

'So what do you want me to do?'

'Get in touch with Moscow at the highest level. I should imagine the last thing they want is the Pope dead, at the hands of someone who can be proved to be a KGB agent, especially after that botched attempt in Rome. Which is exactly what Cussane wants. Warn them that, on this one, we'll brook no interference. And if, by some wild chance, he gets in touch with you, Georgi, you tell me. We're going to get this bastard, make no mistake and he dies, Georgi. No nonsense about a trial or anything like that. There again, I'm sure that's what your people in Moscow will want to hear.'

'I'm sure it is.' Romanov stood up. 'I'd better get back and send a signal.'

'Take a tip from an old chum,' Ferguson told him. 'Make sure you go higher than Maslovsky.'

In view of the importance of the matter, Ferguson had to go to the Director General, who in turn spoke to the Home Secretary. The result was a summons to Downing Street when Ferguson was half-way through his lunch. He rang for his car at once and was there within ten minutes. There was the usual small crowd at the end of the street behind barriers. The policeman on the door saluted. It was opened the moment Ferguson raised a hand to the knocker.

There was a hum of activity inside, but then there would be with the Falklands affair beginning to hot up. He was surprised that she was seeing him personally. His guide led the way up the main staircase to the first floor and Ferguson followed. On the top floor, the young man knocked at a door and led the way in.

'Brigadier Ferguson, Prime Minister.'

She looked up from her desk, elegant as always in a grey tweed dress, blond hair groomed to perfection, and laid down her pen. 'My time is limited, Brigadier. I'm sure you understand.'

'I would have thought that an understatement, Ma'am.'

'The Home Secretary has filled me in on the relevant facts. I simply want an assurance from you that you will stop this man.'

'I can give you that without the slightest hesitation, Prime Minister.'

'If there was any kind of attempt on the Pope's life while he is here, even an unsuccessful one, the consequences in political terms would be disastrous for us.'

'I understand.'

'As head of Group Four, you have special powers, direct from me. Use them, Brigadier. If there is anything else you need, do not hesitate to ask.'

'Prime Minister.'

She picked up her pen and returned to work and Ferguson went out to find the young man waiting for him. As they went downstairs, it occurred to Ferguson, not for the first time in his career, that it was his own head that was on the block as much as Cussane's.

In Moscow, Ivan Maslovsky received another summons to the office of the Minister for State Security, still occupied by Yuri Andropov, whom he found sitting at his desk considering a typed report.

He passed it across. 'Read it, Comrade.'

Maslovsky did so and his heart seemed to turn to stone. When he was finished he handed it back, hands shaking.

'Your man, Maslovsky, is now at large in England, intent on assassinating the Pope, his sole idea apparently being to embarrass us seriously. And there is nothing we can do except sit back and hope that British Intelligence will be one hundred per cent efficient in this matter.'

'Comrade, what can I say?'

'Nothing, Maslovsky. This whole sorry affair was not only ill-advised. It was adventurism of the worst kind.' Andropov pressed a button on his desk, the door opened behind Maslovsky and two young KGB captains in uniform entered. 'You will vacate your office and hand over all official keys and files to the person I designate. You will then be taken to the Lubianka to await trial for crimes against the State.'

The Lubianka, how many people had he sent there himself? Suddenly, Maslovsky found difficulty in breathing and there was a pain in both arms, his chest. He started to fall and clutched at the desk. Andropov jumped back in alarm and the two KGB officers rushed and grabbed Maslovsky's arms. He didn't bother to struggle, he had no strength, but he tried to speak as the pain got worse, tried to tell Andropov that there would be no cell in the Lubianka, no state trial. Strangely enough, the last thing he thought of was Tanya, his beloved Tanya seated at the piano playing his favourite piece, Debussy's *La Mer.* Then the music faded and there was only darkness.

Ferguson had a meeting with the Home Secretary, the Commander of C13, Scotland Yard's anti-terrorist squad and the Director General of the Security Services. He was tired when he got back to the flat and found Devlin sitting by the fire reading *The Times*.

'The Pope seems to be taking over from the Falklands at the moment,' Devlin said and folded the paper.

'Yes, well that's as maybe,' Ferguson said. 'He can't go back fast enough for me. You should have been with me at this meeting I've just attended, Liam. Home Secretary himself, Scotland Yard, the Director, and you know what?' He warmed himself, back against the fire. 'They aren't taking it all that seriously.'

'Cussane, you mean?'

'Oh, don't get me wrong. They accept his existence, if you follow me. I showed them the record and his activities in Dublin during the past few days have been bad enough, God knows. Levin, Lubov, Cherny, two IRA gunmen. The man's a butcher.'

'No,' Devlin said. 'I don't think so. To him, it's just part of the job. Something that has to be done. He gets it over with cleanly and expeditiously. He has frequently spared lives over the years. Tanya and myself were a case in point. He goes for the target, that's all.'

'Don't remind me.' Ferguson shuddered, and then the door opened and Harry Fox came in.

'Hello, sir. Liam. I believe things have been happening while I've been away.'

'I think one could say that,' Ferguson told him. 'Did things go well in Paris?'

'Yes, I saw Tony. He's in control.'

'You can tell me later. I'd better fill you in on the latest events.'

Which he did, as quickly as possible, Devlin occasionally making a point. When Ferguson was finished, Harry Fox said, 'What a man. Strange.' He shook his head.

'What is?'

'When I met him the other day, I rather liked him, sir.'

'Not a difficult thing to do,' Devlin said.

Ferguson frowned. 'Let's have no more of that kind of bloody nonsense.' The door opened and Kim entered with tea things on a tray and a plate of toasted crumpets. 'Excellent,' Ferguson said. 'I'm famished.'

Fox said, 'What about Tanya Voroninova?'

'I've fixed her up with a safe house for the moment.'

'Which one, sir?'

'The Chelsea Place apartment. The Directorate supplied a woman operative to stay with her till we get sorted.'

He handed them each a cup of tea. 'So, what's the next move?' Devlin asked.

'The Home Secretary and the Director, and I must say I agree with them, don't feel we should make too public an issue of this at the moment. The whole purpose of the Pope's visit is sweetness and light. A genuine attempt to help bring about the end of the war in the South Atlantic. Imagine how it would look on the front pages of the nationals. The first visit ever of a Pope to England and a mad-dog killer on the loose.'

'And a priest to boot, sir.'

'Yes, well we can discount that, especially as we know what he really is.'

Devlin said, 'Discount nothing. Let me, as a not very good Catholic, fill you in on a few things. In the eyes of the Church, Harry Cussane was ordained priest at Vine Landing, Connecticut, twenty-one years ago and still is a priest. Haven't you read any Graham Greene lately?'

'All right,' Ferguson said testily. 'Be that as it may, the Prime Minister doesn't see why we should give Cussane front-page publicity. It won't do any of us any good.'

'It could catch him quickly, sir,' Fox said mildly.

'Yes, well they all expect us to do that anyway. Special Branch in Dublin have lifted his prints for us at his cottage. They've gone into the Dublin computer which, as you know, is linked with the security services' computer at Lisburn which, in turn, is linked to our computer here and at Central Records, Scotland Yard.'

'I didn't realize you had that kind of hook-up,' Devlin said.

'Miracle of the micro-chip,' Ferguson said. 'Eleven million people in there. Criminal records, schooling, professions, sexual preferences. Personal habits. Where they buy their furniture.'

'You've got to be joking.'

'No. Caught one of your lot over here from Ulster last year because he always shopped at the Co-Op. Had an excellent cover, but couldn't change the habit of a lifetime. Cussane is in there now and not only his fingerprints but everything we know about him, and as most of the big provincial police forces have what we call visual display characteristics on their computer system, they can plug in to our central bank and punch out his photo.'

'God Almighty!'

'Actually, they can do the same with you. As regards Cussane, I've instructed them to insert a deliberately amended record. No mention of the KGB or anything like that. Poses as a priest, known connections with the IRA. Extremely violent – approach with care. You get the picture.'

'Oh, I do.'

'To that end, we're releasing his picture to the press and quoting very much the details I've just given you. Some evening papers will manage to get it out, but all the national newspapers will have it in tomorrow's editions.'

'And you think that will be enough, sir?' Fox asked.

'Very possibly. We'll have to wait and see, won't we? One thing is certain.' Ferguson walked to the window and glanced out. 'He's out there somewhere.'

'And the thing is,' Devlin said, 'no one can do a damn thing about it till he surfaces.'

'Exactly.' Ferguson went back to the tray and picked up the pot. 'This tea is really quite delicious. Anyone like another cup?'

A little later that afternoon His Holiness Pope John Paul II sat at a desk in the small office adjacent to his bedchamber and examined the report which had just been handed to him. The man who stood before him wore the plainest of black habits and in appearance might have been a simple priest. He was, in fact, Father General of the Society of Jesus, that most illustrious of all orders within the Catholic Church. The Jesuits were proud to be known as Soldiers of Christ and had been responsible, behind the scenes, for the Pope's security for centuries now. All of which explained why the Father General had hastened from his office at the Collegio di San Roberto Bellarmino on the Via del Seminario to seek audience with His Holiness.

Pope John Paul put the report down and looked up. He spoke in excellent Italian, only a trace of his Polish native tongue coming through. 'You received this when?'

'The first report from the Secretariat in Dublin came three hours ago, then the news from London a little later. I have spoken personally to the British Home Secretary who has given me every assurance for your safety and referred me to Brigadier Ferguson, mentioned in the report as being directly responsible.'

'But are you worried?'

'Holiness, it is almost impossible to prevent a lone assassin from reaching his target, especially if he does not care about his own safety and this man Cussane has proved his abilities on too many occasions in the past.'

'Father Cussane.' His Holiness got up and paced to the window. 'Killer he may have been, may still be, but priest he is and God, my friend, will not allow him to forget that.'

The Father General looked into that rough hewn face, the face that might have belonged to any one of a thousand ordinary working men. It was touched with a strange simplicity, a certainty. As had happened on other occasions the Father General, for all his intellectual authority, wilted before it.

'You will go to England, Holiness?'

'To Canterbury, my friend, where Blessed Thomas Beckett died for God's sake.'

The Father General reached to kiss the ring on the extended hand. 'Then your Holiness will excuse me. There is much to do.'

He went out. John Paul stood at the window for a while, then crossed the room, opened a small door and entered his private chapel. He knelt at the altar, hands clasped, a certain fear in his heart as he remembered the assassin's bullet that had almost ended his life, the months of pain. But he pushed that away from him and concentrated on all that was important: his prayers for the immortal soul of Father Harry Cussane and for all sinners everywhere, whose actions only cut them off from the infinite blessing of God's love.

Ferguson put down the phone and turned to Devlin and Fox. 'That was the Director General. His Holiness has been informed in full about Cussane and the threat he poses. It makes no difference.'

'Well, it wouldn't, would it?' Devlin said. 'You're talking about a man who worked for years in the Polish underground against the Nazis.'

'All right,' Ferguson said. 'Point taken. Anyway, you'd better get kitted out. Take him along to the Directorate, Harry. Grade A Security Pass. Not just another piece of plastic with your photo on it,' he said to Devlin. 'Very few people have this particular one. It'll get you in anywhere.'

He moved to his desk and Devlin said, 'Will it entitle me to a gun? A Walther wouldn't come amiss. I'm one of nature's pessimists, as you know.'

'Out of favour with most of our people since that idiot tried to shoot Princess Anne and her bodyguard's Walther jammed. Revolvers never do. Take my advice.'

He picked up some papers and they went into the study and got their coats. 'I still prefer a Walther,' Devlin said.

'One thing's for sure,' Fox said. 'Whatever it is, it had better not jam, not if you're facing Harry Cussane,' and he opened the door and they went out to the lift.

Harry Cussane had a plan of sorts. He knew the end in view on Saturday at Canterbury, but that left the best part of three days and three nights, in which he had to hide out. Danny Malone had mentioned a number of people in the criminal world who provided the right kind of help at a price. Plenty in London of course or Leeds or Manchester, but the Mungo brothers and their farm in Galloway had particularly interested him. It was the remoteness which appealed. The last place anyone would look for him would be Scotland and yet the British Airways shuttle from Glasgow to London took only an hour and a quarter.

Time to fill, that was the thing. No need to be in Canterbury until the last moment. Nothing to organize. That amused him, sitting there in the bus speeding up the motorway to Carlisle. One could imagine the preparation at Canterbury Cathedral, every possible entry point guarded, police marksmen everywhere, probably even the SAS in plain clothes dispersed in the crowd. And all for nothing. It was like chess, as he used to tell Devlin, the world's worst player. It wasn't the present move that counted. It was the final move. It was rather like a stage magician. You believed what he did with his right hand, but it was what he did with his left that was important.

He slept for quite a while and, when he awakened, there was the sea shining in the afternoon light on his left. He leaned over and spoke to the old woman in front of him. 'Where are we?'

'Just past Annan.' She had a thick Glasgow accent. 'Dumfries next. Are you a Catholic?'

'I'm afraid so,' he said warily. The Scottish Lowlands had always been traditionally Protestant.

'That's lovely. I'm Catholic myself. Glasgow-Irish, Father.' She took his hand and kissed it. 'Bless me, Father. You're from the old country.'

'I am indeed.'

He thought she might prove a nuisance, but strangely enough, she simply turned her head and settled back in her seat. Outside, the sky was very dark and it started to rain, thunder rumbling ominously and soon the rain had increased into a monsoon-like force that drummed loudly on the roof of the bus. They stopped in Dumfries to drop two passengers and then moved on through streets washed clean of people, out into the country again.

Not long now. No more than fifteen miles to his dropping-off point at Dunhill. From there, a few miles on a side road to a hamlet called Larwick and the Mungos' place, a mile or two outside Larwick in the hills.

The driver had been speaking into the mike on his car radio and now he switched over to the coach's loudspeaker system. 'Attention, ladies and gentlemen. I'm afraid we've got trouble up ahead just before Dunhill. Bad flooding on the road. A lot of vehicles already stuck in it.'

The old woman in front of Cussane called, 'What are we supposed to do? Sit in the bus all night?'

'We'll be in Corbridge in a few minutes. Not much of a place, but there's a milk stop there on the railway line. They're making arrangements to stop the next train for Glasgow.'

'Three times the fare on the railway,' the old woman called.

'The company pays,' the driver told her cheerfully. 'Don't worry, love.'

'Will the train stop at Dunhill?' Cussane asked.

'Perhaps. I'm not sure. We'll have to see.'

Lag's Luck, they called it in prison circles. Danny Malone had told him that. No matter how well you planned, it was always something totally unforeseeable that caused the problem. No point in wasting energy in dwelling on that. The thing to do was examine alternatives.

A white sign, Corbridge etched on it in black, appeared on the left and then the first houses loomed out of the heavy rain. There was a general store, a newsagents, the tiny railway station opposite. The driver turned the coach into the forecourt.

'Best wait in here while I check things out.' He jumped down and went into the railway station.

The rain poured down relentlessly. There was a gap between the pub and the general store, beams stretching between to shore them up. Obviously the building which had stood there had just been demolished. A small crowd had gathered. Cussane watched idly, reached for the packet of cigarettes in his pocket and found it empty. He hesitated, then picked up his bag, got off the coach and ran across the road to the newsagents. He asked the young woman standing in the entrance for a couple of packs of cigarettes and an ordnance survey map of the area if she had it. She did.

'What's going on?' Cussane asked.

'They've been pulling down the old grain store for a week now. Everything was fine until this rain started. They've got trouble in the cellars. A roof fall or something.'

They moved out into the entrance again and watched. At that moment, a police car appeared from the other end of the village and pulled in. There was only one occupant, a large heavily-built man who wore a navy-blue anorak with sergeant's stripes on it. He forced his way through the crowd and disappeared.

The young woman said, 'The cavalry's arrived.'

'Isn't he from round here?' Cussane asked.

'No police station in Corbridge. He's from Dunhill. Sergeant Brodie – Lachlan Brodie.' The tone of her voice was enough.

'Not popular?' Cussane asked.

'Lachlan's the kind who likes nothing better than finding three drunks together at the same time on a Saturday night to beat up. He's built like the rock of ages and likes to prove it. You wouldn't be Catholic, by any chance?'

'I'm afraid so.'

'To Lachlan, that means antichrist. He's the kind of Baptist who thinks music is a sin. A lay preacher as well.'

A workman came through the crowd in helmet and orange safety jacket. His face was streaked with mud and water. He leaned against the wall, 'It's a sod down there.'

'That bad?' the woman said.

'One of my men is trapped. A wall collapsed. We're doing our best, but there isn't much room to work in and the water's rising.' He frowned and said to Cussane, 'You wouldn't be Catholic by any chance?'

'Yes.'

The man grabbed his arm. 'My name's Hardy. I'm the foreman. The man down there is as Glaswegian as me, but Italian. Gino Tisini. He thinks he's going to die. Begged me to get him a priest. Will you come, Father?'

'But of course,' Cussane said without hesitation, and handed his bag to the woman. 'Would you look after that for me?'

'Certainly, Father.'

He followed Hardy through the crowd and down into the excavation. There was a gaping hole, cellar steps descending. Brodie, the police sergeant, was holding people back. Hardy started down and as Cussane followed, Brodie caught his arm. 'What's this?'

'Let him by,' Hardy called. 'He's a priest.'

The hostility was immediate in Brodie's eyes, the dislike plain. It was an old song to Cussane, Belfast all over again. 'I don't know you,' Brodie said.

'My name's Fallon. I came in on the bus on the way to Glasgow,' Cussane told him calmly.

He took the policeman's wrist, loosening the grip on his arm, and

Brodie winced at the strength of it as Cussane pushed him to one side and went down the steps. He was knee-deep in water at once and ducked under a low roof and followed Hardy into what must have been a narrow passageway. There was a certain amount of light from an extension lamp and it illuminated a chaos of jumbled masonry and planking. There was a narrow aperture and as they reached it, two men stumbled out, both soaked to the skin and obviously at exhaustion point.

'It's no good,' one of them said. 'His head will be under the water in a matter of minutes.'

Hardy brushed past and Cussane went after them. Gino Tisini's white face loomed out of the darkness as they crouched to go forward. Cussane put out a hand to steady himself and a plank fell and several bricks.

'Watch it!' Hardy said. 'The whole thing could go like a house of cards.'

There was the constant gurgle of water as it poured in. Tisini managed a ghastly smile. 'Come to hear my confession, Father? It would take a year and a day.'

'We haven't got that long. Let's get you out,' Cussane said.

There seemed to be a sudden extra flow of water; it washed over Tisini's face and he panicked. Cussane moved behind him, supporting the man's head above the water, crouching over him protectively.

Hardy felt under the water. 'There's a lot moved here,' he said. 'That's where the inflow of water helps. There's just one beam pinning him down now, but it leads into the wall. If I put any kind of force on it, it could bring the lot in on us.'

'If you don't, he drowns within the next couple of minutes,' Cussane said.

'You could be in trouble too, Father.'

'And you,' Cussane said, 'so get on with it.'

'Father!' Tisini cried. 'In the name of God, absolve me!'

Cussane said in a firm clear voice, 'May Our Lord Jesus Christ absolve you and I, by His authority, absolve you from your sins in the name of the Father and the Son and of the Holy Spirit.' He nodded to Hardy. 'Now!'

The foreman took a breath and dipped under the surface, his hands gripping the edges of the beam. His shoulders seemed to swell, he came up out of the water, the beam with him and Tisini screamed and floated free in Cussane's hands. The wall started to bulge. Hardy pulled Tisini up and dragged him towards the entrance, Cussane pushing from the rear as the walls crumbled around them. He put an arm up to protect his head and shoulders, was aware that they were at the steps now, willing hands reaching down to help, and then a brick struck him a glancing blow on the head. He tried to go up the steps, fell on his knees, and there was only darkness.

12

He came awake slowly to find the young woman from the shop crouching over him. He was lying on a rug in front of a coal fire and she was wiping his face.

'Easy,' she said. 'You'll be fine. Remember me? I'm Moira McGregor. You're in my shop.'

'What about the Italian and that fellow Hardy?'

'They're upstairs. We've sent for a doctor.'

He was still confused and found it difficult to think straight. 'My bag?' he said slowly. 'Where is it?'

The big policeman, Brodie, loomed over them. 'Back in the land of the living, are we?' There was an edge to his voice. An unpleasantness. 'Worth a couple of dozen candles to the Virgin, I suppose.'

He went out. Moira McGregor smiled at Cussane. 'Take no notice. You saved that man's life, you and Hardy. I'll get you a cup of tea.'

She went into the kitchen and found Brodie standing by the table. 'I could do with a touch of something stronger myself,' he said.

She took a bottle of Scotch and a glass from a cupboard and put them on the table without a word. He reached for a chair and pulled it forward, not noticing Cussane's bag which fell to the floor. The top being unzipped, several items tumbled out, a couple of shirts and the pyx and the violet stole amongst them.

'This his bag?' Brodie asked.

She turned from the stove, a kettle in her hand. 'That's right.'

He dropped to one knee, stuffing the items back into the bag and frowned. 'What's this?'

By some mischance, the false bottom of the bag had become dislodged in the fall. The first thing Brodie discovered was an English passport and he opened it. 'He told me his name was Fallon.'

'So?' Moira said.

'Then how come he has a passport in the name of Father Sean Daly? Good likeness too.' His hand groped further and came up, holding the Stechkin. 'God Almighty!'

Moira McGregor felt sick. 'What does it mean?'

'We'll soon find out.'

Brodie went back into the other room and put the bag down on a chair. Cussane lay quietly, eyes closed. Brodie knelt down beside him, took out a pair of handcuffs and, very gently, eased one bracelet over Cussane's left wrist. Cussane opened his eyes and Brodie seized the other wrist and snapped the steel cuff in place. He pulled the priest to his feet, then shoved him down into a chair.

'What's all this then?' Brodie had the false base up completely now and sifted through the contents. 'Three handguns, assorted passports and a sizeable sum in cash. Bloody fine priest you are. What's it all about?'

'You are the policeman, not me,' Cussane said.

Brodie cuffed him on the side of the head. 'Manners, my little man. I can see I'm going to have to chastise you.'

Watching from the door, Moira McGregor said, 'Don't do that.'

Brodie smiled contemptuously. 'Women – all the same. Fancy him, do you, just because he played the hero?'

He went out. She said to Cussane desperately, 'Who are you?'

He smiled. 'I wouldn't bother your head about that. I could manage a cigarette, though, before bully-boy gets back.'

Brodie had been a policeman for twenty years after five years in the military police. Twenty undistinguished years. He was a sour and cruel man whose only real authority was the uniform, and his religion had the same purpose as the uniform, to give him a spurious authority. He could have rung headquarters in Dumfries, but there was something special about this, he felt it in his bones, so instead, he rang police headquarters in Glasgow.

Glasgow had received photo and full details on Harry Cussane only one hour previously. The case was marked Priority One with immediate referal to Group Four in London. Brodie's telephone call was transferred at once to Special Branch. Within two minutes he found himself talking to a Chief Inspector Trent.

'Tell me all about it again,' Trent told him. Brodie did so. When he was finished, Trent said, 'I don't know how much time you've got in, but you've just made the biggest collar of your career. This man's called

Cussane. A real IRA heavy. You say the passengers on the bus he was on are being transferred to the train?'

'That's right, sir. Flooding on the road. This is only a milk stop, but they're going to stop the Glasgow express.'

'When is it due?'

'About ten minutes, sir.'

'Get on it, Brodie, and bring Chummy with you. We'll meet you in Glasgow.'

Brodie put down the phone, choking with excitement, then he went into the sitting room.

Brodie walked Cussane along the platform, one hand on his arm, the other clutching Cussane's bag. People turned to watch curiously as the priest passed, wrists handcuffed in front of him. They reached the guards van at the rear of the train, the guard standing on the platform beside the open door.

'What's this?'

'Special prisoner for Glasgow.' Brodie pushed Cussane inside. There were some mailbags in the corner and he shoved him down on to them. 'Now you stay quiet like a good boy.'

There was a commotion and Hardy appeared at the door, Moira McGregor behind him. 'I came as soon as I could,' the foreman said. 'I just heard.'

'You can't come in here,' Brodie told him.

Hardy ignored him. 'Look, I don't know what this is about, but if there's anything I can do.'

On the platform, the guard blew his whistle. Cussane said, 'Nothing anyone can do. How is Tisini?'

'Looks like a broken leg.'

'Tell him his luck is good.'

There was a lurch as the train started. 'It suddenly occurs to me that if I hadn't drawn you in to help, you wouldn't be here now,' Hardy said.

He moved out to join Moira on the platform as the guard jumped inside. 'Luck of the draw,' Cussane called. 'Don't worry about it.'

And then Hardy and the woman were swept away into the past as the guard pulled the sliding door shut and the train surged forward.

Trent couldn't resist phoning Ferguson in London and the Directorate-General patched him in to the Cavendish Square phone. Fox and Devlin were out and Ferguson answered himself.

'Trent here, sir, Chief-Inspector, Special Branch, Glasgow. We think we've got your man, Cussane.'

'Have you, by God?' Ferguson said. 'What shape is he in?'

'Well, I haven't actually seen him, sir. He's been apprehended in a village some miles south of here. He's arriving by train in Glasgow within the hour. I'll pick him up myself.'

'Pity the bugger didn't turn up dead,' Ferguson said. 'Still, one can't have everything. I want him down here on the first available plane in the morning, Chief-Inspector. Bring him yourself. This one's too important for any slip-ups.'

'Will do, sir,' said Trent eagerly.

Ferguson put down the receiver, reached for the red phone, but some innate caution stopped him. Much better to phone the Home Secretary when the fish was actually in the net.

Brodie sat on a stool, leaning back in the corner watching Cussane and smoking a cigarette. The guard was checking a list on his desk. He totalled it and put his pen away. 'I'll make my rounds. See you later.'

He went out and Brodie pulled his stool across the baggage car and sat very close to Cussane. 'I've never understood it. Men in skirts. It'll never catch on.' He leaned forward. 'Tell me, you priests – what do you do for it?'

'For what?' Cussane said.

'You know. Is it choirboys? Is that the truth of it?' There were beads of perspiration on the big man's forehead.

'That's a hell of a big moustache you're wearing,' Cussane said. 'Have you got a weak mouth or something?'

Brodie was angry now. 'Cocky bastard. I'll show you.'

He reached forward and touched the end of the lighted cigarette to the back of Cussane's hand. Cussane cried out and fell back against the mailbags.

Brodie laughed and leaned over him. 'I thought you'd like that,' he said and reached to touch the back of the hand again. Cussane kicked him in the crutch. Brodie staggered back clutching at himself and Cussane sprang to his feet. He kicked out expertly, catching the right kneecap, and as Brodie keeled forward, raised his knee into the face.

The police sergeant lay on his back moaning and Cussane searched his pockets, found the key and unlocked his handcuffs. He got his bag, checked that the contents were intact and slipped the Stechkin into his pocket. He pulled back the sliding door and rain flooded in.

The guard, entering the baggage car a moment later, caught a brief glimpse of him landing in heather at the side of the track and rolling over and over down the slope. And then there was only mist and rain.

When the train coasted into Glasgow Central, Trent and half-a-dozen uniformed constables were waiting on platform one. The door of the baggage car slid open and the guard appeared.

'In here.'

Trent paused at the entrance. There was only Lachlan Brodie nursing a bloody and swollen face, sitting on the guard's stool. Trent's heart sank. 'Tell me,' he said wearily. Brodie did the best he could. When he was finished, Trent said. 'He was handcuffed, you say, and you let him take you?'

'It wasn't as simple as it sounds, sir,' Brodie said lamely.

'You stupid, stupid man,' Trent said. 'By the time I'm finished with you, you'll be lucky if they put you in charge of a public lavatory.'

He turned away in disgust and went back along the platform to phone Ferguson.

Cussane at that precise moment was halted in the shelter of some rocks on top of a hill north of Dunhill. He had the ordnance survey map open that he'd purchased from Moira McGregor. He found Larwick with no trouble and the Mungos' farm was just outside. Perhaps fifteen miles and most of that over hill country, and yet he felt cheerful enough as he pressed on.

The mist curling in on either hand, the heavy rain, gave him a safe, enclosed feeling, remote from the world outside, a kind of freedom. He moved on through birch trees and wet bracken that soaked his trouser legs. Occasionally grouse or plover lifted from the heather, disturbed by his passing. He kept on the move, for by now his raincoat was soaked through and he was experienced enough to know the dangers of being in hill country like this in the wrong clothing.

He came over the edge of an escarpment perhaps an hour after leaving the train and looked down into a valley glen below. Darkness was falling, but there was a clearly defined man-made track a few yards away ending at a cairn of rough stones. It was enough; he hurried on with renewed energy and plunged down the hillside.

Ferguson was looking at a large ordnance survey map of the Scottish Lowlands. 'Apparently he got the coach in Morecambe,' he said. 'We've established that.'

'A neat way of getting to Glasgow, sir,' Fox said.

'No,' Ferguson said. 'He took a ticket to a place called Dunhill. What in the hell would he be doing there?'

'Do you know the area?' Devlin asked.

'Had a week's shooting on some chap's estate about twenty years ago. Funny place, the Galloway hills. High forests, ridgebacks and secret little lochs everywhere.'

'Galloway, you said?' Devlin looked closer at the map. 'So that's Galloway?'

Ferguson frowned. 'So what?'

'I think that's where he's gone,' Devlin said. 'I think that's where he was aiming to go all along.'

Fox said, 'What makes you think that?'

He told them about Danny Malone and when he was finished, Ferguson said, 'You could very well have something.'

Devlin nodded. 'Danny mentioned a number of safe houses used by the underworld in various parts of the country, but the fact that he's in the Galloway area must have some connection with this place run by the Mungo brothers.'

'What do we do now, sir?' Fox asked Ferguson. 'Get Special Branch, Glasgow, to lay on a raid on this Mungo place?'

'No, to hell with that,' Ferguson said. 'We've already had a classic example of just how efficient the local police can be; they had him and let him slip through their fingers.' He glanced out of the window at the darkness outside. 'Too late to do anything tonight. Too late for him as well. He'll still be on foot in those hills.'

'Bound to be,' Devlin said.

'So – you and Harry fly up to Glasgow tomorrow. You check out this Mungo place personally. I'm invoking special powers. On this one, Special Branch will do what you want.'

He went out. Fox gave Devlin a cigarette. 'What do you think?'

'They had him, Harry, in handcuffs,' Devlin said, 'and he got away. That's what I think. Now give me a light.'

Cussane went down through birch trees following the course of a pleasant burn which splashed between a jumble of granite boulders. He was beginning to feel tired now in spite of the fact that the going was all downhill.

The burn disappeared over an edge of rock, cascading into a deep pool as it had done several times before and he slithered down through birch trees through the gathering dusk rather faster than he had intended, landing in an untidy heap, still holding on to his bag.

There was a startled gasp and Cussane, coming up on one knee, saw two children crouched at the side of the pool. The girl, on a second look, was older than he had thought, perhaps sixteen, and wore wellingtons and jeans and an old reefer coat that was too big for her. She had a pointed face, wide dark eyes, and a profusion of black hair flowed from beneath a knitted Tam O'Shanter.

The boy was younger, no more than ten, with ragged jersey, cut-down tweed trousers and rubber and canvas running shoes that had seen better days. He was in the act of withdrawing a gaff from the water, a salmon spitted on it.

Cussane smiled. 'Where I come from that wouldn't be considered very sporting.'

'Run, Morag!' the boy cried and lunged at Cussane with the gaff, the salmon still wriggling on the end.

A section of the bank crumbled under his foot and he fell back into the pool. He surfaced, still clutching the gaff, but in an instant, the swift current, swollen by the heavy rain, had him in its grasp and carried him away.

'Donal!' the girl screamed and ran to the edge.

Cussane got a hand to her shoulder and pulled her back, just in time as another section of the bank crumbled. 'Don't be a fool. You'll go the same way.'

She struggled to break free and he dropped his bag, shoved her out of the way, and ran along the bank, pushing through the birches. At that point the water poured through a narrow slot in the rocks with real force, taking the boy with it.

Cussane plunged on, aware of the girl behind him. He pulled off his raincoat and threw it to one side. He cut out across the rocks, trying to get to the end of the slot before the boy, reaching out to grab one end of the outstretched gaff which the boy still clutched, minus the salmon now.

He managed it, was aware of the enormous force of the current and then went in headfirst, a circumstance impossible to avoid. He surfaced in the pool below, the boy a yard or so away and reached out and secured a grip on the jersey. A moment later, the current took them in to a shingle strand. As the girl ran down the bank, the boy was on his feet, shook himself like a terrier and scrambled up to meet her.

A sudden eddy brought Cussane's black hat floating in. He picked it up, examined it and laughed. 'Now that will certainly never be the same again,' and he tossed it out into the pool.

He turned to go up the bank and found himself looking into the muzzle of a sawn-off shotgun held by an old man of at least seventy who stood at the edge of the birch trees, the girl, Morag, and the young Donal beside him. He wore a shabby tweed suit, a Tam O'Shanter that was twin to the girl's, and badly needed a shave.

'Who is he, Granda?' the girl asked. 'No water baillie.'

'With a minister's collar, that would hardly be likely.' The old man's speech was tinged with the soft *blâs* of the highlander. 'Are you a man of the cloth?'

'My name is Fallon,' Cussane told him. 'Father Michael Fallon.' He recalled the name of a village in the area from his examination of the ordnance survey map. 'I was making for Whitechapel, missed the bus and thought I'd try a short-cut over the hill.'

The girl had walked back to pick up his raincoat. She returned and the old man took it from her. 'Away you now, Donal, and get the gentleman's bag.'

So, he must have seen everything from the beginning. The boy scampered away and the old man weighed the raincoat in his hand. He felt in a pocket and produced the Stechkin. 'Would you look at that now? No water baillie, Morag, that's for sure, and a damn strange priest.'

'He saved Donal, Granda?' the girl touched his sleeve.

He smiled slowly down at her. 'And so he did. Away to the camp then, girl. Say that we have company and see that the kettle is on the fire.'

He put the Stechkin back in the raincoat and handed it to Cussane. The girl turned and darted away through the trees and the boy came back with the bag.

'My name is Hamish Finlay and I am in your debt.' He rumpled the boy's hair. 'You are welcome to share what we have. No man can say more.'

They moved up through the trees and started through the plantation. Cussane said, 'This is strange country.'

The old man took out a pipe and filled it from a worn pouch, the shotgun under his arm. 'Aye, the Galloway is that. A man can lose himself here, from other men, if you take my meaning?'

'Oh, I do,' Cussane said. 'Sometimes we all need to do that.'

There was a cry of fear up ahead, the girl's voice raised high. Finlay's gun was in his hands in an instant and as they moved forward, they saw her struggling in the arms of a tall, heavily-built man. Like Finlay, he carried a shotgun and wore an old, patched, tweed suit. His face was brutal and badly needed a shave and yellow hair poked from beneath his cap. He was staring down at the girl as if enjoying her fear, a half smile on his face. Cussane was conscious of real anger, but it was Finlay who handled it.

'Leave her, Murray!'

The other man scowled, hanging on to her, then pushed her away with a forced smile. 'A bit of sport only.' The girl turned and ran away behind him. 'Who's this?'

'Murray, my dead brother's child you are and my responsibility, but did I ever tell you there's a stink to you like bad meat on a summer day?'

The shotgun moved slightly in Murray's grasp and there was hot rage in the eyes. Cussane slipped a hand in his raincoat pocket and found the Stechkin. Calmly, almost contemptuously, the old man lit his pipe and something went out of Murray. He turned on his heel and walked away.

'My own nephew.' Finlay shook his head. 'You know what they say. "Our friends we choose ourselves, but our relations are chosen for us." '

'True,' Cussane said as they started walking again.

'Aye, and you can take your hand off the butt of that pistol. It won't be needed now, Father – or whatever ye are.'

The camp in the hollow was a poor sort of place. The three wagons were old with patched canvas tilts, and the only motor vehicle in view was a jeep of World War Two vintage, painted khaki green. A depressing air of poverty hung over everything, from the ragged clothes of the three women who cooked at the open fire, to the bare feet of the children who played tig amongst the half dozen horses that grazed beside the stream.

Cussane slept well, deep, dreamless sleep that was totally refreshing, and awakened to find the girl, Morag, sitting on the opposite bunk watching him.

Cussane smiled. 'Hello there.'

'That's funny,' she said. 'One minute you were asleep, the next your eyes were open and you were wide awake. How did you learn to do that?'

'The habit of a lifetime.' He glanced at his watch. 'Only six-thirty.'

'We rise early.' She nodded outside the wagon. He could hear voices and smell bacon frying.

'I've dried your clothes,' she said. 'Would you like some tea?'

There was an eagerness to her as if she desperately wanted to please, something infinitely touching. He reached to pull the Tam O'Shanter down more over one ear. 'I like that.'

'My mother knitted it for me.' She pulled it off and looked at it, her face sad.

'That's nice. Is she here?'

'No.' Morag put the Tam O'Shanter back on. 'She ran away with a man called McTavish last year. They went to Australia.'

'And your father?'

'He left her when I was a baby.' She shrugged. 'But I don't care.'

'Is young Donal your brother?'

'No. His father is my cousin, Murray. You saw him earlier.'

'Ah, yes. You don't like him, I think.'

She shivered. 'He makes me feel funny.'

Cussane was conscious of the anger again, but controlled it. 'That tea would be welcome, plus the chance to get dressed.'

Her reply, cynical and far too adult for her age, surprised him. 'Frightened I might corrupt you, Father?' She grinned. 'I'll fetch your tea.' And she darted out.

His suit had been thoroughly brushed and dried. He dressed quickly, omitting the vest and clerical collar and pulling a thin black polo neck sweater over his head instead. He pulled on his raincoat because it was still raining and went out.

Murray Finlay leaned against the side of a wagon smoking a clay pipe, Donal crouched at his feet.

Cussane said, 'Good morning,' but Murray could only manage a scowl.

Morag turned from the fire to offer Cussane tea in a chipped enamel mug and Murray called, 'Don't I get one?'

She ignored him and Cussane asked, 'Where's your grandfather?'

'Fishing by the loch. I'll show you. Bring your tea.'

There was something immensely appealing, a *gamine* quality that was somehow accentuated by the Tam O'Shanter. It was as if she was putting out her tongue at the whole world in spite of her ragged clothes. It was not pleasant to think of such a girl brutalized by contact with the likes of Murray and the squalor of the years to come.

They went over the rise and came to a small loch, a pleasant place where heather flowed down to the shore-line. Old Hamish Finlay stood thigh deep, rod in hand, making one extremely expert cast after another. A wind stirred the water, small black fins appeared and suddenly, a trout came out of the deep water beyond the sandbar, leapt in the air and vanished.

The old man glanced at Cussane and chuckled. 'Would you look at that now? Have you noticed how often the good things in life tend to pop up in the wrong places?'

'Frequently.'

Finlay gave Morag his rod. 'You'll find three fat ones in the basket. Off with you and get the breakfast going.'

She turned back to the camp and Cussane offered the old man a cigarette. 'A nice child.'

'Aye, you could say that.'

Cussane gave him a light. 'This life you lead is a strange one and yet you aren't gypsies, I think?'

'People of the road. Tinkers. People have many names for us and some of them none too kind. The last remnants of a proud clan broken at Culloden. Mind, we have links with other road people on occasion. Morag's mother was an English gypsy.'

'No resting place?' Cussane said.

'None. No man will have us for long enough. There's a village constable at Whitechapel who'll be up here no later than tomorrow. Three days – that's all we get and he'll move us on. But what about you?'

'I'll be on my way this morning as soon as I've eaten.'

The old man nodded. 'I shan't query the collar you wore last night. Your business is your own. Is there nothing I can do for you?'

'Better by far to do nothing,' Cussane told him.

'Like that, is it?' Finlay sighed heavily and, somewhere, Morag screamed.

Cussane came through the trees on the run and found them in a clearing amongst the birches. The girl was on her back, Murray was crouching on top, pinning her down and there was only lust on his face. He groped for one of her breasts, she cried out again in revulsion and Cussane arrived. He got a handful of Murray's long yellow hair, twisting it cruelly so that it was the big man's turn to cry out. He came to his feet and Cussane turned him round, held him for a moment, then pushed him away.

'Don't touch her again!'

Old Hamish Finlay arrived at that moment, shotgun at the ready. 'Murray, I warned you.'

But Murray ignored him and advanced on Cussane, glaring ferociously. 'I'm going to smash you, you little worm!'

He came in fast, arms raised to destroy. Cussane pivoted to one side and delivered a left to Murray's kidneys as he lurched past. Murray went down on one knee, stayed there for a moment, then got up and swung the wildest of punches. Cussane sank a left under his ribs followed by a right hook to the cheek, splitting flesh.

'Murray, my God is a God of Wrath when the occasion warrants it.' He punched the big man in the face a second time. 'Touch this girl and I'll kill you, understand?'

Cussane kicked Murray under the kneecap. The big man went down on his knees and stayed there.

Old Finlay moved in. 'I've given you your last warning, you bastard.' He prodded Murray with the shotgun. 'You'll leave my camp this day and go your own way.'

Murray lurched painfully to his feet and turned and hobbled away towards the camp. Finlay said, 'By God, man, you don't do things by halves.'

'I could never see the point,' Cussane told him.

Morag had picked up the rod and fishbasket. She stood looking at him, a kind of wonder in her eyes. And then she backed away. 'I'll see to the breakfast,' she said in a low voice, turned and ran towards the camp.

There was the sound of the jeep's engine starting up, it moved away. 'He hasn't wasted much time,' Cussane said.

Finlay said, 'Good riddance. Now let's to breakfast.'

Murray Finlay pulled up the jeep in front of the newsagents in Whitechapel and sat there thinking. Young Donal sat beside him. He hated and feared his father, had not wanted to come, but Murray had given him no option.

'Stay there,' Murray told him. 'I need tobacco.'

He went to the door of the newsagents' shop which obstinately stayed closed when he tried to push it open. He cursed and started to turn away, then paused. The morning papers were stacked in the shop doorway and his attention was caught by a photo on the front page of one of them. He took out a knife, cut the string which tied the bundle and picked up the top copy.

'Would you look at that? I've got you now, you bastard.' He turned, hurried across the street to the police cottage and opened the garden gate.

Young Donal, puzzled, got out of the jeep, picked up the next paper and found himself looking at a reasonably good photo of Cussane. He stood staring for a moment at the photo of the man who had saved his life, then turned and ran up the road as fast as he could.

Morag was stacking the tin plates after breakfast when Donal arrived on the run.

'What is it?' she cried, for his distress was obvious.

'Where's the Father?'

'Walking in the woods with Granda. What is it?'

There was the sound of the jeep approaching. Donal showed her the paper wildly. 'Look at that. It's him.'

Which it undeniably was. The description, as Ferguson had indicated, had Cussane only posing as a priest and made him out to be not only IRA, but a thoroughly dangerous man.

The jeep roared into the camp, and Murray jumped out holding his shotgun, followed by the village constable who was in uniform but had obviously not had time to shave.

'Where is he?' Murray demanded, and grabbed the boy by the hair and shook him. 'Tell me, you little scut!'

Donal screamed in pain. 'In the wood.'

Murray pushed him away and nodded to the constable. 'Right, let's get him.' He turned and hurried towards the plantation.

Morag didn't think, simply acted. She ducked into the wagon, found Cussane's bag and threw it into the jeep. Then she climbed behind the wheel and pressed the starter. She had driven it often and knew what she was doing. She took the jeep away, wheels spinning across the rough ground. She turned away to one side of Murray and the constable. Murray turned, she was aware of the rage in his face, the flat bang of the shotgun. She swung the wheel, brushing him to one side and took the jeep straight into the forest of young birch trees. Cussane and Finlay, alerted by the commotion, were running towards the camp when the jeep came crashing through the trees and stopped.

'What is it, lass?' Finlay cried.

'Murray got the police. Get in! Get in!' she said to Cussane.

He didn't argue, simply vaulted in beside her, and she took the jeep round in a circle, crashing through the trees. Murray came limping towards them, the constable beside him and the two men dived to one side. The jeep burst out of the trees, bumped across the rough ground past the camp and turned on to the road.

She braked to a halt. 'Whitechapel won't be right. Won't they block the road?'

'They'll block all the bloody roads,' he said.

'So where do we go?'

'We?' Cussane said.

'Don't argue, Mr Cussane. If I stay, they'll arrest me for helping you.'

She passed him the newspaper Donal had given her. He looked at his photo and read the salient facts quickly. He smiled wryly. Someone had been on to him a damn sight more quickly than he would ever have imagined.

'So where to?' she asked impatiently.

He made his decision then. 'Turn left and keep climbing. We're going to try and reach a farm outside a village called Larwick on the other side of those hills. They tell me these things will go anywhere, so who needs roads? Can you handle it?'

'Just watch me!' she said, and drove away.

13

The glen was mainly national forest and they left the road and followed a track through pine trees, climbing higher and higher beside a burn swollen by the heavy rain. Finally, they came up out of the trees at the head of the glen and reached a small plateau.

He touched her arm. 'This will do,' he called above the roaring of the engine.

She braked to a halt and switched off. Rolling hills stretched on either side, fading into mist and heavy rain. He got out the ordnance survey map and went forward to study the terrain. The map was as accurate as only a government survey could make it. He found Larwick with no difficulty. Glendhu, that was where Danny Malone had said the Mungos' farm was, a couple of miles outside the village. The Black Glen it meant in Gaelic and there was only one farm marked. It had to be the place. He spent a few more minutes studying the lie of the land below him in conjunction with the map and then went back to the jeep.

Morag looked up from the newspaper. 'Is it true, all this stuff about you and the IRA?'

He got in out of the rain. 'What do you think?'

'It says here you often pose as a priest. That means you aren't one?'

It was a question as much as anything else and he smiled. 'You know what they say. If it's in the papers it must be true. Why, does it worry you being in the company of such a desperate character?'

She shook her head. 'You saved Donal at the burn and you didn't need to. You helped me – saved me from Murray.' She folded the paper and tossed it into the back of the jeep, a slight frown of bewilderment on her face. 'There's the man in the paper and then there's you. It's like two different people.'

'Most of us are at least three people,' he said. 'There's who I think I am, then the person you think I am.'

'Which only leaves who you really are,' she cut in.

'True, except that some people can only survive by continuously adapting. They become many people, but for it to work, they must really live the part.'

'Like an actor?' she said.

'That's it exactly, except that like any good actor, they must believe in the role they are playing at that particular time.'

She lay back in the seat, half-turned towards him, arms folded, listening intently and it struck him then that, in spite of her background and the sparseness of any formal education in her life, she was obviously highly intelligent.

'I see,' she said. 'So when you pose as a priest, you actually become a priest.'

The directness was disturbing. 'Something like that.' They sat there in silence for a few moments before he said softly, 'You saved my hide back there. If it hadn't been for you, I'd have been in handcuffs again.'

'Again?' she said.

'I was picked up by the police yesterday. They were taking me to Glasgow in the train, but I managed to jump for it. Walked over the hill from there and met you.'

'Lucky for Donal,' she said. 'Lucky for me, if it comes to that.'

'Murray, you mean? Has he been a problem for long?'

'Since I was about thirteen,' she said calmly. 'It wasn't so bad while my Mam was still with us. She kept him in check. But after she left . . .' She shrugged. 'He's never had his way with me, but lately, it got worse. I'd been thinking of leaving.'

'Running away? But where would you go?'

'My grandma. My mother's mother. She's a true gypsy. Her name's Brana – Brana Smith, but she calls herself Gypsy Rose.'

'I seem to have heard a name like that before,' Cussane said, smiling.

'She has the gift,' Morag told him seriously. 'Second sight in all things, with the palm, the crystal or the Tarot cards. She has a house in Wapping in London, on the river, when she isn't working the fairgrounds with the travelling shows.'

'And you'd like to go to her?'

'Granda always said I could when I was older.' She pushed herself up. 'What about you? Do you intend to make for London?'

'Perhaps,' he said slowly.

'Then we could go together.' This she said to him calmly and without emotion, as if it was the most natural thing in the world.

'No,' he said flatly. 'I don't think so. For one thing, it would only get you deeper in trouble. For another, I have to travel light. No excess baggage. When I have to run, I have to run fast. No time to think of anyone but me.'

There was something in her eyes, a kind of hurt, but she showed no emotion, simply got out of the jeep and stood at the side of the track, hands in pockets. 'I understand. You go on from here. I'll walk back down the glen.'

He had a momentary vision of the wretched encampment, imagined the slow and inevitable brutalization of the years. And she was worth more than that. Much more.

'Don't be stupid,' he said. 'Get in!'

'What for?'

'I need you to drive the jeep, don't I, while I follow the map? Down through the glen below and over that centre hill. There's a farm in a place called Glendhu outside Larwick.'

She got behind the wheel quickly, smiling. 'Have you friends there?'

'Not exactly.' He reached for his bag, opened it, pulled open the false bottom and took out the bundle of banknotes. 'This is the kind of stuff they like. What most people like if it comes to that.' He pulled several notes off, folded them and put them in the breast pocket of her old reefer coat. 'That should keep you going till you find your grannie.'

Her eyes were round in astonishment. 'I can't take that.'

'Oh yes, you can. Now get this thing moving.'

She selected a low gear and started down the track carefully. 'And what happens when we get there? To me, I mean?'

'We'll have to see. Maybe you could catch a train. On your own, you'd probably do very well. I'm the one they're really after, so your only real danger is in being with me.'

She didn't say anything to that and he studied the map in silence. Finally, she spoke again. 'The business about me and Murray. Does that disgust you? I mean, the wickedness of it?'

'Wickedness?' He laughed softly. 'My dear girl, you have no conception of what true wickedness, real evil, is like, although Murray is probably animal enough to come close. A priest hears more of sin in a week than most people experience in a lifetime.'

She glanced at him briefly. 'But I thought you said you only posed as a priest.'

'Did I?' Cussane lit another cigarette and leaned back in the seat, closing his eyes.

As the police car turned out of the carpark at Glasgow Airport, Chief Inspector Trent said to the driver, 'You know where we're going. We've only got thirty-five minutes so step on it.' Devlin and Fox sat in the rear of the car and Trent turned towards them. 'Did you have a good flight?'

'It was fast, that was the main thing,' Fox said. 'What's the present position?'

'Cussane turned up again, at a gypsy encampment in the Galloway Hills. I got the news on the car radio just before you got in.'

'And got away again, I fancy?' Devlin said.

'As a matter of fact, he did.'

'A bad habit he has.'

'Anyway, you said you wanted to be in the Dunhill area. We're going straight to Glasgow Central Railway Station now. The main road is still flooded, but I've made arrangements for us to board the Glasgow to London express. They'll drop us at Dunhill. We'll also have the oaf who had Cussane and lost him in the first place, Sergeant Brodie. At least he knows the local area.'

'Fine,' Devlin said. 'That takes care of everything from the sound of it. You're armed, I hope?'

'Yes. Am I permitted to know where we're going?' Trent asked.

Fox said, 'A village called Larwick not far from this Dunhill place. There's a farm outside which, according to our information, operates as a safe house for criminals on the run. We think our man could be there.'

'But in that case, you should let me call in reinforcements.'

'No,' Devlin told him. 'We understand the farm in question is in an isolated area. The movement of people in any kind of numbers, never mind men in uniform, would be bound to be spotted. If our man is there, he'd run for it again.'

'So we'd catch him,' Trent said.

Devlin glanced at Fox who nodded, and the Irishman turned back to Trent. 'The night before last, three gunmen of the Provisional IRA tried to take him on the other side of the water. He saw them all off.'

'Good God!'

'Exactly. He'd see off a few of your chaps, too, before they got to him. Better to try it our way, Chief Inspector,' Harry Fox said. 'Believe me.'

From the crest of the hill above Glendhu, Cussane and Morag crouched in the wet bracken and looked down. The track had petered out, but in any case, it had seemed politic to Cussane to leave the jeep up there out of sight. There was nothing like an ace in the hole if anything went sour. Better the Mungos didn't know about that.

'It doesn't look much,' Morag said.

Which was an understatement, for the farm presented an unlovely picture. One barn without its roof, tiles missing from the roof of the main building. There were potholes in the yard filled with water, a truck minus its wheels, a decaying tractor, red with rust.

The girl shivered suddenly. 'I've got a bad feeling. I don't like that place.'

He stood up, picked up his bag, and took the Stechkin from his pocket. 'I've got this. There's no need to worry. Trust me.'

'Yes,' she said and there was a kind of passion in her voice. 'I do trust you.'

She took his arm and together they started down through the bracken towards the farm.

Hector Mungo had driven down to Larwick early that morning, mainly because he'd run out of cigarettes although come to think of it, they'd run out of almost everything. He purchased bacon, eggs, various canned foods, a carton of cigarettes and a bottle of Scotch and told the old lady who ran the general store, to put it on the bill, which she did because she was afraid of Mungo and his brother. Everyone was afraid of them. On his way out, Hector helped himself to a morning paper as an afterthought, got into the old van and drove away.

He was a hard-faced man of sixty-two, sullen and morose in an old flying jacket and tweed cap, a grey stubble covering his chin. He turned the van into the yard, pulled up and got out with the cardboard box filled with his purchases and ran for the door through the rain, kicking it open.

The kitchen he entered was indescribably filthy, the old stone sink piled high with dirty pots. His brother, Angus, sat at the table, head in hands, staring into space. He was younger than his brother, forty-five, with cropped hair and a coarse and brutal face that was rendered even more ugly by the old scar that bisected the right eye which had been left milky white.

'I thought you'd never come.' He reached in the box as his brother put it down and found the whisky, opening it and taking a long swallow. Then he found the cigarettes.

'You idle bastard,' Hector told him. 'You might have put the fire on.'

Angus ignored him, simply took another pull at the bottle, lit a cigarette and opened the newspaper. Hector moved across to the sink and found a match to light the Calor gas stove beside it. He paused, looking out into the yard as Cussane and Morag appeared and approached the house.

'We've got company,' he said.

Angus moved to join him. He stiffened. 'Just a minute.' He laid the newspaper down on the draining board. 'That looks damn like him right there on the front page to me.'

Hector examined the newspaper report quickly. 'Jesus, Angus, we've got a right one here. Real trouble.'

'Just another little Mick straight out of the bogs,' Angus said contemptuously. 'Plenty of room for him at the bottom of the well, just like the others.'

'That's true.' Hector nodded solemnly.

'But not the girl.' Angus wiped his mouth with the back of one hand. 'I like the look of her. She's mine, you old bastard. Just remember that. Now let them in,' he added, as there came a knock at the door.

'You know the Mungo brothers then, Sergeant?' Fox asked Brodie.

They were in the guard's van at the back of the speeding train, the four of them: Devlin, Fox, Trent and the big sergeant.

'They're animals,' Brodie said. 'Everyone in the district is terrified of them. I don't know how they make a living up there. They've both done prison time, Hector for operating an illegal whisky still. He's been inside three times for that. Angus has a string of minor offences to his name and then he killed a man in a fist fight some time back. Sentenced to five years, but they let him out in three. And twice he's been accused of rapes and then the women concerned have dropped the charges. The suggestion that they operate a safe house doesn't surprise me, but I've no knowledge of it and it certainly has never been mentioned in their files.'

'How close can we get to their farm without being spotted?' Trent asked.

'About a quarter of a mile. The road up Glendhu only goes to their place.'

'No other way out?' Fox asked.

'On foot, I suppose, up the glen, over the hill.'

Devlin said, 'We've got to allow for one important point. If Cussane did mean to stay with the Mungos, his plans were badly disrupted. Being taken by the Sergeant here, jumping from the train, that gypsy encampment, were not on the agenda. That could have changed his plans.'

'True,' Harry Fox said. 'And there's the girl too.'

Trent said, 'They could still be back there in the hills. On the other hand, they've got to pass through Larwick to get to the farm if they're still in that jeep. In a village that size, somebody must have seen it.'

'Let's hope so,' Devlin said and the express started to slow as they came into Dunhill.

'Danny Malone.' Hector Mungo poured strong tea into dirty mugs and added milk. 'A long time since we had Danny here, isn't it, Angus?'

'Aye, it is that.' Angus sat with a glass in his hand, ignoring the other two and staring at Morag who did her best to avoid his gaze.

Cussane was already aware that he had made a big mistake. The service the Mungo brothers had offered people like Danny years before must have been very different from what was available now. He ignored the tea and sat there, one hand on the butt of the Stechkin. He wasn't sure what his next move should be. The script seemed to be writing itself this time.

'Actually, we were reading about you just before you arrived.' Hector Mungo shoved the paper across. 'No mention of the girl, you see.'

Cussane ignored the paper. 'There wouldn't be.'

'So what can we do for you? You want to hole up here for a while?'

'Just for the day,' Cussane said. 'Then tonight, when it's dark, one of you can take us south in that old van of yours. Fill it up with stuff from around the farm, hide us in the back.'

Hector nodded gravely. 'I don't see why not. Where to? Dumfries?'

'How far to Carlisle where the motorway begins?'

'Sixty miles. It'll cost you though.'

'How much?'

Hector glanced at Angus and licked dry lips nervously. 'A thousand. You're hot, my friend. Very hot.'

Cussane opened his case, took out the wad of banknotes and peeled ten off. He laid them on the table. 'Five hundred.'

'Well, I don't know,' Hector began.

'Don't be stupid,' Angus said. 'That's more money in one piece than you've seen at any time during the past six months.' He turned to Cussane. 'I'll drive you to Carlisle myself.'

'That's settled then.' Cussane got up. 'You've got a room we can use, I suppose.'

'No problem.' Hector was all eagerness. 'One to spare for the young lady, too.'

'One will do just fine,' Cussane said as they followed him out into the stone-flagged corridor and up the rickety stairs.

He opened the first door on the landing and led the way into a large bedroom. There was a murky, unpleasant smell and the flowered wallpaper was stained with damp. There was an old brass double bed with a mattress that had seen better days, army surplus blankets stacked on top of it.

'There's a lavatory next door,' Hector said. 'I'll leave you to it then.'

He went out, closing the door. They heard him go back down stairs. There was an old rusting bolt on the door. Cussane rammed it home. There was another door on the opposite side of the room with a key in the lock. He opened it and looked out on a stone staircase against the side of the house going down to the yard. He closed the door and locked it again.

He turned to the girl. 'All right?'

'The one with the bad eye.' She shuddered. 'He's worse than Murray.' She hesitated. 'Can I call you Harry?'

'Why not?'

He quickly unfolded the blankets and spread them on the mattress. 'What are we going to do?' she asked.

'Rest,' he said. 'Get a little sleep. No one can get in. Not at the moment.'

'Do you think they'll take us to Carlisle?'

'No, but I don't think they'll try anything until it's dark and we're ready to leave.'

'How can you be sure they will try?'

'Because that's the kind of men they are. Now lie down and try and get some sleep.'

He got on the bed without taking off his coat, the Stechkin in his right hand. She lay down on the other side of the bed. For a while, she stayed there and then she rolled over and cuddled against him.

'I'm frightened.'

'Hush.' His arm went around her. 'Be still now. I am here. Nothing will touch you in this place.'

Her breathing became slow and heavy. He lay there holding her, thinking about things. She was already a liability and how long he could sustain that, he wasn't sure. On the other hand, he owed her. There was a moral debt in that, surely. He looked down at the purity of the young face, still untouched by life. Something good in a bad world. He closed his eyes, thinking of that, and finally slept.

'Did you see all that cash?' Hector asked.

'Yes,' Angus said. 'I saw it.'

'He's locked the door. I heard him.'

'Of course he has. He's no fool. Not that it matters. He's got to come out sooner or later. We'll take him then.'

'Good,' Hector said.

His brother poured another whisky. 'And don't forget. I get the girl.'

Devlin, Fox, Trent and Brodie drove up to Larwick from Dunhill in an old blue Ford van which the police sergeant had borrowed from a local garage. He parked it outside the general store in the village and went in while the others waited. He returned five minutes later and got behind the wheel of the Ford.

'Hector Mungo was in earlier for groceries. The old girl in there runs the saloon bar at the pub in the evenings. She says both of them are around, but no strangers, and they'd stick out like a sore thumb in a place like this.'

Devlin looked out of one of the rear windows in the van doors. There was really only one street, a row of granite cottages, a pub, the store and the hills lifting steeply above. 'I see what you mean.'

Brodie started the engine and drove away, following a narrow road between grey stone walls. 'The only road and the farm at the end of it.' A few minutes later he said, 'Right, this is about as far as we can go without being seen.'

He pulled in under some trees and they all got out. 'How far?' Trent asked.

'Less than a quarter of a mile. I'll show you.'

He led the way up through the trees at the side of the road, scrambling up through ferns and bracken and paused cautiously on the ridge line. 'There you are.'

The farm was below in the hollow a few hundred yards away. 'Cannery Row,' Devlin murmured.

'Yes, it does look a bit like that,' Fox replied. 'No sign of life.'

'What's more important, no sign of the jeep,' Devlin said. 'Maybe I was wrong after all.'

At that moment, both the Mungo brothers came out of the kitchen door and crossed the yard. 'That's them presumably.' Fox took a small pair of Zeiss fieldglasses from his pocket and focused them. 'Nasty looking couple,' he added, as they went into the barn.

A moment later Morag Finlay came into view.

Trent said excitedly, 'It's the girl. Has to be. Reefer coat, Tam O'Shanter. Fits the description exactly.'

'Jesus, Mary and Joseph,' Devlin said softly. 'I was right. Harry must be in the house.'

Trent said, 'How are we going to handle this?'

'You've both got personal radios?' Fox asked.

'Sure.'

'Right, give me one of them. Devlin and I will go in from the rear of the farm. With any kind of luck, we'll take them by surprise. You go back and wait in the van. The moment I give you the good word, you come up that road like an express train.'

'Fine.'

Trent and Brodie went back towards the road. Devlin took a Walther PPK from his pocket and cocked it. Fox did the same.

The Irishman smiled. 'Just remember one thing. Harry Cussane isn't the kind of man to give any kind of a chance to.'

'Don't worry,' Fox said grimly. 'I shan't.' He started down the slope through the wet bracken and Devlin followed.

Morag came awake and lay staring up at the ceiling blankly, and then she remembered where she was and turned to look at Cussane beside her. He slept quietly, his breathing light, the face in repose, very calm. He still clutched the Stechkin in his right hand. She gently eased her feet to the floor, stood up and stretched, then she walked to the window. As she looked out, Hector and Angus Mungo crossed the yard and went into the barn opposite. She opened the door and stood at the top of the stone stairs and was aware of some sort of engine starting up. She frowned, listening intently and then quickly went down the steps and crossed the yard.

In the bedroom, Cussane stirred, stretched, then opened his eyes, instantly awake as usual. He was aware of the girl's absence at once, was on his feet in a second. Then he noticed the open door.

The barn was filled with the sour-sweet smell of mash for the Mungos operated their still in there. Hector switched on the old petrol engine and pump that provided their power supply, then checked the vat.

'We need more sugar,' he said.

Angus nodded. 'I'll get some.'

He opened a door that led into a hut built on the side of the barn. There were various supplies in there, all necessary ingredients of their illegal work, and several sacks of sugar. He was about to pick one up when through a broken plank, he saw Morag Finlay outside, peering in through a window at what was going on in the barn. He smiled delightedly, put down the sack and crept out.

Morag was not even aware of his approach. A hand was clamped over her mouth, stifling her cry and she was lifted in strong arms and carried, kicking and struggling, into the barn.

Hector turned from stirring the vat. 'What's this?'

'A little nosey-parker that needs teaching its manners,' Angus said.

He put her down and she struck at him wildly. He slapped her back-handed and then again with enough force to send her sprawling on a pile of sacks.

He stood over her and started to unbuckle his belt. 'Manners,' he said. 'That's what I'm going to teach you.'

'Angus!' Harry Cussane called from just inside the door. 'Are you a bastard by nature or do you really have to work at it?'

He stood there, hands negligently in the pockets of his raincoat, and Angus turned to face him. He bent down to pick up a shovel. 'You little squirt, I'm going to split your skull.'

'Something I picked up from the IRA,' Cussane said. 'A special punishment for special bastards like you.'

The Stechkin came out of his pocket, there was a dull thud and a bullet splintered Angus Mungo's right kneecap. He screamed, fell back against the petrol motor and rolled over, clutching at his knee with both hands, blood pumping between his fingers. Hector Mungo gave a terrible cry of fear, turned and ran headlong for the side door, arms up in a futile gesture of protection. He burst through and disappeared.

Cussane ignored Angus and pulled Morag to her feet. 'Are you all right?'

She turned and looked down at Angus, rage and humiliation on her face. 'No thanks to him.'

He took her arm and they went out and crossed the yard to the kitchen door. As the girl opened it, Harry Fox called, 'Hold it right there, Cussane!' and moved from behind the parked van.

Cussane recognized the voice instantly, sent the girl staggering through the door, turned and fired, all in one smooth motion. Fox fell back against the van, the gun jumping from his hand. In the same moment, Devlin came round the corner and fired twice. The first bullet ripped Cussane's left sleeve, the second caught him in the shoulder, spinning him round. He went through the kitchen door headfirst, kicked it closed behind him, turned and rammed home the bolt.

'You're hit!' Morag cried.

He shoved her ahead of him. 'Never mind that! Let's get out of here!' He pushed her up the stairs towards the bedroom. 'You take the bag,' he urged her, and ran across to the open door and peered out.

The van, with Fox and Devlin, was just round the corner. He put a finger to his lips, nodding to Morag, and went down the stone staircase quietly, the girl following. At the bottom, he led the way round to the back garden, ducked behind the wall and started along the track through the bracken that led to the head of Glendhu.

Devlin opened Fox's shirt and examined the wound just below the breast on the left. Fox's breathing was bad, his eyes full of pain. 'You were right,' he whispered. 'He's good.'

'Take it easy,' Devlin said. 'I've called in Trent and Brodie.'

He could already hear the Ford approaching. Fox said, 'Is he still in the house?'

'I doubt it.'

Fox sighed. 'We cocked it, Liam. There'll be hell to pay over this. We had him and he got away.'

'A bad habit he has,' Devlin said again, and the Ford entered the farmyard and skidded to a halt.

Cussane sat sideways in the passenger seat of the jeep, feet on the ground. He was stripped to the waist. There wasn't a great deal of blood, just the ugly puckered lips of the wound. He knew that was a bad sign, but there was no point in telling her that. She carefully poured sulphur powder on the wound from his small medical kit and affixed one of the field service dressing packs under his instructions.

'How do you feel?' she asked anxiously.

'Fine.' Which was a lie, for now that the initial shock was wearing off, he was in considerable pain. He found one of the morphine ampoules. They were of the kind used on the battlefield. He gave himself an injection and the pain started to ease quite quickly.

'Good,' he said. 'Now pass me a clean shirt. There should still be one left.'

She helped him on with it and then his jacket and raincoat. 'You'll be needing a doctor.'

'Oh, sure,' he said. 'Please help me. I've got a bullet in the shoulder. The first thing he'd reach for would be a telephone.'

'Then what do we do? They'll really start hunting you now. All the roads covered.'

'I know,' he said. 'Let's have a look at the map.' After a while, he said, 'The Solway Firth between us and England. Only one main route through to Carlisle via Dumfries and Annan. Not much road to plug.'

'So we're trapped?'

'Not necessarily. There's the railway. There might be some sort of chance there. Let's get moving and find out.'

Ferguson said, 'It's a mess. Couldn't be worse. How's Harry Fox?'

'He'll live, as they say. At least that's the local doctor's opinion. They've got him here in Dumfries at the general hospital.'

'I'll make arrangements to have him shipped down here to London as soon as possible. I want him to have the best. Where are you phoning from?'

'Police headquarters in Dumfries. Trent's here with me. They're turning out all the men they can. Road blocks and so on. The weather isn't helping. Still raining like hell.'

'What do you think, Liam?'

'I think he's gone.'

'You don't think they are going to net him up there?'

'Not a chance in the wide world.'

Ferguson sighed. 'Yes, frankly, that's how I feel. Stay for a while with Harry, just to make sure, then come back.'

'Now – this evening?'

'Get the night train to London. The Pope flies into Gatwick Airport at eight o'clock tomorrow morning. I want you with me.'

Cussane and Morag left the jeep in a small quarry in a wood above Dunhill and walked down towards the railway line. At that end of the small town, the streets were deserted in the heavy rain and they crossed the road, passed a ruined warehouse with boarded-up windows and squeezed through a gap in the fence above the railway line. A goods train stood in the siding. Cussane crouched down and watched as a driver in overalls walked along the track and pulled himself up into the engine.

'But we don't know where it's going,' Morag said.

Cussane smiled. 'It's pointing south, isn't it?' He grabbed her arm. 'Come on!'

They went down the bank through the gathering dusk, crossed the line as the train started to move. Cussane broke into a trot, reached up and pushed back a sliding door. He tossed in the bag, pulled himself up, turned and reached for the girl's hand. A moment later and she was with him. The wagon was almost filled with packing cases, some of them stencilled with the address of a factory in Penrith.

'Where's that?' Morag asked.

'South of Carlisle. Even if we don't go further than that, we're on our way.'

He sat down, feeling reasonably elated, and lit a cigarette. His left arm worked, but it felt as if it didn't belong to him. Still, the morphine had taken care of the pain. Morag snuggled beside him and he put an arm around her. A long time since he had felt protective towards anyone. To be even more blunt, a long time since he had cared.

She had closed her eyes and seemed to sleep. Thanks to the morphine, the pain had not returned and he could cope when it did. There were several ampoules in his kit. Certainly enough to keep him going. With the bullet in him and no proper medical attention, sepsis would only be a matter of time, but all he needed now was thirty-six hours. The Holy Father flew into Gatwick in the morning. And the day after that, Canterbury.

As the train started to coast along the track he leaned back, his good arm around the girl, and drifted into sleep.

14

Morag came awake with a start. The train seemed to be skidding to a halt. They were passing through some sort of siding and light from the occasional lamp drifted in through the slats, picking Cussane's face out of the darkness. He was asleep, the face wiped clean of any expression. When she gently touched his forehead it was damp with sweat. He groaned and turned on one side and his arm swung across his body. She saw that he was clutching the Stechkin.

She was cold. She turned up the collar of the reefer coat, put her hands in her pockets and watched him. She was a simple girl, uncomplicated in spite of the life she had known, but blessed with a quick mind and a fund of sound common sense.

She had never known anyone like Cussane. It was not just the gun in his hand, the quick, cold violence of the man. She had no fear of him. Whatever else he was, he was not cruel. Most important of all, he had helped her and that was something she was not used to. Even her grandfather had difficulty in protecting her from Murray's brutality. Cussane had saved her from that, and she was enough of a woman to realize he'd saved her from far worse. That she had helped him simply did not occur to her. For the first time in her life, she was filled with a sense of freedom.

The wagon jolted again, Cussane's eyes opened and he turned quickly, up on one knee, and checked his watch. 'One-thirty. I must have slept for a long time.'

'You did.'

He peered out through the slats and nodded. 'We must be moving into the sidings at Penrith. Where's my bag?'

She pushed it across. He rummaged inside, found the medical kit and gave himself another morphine injection. 'How is it?' she asked.

'Fine,' he said. 'No trouble. I'm just making sure.'

He was lying, for the pain, on waking, had been very real. He slid back the door and peered out and a sign for Penrith loomed out of the dark. 'I was right,' he said.

'Are we getting out here?'

'No guarantee this train goes any further and it's not much of a walk to the motorway.'

'Then what?'

'There'll be a service centre, a café, shops, parked cars, trucks. Who knows?' The pain had faded again now and he managed a smile. 'An infinite possibility to things. Now give me your hand, wait till we slow right down, and jump.'

It was a longer walk than Cussane had anticipated so that it was three o'clock when they turned into the carpark of the nearest service centre on the M6 and approached a café. A couple of cars moved in off the motorway and then a truck, a freightliner so massive that Cussane didn't see the police car until the last moment. He pulled Morag down behind a van and the police car stopped, the light on top of it lazily turning.

'What shall we do?' she whispered.

'Wait and see.'

The driver stayed behind the wheel, the other policeman got out and went in the café. They could see him clearly through the plate glass windows. There were perhaps twenty or thirty people in there, scattered amongst the tables. He took a good look round and came out again. He got back in the car and was speaking on the radio as it drove away.

'They were looking for us,' Morag said.

'What else?' He took the Tam O'Shanter off her head and stuffed it in a nearby waste bin. 'That's better. Too much like advertising.' He fumbled in his pocket and found a five pound note which he gave to her. 'They do take-outs in these places. Get some hot tea and sandwiches. I'll wait here. Safer that way.'

She went up the ramp and into the café. He saw her hesitate at the end of the counter, then pick up a tray. He noticed a bench against a low wall nearby, half-hidden by a large van. He sat down and lit a cigarette and waited, thinking about Morag Finlay.

Strange how right it seemed to think of her. It occurred to him wryly, with the usual priest's habit of self-doubt, that he should not be doing so. She was only a child. He had been celibate for more than twenty years, had never found it in the slightest degree difficult to manage without women. How absurd it would be, to fall in love at the end of the day with a little sixteen-year-old gypsy girl.

She came round the van with a plastic tray and put it on the bench.

‘Tea and ham sandwiches and what do you think of this? We’re in the paper. There was a stand by the door.’

He drank the scalding hot tea carefully from one of the plastic cups and unfolded the paper on his knee, reading it in the dim light falling across the carpark from the café. The newspaper was a local paper, printed in Carlisle the previous evening. They had Cussane on the front page, a separate picture of Morag beside him.

‘You look younger,’ he said.

‘That was a snap my mother took last year. Granda had it on the wall in his caravan. They must have taken it. He’d never have given it to them.’

‘If a local paper had this last night, I’d say we’ll be in every national newspaper’s first edition later on this morning,’ he said.

There was a heavy silence, he lit another cigarette and sat there smoking it, not saying anything.

‘You’re going to leave me, aren’t you?’ she asked.

He smiled gently. ‘My God, you’re about a thousand years old, aren’t you? Yes, I’m going to leave you. We don’t have any choice.’

‘You don’t have to explain.’

But he did. ‘Newspaper photos can be meaningless to most people. It’s the unusual that stands out, like you and me together. On your own, you’d stand a very good chance of going anywhere you want. You’ve got the money I gave you?’

‘Yes.’

‘Then go in the café. Sit in the warm and wait. The express buses stop in here. I should know. I came up on one the other day going the opposite way. You should get one to Birmingham and on to London from there with no trouble.’

‘And you?’

‘Never mind about me. If they do lay their hands on you, tell them I forced you to help me. Enough people will believe that to make it true.’ He picked up his bag and put a hand to her face. ‘You’re a special person. Don’t ever let anyone put you down again. Promise me?’

‘I will.’ She found herself choking, reached up to kiss his cheek, then turned and ran away.

She had learned, in a hard school, not to cry, but there was a hot prickly feeling at the back of her eyes as she went into the café. She brushed past a table. A hand caught her sleeve and she turned to look down at a couple of youths in motor cyclists’ black leathers, hard, vicious looking young men with cropped hair. The one who had her sleeve was blonde with a Nazi Iron Cross on his breast.

He said, 'What's your problem, darling? Nothing a ride on the back of my bike wouldn't fix.'

She pulled away, not even angry, went and got a cup of tea and sat at a table, hands wrapped around its healing warmth. He had come into her life, he had gone from it and nothing would ever be the same again. She started to cry, slow bitter tears, the first in years.

Cussane had two choices: to take his chance on thumbing a lift or to steal a car. The second gave him more freedom, more personal control, but it would only work if the vehicle wouldn't be missed for some time. There was a motel on the other side of the motorway. Anything parked there would belong to people staying overnight. Three to four hours at least before any of those would be missed, and by then he would be long gone.

He went up the steps to the flyover, thinking about Morag Finlay, wondering what would happen to her. But that wasn't his problem. What he had said to her made perfect sense. Together, they stuck out like a sore thumb. He paused on the bridge, lit another cigarette, trucks swishing past beneath him on the motorway. All perfectly sensible and logical, so why did he feel so rotten about it?

'Dear God, Harry,' he said softly, 'you're being corrupted by honesty and decency and innocence. It's not possible to soil that girl. She'll always remain untouched by the rottenness of life.'

And yet . . .

Someone moved up beside her and a soft voice said, 'You okay, kid? Anything I can do?'

He was West Indian, she knew that, with dark, curling hair, a little grey at the edges. He was perhaps forty-five and wore a heavy driving coat with fur collar, all much stained with grease, and carried a plastic sandwich box and a thermos flask. He smiled, the kind of smile that told her instantly that she was okay, and sat down.

'What's the problem?'

'Life,' she said.

'Heh, that's really profound for a chick as young as you.' But the smile was sympathetic. 'Can I do anything?'

'I'm waiting for the bus.'

'To where?'

'London.'

He shook his head. 'It's always London you kids make for when you run away from home.'

'My grandmother lives in London,' she said wearily. 'Wapping.'

He nodded and frowned as if considering the matter, then stood up. 'Okay, I'm your man.'

'What do you mean?'

'I drive a freightliner and London is my home base. The long way round, mind you, 'cause when I hit Manchester, I've got to take the Pennine motorway to Leeds to drop something off, but we should be in London by the early afternoon.'

'I don't know.' She hesitated.

'Bus won't be through here for another five hours, so what have you got to lose? If it helps, I've got three girls of my own, all older than you, and my name is Earl Jackson.'

'All right,' she said, making her decision, and went out at his side.

They walked down the ramp and started across the carpark. The freightliner also towed a huge trailer. 'Here we are,' he said. 'All the comforts of home.'

There was a footstep and as they turned, the blond biker from the café moved round from behind another truck. He came forward and stood there, hands on hips. 'Naughty girl,' he said. 'I told you you'd be better off on the back seat of my bike and what do I find? You're flying off into the night with Rastus here. Now that's definitely out of order.'

'Oh, dear,' Earl Jackson said. 'It talks and everything. Probably wets if you give it water.'

He leaned down to put his sandwich box and thermos on the ground and the other biker ducked from under the truck and booted him so that he staggered forward losing his balance. The blond one lifted a knee in his face. The one behind pulled Jackson to his feet, an arm round his throat and the other flexed his hands, tightening his gloves.

'Hold him, Sammy. He's my meat now.'

Sammy screamed as a fist swung into his kidneys. He jerked in agony, releasing his grip on Jackson and Cussane hit him again, sending him to his knees.

He slipped past Jackson to confront the other biker. 'You really should have stayed under your stone.'

The youth's hand came out of his pocket and, as Morag cried a warning, there was a click as a blade sprang into view, flashing in the pale light. Cussane dropped his bag, swayed to one side, grabbed for the wrist with both hands, twisted it round and up, locking the arm, and ran the blond headfirst into the side of the truck. The youth dropped to his knees, blood on his face, and Cussane pulled him up and reached for the other, who was now standing. He pulled them close.

'I could put you on sticks for a year, but perhaps you'd just rather go?'

They backed off in horror, turned and stumbled away. Cussane was aware of the pain then, so bad that it made him feel sick. He turned, clutching at the canvas side of the trailer, and Morag ran forward and put an arm around him.

'Harry, are you all right?'

'Sure, don't worry.'

Earl Jackson said, 'You saved my hide, man. I owe you.' He turned to Morag. 'I don't think I got the whole story.'

'We were together, then we got separated.' She glanced at Cussane. 'Now we're together again.'

Jackson said, 'Is his destination London, too?'

She nodded. 'Does the offer still hold good?'

He smiled. 'Why not. Climb up in the cab. You'll find a sliding panel behind the passenger seat. An improvement of mine. There's a bunk in there, blankets and so on. It means I can sleep in the carpark and save on hotel bills.'

Morag climbed up. As Cussane made to follow her, Jackson caught his sleeve. 'Look, I don't know what gives here, but she's a nice kid.'

'You don't need to worry,' Cussane told him. 'I think so too.' And he climbed up into the cab.

It was just after 8 a.m. on a fine, bright morning when the Alitalia jet which had brought Pope John Paul from Rome landed at Gatwick Airport. The Pontiff came down the ladder, waving to the enthusiastic crowd. His first act was to kneel and kiss English soil.

Devlin and Ferguson stood on the balcony looking down. The Brigadier said, 'It's at moments like this that I'd welcome my pension.'

'Face facts,' Devlin said. 'If a really determined assassin, the kind who doesn't mind committing suicide, sets his sights on getting the Pope or the Queen of England or whoever, the odds are heavily in his favour.'

Below, the Pope was welcomed by Cardinal Basil Hume and the

Duke of Norfolk on behalf of the Queen. The Cardinal made a speech of welcome and the Pope replied. Then they moved to the waiting cars.

Devlin said, 'What happens now?'

'Mass at Westminster Cathedral. After lunch, a visit to Her Majesty at Buckingham Palace. Then St George's Cathedral at Southwark to anoint the sick. It's going to be all go, I can see that.' Ferguson was unhappy and it showed. 'Dammit, Liam, where is he? Where is that sod, Cussane?'

'Around,' Devlin said. 'Closer than we think, probably. The only certainty is that he'll surface within the next twenty-four hours.'

'And then we get him,' Ferguson said as they walked away.

'If you say so,' was Liam Devlin's only comment.

The yard of the warehouse in Hunslet, Leeds, quite close to the motorway, was packed with trucks. Cussane had the sliding panel open and Jackson said, 'Keep out of sight, man. Passengers are strictly *verboten*. I could lose my licence.'

He got out of the truck to see to the disengagement of the trailer, then went into the freight office to get a signature for it.

The clerk looked up from his desk. 'Hello, Earl, good run?'

'Not bad.'

'I hear they've been having fun over there on the M6. One of the lads rang in from outside Manchester. Had a breakdown. Said they'd had a lot of police activity.'

'I didn't notice anything,' Jackson said. 'What was it about?'

'Looking for some guy that's mixed up with the IRA. Has a girl with him.'

Jackson managed to stay calm and signed the sheets. 'Anything else?'

'No, that's fine, Earl. See you next trip.'

Jackson moved outside. He hesitated beside the truck, then followed his original intention and went out of the yard across the road to the transport café. He gave the girl behind the counter his thermos to fill, ordered some bacon sandwiches and bought a newspaper which he read slowly on the way back to the truck.

He climbed up behind the wheel and passed the thermos and sandwiches through. 'Breakfast and something to read while you eat.'

The photos were those which had appeared in the Carlisle paper and the story was roughly the same. The details on the girl were sparse. It simply said she was in his company.

As they entered the slip road leading up to the motorway, Cussane said, 'Well?'

Jackson concentrated on the road. 'This is heavy stuff, man. Okay, I owe you, but not that much. If you're picked up . . .'

'It would look bad for you.'

'I can't afford that,' Jackson told him. 'I've got form. Been inside twice. Cars were my game till I got smart. I don't want trouble and I definitely don't want to see the inside of Pentonville again.'

'Then the simplest thing to do is keep driving,' Cussane told him. 'Once in London, we drop off and you go on about your business. No one will ever know.'

It was the only solution and Jackson knew it. 'Okay,' he sighed. 'I guess that's it.'

'I'm sorry, Mr Jackson,' Morag told him.

He smiled at her in the mirror. 'Never mind, kid. I should have known better. Now keep inside and close that panel,' and he turned the freightliner on to the motorway.

Devlin was on the phone to the hospital in Dumfries when Ferguson came in from the study.

As the Irishman put down the receiver, the Brigadier said, 'I could do with some good news. Just had advance notice that 2 Para under the command of Colonel H. Jones attacked some place called Goose Green in the Falklands. Turned out to be about three times the Argentinian troops there as anticipated.'

'What happened?'

'Oh, they won the day, but Jones died, I'm afraid.'

'The news on Harry Fox is comforting,' Devlin said. 'They are flying him down from Glasgow this evening. But he's in fair shape.'

'Thank God for that,' Ferguson said.

'I spoke to Trent. They can't get a word out of those tinkers. Nothing helpful anyway. According to the old grandfather, he's no idea where the girl might go. Her mother's in Australia.'

'They're worse than gypsies, tinkers,' Ferguson said. 'I know. I come from Angus, remember. Funny people. Even when they hate each other, they hate the police more. Wouldn't even tell you the way to the public toilet.'

'So what do we do now?'

'We'll go along to St George's to see what His Holiness is up to, then

I think you can take a run down to Canterbury. I'm laying on a police car and driver for you, by the way. I think it will help for you to look as official as possible from now on.'

Morag sat in the corner of the bunk, her back against the wall. 'Why did you come back at Penrith? You haven't told me.'

Cussane shrugged. 'I suppose I decided you weren't fit to be out on your own or something like that.'

She shook her head. 'Why are you so afraid to admit to kindness?'

'Am I?' He lit a cigarette and watched her as she took an old pack of cards from her pocket and shuffled them. They were Tarot. 'Can you use those things?'

'My grandma showed me how years ago when I was quite young. I'm not sure if I have the gift. It's hard to tell.'

She shuffled the cards again. He said, 'The police might be waiting at her place.'

She paused, surprise on her face. 'Why should they? They don't know she exists.'

'They must have asked questions at the camp and someone must have told them something. If not your grandad, there's always Murray.'

'Never,' she said. 'Even Murray wouldn't do a thing like that. You were different – an outsider – but me, that's not the same at all.'

She turned the first card. It was the Tower, the building struck by lightning, two bodies falling. 'The individual suffers through the forces of destiny being worked out in the world,' Morag commented.

'That's me. Oh, that's very definitely me,' Harry Cussane told her and he started to laugh helplessly.

Susan Calder was twenty-three, a small girl, undeniably attractive in the neat navy-blue police uniform with the hat with the black and white checks round the brim. She had trained as a schoolteacher, but three terms of that had very definitely been enough. She had volunteered for the Metropolitan Police and had been accepted. She had served for just over one year. Waiting beside the police car outside the Cavendish Square flat, she presented a pleasing picture, and Devlin's heart lifted. She was polishing the windscreen as he came down the steps.

'Good day to you, *a colleen*, God save the good work.'

She took in the black Burberry, the felt hat slanted across the ears, was about to give him a dusty answer, then paused. 'You wouldn't be Professor Devlin, would you?'

'As ever was. And you?'

'WPC Susan Calder, sir.'

'Have they told you you're mine until tomorrow?'

'Yes, sir. Hotel booked in Canterbury.'

'There *will* be talk back at the station. Let's get moving then,' and he opened the rear door and got in. She slipped behind the wheel and drove away and Devlin leaned back, watching her. 'Have they told you what this is about?'

'You're with Group Four, sir, that's all I know.'

'And that is?'

'Anti-terrorism; intelligence side of things as distinct from the Yard's anti-terrorist squad.'

'Yes, Group Four can employ people like me and get away with it.' He frowned. 'The next sixteen hours will see the making or breaking of this affair and you'll be with me every step of the way.'

'If you say so, sir.'

'So I think you deserve to know what it's about.'

'Should you be telling me, sir?' she asked calmly.

It was one way of getting it all straight in his head.

'No, but I'm going to,' he said and started to talk, telling her everything there was to know about the whole affair from the beginning and especially about Harry Cussane.

When he was finished, she said, 'It's quite a story.'

'And that's an understatement.'

'There is just one thing, sir.'

'And what would that be?'

'My elder brother was killed in Belfast three years ago while serving there as a lieutenant in the Marines. A sniper hit him from a place called the Divis flats.'

'Does that mean I pose a problem for you?' Devlin asked her.

'Not at all, sir. I just wanted you to know,' she said crisply and turned into the main road and drove down towards the river.

Cussane and Morag stood in the quiet street on the edge of Wapping and watched the freightliner turn the corner and disappear.

'Poor Earl Jackson,' Cussane said. 'I bet he can't get away fast enough. What's your grandma's address?'

'Cork Street Wharf. It's five or six years since I was there. I'm afraid I can't remember the way.'

'We'll find it.'

They walked down towards the river which seemed the obvious thing to do. His arm was hurting again and he had a headache, but he made no sign of any of this to the girl. When they came to a grocery shop on a corner, she went in to make enquiries.

She came out quickly. 'It's not far. It's only a couple of streets away.'

They walked to the corner and there was the river and a hundred yards further on, a sign on the wall saying *Cork Street Wharf*.

Cussane said, 'All right, off you go. I'll stay back out of the way, just in case she has visitors.'

'I shan't be long.'

She hurried off down the street and Cussane stepped back through a broken door into a hard half-filled with rubble and waited. He could smell the river. Not many boats now though. This had once been the greatest port in the world, now it was a graveyard of rusting cranes pointing into the sky like primeval monsters. He felt lousy and when he lit a cigarette, his hand shook. There was the sound of running steps and Morag appeared. 'She isn't there. I spoke to the next door neighbour.'

'Where is she?'

'With a touring show. A fairground show. She's in Maidstone this week.'

And Maidstone was only thirty miles from Canterbury. There was an inevitability to things and Cussane said, 'We'd better get going then.'

'You'll take me?'

'Why not?' and he turned and led the way along the street.

He found what he was looking for within twenty minutes, a pay and display parking lot.

'Why is this so important?' she demanded.

'Because people pay in advance for however many hours of parking they want and stick the ticket on the windscreen. A wonderful aid to car thieves. You can tell just how long you've got before the car is missed.'

She scouted around. 'There's one here says six hours.'

'And what time was it booked in?' He checked and took out his pocket knife. 'That'll do. Four hours to go. Dark then anyway.'

He worked on the quarter-light with the knife, forced it and unlocked the door, then he reached under the dashboard and pulled the wires down.

'You've done this before,' she said.

'That's true.' The engine roared into life. 'Okay,' he said, 'Let's get out of here,' and as she scrambled into the passenger seat, he drove away.

15

'Of course, it's hardly surprising the Pope wants to come here, sir,' Susan Calder said to Devlin. 'This is the birthplace of English Christianity. It was St Augustine who founded the cathedral here in Saxon times.'

'Is it now?' They were standing in the magnificent Perpendicular nave of the cathedral, the pillars soaring to the vaulted ceiling high above them. The place was a hive of activity, workmen everywhere.

'It's certainly spectacular,' Devlin said.

'It was even bombed in nineteen-forty-two during the Canterbury blitz. The library was destroyed, but it's been rebuilt. Up here in the north-west transept is where Saint Thomas Beckett was murdered by the three knights eight hundred years ago.'

'I believe the Pope has a particular affinity for him,' Devlin said. 'Let's have a look.'

They moved up the nave to the place of Beckett's martyrdom all those years ago. The precise spot where he was traditionally believed to have fallen was marked by a small square stone. There was a strange atmosphere. Devlin shivered, suddenly cold.

'The Sword's Point,' the girl said simply. 'That's what they call it.'

'Yes, well they would, wouldn't they? Come on, let's get out of here. I could do with a smoke and I've seen enough.'

They went out through the south porch past the police guard. There was plenty of activity outside also, workmen working on stands and a considerable police presence. Devlin lit a cigarette and he and Susan Calder moved out on to the pavement.

'What do you think?' she said. 'I mean, not even Cussane could expect to get in there tomorrow. You've seen the security.'

Devlin took out his wallet and produced the security card Ferguson had given him. 'Have you seen one of these before?'

'I don't think so.'

'Very special. Guaranteed to unlock all doors.'

'So?'

'Nobody has asked to see it. We were totally accepted when we walked in. Why? Because you are wearing police uniform. And don't tell me that's what you are. It isn't the point.'

'I see what you mean.' She was troubled and it showed.

'The best place to hide a tree is in a forest,' he said. 'Tomorrow, there'll be policemen all over the place and church dignitaries so what's another policeman or priest.'

At that moment someone called his name, and they turned to see Ferguson walking towards them with a man in a dark overcoat. Ferguson wore a greatcoat of the kind favoured by Guards officers, and carried a smartly rolled umbrella.

'Brigadier Ferguson,' Devlin told the girl hastily.

'There you are,' the Brigadier said. 'This your driver?'

'WPC Calder, sir,' she saluted smartly.

'This is Superintendent Foster, attached to Scotland Yard's anti-terrorist squad,' Ferguson said. 'I've been going over things with him. Seems pretty watertight to me.'

'Even if your man gets as far as Canterbury, there's no way he'll get in the cathedral tomorrow,' Foster said simply. 'I'd stake my reputation on it.'

'Let's hope you don't have to,' Devlin told him.

Ferguson tugged at Foster's sleeve impatiently. 'Right, let's get inside before the light fails. I'm staying here tonight myself, Devlin. I'll phone you at your hotel later.'

The two men walked up to the great door, a policeman opened it for them and they went inside. 'Do you think he knows them?' Devlin asked her gently.

'God, I don't know. You've got *me* wondering now, sir.' She opened the door of the car for him. He got in and she slid behind the wheel and started the engine. 'One thing.'

'What's that?'

'Even if he did get in and did something, he'd never get out again.'

'But that's the whole point,' Devlin said. 'He doesn't care what happens to him afterwards.'

'God help us then.'

'I wouldn't bank on it. Nothing we can do now, girl dear. We don't control the game any more, it controls us, so get us to that hotel in your own good time and I'll buy you the best dinner the place can offer. Did I tell you, by the way, that I have this terrible thing for women in uniform?'

As she turned out into the traffic she started to laugh.

The caravan was large and roomy and extremely well-furnished. The bedroom section was separate in its own small compartment, twin bunks. When Cussane opened the door and peered in, Morag appeared to be sleeping.

He started to close the door and she called, 'Harry?'

'Yes?' He moved back in. 'What is it?'

'Is Grandma still working?'

'Yes.'

He sat on the edge of the bunk. He was in considerable pain now. It even hurt to breathe. Something was badly wrong, he knew that. She reached up to touch his face and he drew back a little.

She said, 'Remember in Granda's caravan that first day? I asked if you were frightened I might corrupt you.'

'To be precise,' he told her, 'your actual words were: "Are you frightened I might corrupt you, *Father*?" '

She went very still. 'You are a priest then? A real priest? I think I always knew it.'

'Go to sleep,' he said.

She reached for his hand. 'You wouldn't leave without telling me?'

There was genuine fear in her voice. He said gently, 'Now would I do a thing like that to you?' He got up and opened the door. 'Like I said, get some sleep. I'll see you in the morning.'

He lit a cigarette, opened the door and went out. The Maidstone fairground was a comparatively small affair, a number of sideshows, various stalls, bingo stands, several carousels. There were still a number of people around, noisy and good-humoured in spite of the late hour, music loud on the night air. At one end of the caravan was the Land Rover which towed it, at the other the red tent with the illuminated sign that said *Gypsy Rose*. As he watched, a young couple emerged, laughing. Cussane hesitated, then went in.

Brana Smith was at least seventy, a highly-coloured scarf drawing back the hair from the brown parchment face. She wore a shawl over her shoulders, a necklace of gold coins around her neck. The table she was seated at had a crystal ball on it.

'You certainly look the part,' he said.

'That's the general idea. The public like a gypsy to look like a gypsy. Put up the closed sign and give me a cigarette.' He did as he was told, came back and sat opposite her like a client, the crystal between them. 'Is Morag asleep?'

'Yes.' He took a deep breath to control his pain. 'You must never let her go back to that camp, you understand me?'

'Don't worry.' Her voice was dry and very calm. 'We gypsies stick together and we pay our debts. I'll put the word out and one day soon Murray pays for what he's done, believe me.'

He nodded. 'When you saw her picture in the paper today and read the circumstances, you must have been worried. Why didn't you get in touch with the police?'

'The police? You must be joking.' She shrugged. 'In any case, I knew she was coming and I knew she would be all right.'

'Knew?' Cussane said.

She rested a hand lightly on the crystal. 'These are only the trappings, my friend. I have the gift as my mother did before me and hers before her.'

He nodded. 'Morag told me. She read the Tarot cards for me, but she isn't certain of her powers.'

'Oh, she has the gift.' The old woman nodded. 'As yet unformed.' She pushed a pack of cards to him. 'Cut them, then hand them back to me with your left hand.'

He did as he was told and she cut them in turn. 'The cards mean nothing without the gift. You understand this?'

He felt strangely light-headed. 'Yes.'

'Three cards, that will tell all.' She turned the first. It was the Tower. 'He has suffered through the forces of destiny,' she said. 'Others have controlled his life.'

'Morag drew that card,' he said. 'She told me something like that.'

She turned the second card. It showed a young man suspended upside down from a wooden gibbet by his right ankle.

'The Hanged Man. When he strives hardest, it is with his own shadow. He is two people. Himself and yet not himself. Impossible now to go back to the wholeness of youth.'

'Too late,' he said. 'Far too late.'

The third card showed Death in traditional form, his scythe mowing a crop of human bodies.

'But whose?' Cussane laughed a little too loud. 'Death, I mean? Mine or perhaps somebody else's?'

'The card means far more than its superficial image implies. He comes as a redeemer. In this man's death lies the opportunity for rebirth.'

'Yes, but for whom?' Cussane demanded, leaning forward. The light reflected from the crystal seemed very bright.

She touched his forehead, damp with sweat. 'You are ill.'

'I'll be all right. I need to lie down, that's all.' He got to his feet. 'I'll sleep for a while, if that's all right with you, then I'll leave before Morag wakes. That's important. Do you understand me?'

'Oh, yes,' she nodded. 'I understand you very well.'

He went out into the cool night. Most people had gone home now, the stalls, the carousels were closing down. His forehead was burning. He went up the steps into the caravan and lay on the bench seat, looking up at the ceiling. Better to take the morphine now than in the morning. He got up, rummaged in the bag and found an ampoule. The injection worked quite quickly and, after a while, he slept.

He came awake with a start, his head clear. It was morning, light coming in through the windows and the old woman was seated at the table smoking a cigarette and watching him. When he sat up, the pain was like a living thing. For a moment, he thought he was going to stop breathing.

She pushed a cup across to him. 'Hot tea. Drink some.'

It tasted good, better than anything he had ever known, and he smiled and helped himself to a cigarette from her packet, hand shaking. 'What time is it?'

'Seven o'clock.'

'And Morag's still asleep?'

'Yes.'

'Good. I'll get going.'

She said gravely, 'You're ill, Father Harry Cussane. Very ill.'

He smiled gently. 'You have the gift, so you would know.' He took a deep breath. 'Things to get straight before I go. Morag's position in all this. Have you got a pencil?'

'Yes.'

'Good. Take down this number.' She did as she was told. 'The man on the other end is called Ferguson – Brigadier Ferguson.'

'Is he police?'

'In a way. He'd dearly love to get his hands on me. If he isn't there, they'll know how to contact him wherever he is, which is probably Canterbury.'

'Why there?'

'Because I'm going to Canterbury to kill the Pope.' He produced the Stechkin from his pocket. 'With this.'

She seemed to grow small, to withdraw into herself. She believed him, of course, he could see that. 'But why?' she whispered. 'He's a good man.'

'Aren't we all?' he said, 'or at least were, at some time or other in our lives. The important thing is this. When I've gone, you phone Ferguson. Tell him I'm going to Canterbury Cathedral. You'll also tell him I forced Morag to help me. Say she was frightened for her life. Anything.' He laughed. 'Taking it all in all, that should cover it.'

He picked up his bag and walked to the door. She said, 'You're dying, don't you know that?'

'Of course I do.' He managed a smile. 'You said that Death on the Tarot cards means redemption. In my death lies the opportunity for rebirth. That child's in there. That's all that's important.' He opened the bag, took out the bundle of fifty pound notes and tossed them on the table. 'That's for her. I won't be needing it now.'

He went out. The door banged. She sat there listening, aware of the sound of the car starting up and moving away. She stayed like that for a long time, thinking about Harry Cussane himself. She had liked him more than most men she had known, but there was Death in his eyes, she had seen that at the first meeting. And there was Morag to consider.

There was a sound of movement next door where the girl slept – a faint stirring. Old Brana checked her watch. It was eight-thirty. Making her decision, she got up, let herself out of the caravan quietly. Hurried across the fairground to the public phone box and dialled Ferguson's number.

Devlin was having breakfast at the hotel in Canterbury with Susan Calder when he was called to the phone. He was back quite quickly.

'That was Ferguson. Cussane's turned up. Or at least his girl-friend has. Do you know Maidstone?'

'Yes, sir. It can't be more than thirty miles from here. Thirty-five at the most.'

'Then let's get moving,' he said. 'There really isn't much time for any of us now.'

In London, the Pope had left the Pro-Nunciature very early to visit more than 4000 religious: nuns, monks, and priests, Catholic and Anglican, at Digby Stuart Training College in London. Many of them were from enclosed orders. This was the first time they had gone into the outside world in many years. It was a highly emotional moment for all when they renewed their vows in the Holy Father's presence. It was after that that he left for Canterbury in the helicopter provided by British Caledonian Airways.

Stokely Hall was bounded by a high wall of red brick, a Victorian addition to the estate when the family still had money. The lodge beside the great iron gates was Victorian also, though the architect had done his best to make it resemble the early Tudor features of the main house. When Cussane drove by on the main road, there were two police cars at the gates and a police motor-cyclist who had been trailing behind him for the past mile, turned in.

Cussane carried on down the road, the wall on his left, fringed by trees. When the gate was out of sight, he scanned the opposite side of the road and finally noticed a five-barred gate and a track leading into a wood. He drove across quickly, got out, opened the gate, then drove some little way into the trees. He went back to the gate, closed it and returned to the car.

He took off his raincoat, jacket and shirt, awkwardly because of his bad arm. The smell was immediately apparent, the sickly odour of decay. He laughed foolishly and said softly, 'Jesus, Harry, you're falling apart.'

He got his black vest from the bag, his clerical collar and put them on. Finally, the cassock. It seemed a thousand years since he had rolled it up and put it in the bottom of the bag at Kilrea. He reloaded the Stechkin with a fresh clip, put it in one pocket, a spare clip in the other and got in the car as it started to drizzle. No more morphine. The pain would keep him sharp. He closed his eyes and vowed to stay in control.

Brana Smith sat at the table in the caravan, an arm around Morag, who was crying steadily.

'Just tell me exactly what he said,' Liam Devlin told her.

'Grandma . . .' the girl started.

The old woman shook her head. 'Hush, child.' She turned to Devlin. 'He told me he intended to shoot the Pope. Showed me the gun. Then he gave me the telephone number to ring in London. The man Ferguson.'

'And what did he tell you to say?'

'That he would be at Canterbury Cathedral.'

'And that's all?'

'Isn't it enough?'

Devlin turned to Susan Calder standing at the door. 'Right, we'd better get back.'

She opened the door. Brana Smith said, 'What about Morag?'

'That's up to Ferguson.' Devlin shrugged. 'I'll see what I can do.'

He started to go out and she said, 'Mr Devlin?' He turned. 'He's dying.'

'Dying?' Devlin said.

'Yes, from a gunshot wound.'

He went out, ignoring the curious crowd of fairground workers, and got in the front passenger seat beside Susan. As she drove away, he called up Canterbury Police Headquarters on the car radio and asked to be patched through to Ferguson.

'Nothing fresh here,' he told the Brigadier. 'The message was for you and quite plain. He intends to be at Canterbury Cathedral.'

'Cheeky bastard!' Ferguson said.

'Another thing. He's dying. It would seem sepsis must be setting in from the bullet he took at the Mungos' farm.'

'Your bullet?'

'That's right.'

Ferguson took a deep breath. 'All right, get back here fast. The Pope should be here soon.'

Stokely Hall was one of the finest Tudor mansions in England and the Stokelys had been one of the handful of English aristocratic families to maintain its Catholicism after Henry VIII and the Reformation. The thing which distinguished Stokely was the family chapel, the chapel in the wood, reached by tunnel from the main house. It was regarded by most experts as being, in effect, the oldest Catholic church in England. The Pope had expressed a desire to pray there.

Cussane lay back in the passenger seat thinking it over. The pain was a living thing now, his face ice-cold and yet dripping sweat. He managed to find a cigarette and started to light it and then, in the distance, heard the sound of engines up above. He got out of the car and stood listening. A moment later, the blue and white painted helicopter passed overhead.

Susan Calder said, 'You don't look happy, sir.'

'It was Liam last night. And I'm not happy. Cussane's behaviour doesn't make sense.'

'That was then, this is now. What's worrying you?'

'Harry Cussane, my good friend of more than twenty years. The best chess player I ever knew.'

'And what was the most significant thing about him?'

'That he was always three moves ahead. That he had the ability to make you concentrate on his right hand when what was really important was what he was doing with his left. In the present circumstances, what does that suggest to you?'

'That he hasn't any intention of going to Canterbury Cathedral. That's where the action is. That's where everyone is waiting for him.'

'So he strikes somewhere else. But how? Where's the schedule?'

'Back seat, sir.'

He found it and read it aloud. 'Starts off at Digby Stuart College in London, then by helicopter to Canterbury.' He frowned. 'Wait a minute. He's dropping in at some place called Stokely Hall to visit a Catholic chapel.'

'We passed it on the way to Maidstone,' she said. 'About three miles from here. But that's an unscheduled visit. It's not been mentioned in any of the newspapers that I've seen and everything else has. How would Cussane know?'

'He used to run the press office at the Catholic Secretariat in Dublin.' Devlin slammed a fist into his thigh. 'That's it. Has to be. Get your foot down hard and don't stop for anything.'

'What about Ferguson?'

He reached for the mike. 'I'll try and contact him, but it's too late for him to do anything. We'll be there in a matter of minutes. It's up to us now.'

He took the Walther from his pocket, cocked it, then put the safety catch on as the car shot forward.

The road was clear when Cussane crossed it. He moved into the shelter of the trees and walked along the base of the wall. He came to an old iron gate, narrow and rusting, fixed firm in the wall and as he tested it, heard voices on the other side. He moved behind a tree and waited. Through the bars he could see a path and rhododendron bushes. A moment later, two nuns walked by.

He gave them time to pass, then went back to where the ground under the trees rose several feet bringing him almost level with the wall. He reached for a branch that stretched across. It would have been ridiculously easy if it had not been for his shoulder and arm. The pain was appalling, but he hoisted the skirts of his cassock to give him freedom of movement and swung across, pausing on top of the wall for only a moment before dropping to the ground.

He stayed on one knee, fighting for breath, then stood up and ran a hand over his hair. Then he hurried along the path, aware of the nuns' voices up ahead, turned a corner by an old stone fountain and caught up with them. They turned in surprise. One of them was very old, the other younger.

'Good morning, Sisters,' he said briskly. 'Isn't it beautiful here? I couldn't resist taking a little walk.'

'Neither could we, Father,' the older one said.

They walked on side-by-side and emerged from the shrubbery on to an expansive lawn. The helicopter was parked a hundred yards to the right, the crew lounging beside it. There were several limousines in front of the house and two police cars. A couple of policemen crossed the lawn with an Alsatian guard dog on a lead. They passed Cussane and the two nuns without a word and continued down towards the shrubbery.

'Are you from Canterbury, Father?' the old nun enquired.

'No, Sister . . . ?' he paused.

'Agatha – and this is Sister Anne.'

'I'm with the Secretariat in Dublin. A wonderful thing to be invited over here to see His Holiness. I missed him during his Irish trip.'

Susan Calder turned in from the road at the front gate and Devlin showed his security pass as two policemen moved forward. 'Has anyone passed through here in the last few minutes?'

'No, sir,' one officer said. 'A hell of a lot of guests came before the helicopter arrived though.'

'Move!' Devlin said.

Susan went up the drive at some speed. 'What do you think?'

'He's here!' Devlin said. 'I'd stake my life on it.'

'Have you met His Holiness yet, Father?' Sister Anne enquired.

'No, I've only just arrived from Canterbury with a message for him.'

They were crossing the gravel drive now, past the policemen standing beside the cars, up the steps and past the two uniformed security guards and in through the great oak door. The hall was spacious, a central staircase lifting to a landing. Double doors stood open to the right, disclosing a large reception room filled with visitors, many of them church dignitaries.

Cussane and the two nuns walked towards it. 'And where is this famous Stokely chapel?' he asked. 'I've never seen it.'

'Oh, it's so beautiful,' Sister Agatha said. 'So many years of prayer. The entrance is just down the hall, see where the Monsignor is standing?'

They paused at the door of the reception and Cussane said, 'If you'll excuse me for a moment. I may be able to give my message to His Holiness before he joins the reception.'

'We'll wait for you, Father,' Sister Agatha said. 'I think we'd rather go in with you.'

'Of course. I shan't be long.'

Cussane went past the bottom of the stairs and moved into the corner of the hall where the Monsignor was standing, resplendent in scarlet and black. He was an old man with silver hair and spoke with an Italian accent.

'What do you seek, Father?'

'His Holiness.'

'Impossible. He is at prayer.'

Cussane put a hand to the old man's face, turned the handle of the door and forced him through. He closed the door behind him with a foot.

'I'm truly sorry, Father.' He chopped the old priest on the side of the neck and gently lowered him to the floor.

A long narrow tunnel stretched ahead of him, dimly lit, steps leading up to an oaken door at the end. The pain was terrible now, all consuming. But that no longer mattered. He fought for breath momentarily, then took the Stechkin from his pocket and went forward.

Susan Calder swung the car in at the bottom of the steps and as Devlin jumped out, she followed him. His security pass was already in his hand as a police sergeant moved forward.

'Anything out of the way happened? Anyone unusual gone in?'

'No, sir. Lots of visitors before the Pope arrived. Couple of nuns and a priest just went in.'

Devlin went up the steps on the run past the security guards, Susan Calder at his heels. He paused, taking in the scene, the reception on the right, the two nuns waiting by the door. *A priest, the sergeant had said.*

He approached Sisters Agatha and Anne. 'You've just arrived, Sisters?'

Beyond them, the guests talked animatedly, waiters moving amongst them.

'That's right,' Sister Agatha said.

'Wasn't there a priest with you?'

'Oh, yes, the good father from Dublin.'

Devlin's stomach went hollow. 'Where is he?'

'He had a message for His Holiness, a message from Canterbury, but I told him the Holy Father was in the chapel so he went to speak to the Monsignor on the door.' Sister Agatha led the way across the hall and paused. 'Oh, the Monsignor doesn't seem to be there.'

Devlin was running and the Walther was in his hand as he flung open the door and tumbled over the Monsignor on the floor. He was aware of Susan Calder behind him, was even more aware of the priest in the black cassock mounting the steps at the end of the tunnel and reaching for the handle of the oak door.

'Harry!' Devlin called.

Cussane turned and fired without the slightest hesitation, the bullet slamming into Devlin's right forearm, punching him back against the wall. Devlin dropped the Walther as he fell and Susan cried out and flattened herself against the wall.

Cussane stood there, the Stechkin extended in his right hand, but he did not fire. Instead, he smiled a ghastly smile.

'Stay out of it, Liam,' he called. 'Last act!' and he turned and opened the chapel door.

Devlin was sick, dizzy from shock. He reached for the Walther with his left hand, fumbled and dropped it as he tried to stand. He glared up at the girl.

'Take it! Stop him! It's up to you now!'

Susan Calder knew nothing of guns beyond a couple of hours of basic handling experience on her training course. She had fired a few rounds from a revolver on the range, that was all. Now, she picked up the

Walther without hesitation and ran along the tunnel. Devlin got to his feet and went after her.

The chapel was a place of shadows hallowed by the centuries, the sanctuary lamp the only light. His Holiness Pope John Paul II knelt in his white robes before the simple altar. The sound of the silenced Stechkin, muffled by the door, had not alerted him, but the raised voices had. He was on his feet and turning as the door crashed open and Cussane entered.

He stood there, face damp with sweat, strangely medieval in the black cassock, the Stechkin against his thigh.

John Paul said calmly, 'You are Father Harry Cussane.'

'You are mistaken. I am Mikhail Kelly.' Cussane laughed wildly. 'Strolling player of sorts.'

'You are Father Harry Cussane,' John Paul said relentlessly. 'Priest then, priest now, priest eternally. God will not let go.'

'No!' Cussane cried in a kind of agony. 'I refuse it!'

The Stechkin swung up and Susan Calder stumbled in through the door, falling to her knees, skirt riding up, the Walther levelled in both hands. She shot him twice in the back, shattering his spine and Cussane cried out in agony and fell on his knees in front of the Pope. He stayed there for a moment then rolled on his back, still clutching the Stechkin.

Susan stayed on her knees, lowering the Walther to the floor, watching as the Pontiff gently took the Stechkin from Cussane's hand.

She heard the Pope say in English, 'I want you to make an act of contrition. Say after me: O my God who art infinitely good in thyself . . .'

'Oh my God,' Harry Cussane said and died.

The Pope, on his knees, started to pray, hands clasped.

Behind Susan, Devlin crawled in and sat with his back against the wall, holding his wound, blood on his fingers. She dropped the gun and eased against him as if for warmth.

'Does it always feel like this?' she asked him harshly. 'Dirty and ashamed?'

'Join the club, girl dear,' Liam Devlin said, and he put his good arm around her.

EPILOGUE

It was six o'clock on a grey morning, the sky swollen with rain, when Susan Calder turned her mini car in through the gate of St Joseph's Catholic Cemetery, Highgate. It was a poor sort of place with lots of Gothic monuments from an obviously more prosperous past, but now, everything overgrown, nothing but decay.

She was not in uniform and wore a dark headscarf, blue-belted coat and leather boots. She pulled in at the superintendent's lodge and found Devlin standing beside a taxi. He was wearing his usual dark Burberry and black felt hat and his right arm was in a black sling. She got out of the car and he came to meet her.

'Sorry I'm late. The traffic,' she said. 'Have they started?'

'Yes.' He smiled ironically. 'I think Harry would have appreciated this. Like a bad set for a second rate movie. Even the rain makes it another cliché,' he said, as it started to fall in heavy drops.

He told the taxi driver to wait and he and the girl went along the path between gravestones. 'Not much of a place,' she said.

'They had to tuck him away somewhere.' He took out a cigarette with his good hand and lit it. 'Ferguson and the Home Office people felt you should have had some sort of gallantry award.'

'A medal?' There was genuine distaste on her face. 'They can keep it. He had to be stopped, but that doesn't mean I liked doing it.'

'They've decided against it anyway. It would be too public; require an explanation and they can't have that. So much for Harry wanting to leave the KGB with the blame.'

They came to the grave and paused some distance away under a tree. There were two gravediggers, a priest, a woman in black coat and a girl.

'Tanya Voroninova?' Susan asked.

'Yes, and the girl is Morag Finlay,' Devlin said. 'The three women in Harry Cussane's life, together now to see him planted. First, the one he so greatly wronged as a child, then the child he saved at great inconvenience to himself. I find that ironic. Harry the redemptionist.'

'And then there's me,' she said. 'His executioner and I never even met him.'

'Only the once,' Devlin said. 'And that was enough. Strange – the most important people in his life were women and in the end they were the death of him.'

The priest sprinkled the grave and the coffin with Holy Water and incensed them. Morag started to cry and Tanya Voroninova put an arm around her as the priest's voice rose in prayer.

Lord Jesus Christ, Saviour of the world, we commend your servant to you and pray for him.

'Poor Harry,' Devlin said. 'Final curtain and he still didn't get a full house.'

He took her arm and they turned and walked away through the rain.

A Prayer for the Dying

For Philip Williams, the expert

1

Fallon

When the police car turned the corner at the end of the street Fallon stepped into the nearest doorway instinctively and waited for it to pass. He gave it a couple of minutes and then continued on his way, turning up his collar as it started to rain.

He walked on towards the docks keeping to the shadows, his hands pushed deep into the pockets of his dark-blue trenchcoat, a small dark man of five feet four or five who seemed to drift rather than walk.

A ship eased down from the Pool of London sounding its foghorn, strange, haunting – the last of the dinosaurs moving aimlessly through some primeval swamp, alone in a world already alien. It suited his mood perfectly.

There was a warehouse at the end of the street facing out across the river. The sign said *Janos Kristou – Importer*. Fallon opened the little judas gate in the main entrance and stepped inside.

The place was crammed with bales and packing cases of every description. It was very dark, but there was a light at the far end and he moved towards it. A man sat at a trestle table beneath a naked light bulb and wrote laboriously in a large, old-fashioned ledger. He had lost most of his hair and what was left stuck out in a dirty white fringe. He wore an old sheepskin jacket and woollen mittens.

Fallon took a cautious step forward and the old man said without turning round, 'Martin, is that you?'

Fallon moved into the pool of light and paused beside the table. 'Hello, Kristou.'

There was a wooden case on the floor beside him and the top was loose. Fallon raised it and took out a Sterling sub-machine-gun thick with protective grease.

'Still at it, I see. Who's this for? The Israelis or the Arabs or have you actually started taking sides?'

Kristou leaned across, took the Sterling from him and dropped it back into the box. 'I didn't make the world the way it is,' he said.

'Maybe not, but you certainly helped it along the way.' Fallon lit a cigarette. 'I heard you wanted to see me.'

Kristou put down his pen and looked up at him speculatively. His face was very old, the parchment-coloured skin seamed with wrinkles, but the blue eyes were alert and intelligent.

He said, 'You don't look too good, Martin.'

'I've never felt better,' Fallon told him. 'Now what about my passport?'

Kristou smiled amiably. 'You look as if you could do with a drink.' He took a bottle and two paper cups from a drawer. 'Irish whiskey – the best. Just to make you feel at home.'

Fallon hesitated and then took one of the cups. Kristou raised the other. 'May you die in Ireland. Isn't that what they say?'

Fallon swallowed the whiskey down and crushed the paper cup in his right hand. 'My passport,' he said softly.

Kristou said, 'In a sense it's out of my hands, Martin. I mean to say, you turning out to be so much in demand in certain quarters – that alters things.'

Fallon went round to the other side of the table and stood there for a moment, head bowed, hands thrust deep into the pockets of the blue trenchcoat. And then he looked up very slowly, dark empty eyes burning in the white face.

'If you're trying to put the screw on me, old man, forget it. I gave you everything I had.'

Kristou's heart missed a beat. There was a cold stirring in his bowels. 'God help me, Martin,' he said, 'but with a hood on you'd look like Death himself.'

Fallon stood there, eyes like black glass staring through and beyond and then suddenly, something seemed to go out of him. He turned as if to leave.

Kristou said quickly, 'There is a way.'

Fallon hesitated. 'And what would that be?'

'Your passport, a berth on a cargo boat leaving Hull for Australia, Sunday night.' He paused. 'And two thousand pounds in your pocket to give you a fresh start.'

Fallon said incredulously. 'What do I have to do? Kill somebody?'

'Exactly,' the old man answered.

Fallon laughed softly. 'You get better all the time, Kristou. You really do.'

He reached for the whiskey bottle, emptied Kristou's cup on the floor and filled it again. The old man watched him, waiting. Rain tapped against a window as if somebody was trying to get in. Fallon walked across and peered down into the empty street.

A car was parked in the entrance to an alley on his left. No lights – which was interesting. The foghorn sounded again, further downriver this time.

'A dirty night for it.' He turned. 'But that's appropriate.'

'For what, Martin?' Kristou asked.

'Oh, for people like you and me.'

He emptied the cup at a swallow, walked back to the table and put it down in front of Kristou very carefully.

'All right,' he said. 'I'm listening.'

Kristou smiled. 'Now you're being sensible.' He opened a manilla folder, took out a photo and pushed it across the table. 'Take a look at that.'

Fallon picked it up and held it under the light. It had obviously been taken in a cemetery and in the foreground there was a rather curious monument. A bronze figure of a woman in the act of rising from a chair as if to go through the door which stood partly open between marble pillars behind her. A man in a dark overcoat, head bare, knelt before her on one knee.

'Now this.' Kristou pushed another photo across.

The scene was the same except for one important fact. The man in the dark overcoat was now standing, facing the camera, hat in hand. He was massively built, at least six foot two or three, with chest and shoulders to match. He had a strong Slav face with high flat cheekbones and narrow eyes.

'He looks like a good man to keep away from,' Fallon said.

'A lot of people would agree with you.'

'Who is he?'

'His name's Krasko – Jan Krasko.'

'Polish?'

'Originally – but that was a long time ago. He's been here since before the war.'

'And where's here?'

'Up North. You'll be told where at the right time.'

'And the woman in the chair?'

'His mother.' Kristou reached for the photo and looked at it himself. 'Every Thursday morning without fail, wet or fine, there he is with his bunch of flowers. They were very close.'

He put the photos back in the manilla folder and looked up at Fallon again. 'Well?'

'What's he done to deserve me?'

'A matter of business, that's all. What you might call a conflict of interests. My client's tried being reasonable, only Krasko won't play. So he'll have to go; and as publicly as possible.'

'To encourage the others?'

'Something like that.'

Fallon moved back to the window and looked down into the street. The car was still there in the alley. He spoke without turning round.

'And just what exactly is Krasko's line of business?'

'You name it,' Kristou said. 'Clubs, gambling, betting shops . . .'

'Whores and drugs?' Fallon turned round. 'And your client?'

Kristou raised a hand defensively. 'Now you're going too far, Martin. Now you're being unreasonable.'

'Good night, Kristou.' Fallon turned and started to walk away.

'All right, all right,' Kristou called, something close to panic in his voice. 'You win.'

As Fallon moved back to the table, Kristou opened a drawer and rummaged inside. He took out another folder, opened it and produced a bundle of newspaper clippings. He sorted through them, finally found what he was looking for and passed it to Fallon.

The clipping was already yellowing at the edges and was dated eighteen months previously. The article was headed *The English Al Capone*.

There was a photo of a large, heavily-built man coming down a flight of steps. He had a fleshy, arrogant face under a Homburg hat and wore a dark-blue, double-breasted melton overcoat, a handkerchief in the breast pocket. The youth at his shoulder was perhaps seventeen or eighteen and wore a similar coat, but he was bare-headed, an albino, with white shoulder-length hair that gave him the look of some decadent angel.

Underneath the photo it said; *Jack Meehan and his brother Billy leaving Manchester Central Police Headquarters after questioning in connection with the death of Agnes Drew*.

'And who was this Agnes Drew?' Fallon demanded.

'Some whore who got kicked to death in an alley. An occupational hazard. You know how it is?'

'I can imagine.' Fallon glanced at the photo again. 'They look like a couple of bloody undertakers.'

Kristou laughed until the tears came to his eyes. 'That's really very funny, you know that? That's exactly what Mr Meehan is. He runs one of the biggest funeral concerns in the north of England.'

'What, no clubs, no gambling? No whores, no drugs?' Fallon put the clipping down on the table. 'That's not what it says here.'

'All right,' Kristou leaned back, took off his spectacles and cleaned them with a soiled handkerchief. 'What if I told you Mr Meehan is strictly legitimate these days? That people like Krasko are leaning on him. Leaning hard – and the law won't help.'

'Oh, I see it all now,' Fallon said. 'You mean give a dog a bad name?'

'That's it.' Kristou slammed a fist against the table. 'That's it exactly.' He adjusted his spectacles again and peered up at Fallon eagerly. 'It's a deal then?'

'Like hell it is,' Fallon said coldly. 'I wouldn't touch either Krasko or your friend Meehan with a bargepole. I might catch something.'

'For God's sake, Martin, what's one more on the list to you?' Kristou cried as he turned to go. 'How many did you kill over there? Thirty-two? Thirty-four? Four soldiers in Londonderry alone.'

He got up quickly, his chair going backwards, darted round the table and grabbed Fallon by the arm.

Fallon pushed him away. 'Anything I did, I did for the cause. Because I believed it was necessary.'

'Very noble,' Kristou said. 'And the kids in that school bus you blew to a bloody pulp. Was that for your cause?'

He was back across the table, a hand of iron at his throat, staring up into the muzzle of a Browning automatic and behind it Fallon and the white devil's face on him. There was the click of the hammer being cocked.

Kristou almost fainted. He had a partial bowel movement, the stench foul in the cold, sharp air of the warehouse and Fallon pushed him away in disgust.

'Never again, Kristou,' he whispered and the Browning in his left hand was rock-steady. 'Never again.' The Browning disappeared into the right-hand pocket of his trenchcoat. He turned and walked away, his footsteps echoing on the concrete floor. The judas gate banged.

Kristou got up gingerly, tears of rage and shame in his eyes. Someone laughed and a harsh, aggressive Yorkshire voice said from the shadows, 'Now that's what I call really being in the shit, Kristou.'

Jack Meehan walked into the light, his brother Billy at his heels. They were both dressed exactly as they had been in the newspaper photo. It really was quite remarkable.

Meehan picked up the clipping. 'What in the hell did you want to show him that for? I sued the bastard who wrote that article and won.'

'That's right.' Billy Meehan giggled. 'The judge would have made it a farthing damages only there's no such coin any more.' His voice was high-pitched, repellent – nothing masculine about it at all.

Meehan slapped him casually, back-handed across the mouth, and said to Kristou, his nose wrinkling in disgust, 'Go and wipe your backside, for Christ's sake. Then we talk.'

When Kristou returned, Meehan was sitting at the table pouring whiskey into a clean paper cup, his brother standing behind him. He sampled a little, spat it out and made a face. 'All right, I know the Irish still have one foot in the bog, but how can they drink this muck?'

'I'm sorry, Mr Meehan,' Kristou said.

'You'll be a bloody sight sorrier before I'm through with you. You cocked it up proper, didn't you?'

Kristou moistened dry lips and fingered his spectacles. 'I didn't think he'd react that way.'

'What in the hell did you expect? He's a nutcase, isn't he? I mean, they all are over there, going round shooting women and blowing up kids. That's civilised?'

Kristou couldn't think of a thing to say, but was saved by Billy who said carelessly, 'He didn't look much to me. Little half-pint runt. Without that shooter in his fist he'd be nothing.'

Meehan sighed heavily. 'You know there are days when I really despair of you, Billy. You've just seen hell on wheels and didn't recognise it.' He laughed harshly again. 'You'll never come closer, Kristou. He was mad at you, you old bastard. Mad enough to kill and yet that shooter didn't even waver.'

Kristou winced. 'I know, Mr Meehan. I miscalculated. I shouldn't have mentioned those kids.'

'Then what are you going to do about it?'

Kristou glanced at Billy, then back to his brother, frowning slightly. 'You mean you still want him, Mr Meehan?'

'Doesn't everybody?'

'That's true enough.'

He laughed nervously and Meehan stood up and patted him on the face. 'You fix it, Kristou, like a good lad. You know where I'm staying.

If I haven't heard by midnight, I'll send Fat Albert to see you and you wouldn't like that, would you?'

He walked into the darkness followed by his brother and Kristou stood there, terrified, listening to them go. The judas gate opened and Meehan's voice called, 'Kristou?'

'Yes, Mr Meehan.'

'Don't forget to have a bath when you get home. You stink like my Aunt Mary's midden.'

The judas banged shut and Kristou sank down into the chair, fingers tapping nervously. God damn Fallon. It would serve him right if he turned him in.

And then it hit him like a bolt from the blue. The perfect solution and so beautifully simple.

He picked up the telephone, dialled Scotland Yard and asked to be put through to the Special Branch.

It was raining quite heavily now and Jack Meehan paused to turn up his collar before crossing the street.

Billy said, 'I still don't get it. Why is it so important you get Fallon?'

'Number one, with a shooter in his hand he's the best there is,' Meehan said. 'Number two, everybody wants him. The Special Branch, Military Intelligence – even his old mates in the IRA which means – number three – that he's eminently disposable afterwards.'

'What's that mean?' Billy said as they turned the corner of the alley and moved towards the car.

'Why don't you try reading a few books, for Christ's sake?' Meehan demanded. 'All you ever seem to think of is birds.'

They were at the front of the car by now, a Bentley Continental, and Meehan grabbed Billy by the arm and pulled him up quickly.

'Here, what the hell's going on? Where's Fred?'

'A slight concussion, Mr Meehan. Nothing much. He's sleeping it off in the rear seat.'

A match flared in a nearby doorway pulling Fallon's face out of the darkness. There was a cigarette between his lips. He lit it, then flicked the match into the gutter.

Meehan opened the door of the Bentley and switched on the lights. 'What are you after?' he said calmly.

'I just wanted to see you in the flesh, so to speak, that's all,' Fallon said. 'Good night to you.'

He started to move away and Meehan grabbed his arm. 'You know, I like you, Fallon. I think we've got a lot in common.'

'I doubt that.'

Meehan ignored him. 'I've been reading this German philosopher lately. You wouldn't know him. He says that for authentic living what is necessary is the resolute confrontation of death. Would you agree with that?'

'Heidegger,' Fallon said. 'Interesting you should go for him. He was Himmler's bible.'

He turned away again and Meehan moved quickly in front of him. 'Heidegger?' he said. 'You've read Heidegger?' There was genuine astonishment in his voice. 'I'll double up on the original offer and find you regular work. Now I can't say fairer than that, can I?'

'Good night, Mr Meehan,' Fallon said and melted into the darkness.

'What a man,' Meehan said. 'What a hard-nosed bastard. Why, he's beautiful, Billy, even if he is a fucking Mick.' He turned. 'Come on, let's get back to the Savoy. You drive and if you put as much as a scratch on this motor I'll have your balls.'

Fallon had a room in a lodging-house in Hanger Street in Stepney just off the Commercial Road. A couple of miles, no more, so he walked, in spite of the rain. He hadn't the slightest idea what would happen now. Kristou had been his one, his only hope. He was finished, it was as simple as that. He could run, but how far?

As he neared his destination, he took out his wallet and checked the contents. Four pounds and a little silver and he was already two weeks behind with his rent: He went into a cheap wine shop for some cigarettes then crossed the road to Hanger Street.

The newspaper man on the corner had deserted his usual pitch to shelter in a doorway from the driving rain. He was little more than a bundle of rags, an old London-Irishman, totally blind in one eye and only partially sighted in the other.

Fallon dropped a coin in his hand and took a paper. 'Good night to you, Michael,' he said.

The old man rolled one milky white eye towards him, his hand fumbling for change in the bag which hung about his neck.

'Is it yourself, Mr Fallon?'

'And who else? You can forget the change.'

The old man grabbed his hand and counted out his change laboriously. 'You had visitors at number thirteen about twenty minutes ago.'

'The law?' Fallon asked softly.

'Nothing in uniform. They went in and didn't come out again. Two cars waiting at the other end of the street – another across the road.'

He counted a final penny into Fallon's hand. Fallon turned and crossed to the telephone-box on the other corner. He dialled the number of the lodging-house and was answered instantly by the old woman who ran the place. He pushed in the coin and spoke.

'Mrs Keegan? It's Daly here. I wonder if you'd mind doing me a favour?'

He knew at once by the second's hesitation, by the strain in her voice, that old Michael's supposition had been correct.

'Oh, yes, Mr Daly.'

'The thing is, I'm expecting a phone call at nine o'clock. Take the number and tell them I'll ring back when I get in. I haven't a hope in hell of getting there now. I ran into a couple of old friends and we're having a few drinks. You know how it is?'

There was another slight pause before she said as if in response to some invisible prompt, 'Sounds nice. Where are you?'

'A pub called The Grenadier Guard in Kensington High Street. I'll have to go now. See you later.'

He replaced the receiver, left the phone-box and moved into a doorway from which he had a good view of No. 13 halfway down the short street.

A moment later, the front door was flung open. There were eight of them. Special Branch from the look of it. The first one on to the pavement waved frantically and two cars moved out of the shadows at the end of the street. The whole crew climbed inside, the cars moved away at speed. A car which was parked at the kerb on the other side of the main road went after them.

Fallon crossed to the corner and paused beside the old newspaper seller. He took out his wallet, extracting the four remaining pound notes and pressed them into his hand.

'God bless you, Mr Fallon,' Michael said, but Fallon was already on the other side of the road, walking rapidly back towards the river.

This time Kristou didn't hear a thing although he had been waiting for something like an hour, nerves taut. He sat there at the table, ledger open, the pen gripped tightly in his mittened hand. There was the softest of footfalls, wind over grass only, then the harsh, deliberate click as the hammer of the Browning was cocked.

Kristou breathed deeply to steady himself. 'What's the point, Martin?' he said. 'What would it get you?'

Fallon moved round to the other side of the table, the Browning in his hand. Kristou stood up, leaning on the table to stop from shaking.

'I'm the only friend you've got left now, Martin.'

'You bastard,' Fallon said. 'You sicked the Special Branch on to me.'

'I had to,' Kristou said frantically. 'It was the only way I could get you back here. It was for your own good, Martin. You've been like a dead man walking. I can bring you back to life again. Action and passion, that's what you want. That's what you need.'

Fallon's eyes were like black holes in the white face. He raised the Browning at arm's length, touching the muzzle between Kristou's eyes.

The old man closed them. 'All right, if you want to, go ahead. Get it over with. This is a life, the life I lead? Only remember one thing. Kill me, you kill yourself because there *is* no one else. Not one single person in this world that would do anything other than turn you in or put a bullet in your head.'

There was a long pause. He opened his eyes to see Fallon gently lowering the hammer of the Browning. He stood there holding it against his right thigh, staring into space.

Kristou said carefully, 'After all, what is he to you, this Krasko? A gangster, a murderer. The kind who lives off young girls.' He spat. 'A pig.'

Fallon said. 'Don't try to dress it up. What's the next move?'

'One phone call is all it takes. A car will be here in half an hour. You'll be taken to a farm near Doncaster. An out-of-the-way place. You'll be safe there. You make the hit on Thursday morning at the cemetery like I showed you in the photo. Krasko always leaves his goons at the gate. He doesn't like having them around when he's feeling sentimental.'

'All right,' Fallon said. 'But I do my own organising. That's understood.'

'Of course. Anything you want.' Kristou opened the drawer, took out an envelope and shoved it across. 'There's five hundred quid there in fives, to be going on with.'

Fallon weighed the envelope in his hand carefully for a moment, then slipped it into a pocket. 'When do I get the rest?' he said. 'And the passport?'

'Mr Meehan takes care of that end on satisfactory completion.'

Fallon nodded slowly. 'All right, make your phone call.'

Kristou smiled, a mixture of triumph and relief. 'You're doing the wise thing, Martin. Believe me you are.' He hesitated. 'There's just one thing if you don't mind me saying so?'

'And what would that be?'

'The Browning – no good to you for a job like this. You need something nice and quiet.'

Fallon looked down at the Browning, a slight frown on his face. 'Maybe you have a point. What have you got to offer?'

'What would you like?'

Fallon shook his head. 'I've never had a preference for any particular make of handgun. That way you end up with a trademark. Something they can fasten on to and that's bad.'

Kristou unlocked a small safe in the corner, opened it and took out a cloth bundle which he unwrapped on the table. It contained a rather ugly-looking automatic, perhaps six inches long, a curious-looking barrel protruding a further two inches. The bundle also contained a three-inch silencer and two fifty-round cartons of ammunition.

'And what in the hell is this?' Fallon said, picking it up.

'A Czech Ceska,' Kristou told him. 'Seven point five mm. Model twenty-seven. The Germans took over the factory during the war. This is one of theirs. You can tell by the special barrel modification. Made that way to take a silencer.'

'Is it any good?'

'SS Intelligence used them, but judge for yourself.'

He moved into the darkness. A few moments later, a light was turned on at the far end of the building and Fallon saw that there was a target down there of a type much used by the army. A lifesize replica of a charging soldier.

As he screwed the silencer on to the end of the barrel, Kristou rejoined him. 'Any time you're ready.'

Fallon took careful aim with both hands, there was a dull thud that outside would not have been audible above three yards. He had fired at the heart and chipped the right arm.

He adjusted the sight and tried again. He was still a couple of inches out. He made a further adjustment. This time he was dead on target.

Kristou said, 'Didn't I tell you?'

Fallon nodded. 'Ugly, but deadly, Kristou, just like you and me. Did I ever tell you that I once saw a sign on a wall in Derry that said: Is there a life before death? Isn't that the funniest thing you ever heard?'

Kristou stared at him, aghast, and Fallon turned, his arm swung up, he fired twice without apparently taking aim and shot out the target's eyes.

2

Father da Costa

. . . the Lord is my Shepherd, I shall not want. Father Michael da Costa spoke out bravely as he led the way up through the cemetery, his words almost drowned in the rush of heavy rain.

Inside, he was sick at heart. It had rained heavily all night, was raining even harder now. The procession from chapel to graveside was a wretched affair at the best of times, but this occasion was particularly distressing.

For one thing, there were so few of them. The two men from the funeral directors carrying the pitifully small coffin between them and the mother, already on the point of collapse, staggering along behind supported by her husband on one side and her brother on the other. They were poor people. They had no one. They turned inward in their grief.

Mr O'Brien, the cemetery superintendent, was waiting at the graveside, an umbrella over his head against the rain. There was a gravedigger with him who pulled off the canvas cover as they arrived. Not that it had done any good for there was at least two feet of water in the bottom.

O'Brien tried to hold the umbrella over the priest, but Father da Costa waved it away. Instead, he took off his coat and handed it to the superintendent and stood there in the rain at the graveside, the old red and gold cope making a brave show in the grey morning.

O'Brien had to act as server and Father da Costa sprinkled the coffin with holy water and incense and as he prayed, he noticed that the father was glaring across at him wildly like some trapped animal behind bars, the fingers of his right hand clenching and unclenching convulsively. He was a big man – almost as big as da Costa. Foreman on a building site.

Da Costa looked away hurriedly and prayed for the child, face upturned, rain beading his tangled grey beard.

Into your hands, O Lord,
We humbly commend our sister,
Lead her for whom you have
Shown so great a love,
Into the joy of the heavenly paradise.

Not for the first time, the banality of what he was saying struck him. How could he explain to any mother on this earth that God needed her eight-year-old daughter so badly that it had been necessary for her to choke to death in the stinking waters of an industrial canal. To drift for ten days before being found.

The coffin descended with a splash and the gravedigger quickly pulled the canvas sheet back in place. Father da Costa said a final prayer, then moved round to the woman who was now crying bitterly.

He put a hand on her shoulder. 'Mrs Dalton – if there's anything I can do.'

The father struck his arm away wildly. 'You leave her alone!' he cried. 'She's suffered enough. You and your bloody prayers. What good's that? I had to identify her, did you know that? A piece of rotting flesh that was my daughter after ten days in the canal. What kind of a God is it that could do that to a child?'

O'Brien moved forward quickly, but Father da Costa put up an arm to hold him back. 'Leave it,' he said calmly.

A strange, hunted look appeared on Dalton's face as if he suddenly realised the enormity of his offence. He put an arm about his wife's shoulders and he and her brother hurried her away. The two funeral men went after them.

O'Brien helped da Costa on with his coat. 'I'm sorry about that, Father. A bad business.'

'He has a point, poor devil,' da Costa said. 'After all, what am I supposed to say to someone in his position?'

The gravedigger looked shocked, but O'Brien simply nodded slowly. 'It's a funny old life sometimes.' He opened his umbrella. 'I'll walk you back to the chapel, Father.'

Da Costa shook his head. 'I'll take the long way round if you don't mind. I could do with the exercise. I'll borrow the umbrella if I may.'

'Certainly, Father.'

O'Brien gave it to him and da Costa walked away through the wilderness of marble monuments and tombstones.

The gravedigger said, 'That was a hell of an admission for a priest to make.'

O'Brien lit a cigarette. 'Ah, but then da Costa is no ordinary priest. Joe Devlin, the sacristan at St Anne's, told me all about him. He was some sort of commando or other during the war. Fought with Tito and the Jugoslav partisans. Afterwards, he went to the English College in Rome. Had a brilliant career there – could have been anything. Instead, he decided to go into mission work after he was ordained.'

'Where did they send him?'

'Korea. The Chinese had him for nearly five years. Afterwards they gave him some administrative job in Rome to recuperate, but he didn't like that. Got them to send him to Mozambique. I think it was his grandfather who was Portuguese. Anyway, he speaks the language.'

'What happened there?'

'Oh, he was deported. The Portuguese authorities accused him of having too much sympathy with the rebels.'

'So what's he doing here?'

'Parish priest at Holy Name.'

'That pile of rubble?' the gravedigger said incredulously. 'Why, it's only standing up because of the scaffolding. If he gets a dozen for Mass on a Sunday he'll be lucky.'

'Exactly,' O'Brien said.

'Oh, I get it.' The gravedigger nodded sagely. 'It's their way of slapping his wrist.'

'He's a good man,' O'Brien said. 'Too good to be wasted.'

He was suddenly tired of the conversation and, for some strange reason, unutterably depressed. 'Better get that grave filled in.'

'What, now, in this rain?' The gravedigger looked at him bewildered. 'It can wait till later, can't it?'

'No, it damn well can't.'

O'Brien turned on heel and walked away and the grave-digger, swearing softly, pulled back the canvas sheet and got to work.

Father da Costa usually enjoyed a walk in the rain. It gave him a safe, enclosed feeling. Some psychological thing harking back to childhood, he supposed. But not now. Now, he felt restless and ill at ease. Still disturbed by what had happened at the graveside.

He paused to break a personal vow by lighting a cigarette, awkwardly because of the umbrella in his left hand. He had recently reduced his consumption to five a day, and those he smoked only during the evening, a pleasure to be savoured by anticipation, but under the circumstances . . .

He moved on into the oldest part of the cemetery, a section he had discovered with delight only a month or two previously. Here amongst the pines and the cypresses were superb Victorian-Gothic tombs, winged angels in marble, bronzed effigies of Death. Something different on every hand and on each slab a pious, sentimental, implacable belief in the hereafter was recorded.

He didn't see a living soul until he went round a corner between rhododendron bushes and paused abruptly. The path divided some ten yards in front of him and at the intersection stood a rather interesting grave. A door between marble pillars, partially open. In front of it the bronze figure of a woman in the act of rising from a chair.

A man in a dark overcoat, head bare, knelt before her on one knee. It was very quiet – only the rushing of the rain into wet earth and Father da Costa hesitated for a moment, unwilling to intrude on such a moment of personal grief.

And then an extraordinary thing happened. A priest stepped in through the eternity door at the back of the grave. A youngish man who wore a dark clerical raincoat over his cassock and a black hat.

What took place then was like something out of a nightmare, frozen in time, no reality to it at all. As the man in the dark overcoat glanced up, the priest produced an automatic with a long black silencer on the end. There was a dull thud as he fired. Fragments of bone and brain sprayed out from the rear of his victim's skull as he was slammed back against the gravel.

Father da Costa gave a hoarse cry, already seconds too late, 'For God's sake no!'

The young priest, in the act of stepping towards his victim, looked up, aware of da Costa for the first time. The arm swung instantly as he took deliberate aim and da Costa looked at Death, at the white devil's face on him, the dark, dark eyes.

And then, unaccountably, as his lips moved in prayer, the gun was lowered. The priest bent down to pick something up. The dark eyes stared into his for a second longer and then he slipped back through the door and was gone.

Father da Costa threw the umbrella to one side and dropped to his knees beside the man who had been shot. Blood trickled from the nostrils, the eyes were half-closed and yet, incredibly, there was still the sound of laboured breathing.

He began to recite in a firm voice, the prayers for the dying. *Go, Christian Soul, from this world, in the Name of God the Father Almighty who created thee* and then, with a hoarse rattle, the breathing stopped abruptly.

Fallon followed the path at the north end of the cemetery, walking fast, but not too fast. Not that it mattered. He was well screened by rhododendron bushes and it was unlikely that there would be anyone about in such weather.

The priest had been unfortunate. One of those time and chance things. It occurred to him, with something like amusement and not for the first time in his life, that no matter how well you planned, something unexpected always seemed to turn up.

He moved into a small wood and found the van parked in the track out of sight as he had left it. There was no one in the driver's seat and he frowned.

'Varley, where are you?' he called softly.

A small man in a raincoat and cloth cap came blundering through the trees, mouth gaping, clutching a pair of binoculars in one hand. He leaned against the side of the van, fighting for breath.

Fallon shook him roughly by the shoulder. 'Where in the hell have you been?'

'I was watching,' Varley gasped. He raised the binoculars. 'Mr Meehan's orders. That priest. He saw you. Why didn't you give it to him?'

Fallon opened the van door and shoved him in behind the wheel. 'Shut up and get driving!'

He went round to the rear, opened the doors, got in and closed them again as the engine roared into life and they lurched away along the rough track.

He opened the small window at the rear of the driver's compartment. 'Steady,' he said. 'Easy does it. The slower the better. A friend of mine once robbed a bank and made his escape in an ice-cream van that couldn't do more than twenty miles an hour. They expect you to move like hell after a killing so do the other thing.'

He started to divest himself of the raincoat and cassock. Underneath he wore a dark sweater and grey slacks. His navy blue trenchcoat was ready on the seat and he pulled it on. Then he took off the rubber galoshes he was wearing.

Varley was sweating as they turned into the dual carriageway. 'Oh, God,' he moaned. 'Mr Meehan will have our balls for this.'

'Let me worry about Meehan.' Fallon bundled the priest's clothing into a canvas holdall and zipped it shut.

'You don't know him, Mr Fallon,' Varley said. 'He's the devil himself when he's mad. There was a fella called Gregson a month or two back. Professional gambler. Bent as a cork-screw. He took one of Mr Meehan's clubs for five grand. When the boys brought him in, Mr Meehan nailed his hands to a table top. Did it himself, too. Six-inch nails and a five-pound hammer. Left him like that for five hours. To consider the error of his ways, that's what he said.'

'What did he do to him after that?' Fallon asked.

'I was there when they took the nails out. It was horrible. Gregson was in a terrible state. And Mr Meehan, he pats him on the cheek and tells him to be a good boy in future. Then he gives him a tenner and sends him to see this Paki doctor he uses.' Varley shuddered. 'I tell you, Mr Fallon, he's no man to cross.'

'He certainly seems to have his own special way of winning friends and influencing people,' Fallon said. 'The priest back there? Do you know him?'

'Father da Costa?' Varley nodded. 'Has a broken-down old church near the centre of the city. Holy Name, it's called. He runs the crypt as a kind of doss house for down-and-outs. About the only congregation he gets these days. One of these areas where they've pulled down all the houses.'

'Sounds interesting. Take me there.'

The car swerved violently, so great was Varley's surprise and he had to fight to regain control of the wheel. 'Don't be crazy. My orders were to take you straight back to the farm.'

'I'm changing them,' Fallon said simply and he sat back and lit a cigarette.

The Church of the Holy Name was in Rockingham Street, sandwiched between gleaming new cement and glass office blocks on the one hand and shabby, decaying warehouses on the other. Higher up the street there was a vast brickfield where old Victorian slum houses had been cleared. The bull-dozers were already at work digging the foundation for more tower blocks.

Varley parked the van opposite the church and Fallon got out. It was a Victorian-Gothic monstrosity with a squat, ugly tower at its centre, the whole networked with scaffolding although there didn't seem to be any work in progress.

'It isn't exactly a hive of industry,' Fallon said.

'They ran out of money. The way I hear it the bloody place is falling down.' Varley wiped sweat from his brow nervously. 'Let's get out of it, Mr Fallon – please.'

'In a minute.'

Fallon crossed the road to the main entrance. There was the usual board outside with da Costa's name there and the times of Mass. Confession was at one o'clock and five on weekdays. He stood there, staring at the board for a moment and then he smiled slowly, turned and went back to the van.

He leaned in the window. 'This funeral place of Meehan's – where is it?'

'Paul's Square,' Varley said. 'It's only ten minutes from here on the side of the town hall.'

'I've got things to do,' Fallon said. 'Tell Meehan I'll meet him there at two o'clock.'

'For Christ's sake, Mr Fallon,' Varley said frantically. 'You can't do that,' but Fallon was already halfway across the road going back towards the church.

Varley moaned, 'You bastard!' and he moved into gear and drove away.

Fallon didn't go into the church. Instead, he walked up the side street beside a high, greystone wall. There was an old cemetery inside, flat tombstones mainly and a house in one corner, presumably the presbytery. It looked to be in about the same state as the church.

It was a sad, grey sort of place, the leafless trees black with a century of city soot that even the rain could not wash away and he was filled with a curious melancholy. This was what it all came to in the end whichever way you looked at it. Words on cracked stones. A gate clicked behind him and he turned sharply.

A young woman was coming down the path from the presbytery, an old trenchcoat over her shoulders against the rain. She carried an ebony walking stick in one hand and there was a bundle of sheet music under the other arm.

Fallon judged her to be in her late twenties with black shoulder-length hair and a grave, steady face. One of those plain faces that for some strange reason you found yourself looking at twice.

He got ready to explain himself as she approached, but she stared straight through him as if he wasn't there. And then, as she went by, he noticed the occasional tap with the stick against the end of a tomb – familiar friends.

She paused and turned, a slight, uncertain frown on her face. 'Is anyone there?' she called in a calm, pleasant voice.

Fallon didn't move a muscle. She stayed there for a moment longer, then turned and continued along the path. When she reached a small door at the end of the church, she took out a yale key, opened it and went inside.

Fallon went out through the side gate and round to the main entrance. When he pushed open the door and went inside he was conscious of the familiar odour and smiled wryly.

'Incense, candles and the holy water,' he said softly and his fingers dipped in the bowl as he went past in a kind of reflex action.

It had a sort of charm and somewhere in the dim past, somebody had obviously spent a lot of money on it. There was Victorian stained glass and imitation mediaeval carvings everywhere. Gargoyles, skulls, imagination running riot.

Scaffolding lifted in a spider's web to support the nave at the altar end and it was very dark except for the sanctuary lamp and candles flickering before the Virgin.

The girl was seated at the organ behind the choir stalls. She started to play softly. Just a few tentative chords at first and then, as Fallon started to walk down the centre aisle, she moved into the opening of the Bach Prelude and Fugue in D Major.

And she was good. He stood at the bottom of the steps listening, then started up. She stopped at once and swung round.

'Is anyone there?'

'I'm sorry if I disturbed you,' he told her. 'I was enjoying listening.'

There was that slight, uncertain smile on her face again. She seemed to be waiting, so he carried on. 'If I might make a suggestion?'

'You play the organ?'

'Used to. Look, that trumpet stop is a reed. Unreliable at the best of times, but in a damp atmosphere like this –' he shrugged. 'It's so badly out of tune it's putting everything else out. I'd leave it in if I were you.'

'Why, thank you,' she said. 'I'll try that.'

She turned back to the organ and Fallon went down the steps to the rear of the church and sat in a pew in the darkest corner he could find.

She played the Prelude and Fugue right through and he sat there, eyes closed, arms folded. And his original judgement still stood. She *was* good – certainly worth listening to.

When she finished after half an hour or so, she gathered up her things and came down the steps. She paused at the bottom and waited, perhaps sensing that he was still there, but he made no sign and after a moment, she went into the sacristy.

And in the darkness at the back of the church, Fallon sat waiting.

3

Miller

Father da Costa was just finishing his second cup of tea in the cemetery superintendent's office when there was a knock at the door and a young police constable came in.

'Sorry to bother you again, Father, but Mr Miller would like a word with you.'

Father da Costa stood up. 'Mr Miller?' he said.

'Detective-Superintendent Miller, sir. He's head of the CID.'

It was still raining heavily when they went outside. The forecourt was crammed with police vehicles and as they walked along the narrow path, there seemed to be police everywhere, moving through the rhododendron bushes.

The body was exactly where he had left it although it was now partially covered with a groundsheet. A man in an overcoat knelt on one knee beside it making some sort of preliminary examination. He was speaking in a low voice into a portable dictaphone and what looked like a doctor's bag was open on the ground beside him.

There were police here everywhere, too, in uniform and out. Several of them were taking careful measurements with tapes. The others were searching the ground area.

The young detective-inspector who had his statement, was called Fitzgerald. He was standing to one side, talking to a tall, thin, rather scholarly-looking man in a belted raincoat. When he saw da Costa, he came across at once.

'There you are, Father. This is Detective-Superintendent Miller.'

Miller shook hands. He had a thin face and patient brown eyes. Just now he looked very tired.

He said, 'A bad business, Father.'

'It is indeed,' da Costa said.

'As you can see, we're going through the usual motions and Professor

Lawlor here is making a preliminary report. He'll do an autopsy this afternoon. On the other hand, because of the way it happened you're obviously the key to the whole affair. If I might ask you a few more questions?'

'Anything I can do, of course, but I can assure you that Inspector Fitzgerald was most efficient. I don't think there can be anything he overlooked.'

Fitzgerald looked suitably modest and Miller smiled. 'Father, I've been a policeman for nearly twenty-five years and if I've learned one thing, it's that there's always something and it's usually that something which wins cases.'

Professor Lawlor stood up. 'I've finished here, Nick,' he said. 'You can move him.' He turned to da Costa. 'You said, if I got it right from Fitzgerald, that he was down on his right knee at the edge of the grave.' He walked across. 'About here?'

'That's correct.'

Lawlor turned to Miller. 'It fits, he must have glanced up at the crucial moment and his head would naturally be turned to the right. The entry wound is about an inch above the outer corner of the left eye.'

'Anything else interesting?' Miller asked.

'Not really. Entry wound a quarter of an inch in diameter. Very little bleeding. No powder marking. No staining. Exterior wound two inches in diameter. Explosive type with disruptions of the table of the skull and lacerations of the right occipital lobe of the brain. The wound is two inches to the right of the exterior occipital protruberance.'

'Thank you, Doctor Kildare,' Miller said.

Professor Lawlor turned to Father da Costa and smiled. 'You see, Father, medicine has its jargon, too, just like the Church. What I'm really trying to say is that he was shot through the skull at close quarters – but not too close.'

He picked up his bag. 'The bullet shouldn't be too far away, or what's left of it,' he said as he walked off.

'Thank you for reminding me,' Miller called ironically.

Fitzgerald had crossed to the doorway and now he came back, shaking his head. 'They're making a plaster cast of those footprints, but we're wasting our time. He was wearing galoshes. Another thing, we've been over the appropriate area with a tooth comb and there isn't a sign of a cartridge case.'

Miller frowned and turned to da Costa. 'You're certain he was using a silencer?'

'Absolutely.'

'You seem very sure.'

'As a young man I was a lieutenant in the Special Air Service, Superintendent,' da Costa told him calmly. 'The Aegean Islands – Jugoslavia. That sort of thing. I'm afraid I had to use a silenced pistol myself on more than one occasion.'

Miller and Fitzgerald glanced at each other in surprise and then Father da Costa saw it all in a flash of blinding light. 'But of course,' he said. 'It's impossible to use a silencer with a revolver. It has to be an automatic pistol which means the cartridge case would have been ejected.' He crossed to the doorway. 'Let me see, the pistol was in his right hand so the cartridge case should be somewhere about here.'

'Exactly,' Miller said. 'Only we can't find it.'

And then da Costa remembered. 'He dropped to one knee and picked something up, just before he left.'

Miller turned to Fitzgerald who looked chagrined. 'Which wasn't in your report.'

'My fault, Superintendent,' da Costa said. 'I didn't tell him. It slipped my mind.'

'As I said, Father, there's always something.' Miller took out a pipe and started to fill it from a worn leather pouch. 'I know one thing. This man's no run-of-the-mill tearaway. He's a professional right down to his fingertips, and that's good.'

'I don't understand,' Father da Costa said.

'Because there aren't many of that calibre about, Father. It's as simple as that. Let me explain. About six months ago somebody got away with nearly a quarter of a million from a local bank. Took all weekend to get into the vault. A beautiful job – too beautiful. You see we knew straight away that there were no more than five or six men in the country capable of that level of craftsmanship and three of them were in jail. The rest was purely a matter of mathematics.'

'I see,' da Costa said.

'Now take my unknown friend. I know a hell of a lot about him already. He's an exceptionally clever man because that priest's disguise was a touch of genius. Most people think in stereotypes. If I ask them if they saw anyone they'll say no. If I press them, they'll remember they saw a postman or – as in this case – a priest. If I ask them what he looked like, we're in trouble because all they can remember is that he looked like a priest – any priest.'

'I saw his face,' da Costa said. 'Quite clearly.'

'I only hope you'll be as certain if you see a photo of him dressed differently.' Miller frowned. 'Yes, he knew what he was doing all right. Galoshes to hide his normal footprints, probably a couple of sizes too large, and a crack shot. Most people couldn't hit a barn door with a handgun at twelve feet. He only needed one shot and that's going some, believe me.'

'And considerable nerve,' Father da Costa said. 'He didn't forget to pick up that cartridge case, remember, in spite of the fact that I had appeared on the scene.'

'We ought to have you in the Department, Father.' Miller turned to Fitzgerald. 'You carry on here. I'll take Father da Costa down town.'

Da Costa glanced at his watch. It was twelve-fifteen and he said quickly, 'I'm sorry, Superintendent, but that isn't possible. I hear confessions at one o'clock. And my niece was expecting me for lunch at twelve. She'll be worried.'

Miller took it quite well. 'I see. And when will you be free?'

'Officially at one-thirty. It depends, of course.'

'On the number of customers?'

'Exactly.'

Miller nodded good-humouredly. 'All right Father, I'll pick you up at two o'clock. Will that be all right?'

'I should imagine so,' da Costa said.

'I'll walk you to your car.'

The rain had slackened just a little as they went along the path through the rhododendron bushes. Miller yawned several times and rubbed his eyes.

Father da Costa said, 'You look tired, Superintendent.'

'I didn't get much sleep last night. A car salesman on one of the new housing estates cut his wife's throat with a bread knife, then picked up the phone and dialled nine-nine-nine. A nice, straightforward job, but I still had to turn out personally. Murder's important. I was in bed again by nine o'clock and then they rang through about this little lot.'

'You must lead a strange life,' da Costa said. 'What does your wife think about it?'

'She doesn't. She died last year.'

'I'm sorry.'

'I'm not. She had cancer of the bowel,' Miller told him calmly, then frowned slightly. 'Sorry, I know you don't look at things that way in your Church.'

Father da Costa didn't reply to that one because it struck him with startling suddenness that in Miller's position, he would have very probably felt the same way.

They reached his car, an old grey Mini van in front of the chapel, and Miller held the door open for him as he got in.

Da Costa leaned out of the window. 'You think you'll get him, Superintendent? You're confident?'

'I'll get him all right, Father,' Miller said grimly. 'I've got to if I'm to get the man I really want – the man behind him. The man who set this job up.'

'I see. And you already know who that is?'

'I'd put my pension on it.'

Father da Costa switched on the ignition and the engine rattled noisily into life. 'One thing still bothers me,' he said.

'What's that, Father?'

'This man you're looking for – the killer. If he's as much a professional as you say, then why didn't he kill me when he had the chance?'

'Exactly,' Miller said. 'Which is why it bothers me too. See you later, Father.'

He stood back as the priest drove away and Fitzgerald appeared round the corner of the chapel.

'Quite a man,' he said.

Miller nodded. 'Find out everything you can about him and I mean everything. I'll expect to hear from you by a quarter to two.' He turned on the astonished Fitzgerald. 'It should be easy enough for you. You're a practising Catholic, aren't you, and a Knight of St Columba or whatever you call it, or is that just a front for the IRA?'

'It damn well isn't,' Fitzgerald told him indignantly.

'Good. Try the cemetery superintendent first and then there's the Cathedral. They should be able to help. They'll talk to you.'

He put a match to his pipe and Fitzgerald said despairingly, 'But why, for God's sake?'

'Because another thing I've learned after twenty-five years of being a copper is never to take anything or anyone at face value,' Miller told him.

He walked across to his car, climbed in, nodded to the driver and leaned back. By the time they reached the main road, he was already asleep.

4

Confessional

Anna da Costa was playing the piano in the living-room of the old presbytery when Father da Costa entered. She swung round on the piano stool at once and stood up.

'Uncle Michael, you're late. What happened?'

He kissed her cheek and led her to a chair by the window. 'You'll hear soon enough so I might as well tell you now. A man was murdered this morning at the cemetery.'

She gazed up at him blankly, those beautiful, useless, dark eyes fixed on some point beyond, and there was a complete lack of comprehension on her face.

'Murdered? I don't understand.'

He sat down beside her and took both her hands in his. 'I saw it, Anna. I was the only witness.'

He got up and started to pace up and down the room. 'I was walking through the old part of the cemetery. Remember, I took you there last month?'

He described what had happened in detail, as much for himself as for her, because for some reason it seemed suddenly necessary.

'And he didn't shoot me, Anna!' he said. 'That's the strangest thing of all. I just don't understand it. It doesn't make any kind of sense.'

She shuddered deeply. 'Oh, Uncle Michael, it's a miracle you're here at all.'

She held out her hands and he took them again, conscious of a sudden, overwhelming tenderness. It occurred to him, and not for the first time, that in some ways she was the one creature he truly loved in the whole world, which was a great sin, for a priest's love, after all, should be available to all. But then, she was his dead brother's only child, an orphan since her fifteenth year.

The clock struck one and he patted her head. 'I'll have to go. I'm already late.'

'I made sandwiches,' she said. 'They're in the kitchen.'

'I'll have them when I get back,' he said. 'I won't have much time. I'm being picked up by a detective-superintendent called Miller at two o'clock. He wants me to look through some photos to see if I can recognise the man I saw. If he's early, give him a cup of tea or something.'

The door banged. It was suddenly very quiet. She sat there, thoroughly bewildered by it all, unable to comprehend what he had told her. She was a quiet girl. She knew little of life. Her childhood had been spent in special schools for the blind. After the death of her parents, music college. And then Uncle Michael had returned and for the first time in years, she had somebody to care about again. Who cared about her.

But as always, there was solace in her music and she turned back to the piano, feeling expertly through the Braille music transcripts for the Chopin Prelude she was working on. It wasn't there. She frowned in bewilderment and then suddenly remembered going across to the church earlier to play the organ and the stranger who'd spoken to her. She must have left the piece she wanted over there with her organ transcripts.

She went out into the hall, found a raincoat and a walking stick and let herself out of the front door.

It was still raining hard as Father da Costa hurried through the churchyard and unlocked the small door which led directly into the sacristy. He put on his alb, threw a violet stole over his shoulder and went to hear confession.

He was late – not that it mattered very much. Few people came at that time of day. Perhaps the odd shopper or office worker who found the old church convenient. On some days he waited the statutory half an hour and no one came at all.

The church was cold and smelt of damp, which wasn't particularly surprising as he could no longer meet the heating bill. A young woman was just lighting another candle in front of the Virgin, and as he moved past he was aware of at least two other people sitting waiting by the confessional box.

He went inside, murmured a short prayer and settled himself. The prayer hadn't helped, mainly because his mind was still in a turmoil, obsessed with what he had seen at the cemetery.

The door clicked on the other side of the screen and a woman started to speak. Middle-aged from the sound of her. He hastily forced himself back to reality and listened to what she had to say. It was nothing very much. Sins of omission in the main. Some minor dishonesty concerning a grocery bill. A few petty lies.

The next was a young woman, presumably the one he had seen lighting the candle to the Virgin. She started hesitantly. Trivial matters on the whole. Anger, impure thoughts, lies. And she hadn't been to Mass for three months.

'Is that all?' he prompted her in the silence.

It wasn't, of course, and out it came. An affair with her employer, a married man.

'How long has this been going on?' da Costa asked her.

'For three months, Father.'

The exact period since she had last been to Mass.

'This man has made love to you?'

'Yes, Father.'

'How often?'

'Two or three times a week. At the office. When everyone else has gone home.'

There was a confidence in her voice now, a calmness. Of course bringing things out into the open often made people feel like that, but this was different.

'He has children?'

'Three, Father.' There was a pause. 'What can I do?'

'The answer is so obvious. Must be. Leave this place, find another job. Put him out of your mind.'

'I can't do that.'

'Why?' he said, and added with calculated brutality, 'Because you enjoy it?'

'Yes, Father,' she said simply.

'And you're not prepared to stop?'

'I can't!' For the first time she cracked, just a little, but there was panic there now.

'Then why have you come here?'

'I haven't been to Mass in three months, Father.'

He saw it all then and it was really so beautifully simple, so pitifully human.

'I see,' he said. 'You can't do without God either.'

She started to cry quietly. 'This is a waste of time, Father, because I can't say I won't go with him again when I know damn well my body will betray me every time I see him. God knows that. If I said any different I'd be lying to him as well as you and I couldn't do that.'

How many people were that close to God? Father da Costa was filled with a sense of incredible wonder. He took a deep breath to hold back the lump that rose in his throat and threatened to choke him.

He said in a firm, clear voice, 'May Our Lord Jesus Christ absolve you, and I, by his authority, absolve you from every bond of excommunication and interdict, so far as I can, and you have need. Therefore, I absolve you from your sins in the name of the Father and of the Son and of the Holy Spirit.'

There was silence for a moment and then she said, 'But I can't promise I won't see him again.'

'I'm not asking you to,' da Costa said. 'If you feel you owe me anything, find another job, that's all I ask. We'll leave the rest up to God.'

There was the longest pause of all now and he waited, desperately anxious for the right answer, aware of an unutterable sense of relief when it came. 'Very well, Father, I promise.'

'Good. Evening Mass is at six o'clock. I never get more than fifteen or twenty people. You'll be very welcome.'

The door clicked shut as she went and he sat there feeling suddenly drained. With any luck, he'd said the right thing, handled it the right way. Only time would tell.

It was a change to feel useful again. The door clicked, there was the scrape of the chair being moved on the other side of the grille.

'Please bless me, Father.'

It was an unfamiliar voice. Soft. Irish – an educated man without a doubt.

Father da Costa said, 'May our Lord Jesus bless you and help you to tell your sins.'

There was a pause before the man said, 'Father, are there any circumstances under which what I say to you now could be passed on to anyone else?'

Da Costa straightened in his chair. 'None whatsoever. The secrets of the confessional are inviolate.'

'Good,' the man said. 'Then I'd better get it over with. I killed a man this morning.'

Father da Costa was stunned. 'Killed a man?' he whispered. 'Murdered, you mean?'

'Exactly.'

With a sudden, terrible premonition, da Costa reached forward, trying to peer through the grille. On the other side, a match flared in the darkness and for the second time that day, he looked into the face of Martin Fallon.

The church was still when Anna da Costa came out of the sacristy and crossed to the choir stalls. The Braille transcripts were where she had left them. She found what she was looking for with no difficulty. She put the rest back on the stand and sat there for a few moments, remembering the stranger with the soft Irish voice.

He'd been right about the trumpet stop. She put out a hand and touched it gently. One thing putting everything else out of joint. How strange. She reached for her walking stick and stood up and somewhere below her in the body of the church, a door banged and her uncle's voice was raised in anger. She froze, standing perfectly still, concealed by the green curtains which hung beside the organ.

Father da Costa erupted from the confessional box, flinging the door wide. She had never heard such anger in his voice before.

'Come out – come out, damn you, and look me in the face if you dare!'

Anna heard the other door in the confessional box click open, there was the softest of footfalls and then a quiet voice said, 'Here we are again then, Father.'

Fallon stood beside the box, hands in the pockets of the navy blue trenchcoat. Father da Costa moved closer, his voice a hoarse whisper.

'Are you a Catholic?'

'As ever was, Father.' There was a light, mocking note in Fallon's voice.

'Then you must know that I cannot possibly grant you absolution in this matter. You murdered a man in cold blood this morning. I saw you do it. We both know that.' He drew himself up. 'What do you want with me?'

'I've already got it, Father. As you said, the secrets of the confessional are inviolate. That makes what I told you privileged information.'

There was an agony in Father da Costa's voice that cut into Anna's heart like a knife. 'You used me!' he cried. 'In the worst possible way. You've used this church.'

'I could have closed your mouth by putting a bullet between your eyes. Would you have preferred that?'

'In some ways I think I would.' Father da Costa had control of himself again now. He said, 'What is your name?'

'Fallon – Martin Fallon.'

'Is that genuine?'

'Names with me are like the Book of the Month. Always changing. I'm not wanted as Fallon. Let's put it that way.'

'I see,' Father da Costa said. 'An interesting choice. I once knew a priest of that name. Do you know what it means in Irish?'

'Of course. Stranger from outside the campfire.'

'And you consider that appropriate?'

'I don't follow you.'

'I mean, is that how you see yourself? As some romantic desperado outside the crowd?'

Fallon showed no emotion whatsoever. 'I'll go now. You won't see me again.'

He turned to leave and Father da Costa caught him by the arm. 'The man who paid you to do what you did this morning, Fallon? Does he know about me?'

Fallon stared at him for a long moment, frowning slightly, and then he smiled. 'You've nothing to worry about. It's taken care of.'

'For such a clever man, you really are very foolish,' Father da Costa told him.

The door at the main entrance banged open in the wind. An old woman in a headscarf entered. She dipped her fingers in the holy water, genuflected and came up the aisle.

Father da Costa took Fallon's arm firmly. 'We can't talk here. Come with me.'

At one side of the nave there was an electric cage hoist, obviously used by workmen for access to the tower. He pushed Fallon inside and pressed the button. The cage rose through the network of scaffolding, passing through a hole in the roof.

It finally jerked to a halt and da Costa opened the gate and led the way out on to a catwalk supported by scaffolding that encircled the top of the tower like a ship's bridge.

'What happened here?' Fallon asked.

'We ran out of money,' Father da Costa told him and led the way along the catwalk in the rain.

Neither of them heard the slight whirring of the electric motor as the cage dropped back to the church below. When it reached ground level, Anna da Costa entered, closed the gate and fumbled for the button.

The view of the city from the catwalk was magnificent although the grey curtain of the rain made things hazy in the middle distance. Fallon gazed about him with obvious pleasure. He had changed in some subtle, indefinable way and smiled slightly.

'Now this I like. Earth hath not anything to show more fair: isn't that what the poet said?'

'Great God in heaven, I bring you up here to talk seriously and you quote Wordsworth to me? Doesn't anything touch you at all?'

'Not that I can think of.' Fallon took out a packet of cigarettes. 'Do you use these?'

Father da Costa hesitated, then took one angrily. 'Yes, I will, damn you.'

'That's it, Father, enjoy yourself while you can,' Fallon said as he struck a match and gave him a light. 'After all, we're all going to hell the same way.'

'You actually believe that?'

'From what I've seen of life it would seem a reasonable conclusion to me.'

Fallon leaned on the rail, smoking his cigarette, and Father da Costa watched him for a moment, feeling strangely helpless. There was obvious intelligence here – breeding, strength of character – all the qualities and yet it seemed impossible to reach through and touch the man in any way.

'You're not a practising Catholic?' he said at last.

Fallon shook his head. 'Not for a long time.'

'Can I ask why?'

'No,' Fallon told him calmly.

Father da Costa tried again. 'Confession, Fallon, is a Sacrament. A Sacrament of Reconciliation.'

He suddenly felt rather silly, because this was beginning to sound dangerously like one of his Confirmation classes at the local Catholic school, but he pressed on.

'When we go to confession we meet Jesus who takes us to himself and, because we are in him and because we are sorry, God our Father forgives us.'

'I'm not asking for any forgiveness,' Fallon said. 'Not from anybody.'

'No man can damn himself for all eternity in this way,' Father da Costa said sternly. 'He has not the right.'

'Just in case you hadn't heard, the man I shot was called Krasko and he was the original thing from under a stone. Pimp, whoremaster, drug-pusher. You name it, he had a finger in it. And you want me to say sorry? For him?'

'Then he was the law's concern.'

'The law!' Fallon laughed harshly. 'Men like him are above the law. He's been safe for years behind a triple wall of money, corruption and lawyers. By any kind of logic I'd say I've done society a favour.'

'For thirty pieces of silver?'

'Oh, more than that, Father. Much more,' Fallon told him. 'Don't worry, I'll put something in the poor box on the way out. I can afford it.' He flicked his cigarette out into space. 'I'll be going now.'

He turned and Father da Costa grabbed him by the sleeve, pulling him round. 'You're making a mistake, Fallon. I think you'll find that God won't let you have it your way.'

Fallon said coldly, 'Don't be stupid, Father.'

'In fact, he's already taken a hand,' Father da Costa continued. 'Do you think I was there in that cemetery at that particular moment by accident?' He shook his head. 'Oh, no, Fallon. You took one life, but God has made you responsible for another – mine.'

Fallon's face was very pale now. He took a step back, turned and walked towards the hoist without a word. As he drew abreast of a buttress, some slight noise caused him to look to his left and he saw Anna da Costa hiding behind it.

He drew her out gently, but in spite of that fact, she cried out in fear. Fallon said softly. 'It's all right. I promise you.'

Father da Costa hurried forward and pulled her away from him. 'Leave her alone.'

Anna started to weep softly as he held her in his arms. Fallon stood looking at them, a slight frown on his face. 'Perhaps she's heard more than was good for her.'

Father da Costa held Anna away from him a little and looked down at her. 'Is that so?'

She nodded, whispering, 'I was in the church.' She turned reaching out her hands, feeling her way to Fallon. 'What kind of man are you?'

One hand found his face as he stood there as if turned to stone. She drew back hastily as if stung and da Costa put a protective arm about her again.

'Leave us!' she whispered hoarsely to Fallon. 'I'll say nothing of what I heard to anyone, I promise, only go away and don't come back. Please!' There was a passionate entreaty in her voice.

Father da Costa held her close again and Fallon said, 'Does she mean it?'

'She said it, didn't she?' Father da Costa told him. 'We take your guilt on our souls, Fallon. Now get out of here.'

Fallon showed no emotion at all. He turned and walked to the hoist. As he opened the gate, da Costa called, 'Two of us now, Fallon. Two lives to be responsible for. Are you up to that?'

Fallon stood there for a long moment, a hand on the open gate. Finally, he said softly, 'It will be all right. I gave you my word. My own life on it, if you like.'

He stepped into the hoist and closed the gate. There was the gentle whirring of the electric motor, a dull echo from below as the cage reached the ground floor.

Anna looked up. 'He's gone?' she whispered.

Father da Costa nodded. 'It's all right now.'

'He was in the church earlier,' she said. 'He told me what was wrong with the organ. Isn't that the strangest thing?'

'The organ?' Da Costa stared down at her in bewilderment and then he sighed, shaking his head and turned her gently round. 'Come on, now, I'll take you home. You'll catch your death.'

They stood at the cage, waiting for the gate to come up after he had pressed the button. Anna said slowly, 'What are we going to do, Uncle Michael?'

'About Martin Fallon?' He put an arm about her shoulder. 'For the moment, nothing. What he told me in the church spilled over from the confessional box because of my anger and impatience so that what you overheard was still strictly part of that original confession. I'm afraid I can't look at it in any other way.' He sighed. 'I'm sorry, Anna. I know this must be an intolerable burden for you, but I must ask you to give me your promise not to speak of this to anyone.'

'But I already have,' she said. 'To him.'

A strange thing to say and it troubled him deeply as the cage arrived and they moved inside and made the quick descent to the church.

Alone in his study, he did a thing he seldom did so early in the day and poured himself a glass of whisky. He sipped it slowly and stood, one hand on the marble mantelpiece and stared down into the flames of the small coal fire.

'And what do we do now, Michael?' he asked himself softly.

It was an old habit, this carrying on a conversation with his inner self. A relic of three years of solitary confinement in a Chinese prison cell in North Korea. Useful in any situation where he needed to be as objective as possible about some close personal problem.

But then, in a sense, this wasn't his problem, it was Fallon's, he saw that suddenly with startling clarity. His own situation was such that his hands were tied. There was little that he could do or say. The next move would have to be Fallon's.

There was a knock at the door and Anna appeared. 'Superintendent Miller to see you, Uncle Michael.'

Miller moved into the room, hat in hand. 'There you are, Superintendent,' da Costa said. 'Have you met my niece?'

He made a formal introduction. Anna was remarkably controlled. In fact she showed no nervousness at all, which surprised him.

'I'll leave you to it.' She hesitated, the door half-open. 'You'll be going out, then?'

'Not just yet,' Father da Costa told her.

Miller frowned. 'But I don't understand, Father, I thought . . .'

'A moment, please, Superintendent,' Father da Costa said and glanced at Anna. She went out, closing the door softly and he turned again to Miller. 'You were saying?'

'Our arrangement was that you were to come down to the Department to look at some photos,' Miller said.

'I know, Superintendent, but that won't be possible now.'

'May I ask why not, Father?' Miller demanded.

Father da Costa had given considerable thought to his answer, yet in the end could manage nothing more original than, 'I'm afraid I wouldn't be able to help you, that's all.'

Miller was genuinely puzzled and showed it. 'Let's start again, Father. Perhaps you didn't understand me properly. All I want you to do is to come down to the Department to look at some photos in the hope that you might recognise our friend of this morning.'

'I know all that,' Father da Costa told him.

'And you still refuse to come?'

'There wouldn't be any point.'

'Why not?'

'Because I can't help you.'

For a moment, Miller genuinely thought he was going out of his mind. This couldn't be happening. It just didn't make any kind of sense, and then he was struck by a sudden, dreadful suspicion.

'Has Meehan been getting at you in some way?'

'Meehan?' Father da Costa said, his genuine bewilderment so perfectly obvious that Miller immediately dropped the whole idea.

'I could have you brought in formally, Father, as a material witness.'

'You can take a horse to water but you can't make him drink, Superintendent.'

'I can have a damn good try,' Miller told him grimly. He walked to the door and opened it. 'Don't make me take you in formally, sir. I'd rather not but I will if I have to.'

'Superintendent Miller,' Father da Costa said softly, 'men of a harsher disposition than you have tried to make me speak in circumstances where it was not appropriate. They did not succeed and neither will you, I can assure you. No power on earth can make me speak on this matter if I do not wish to.'

'We'll see about that, sir. I'll give you some time to think this matter over, then I'll be back.' He was about to walk out when a sudden wild thought struck him and he turned, slowly, 'Have you see him again, sir, since this morning? Have you been threatened? Is your life in any kind of danger?'

'Goodbye, Superintendent,' Father da Costa said.

The front door banged. Father da Costa turned to finish his whisky and Anna moved silently into the room. She put a hand on his arm.

'He'll go to Monsignor O'Halloran.'

'The bishop being at present in Rome, that would seem the obvious thing to do,' he said.

'Hadn't you better get there first?'

'I suppose so.' He emptied his glass and put it on the mantelpiece. 'What about you?'

'I want to do some more organ practice. I'll be all right.'

She pushed him out into the hall and reached for his coat from the stand with unerring aim. 'What would I do without you?' he said.

She smiled cheerfully. 'Goodness knows. Hurry back.'

He went out, she closed the door after him. When she turned, the smile had completely disappeared. She went back into his study, sat down by the fire and buried her face in her hands.

Nick Miller had been a policeman for almost a quarter of a century. Twenty-five years of working a three-shift system. Of being disliked by his neighbours, of being able to spend only one weekend in seven at home with his family and the consequent effect upon his relationship with his son and daughter.

He had little formal education but he was a shrewd, clever man with the ability to cut through to the heart of things, and this, coupled with an extensive knowledge of human nature gained from a thousand long, hard Saturday nights on the town, had made him a good policeman.

He had no conscious thought or even desire to help society. His job was in the main to catch thieves, and society consisted of the civilians who sometimes got mixed up in the constant state of guerrilla warfare which existed between the police and the criminal. If anything, he preferred the criminal. At least you knew where you were with him.

But Dandy Jack Meehan was different. One corruption was all corruption, he'd read that somewhere and if it applied to any human being, it applied to Meehan.

Miller loathed him with the kind of obsessive hate that was in the end self-destructive. To be precise, ten years of his life had gone to Dandy Jack without the slightest hint of success. Meehan had to be behind the Krasko killing, that was a fact of life. The rivalry between the two men had been common knowledge for at least two years.

For the first time in God knows how long he'd had a chance and now, the priest . . .

When he got into the rear of the car he was shaking with anger, and on a sudden impulse he leaned across and told his driver to take him to the headquarters of Meehan's funeral business. Then he sat back and tried to light his pipe with trembling fingers.

5

Dandy Jack

Paul's Square was a green lung in the heart of the city, an acre of grass and flower-beds and willow trees with a fountain in the centre surrounded on all four sides by Georgian terrace houses, most of which were used as offices by barristers, solicitors or doctors and beautifully preserved.

There was a general atmosphere of quiet dignity and Meehan's funeral business fitted in perfectly. Three houses on the north side had been converted to provide every possible facility from a flower shop to a Chapel of Rest. A mews entrance to one side gave access to a car park and garage area at the rear surrounded by high walls so that business could be handled as quietly and as unobtrusively as possible, a facility which had other uses on occasion.

When the big Bentley hearse turned into the car park shortly after one o'clock, Meehan was sitting up front with the chauffeur and Billy. He wore his usual double-breasted melton overcoat and Homburg hat and a black tie for he had been officiating personally at a funeral that morning.

The chauffeur came round to open the door and Meehan got out followed by his brother. 'Thanks, Donner,' he said.

A small grey whippet was drinking from a dish at the rear entrance. Billy called, 'Here, Tommy!' It turned, hurled itself across the yard and jumped into his arms.

Billy fondled its ears and it licked his face frantically. 'Now then, you little bastard,' he said with genuine affection.

'I've told you before,' Meehan said. 'He'll ruin your coat. Hairs all over the bloody place.'

As he moved towards the rear entrance, Varley came out of the garage and stood waiting for him, cap in hand. A muscle twitched nervously in his right cheek, his forehead was beaded with sweat. He seemed almost on the point of collapse.

Meehan paused, hands in pockets and looked him over calmly. 'You look awful, Charlie. You been a bad lad or something?'

'Not me, Mr Meehan,' Varley said. 'It's that sod, Fallon. He . . .'

'Not here, Charlie,' Meehan said softly. 'I always like to hear bad news in private.'

He nodded to Donner who opened the rear door and stood to one side. Meehan went into what was usually referred to as the receiving-room. It was empty except for a coffin on a trolley in the centre.

He put a cigarette in his mouth and bent down to read the brass nameplate on the coffin.

'When's this for?'

Donner moved to his side, a lighter ready in his hand. 'Three-thirty, Mr Meehan.'

He spoke with an Australian accent and had a slightly twisted mouth, the scar still plain where a hair lip had been cured by plastic surgery. It gave him a curiously repellent appearance, modified to a certain extent by the hand-tailored, dark uniform suit he wore.

'Is it a cremation?'

Donner shook his head. 'A burial, Mr Meehan.'

Meehan nodded. 'All right, you and Bonati better handle it. I've an idea I'm going to be busy.'

He turned, one arm on the coffin. Billy leaned against the wall, fondling the whippet. Varley waited in the centre of the room, cap in hand, the expression on his face that of a condemned man waiting for the trap to open beneath his feet at any moment and plunge him into eternity.

'All right, Charlie,' Meehan said. 'Tell me the worst.'

Varley told him, the words falling over themselves in his eagerness to get them out. When he had finished, there was a lengthy silence. Meehan had shown no emotion at all.

'So he's coming here at two o'clock?'

'That's what he said, Mr Meehan.'

'And the van? You took it to the wrecker's yard like I told you?'

'Saw it go into the crusher myself, just like you said.'

Varley waited for his sentence, face damp with sweat. Meehan smiled suddenly and patted him on the cheek. 'You did well, Charlie. Not your fault things went wrong. Leave it to me. I'll handle it.'

Relief seemed to ooze out of Varley like dirty water. He said weakly, 'Thanks, Mr Meehan. I did my best. Honest I did. You know me.'

'You have something to eat,' Meehan said. 'Then get back to the car wash. If I need you, I'll send for you.'

Varley went out. The door closed. Billy giggled as he fondled the whippet's ears. 'I told you he was trouble. We could have handled it ourselves only you wouldn't listen.'

Meehan grabbed him by the long white hair, the boy cried out in pain, dropping the dog. 'Do you want me to get nasty, Billy?' he said softly. 'Is that what you want?'

'I didn't mean any harm, Jack,' the boy whined.

Meehan shoved him away. 'Then be a good boy. Tell Bonati I want him, then take one of the cars and go and get Fat Albert.'

Billy's tongue flicked nervously between his lips. 'Albert?' he whispered. 'For God's sake, Jack, you know I can't stand being anywhere near that big creep. He frightens me to death.'

'That's good,' Meehan said. 'I'll remember that next time you step out of line. We'll call Albert in to take you in hand.' He laughed harshly. 'Would you like that?'

Billy's eyes were wide with fear. 'No, please, Jack,' he whispered. 'Not Albert.'

'Be a good lad, then.' Meehan patted his face and opened the door. 'On your way.'

Billy went out and Meehan turned to Donner with a sigh. 'I don't know what I'm going to do with him, Frank. I don't really.'

'He's young, Mr Meehan.'

'All he can think about is birds,' Meehan said. 'Dirty little tarts in mini skirts showing all they've got.' He shivered in genuine disgust. 'I even found him having it off with the cleaning woman one afternoon. Fifty-five if she was a day – and on my bed.'

Donner kept a diplomatic silence and Meehan opened an inner door and led the way through into the Chapel of Rest. The atmosphere was cool and fresh thanks to air-conditioning, and scented with flowers. Taped organ music provided a suitably devotional background.

There were half-a-dozen cubicles on either side. Meehan took off his hat and stepped into the first one. There were flowers everywhere and an oak coffin stood on a draped trolley.

'Who's this?'

'That young girl. The student who went through the windscreen of the sports car,' Donner told him.

'Oh yes,' Meehan said. 'I did her myself.'

He lifted the face cloth. The girl was perhaps eighteen or nineteen, eyes closed, lips slightly parted, the face so skilfully made up that she might only have been sleeping.

'You did a good job there, Mr Meehan,' Donner said.

Meehan nodded complacently. 'I've got to agree with you there, Frank. You know something. There was no flesh left on her left cheek when she came to me. That girl's face was mincemeat, I'm telling you.'

'You're an artist, Mr Meehan,' Donner said, genuine admiration in his voice. 'A real artist. It's the only word for it.'

'It's nice of you to say so, Frank. I really appreciate that.' Meehan switched off the light and led the way out. 'I always try to do my best, of course, but a case like that – a young girl. Well, you got to think of the parents.'

'Too true, Mr Meehan.'

They moved out of the chapel area into the front hall, the original Georgian features still beautifully preserved, blue and white Wedgewood plaques on the walls. There was a glass door leading to the reception office on the right. As they approached, they could hear voices and someone appeared to be crying.

The door opened and a very old woman appeared, sobbing heavily. She wore a headscarf and a shabby woollen overcoat bursting at the seams. She had a carrier bag over one arm and clutched a worn leather purse in her left hand. Her face was swollen with weeping.

Henry Ainsley, the reception clerk, moved out after her. He was a tall, thin man with hollow cheeks and sly, furtive eyes. He wore a neat, clerical-grey suit and sober tie and his hands were soft.

'I'm sorry, madam,' he was saying sharply, 'but that's the way it is. Anyway, you can leave everything in our hands from now on.'

'That's the way what is?' Meehan said, advancing on them. He put his hands on the old lady's shoulders. 'We can't have this, love. What's up?'

'It's all right, Mr Meehan. The old lady was just a bit upset. She's just lost her husband,' Ainsley said.

Meehan ignored him and drew the old lady into the office. He put her in a chair by the desk. 'Now then, love, you tell me all about it.'

He took her hand and she held on tight. 'Ninety, he was. I thought he'd last for ever and then I found him at the bottom of the stairs when I got back from chapel, Sunday night.' Tears streamed down her face. 'He was that strong, even at that age. I couldn't believe it.'

'I know, love, and now you've come here to bury him?'

She nodded. 'I don't have much, but I didn't want him to have a state funeral. I wanted it done right. I thought I could manage nicely what with the insurance money and then this gentleman here, he told me I'd need seventy pound.'

'Now look, Mr Meehan, it was like this,' Ainsley cut in.

Meehan turned and glanced at him bleakly. Ainsley faltered into silence. Meehan said, 'You paid cash, love?'

'Oh yes,' she said. 'I called at the insurance office on the way and they paid me out on the policy. Fifty pounds, I thought it would be enough.'

'And the other twenty?'

'I had twenty-five pounds in the Post Office.'

'I see.' Meehan straightened. 'Show me the file,' he said.

Ainsley stumbled to the desk and picked up a small sheaf of papers which shook a little as he held them out. Meehan leafed through them. He smiled delightedly and put a hand on the old woman's shoulders.

'I've got good news for you, love. There's been a mistake.'

'A mistake?' she said.

He took out his wallet and extracted twenty-five pounds. 'Mr Ainsley was forgetting about the special rate we've been offering to old age pensioners this autumn.'

She looked at the money, a dazed expression on her face. 'Special rate. Here, it won't be a state funeral will it? I wouldn't want that.'

Meehan helped her to her feet. 'Not on your life. Private. The best. I guarantee it. Now let's go and see about your flowers.'

'Flowers?' she said. 'Oh, that would be nice. He loved flowers, did my Bill.'

'All included, love.' Meehan glanced over his shoulder at Donner. 'Keep him here. I'll be back.'

A door had been cut through the opposite wall giving access to the flower shop next door. When Meehan ushered the old lady in, they were immediately approached by a tall, willowy young man with shoulder-length dark hair and a beautiful mouth.

'Yes, Mr Meehan. Can I be of service?' He spoke with a slight lisp.

Meehan patted his cheek. 'You certainly can, Rupert. Help this good lady choose a bunch of flowers. Best in the shop and a wreath. On the firm, of course.'

Rupert accepted the situation without the slightest question. 'Certainly, Mr Meehan.'

'And Rupert, see one of the lads runs her home afterwards.' He turned to the old lady. 'All right, love?'

She reached up and kissed his cheek. 'You're a good man. A wonderful man. God bless you.'

'He does, my love,' Dandy Jack Meehan told her. 'Every day of my life.' And he walked out.

'Death is something you've got to have some respect for,' Meehan said. 'I mean, this old lady. According to the form she's filled in, she's eighty-three. I mean, that's a wonderful thing.'

He was sitting in the swing chair in front of the desk. Henry Ainsley stood in front of him, Donner was by the door.

Ainsley stirred uneasily and forced a smile, 'Yes, I see what you mean, Mr Meehan.'

'Do you, Henry? I wonder.'

There was a knock at the door and a small, dapper man in belted continental raincoat entered. He looked like a Southern Italian, but spoke with a South Yorkshire accent.

'You wanted me, Mr Meehan?'

'That's it, Bonati. Come in.' Meehan returned to Ainsley. 'Yes, I really wonder about you, Henry. Now the way I see it, this was an insurance job. She's strictly working class. The policy pays fifty and you price the job at seventy and the old dear coughs up because she can't stand the thought of her Bill having a state funeral.' He shook his head. 'You gave her a receipt for fifty, which she's too tired and old to notice, and you enter fifty in the cash book.'

Ainsley was shaking like a leaf. 'Please, Mr Meehan, please listen. I've had certain difficulties lately.'

Meehan stood up. 'Has he been brought in, her husband?'

Ainsley nodded. 'This morning. He's in number three. He hasn't been prepared yet.'

'Bring him along,' Meehan told Donner and walked out.

He went into cubicle number three in the Chapel of Rest and switched on the light and the others followed him in. The old man was laying in an open coffin with a sheet over him and Meehan pulled it away. He was quite naked and had obviously been a remarkably powerful man in his day with the shoulders and chest of a heavyweight wrestler.

Meehan looked at him in awe. 'He was a bull this one and no mistake. Look at the dick on him.' He turned to Ainsley. 'Think of the women he pleasured. Think of that old lady. By God, I can see why she loved him. He was a man, this old lad.'

His knee came up savagely. Henry Ainsley grabbed for his privates too late and he pitched forward with a choked cry.

'Take him up to the coffin room,' Meehan told Donner. 'I'll join you in five minutes.'

When Henry Ainsley regained his senses, he was lying flat on his back, arms outstretched, Donner standing on one hand, Bonati on the other.

The door opened and Meehan entered. He stood looking down at him for a moment, then nodded. 'All right, pick him up.'

The room was used to store coffins which weren't actually made on the premises, but there were a couple of workbenches and a selection of carpenter's tools on a rack on the wall.

'Please, Mr Meehan,' Ainsley begged him.

Meehan nodded to Donner and Bonati dragged Ainsley back across one of the workbenches, arms outstretched, palms uppermost.

Meehan stood over him. 'I'm going to teach you a lesson, Henry. Not because you tried to fiddle me out of twenty quid. That's one thing that's definitely not allowed, but it's more than that. You see, I'm thinking of that old girl. She's never had a thing in her life. All she ever got was screwed into the ground.'

His eyes were smoking now and there was a slightly dreamy quality to his voice. 'She reminded me of my old mum, I don't know why. But I know one thing. She's earned some respect just like her old fella's earned something better than a state funeral.'

'You've got it wrong, Mr Meehan,' Ainsley gabbled.

'No, Henry, you're the one who got it wrong.'

Meehan selected two bradawls from the rack on the wall. He tested the point of one on his thumb then drove it through the centre of Ainsley's right palm pinning his hand to the bench. When he repeated the process with the other hand Ainsley fainted.

Meehan turned to Donner. 'Five minutes, then release him and tell him if he isn't in the office on time in the morning, I'll have his balls.'

'All right, Mr Meehan,' Donner said. 'What about Fallon?'

'I'll be in the preparation room. I've got some embalming to do. When Fallon comes, keep him in the office till I've had a chance to get up to the flat, then bring him up. And I want Albert up there as soon as he comes in.'

'Kid glove treatment, Mr Meehan?'

'What else, Frank? What else?'

Meehan smiled, patted the unconscious Ainsley on the cheek and walked out.

The preparation room was on the other side of the Chapel of Rest and when Meehan went in he closed the door. He liked to be alone on such occasions. It aided concentration and made the whole thing somehow much more personal.

A body waited for him on the table in the centre of the room covered with a sheet. Beside it on a trolley the tools of his trade were laid out neatly on a white cloth. Scalpels, scissors, forceps, surgical needles of various sizes, artery tubes, a large rubber bulb syringe and a glass jar containing a couple of gallons of embalming fluid. On a shelf underneath was an assortment of cosmetics, make-up creams and face powders, all made to order.

He pulled away the sheet and folded it neatly. The body was that of a woman of forty – handsome, dark-haired. He remembered the case. A history of heart trouble. She'd died in mid-sentence while discussing plans for Christmas with her husband.

There was still that look of faint surprise on her face that many people show in death; jaw dropped, mouth gaping as if in amazement that this should be happening to her of all people.

Meehan took a long curved needle and skilfully passed a thread from behind the lower lip, up through the nasal septum and down again, so that when he tightened the thread and tied it off, the jaw was raised.

The eyeballs had fallen into their sockets. He compensated for that by inserting a circle of cotton wool under each eyelid before closing it and cotton wool between the lips and gums and in the cheeks to give a fuller, more natural appearance.

All this he did with total absorption, whistling softly between his teeth, a frown of concentration on his face. His anger at Ainsley had disappeared totally. Even Fallon had ceased to exist. He smeared a little cream on the cold lips with one finger, stood back and nodded in satisfaction. He was now ready to start the embalming process.

The body weighed nine and a half stones which meant that he needed about eleven pints of fluid of the mixture he habitually used. Formaldehyde, glycerine, borax with a little phenol added and some sodium citrate as an anti-coagulant.

It was a simple enough case with little likelihood of complications so he decided to start with the axillary artery as usual. He extended the left arm at right angles to the body, the elbow supported on a wooden block, reached for a scalpel and made his first incision halfway between the mid-point of the collar-bone and the bend of the elbow.

It was perhaps an hour later as he tied off the last stitch that he became aware of some sort of disturbance outside. Voices were raised in anger and then the door flew open. Meehan glanced over his shoulder. Miller was standing there. Billy tried to squeeze past him.

'I tried to stop him, Jack.'

'Make some tea,' Meehan told him. 'I'm thirsty. And close that door. You'll ruin the temperature in here. How many times have I told you?'

Billy retired, the door closing softly behind him and Meehan turned back to the body. He reached for a jar of foundation cream and started to rub some into the face of the dead woman with infinite gentleness, ignoring Miller completely.

Miller lit a cigarette, the match rasping in the silence and Meehan said without turning round, 'Not in here. In here we show a little respect.'

'Is that a fact?' Miller replied, but he still dropped the cigarette on the floor and stepped on it.

He approached the table. Meehan was now applying a medium red cream rouge to the woman's cheekbones, his fingers bringing her back to life by the minute.

Miller watched for a moment in fascinated horror. 'You really like your work, don't you, Jack?'

'What do you want?' Meehan asked calmly.

'You.'

'Nothing new in that, is there?' Meehan replied. 'I mean, anybody falls over and breaks a leg in this town you come to me.'

'All right,' Miller said. 'So we'll go through the motions. Jan Krasko went up to the cemetery this morning to put flowers on his mother's grave. He's been doing that for just over a year now – every Thursday without fail.'

'So the bastard has a heart after all. Why tell me?'

'At approximately ten past eleven somebody put a bullet through his skull. A real pro job. Nice and public, so everyone would get the message.'

'And what message would that be?'

'Toe the Meehan line or else.'

Meehan dusted the face with powder calmly. 'I had a funeral this morning,' he said. 'Old Marcus the draper. At ten past eleven I was sitting in St Saviour's listening to the vicar say his piece. Ask Billy – he was with me. Along with around a couple of hundred other people including the mayor. He had a lot of friends had old Mr Marcus, but then he was a gentleman. Not many of his kind left these days.'

He brightened the eyebrows and lashes with Vaseline and coloured the lips. The effect was truly remarkable. The woman seemed only to sleep.

Miller said, 'I don't care where you were. It was your killing.'

Meehan turned to face him, wiping his hands on a towel. 'Prove it,' he said flatly.

All the frustration of the long years, all the anger, welled up in Miller threatening to choke him so that he pulled at his tie, wrenching open his collar.

'I'll get you for this, Meehan,' he said. 'I'll lay it on you if it's the last thing I do. This time you've gone too far.'

Meehan's eyes became somehow luminous, his entire personality assumed a new dimension, power seemed to emanate from him like electricity.

'You – touch me?' He laughed coldly, turned and gestured to the woman. 'Look at her, Miller. She was dead. I've given her life again. And you think you can touch me?'

Miller took an involuntary step back and Meehan cried, 'Go on, get the hell out of it!'

And Miller went as if all the devils in hell had been snapping at his heels.

It was suddenly very quiet in the preparation room. Meehan stood there, chest heaving, and then reached for the tin of vanishing cream and turned to the woman.

'I gave you life again,' he whispered. 'Life.'

He started to rub the cream firmly into the body.

6

Face to Face

It was still raining when Fallon crossed Paul's Square and went up the steps to the main entrance. When he tried the office it was empty and then Rupert appeared, having noticed him arrive through the glass door of the flower shop.

'Can I help you, sir?'

'Fallon's the name. Meehan's expecting me.'

'Oh yes, sir.' Rupert was exquisitely polite. 'If you'd like to wait in the office I'll just see where he is.'

He went out and Fallon lit a cigarette and waited. It was a good ten minutes before Rupert reappeared.

'I'll take you up now, sir,' he said, and with a flashing smile led the way out into the hall.

'And where would up be?' Fallon asked him.

'Mr Meehan's had the attics of the three houses knocked together into a penthouse suite for his personal use. Beautiful.'

They reached a small lift and as Rupert opened the door Fallon said, 'Is this the only way?'

'There's the back stairs.'

'Then the back stairs it is.'

Rupert's ready smile slipped a little. 'Now don't start to play games, ducky. It'll only get Mr Meehan annoyed, which means I'll end up having one hell of a night and to be perfectly frank, I'm not in the mood.'

'I'd have thought you'd have enjoyed every golden moment,' Fallon said and kicked him very hard on the right shin.

Rupert cried out and went down on one knee and Fallon took the Ceska out of his right-hand pocket. He had removed the silencer, but it was still a deadly-looking item in every way. Rupert went white, but he was game to the last.

'He'll crucify you for this. Nobody mixes it with Jack Meehan and passes the post first.'

Fallon put the Ceska back in his pocket. 'The stairs,' he said softly.

'All right,' Rupert leaned down to rub his shin. 'It's your funeral, ducky.'

The stairway started beside the entrance to the Chapel of Rest and they climbed three flights, Rupert leading the way. There was a green baize door at the top and he paused a few steps below. 'That leads directly into the kitchen.'

Fallon nodded. 'You'd better go back to minding the shop then, hadn't you?'

Rupert needed no second bidding and went back down the stairs quickly. Fallon tried the door which opened to his touch. As Rupert had said, a kitchen was on the other side. The far door stood ajar and he could hear voices.

He crossed to it on tiptoe and looked into a superbly furnished lounge with broad dormer windows at either end. Meehan was sitting in a leather club chair, a book in one hand, a glass of whisky in the other. Billy, holding the whippet, stood in front of an Adam fireplace in which a log fire was burning brightly. Donner and Bonati waited on either side of the lift.

'What's keeping him, for Christ's sake?' Billy demanded.

The whippet jumped from his arms and darted across to the kitchen door. It stood there, barking, and Fallon moved into the lounge and crouched down to fondle its ears, his right hand still in his coat pocket.

Meehan dropped the book on the table and slapped a hand against his thigh. 'Didn't I tell you he was a hard-nosed bastard?' he said to Billy.

The telephone rang. He picked it up, listened for a moment and smiled. 'It's all right, sweetheart, you get back to work. I can handle it.' He replaced the receiver. 'That was Rupert. He worries about me.'

'That's nice,' Fallon said.

He leaned against the wall beside the kitchen door, hands in pockets. Donner and Bonati moved in quietly and stood behind the big leather couch facing him. Meehan sipped a little of his whisky and held up the book. It was *The City of God* by St Augustine.

'Read this one, have you, Fallon?'

'A long time ago.' Fallon reached for a cigarette with his left hand.

'It's good stuff,' Meehan said. 'He knew what he was talking about. God and the Devil, good and evil. They all exist. And sex.' He emptied his glass and belched. 'He really puts the record straight there. I mean, women just pump a man dry, like I keep trying to tell my little brother here only he won't listen. Anything in a skirt, he goes for. You ever seen a dog after a bitch in heat with it hanging half out? Well, that's our Billy twenty-four hours a day.'

He poured himself another whisky and Fallon waited. They all waited. Meehan stared into space. 'No, these dirty little tarts are no good to anybody and the boys are no better. I mean, what's happened to all the nice clean-cut lads of sixteen or seventeen you used to see around? These days, most of them look like birds from the rear.'

Fallon said nothing. There was a further silence and Meehan reached for the whisky bottle again. 'Albert!' he called. 'Why don't you join us?'

The bedroom door opened, there was a pause and a man entered the room who was so large that he had to duck his head to come through the door. He was a walking anachronism. Neanderthal man in a baggy grey suit and he must have weighed at least twenty stone. His head was completely bald and his arms were so long that his hands almost reached his knees.

He shambled into the room, his little pig eyes fixed on Fallon. Billy moved out of the way nervously and Albert sank into a chair on the other side of Meehan, next to the fire.

Meehan said, 'All right, Fallon. You cocked it up.'

'You wanted Krasko dead. He's on a slab in the mortuary right now,' Fallon said.

'And the priest who saw you in action? This Father da Costa?'

'No problem.'

'He can identify you, can't he? Varley says he was close enough to count the wrinkles on your face.'

'True enough,' Fallon said. 'But it doesn't matter. I've shut his mouth.'

'You mean you've knocked him off?' Billy demanded.

'No need.' Fallon turned to Meehan. 'Are you a Catholic?'

Meehan nodded, frowning. 'What's that got to do with it?'

'When did you last go to confession?'

'How in the hell do I know? It's so long ago I forget.'

'I went today,' Fallon said. 'That's where I've been. I waited my turn at da Costa's one o'clock confession. When I went in, I told him I'd shot Krasko.'

Billy Meehan said quickly, 'But that's crazy. He'd seen you do it himself, hadn't he?'

'But he didn't know it was me in that confessional box – not until he looked through the grille and recognised me and that was after I'd confessed.'

'So what, for Christ's sake?' Billy demanded.

But his brother was already waving him down, his face serious. 'I get it,' he said. 'Of course. Anything said to a priest at confession's got to be kept a secret. I mean, they guarantee that, don't they?'

'Exactly,' Fallon said.

'It's the biggest load of cobblers I've ever heard,' Billy said. 'He's alive, isn't he? And he knows. What guarantee do you have that he won't suddenly decide to shoot his mouth off?'

'Let's just say it isn't likely,' Fallon said. 'And even if he did, it wouldn't matter. I'm being shipped out from Hull Sunday night – or have you forgotten?'

Meehan said, 'I don't know. Maybe Billy has a point.'

'Billy couldn't find his way to the men's room unless you took him by the hand,' Fallon told him flatly.

There was a dead silence. Meehan gazed at him impassively and Albert picked a steel and brass poker out of the fireplace and bent it into a horseshoe shape between his great hands, his eyes never leaving Fallon's face.

Meehan chuckled unexpectedly. 'That's good – that's very good. I like that.'

He got up, walked to a desk in the corner, unlocked it and took out a large envelope. He returned to his chair and dropped the envelope on the coffee table.

'There's fifteen hundred quid in there,' he said. 'You get another two grand on board ship Sunday night plus a passport. That clears the account.'

'That's very civil of you,' Fallon said.

'Only one thing,' Meehan told him. 'The priest goes.'

Fallon shook his head. 'Not a chance.'

'What's wrong with you, then?' Meehan jeered. 'Worried, are you? Afraid the Almighty might strike you down? They told me you were big stuff over there, Fallon, running round Belfast, shooting soldiers and blowing up kids. But a priest is different, is that it?'

Fallon said, in what was little more than a whisper, 'Nothing happens to the priest. That's the way I want it. That's the way it's going to be.'

'The way *you* want it?' Meehan said and the anger was beginning to break through now.

Albert tossed the poker into the fireplace and stood up. He spoke in a rough, hoarse voice. 'Which arm shall I break first, Mr Meehan? His left or his right?'

Fallon pulled out the Ceska and fired instantly. The bullet splintered Albert's right kneecap and he went back over the chair. He lay there cursing, clutching his knee with both hands, blood pumping between his fingers.

For a moment, nobody moved and then Meehan laughed out loud. 'Didn't I tell you he was beautiful?' he said to Billy.

Fallon picked up the envelope and stowed it away in his raincoat. He backed into the kitchen without a word, kicked the door shut as Meehan called out to him and started down the stairs.

In the lounge, Meehan grabbed his coat and made for the lift. 'Come on, Billy!'

As he got the door open, Donner called, 'What about Albert?'

'Call that Pakistani doctor. The one who was struck off. He'll fix him up.'

As the lift dropped to the ground floor Billy said, 'Look, what are we up to?'

'Just follow me and do as you're bleeding well told,' Meehan said.

He ran along the corridor, through the hall and out of the front door. Fallon had reached the other side of the road and was taking one of the paths that led across the green centre of the square.

Meehan called to him and ran across the road, ignoring the traffic. The Irishman glanced over his shoulder but kept on walking and had reached the fountain before Meehan and Billy caught up with him.

He turned to face them, his right hand in his pocket and Meehan put up a hand defensively. 'I just want to talk.'

He dropped on to a bench seat, slightly breathless, and took out a handkerchief to wipe his face. Billy arrived a moment later just as the rain increased suddenly from a steady drizzle into a solid downpour.

He said, 'This is crazy. My bloody suit's going to be ruined.'

His brother ignored him and grinned up at Fallon disarmingly. 'You're hell on wheels, aren't you, Fallon? There isn't a tearaway in town who wouldn't run from Fat Albert, but you.' He laughed uproariously. 'You put him on sticks for six months.'

'He shouldn't have joined,' Fallon said.

'Too bloody true, but to hell with Albert. You were right, Fallon, about the priest, I mean.' Fallon showed no emotion at all, simply stood there watching him and Meehan laughed. 'Scout's honour. I won't lay a glove on him.'

'I see,' Fallon said. 'A change of heart?'

'Exactly, but it still leaves us with a problem. What to do with you till that boat leaves Sunday. I think maybe you should go back to the farm.'

'No chance,' Fallon said.

'Somehow I thought you might say that.' Meehan smiled good-humouredly. 'Still, we've got to find you something.' He turned to Billy. 'What about Jenny? Jenny Fox. Couldn't she put him up?'

'I suppose so,' Billy said sullenly.

'A nice kid,' Meehan told Fallon. 'She's worked for me in the past. I helped her out when she was having a kid. She owes me a favour.'

'She's a whore,' Billy said.

'So what?' Meehan shrugged. 'A nice, safe house and not too far away. Billy can run you up there.'

He smiled genially – even the eyes smiled – but Fallon wasn't taken in for a moment. On the other hand, the sober truth was that he did need somewhere to stay.

'All right,' he said.

Meehan put an arm around his shoulders. 'You couldn't do better. She cooks like a dream, that girl, and when it comes to dropping her pants she's a little firecracker, I can tell you.'

They went back across the square and followed the mews round to the car park at the rear. The whippet was crouched at the entrance, shivering in the rain. When Billy appeared, it ran to heel and followed him into the garage. When he drove out in a scarlet Scimitar, it was sitting in the rear.

Fallon slipped into the passenger seat and Meehan closed the door. 'I'd stick pretty close to home if I were you. No sense in running any needless risks at this stage, is there?'

Fallon didn't say a word and Billy drove away. The door to the reception room opened and Donner came out. 'I've rung for that quack, Mr Meehan. What happened to Fallon?'

'Billy's taking him up to Jenny Fox's place,' Meehan said. 'I want you to go over to the car wash and get hold of Varley. I want him outside Jenny's place within half an hour. If Fallon leaves, he follows and phones in whenever he can.'

'I don't follow, Mr Meehan.' Donner was obviously mystified.

'Just till we sort things out, Frank,' Meehan told him. 'Then we drop both of them. Him *and* the priest.'

Donner grinned as a great light dawned. 'That's more like it.'

'I thought you'd approve,' Meehan smiled, opened the door and went inside.

Jenny Fox was a small, rather hippy girl of nineteen with good breasts, high cheekbones and almond-shaped eyes. Her straight black hair hung shoulder-length in a dark curtain and the only flaw in the general picture was the fact that she had too much make-up on.

When she came downstairs she was wearing a simple, white blouse, black pleated mini skirt and high-heeled shoes and she walked with a sort of general and total movement of the whole body that most men found more than a little disturbing.

Billy Meehan waited for her at the bottom of the stairs and when she was close enough, he slipped a hand up her skirt. She stiffened slightly and he shook his head, a sly, nasty smile on his face.

'Tights again, Jenny. I told you I wanted you to wear stockings.'

'I'm sorry, Billy.' There was fear in her eyes. 'I didn't know you'd be coming today.'

'You'd better watch it, hadn't you, or you'll be getting one of my specials.' She shivered slightly and he withdrew his hand. 'What about Fallon? Did he say anything?'

'Asked me if I had a razor he could borrow. Who is he?'

'None of your business. He shouldn't go out, but if he does, give Jack a ring straight away. And try to find out where he's going.'

'All right, Billy.' She opened the front door for him.

He moved in close behind her, his arms about her waist. She could feel his hardness pressed against her buttocks and the hatred, the loathing rose like bile in her throat, threatening to choke her. He said softly, 'Another thing. Get him into bed. I want to see what makes him tick.'

'And what if he won't play?' she said.

'Stocking tops and suspenders. That's what blokes of his age go for. You'll manage.' He slapped her bottom and went out. She closed the door, leaning against it for a moment, struggling for breath. Strange how he always left her with that feeling of suffocation.

She went upstairs, moved along the corridor and knocked softly on Fallon's door. When she went in, he was standing in front of the washbasin in the corner by the window, drying his hands.

'I'll see if I can find you that razor now,' she said.

He hung the towel neatly over the rail and shook his head. 'It'll do later. I'm going out for a while.'

She was gripped by a sudden feeling of panic. 'Is that wise?' she said. 'I mean, where are you going?'

Fallon smiled as he pulled on his trenchcoat. He ran a finger down her nose in a strangely intimate gesture that brought a lump to her throat.

'Girl dear, do what you have to, which I presume means ringing Jack Meehan to say I'm taking a walk, but I'm damned if I'll say where to.'

'Will you be in for supper?'

'I wouldn't miss it for all the tea in China.' He smiled and was gone.

It was an old-fashioned phrase. One her grandmother had used frequently. She hadn't heard it in years. Strange how it made her want to cry.

When Miller went into the Forensic Department at police headquarters, he found Fitzgerald in the side laboratory with Johnson, the ballistics specialist. Fitzgerald looked excited and Johnson seemed reasonably complacent.

Miller said, 'I hear you've got something for me.'

Johnson was a slow, cautious Scot. 'That just could be, Superintendent.' He picked up a reasonably misshapen piece of lead with a pair of tweezers. 'This is what did all the damage. They found it in the gravel about three yards from the body.'

'Half an hour after you left, sir,' Fitzgerald put in.

'Any hope of making a weapon identification?' Miller demanded.

'Oh, I've pretty well decided that now.' There was a copy of *Small Arms of the World* beside Johnson. He flipped through it quickly, found the page he was searching for and pushed it across to Miller. 'There you are.'

There was a photo of the Ceska in the top right-hand corner. 'I've never even heard of the damn thing,' Miller said. 'How can you be sure?'

'Well, I've some more tests to run, but it's pretty definite. You see there are four factors which are constant in the same make of weapon. Groove and land marks on the bullet, their number and width, their direction, which means are they twisting to the right or left, and the rate of that twist. Once I have those facts, I simply turn to a little item entitled the *Atlas of Arms*, and thanks to the two German gentlemen who so painstakingly put the whole thing together, it's possible to trace the weapon which fits without too much difficulty.'

Miller turned to Fitzgerald. 'Get this information to CRO at Scotland Yard straight away. This Ceska's an out-of-the-way gun. If they feed that into the computer, it might throw out a name. Somebody who's used one before. You never know. I'll see you back in my office.'

Fitzgerald went out quickly and Miller turned to Johnson. 'Anything else, let me know at once.' He went back to his office where he found a file on his desk containing a résumé of Father da Costa's career. Considering the limited amount of time Fitzgerald had had, it was really very comprehensive.

He came in as Miller finished reading the file and closed it. 'I told you he was quite a man, sir.'

'You don't know the half of it,' Miller said and proceeded to tell him what had happened at the presbytery.

Fitzgerald was dumbfounded. 'But it doesn't make any kind of sense.'

'You don't think he's been got at?'

'By Meehan?' Fitzgerald laughed out loud. 'Father da Costa isn't the kind of man who can be got at by anybody. He's the sort who's always spoken up honestly. Said exactly how he felt, even when the person who was hurt most was himself. Look at his record. He's a brilliant scholar. Two doctorates. One in languages, the other in philosophy, and where's it got him? A dying parish in the heart of a rather unpleasant industrial city. A church that's literally falling down.'

'All right, I'm convinced,' Miller said. 'So he speaks up loud and clear when everyone else has the good sense to keep their mouths shut.' He opened the file again. 'And he's certainly no physical coward. During the war he dropped into Jugoslavia by parachute three times and twice into Albania. DSO in 1944. Wounded twice.' He shrugged impatiently. 'There's got to be an explanation. There must be. It doesn't make any kind of sense that he should refuse to come in like this.'

'But did he actually refuse?'

Miller frowned, trying to remember exactly what the priest had said. 'No, come to think of it, he didn't. He said there was no point to coming in, as he wouldn't be able to help.'

'That's a strange way of putting it,' Fitzgerald said.

'You're telling me. There was an even choicer item. When I told him I could always get a warrant, he said that no power on earth could make him speak on this matter if he didn't want to.'

Fitzgerald had turned quite pale. He stood up and leaned across the desk. 'He said that? You're sure?'

'He certainly did.' Miller frowned. 'Does it mean something?'

Fitzgerald turned away and moved across the room to the window. 'I can only think of one circumstance in which a priest would speak in such a way.'

'And what would that be?'

'If the information he had at his disposal had been obtained as part of confession.'

Miller stared at him. 'But that isn't possible. I mean, he actually saw this character up there at the cemetery. It wouldn't apply.'

'It could,' Fitzgerald said, 'if the man simply went into the box and confessed. Da Costa wouldn't see his face, remember – not then.'

'And you're trying to tell me that once the bloke has spilled his guts, da Costa would be hooked?'

'Certainly he would.'

'But that's crazy.'

'Not to a Catholic it isn't. That's the whole point of confession. That what passes between the priest and individual involved, no matter how vile, must be utterly confidential.' He shrugged. 'Just as effective as a bullet, sir.' Fitzgerald hesitated. 'When we were at the cemetery, didn't he tell you he was in a hurry to leave because he had to hear confession at one o'clock?'

Miller was out of his chair and already reaching for his raincoat. 'You can come with me,' he said. 'He might listen to you.'

'What about the autopsy?' Fitzgerald reminded him. 'I thought you wanted to attend personally.'

Miller glanced at his watch. 'There's an hour yet. Plenty of time.'

The lifts were all busy and he went down the stairs two at a time, heart pounding with excitement. Fitzgerald had to be right – it was the only explanation that fitted. But how to handle the situation? That was something else again.

When Fallon turned down the narrow street beside Holy Name, Varley was no more than thirty yards in the rear. Fallon had been aware of his presence within two minutes of leaving Jenny's place – not that it mattered. He entered the church and Varley made for the phone-box on the corner of the street and was speaking to Meehan within a few moments.

'Mr Meehan? It's me. He's gone into a church in Rockingham Street. The Church of the Holy Name.'

'I'll be there in five minutes,' Meehan said and slammed down the receiver.

He arrived in the scarlet Scimitar with Billy at the wheel to find Varley standing on the street corner, miserable in the rain. He came to meet them as they got out.

'He's still in there, Mr Meehan. I haven't been in myself.'

'Good lad,' Meehan said and glanced up at the church. 'Bloody place looks as if it might fall down at any moment.'

'They serve good soup,' Varley said. 'To dossers. They use the crypt as a day refuge. I've been in. The priest, he's Father da Costa, and his niece, run it between them. She's a blind girl. A real smasher. Plays the organ here.'

Meehan nodded. 'All right, you wait in a doorway. When he comes out, follow him again. Come on, Billy.'

He moved into the porch and opened the door gently. They passed inside and he closed it again quickly.

The girl was playing the organ, he could see the back of her head beyond the green baize curtain. The priest knelt at the altar rail in prayer. Fallon sat at one end of a pew halfway along the aisle.

There was a small chapel to St Martin de Porres on the right. Not a single candle flickered in front of his image, leaving the chapel in semi-darkness. Meehan pulled Billy after him into the concealing shadows and sat down in the corner.

'What in the hell are we supposed to be doing?' Billy whispered.

'Just shut up and listen.'

At that moment, Father da Costa stood up and crossed himself. As he turned he saw Fallon.

'There's nothing for you here, you know that,' he said sternly.

Anna stopped playing. She swung her legs over the seat as Fallon advanced along the aisle and Billy whistled softly. 'Christ, did you see those legs?'

'Shut up!' Jack hissed.

'I told you I'd see to things and I have done,' Fallon said as he reached the altar rail. 'I just wanted you to know that.'

'What am I supposed to do, thank you?' Father da Costa said.

The street door banged open, candles flickered in the wind as it closed again and to Jack Meehan's utter astonishment, Miller and Fitzgerald walked up the aisle towards the altar.

'Ah, there you are, Father,' Miller called. 'I'd like a word with you.'

'My God,' Billy Meehan whispered in panic. 'We've got to get out of here.'

'Like hell we do,' Meehan said and his hand gripped Billy's right knee like a vice. 'Just sit still and listen. This could be very interesting.'

7

Prelude and Fugue

Fallon recognised Miller for what he was instantly and waited, shoulders hunched, hands in the pockets of his trenchcoat, feet apart, ready to make whatever move was necessary. There was an elemental force to the man that was almost tangible. Father da Costa could feel it in the very air and the thought of what might happen here filled him with horror.

He moved forward quickly to place himself between Fallon and the two policemen as they approached. Anna paused uncertainly a yard or two on the other side of the altar rail.

Miller stopped, hat in hand, Fitzgerald a pace or two behind him. There was a slight, awkward silence and da Costa said, 'I think you've met my niece, Superintendent. He has Inspector Fitzgerald with him, my dear.'

'Miss da Costa,' Miller said formally and turned to Fallon.

Father da Costa said, 'And this is Mr Fallon.'

'Superintendent,' Fallon said easily.

He waited, a slight, fixed smile on his mouth and Miller, looking into that white, intense face, those dark eyes, was aware of a strange, irrational coldness as if somewhere, someone had walked over his grave, which didn't make any kind of sense – and then a sudden, wild thought struck him and he took an involuntary step backwards. There was a silence. Everyone waited. Rain drummed against a window.

It was Anna who broke the spell by taking a blind step towards the altar rail and stumbling. Fallon jumped to catch her.

'Are you all right, Miss da Costa?' he said easily.

'Thank you, Mr Fallon. How stupid of me.' Her slight laugh sounded very convincing as she looked in Miller's general direction. 'I've been having trouble with the organ. I'm afraid that, like the church, it's past its best. Mr Fallon has kindly agreed to give us the benefit of his expert advice.'

'Is that so?' Miller said.

She turned to Father da Costa. 'Do you mind if we start, Uncle? I know Mr Fallon's time is limited.'

'We'll go into the sacristy, if that's all right with you, Superintendent,' Father da Costa said. 'Or up to the house if you prefer.'

'Actually, I'd rather like to hang on here for a few minutes,' Miller told him. 'I'm a pianist myself, but I've always been rather partial to a bit of organ music. If Mr Fallon has no objection.'

Fallon gave him an easy smile. 'Sure and there's nothing like an audience, Superintendent, for bringing out the best in all of us,' and he took Anna by the arm and led her up through the choir stalls.

From the darkness at the rear of the little chapel to St Martin de Porres, Meehan watched, fascinated. Billy whispered, 'I said he was a nutter, didn't I? So how in the hell is he going to talk his way out of this one?'

'With his fingers, Billy, with his fingers,' Meehan said. 'I'd put a grand on it.' There was sincere admiration in his voice when he added. 'You know something. I'm enjoying every bleeding minute of this. It's always nice to see a real pro in action.' He sighed. 'There aren't many of us left.'

Fallon took off his trenchcoat and draped it over the back of a convenient choir stall. He sat down and adjusted the stool so that he could reach the pedals easily. Anna stood at his right hand.

'Have you tried leaving the trumpet in as I suggested?' he asked.

She nodded. 'It made quite a difference.'

'Good. I'll play something pretty solid and we'll see what else we can find wrong. What about the Bach Prelude and Fugue in D Major?'

'I only have it in Braille.'

'That's all right. I know it by heart.' He turned and looked down at Father da Costa and the two policemen on the other side of the altar rail. 'If you're interested, this is reputed to have been Albert Schweitzer's favourite piece.'

No one said a word. They stood there, waiting, and Fallon swung round to face the organ. It had been a long time – a hell of a long time and yet, quite suddenly and in some strange, incomprehensible way, it was only yesterday.

He prepared the swell organ, hands moving expertly – all stops except the Vox Humana and the Celeste and on the Great Organ, Diapasons and a four foot Principal.

He looked up at Anna gravely. 'As regards the Pedal Organ, I'd be disinclined to use any reed stops on this instrument. Only the sixteen-foot Diapason and the Bourdon and maybe a thirty-two-foot stop to give a good, solid tone. What do you think?'

She could not see the corner of his mouth lifted in a slight, sardonic smile and yet something of that smile was in his voice. She put a hand on his shoulder and said clearly, 'An interesting beginning, anyway.'

To her horror he said very softly, 'Why did you interfere?'

'Isn't that obvious?' she answered in a low voice. 'For Superintendent Miller and his inspector's sake. Now play.'

'God forgive you, but you're a terrible liar,' Fallon told her, and started.

He opened with a rising scale, not too fast, allowing each note to be heard, heeling and toeing with his left foot in a clear, bold, loud statement, playing with such astonishing power that Miller's wild surmise died on the instant for it was a masterly performance by any standard.

Father da Costa stood at the altar rail as if turned to stone, caught by the brilliance of Fallon's playing as he answered the opening statement with the chords of both hands on the sparkling Great Organ. He repeated, feet, then hands again, manual answering pedals until his left toe sounded the long four bar bottom A and his hands traced the brilliant passages announced by the pedals.

Miller tapped Father da Costa on the shoulder and whispered in his ear, 'Brilliant, but I'm running out of time, Father. Can we have our chat now?'

Father da Costa nodded reluctantly and led the way across to the sacristy. Fitzgerald was the last in and the door banged behind him in a sudden gust of wind.

Fallon stopped playing. 'Have they gone?' he asked softly.

Anna da Costa stared blindly down at him, a kind of awe on her face, reached out to touch his cheek. 'Who are you?' she whispered. 'What are you?'

'A hell of a question to ask any man,' he said and, turning back to the organ, he moved into the opening passage again.

The music could be heard in the sacristy, muted yet throbbing through the old walls with a strange power. Father da Costa sat on the edge of the table.

'Cigarette, sir?' Fitzgerald produced an old, silver case. Father da Costa took one and the light that followed.

Miller observed him closely. The massive shoulders, that weathered, used-up face, the tangled grey beard, and suddenly realised with something close to annoyance that he actually liked the man. It was precisely for this reason that he decided to be as formal as possible.

'Well, Superintendent?' Father da Costa said.

'Have you changed your mind, sir, since we last spoke?'

'Not in the slightest.'

Miller fought hard to control his anger and Fitzgerald moved in smoothly. 'Have you been coerced in any way since this morning, sir, or threatened?'

'Not at all, Inspector,' Father da Costa assured him with complete honesty.

'Does the name Meehan mean anything to you, sir?'

Father da Costa shook his head, frowning slightly, 'No, I don't think so. Should it?'

Miller nodded to Fitzgerald, who opened the briefcase he was carrying and produced a photo which he passed to the priest. 'Jack Meehan,' he said. 'Dandy Jack to his friends. That one was taken in London on the steps of West End Central police station after he was released for lack of evidence in an East End shooting last year.'

Meehan, wearing his usual double-breasted overcoat, smiled out at the world hugely, waving his hat in his right hand, his left arm encircling the shoulders of a well-known model girl.

'The girl is strictly for publicity purposes,' Fitzgerald said. 'In sexual matters his tastes run elsewhere. What you read on the sheet pinned to the back is all we have on him officially.'

Father da Costa read it with interest. Jack Meehan was forty-eight and had joined the Royal Navy in 1943 at eighteen, serving on minesweepers until 1945 when he had been sentenced to a year's imprisonment and discharged with ignominy for breaking a Petty Officer's jaw in a brawl. In 1948 he had served six months on a minor smuggling charge and in 1954 a charge of conspiracy to rob the mails had been dropped for lack of evidence. Since then, he had been questioned by the police on over forty occasions in connection with indictable offences.

'You don't seem to be having much success,' Father da Costa said with a slight smile.

'There's nothing funny about Jack Meehan,' Miller said. 'In twenty-five years in the police force he's the nastiest thing I've ever come across. Remember the Kray brothers and the Richardson torture gang? Meehan's worse than the whole damn lot of them put together. He has an undertaking business here in the city, but behind that façade of respectability he heads an organisation that controls drug-pushing, prostitution, gambling and protection in most of the big cities in the north of England.'

'And you can't stop him? I find that surprising.'

'Rule by terror, Father. The Krays got away with it for years. Meehan makes them look like beginners. He's had men shot on many occasions – usually the kind of shotgun blast in the legs that doesn't kill, simply cripples. He likes them around as an advertisement.'

'You know this for a fact?'

'And couldn't prove it. Just as I couldn't prove he was behind the worst case of organised child prostitution we ever had or that he disciplined one man by crucifying him with six-inch nails and another by making him eat his own excreta.'

For the briefest of moments, Father da Costa found himself back in that camp in North Korea – the first one where the softening up was mainly physical – lying half-dead in the latrine while a Chinese boot ground his face into a pile of human ordure. The guard had tried to make him eat, too, and he had refused, mainly because he thought he was dying anyway.

He pulled himself back to the present with an effort. 'And you think Meehan is behind the killing of Krasko this morning?'

'He has to be,' Miller told him. 'Krasko was, to put it politely, a business rival in every sense of the word. Meehan tried to take him under his wing and he refused. In Meehan's terms, he wouldn't see reason.'

'And a killer was brought in to execute him publicly?'

'To encourage the others,' Miller said. 'In a sense, the very fact that Meehan dares to do such a thing is a measure of just how sick he is. He knows that *I* know he's behind the whole thing. But he wants me to know – wants everyone to know. He thinks nothing can touch him.'

Father da Costa looked down at the photo, frowning, and Fitzgerald said, 'We could get him this time, Father, with your help.'

Father da Costa shook his head, his face grave. 'I'm sorry, Inspector. I really am.'

Miller said in a harsh voice, 'Father da Costa, the only inference we can draw from your strange conduct is that you are aware of the identity of the man we are seeking. That you are in fact protecting him. Inspector Fitzgerald here, himself a Catholic, has suggested a possible explanation to me. That your knowledge is somehow bound up with the secrets of the confessional, if that is the term. Is there any truth in that supposition?'

'Believe me, Superintendent, if I could help you I would,' Father da Costa told him.

'You still refuse?'

'I'm afraid so.'

Miller glanced at his watch. 'All right, Father, I have an appointment in twenty minutes and I'd like you to come with me. No threats – no coercion. Just a simple request.'

'I see,' Father da Costa said. 'May I be permitted to ask where we are going?'

'To attend the post mortem of Janos Krasko at the city mortuary.'

'I see,' Father da Costa said. 'Tell me, Superintendent, is this supposed to be a challenge?'

'That's up to you, Father.'

Father da Costa stood up, suddenly weary. His will to resist was at a new low. He was sick of the whole wretched business. Strangely enough the only thing of which he was aware with any clarity was the sound of the organ, muted and far away.

'I have evening Mass, Superintendent, and supper at the refuge afterwards. I can't be long.'

'An hour at the most, sir. I'll have you brought back by car, but we really will have to leave now.'

Father da Costa opened the sacristy door and led the way back into the church. He paused at the altar. 'Anna?' he called.

Fallon stopped playing and the girl turned to face him. 'I'm just going out, my dear, with Superintendent Miller.'

'What about Mass?' she said.

'I won't be long. As for the organ,' he added, 'perhaps Mr Fallon would come back after Mass? We could discuss it then.'

'Glad to, Father,' Fallon called cheerfully.

Father da Costa, Miller and Inspector Fitzgerald walked down the aisle, past the chapel of St Martin de Porres, where Jack Meehan and his brother still sat in the shadows, and out of the front door.

It banged in the wind. There was silence. Fallon said softly,

'Well now, at a rough estimate, I'd say you've just saved my neck. I think he suspected something, the good Superintendent Miller.'

'But not now,' she said. 'Not after such playing. You were brilliant.'

He chuckled softly. 'That might have been true once, as I'll admit with becoming modesty, but not any more. My hands aren't what they were, for one thing.'

'Brilliant,' she said. 'There's no other word for it.'

She was genuinely moved and for the moment it was as if she had forgotten that other darker side. She groped for his hands, a smile on her face.

'As for your hands – what nonsense.' She took them in hers, still smiling, and then that smile was wiped clean. 'Your fingers?' she whispered, feeling at them. 'What happened?'

'Oh, those.' He pulled his hands free and examined the ugly, misshapen finger-ends. 'Some unfriends of mine pulled out my nails. A small matter on which we didn't quite see eye to eye.'

He stood up and pulled on his coat. She sat there, horror on her face and reached out a hand as if to touch him, pawing at space. He helped her to her feet and placed her coat about her shoulders.

'I don't understand,' she said.

'And please God, you never should,' he told her softly. 'Come on now and I'll take you home.'

They went down the altar steps and out through the sacristy. The door closed behind them. There was a moment of silence and then Billy Meehan stood up.

'Thank God for that. Can we kindly get the hell out of here now?'

'You can, not me,' Meehan told him. 'Find Fallon and stick to him like glue.'

'But I thought that was Varley's job?'

'So now I'm putting you on to it. Tell Varley to wait outside.'

'And what about you,' Billy said sullenly.

'Oh, I'll wait here for the priest to get back. Time we had a word.' He sighed and stretched his arms. 'I like it here. Nice and peaceful in the dark with all those candles flickering away there. Gives a fella time to think.' Billy hesitated as if trying to find some suitable reply and Meehan said irritably, 'Go on, piss off out of it for Christ's sake. I'll see you later.'

He leaned back, arms folded, and closed his eyes and Billy left by the front entrance to do as he was told.

It was raining hard in the cemetery. As they moved along the path to the presbytery, Fallon slipped her arm in his.

'Sometimes I think it's never going to stop,' she said. 'It's been like this for days.'

'I know,' he said.

They reached the front door, she opened it and paused in the porch while Fallon stood at the bottom of the steps looking up at her.

'Nothing seems to make sense to me any longer,' she said. 'I don't understand you or what's happened today or any part of it – not after hearing you play. It doesn't make sense. It doesn't fit.'

He smiled up at her gently. 'Go in now, girl dear, out of the cold. Stay safe in your own small world.'

'Not now,' she said. 'How can I? You've made me an accessory now, isn't that what they call it? I could have spoken up, but I didn't.'

It was the most terrible thing she could have said to him. He said hoarsely, 'Then why didn't you?'

'I gave my uncle my word, had you forgotten? And I would not hurt him for worlds.'

Fallon moved back into the rain very softly. She called from the porch, 'Mr Fallon, are you there?'

He didn't reply. She stood there for a moment longer, uncertainty on her face, then went in and closed the door. Fallon turned and moved back along the path.

Billy had been watching them from the shelter of a large Victorian mausoleum, or rather, he had been watching Anna. She was different from the girls he was used to. Quiet, lady-like and yet she had an excellent figure. There was plenty of warmth beneath that cool exterior, he was certain of that, and the fact of her blindness made his stomach churn, exciting some perversity inside him and he got an almost instant erection.

Fallon paused, hands cupped to light a cigarette, and Billy drew back out of sight.

Fallon said, 'All right, Billy, I'm ready to go home now. Since you're here, you can drive me back to Jenny's place.'

Billy hesitated, then stepped reluctantly into the open. 'Think you're bleeding smart, don't you?'

'To be smarter than you doesn't take much, sonny,' Fallon told him. 'And another thing. If I catch you hanging around here again, I'll be very annoyed.'

'Why don't you go stuff yourself,' Billy told him furiously.

He turned and walked rapidly towards the gate. Fallon was smiling as he went after him.

The city mortuary was built like a fort and encircled by twenty-foot walls of red brick to keep out prying eyes. When Miller's car reached the main entrance the driver got out and spoke into a voice box on the wall. He climbed back behind the wheel. A moment later the great steel gate slid back automatically and they passed into an inner courtyard.

'Here we are, Father,' Miller said. 'The most modern mortuary in Europe, or so they say.'

He and Fitzgerald got out first and Father da Costa followed them. The inner building was all concrete and glass. Functional, but rather beautiful in its own way. They went up a concrete ramp to the rear entrance and a technician in white overalls opened the door for them.

'Good morning, Superintendent,' he said. 'Professor Lawlor said he'd meet you in the dressing-room. He's very anxious to get started.'

There was the constant low hum of the air-conditioning plant as they followed him along a maze of narrow corridors. Miller glanced over his shoulder at Father da Costa and said casually, 'They boast the purest air in the city up here. If you can breathe it at all, that is.'

It was the kind of remark that didn't seem to require an answer and Father da Costa made no attempt to make one. The technician opened a door, ushered them inside and left.

There were several washbasins, a shower in the corner, white hospital overalls and robes hanging on pegs on one wall. Underneath was a row of white rubber boots in various sizes. Miller and Fitzgerald removed their raincoats and the Superintendent took down a couple of white robes and passed one to Father da Costa.

'Here, put this on. You don't need to bother about boots.'

Father da Costa did as he was told and then the door opened and Professor Lawlor entered. 'Come on, Nick,' he said. 'You're holding me up.' And then he saw the priest and his eyes widened in surprise. 'Hello, Father.'

'I'd like Father da Costa to observe, if you've no objection,' Miller said.

Professor Lawlor was wearing white overalls and boots and long pale-green rubber gloves, which he pulled at impatiently, 'As long as he doesn't get in the way. But do let's get on with it. I've got a lecture at the medical school at five.'

He led the way out and they followed along a short corridor and through a rubber swing door into the post mortem room. It was lit by fluorescent lighting so bright that it almost hurt the eyes and there was a row of half-a-dozen stainless steel operating tables.

Janos Krasko lay on his back on the one nearest the door, head raised on a wooden block. He was quite naked. Two technicians stood ready beside a trolley on which an assortment of surgical instruments was laid out neatly. The greatest surprise for Father da Costa were the closed circuit television cameras, one set close up to the operating table, the other waiting nearby on a movable trolley.

'As you can see, Father, science marches on,' Miller said. 'These days in a case like this everything's videotaped and in colour.'

'Is that necessary?' Father da Costa asked him.

'It certainly is. Especially when you get the kind of defence council who hasn't got much to go on and tries bringing in his own expert witness. In other words, some other eminent pathologist with his own particular theory about what happened.'

One of the technicians was fastening a throat mike around Lawlor's throat and Miller nodded. 'The medical profession are great on opinions, Father, I've learned that the hard way.'

Lawlor smiled frostily. 'Don't get bitter in your old age, Nick. Have you witnessed a post mortem before, Father?'

'Not in your terms, Professor.'

'I see. Well, if you feel sick, you know where the dressing-room is and please stand well back – all of you.' He turned and addressed the camera men and technicians. 'Right, gentlemen, let's get started.'

It should have been like something out of a nightmare. That it wasn't was probably due to Lawlor as much as anything else. That and the general atmosphere of clinical efficiency.

He was really quite brilliant. More than competent in every department. An artist with a knife who kept up a running commentary in that dry, precise voice of his during the entire proceedings.

'Everything he says is recorded,' Miller whispered. 'To go with the video.'

Father da Costa watched, fascinated, as Lawlor drew a scalpel around the skull. He grasped the hair firmly and pulled the entire face forward, eyeballs and all, like a crumpled rubber mask.

He nodded to the technician who handed him a small electric saw and switched on. Lawlor began to cut round the top of the skull very carefully.

'They call it a de Soutter,' Miller whispered again. 'Works on a vibratory principle. A circular saw would cut too quickly.'

There was very little smell, everything being drawn up by extractor fans in the ceiling above the table. Lawlor switched off the saw and handed it to the technician. He lifted off the neat skullcap of bone and placed it on the table, then carefully removed the brain and put it in a rather commonplace red, plastic basin which one of the technicians held ready.

The technician carried it across to the sink and Lawlor weighed it carefully. He said to Miller, 'I'll leave my examination of this until I've finished going through the motions on the rest of him. All right?'

'Fine,' Miller said.

Lawlor returned to the corpse, picked up a large scalpel and opened the entire body from throat to belly. There was virtually no blood, only a deep layer of yellow fat, red meat underneath. He opened the body up like an old overcoat, working fast and efficiently, never stopping for a moment.

Father da Costa said, 'Is this necessary? The wound was in the head. We know that.'

'The Coroner will demand a report that is complete in every detail,' Miller told him. 'That's what the law says he's entitled to and that's what he expects. It's not as cruel as you think. We had a case the other year. An old man found dead at his home. Apparent heart failure. When Lawlor opened him up he was able to confirm that, and if he'd stopped at the heart that would have been the end of the matter.'

'There was more?'

'Fractured vertebrae somewhere in the neck area. I forget the details, but it meant the old boy had been roughly handled by someone, which led us to a character who'd been making a nuisance of himself preying on old people. The sort who knocks on the door, insists he was told to clean the drains and demands ten quid.'

'What happened to him?'

'The court accepted a plea of manslaughter. Gave him five years so he's due out soon. A crazy world, Father.'

'And what would you have done with him?'

'I'd have hung him,' Miller said simply. 'You see, for me, it's a state of war now. A question of survival. Liberal principles are all very fine as long as they leave you with something to have principles about.'

Which made sense in its own way and it was hard to argue. Father da Costa moved to one side as the technicians carried the various organs across to the sink in more plastic basins. Each item was weighed, then passed to Lawlor who sliced it quickly into sections on a wooden block with a large knife. Heart, lungs, liver, kidneys, intestines – they all received the same treatment with astonishing speed and the camera on the trolley recorded everything at his side.

Finally he was finished and put down his knife. 'That's it,' he said to Miller. 'Nothing worth mentioning. I'll go to town on the brain after I've had a cigarette.' He smiled at da Costa, 'Well, what did you think?'

'An extraordinary experience,' Father da Costa said. 'Disquieting more than anything else.'

'To find that man is just so much raw meat?' Professor Lawlor said.

'Is that what you think?'

'See for yourself.'

Lawlor crossed to the operating table, and Father da Costa went with him. The body was open to the view and quite empty. Gutted. Nothing but space from inside the rib-cage and down into the penis.

'Remember that poem of Eliot's The Hollow Men? Well, this is what he was getting at or so it's always seemed to me.'

'And you think that's all there is?'

'Don't you?' Lawlor demanded.

One of the technicians replaced the skullcap of bone and pulled the scalp back into place. Amazing how easily the face settled into position again. Quite remarkable.

Father da Costa said, 'A superb piece of engineering, the human body. Infinitely functional. There seems to be no task that a man cannot cope with if he so desires. Wouldn't you agree, Professor?'

'I suppose so.'

'Sometimes I find the mystery of it quite terrifying. I mean, is this all that's left in the end of an Einstein, let's say, or a Picasso? A gutted body, a few scraps of raw meat swilling about in the bottom of a plastic bucket?'

'Ah no you don't.' Lawlor grinned tiredly. 'No metaphysics, if you please, Father, I've got other things to do.' He turned to Miller. 'Have you seen enough?'

'I think so,' Miller said.

'Good, then get this Devil's Advocate out of here and leave me in peace to finish. It will be the morning before you get the full report now.' He grinned at Father da Costa again. 'I won't shake hands for obvious reasons, but any time you're passing just drop in. There's always someone here.'

He laughed at his own joke, was still laughing when they went back to the dressing-room. One of the technicians went with them to make sure that the robes they had worn went straight into the dirty laundry basket, so there was no opportunity to talk.

Miller led the way back outside, feeling tired and depressed. He had lost, he knew that already. The trouble was he didn't really know what to do next, except to take the kind of official action he'd been hoping to avoid.

It was still raining when they went out into the courtyard. When they reached the car, Fitzgerald opened the door and Father da Costa climbed in. Miller followed him. Fitzgerald sat in the front with the driver.

As they moved out into the city traffic, Miller said, 'I wanted you to see the reality of it and it hasn't made the slightest difference, has it?'

Father da Costa said, 'When I was twenty years of age, I dropped into the Cretan mountains by parachute, dressed as a peasant. All very romantic. Action by night – that sort of thing. When I arrived at the local village inn I was arrested at gunpoint by a German undercover agent. A member of the Feldgendarmerie.'

Miller was interested in spite of himself. 'You'd been betrayed?'

'Something like that. He wasn't a bad sort. Told me he was sorry, but that he'd have to hold me till the Gestapo got there. We had a drink together. I managed to hit him on the head with a wine bottle.'

Father da Costa stared back into the past and Miller said gently. 'What happened?'

'He shot me in the left lung and I choked him to death with my bare hands.' Father da Costa held them up. 'I've prayed for him every day of my life since.'

They turned into the street at the side of the church and Miller said wearily, 'All right, I get the picture.' The car pulled in at the kerb and there was a new formality in his voice when he said, 'In legal terms, your attitude in this matter makes you an accessory after the fact. You understand that?'

'Perfectly,' da Costa told him.

'All right,' Miller said. 'This is what I intend to do. I shall approach your superiors in a final effort to make you see sense.'

'Monsignor O'Halloran is the man you want. I tried to see him myself earlier, but he's out of town. He'll be back in the morning – but it won't do you any good.'

'Then I'll apply to the Director of Public Prosecutions for a warrant for your arrest.'

Father da Costa nodded soberly. 'You must do what you think is right. I see that, Superintendent.' He opened the door and got out. 'I'll pray for you.'

'Pray for me!' Miller ground his teeth together as the car moved away. 'Have you ever heard the like?'

'I know, sir,' Fitzgerald said. 'He's quite a man, isn't he?'

It was cold in the church and damp as Father da Costa opened the door and moved inside. Not long till Mass. He felt tired – wretchedly tired. It had been an awful day – the worst he could remember in a great many years – since the Chinese prison camp at Chong Sam. If only Fallon and Miller – all of them – would simply fade away, cease to exist.

He dipped his fingers in the Holy Water and on his right a match flared in the darkness of the little side chapel to St Martin de Porres as someone lit a candle, illuminating a familiar face.

There was a slight pause and then the Devil moved out of the darkness and Father da Costa girded up his loins to meet him.

8

The Devil and all his Works

'What do you want here, Mr Meehan?' Father da Costa said.

'You know who I am?'

'Oh, yes,' Father da Costa told him. 'I was taught to recognise the Devil from a very early age.'

Meehan stared at him for a moment in genuine amazement and then he laughed harshly, his head thrown back, and the sound echoed up into the rafters.

'That's good. I like that.' Father da Costa said nothing and Meehan shrugged and turned to look down towards the altar. 'I used to come here when I was a kid. I was an acolyte.' He turned and there was a challenge in his voice. 'You don't believe me?'

'Shouldn't I?'

Meehan nodded towards the altar. 'I've stood up there many a time when it was my turn to serve at Mass. Scarlet cassock, white cotta. My old lady used to launder them every week. She loved seeing me up there. Father O'Malley was the priest in those days.'

'I've heard of him,' Father da Costa said.

'Tough as old boots.' Meehan was warming to his theme now – enjoying himself. 'I remember one Saturday evening, a couple of drunken Micks came in just before Mass and started turning things upside down. Duffed them up proper, he did. Straight out on their ear. Said they'd desecrated God's house and all that stuff.' He shook his head. 'A real old sod, he was. He once caught me with a packet of fags I'd nicked from a shop round the corner. Didn't call the law. Just took a stick to me in the sacristy.' He chuckled. 'Kept me honest for a fortnight that, Father. Straight up.'

Father da Costa said quietly, 'What do you want here, Mr Meehan?'

Meehan made a sweeping gesture with one arm that took in the whole church. 'Not what it was, I can tell you. Used to be beautiful, a real picture, but now . . .' He shrugged. 'Ready to fall down any time. This restoration fund of yours? I hear you've not been getting very far.'

Father da Costa saw it all. 'And you'd like to help, is that it?'

'That's it, Father, that's it exactly.'

The door opened behind them, they both turned and saw an old lady with a shopping-bag enter. As she genuflected, Father da Costa said, 'We can't talk here. Come with me.'

They went up in the hoist to the top of the tower. It was still raining as he led the way out along the catwalk, but the mist had lifted and the view of the city was remarkable. In the far distance, perhaps four or five miles away, it was even possible to see the edge of the moors smudging the grey sky.

Meehan was genuinely delighted. 'Heh, I was up here once when I was a kid. Inside the belfry. It was different then.' He leaned over the rail and pointed to where the bulldozers were excavating in the brick-field. 'We used to live there. Thirteen, Khyber Street.'

He turned to Father da Costa who made no reply. Meehan said softly, 'This arrangement between you and Fallon? You going to stick to it?'

Father da Costa said, 'What arrangement would that be?'

'Come off it,' Meehan replied impatiently. 'This confession thing. I know all about it. He told me.'

'Then, as a Catholic yourself, you must know that there is nothing I can say. The secrets of the confessional are absolute.'

Meehan laughed harshly, 'I know. He's got brains, that Fallon. He shut you up good, didn't he?'

A small, hot spark of anger moved in Father da Costa and he breathed deeply to control it. 'If you say so.'

Meehan chuckled. 'Never mind, Father, I always pay my debts. How much?' His gesture took in the church, the scaffolding, everything. 'To put all this right?'

'Fifteen thousand pounds,' Father da Costa told him. 'For essential preliminary work. More would be needed later.'

'Easy,' Meehan said. 'With my help you could pick that up inside two or three months.'

'Might I ask how?'

Meehan lit a cigarette. 'For a start, there's the clubs. Dozens of them all over the north. They'll all put the old collecting-box round if I give the word.'

'And you actually imagine that I could take it?'

Meehan looked genuinely bewildered. 'It's only money, isn't it?

Pieces of paper. A medium of exchange, that's what the bright boys call it. Isn't that what you need?'

'In case you've forgotten, Mr Meehan, Christ drove the money-lenders *out* of the Temple. He didn't ask them for a contribution to the cause.'

Meehan frowned. 'I don't get it.'

'Then let me put it this way. My religion teaches me that reconciliation with God is always possible. That no human being, however degraded or evil, is beyond God's mercy. I had always believed that until now.'

Meehan's face was pale with fury. He grabbed da Costa's arm and pushed him towards the rail, pointing down at the brickfield.

'Thirteen, Khyber Street. A back-to-back rabbit hutch. One room downstairs, two up. One stinking lavatory to every four houses. My old man cleared off when I was a kid – he had sense. My old lady – she kept us going by cleaning when she could get it. When she couldn't, there were always ten bob quickies behind the boozer on a Saturday night. A bloody whore, that's all she was.'

'Who found time to clean and iron your cassock and cotta each week?' Father da Costa said. 'Who fed you and washed you and sent you to this church?'

'To hell with that,' Meehan said wildly. 'All she ever got – all anybody from Khyber Street ever got – was screwed into the ground, but not me. Not Jack Meehan. I'm up here now. I'm on top of the world where nobody can touch me.'

Father da Costa felt no pity, only a terrible disgust. He said calmly, 'I believe you to be the most evil and perverted creature it has ever been my misfortune to meet. If I could, I would hand you over to the proper authorities gladly. Tell them everything, but for reasons well known to you, this is impossible.'

Meehan seemed to be more in control of himself again. He said, with a sneer, 'That's good, that is. Me, you wouldn't touch with a ten-foot pole, but Fallon, he's different, isn't he? I mean, he only murders women and children.'

For a moment, Father da Costa had to fight for breath. When he spoke, it was with difficulty, 'What are you talking about?'

'Don't say he hasn't told you,' Meehan jeered. 'Nothing about Belfast or Londonderry or that bus full of schoolkids he blew up?' He leaned forward, a strange intent look on his face and then he smiled softly. 'You don't like that, do you? Fell for his Irish charm. Did you fancy him, then? I've heard some of you priests . . .'

There was a hand at his throat, a hand of iron and he was back against the cage of the hoist, fighting for his very life, the priest's eyes sparking fire. Meehan tried to bring up a knee and found only a thigh turned expertly to block it. Father da Costa shook him like a rat, then opened the door and threw him inside.

The cage door slammed as Meehan picked himself up. 'I'll have you for this,' he said hoarsely. 'You're dead meat.'

'My God, Mr Meehan,' Father da Costa said softly through the bars of the cage, 'is a God of Love. But he is also a God of Wrath. I leave you in his hands.'

He pressed the button and the cage started to descend.

As Meehan emerged from the church porch, a sudden flurry of wind dashed rain in his face. He turned up his collar and paused to light a cigarette. It was beginning to get dark and as he went down the steps he noticed a number of men waiting by a side door, sheltering against the wall from the rain. Human derelicts, most of them, in tattered coats and broken boots.

He moved across the street and Varley came out of the doorway of the old warehouse on the corner. 'I waited, Mr Meehan, like Billy said.'

'What happened to Fallon?'

'Went off in the car with Billy.'

Meehan frowned, but for the moment, that could wait and he turned his attention to the queue again. 'What are they all waiting for? This bleeding soup kitchen to open?'

'That's right, Mr Meehan. In the crypt.'

Meehan stared across at the queue for a while and then smiled suddenly. He opened his wallet and extracted a bundle of one-pound notes.

'I make it twenty-two in that queue, Charlie. You give them a quid apiece with my compliments and tell them the pub on the corner's just opened.'

Varley, mystified, crossed the street to distribute his largesse and within seconds, the queue was breaking up, several of the men touching their caps to Meehan who nodded cheerfully as they shuffled past. When Varley came back, there was no one left outside the door.

'He's going to have a lot of bleeding soup on his hands tonight,' Meehan said, grinning.

'I don't know about that, Mr Meehan,' Varley pointed out. 'They'll only come back when they've spent up.'

'And by then they'll have a skinful, won't they, so they might give him a little trouble. In fact, I think we'll make sure they do. Get hold of that bouncer from the Kit Kat Club. The Irishman, O'Hara.'

'Big Mick, Mr Meehan?' Varley stirred uneasily. 'I'm not too happy about that. He's a terrible man when he gets going.'

Meehan knocked off his cap and grabbed him by the hair. 'You tell him to be outside that door with one of his mates at opening time. Nobody goes in for the first hour. Nobody. He waits for at least a dozen drunks to back him, then he goes in and smashes the place up. If he does it right, it's worth twenty-five quid. If the priest breaks an arm, accidental like, it's worth fifty.'

Varley scrambled for his cap in the gutter. 'Is that all, Mr Meehan?' he asked fearfully.

'It'll do for starters.' Meehan was chuckling to himself as he walked away.

Father da Costa could count on only three acolytes for evening Mass. The parish was dying, that was the trouble. As the houses came down, the people moved away to the new estates, leaving only the office blocks. It was a hopeless task, he had known that when they sent him to Holy Name. His superiors had known. A hopeless task to teach him humility, wasn't that what the bishop had said? A little humility for a man who had been arrogant enough to think he could change the world. Remake the Church in his own image.

Two of the boys were West Indians, the other English of Hungarian parents. All a product of the few slum streets still remaining. They stood in the corner waiting for him, whispering together, occasionally laughing, newly-washed, hair combed, bright in their scarlet cassocks and white cottas. Had Jack Meehan looked like that once?

The memory was like a sword in the heart. The fact of his own violence, the killing rage. The violence that had been so often his undoing through the years. The men he had killed in the war – that was one thing, but after . . . The Chinese soldier in Korea machine-gunning a column of refugees. He had picked up a rifle and shot the man through the head at two hundred yards. Expertly, skilfully, the old soldier temporarily in control. Had he been wrong? Had it really been wrong when so many lives had been saved? And that Portuguese Captain in Mozambique stringing up guerrillas by their ankles. He had beaten the man half to death, the incident that had finally sent him home in disgrace.

'The days when bishops rode into battle with a mace in one hand are over, my friend.' The Bishop's voice echoed faintly. 'Your task is to save souls.'

Violence for violence. That was Meehan's way. Sick and disgusted, Father da Costa took off the violet stole he had worn for confession and put on a green one, crossing it under his girdle to represent Christ's passion and death. As he put on an old rose-coloured cope, the outer door opened and Anna came in, her stick in one hand, a raincoat over her.

He moved to take the raincoat, holding her shoulders briefly. 'Are you all right?'

She turned at once, concern on her face. 'What is it? You're upset. Has anything happened?'

'I had an unpleasant interview with the man Meehan,' he replied in a low voice. 'He said certain things concerning Fallon. Things which could explain a great deal. I'll tell you later.'

She frowned slightly, but he led her to the door and opened it, pushing her through into the church. He waited for a few moments to give her time to reach the organ, then nodded to the boys. They formed into their tiny procession, one of them opening the door, and as the organ started to play, they moved into the church.

It was a place of shadows, candlelight and darkness alternating, cold and damp. There were perhaps fifteen people in the congregation, no more. He had never felt so dispirited, so close to the final edge of things, not since Korea, and then he looked across at the figure of the Virgin. She seemed to float there in the candlelight, so calm, so serene and the slight half-smile on the parted lips seemed somehow for him alone.

'*Asperges me*,' he intoned and moved down the aisle, one of the West Indian boys carrying the bucket of holy water in front of him, Father da Costa sprinkling the heads of his congregation as he passed, symbolically washing them clean.

'And who will cleanse me?' he asked himself desperately. 'Who?'

In the faded rose cope, hands together, he commenced the mass. 'I confess to Almighty God, and to you, my brothers and sisters, that I have sinned through my own fault.' Here, he struck his breast once as ritual required. 'In my thoughts and in my words, in what I have done, and in what I have failed to do.'

The voices of the congregation swelled up in unison behind him.

There were tears on his face, the first in many years, and he struck his breast again.

'Lord, have mercy on me,' he whispered. 'Help me. Show me what to do.'

9

The Executioner

The wind howled through the city like a living thing, driving rain before it, clearing the streets, rattling old window frames, tapping at the glass like some invisible presence.

When Billy Meehan went into Jenny Fox's bedroom, she was standing in front of the mirror combing her hair. She was wearing the black pleated mini skirt, dark stockings, patent-leather, high-heeled shoes and a white blouse. She looked extremely attractive.

As she turned, Billy closed the door and said softly, 'Nice, very nice. He's still in his room, isn't he?'

'He said he was going out again, though.'

'We'll have to change his mind then, won't we?' Billy went and sat on the bed. 'Come here.'

She fought to control the instant panic that threatened to choke her, the disgust that made her flesh crawl as she moved towards him.

He slipped his hands under her skirt, fondling the warm flesh at the top of the stockings. 'That's a good girl. He'll like that. They always do.' He stared up at her, that strange, dreamy look in his eyes again. 'You muck this up for me, you'll be in trouble. I mean, I'd have to punish you and you wouldn't like that, would you?'

Her heart thudded painfully. 'Please, Billy! Please!'

'Then do it right. I want to see what makes this guy tick.'

He pushed her away, got up and moved to a small picture on the wall. He removed it carefully. There was a tiny peephole underneath, skilfully placed and he peered through.

After a few moments, he turned and nodded. 'Just taken his shirt off. Now you get in there and remember – I'll be watching.'

His mouth was slack, his hands trembling a little and she turned, choking back her disgust, opened the door and slipped outside.

Fallon was standing at the washbasin, stripped to the waist, lather on his face, when she knocked on the door and went in. He turned to greet her, a bone-handled cut-throat razor in one hand.

She leaned against the door. 'Sorry about the razor. It was all I could find.'

'That's all right.' He smiled. 'My father had one of these. Wouldn't use anything else till the day he died.'

A line of ugly, puckered scars cut across his abdomen down into the left hip. Her eyes widened. 'What happened?'

He glanced down. 'Oh, that – a machine-gun burst. One of those times I should have moved faster than I did.'

'Were you in the army?'

'In a manner of speaking.'

He turned back to the mirror to finish shaving. She moved across and stood beside him. He smiled sideways, crookedly, stretching his mouth for the razor.

'You look nice enough to eat. Going somewhere?'

There was that warmth again, that pricking behind her eyes and she suddenly realised, with a sense of wonder, just how much she had come to like this strange, small man, and in the same moment remembered Billy watching her every move on the other side of that damned wall.

She smiled archly and ran a finger down his bare arm. 'I thought I might stay in tonight. What about you?'

Fallon's eyes flickered towards her once, something close to amusement in them. 'Girl dear, you don't know what you'd be getting into. And me twice your age.'

'I've got a bottle of Irish whiskey in.'

'God save us and isn't that enough to tempt the Devil himself?'

He continued his shaving and she moved across to the bed and sat down. It wasn't going right – it wasn't going right at all and at the thought of Billy's anger, she turned cold inside. She summoned up all her resources and tried again.

'Mind if I have a cigarette?'

There was a packet on the bedside table and a box of matches. She took one, lit it and leaned back on the bed, a pillow behind her shoulders.

'Have you really got to go out?'

She raised one knee so that the skirt slid back provocatively exposing bare flesh at the top of dark stockings, sheer black nylon briefs.

Fallon sighed heavily, put down the razor and picked up a towel. He wiped the foam from his face as he crossed to the bed and stood looking down at her.

'You'll catch cold.' He smiled softly and pulled down her skirt. 'If you're not careful. And I'm still going out, but I'll have a glass with you before I do, so be off now and open the bottle.'

He pulled her up from the bed and pushed her firmly across the room. She turned at the door, fear in her eyes. 'Please?' she said fiercely. 'Please?'

He frowned slightly and then a brief, sad smile touched his mouth. He kissed her gently on the lips and shook his head. 'Not me, girl dear, not me in the whole wide world. You need a man . . . I'm just a corpse walking.'

It was such a terrible remark, so dreadful in its implication, that for the moment it drove every other thought from her mind. She stared up at him, eyes wide, and he opened the door and pushed her outside.

Fear possessed her now, such fear as she had never known. She couldn't face what awaited her in her bedroom. If she could only get downstairs – but it was already too late for as she tiptoed past, the door opened and Billy pulled her so violently into the bedroom that she stumbled, losing a shoe and went sprawling across the bed.

She turned fearfully and found him already unbuckling his belt. 'You cocked it up, didn't you?' he said softly. 'And after all I've done for you.'

'Please, Billy. Please don't,' she said. 'I'll do anything.'

'You can say that again. You going to get one of my specials, just to keep you in line, and maybe next time I tell you to do something, you'll bloody well make sure it gets done.' He started to unfasten his trousers. 'Go on, turn over.' She was almost choking and shook her head dumbly. His face was like a mirror breaking, madness staring at her from those pale eyes and he struck her heavily across the face.

'You do as you're bloody well told, you bitch.'

He grabbed her by the hair, forcing her round until she sprawled across the edge of the bed, face down. His other hand tore at her briefs, pulling them down. And then, as she felt his hardness, as he forced himself between her buttocks like some animal, she screamed at the top of her voice, head arched back in agony.

The door opened so violently that it splintered against the wall and Fallon stood there, one side of his face still lathered, the cut-throat razor open in his right hand.

Billy turned from the girl, mouthing incoherently, clutching at his trousers, and as he stood up Fallon took two quick paces into the room and kicked him in the privates. Billy went down like a stone and lay there twitching, knees drawn up to his chest in a foetal position.

The girl adjusted her clothes as best she could and got up, every last shred of decency stripped from her, tears pouring down her face. Fallon wiped lather from his cheek mechanically with the back of his hand and his eyes were very dark.

She could hardly speak for sobbing. 'He made me go into your room tonight. He was watching.'

She gestured towards the wall and Fallon crossed to the peephole. He turned slowly. 'Does this kind of thing happen often?'

'He likes to watch.'

'And you? What about you?'

'I'm a whore,' she said and suddenly it erupted from her. All the disgust, the self-hate, born of years of degradation. 'Have you any idea what that means? He started me early, his brother.'

'Jack Meehan?'

'Who else? I was thirteen. Just right for a certain kind of client, and from then on it's been downhill all the way.'

'You could leave?'

'Where would I go to?' She had regained some of her composure now. 'It takes money. And I have a three-year-old daughter to think of.'

'Here – in this place?'

She shook her head. 'I board her out with a woman. A nice woman in a decent part of town, but Billy knows where she is.'

At that moment he stirred and pushed himself up on one elbow. There were tears in his eyes and his mouth was flecked with foam.

'You've had it,' he said faintly. 'When my brother hears about this you're a dead man.'

He started to zip up his trousers and Fallon crouched down beside him. 'My grandfather,' he began in a conversational tone, 'kept a farm back home in Ireland. Sheep mostly. And every year, he'd geld a few to improve the flavour of the mutton or make the wool grow more – something like that. Do you know what geld means, Billy boy?'

'Like hell I do. You're crackers,' Billy said angrily. 'Like all the bloody Irish.'

'It means he cut off their balls with a pair of sheep shears.'

An expression of frozen horror appeared on the boy's face and Fallon said softly, 'Touch this girl in any way from now on,' he held up the cut-throat razor, 'and I will attend to you personally. My word on it.'

The boy scrambled away from him and pushed himself up against the wall, clutching at his trousers. 'You're mad,' he whispered. 'Raving mad.'

'That's it, Billy,' Fallon said. 'Capable of anything and don't you forget it.'

The boy ducked out through the open door, his feet thundered on the stairs. The front door banged.

Fallon turned, a hand to his cheek. 'Could I finish my shaving now, do you suppose?'

She ran forward, gripping his arms fiercely. 'Please don't go out. Please don't leave me.'

'I must,' he said. 'He won't be back, not as long as I'm staying here.'

'And afterwards?'

'We'll think of something.'

She turned away and he grabbed her hand quickly. 'I'll be an hour, no more, I promise, and then we can have that glass of whiskey. How's that?'

She turned, peering at him uncertainly. The tears had streaked her make-up, making her somehow seem very young. 'You mean it?'

'On the word of an Irish gentleman.'

She flung her arms about his neck in delight. 'Oh, I'll be good to you. I really will.'

He put a finger on her mouth. 'There's no need. No need at all.' He patted her cheek. 'I'll be back, I promise. Only do one thing for me.'

'What's that?'

'Wash your face, for God's sake.'

He closed the door gently as he went out and she moved across to the washbasin and looked into the mirror. He was right. She looked terrible and yet for the first time in years, the eyes were smiling. Smiling through that streaked whore's mask. She picked up a flannel and some soap and started to wash her face thoroughly.

Father da Costa couldn't understand it. The refuge had been open for just over an hour without a single customer. In all the months he had been operating from the old crypt he had never known such a thing.

It wasn't much of a place, but the stone walls had been neatly whitewashed, there was a coke fire in the stove, benches and trestle tables. Anna sat behind one of them, knitting a sweater. The soup was in front of her in a heat-retaining container, plates piled beside it. There were several loaves of yesterday's bread supplied free by arrangement with a local bakery.

Father da Costa put more coke on the stove and stirred it impatiently with the poker. Anna stopped knitting. 'What do you think has happened?'

'God knows,' he said. 'I'm sure I don't.' He walked to the door and went out to the porch. The street was apparently deserted. The rain had declined into a light drizzle. He went back inside.

The Irishman, O'Hara, the one Varley had referred to as Big Mick, moved out of the entrance to a small yard halfway up the street and stood under a lamp. He was a tall, broad-shouldered man, six foot three or four at least, with curling, black hair and a perpetual smile. The man who moved out of the shadows to join him was two or three inches shorter and had a broken nose.

It was at this moment that Fallon turned into the end of the street. He approached silently, pausing in the darkness to take stock of the situation when he saw O'Hara and his friend. When the Irishman started speaking, Fallon moved into a convenient doorway and listened.

'Sure and I think the reverend gentleman's just about ready for it, Daniel,' O'Hara said. 'How many have we got in there now?'

Daniel snapped his fingers and several shadowy figures emerged from the darkness. He counted them quickly. 'I make it eight,' he said. 'That's ten including us.'

'Nine,' O'Hara said. 'You stay outside and watch the door, just in case. They all know what to do?'

'I've seen to that,' Daniel said. 'For a quid apiece they'll take the place apart.'

O'Hara turned to address the shadowy group. 'Remember one thing. Da Costa – he's mine.'

Daniel said, 'Doesn't that worry you, Mick? I mean you being an Irishman and so on. After all, he's a priest.'

'I've a terrible confession to make, Daniel.' O'Hara put a hand on his shoulder. 'Some Irishmen are Protestants and I'm one of them.' He turned to the others. 'Come on, lads,' he said and crossed the road.

They went in through the door and Daniel waited by the railings, his ear cocked for the first sound of a disturbance from inside. There was a slight, polite cough from behind and when he turned, Fallon was standing a yard or two away, hands in pockets.

'Where in hell did you spring from?' Daniel demanded.

'Never mind that,' Fallon said. 'What's going on in there?'

Daniel knew trouble when he saw it, but completely miscalculated his man. 'You little squirt,' he said contemptuously. 'Get the hell out of it.'

He moved in fast, his hands reaching out to destroy, but they only fastened on thin air as his feet were kicked expertly from beneath him.

He thudded against the wet pavement and scrambled to his feet, mouthing obscenities. Fallon seized his right wrist with both hands, twisting it up and around. Daniel gave a cry of agony as the muscle started to give. Still keeping that terrible hold in position, Fallon ran him headfirst into the railings.

Daniel pulled himself up off his knees, blood on his face, one hand out in supplication. 'No more, for Christ's sake.'

'All right,' Fallon said. 'Answers then. What's the game?'

'They're supposed to turn the place over.'

'Who for?' Daniel hesitated and Fallon kicked his feet from under him. 'Who for?'

'Jack Meehan,' Daniel gabbled.

Fallon pulled him to his feet and stood back. 'Next time you get a bullet in the kneecap. That's a promise. Now get out of it.'

Daniel turned and staggered into the darkness.

At the first sudden noisy rush, Father da Costa knew he was in trouble. As he moved forward, a bench went over and then another. Hands pawed at him, someone pulled his cassock. He was aware of Anna crying out in alarm and turning, saw O'Hara grab her from behind, arms about her waist.

'Now then, darlin', what about a little kiss?' he demanded.

She pulled away from him in a panic, hands reaching out blindly and cannoned into the trestle table, knocking it over, soup spilling out across the floor, plates clattering.

As Father da Costa fought to get towards her, O'Hara laughed out loud. 'Now look what you've done.'

A soft, quiet voice called from the doorway, cutting through the noise.

'Mickeen O'Hara. Is it you I see?'

The room went quiet. Everyone waited. O'Hara turned, an expression of disbelief on his face that seemed to say this couldn't be happening. The expression was quickly replaced by one that was a mixture of awe and fear.

'God in heaven,' he whispered. 'Is that you, Martin?'

Fallon went towards him, hands in pockets and everyone waited. He said softly, 'Tell them to clean the place up, Mick, like a good boy, then wait for me outside.'

O'Hara did as he was told without hesitation and moved towards the door. The other men started to right the tables and benches, one of them got a bucket and mop and started on the floor.

Father da Costa had moved to comfort Anna and Fallon joined them. 'I'm sorry about that, Father,' he said. 'It won't happen again.'

'Meehan?' Father da Costa asked.

Fallon nodded. 'Were you expecting something like this?'

'He came to see me earlier this evening. You might say we didn't get on too well.' He hesitated. 'The big Irishman. He knew you.'

'Little friend of all the world, that's me.' Fallon smiled. 'Good night to you,' he said and turned to the door.

Father da Costa reached him as he opened it and put a hand on his arm. 'We must talk, Fallon. You owe me that.'

'All right,' Fallon said. 'When?'

'I'll be busy in the morning, but I don't have a lunchtime confession tomorrow. Will one o'clock suit you? At the presbytery.'

'I'll be there.'

Fallon went out, closing the door behind him and crossed the street to where O'Hara waited nervously under the lamp. As Fallon approached he turned to face him.

'Before God, if I'd known you were mixed up in this, Martin, I wouldn't have come within a mile of it. I thought you were dead by now – we all did.'

'All right,' Fallon said. 'How much was Meehan paying you?'

'Twenty-five quid. Fifty if the priest got a broken arm.'

'How much in advance?'

'Not a sou.'

Fallon opened his wallet, took out two ten-pound notes and handed them to him. 'Travelling money – for old times' sake. I don't think it's going to be too healthy for you round here. Not when Jack Meehan finds out you've let him down.'

'God bless you, Martin, I'll be out of it this very night.' He started to turn away, then hesitated. 'Does it bother you any more, Martin, what happened back there?'

'Every minute of every hour of every day of my life,' Fallon said with deep conviction and he turned and walked away up the side street.

From the shelter of the porch, Father da Costa saw O'Hara cross the main road. He made for the pub on the corner, going in at the saloon bar entrance and Father da Costa went after him.

It was quiet in the saloon bar which was why O'Hara had chosen it. He was still badly shaken and ordered a large whisky which he swallowed at once. As he asked for another, the door opened and Father da Costa entered.

O'Hara tried to brazen it out. 'So there you are, Father,' he said. 'Will you have a drink with me?'

'I'd sooner drink with the Devil.' Father da Costa dragged him across to a nearby booth and sat opposite him. 'Where did you know Fallon?' he demanded. 'Before tonight, I mean?'

O'Hara stared at him in blank astonishment, glass half-raised to his lips. 'Fallon?' he said. 'I don't know anyone called Fallon.'

'Martin Fallon, you fool,' Father da Costa said impatiently. 'Haven't I just seen you talking together outside the church?'

'Oh, you mean Martin,' O'Hara said. 'Fallon – is that what he's calling himself now?'

'What can you tell me about him?'

'Why should I tell you anything?'

'Because I'll ring for the police and put you in charge for assault if you don't. Detective-Superintendent Miller is a personal friend. He'll be happy to oblige, I'm sure.'

'All right, Father, you can call off the dogs.' O'Hara, mellowed by two large whiskies, went to the bar for a third and returned. 'What do you want to know for?'

'Does that matter?'

'It does to me. Martin Fallon, as you call him, is probably the best man I ever knew in my life. A hero.'

'To whom?'

'To the Irish people.'

'Oh, I see. Well, I don't mean him any harm, I can assure you of that.'

'You'll give me your word on it?'

'Of course.'

'All right, I won't tell you his name, his real name. It doesn't matter anyway. He was a lieutenant in the Provisional IRA. They used to call him the Executioner in Derry. I've never known the likes of him with a gun in his hand. He'd have killed the Pope if he'd thought it would advance the cause. And brains.' He shook his head. 'A university man, Father, would you believe it? Trinity College, no less. There were days when it all poured out of him. Poetry – books. That sort of thing – and he played the piano like an angel.' O'Hara hesitated, fingering a cigarette, frowning back into the past. 'And then there were other times.'

'What do you mean?' Father da Costa asked him.

'Oh, he used to change completely. Go right inside himself. No emotion, no response. Nothing. Cold and dark.' O'Hara shivered and stuck the cigarette into the corner of his mouth. 'When he was like that, he scared the hell out of everybody, including me, I can tell you.'

'You were with him long?'

'Only for a time. They never really trusted me. I'm a Prod, you see, so I got out.'

'And Fallon?'

'He laid this ambush for a Saracen armoured car, somewhere in Armagh. Mined the road. Someone had got the time wrong. They got a school bus instead with a dozen kids on board. Five killed, the rest crippled. You know how it is. It finished Martin. I think he'd been worrying about the way things were going for a while. All the killing and so on. The business with the bus was the final straw, you might say.'

'I can see that it would be,' Father da Costa said without irony.

'I thought he was dead,' O'Hara said. 'Last I heard, the IRA had an execution squad out after him. Me, I'm no account. Nobody worries about me, but for someone like Martin, it's different. He knows too much. For a man like him, there's only one way out of the movement and that's in a coffin.'

He got to his feet, face flushed. 'Well, Father, I'll be leaving you now. This town and I are parting company.'

He walked to the door and Father da Costa went with him. As rain drifted across the street, O'Hara buttoned up his coat and said cheerfully, 'Have you ever wondered what it's all about, Father? Life, I mean?'

'Constantly,' Father da Costa told him.

'That's honest, anyway. See you in hell, Father.'

He moved off along the pavement, whistling, and Father da Costa went back across the road to the Holy Name. When he went back into the crypt, everything was in good order again. The men had gone and Anna waited patiently on one of the bench seats.

'I'm sorry I had to leave you,' he said, 'but I wanted to speak to the man who knew Fallon. The one who started all the trouble. He went into the pub on the corner.'

'What did you find out?'

He hesitated, then told her. When he was finished, there was pain on her face. She said slowly, 'Then he isn't what he seemed at first.'

'He killed Krasko,' Father da Costa reminded her. 'Murdered him in cold blood. There was nothing romantic about that.'

'You're right, of course.' She groped for her coat and stood up. 'What are you going to do now?'

'What on earth do you expect me to do?' he said half-angrily. 'Save his soul?'

'It's a thought,' she said, slipping her hand into his arm and they went out together.

There was an old warehouse at the rear of Meehan's premises in Paul's Square and a fire escape gave easy access to its flat roof.

Fallon crouched behind a low wall as he screwed the silencer on to the barrel of the Ceska and peered across through the rain. The two dormer windows at the rear of Meehan's penthouse were no more than twenty yards away and the curtains weren't drawn. He had seen Meehan several times pacing backwards and forwards, a glass in his hand. On one occasion, Rupert had joined him, putting an arm about his neck, but Meehan had shoved him away and angrily from the look of it.

It was a difficult shot at that distance for a handgun, but not impossible. Fallon crouched down, holding the Ceska ready in both hands, aiming at the left-hand window. Meehan appeared briefly and paused, raising a glass to his lips. Fallon fired the silenced pistol once.

In the penthouse, a mirror on the wall shattered and Meehan dropped to the floor. Rupert, who was lying on the couch watching television, turned quickly. His eyes widened.

'My God, look at the window. Somebody took a shot at you.'

Meehan looked up at the bullet hole, the spider's web of cracks, then across at the mirror. He got up slowly.

Rupert joined him. 'You want to know something, ducky? You're getting to be too damn dangerous to know.'

Meehan shoved him away angrily. 'Get me a drink, damn you. I've got to think this thing out.'

A couple of minutes later the phone rang. When he picked up the receiver, he got a call-box signal and then the line cleared as a coin went in at the other end.

'That you, Meehan?' Fallon said. 'You know who this is?'

'You bastard,' Meehan said. 'What are you trying to do?'

'This time I missed because I meant to,' Fallon said. 'Remember that and tell your goons to stay away from Holy Name – and that includes you.'

He put down the receiver and Meehan did the same. He turned, his face white with fury, and Rupert handed him a drink. 'You don't look too good, ducky, bad news?'

'Fallon,' Meehan said between his teeth. 'It was that bastard Fallon and he missed because he wanted to.'

'Never mind, ducky,' Rupert said. 'After all, you've always got me.'

'That's right,' Meehan said. 'So I have. I was forgetting,' and he hit him in the stomach with his clenched fist.

It was late when Fallon got back, much later than he had intended, and there was no sign of Jenny. He took off his shoes and went up the stairs and along the landing to his room quietly.

He undressed, got into bed and lit a cigarette. He was tired. It had certainly been one hell of a day. There was a slight, timid knock on the door. It opened and Jenny came in.

She wore a dark-blue nylon nightdress, her hair was tied back with a ribbon and her face was scrubbed clean. She said, 'Jack Meehan was on the phone about half an hour ago. He says he wants to see you in the morning.'

'Did he say where?'

'No, he just said to tell you it couldn't be more public so you've nothing to worry about. He'll send a car at seven-thirty.'

Fallon frowned. 'A bit early for him, isn't it?'

'I wouldn't know.' She hesitated. 'I waited. You said an hour. You didn't come.'

'I'm sorry,' he said. 'It couldn't be helped, believe me.'

'I did,' she said. 'You were the first man in years who didn't treat me like something you'd scrape off your shoe.'

She started to cry. Wordless, he pulled back the covers and held out a hand. She stumbled across the room and got in beside him.

He switched off the lamp. She lay there, her face against his chest, sobbing, his arm about her. He held her close, stroking her hair with his other hand and after a while, she slept.

10

Exhumation

The car that called to pick Fallon up the following morning at seven-thirty was a black, funeral limousine. Varley was at the wheel dressed in a neat blue serge suit and peaked cap. There was no other passenger.

Fallon climbed into the rear and closed the door. He reached across and slid back the glass window between the driver's compartment and the rest of the car.

'All right,' he said, as Varley moved into gear and drove away. 'Where are we going?'

'The Catholic cemetery.' Fallon, in the act of lighting his first cigarette of the day, started, and Varley said soothingly, 'Nothing to worry about, Mr Fallon. Honest. It's just that Mr Meehan has an exhumation first thing this morning.'

'An exhumation?' Fallon said.

'That's right. They don't come along very often and Mr Meehan always likes to see to a thing like that personally. He's very particular about his funeral work.'

'I can believe that,' Fallon said. 'What's so special about this case?'

'Nothing really. I suppose he thought you might find it interesting. The man they're digging up is a German. Died about eighteen months ago. His wife couldn't afford to take him back to Germany then, but now she's come into a bit of money, and wants to bury him in Hamburg.' He swung the car out into the main road and added cheerfully, 'It's a fascinating game, the funeral business, Mr Fallon. Always something new happening.'

'I just bet there is,' Fallon said.

They reached the cemetery in ten minutes, and Varley turned in through the gate and drove up the drive, past the chapel and the superintendent's office, following a narrow track.

The grave they were seeking was on top of the hill covered by a canvas awning. At least a dozen people were grouped around it and there was a truck and a couple of cars. Meehan was standing beside one of them talking to a grey-haired man in rubber boots and an oilskin mac. Meehan wore a Homburg hat and his usual melton overcoat and Donner stood beside him holding an umbrella over his head.

As Fallon got out and splashed through the heavy rain towards them, Meehan turned and smiled. 'Ah, there you are. This is Mr Adams, the Public Health Inspector. Mr Fallon is a colleague of mine.'

Adams shook hands and turned back to Meehan. 'I'll see how they're getting on, Mr Meehan.'

He moved away and Fallon said, 'All right, what game are we playing now?'

'No games,' Meehan said. 'This is strictly business and I've a funeral afterwards so I'm busy all morning, but we obviously need to talk. We can do it in the car on the way. For the moment, just stick close to me and pretend to be a member of the firm. This is a privileged occasion. The cemetery superintendent wouldn't be too pleased if he thought an outsider had sneaked in.'

He moved towards the grave, Donner keeping pace with the umbrella, and Fallon followed. The smell was terrible – like nothing he had ever smelt before and when he peered down into the open grave, he saw that it had been sprinkled with lime.

'Two feet of water down there, Mr Meehan,' the Public Health Inspector called. 'No drainage. Too much clay. Means the coffin's going to be in a bad state. Probably come to pieces.'

'All in the game,' Meehan said. 'Better have the other one ready.'

He nodded and two of the gravediggers standing by lifted a large oaken coffin out of the back of the truck and put it down near the grave. When they opened it, Fallon saw that it was zinc lined.

The old coffin drops inside and we close the lid,' Meehan said. 'Nothing to it. The lid has to be welded into place, mind you, in front of the Public Health Inspector, but that's what the law says if you want to fly a corpse from one country to another.'

Just then there was a sudden flurry of movement, and as they turned, the half-dozen men grouped around the grave heaved up the coffin. Webbing bands had been passed underneath, which to a certain extent held things together, but as the coffin came into view, the end broke away and a couple of decaying feet poked through minus their toes.

The smell was even worse now as the half-dozen unfortunate gravediggers lurched towards the new coffin clutching the old. Meehan seemed to enjoy the whole thing hugely and moved in close, barking orders.

'Watch it, now! Watch it! A little bit more to the left. That's it.'

The old coffin dropped into the new, the lid was closed. He turned triumphantly to Fallon. 'I told you there was nothing to it, didn't I? Now let's get moving. I've got a cremation at nine-thirty.'

The gravediggers seemed badly shaken. One of them lit a cigarette, hands trembling, and said to Fallon in a Dublin accent, 'Is it a fact that they're flying him over to Germany this afternoon?'

'So I understand,' Fallon said.

The old man made a wry face. 'Sure and I hope the pilot remembers to wind the windows down.'

Which at least sent Fallon to the car laughing helplessly to himself.

Donner drove and Meehan and Fallon sat in the back seat. Meehan opened a cupboard in the bottom half of the partition between the driver's compartment and the rear and took out a Thermos flask and a half-bottle of Cognac. He half filled a cup with coffee, topped it up with Cognac and leaned back.

'Last night. That was very silly. Not what I'd call a friendly gesture at all. What did you have to go and do a thing like that for?'

'You said the priest would be left alone,' Fallon told him, 'then sent O'Hara to the crypt to smash it up. Lucky I turned up when I did. As for O'Hara – he and I are old comrades in a manner of speaking. He's cleared off, by the way. You won't be seeing him around here any more.'

'You have been busy.' Meehan poured more Cognac into his coffee. 'I do admit I got just a little bit annoyed with Father da Costa. On the other hand he wasn't very nice when I spoke to him yesterday evening and all I did was offer to help him raise the money to stop that church of his from falling down!'

'And you thought he'd accept?' Fallon laughed out loud. 'You've got to be joking.'

Meehan shrugged. 'I still say that bullet was an unfriendly act.'

'Just like Billy playing Peeping Tom at Jenny Fox's place,' Fallon said. 'When are you going to do something about that worm, anyway! He isn't fit to be out without his keeper.'

Meehan's face darkened. 'He's my brother,' he said. 'He has his faults, but we all have those. Anyone hurts him, they hurt me too.'

Fallon lit a cigarette and Meehan smiled expansively. 'You don't really know me, do you, Fallon? I mean, the other side of me, for instance? The funeral game.'

'You take it seriously.'

It was a statement of fact, not a question and Meehan nodded soberly. 'You've got to have some respect for death. It's a serious business. Too many people are too off-hand about it these days. Now me, I like to see things done right.'

'I can imagine.'

Meehan smiled. 'That's why I thought it might be a good idea to get together like this this morning. You could find it very interesting. Who knows, you might even see some future in the business.'

He put a hand on Fallon's knee and Fallon eased away. Meehan wasn't in the least embarrassed. 'Anyway, we'll start you off with a cremation,' he said. 'See what you make of that.'

He poured another coffee, topped it up with more Cognac and leaned back with a contented sigh.

The crematorium was called Pine Trees and when the car turned in through the gate, Fallon was surprised to see Meehan's name in gold leaf on the notice-board, one of half-a-dozen directors.

'I have a fifty-one per cent holding in this place,' Meehan said. 'The most modern crematorium in the north of England. You should see the gardens in spring and summer. Costs us a bomb, but it's worth it. People come from all over.'

The superintendent's house and the office were just inside the gate. They drove on and came to a superb, colonnaded building. Meehan tapped on the glass and Donner braked to a halt.

Meehan wound down the window. 'This is what they call a columbarium,' he said. 'Some people like to store the ashes in an urn and keep it on display. There are niches in all the walls, most of them full. We try to discourage it these days.'

'And what would you recommend?' Fallon demanded, irony in his voice.

'Strewing,' Meehan said seriously. 'Scattering the ashes on the grass and brushing them in. We come out of the earth, we go back to it. I'll show you if you like, after the funeral.'

Fallon couldn't think of a single thing to say. The man took himself so seriously. It was really quite incredible. He sat back and waited for what was to come.

The chapel and the crematorium were in the centre of the estate and several hundred yards from the main gate for obvious reasons. There were several cars parked there already and a hearse waited with a coffin at the back, Bonati at the wheel.

Meehan said, 'We usually bring the hearse on ahead of the rest of the party if the relations agree. You can't have a cortège following the coffin these days, not with present day traffic. The procession gets split wide open.'

A moment later, a limousine turned out of the drive followed by three more. Billy was sitting up front, beside the driver.

Meehan got out of the car and approached, hat in hand, to greet the mourners.

It was quite a performance and Fallon watched, fascinated, as Meehan moved from one group to the next, his face grave, full of concern. He was particularly good with the older ladies.

The coffin was carried into the chapel and the mourners followed it in. Meehan joined on at the end and pulled at Fallon's sleeve. 'You might as well go in. See the lot.'

The service was painfully brief, almost as synthetic as the taped religious music with its heavenly choir background. Fallon was relieved when the proceedings came to an end and some curtains were closed by an automatic device, hiding the coffin from view.

'They pull it through into the funeral room on a movable belt,' Meehan whispered. 'I'll take you round there when they've all moved off.'

He did a further stint with the relatives when they got outside. A pat on the back where it was needed, an old lady's hand held for an instant. It was really quite masterly. Finally, he managed to edge away and nodded to Fallon. They moved round to the rear of the building, he opened a door and led the way in.

There were four enormous cylindrical furnaces. Two were roaring away, another was silent. The fourth was being raked out by a man in a white coat.

Meehan nodded familiarly. 'Arthur's all we need in here,' he said. 'Everything's fully automatic. Here, I'll show you.'

The coffin Fallon had last seen in the chapel stood waiting on a trolley. 'Rubber doors in the wall,' Meehan explained. 'It comes straight through on the rollers and finishes on the trolley.'

He pushed it across to the cold oven and opened the door. The coffin was at exactly the right height and moved easily on the trolley rollers when he pushed it inside. He closed the door and flicked a red switch. There was an immediate roar and through the glass peep-hole, Fallon could see flames streak into life inside.

'That's all it needs,' Meehan said. 'These ovens operate by radiant heat and they're the last word in efficiency. An hour from beginning to end and you don't need to worry about pre-heating. The moment it reaches around a thousand degrees centigrade, that coffin will go up like a torch.'

Fallon peered through the glass and saw the coffin suddenly burst into flames. He caught a glimpse of a head, hair flaming, and looked away hurriedly.

Meehan was standing beside the oven where Arthur was busily at work with his rake. 'Have a look at this. This is what you're left with.'

All that remained was a calcined bony skeleton in pieces. As Arthur pushed at it with the rake, it broke into fragments falling through the bars into the large tin box below which already contained a fair amount of ash.

Meehan pulled it out, picked it up and carried it across to a contraption on a bench by the wall. 'This is the pulveriser,' he said, emptying the contents of the tin box into the top. He clamped down the lid. 'Just watch. Two minutes is all it takes.'

He flicked a switch and the machine got to work, making a terrible grinding noise. When Meehan was satisfied, he switched off and unscrewed a metal urn on the underside and showed it to Fallon, who saw that it was about three-quarters full of powdery grey ash.

'You notice there's a label already on the urn?' Meehan said. 'That's very important. We do everything in strict rotation. No possibility of a mistake.' He pulled open a drawer in a nearby desk and took out a white card edged in black. 'And the next of kin get one of these with the plot number on. What we call a Rest-in-Peace card. Now come outside and I'll show you the final step.'

It was still raining as they moved along the path at the back of the building between cypress trees. They came out into a lawned area, criss-crossed by box hedges. The edges of the paths were lined with numbered plates.

A gardener was working away beside a wheelbarrow hoeing a flower-bed and Meehan called, 'More work for the undertaker, Fred. Better note it down in your little black book.'

The gardener produced a notebook into which he entered the particulars typed on the urn label. 'Number five hundred and thirty-seven, Mr Meehan,' he said when he'd finished.

'All right, Fred, get it done,' Meehan told him.

The gardener moved to the plate with the correct number and strewed the ashes across the damp grass. Then he got a besom and brushed them in.

Meehan turned to Fallon. 'That's it. The whole story. Ashes to ashes. A Rest-in-Peace card with the right number on it is all that's left.'

They walked back towards the chapel. Meehan said, 'I'd rather be buried myself. It's more fitting, but you've got to give people what they want.'

They went round to the front of the chapel. Billy and Bonati had gone, but Donner was still there and Varley had arrived in the other limousine. The crematorium superintendent appeared, wanting a word with Meehan, and Fallon was for the moment left alone.

The stench of that open grave was still in his nostrils. Just inside the main door to the chapel there was a toilet and he went inside and bathed his face and hands in cold water.

A pane of glass in the small window above the basin was missing and rain drifted through. He stood there for a moment, suddenly depressed. The open grave, the toeless feet protruding from that rotting coffin had been a hell of a start to the day and now this. A man came down to so little in the end. A handful of ashes.

When he went outside, Meehan was waiting for him. 'Well, that's it,' he said. 'Do you want to see another one?'

'Not if I can help it.'

Meehan chuckled. 'I've got two more this morning, but never mind. Varley can take you back to Jenny's place.' He grinned broadly. 'Not worth going out on a day like this unless you have to. I'd stay in if I were you. I mean, it could get interesting. She's a real little firecracker when she gets going is our Jenny.'

'I know,' Fallon said. 'You told me.'

He got into the rear seat of the limousine and Varley drove away.

Instead of going down to the main gate, he followed a track that was barely wide enough for the car and round to the right through trees.

'I hope you don't mind, Mr Fallon, but it saves a good mile and a half this way.'

They came to a five-barred gate. He got out, opened it, drove through and got out to close the gate again. The main road was fifty yards further on at the end of the track.

As they moved down towards the centre of the city, Fallon said, 'You can drop me anywhere here, Charlie.'

'But you can't do that, Mr Fallon. You know you can't,' Varley groaned. 'You know what Mr Meehan said. I've got to take you back to Jenny's place.'

'Well, you tell Mr Meehan, with my compliments, that he can do the other thing.'

They were moving along Rockingham Street now and as they came to the Holy Name, Fallon leaned over suddenly and switched off the ignition. As the car coasted to a halt, he opened the door, jumped out and crossed the road. Varley watched him go into the side entrance of the church, then drove rapidly away to report.

11

The Gospel according to Fallon

The Right Reverend Monsignor Canon O'Halloran, administrator of the pro-cathedral, was standing at his study window when Miller and Fitzgerald were shown in. He turned to greet them, moving towards his desk, leaning heavily on a stick, his left leg dragging.

'Good morning, gentlemen, or is it? Sometimes I think this damned rain is never going to stop.'

He spoke with a Belfast accent and Miller liked him at once and for no better reason than the fact that in spite of his white hair, he looked as if he'd once been a useful heavyweight fighter and his nose had been broken in a couple of places.

Miller said, 'I'm Detective-Superintendent Miller, sir. I believe you know Inspector Fitzgerald.'

'I do indeed. One of four Knights of St Columba stalwarts.' Monsignor O'Halloran eased himself into the chair behind the desk. 'The bishop is in Rome, I'm afraid, so you'll have to make do with me.'

'You got my letter, sir?'

'Oh yes, it was delivered by hand last night.'

'I thought that might save time.' Miller hesitated and said carefully, 'I did ask that Father da Costa should be present.'

'He's waiting in the next room.' Monsignor O'Halloran filled his pipe from an old pouch methodically. 'I thought I'd hear what the prosecution had to say first.'

Miller said, 'You've got my letter. It says it all there.'

'And what do you expect me to do?'

'Make Father da Costa see reason. He must help us in this matter. He must identify this man.'

'If your supposition is correct, the Pope himself couldn't do that, Superintendent,' Monsignor O'Halloran said calmly. 'The secret nature of the confessional is absolute.'

'In a case like this?' Miller said angrily. 'That's ridiculous and you know it.'

Inspector Fitzgerald put a restraining hand on his arm, but Monsignor O'Halloran wasn't in the least put out. He said mildly, 'To a Protestant or a Jew, or indeed to anyone outside the Catholic religion, the whole idea of confession must seem absurd. An anachronism that has no place in this modern world. Wouldn't you agree, Superintendent?'

'When I consider this present situation then I must say I do,' Miller told him.

'The Church has always believed confession to be good for the soul. Sin is a terrible burden and through the medium of confession people are able to relieve themselves of that burden and start again.'

Miller stirred impatiently, but O'Halloran continued in the same calm voice. He was extraordinarily persuasive. 'For a confession to be any good as therapy, it has to be told to someone, which is where the priest comes in. Only as God's intermediary, of course, and one can only expect people to unburden themselves when they know that what they say is absolutely private and will never be revealed on any account.'

'But this is murder we're talking about, Monsignor,' Miller said. 'Murder and corruption of a kind that would horrify you.'

'I doubt that.' Monsignor O'Halloran laughed shortly and put another match to his pipe. 'It's a strange thing, but in spite of the fact that most people believe priests to be somehow cut off from the real world, I come face to face with more human wickedness in a week than the average man does in a lifetime.'

'Very interesting,' Miller said, 'but I fail to see the relevance.'

'Very well, Superintendent. Try this. During the last war, I was in a German prisoner-of-war camp where escape plans were constantly being frustrated because somebody was keeping the German authorities informed of every move that was made.' He heaved himself up out of his seat and hobbled to the window. 'I knew who it was, knew for months. The man involved told me at confession.'

'And you did nothing?' Miller was genuinely shocked.

'Oh, I tried to reason with him privately, but there was nothing else I could do. No possibility of my even hinting to the others what was going on.' He turned, a weary smile on his face. 'You think it easy carrying that kind of burden, Superintendent? Let me tell you something. I hear confessions at the cathedral regularly. Not a week passes that someone doesn't tell me something for which they could be criminally liable at law.'

Miller stood up. 'So you can't help us then?'

'I didn't say that. I'll talk to him. Hear what he has to say. Would you wait outside for a few minutes?'

'Certainly, but I'd like to see him again in your presence before we leave.'

'As you wish.'

They went out and Monsignor O'Halloran pressed a button on the intercom on his desk. 'I'll see Father da Costa now.'

It was a bad business and he felt unaccountably depressed in a personal sense. He stared out at the rainswept garden wondering what on earth he was going to say to da Costa and then the door clicked open behind him.

He turned slowly as da Costa crossed to the desk. 'Michael, what on earth am I going to do with you?'

'I'm sorry, Monsignor,' Father da Costa said formally, 'but this situation was not of my choosing.'

'They never are,' Monsignor O'Halloran said wryly as he sat down. 'Is it true what they suppose? Is this business connected in some way with the confessional?'

'Yes,' Father da Costa said simply.

'I thought so. The Superintendent was right, of course. As he said in his letter, it was the only explanation that made any kind of sense.' He sighed heavily and shook his head. 'I would imagine he intends to take this thing further. Are you prepared for that?'

'Of course,' Father da Costa answered calmly.

'Then we'd better get it over with,' Monsignor O'Halloran pressed the button on the intercom again. 'Send in Superintendent Miller and Inspector Fitzgerald.' He chuckled. 'It has a certain black humour, this whole business. You must admit.'

'Has it, Monsignor?'

'But of course. They sent you to Holy Name as a punishment, didn't they? To teach you a little humility and here you are, up to your ears in scandal again.' He smiled wryly, 'I can see the expression on the bishop's face now.'

The door opened and Miller and Fitzgerald were ushered in again. Miller nodded to da Costa. 'Good morning, Father.'

Monsignor O'Halloran pushed himself up on to his feet again, conscious that somehow the situation demanded it. He said, 'I've discussed this matter with Father da Costa, Superintendent. To be perfectly frank, there doesn't seem to be a great deal I can do.'

'I see, sir.' Miller turned to Father da Costa, 'I'll ask you again, Father, and for the last time. Are you prepared to help us?'

'I'm sorry, Superintendent,' Father da Costa told him.

'So am I, Father.' Miller was chillingly formal now. 'I've discussed the situation with my chief constable and this is what I've decided to do. A report on this whole affair and your part in it goes to the Director of Public Prosecutions today to take what action he thinks fit.'

'And where do you think that will get you?' Monsignor O'Halloran asked him.

'I should think there's an excellent chance that they'll issue a warrant for the arrest of Father da Costa on a charge of being an accessory after the fact to murder.'

Monsignor O'Halloran looked grave and yet he shook his head slowly. 'You're wasting your time, Superintendent. They won't play. They'll never issue such a warrant.'

'We'll see, sir,' Miller turned and went out followed by Fitzgerald.

Monsignor O'Halloran sighed heavily and sat down. 'So there we are. Now we wait.'

'I'm sorry, Monsignor,' Father da Costa said.

'I know, Michael, I know.' O'Halloran looked up at him. 'Is there anything I can do for you? Anything at all?'

'Will you hear my confession, Monsignor?'

'Of course.'

Father da Costa moved round to the side of the desk and knelt down.

When Fallon went into the church, Anna was playing the organ. It was obviously a practice session. Hymns in the main – nothing complicated. He sat in the front pew listening and after a while she stopped playing abruptly.

He walked up the steps between the choir stalls. 'The curse of the church organist's life, hymns,' he said.

She swung round to face him. 'You're early. Uncle Michael said one o'clock.'

'I'd nothing else to do.'

She stood up. 'Would you like to play?'

'Not at the moment.'

'All right,' she said. 'Then you can take me for a walk. I could do with some air.'

Her trenchcoat was in the sacristy. He helped her on with it. It was raining heavily when they went outside, but she didn't seem concerned.

'Where would you like to go?' he asked her.

'Oh, this will do fine. I like churchyards. I find them very restful.'

She took his arm and they followed the path between the old Victorian monuments and gravestones. The searching wind chased leaves from amongst the stones so that they seemed like living things crawling along the path in front of them.

They paused beside an old marble mausoleum for Fallon to light a cigarette and it was at that precise moment that Billy Meehan and Varley appeared at the side gate. They saw Fallon and the girl at once and ducked back out of sight.

'See, he's still here,' Varley said. 'Thank God for that.'

'You go back to Paul's Square and wait for Jack,' Billy said. 'Tell him where I am. I'll keep watch here.'

Varley moved away and Billy slipped in through the gate and worked his way towards Fallon and Anna, using the monuments for cover.

Anna said, 'I'd like to thank you for what you did last night.'

'It was nothing.'

'One of the men involved was an old friend of yours. O'Hara, wasn't that his name?'

Fallon said quickly, 'No, you've got it wrong.'

'I don't think so,' she insisted. 'Uncle Michael spoke to him after you'd left, in the pub across the road. He told him a great deal about you. Belfast, Londonderry – the IRA.'

'The bastard,' Fallon said bitterly. 'He always had a big mouth, that one. Somebody will be closing his eyes with pennies one of these fine days if he isn't careful.'

'I don't think he meant any harm. Uncle Michael's impression was that he thought a great deal about you.' She hesitated and said carefully, 'Things happen in war sometimes that nobody intends.'

Fallon cut in on her sharply. 'I never go back to anything in thought or deed. It doesn't pay.' They turned into another path and he looked up at the rain. 'God, is it never going to stop? What a world. Even the bloody sky can't stop weeping.'

'You have a bitter view of life, Mr Fallon.'

'I speak as I find and as far as I am concerned, life is one hell of a name for the world as it is.'

'And is there nothing, then?' she demanded. 'Not one single solitary thing worth having in this world of yours?'

'Only you,' he said.

They were close to the presbytery now and Billy Meehan observed them closely with the aid of a pair of binoculars from behind a mausoleum.

Anna stopped walking and turned to face Fallon. 'What did you say?'

'You've no business here.' He made a sweeping gesture with one arm encompassing the whole cemetery. 'This place belongs to the dead and you're still alive.'

'And you?'

There was a long pause and then he said calmly, 'No, it's different for me. I'm a dead man walking. Have been for a long time now.'

She was to remember that remark always as one of the most terrible things she had ever heard in her life.

She stared up at him, those calm, blind eyes fixed on some point in space, and then she reached up and pulled down his head and kissed him hard, her mouth opening in a deliberately provocative gesture.

She pulled away. 'Did you feel that?' she demanded fiercely. 'Did I break through?'

'I think you could say that,' he said in some amazement.

'Good,' she said. 'I'm going in now. I want to change and then I have lunch to get ready. You'd better play the organ or something until my uncle gets back.'

'All right,' Fallon said and turned away.

He had only taken a few steps when she called, 'Oh, and Fallon?' When he turned she was standing in the porch, the door half-open. 'Think of me. Remember me. Concentrate on that. I exist. I'm real.'

She went in and closed the door and Fallon turned and walked away quickly.

It was only when he was out of sight that Billy moved from the shelter of the mausoleum holding his binoculars in one hand. *Fallon and the priest's niece.* Now that was interesting.

He was about to turn away when a movement at one of the presbytery windows caught his eye. He moved back into cover and raised the binoculars.

Anna was standing at the window and as he watched, she started to unbutton her blouse. His mouth went dry, a hand seemed to squeeze his insides and when she unzipped her skirt and stepped out of it, his hands, clutching the binoculars, started to shake.

The bitch, he thought, and she's Fallon's woman. Fallon's. The ache between his thighs was almost unbearable and he turned and hurried away.

Fallon had been playing the organ for just over an hour when he paused for breath. It had been a long time and his hands were aching, but it was good to get down to it again.

He turned and found Father da Costa sitting in the front pew watching him, arms folded. 'How long have you been there?' Fallon got up and started down the steps between the choir stalls.

'Half an hour, maybe more,' Father da Costa said. 'You're brilliant, you know that, don't you?'

'Used to be.'

'Before you took up the gun for dear old mother Ireland and that glorious cause?'

Fallon went very still. When he spoke, it was almost in a whisper. 'That's of no interest to you.'

'It's of every interest,' Father da Costa told him. 'To me in particular, for obvious reasons. Good God, man, how could you do what you've done and you with so much music in you?'

'Sir Philip Sidney was reputed to be the most perfect of all knights at the court of Elizabeth Tudor,' Fallon said. 'He composed music and wrote poetry like an angel. In his lighter moments, he and Sir Walter Raleigh herded Irishmen together into convenient spots and butchered them like cattle.'

'All right,' Father da Costa said. 'Point taken. But is that how you see yourself? As a soldier?'

'My father was.' Fallon sat back on the altar rail. 'He was a sergeant in the Parachute Regiment. Killed at Arnhem fighting for the English. There's irony for you.'

'And what happened to you?'

'My grandfather raised me. He had a hill farm in the Sperrins. Sheep mostly – a few horses. I ran happily enough, wild and barefooted, till the age of seven when the new schoolmaster, who was also organist of the church, discovered I had perfect pitch. Life was never the same after that.'

'And you went to Trinity College?'

Fallon frowned slightly. 'Who told you that?'

'Your friend O'Hara. Did you take a degree?'

There was sudden real humour in Fallon's eyes. 'Would you believe me, now, Father, if I told you the farm boy became a doctor of music, no less?'

'Why not?' da Costa replied calmly. 'Beethoven's mother was a cook, but never mind that. The other? How did that start?'

'Time and chance. I went to stay with a cousin of mine in Belfast one weekend in August 1969. He lived in the Falls Road. You may remember what happened.'

Father da Costa nodded gravely. 'I think so.'

'An Orange mob led by B Specials swarmed in bent on burning every Catholic house in the area to the ground. They were stopped by a handful of IRA men who took to the streets to defend the area.'

'And you became involved.'

'Somebody gave me a rifle, let's put it that way, and I discovered a strange thing. What I aimed at, I hit.'

'You were a natural shot.'

'Exactly.' Fallon's face was dark and suddenly, he took the Ceska out of his pocket. 'When I hold this, when my finger's on the trigger, a strange thing happens. It becomes an extension, an extension of me personally. Does that make sense?'

'Oh, yes,' Father da Costa said. 'But of the most horrible kind. So you continued to kill.'

'To fight,' Fallon said, his face stony, and he slipped the Ceska back inside his pocket. 'As a soldier of the Irish Republican Army.'

'And it became easier? Each time it became easier.'

Fallon straightened slowly. His eyes were very dark. He made no reply.

Father da Costa said, 'I've just come from a final showdown with Superintendent Miller. Would you be interested to know what he intends?'

'All right, tell me.'

'He's laying the facts before the Director of Public Prosecutions and asking him for a warrant charging me with being an accessory after the fact to murder.'

'He'll never make it stick.'

'And what if he succeeds? Would it cause you the slightest concern?'

'Probably not.'

'Good, honesty at last. There's hope for you yet. And your cause, Fallon. Irish unity or freedom or hatred of the bloody English or whatever it was. Was it worth it? The shooting and bombings. People dead, people crippled?'

Fallon's face was very white now, the eyes jet black, expressionless. 'I enjoyed every golden moment,' he said calmly.

'And the children?' Father da Costa demanded. 'Was it worth that?'

'That was an accident,' Fallon said hoarsely.

'It always is, but at least there was some semblance of reason to it, however mistaken. But Krasko was plain, cold-blooded murder.'

Fallon laughed softly, 'All right, Father, you want answers. I'll try and give you some.' He walked to the altar rail and put a foot on it, leaning an elbow on his knee, chin in hand. 'There's a poem by Ezra Pound I used to like. "Some quick to arm," it says, and then later, "walked eye-deep in hell, believing in old men's lies." Well, that was my cause at the final end of things. Old men's lies. And for that, I personally killed over thirty people and assisted at the end of God knows how many more.'

'All right, so you were mistaken. In the end, violence in that sort of situation gains you nothing. I could have told you that before you started. But Krasko.' Father da Costa shook his head. 'That, I don't understand.'

'Look, we live in different worlds,' Fallon told him. 'People like Meehan – they're renegades. So am I. I engage in a combat that's nothing to do with you and the rest of the bloody civilians. We inhabit our own world. Krasko was a whoremaster, a pimp, a drug-pusher.'

'Whom you murdered,' Father da Costa repeated inexorably.

'I fought for my cause, Father,' Fallon said. 'Killed for it, even when I ceased to believe it worth a single human life. That was murder. But now? Now, I only kill pigs.'

The disgust, the self-loathing were clear in every word he spoke. Father da Costa said with genuine compassion, 'The world can't be innocent with Man in it.'

'And what in the hell is that pearl of wisdom supposed to mean?' Fallon demanded.

'Perhaps I can explain best by telling you a story,' Father da Costa said. 'I spent several years in a Chinese Communist prison camp after being captured in Korea. What they called a special indoctrination centre.'

Fallon could not help but be interested. 'Brainwashing?' he said.

'That's right. From their point of view, I was a special target, the Catholic Church's attitude to Communism being what it is. They have an extraordinarily simple technique and yet it works so often. The original concept is Pavlovian. A question of inducing guilt or rather of magnifying the guilt that is in all of us. Shall I tell you the first thing my instructor asked me? Whether I had a servant at the mission to clean my room and make the bed. When I admitted that I had, he expressed surprise, produced a Bible and read to me that passage in which Our Lord speaks of serving others. Yet here was I allowing one of those I had come to help to serve me. Amazing how guilty that one small point made me feel.'

'And you fell for that?'

'A man can fall for almost anything when he's half-starved and kept in solitary confinement. And they were clever, make no mistake about that. To use the appropriate Marxian terminology, each man has his thesis and his antithesis. For a priest, his thesis is everything he believes in. Everything he and his vocation stand for.'

'And his antithesis?'

'His darker side. The side which is present in all of us. Fear, hate, violence, aggression, the desires of the flesh. This is the side they work on, inducing guilt feelings to such a degree in an attempt to force a complete breakdown. Only after that can they start their own particular brand of re-education.'

'What did they try on you?'

'With me it was sex.' Father da Costa smiled. 'A path they frequently follow where Catholic priests are concerned, celibacy being a state they find quite unintelligible.'

'What did they do?'

'Half-starved me, left me on my own in a damp cell for three months, then put me to bed between two young women who were presumably willing to give their all for the cause, just like you.' He laughed. 'It was rather childish really. The idea was, I suppose, that I should be racked with guilt because I experienced an erection, whereas I took it to be a chemical reaction perfectly understandable in the circumstances. It seemed to me that would be God's view also.'

'So, no sin in you then. Driven snow. Is that it?'

'Not at all. I am a very violent man, Mr Fallon. There was a time in my life when I enjoyed killing. Perhaps if they'd worked on that they would have got somewhere. It was to escape that side of myself that I entered the Church. It was, still is, my greatest weakness, but at least I acknowledge its existence.' He paused and then said deliberately, 'Do you?'

'Any man can know about things,' Fallon said. 'It's knowing the significance of things that's important.'

He paused and Father da Costa said, 'Go on.'

'What do you want me to do, drain the cup?' Fallon demanded. 'The gospel according to Fallon? All right, if that's what you want.'

He mounted the steps leading up to the pulpit and stood at the lectern.

'I never realised you had such a good view. What do you want me to say?'

'Anything you like.'

'All right. We are fundamentally alone. Nothing lasts. There is no purpose to any of it.'

'You are wrong,' Father da Costa said. 'You leave out God.'

'God?' Fallon cried. 'What kind of a God allows a world where children can be happily singing one minute –' here, his voice faltered for a moment – 'and blown into strips of bloody flesh the next. Can you honestly tell me you still believe in a God after what they did to you in Korea? Are you telling me you never faltered, not once?'

'Strength comes from adversity always,' Father da Costa told him. 'I crouched in the darkness in my own filth for six months once, on the end of a chain. There was one day, one moment, when I might have done anything. And then the stone rolled aside and I smelled the grave, saw him walk out on his own two feet and I knew, Fallon! I knew!'

'Well, all I can say is, that if he exists, your God, I wish to hell you could get him to make up his mind. He's big on how and when. Not so hot on why.'

'Have you learned nothing, then?' Father da Costa demanded.

'Oh yes,' Fallon said. 'I've learned to kill with a smile, Father, that's very important. But the biggest lesson of all, I learned too late.'

'And what might that be?'

'That nothing is worth dying for.'

It was suddenly very quiet, only the endless rain drifting against the windows. Fallon came down the steps of the pulpit buckling the belt of his trenchcoat. He paused beside Father da Costa.

'And the real trouble is, Father, that nothing's worth living for either.'

He walked away down the aisle, his footsteps echoing. The door banged, the candles flickered. Father da Costa knelt down at the altar rail, folded his hands and prayed as he had seldom prayed before.

After a while, a door clicked open and a familiar voice said, 'Uncle Michael? Are you there?'

He turned to find Anna standing outside the sacristy door. 'Over here,' he called.

She moved towards him and he went to meet her, reaching for her outstretched hands. He took her across to the front pew and they sat down. And as usual she sensed his mood.

'What is it?' she said, her face full of concern, 'Where's Mr Fallon?'

'Gone,' he said. 'We had quite a chat. I think I understand him more now.'

'He's dead inside,' she said. 'Everything frozen.'

'And racked by self-hate. He hates himself, so he hates all of life. He has no feelings left, not in any normal sense. In fact it is my judgement that the man is probably seeking death. One possible reason for him to continue to lead the life he does.'

'But I don't understand,' she said.

'He put his whole life on the scales, gave himself for a cause he believed was an honourable one – gave everything he had. A dangerous thing to do, because if anything goes wrong, if you find that in the final analysis your cause is as worthless as a bent farthing, you're left with nothing.'

'He told me he was a dead man walking,' she said.

'I think that's how he sees himself.'

She put a hand on his arm. 'But what can you do?' she said. 'What can anyone do?'

'Help him find himself. Save his soul, perhaps. I don't really know. But I must do something. I must!'

He got up, walked across to the altar rail, knelt down and started to pray.

12

More Work for the Undertaker

Fallon was in the kitchen having tea with Jenny when the doorbell rang. She went to answer it. When she came back, Jack Meehan and Billy followed her into the room.

'All right, sweetheart,' Meehan told her. 'Make yourself scarce. This is business.'

She gave Fallon a brief troubled look, hesitated, then went out. 'She's taken a shine to you, I can see that,' Meehan commented.

He sat on the edge of the table and poured himself a cup of tea. Billy leaned against the wall by the door, hands in his pockets, watching Fallon sullenly.

'She's a nice kid,' Fallon said, 'but you haven't come here to discuss Jenny.'

Meehan sighed. 'You've been a naughty boy again, Fallon. I told you when I left you this morning to come back here and keep under cover and what did you do at the first opportunity? Gave poor old Varley the slip again and that isn't nice because he knows how annoyed I get and he has a weak heart.'

'Make your point.'

'All right. You went to see that bloody priest again.'

'Like hell he did,' Billy put in from the doorway. 'He was with that da Costa bird in the churchyard.'

'The blind girl?' Meehan said.

'That's right. She kissed him.'

Meehan shook his head sorrowfully. 'Leading the poor girl on like that and you leaving the country after tomorrow.'

'She's a right whore,' Billy said viciously. 'Undressing at the bloody window, she was. Anybody could have seen her.'

'That's hardly likely,' Fallon said. 'Not with a twenty-foot wall round the churchyard. I thought I told you to stay away from there.'

'What's wrong?' Billy jeered. 'Frightened I'll queer your pitch? Want to keep it all for yourself?'

Fallon stood up slowly and the look on his face would have frightened the Devil himself. 'Go near that girl again, harm her in any way, and I'll kill you,' he said simply and his voice was the merest whisper.

Jack Meehan turned and slapped his brother across the face back-handed. 'You randy little pig,' he said. 'Sex, that's all you can think about. As if I don't have enough troubles. Go on, get out of it!'

Billy got the door open and glared at Fallon, his face white with passion. 'You wait, you bastard. I'll fix you, you see if I don't. You and your posh bird.'

'I said get out of it!' Meehan roared and Billy did just that, slamming the door behind him.

Meehan turned to Fallon, 'I'll see he doesn't step out of line, don't you worry.'

Fallon put a cigarette between his lips and lit it with a taper from the kitchen fire. 'And you?' he said. 'Who keeps you in line?'

Meehan laughed delightedly. 'Nothing ever throws you, does it? I mean, when Miller walked into the church yesterday and found you talking to the priest, I was worried, I can tell you. But when you sat down at that organ.' He shook his head and chuckled. 'That was truly beautiful.'

There was a slight frown on Fallon's face. 'You were there?'

'Oh yes, I was there all right.' Meehan lit a cigarette. 'There's one thing I don't understand.'

'And what would that be?'

'You could have put a bullet in my head last night instead of into that mirror. Why didn't you? I mean, if da Costa is so important to you and you think I'm some sort of threat to him, it would have been the logical thing to do.'

'And what would have happened to my passport and passage on that boat out of Hull Sunday night?'

Meehan chuckled. 'You don't miss a trick, do you? We're a lot alike, Fallon, you and me.'

'I'd rather be the Devil himself,' Fallon told him with deep conviction.

Meehan's face darkened. 'Coming the superior bit again, are we? My life for Ireland. The gallant rebel, gun in hand?' There was anger in his voice now. 'Don't give me that crap, Fallon. You enjoyed it for its own sake, running around in a trenchcoat with a gun in your pocket like something out of an old movie. You enjoyed the killing. Shall I tell you how I know? Because you're too bloody good at it not to have done.'

Fallon sat there staring at him, his face very white, and then, by some mysterious alchemy, the Ceska was in his hand.

Meehan laughed harshly. 'You need me, Fallon, remember? Without me there's no passport and no passage out of Hull Sunday so put it away like a good boy.'

He walked to the door and opened it. Fallon shifted his aim slightly, following him, and Meehan turned to face him. 'All right then, let's see you pull that trigger.'

Fallon held the gun steady. Meehan stood there waiting, hands in the pockets of his overcoat. After a while he turned slowly and went out, closing the door behind him.

For a moment or so longer Fallon held the Ceska out in front of him, staring into space, and then, very slowly, he lowered it, resting his hand on the table, his finger still on the trigger.

He was still sitting there when Jenny came in. 'They've gone,' she said.

Fallon made no reply and she looked down at the gun with distaste. 'What did you need that thing for? What happened?'

'Nothing much,' he said. 'He held up a mirror, that's all, but there was nothing there that I hadn't seen before.' He pushed back his hair and stood up. 'I think I'll get a couple of hours' sleep.'

He moved to the door and she said diffidently, 'Would you like me to come up?'

It was as if he hadn't heard her and went out quietly, trapped in some dark world of his own. She sat down at the table and buried her face in her hands.

When Fitzgerald went into Miller's office, the Superintendent was standing by the window reading a carbon copy of a letter.

He offered it to Fitzgerald. 'That's what we sent to the Director of Public Prosecutions.'

Fitzgerald read it quickly. 'That seems to sum up the situation pretty adequately to me, sir,' he said as he handed the letter back. 'When can we expect a decision?'

'That's the trouble, they'll probably take a couple of days. Unofficially, I've already spoken to the man who'll be handling it by telephone.'

'And what did he think, sir?'

'If you really want to know, he wasn't too bloody hopeful.'

Miller's frustration was a tangible thing. 'Anything to do with religion, you know what people are like. That's the English for you.'

'I see, sir,' Fitzgerald said slowly.

It was only then that Miller noticed that the Inspector was holding a flimsy in his right hand. 'What have you got there?'

Fitzgerald steeled himself, 'Bad news, I'm afraid, sir. From CRO about that Ceska.'

Miller sat down wearily. 'All right, tell me the worst.'

'According to the computer, the last time a Ceska was used to kill someone in this country was in June, nineteen fifty-two, sir. A Polish ex-serviceman shot his wife and her lover to death. They hanged him three months later.'

'Marvellous,' Miller said bitterly. 'That's all I needed.'

'Of course they're circulating arms dealers in the London area for us,' Fitzgerald said. 'It will take time, but something could come out of that line of enquiry.'

'I know,' Miller said bitterly. 'Pigs might also fly.' He pulled on his raincoat. 'Do you know what the unique feature of this case is?'

'I don't think so, sir.'

'Then I'll tell you. There's nothing to solve. We already know who's behind the killing. Jack Meehan, and if that damned priest would only open his mouth I could have his head on a platter.'

Miller turned angrily and walked out, banging the door so hard that the glass panel cracked.

Fallon had only taken off his shoes and jacket and had lain on top of the bed. He awakened to find the room in darkness. He had been covered with an eiderdown which meant that Jenny must have been in. It was just after eight when he checked his watch and he pulled on his shoes hurriedly, grabbed his jacket and went downstairs.

Jenny was doing some ironing when he went into the kitchen. She glanced up. 'I looked in about three hours ago, but you were asleep.'

'You should have wakened me,' he said and took down his raincoat from behind the door.

'Jack Meehan said you weren't to go out.'

'I know.' He transferred the Ceska to the pocket of his raincoat and fastened the belt.

'It's that girl, isn't it?' she said. 'You're worried about her.' He frowned slightly and she rested the iron. 'Oh, I was listening outside the door. I heard most of what went on. What's she like?'

'She's blind,' Fallon said. 'That means she's vulnerable.'

'And you're worried about Billy? You think he might try to pay you off for what happened last night by getting at her?'

'Something like that.'

'I don't blame you.' She started to iron a crisp white blouse. 'Let me tell you about him so you know what you're up against. At twelve, most boys are lucky if they've learnt how to make love to their hand, but not our Billy. At that age, he was having it off with grown women. Whores mostly, working for Jack Meehan, and Billy was Jack's brother, so they didn't like to say no.' She shook her head. 'He never looked back. By the time he was fifteen he was a dirty, sadistic little pervert. It was downhill all the way after that.' She rested the iron again. 'So if I were you, I'd worry all right where he's concerned.'

'Thanks,' he said. 'Don't wait up for me.'

The door banged and he was gone. She stood there for a moment, staring into space sadly and then she returned to her ironing.

Anna da Costa was about to get into the bath when she heard the phone ringing. She put on a robe and went downstairs, arriving in the hall as her uncle replaced the receiver.

'What is it?' she asked.

'The Infirmary. The old Italian lady I visited the other day. She's had a relapse. They expect her to die some time tonight. I'll have to go.'

She took down his coat from the hallstand and held it out for him. He opened the front door and they moved out into the porch. The rain was pouring down.

'I'll walk,' he said. 'It's not worth taking the van. Will you be all right?'

'Don't worry about me,' she said. 'How long will you be?'

'God knows, probably several hours. Don't wait up for me.'

He plunged into the rain and hurried down the path passing a magnificent Victorian mausoleum, the pride of the cemetery with its bronze doors and marble porch. Billy Meehan dropped back into the shadows of the porch quickly, but when the priest had gone past, he moved forward again.

He had heard the exchange at the door and a cold finger of excitement moved in his belly. He had already had intercourse twice that night with a prostitute, not that it had been any good. He didn't seem to be able to get any satisfaction any more. He'd intended going home and then he'd remembered Anna – Anna at the window undressing.

He'd only been lurking in the shadows of that porch for ten minutes, but he was already bitterly cold and rain drifted in on the wind. He thought of Fallon, the humiliation of the previous night, and his face contorted.

'The bastard,' he said softly. 'The little Mick bastard. I'll show him.'

He produced a half-bottle of Scotch from his pocket and took a long pull.

Father da Costa hurried into the church. He took a Host out of the ciborium and hung it in a silver pyx around his neck. He also took holy oils with him to anoint the dying woman's ears, nose, mouth, hands and feet and went out quietly.

The church was still and quiet, only the images floating in candlelight, the drift of rain against the window. It was perhaps five minutes after Father da Costa's departure that the door creaked open eerily and Fallon entered.

He looked about him to make sure that no one was there, then hurried down the aisle, went inside the cage and pressed the button to ascend. He didn't go right up to the tower, stopping the cage on the other side of the canvas sheet covering the hole in the roof of the nave.

It only sloped slightly and he walked across the sheeted lead and paused at the low retaining wall, sheltering in the angle of a buttress with the tower.

From here, his view of the presbytery was excellent and two tall concrete lamp-posts in the street to the left towered above the cemetery walls, throwing a band of light across the front of the house.

There was a light in one of the bedroom windows and he could see right inside the room. A wardrobe, a painting on the wall, the end of a bed and then Anna suddenly appeared wrapped in a large white towel.

From the look of things she had obviously just got out of the bath. She didn't bother to draw the curtains, probably secure in the knowledge that she was cut off from the street by twenty-foot high walls or perhaps it was something to do with her blindness.

As Fallon watched she started to dry herself off. Strange how few women looked at their best in the altogether, he told himself, but she was more than passable. The black hair almost reached the pointed breasts and a narrow waist swelled to hips that were perhaps a trifle too large for some tastes.

She pulled on a pair of hold-up stockings, black bra and pants and a green, silk dress with a pleated skirt and started to brush her hair, perhaps the most womanly of all actions. Fallon felt strangely sad, no desire in him at all, certainly not for anything physical. Just the sudden terrible knowledge that he was looking at something he could never have on top of this earth and there was no one to blame but himself. She tied her hair back with a black ribbon and moved out of sight. A second later, the light went off.

Fallon shivered as the wind drove rain in his face and turned up his collar. It was very quiet, only the occasional sound of a car muted in the distance, and then, quite clearly, he heard the crunch of a foot in the gravel of the path below.

As he peered down, a figure moved out of the shadows into the light, the white shoulder-length hair identifying him at once. *Billy Meehan.* As Fallon leaned forward, the boy mounted the steps to the front door and tried the handle. It opened to his touch and he passed inside.

Fallon turned and scrambled back across the roof to the hoist. He jumped inside the cage, closed the gate and pressed the button to descend, his heart racing.

The sight of Anna at the window had excited Billy Meehan to a state where he could no longer contain himself. The ache between his legs was unbearable and the half-bottle of whisky which he had consumed had destroyed completely any last vestige of self-control.

He moved into the porch and tried the door and when it opened to his touch, he almost choked with excitement. He tiptoed inside, closing it behind him, and pushed the bolt home.

He could hear someone singing softly from a room at the end of the passage. He approached quietly and peered in through the partly opened door.

Anna was sitting at one end of a Victorian sofa, a small table at her elbow and the large sewing-box which stood on it was open. She was sewing a button on a shirt and as he watched, she reached into the mending-box, fumbled for a pair of scissors and cut the thread.

Billy took off his overcoat, dropped it to the floor and moved towards her, shaking with excitement. She was aware first of the coat dropping and then the faint sound of his approach and frowned, her face turned towards him.

'Who is it? Is anyone there?'

He paused momentarily and she stood up. Billy approached on tiptoe and as she half-turned, clutching the shirt to her, a needle in the other hand, he circled behind her.

'Who is it?' she demanded, fear in her voice.

He slipped a hand up her skirt from the rear, cupping it between her thighs and giggled. 'That's nice. You like that, don't you? Most girls like what I do to them.'

She gave a cry of horror, pulling away, turning to face him at the same moment and he reached forward and slipped a hand inside the neck of her dress feeling for a breast.

Anna cried out, her face a mask of horror. 'No, please – in the name of God! Who is it?'

'Fallon!' he said. 'It's me, Fallon!'

'Liar!' she screamed. 'Liar!' and lashed out blindly, catching him across the face.

Billy slapped her back-handed. 'I'll teach you, you bitch. I'll make you crawl.'

He knocked her back across the sofa tearing at her pants, forcing her thighs apart brutally, crushing his mouth on hers. Through the unbelievable horror of it, the nameless disgust, she was aware of his hand between his legs fumbling with the zip of his trousers and then the hardness pushing against her.

She screamed, he slapped her again, forcing her head back across the end of the sofa and her right hand, grabbing at the table for support, fastened upon the scissors. She was almost unconscious by then so that as the darkness flooded over her, she was not aware of her hand swinging convulsively, driving the scissors up under the ribs with all the force of which she was capable, piercing the heart and killing him instantly.

Finding the front door barred, Fallon had only been able to gain entry by breaking a kitchen window. He arrived in the sitting-room to find Billy Meehan sprawled across the unconscious girl and hurled himself on him. It was only in dragging him away that he saw the handle of the scissors protruding beneath the ribs.

He picked her up in his arms and carried her upstairs. The first room he tried was obviously her uncle's, but the second was hers and he laid her on the bed and covered her with an eiderdown.

He sat there holding her hand and after a while her eyelids flickered. She started violently and tried to pull her hands away.

Fallon said soothingly, 'There, now, it's me – Martin Fallon. You're all right now. You've nothing to worry about.'

She gave a great shuddering sigh. 'Thank God! Thank God! What happened?'

'Can't you remember?'

'Only this dreadful man. He said he was you and then he tried to . . . he tried to . . .' She shuddered. 'Oh, God, the feel of his hands. It was horrible. Horrible. I fainted, I think.'

'That's right,' Fallon said calmly. 'Then I arrived and he ran away.'

She turned her face to him, those blind eyes focusing to one side. 'Did you see who it was?'

'I'm afraid not.'

'Was it . . .' She hesitated. 'Do you think Meehan was behind it?'

'I should imagine so.'

She closed her eyes and when Fallon gently took her hand, she pulled it away convulsively. It was as if for the moment she could not bear the touch of a man – any man.

He steeled himself for the obvious question. 'Did he have his way with you?'

'No, I don't think so.'

'Would you like me to get you a doctor?'

'For God's sake, no, not that. The very idea that anyone should know fills me with horror.'

'And your uncle?'

'He's attending a dying woman at the Infirmary. He could be hours.'

Fallon stood up. 'All right – stay here and rest. I'll bring you a brandy.'

She closed her eyes again. The lids were pale, translucent. She seemed very vulnerable and Fallon went down the stairs full of controlled, ice-cold anger.

He dropped to one knee beside Billy Meehan, took out a handkerchief, wrapped it around the handle of the scissors and pulled them out. There was very little blood and obviously most of the bleeding was internal.

He cleaned the scissors, then went to the door and picked up the boy's overcoat. Some car keys fell to the floor. He picked them up mechanically, then draped the coat across the body.

As he looked down at it, he was conscious only of disgust and loathing. The world was well rid of Billy Meehan. His ending had been richly deserved, but could Anna da Costa live with the knowledge that she had killed him? And even if the verdict of the court was as it should be – even if she were exonerated, the whole world would know. At the thought of the shame, the humiliation for that gentle creature, Fallon's anger was so great that he kicked the corpse in the side.

And in the same moment, a thought came to him that was so incredible it almost took his breath away. What if she didn't have to know, now or ever? What if Billy Meehan vanished utterly and completely from the face of the earth as if he had never existed? There was a way. It could be done. In any event, he owed it to her to try.

The keys which had fallen from the overcoat pocket indicated the presence of Billy's car somewhere in the vicinity and if it was the red Scimitar, it should be easy enough to find. Fallon let himself out of the front door, hurried through the cemetery to the side gate.

The Scimitar was parked at the kerb only a few yards away. He unlocked the tailgate and when he opened it, Tommy, the grey whippet, barked once, then nuzzled his hand. The presence of the dog was unfortunate, but couldn't be helped. Fallon closed the tailgate and hurried back to the presbytery.

He pulled off the overcoat and went through the boy's pockets systematically, emptying them of everything they held. He removed a gold medallion on a chain around the neck, a signet ring and a wrist-watch and put them in his pocket, then he wrapped the body in the overcoat, heaved it over his shoulder and went out.

He paused at the gate to make sure that the coast was clear, but the street was silent and deserted. He crossed to the Scimitar quickly, heaved up the tailgate with one hand and dumped the body inside. The whippet started to whine almost immediately and he closed the tailgate quickly and went back to the presbytery.

He washed the scissors thoroughly in hot water in the kitchen, went back to the sitting-room and replaced them in the mending-box. Then he poured a little brandy in a glass and took it upstairs.

She was already half asleep, but sat up to drink the brandy. Fallon said, 'What about your uncle? Do you want him to know what happened?'

'Yes – yes, I think so. It's right that he should know.'

'All right,' Fallon said, and he tucked the quilt around her. 'Go to sleep now. I'll be downstairs. You've nothing to worry about. I'll wait till your uncle comes back.'

'He might be hours,' she said sleepily.

'That's all right.'

He walked to the door, 'I'm sorry to be such a nuisance,' she whispered.

'I brought you to this,' he said. 'If it hadn't been for me none of this would have happened.'

'It's pointless to talk like that,' she said. 'There's a purpose to everything under heaven – a reason – even for my blindness. We can't always see it because we're such little people, but it's there.'

He was strangely comforted by her words, God knows why, and said softly, 'Go to sleep now,' and closed the door.

Time, now, was the critical factor and he quietly let himself out of the front door and hurried through the churchyard to the Scimitar.

Strangely enough, the whippet gave him no trouble during the drive. It crouched in the rear beside the body, whining only occasionally, although when he put a hand on it, it was trembling.

He approached Pine Trees Crematorium by the back lane Varley had used that morning, getting out of the car to open the five-barred gate that led into the estate. He followed the same narrow track down through the cypress trees, cutting the engine for the last hundred yards which was slightly downhill. Not that it mattered, for as he remembered it, the superintendent's house and the main gate were a good quarter of a mile from the crematorium itself, so noise was really no problem.

He left the Scimitar at the side of the chapel and gained access by reaching in through the broken pane in the lavatory which he had noticed during his visit that morning and unfastening the window itself.

The chapel door had a Yale lock so opened easily enough from the inside. He returned to the Scimitar. There was a torch in the glove compartment which he slipped into his pocket, then he raised the tailgate and heaved the body over his shoulder. The whippet tried to follow, but he managed to shove it back inside with his free hand and closed the tailgate again.

He gained access to the furnace room by sliding the body along the rollers of the movable belt and crawling through after it himself, following the route the coffin had taken that morning.

The furnaces were cold and dark. He opened the door of the first one and shoved the body inside. Next he produced the various items he had taken from Billy Meehan's pockets and examined them in the light of the torch. Those things which would burn, he placed on top of the body. The ring, the watch and the medal he put back in his pocket. Then he closed the oven door and pressed the switch.

He could hear the muted rumble of the gas jets as they roared into life and peered inside. What was it Meehan had said? An hour at the most. He lit a cigarette, opened the back door and went outside.

The sound of the furnace in operation was barely discernible outside the building. Not at all when he moved a few yards away. He went back inside to see what was happening. The gauge was just coming up to the thousand degrees centigrade mark and as he peered through the observation panel in the door, the wallet he had left on the body's chest burst into flames. The clothing was already smouldering, there was a sudden bright flash and the whole body started to burn.

He lit another cigarette, went and stood at the back door and waited.

At the end of the specified period he switched off. There was part of the skull, the pelvic girdle and some of the limbs clearly visible, and much of this crumbled into even smaller pieces at the first touch of the rake.

He filled the tin box, found a handbrush and shovel, carefully swept up every trace of ash that he could see, then closed the furnace door leaving it exactly as he had found it. Certainly all heat would be dissipated again before the morning.

He found an empty urn, screwed it on the bottom of the pulveriser then poured in the contents of the tin box. He clamped down the lid and switched on. While he was waiting, he opened the desk drawer and helped himself to a blank Rest-in-Peace card.

When he switched off about two minutes later and unscrewed the urn, all that was left of Billy Meehan was about five pounds of grey ash.

He walked along the path to the point Meehan had taken him to that morning until he came across a gardener's wheelbarrow and various tools, indicating where the man had stopped work that afternoon.

Fallon checked the number plate and strewed the ashes carefully.

Then he took a besom from the wheelbarrow and worked them well in. When he was satisfied, he replaced the besom exactly as he had found it, turned and walked away.

It was when he reached the Scimitar that he ran into his first snag for as he opened the door to get behind the wheel, the whippet slipped through his legs and scampered away.

Fallon went after it fast. It went round the corner of the chapel and followed the path he had just used. When he reached the place where he had strewn the ashes, the whippet was crouching in the wet grass, whining very softly.

Fallon picked him up and fondled his ears, talking softly to him as he walked back. When he got behind the wheel this time, he held on to the animal until he had closed the door. He put it in the rear seat and drove away quickly.

It was only after he had closed the five-barred gate behind him and turned into the main road again that he allowed that iron composure of his to give a little. He gave a long shuddering sigh, a partial release of tension, and when he lit a cigarette his hands were trembling.

It had worked and there was a kind of elation in that. For a while it had seemed that Billy Meehan might prove to be just as malignant an influence in death as he had been in life, but not now. He had ceased to exist, had been wiped clean off the face of the earth, and Fallon felt not even a twinge of compunction.

As far as he was concerned, Billy Meehan had been from under a stone, not to wipe Anna da Costa's shoes. Let be.

When he reached Paul's Square, he turned into the mews entrance cautiously, but luck was with him to the very end. The yard was deserted. He ran the Scimitar into the garage, left both the keys and the whippet inside and walked rapidly away.

When he got back to the presbytery, there was no sign of Father da Costa. Fallon went upstairs on tiptoe and peered into Anna's bedroom. She was sleeping soundly so he closed her door and went back downstairs.

He went into the sitting-room and checked the carpet carefully, but there was no sign of blood. So that was very much that. He went to the sideboard and poured himself a large whisky. As he was adding a dash of soda, the front door opened.

Fallon turned round as Father da Costa entered the room. The priest stopped short in amazement. 'Fallon, what are you doing here?' And then he turned very pale and said, 'Oh, dear God! Anna!'

He turned and moved to the stairs and Fallon went after him. 'She's all right. She's sleeping.'

Father da Costa turned slowly. 'What happened?'

'There was an intruder,' Fallon said. 'I arrived in time to chase him away.'

'One of Meehan's men?'

Fallon shrugged. 'Maybe – I didn't get a good look at him.'

Father da Costa paced up and down the hall, fingers intertwined so tightly that the knuckles turned white. 'Oh, my God!' he said. 'When will it all end?'

'I'm leaving on Sunday night,' Fallon told him. 'They've arranged passage for me on a ship out of Hull.'

'And you think that will finish it?' Father da Costa shook his head. 'You're a fool, Fallon. Jack Meehan will never feel safe while I am still in the land of the living. Trust, honour, truth, the sanctity of the given word. None of these exist for him personally so why should he believe that they have a meaning for someone else?'

'All right,' Fallon said. 'It's all my fault. What do you want me to do?'

'There's only one thing you can do,' Father da Costa said. 'Set me free in the only way possible.'

'And spend my life in a maximum security cell?' Fallon shook his head. 'I'm not that kind of hero.'

He walked to the front door and Father da Costa said, 'She *is* all right?'

Fallon nodded soberly. 'A good night's rest is all she needs. She's a much stronger person than you realise. In every way.'

He turned to go out and Father da Costa said, 'That you arrived when you did was most fortuitous.'

'All right,' Fallon said. 'So I was watching the house.'

Father da Costa shook his head sadly. 'You see, my friend, good deeds in spite of yourself. You are a lost man.'

'Go to hell!' Fallon said and he plunged out into the rain and walked rapidly away.

13

The Church Militant

Father da Costa was packing his vestments into a small suitcase when Anna went into the study. It was a grey morning, that eternal rain still tapping at the window. She was a little paler than usual, but otherwise seemed quite composed. Her hair was tied back with a black ribbon and she wore a neat grey skirt and sweater.

Father da Costa took both her hands and led her to the fire. 'Are you all right?'

'I'm fine,' she said. 'Truly I am. Are you going out?'

'I'm afraid I have to. One of the nuns at the convent school of Our Lady of Pity died yesterday. Sister Marie Gabrielle. They've asked me to officiate.' He hesitated. 'I don't like leaving you.'

'Nonsense,' she said. 'I'll be all right. Sister Claire will be bringing up the children from the junior school for choir practice at ten-thirty. I have a private lesson after that until twelve.'

'Fine,' he said. 'I'll be back by then.'

He picked up his case and she took his arm and they went through to the hall together. 'You'll need your raincoat.'

He shook his head. 'The umbrella will be enough.' He opened the door and hesitated, 'I've been thinking, Anna. Perhaps you should go away for a while. Just until this thing is settled one way or the other.'

'No!' she said firmly.

He put down his case and took her by the shoulders standing there in the half-open doorway. 'I've never felt so helpless. So confused. After what happened last night, I thought of speaking to Miller.'

'But you can't do that,' she said quickly – too quickly. 'Not without involving Fallon.'

He gazed at her searchingly, 'You like him, don't you?'

'It's not the word I would choose,' she said calmly. 'I feel for him. He has been marked by life. No, used by life in an unfair way. Spoiled utterly.' There was a sudden passion in her voice. 'No one could have the music in him that man has and have no soul. God could not be so inhuman.'

'The greatest gift God gave to man was free will, my dear. Good and evil. Each man has a free choice in the matter.'

'All right,' she said fiercely. 'I only know one thing with any certainty. When I needed help last night, more than I have ever needed it in my life before, it was Fallon who saved me.'

'I know,' Father da Costa told her. 'He was watching the house.'

Her entire expression changed, colour touched those pale cheeks. 'And you don't care what happens to him?'

'Oh, I care,' Father da Costa said gravely. 'More than you perhaps understand. I see a man of genius brought down to the level of the gutter. I see a human being – a fine human being – committing, for his own dark reasons, a kind of personal suicide.'

'Then help him,' she said.

'To help himself?' Father da Costa shook his head sadly. 'That only works in books. Seldom in life. Whoever he is, this man who calls himself Martin Fallon, one thing is certain. He hates himself for what he has done, for what he has become. He is devoured by self-loathing.'

But by now she looked completely bewildered. 'I don't understand this – not any of it.'

'He is a man who seeks Death at every turn, Anna. Who would welcome him with open arms.' He shook his head. 'Oh yes, I care what happens to Martin Fallon – care passionately. The tragedy is that he does not.'

He turned and left her there in the porch and hurried away through the churchyard, head down against the rain, not bothering to raise his umbrella. When he moved into the side porch to unlock the sacristy door, Fallon was sitting on the small bench leaning against the corner, head on his chest, hands in the pockets of his trenchcoat.

Father da Costa shook him by the shoulder and Fallon raised his head and opened his eyes instantly. He badly needed a shave and the skin of his face seemed to have tightened over the cheekbones and the eyes were vacant.

'A long night,' Father da Costa said gently.

'Time to think,' Fallon said in a strange, dead voice. 'About a lot of things.'

'Any conclusions?'

'Oh yes.' Fallon stood up and moved out into the rain. 'The right place for me, a cemetery.' He turned to face da Costa, a slight smile on his lips. 'You see, Father, I've finally realised one very important thing.'

'And what's that?' Father da Costa asked him.

'That I can't live with myself any more.'

He turned and walked away very quickly and Father da Costa moved out into the rain, one hand extended as if he would pull him back.

'Fallon,' he called hoarsely.

A few rooks lifted out of a tree on the other side of the churchyard, fluttering in the wind like a handful of dirty black rags, calling angrily. As they settled again, Fallon turned the corner of the church and was gone.

When Anna closed the front door of the presbytery and went down the steps, she was instantly aware of the organ. She stood quite still, looking across the cemetery towards the church, head slightly turned as she listened. The playing, of course, was quite unmistakable. The heart quickened inside her, she hurried along the path as fast as she dared, tip-tapping with her stick.

When she opened the sacristy door, the music seemed to fill the church. He was playing *Pavane for a Dead Infanta*, infinitely moving, touching the very heart of things, the deep places of life, brilliant technique and emotion combining in a way she would never have thought possible.

He finished on a dying fall and sat, shoulders hunched for a long moment as the last echoes died away. When he swung round on the stool, she was standing at the altar rail.

'I've never heard such playing,' she told him.

He went down through the choir stalls and stood on the other side of the rail from her. 'Good funeral music.'

His words touched the heart in her like a cold finger. 'You mustn't speak like that.' She forced a smile. 'Did you want to see me?'

'Let's say I hoped you'd come.'

'Here I am, then.'

'I want you to give your uncle a message. Tell him I'm sorry, more sorry than I can say, but I intend to put things right. You'll have nothing more to worry about, either of you. He has my word on that.'

'But how?' she said. 'I don't understand.'

'My affair,' Fallon told her calmly. 'I started it, I'll finish it. Goodbye, Anna da Costa. You won't see me again.'

'I never have,' she said sadly, and put a hand on his arm as he went by. 'Isn't that a terrible thing?'

He backed away slowly and delicately, making not the slightest sound. Her face changed. She put out a hand uncertainly. 'Mr Fallon?' she said softly. 'Are you there?'

Fallon moved quickly towards the door. It creaked when he opened it and as he turned to look at her for the last time, she called, 'Martin, come back!' and there was a terrible desperation in her voice.

Fallon went out, the door closed with a sigh and Anna da Costa, tears streaming down her face, fell on her knees at the altar rail.

The Little Sisters of Pity were not only teachers. They also had an excellent record in medical missionary work overseas, which was where Father da Costa had first met Sister Marie Gabrielle in Korea in nineteen fifty-one. A fierce little French-woman who was probably the kindest, most loving person he had met in his entire life. Four years in a communist prison camp had ruined her health, but that indomitable spirit, that all-embracing love, had not been touched in the slightest.

Some of the nuns, being human, were crying as they sang the offertory; '*Domine Jesu Christ, Rex Gloriae, libera animas omnium fidelium* . . .'

Their voices rose sweetly to the rafters of the tiny convent chapel as Father da Costa prayed for the repose of Sister Marie Gabrielle's soul, for all sinners everywhere whose actions only cut them off from the infinite blessing of God's love. For Anna, that she might come to no harm. For Martin Fallon that he might face what must be done and for Dandy Jack Meehan . . .

But here, a terrible thing happened, for his throat went dry and he seemed to choke on the very name.

Once the Mass was over and the absolutions given, the nuns carried the coffin out through the rain to the small private cemetery in a corner between the inner and outer walls of the convent.

At the graveside Father da Costa sprinkled the grave and the coffin with holy water and incensed them and after he had prayed, some of the nuns lit candles, with some difficulty because of the rain, to symbolise Sister Marie Gabrielle's soul, with God now and shining still, and they sang together, very sweetly, the twenty-third psalm which had been her favourite.

Father da Costa remembered her, for a moment, during those last days, the broken body racked with pain. Oh God, he thought, why is it the good who suffer? People like Sister Marie Gabrielle?

And then there was Anna. So gentle, so loving, and at the thought of what had taken place the night before, black rage filled his heart.

Try as he might, the only thought that would come to mind as he looked down into the open grave was that Meehan's firm had probably made the coffin.

Jenny Fox had taken two sleeping pills the previous night and overslept. It was after eleven when she awakened and she put on her dressing-gown and went downstairs. She went into the kitchen and found Fallon sitting at the table, the bottle of Irish whiskey in front of him, a half-filled tumbler at his elbow. He had taken the Ceska to pieces and was putting it carefully together again. The silencer was also on the table next to the whiskey bottle.

'You're starting early,' she commented.

'A long time since I had a drink,' he said. 'A real drink. Now I've had four. I had some thinking to do.'

He emptied his glass in a single swallow, rammed the magazine into the butt of the Ceska and screwed the silencer on the end of the barrel.

Jenny said warily, 'Did you come to any conclusions?'

'Oh yes, I think you could say that.' He poured himself another whiskey and tossed it down. 'I've decided to start a Jack Meehan-must-go campaign. A sort of one man crusade, if you like.'

'You must be crazy,' she said. 'You wouldn't stand a chance.'

'He'll be sending for me some time today, Jenny. He has to because he's shipping me out from Hull tomorrow night so we've got things to discuss.'

He squinted along the barrel of the gun and Jenny whispered, 'What are you going to do?'

'I'm going to kill the bastard,' he said simply. 'You know what Shakespeare said. A good deed in a naughty world.'

He was drunk, she realised that, but in his own peculiar way. She said desperately, 'Don't be a fool. Kill him and there'll be no passage out of Hull for you. What happens then?'

'I couldn't really care less.'

He flung up his arm and fired. There was a dull thud and a small china dog on the top shelf above the refrigerator shattered into fragments.

'Well now,' he said. 'If I can hit that at this range after half-a-bottle of whiskey, I don't see how I can very well miss Dandy Jack.'

He stood up and picked up the bottle of whiskey. Jenny said, 'Martin, listen to me for God's sake.'

He walked past her to the door. 'I didn't go to bed last night so I will now. Wake me if Meehan calls, but whatever happens, don't let me sleep past five o'clock. I've got things to do.'

He went out and she stood there listening as he mounted the stairs. She heard the door to his bedroom open and close and only then did she move, going down on her hands and knees wearily to pick up the shattered fragments of the china dog.

The Bull and Bell yard was not far from Paul's Square, a dirty and sunless cobbled alley named after the public house which had stood there for two hundred years or more. Beside the entrance to the snug stood several overflowing dustbins and cardboard boxes and packing cases were thrown together in an untidy heap.

The Bull and Bell itself did most of its trade in the evening, which was why Jack Meehan preferred to patronise it in the afternoon. For one thing it meant that he could have the snug to himself, which was handy for business of a certain kind.

He sat on a stool, a tankard of beer at his elbow, finishing a roast beef sandwich and reading the *Financial Times*. Donner was sitting in the window seat playing solitaire.

Meehan emptied his tankard and pushed it across the bar. 'Same again, Harry.'

Harry was a large, hefty young man who, in spite of his white apron, had the physique of a professional Rugby player. He had long dark sideburns and a cold, rather dangerous-looking face.

As he filled the tankard and pushed it across, the door opened and Rupert and Bonati came in. Rupert was wearing a sort of caped, ankle-length highwayman's coat in large checks.

He shook himself vigorously and unbuttoned his coat. 'When's it going to stop, that's what I'd like to know.'

Meehan drank some more beer and belched. He said, 'What in the hell do you want? Who's minding the shop?'

Rupert slid gracefully on to the stool next to him and put a hand on his thigh. 'I do have to eat some time, ducky. I mean, I need to keep my strength up, don't I?'

'All right, Harry.' Meehan said, 'Give him his Bloody Mary.'

Rupert said, 'By the way, does anyone know where Billy is?'

'I haven't seen him since last night,' Meehan told him. 'Who wants him, anyway?'

'The superintendent at Pine Trees phoned into the office just before I left.'

'And what did he want?'

'It seems they found Billy's whippet wandering about up there. Soaked to the skin and trembling like a leaf apparently. Wanted to know what to do with him.'

Meehan frowned. 'What in the hell would it be doing up there?'

Donner said, 'Last I saw of it, was about half eight this morning when I went into the garage. It was inside the Scimitar. I figured Billy had forgotten about it when he came in last night so I let it out. I mean, he's done that before when he's been pissed or something. Left Tommy in the car, I mean.'

'He still hadn't come in when I came out this morning,' Meehan said, 'and if he left his car in the garage, that means he went to one of the city centre clubs. Probably still in bed with some whore, the dirty little bastard.' He turned to Bonati. 'You'd better go up to Pine Trees and get it. Take it back home and give it something to eat.'

'All right, Mr Meehan,' Bonati said and went out.

Meehan swallowed some more beer. 'Inconsiderate little swine. I'll kick his arse for him when I see him.'

'He's young, Mr Meehan,' Harry said. 'He'll learn.'

He picked up a bucket of slops, moved from behind the bar, and opened the door and went out into the yard. As he emptied the bucket across the cobbles, Father da Costa entered the yard. He was wearing his cassock and held the umbrella over his head against the rain.

Harry looked him over in some amazement and Father da Costa said politely, 'I'm looking for Mr Meehan – Mr Jack Meehan. They told me at his office that I might find him here.'

'Inside,' Harry said.

He moved into the snug and Father da Costa followed, pausing just inside the door to put down his umbrella.

It was Rupert who saw him first in the mirror behind the bar. 'Good God Almighty!' he said.

There was a long silence and Meehan turned on his stool very slowly.

'And what in the hell are you doing there? Rattling the box for Christmas or something? Will a quid get rid of you?'

He took out his wallet ostentatiously and Father da Costa said quietly, 'I was hoping we might have a few words in private.'

He stood there with the umbrella in his hand, the skirts of his cassock soaking wet from the long grass of the convent cemetery, mud on his shoes, grey beard tangled, waiting for some sort of response.

Meehan laughed out loud. 'God, but I wish you could see yourself. You look bloody ridiculous. Men in skirts.' He shook his head. 'It'll never catch on.'

Father da Costa said patiently, 'I don't expect it will. Now can we talk?'

Meehan indicated Donner and Rupert with a wave of the hand. 'There's nothing you can say to me that these two can't hear.'

'Very well,' Father da Costa said. 'It's simple enough. I want you to stay away from Holy Name and I don't want any repetition of what happened at the presbytery last night.'

Meehan frowned, 'What in the hell are you talking about?'

'All right, Mr Meehan,' Father da Costa said wearily. 'Last night, someone broke into the presbytery when I was out and attacked my niece. If Fallon hadn't arrived at the right moment and chased the man away anything might have happened to her. On the other hand, I suppose you'll now tell me that you know nothing about it.'

'No, I bloody well don't,' Meehan shouted.

Father da Costa struggled to contain his anger. 'You're lying,' he said simply.

Meehan's face was suffused with blood, the eyes bulging. 'Who in the hell do you think you are?' he demanded hoarsely.

'It's my final warning,' Father da Costa said. 'When we last spoke I told you my God was a God of Wrath as well as of Love. You'd do well to remember that.'

Meehan's face was purple with rage and he turned to the barman in fury. 'Get him out of here!'

Harry lifted the bar flap and moved out. 'Right, on your way, mate.'

'I'll go when I'm ready,' Father da Costa told him.

Harry's right hand fastened on his collar, the other on his belt and they went through the door on the run to a chorus of laughter from Donner and Rupert. They crowded to the door to see the fun and Meehan joined them.

Father da Costa was on his hands and knees in the rain in a puddle of water. 'What's up, ducky?' Rupert called. 'Have you pissed yourself or something?'

It was a stupid remark, childish in its vulgarity, and yet it was some sort of final straw that set black rage boiling inside Father da Costa so that when Harry dragged him to his feet, an arm about his throat, he reacted as he had been taught to react thirty years earlier in that hard, brutal school of guerrilla warfare and action by night.

Harry was grinning widely. 'We don't like fancy sods like you coming round here annoying the customers.'

He didn't get a chance to say anything else. Father da Costa's right elbow swung back into his ribs and he pivoted on one foot as Harry reeled back, gasping.

'You should never let anyone get that close. They haven't been teaching you properly.'

Harry sprang forward, his right fist swinging in a tremendous punch. Father da Costa swayed to one side, grabbed for the wrist with both hands, twisted it round and up, locking the arm and ran him headfirst into the stack of packing cases.

As Father da Costa turned, Donner came in fast and received a kick under the right kneecap, perfectly delivered, that doubled him over in pain and Father da Costa followed with a knee in the face that lifted him back against the wall.

Rupert gave a cry of dismay and in his haste to regain the safety of the snug, slipped on the top step, bringing Meehan down with him. As Meehan started to get up, Father da Costa punched him in the face, a good, solid right hand that carried all his rage, all his frustration with it. Bone crunched, Meehan's nose flattened beneath Father da Costa's knuckles and he fell back into the snug with a groan, blood gushing from his nostrils.

Rupert scrambled behind the bar on his hands and knees and Father da Costa stood over Meehan, the killing rage still on him, his fists clenched. And then he looked down at his hands, saw the blood on them and an expression of horror appeared on his face.

He backed slowly out into the yard. Harry lay on his face amongst the packing cases, Donner was being sick against the wall. Father da Costa looked in horror once again at the blood on his hands, turned and fled.

When he went into his study at the presbytery, Anna was sitting by the fire knitting. She turned her face towards him. 'You're late. I was worried.'

He was still extremely agitated and had to force himself to sound calm. 'I'm sorry. Something came up.'

She put down her knitting and stood up. 'After you'd gone, when I went down to the church to get ready for choir practice, Fallon was playing the organ.'

He frowned. 'Did he say anything? Did you speak with him?'

'He gave me a message for you,' she told him. 'He said to tell you that it had all been his fault and he was sorry.'

'Was there anything else?'

'Yes, he said that there was no need to worry from now on. That he'd started it, so he'd finish it. And he told me we wouldn't be seeing him again. What did he mean? Do you think he intends to give himself up?'

'God knows,' Father da Costa forced a smile and put a hand on her shoulder, a gesture of reassurance. 'I'm just going down to the church. Something I have to do. I won't be long.'

He left her there and hurried down through the cemetery, entering the church by way of the sacristy. He dropped on his knees at the altar rail, hands clenched together and looked up at Christ on the cross.

'Forgive me,' he pleaded. 'Heavenly Father, forgive me.'

He bowed his head and wept, for in his heart, he knew there was not one single particle of regret for what he had done to Jack Meehan. Worse than that, much worse, was the still, small voice that kept telling him that by wiping Meehan off the face of the earth he would be doing mankind a favour.

Meehan came out of the bathroom at the penthouse wearing a silk kimono and holding an ice-bag to his face. The doctor had been and gone, the bleeding had stopped, but his nose was an ugly, swollen, bruised hump of flesh that would never look the same again. Donner, Bonati and Rupert waited dutifully by the door. Donner's mouth was badly bruised and his lower lip was twice its usual size.

Meehan tossed the ice-bag across the room. 'No bloody good at all, that thing. Somebody get me a drink.'

Rupert hurried to the drinks trolley and poured a large brandy. He carried it across to Meehan who was standing at the window, staring out in the square, frowning slightly.

He turned, suddenly and mysteriously his old self again. He said to Donner, 'Frank, what was the name of that old kid who was so good with explosives?'

'Ellerman, Mr Meehan, is he the one you're thinking of?'

'That's him. He isn't inside, is he?'

'Not that I know of.'

'Good, then I want him here within the next hour. You go get him and you can tell him there's a couple of centuries in it for him.'

He swallowed some more of his brandy and turned to Rupert. 'And you, sweetheart – I've got just the job for you. You can go and see Jenny for me. We're going to need her, too, for what I have in mind.'

Rupert said, 'Do you think she'll play? She can be an awkward bitch, when she feels like it.'

'Not this time.' Meehan chuckled. 'I'll give you a proposition to put to her that she can't refuse.'

He laughed again as if it was a particularly good joke and Rupert glanced uncertainly at Donner. Donner said carefully, 'What's it all about, Mr Meehan?'

'I've had enough,' Meehan said. 'That's what it's all about. The priest, Fallon, the whole bit. I'm going to clean the slate once and for all. Take them both out this very night and here's how we're going to do it.'

Harvey Ellerman was fifty years of age and looked ten years older, which came of having spent twenty-two years of his life behind bars if he added his various sentences together.

He was a small diffident individual who habitually wore a tweed cap and brown raincoat and seemed crushed by life, yet this small, anxious-looking man was reputed to know more about explosives than any man in the north of England. In the end, his own genius had proved his undoing, for such was the uniqueness of his approach to the task in hand that it was as if he had signed his own name each time he did a job, and for some years the police had arrested him with monotonous regularity the moment he put a foot wrong.

He came out of the lift into the penthouse, followed by Donner, holding a cheap fibre suitcase in one hand that was bound together by a leather strap. Meehan went to meet him, hand extended, and Ellerman put the suitcase down.

'Great to see you, Harvey,' Meehan said. 'Hope you'll be able to help. Did Frank explain what I'm after?'

'He did, Mr Meehan, in a manner of speaking.' Ellerman hesitated. 'You won't want me personally on this thing, Mr Meehan? There's no question of that?'

'Of course not,' Meehan told him.

Ellerman looked relieved. 'It's just that I've retired from active participation in anything, Mr Meehan,' he said. 'You know how it is?'

'Too true, I do, Harvey. You were too bloody good for them.' He picked up Ellerman's suitcase and put it down on the table. 'Okay, let's see what you've got.'

Ellerman unfastened the strap and opened the suitcase. It contained a varied assortment of explosives carefully packed in tins, a selection of fuses and detonators, neat coils of wire and a rack of tools.

'Frank told me you wanted something similar to the sort of thing the IRA have been using in Ireland.'

'Not just similar, Harvey. I want it to be exactly the same. When the forensic boys get to examine what's left of this bomb I don't want there to be the slightest doubt in their minds where it's come from.'

'All right, Mr Meehan,' Ellerman said in his flat, colourless voice. 'Just as you say.' He produced a tin from the case. 'We'll use this, then. A Waverley biscuit tin. Made in Belfast. Packed with plastic gelignite. Say twenty pounds. That should do the trick.'

'What about a fuse?'

Ellerman held up a long, slim, dark pencil. 'They've been using a lot of these things lately. Chemical fuse of Russian manufacture. Virtually foolproof. Once you break the cap seal you've got twenty minutes.'

'Just the job,' Meehan rubbed his hands together. 'You'd better get started, then.'

He turned and walked across to the window, whistling happily.

14

Grimsdyke

Fallon came awake to find Jenny shaking him by the shoulder. 'Wake up!' she kept saying insistently. 'Wake up!'

There was a slight persistent throbbing ache behind his right eye, but otherwise he felt strangely light-headed. He sat up, swinging his legs to the floor, and ran his hands over his stubbled chin.

'What time is it?' he asked her.

'About four. Your friend, Father da Costa, was on the phone. He wants to see you.'

Fallon straightened slowly and looked at her, a slight, puzzled frown on his face. 'When was this?'

'About ten minutes ago. I wanted to come and get you, but he said there wasn't time.'

'And where does he want to see me? At Holy Name?'

She shook her head. 'No, he said he was taking his niece into the country. He thought it would be safer for her. A little place called Grimsdyke. It's about twenty miles from here in the marshes. He wants you to meet him there as soon as possible.'

'I see,' Fallon said. 'Do you know where this place is?'

She nodded. 'I used to go there for picnics when I was a kid. I've never been to this place he's going to, Mill House, he called it, but he told me how to get there.'

Fallon nodded slowly. 'And you'd take me?'

'If you like. We could go in my car. It wouldn't take much more than half an hour.'

He stared at her, the eyes very dark, no expression there at all. She glanced away nervously, unable to meet his gaze, and flushed angrily. 'Look, it's no skin off my nose. Do you want to go or don't you?'

He knew she was lying, yet it didn't seem to matter because for some strange reason he knew beyond any shadow of a doubt that she was leading him in the right direction.

'All right,' he said. 'Fine. Just give me a couple of minutes to get cleaned up. I'll meet you downstairs.'

As soon as she had gone he took the Ceska from his jacket pocket, ejected the magazine, reloaded carefully with eight rounds and slipped it into the right-hand pocket of his trenchcoat.

He moved across to the window, dropped to one knee and raised the carpet to disclose the Browning automatic he had used at his first meeting with Kristou in London. Underneath it was a large buff envelope containing the best part of two thousand pounds in ten-pound notes, the bulk of the money he had received from Meehan. He slipped the envelope into his breast pocket and checked the Browning quickly.

He found a roll of surgical tape in the cabinet over the washbasin and cut off a couple of lengths, using the razor Jenny had loaned him, then taped the Browning to the inside of his left leg just above the anklebone, covering it with his sock.

He buttoned his trenchcoat as he went downstairs. Jenny was waiting in the hall dressed in a red plastic mac. She gave him a tight smile as she pulled on her gloves. 'Ready to go, then?'

He opened the front door, but stopped her with a hand on her shoulder as she was about to step outside. 'There isn't anything else, is there? Anything you've forgotten to tell me?'

She flushed and the anger was there in her voice again. 'Would I be likely to do a thing like that?'

'That's all right, then.' He smiled calmly. 'We'd better get going.'

He closed the door and followed her down the steps to the Mini-Cooper parked at the bottom.

The marsh at Grimsdyke on the river estuary was a wild, lonely place of sea-creeks and mud flats and great, pale barriers of reeds higher than a man's head. Since the beginning of history men had come here for one purpose or another, Roman, Saxon, Dane, Norman, but now it was a place of ghosts. An alien world inhabited mainly by the birds, curlew and redshank and brent geese coming south from Siberia for the winter on the mud flats.

They passed through the village, a pleasant enough little place. Thirty or forty houses, a garage and pub, and then they were out on the other side. It was raining quite hard, the wind driving it in off the sea and across the marshes in great clouds.

'Half a mile beyond the village on the right.' Jenny glanced at Fallon briefly. 'That's what the man said.'

'This looks like it,' Fallon told her.

She turned the Cooper off the main road and followed a track no wider than a farm cart that was little more than a raised causeway of grass. On either side miles of rough marsh grass and reeds marched into the heavy rain and a thin sea mist was drifting before the wind.

Fallon lowered the window on his side and took a deep breath of the pungent salt air. 'Quite a place.'

'I used to love coming here when I was a kid,' she said. 'It was like nowhere else on earth. A different world after the city.'

The closer they got to the estuary, the more the mist seemed to close in on them and then they topped a rise and saw what was very obviously the mill sticking up above a clump of trees about a hundred yards to the south of them.

Fallon put a hand on her arm and she braked to a halt. 'Now what?'

'We'll walk from here.'

'Is that necessary?'

'If I've learned anything in life it's never to take anything for granted.'

She shrugged, but got out of the car without further argument and Fallon left the track and forced his way through a fir plantation towards the mill, dimly seen through the trees.

He crouched under a bush, pulling Jenny down beside him, and examined the place carefully. There was a three-storeyed stone tower, roof open to the sky. At one end there was an extension made of wood which looked like a barn and seemed to be in a better state of repair than the rest of the building. A thin trickle of smoke drifted up from an iron chimney.

At the other side there was an immense water-wheel and it was moving round now with an unearthly creaking and groaning, forced by the rushing waters of the flooded stream.

'No sign of his Mini van,' Fallon said softly.

'He'll have it inside that barn, won't he?' Jenny replied, and then added impatiently, 'For goodness sake, make your mind up. Are we going on or aren't we? I'm getting wet.'

She seemed angry and yet the fingers of her left hand trembled slightly. He said, 'You go. Give me a call if everything is all right.'

She glanced at him with a certain surprise in her eyes, then shrugged, stood up and walked out into the open. He watched her go, all the way to the barn. She turned to look at him once, then opened the big double door and went in.

She reappeared a moment later and called, 'It's all right. Everything's fine. Come on.'

Fallon hesitated for a moment and then shrugged and walked out into the clearing, a slight, fixed smile on his face. When he was four or five yards from the door, Jenny said, 'They're here,' and she went back inside.

He followed her in without hesitation. The place smelled of old hay and mice. There was a decrepit cart in one corner and a large loft ran round three sides of the building with round glassless windows letting in light. A fire was burning in an old iron stove in the corner.

There was no sign of Father da Costa or Anna, not that Fallon had really expected there to be. Only Jenny, standing alone beside a small iron cot bed against the far wall on which a little fair-haired girl was apparently sleeping, covered by a blanket.

'I'm sorry, Martin,' she said, and there was genuine distress in her face now. 'I didn't have any choice.'

'Up here, Fallon,' a voice called.

Fallon looked up and saw Donner on the edge of the loft holding an Armalite rifle. Rupert was standing beside him clutching a sawn-off shotgun and Harry, the barman from the Bull and Bell, appeared in the loft at the other side of the building, some sort of revolver in his right hand.

Donner raised the Armalite a little. 'They tell me that a bullet from one of these things goes in at the front and out at the back and takes a sizeable piece of you with it on the way, so I'd advise you to stay very still.'

'Oh, I will,' Fallon assured him without irony. And he raised his hands.

Harry came down the ladder from the loft first. He looked terrible. His left eye was completely closed and one side of his face was very badly bruised. He stood a yard or two away, covering Fallon with his revolver while Rupert followed him down the ladder. When they were both in position, Donner lowered the Armalite and joined them.

'Never trust a woman, ducky,' Rupert said with a mocking smile. 'I'd have thought you'd have learnt that. Unreliable bitches, the lot of them. Ruled by the moon. Now me, for instance . . .'

Donner kicked him in the leg. 'Shut up and search him. He'll probably have the shooter in his right-hand pocket.'

Rupert found the Ceska at once and the buff envelope containing the money. Donner looked inside and whistled softly. 'How much?' he demanded.

'Two thousand,' Fallon said.

Donner grinned. 'That must be what they mean by an unexpected bonus.'

He put the envelope in his inside pocket and Rupert started to run his hands over Fallon's body. 'Lovely,' he breathed. 'I could really go for you, ducky,' and he patted Fallon's cheek.

Fallon sent him staggering back with a stiff right arm. 'Put a hand on me again, and I'll break your neck.'

Rupert's eyes glittered and he picked up the sawn-off shot-gun and thumbed back the hammer. 'My, my, aren't we butch?' he said softly. 'But I can soon fix that.'

Donner kicked him in the backside. 'You bloody stupid little bitch,' he cried. 'What are you trying to do? Ruin everything at this stage?' He shoved him violently away. 'Go on and make some tea. It's all you're fit for.'

Rupert moved over to the stove sullenly, stili clutching his shotgun, and Donner took a pair of regulation police handcuffs from his pocket. He snapped them around Fallon's wrists, locked them and slipped the key into his breast pocket.

'You can have it the hard way or you can have it easy,' he said. 'It's all one to me. Understand?'

'I always try to,' Fallon said.

'Right, go and sit down by the bird where I can keep an eye on both of you.'

Fallon moved across to the cot and sat down beside it, his back against the wall. He looked at the child. Her eyes were closed, the breathing easy.

'The daughter you told me about?' he said. 'Is she all right?'

She nodded. 'They gave her a sedative, that's all.' Her eyes were bright with tears. 'I'm sorry, Martin, I didn't have any choice. I collected her after lunch like I do every Saturday and took her to the playground in the local park. That's where Rupert and that creep Harry picked us up.'

'And they threatened you?'

'They said they'd hang on to Sally. That I could have her back if I managed to get you out here.' She put a hand on his arm. 'What else could I do? I was terrified. You don't know Jack Meehan like I do. He's capable of anything – just like Billy.'

'Billy will never bother you again,' Fallon said. 'I killed him last night.'

She stared at him, eyes wide. 'You what?'

'Just as I intend to kill Dandy Jack,' Fallon said calmly. 'There's a packet of cigarettes in my left-hand jacket pocket, by the way. Light me one, will you, like a good girl?'

She seemed stunned by the enormity of what he had said but did as she was told. She put a cigarette in his mouth and as she struck a match, Donner joined them. He was carrying a tartan bag in one hand and squatted down in front of Fallon and unzipped it. One by one he produced three bottles of Irish whiskey and placed them on the ground.

'Jameson,' Fallon said. 'My favourite. How did you guess?'

'And all for you,' Donner told him. 'All three bottles.'

'I must say it sounds like an interesting idea,' Fallon said. 'Tell me more.'

'Why not?' Donner said. 'Actually, it's very good. I think you'll like it. You see, we have three problems, Fallon. The priest and his niece, because they know more than what's good for them.'

'And me?' Fallon said.

'Exactly.' Donner helped himself to a cigarette. 'Anyway, Mr Meehan had this rather nice idea. It's beautifully simple. We get rid of da Costa and his niece and put the blame on you.'

'I see,' said Fallon. 'And just how do you propose to do that?'

'You were a big man with a bomb in your hand over there in Ulster, weren't you? So it would make sense if you used the same method when you wanted to knock someone off over here.'

'My God,' Jenny said.

Donner ignored her and he was obviously enjoying himself. He said, 'Evening Mass at Holy Name is at six o'clock. When it's over, Mr Meehan and Bonati will pick up Father da Costa and his niece and take 'em up that tower, together with about twenty pounds of plastic gelignite and a chemical fuse packed in a Waverley biscuit tin. When that little lot goes up, they go with it and the church comes down.'

'I see,' Fallon said. 'And me – what about me?'

'That's easy. Bonati drives out here in da Costa's Mini van. You get three bottles of Irish whiskey poured down your throat, we put you behind the wheel and send you for a drive. There's a hill called Cullen's Bend about three miles from here. A terrible place for accidents.'

'And you think that will wrap things up?' Fallon asked him.

'As neat as a Christmas parcel. When they check what's left of that van they'll find bomb-making equipment and a few sticks of gelignite from the same batch the church bomb was manufactured from, not to mention the gun that was used to kill Krasko. The forensic boys will have a field day and let's face it – the Special Branch and Intelligence have been after you for years. They'll be delighted.'

'Miller won't buy it for a second,' Fallon said. 'He knows Meehan was behind the Krasko killing.'

'Perhaps he does, but there won't be a thing he can do about it.'

Jenny said in a whisper, 'It's murder. Cold-blooded murder. You can't do it.'

'Shut your mouth!' Donner said.

She backed away fearfully and then she noticed an extraordinary thing. Fallon's eyes seemed to have changed colour slightly, the dark flecked with light, and when he looked up at her there was a power in him that was almost physical, a new authority. Somehow it was as if he had been asleep and was now awake. He glanced across at the other two. Harry was examining the old cart, his back to them, and Rupert stood beside the stove fingering the shotgun.

'That's it then?' he said softly.

Donner shook his head in mock sorrow. 'You should have stayed back home in the bogs, Fallon. You're out of your league.'

'So it would appear,' Fallon said.

Donner leaned across to help himself to another cigarette. Fallon got both hands to the butt of the Browning he had taped so carefully to the inside of his left leg above the ankle, tore it free and shot Donner through the heart at point blank range.

The force of the shot lifted Donner off his feet, slamming him back against the ground, and in the same instant Fallon shot Harry in the back before he could turn, the bullet shattering his spine, driving him head first into the cart.

And as Jenny screamed, Fallon knocked her sideways, on his feet now, the Browning arcing towards Rupert as he turned in alarm, already too late, still clutching the shotgun in both hands.

His mouth opened in a soundless scream as Fallon's third bullet caught him squarely in the forehead. Blood and brains sprayed across the grey stones as the skull disintegrated and Rupert was knocked back against the wall, his finger tightening convulsively on the trigger of the shotgun in death, discharging both barrels.

Jenny sprawled protectingly across the child, still deep in her drugged sleep. There was silence. She looked up fearfully and saw that Fallon was standing quite still, legs apart, perfectly balanced, the Browning held out in front of him in both hands. His face was very white, wiped clean of all expression, the eyes dark.

His right sleeve was torn and blood dripped to the floor. She got to her feet unsteadily. 'You're hurt.'

He didn't seem to hear her, but walked to the cart where Harry sprawled on his face and stirred him with his foot. Then he crossed to Rupert.

Jenny moved to join him. 'Is he dead?' she whispered, and then she saw the back of the skull and turned away, stomach heaving, clutching at the wall to steady herself.

When she turned again, Fallon was on his knees beside Donner, fumbling in the dead man's breast pocket. He found the key he was looking for and stood up.

'Get me out of these things.'

The stench of that butcher's shop filled her nostrils, seeped into her very brain, and when she walked towards him, dazed and frightened, she stumbled and almost fell down.

He grabbed her by one arm and held her up. 'Steady, girl. Don't let go now. I need you.'

'I'm fine,' she said. 'Really I am.'

She unlocked the handcuffs. Fallon threw them to one side, dropped to one knee again and took the buff envelope from Donner's inside pocket.

As he stood up, Jenny said wearily, 'You'd better let me have a look at that arm.'

'All right,' Fallon said.

He took off his jacket and sat on the edge of the bed, smoking a cigarette while she did what she could for him.

The arm was a mess. Three or four nasty wounds where steel buckshot had ripped into the flesh. She bandaged it as best she could, with the handkerchief from Donner's breast pocket. Fallon picked up one of the bottles of Jameson, pulled the cork with his teeth and took a long swallow.

When she was finished, she sat on the bed beside him and looked around the barn. 'How long did it take? Two – maybe three seconds?' She shivered. 'What kind of man are you, Martin?'

Fallon pulled on his jacket awkwardly, 'You heard Donner, didn't you? A little Mick out of his league, who should have stayed back home in the bogs.'

'He was wrong, wasn't he?'

'Where I come from, he wouldn't have lasted a day,' Fallon said dispassionately. 'What time is it?'

She glanced at her watch. 'Five-thirty.'

'Good.' He stood up and reached for his trenchcoat. 'Evening Mass at Holy Name starts at six and finishes around seven. You take me there – now.'

She helped him on with the trenchcoat. 'That boat,' she said. 'The one you were supposed to leave on from Hull? I heard the name. Donner and Rupert were talking. You could still go.'

'Without a passport?'

He turned, trying to belt his coat, awkwardly because of his wounded arm, and she did it for him.

'Money talks,' she said. 'And you've got plenty in that envelope.'

She stood very close, her hands around his waist, looking up at him. Fallon said calmly, 'And you'd like to come with me, I suppose?'

She shook her head. 'You couldn't be more wrong. It's too late for me to change now. It was too late the day I started. It's you I'm thinking of. You're the only man I've ever known who gave me more than a quick tumble and the back of his hand.'

Fallon stared at her sombrely for a long moment and then said quietly, 'Bring the child.'

He walked to the door. Jenny picked up her daughter, wrapped her in a blanket and followed. When she went outside, he was standing, hands in pockets, staring up into the rain where brent geese passed overhead in a V formation.

He said quietly, 'They're free and I'm not, Jenny. Can you understand that?'

When he took his right hand out of his pocket, blood dripped from the fingers. She said, 'You need a doctor.'

'I need Dandy Jack Meehan and no one else,' he said. 'Now let's get out of here.' And he turned and led the way back along the track to the car.

15

The Wrath of God

Meehan was feeling pleased with himself, in spite of his broken nose, as he and Bonati walked past the town hall. Pleased and excited. His Homburg was set at a jaunty angle, the collar of his double-breasted melton overcoat was turned up against the wind, and he carried a canvas holdall containing the bomb in his right hand.

'I know one thing,' he said to Bonati as they crossed the road. 'I'd like to know where our Billy is right now. I'll have the backside off him for this when I see him.'

'You know what it's like for these young lads when they get with a bird, Mr Meehan,' Bonati said soothingly. 'He'll turn up.'

'Bloody little tarts,' Meehan said in disgust. 'All that lad ever thinks of is his cock-end.'

He turned the corner into Rockingham Street and received his first shock when he heard the organ playing at Holy Name and voices raised in song.

He dodged into a doorway out of the rain and said to Bonati, 'What in the hell goes on here? Evening Mass starts at six. I only make it ten to.'

'Search me, Mr Meehan.'

They crossed the street, heads down in a flurry of rain, and paused at the notice board. Bonati peered up, reading it aloud. 'Evening Mass, six o'clock, Saturdays, five-thirty.'

Meehan swore softly. 'A bloody good job we were early. Come on, let's get inside.'

It was cold in the church and damp and the smell of the candles was very distinctive. There were only a dozen people in the congregation. Father da Costa was up at the altar praying and on the other side of the green baize curtain, Meehan could see Anna da Costa's head as she played the organ.

He and Bonati sat down at one side, partially hidden by a pillar, and he put the canvas holdall between his feet. It was really quite pleasant sitting there in the half-darkness, Meehan decided, with the candles flickering and the organ playing. The four acolytes in their scarlet cassocks and white cottas reminded him nostalgically of his youth. Strangest thing of all, he found that he could remember some of the responses.

'I confess to Almighty God, and to you, my brothers and sisters,' said Father da Costa, 'that I have sinned through my own fault.'

He struck his breast and Meehan joined in enthusiastically, asking blessed Mary ever Virgin, all the angels and saints and the rest of the congregation to pray for him to the Lord our God.

As they all stood for the next hymn it suddenly struck him, with something like surprise, that he was thoroughly enjoying himself.

As the Cooper went over a humped-back bridge, Fallon, who had been sitting with his head forward on his chest, sat up with a start.

'Are you all right?' Jenny asked him anxiously.

'I'm fine,' he said and his voice was calm and perfectly controlled.

He touched his right arm gingerly. The shock effects were wearing off now and it was beginning to hurt like hell. He winced and Jenny noticed at once.

'I think I should take you straight to the Infirmary.'

He ignored the remark and turned to looked at the child who lay on the back seat, still in her drugged sleep, wrapped in the blanket in which Jenny had carried her from the mill.

'She's a nice kid,' he said.

The road was dangerous now in the heavy rain as darkness fell and needed all her attention, yet there was something in his voice that caused her to glance warily at him.

He lit a cigarette one-handed and leaned back against the seat. 'I'd like you to know something,' he said. 'What Donner said back there about me being bomb-happy wasn't true. Those kids in that school bus – it was an accident. They walked into an ambush we'd laid for a Saracen armoured car. It was a mistake.'

He hammered his clenched fist against his right knee in a kind of frenzy.

'I know,' Jenny told him. 'I understand.'

'That's good, that's marvellous,' he said. 'Because I never have.'

The agony in his voice was more than she could bear and she concentrated on the road, tears in her eyes.

As the congregation moved out, Anna continued to play and Father da Costa went into the sacristy with the acolytes. He took off his cope as the boys got out of their cassocks and into their street clothes. He saw them out of the side door, bidding each one of them good night.

Anna was still playing, something more powerful now, which meant that the last of the congregation had left. She always seemed to sense that moment. It was Bach again from the sound of it. The piece Fallon had played. She stopped abruptly. Father da Costa paused in the act of pulling off his alb and waited, but she did not start playing again. He frowned, opened the sacristy door and went into the church.

Anna was standing at the altar rail and Jack Meehan was holding her firmly by the arm. Father da Costa took an angry step forward and Bonati moved from behind a pillar holding a Luger in his left hand.

It stopped Father da Costa dead in his tracks and Meehan smiled. 'That's better. Now we're all going to take a little ride in the cage up to the catwalk. There's only room for two at a time so we'll have to split up. I'll stick with the girl, you go with Bonati, Father, and remember one thing. Anything you try that's the slightest bit out of turn will be reflected in the girl's treatment, so keep your hands to yourself and don't try any rough stuff.'

'All right, Mr Meehan,' Father da Costa said. 'What do you want with me?'

'All in good time.' Meehan pushed Anna across to the hoist, opened the cage door and followed her inside. As they started to rise he looked out at Father da Costa. 'Remember what I told you,' he said. 'So don't try anything funny.'

Father da Costa waited, the black, killing rage in him again and he fought to control it. What on earth did the man want? What was it all about? When the hoist descended again, he rushed inside eagerly and Bonati followed him and pressed the button.

When it jolted to a halt, Father da Costa opened the gate at once and stepped out. Meehan had switched the light on and the boards of the catwalk, wet with rain, glistened in the darkness.

Anna was standing, one hand on the rail, complete uncertainty on her face. Father da Costa took a step towards her and Meehan produced a Browning from his pocket. 'Stay where you are!' He nodded to Bonati. 'Tie his wrists together.'

There was little that Father da Costa could do except comply and he put his arms behind him. Bonati lashed his wrists together quickly with a piece of thin twine.

'Now the girl,' Meehan said.

Anna didn't say a word as Bonati repeated the performance. As he finished, her uncle moved to join her. 'Are you all right?' he asked her in a low voice.

'I think so,' she said. 'What's going to happen to us?'

'I'm afraid you'll have to address that question to Mr Meehan personally,' he said. 'I'm sure I don't know.'

Meehan unzipped the holdall, slipped his hand inside and broke the detonating cap on the chemical fuse, then he zipped the bag up again and put it down casually at the side of the catwalk in the shadows.

'All right, Father, I'll tell you what I'm going to do with you. I'm going to leave you and your niece up here on your own for fifteen minutes to meditate. When I return, I hope to find you in a more reasonable frame of mind. If not, then . . .'

'But I don't understand,' Father da Costa interrupted. 'What on earth are you hoping to accomplish?'

At that moment, the organ in the church below broke into the opening bars of the Bach Prelude and Fugue in D major.

The astonishment on Meehan's face was something to see. 'It's Fallon,' he whispered.

'It can't be,' Bonati said.

'Then who the hell am I listening to – a ghost playing?' Meehan's anger overflowed like white-hot lava. 'Go and get him,' he raved. 'Bring the bastard up here. Tell him the girl gets it if he doesn't come.'

Bonati hurriedly stepped into the cage, closed the gate and started down. When he was halfway there, the organ stopped playing. The cage juddered to a halt. It was suddenly very quiet. He cocked the Luger, kicked the gate open and stepped out.

When the Cooper turned into Rockingham Street and pulled up opposite Holy Name, Fallon was leaning in the corner, eyes closed. At first Jenny thought he was unconscious, or, at the very least, asleep, but when she touched him gently he opened his eyes at once and smiled at her.

'Where are we?'

'Holy Name,' she said.

He took a deep breath and straightened up. 'Good girl.' He put a hand inside his coat and produced the buff envelope and passed it across to her. 'There's nearly two thousand pounds in there. The money I received from Jack Meehan on account and hard earned. I won't need it where I'm going. Go off somewhere. Somewhere you've never even heard of. Take the kid with you and try again.'

The envelope was slippery with blood as she examined it in the light from the instrument panel. 'Oh my God,' she said, and then she switched on the interior light and turned to look at him. 'Oh, Martin,' she said in horror. 'There's blood all over you.'

'It doesn't matter,' he said, and he opened the car door.

She got out on her side. 'He'll kill you,' she said desperately. 'You don't know him like I do. You don't stand a chance. Let me get the police. Let Mr Miller handle him.'

'God save us, but I've never asked a policeman for help in my life.' A slight, ironic smile touched Fallon's mouth fleetingly. 'Too late to start now.' He patted her face gently. 'You're a nice girl, Jenny. A lovely girl. It didn't touch you, any of it. Always believe that. Now get the hell out of it and God bless you.'

He turned and crossed the road to Holy Name. Jenny got into the Cooper and started the engine. He was going to his death, she was convinced of that, and the compulsion to save him was something that she was unable to deny.

Suddenly resolute, she drove round the corner, stopped at the first telephone-box she came to and dialled nine-nine-nine. When they put her through to the main switchboard at police headquarters, she asked for Detective-Superintendent Miller.

There were still lights at the windows, but it was the absence of music that Fallon found puzzling until, gazing up at the noticeboard, he made the same discovery that Jack Meehan had about the time of evening Mass on a Saturday.

Panic moved inside him. Oh my God, he thought. I'm too late.

The door went back against the wall with a crash that echoed throughout the silent building, but the church was empty. Only the eternal ruby light of the sanctuary lamp, the flickering candles, the Virgin smiling sadly down at him, Christ high on his cross down there by the altar.

He ran along the centre aisle and reached the hoist. The cage was not there. They were still on top and he was conscious of a fierce joy. He pressed the button to bring the cage down, but nothing happened. He pressed it again with the same result. *Which meant that the cage was standing open up there.*

He hammered his clenched fist against the wall in despair. There had to be a way to bring Meehan down. There had to be.

And there was, of course, and it was so beautifully simple that he laughed out loud, his voice echoing up into the nave as he turned and moved towards the altar rail and went up through the choir stalls.

He sat down on the organ stool, switched on and pulled out an assortment of stops feverishly. There was blood on the keys, but that didn't matter and he moved into the opening of the Bach Prelude in D Major. The glorious music echoed between the walls as he gave it everything he had, ignoring the pain in his right hand and arm.

'Come on, you bastard!' he shouted aloud. 'Let's be having you.'

He stopped playing and was immediately aware of the slight clanging the cage made on its descent. He got up and went down the steps through the choir stalls, drawing the Ceska from his pocket and screwing the silencer into place with difficulty, arriving at the correct vantage point as the cage reached ground level.

Fallon flattened himself against the wall and waited, the Ceska ready. The cage door was kicked open and Bonati stepped out, clutching the Luger. Fallon shot him through the hand and Bonati dropped the Luger with a sharp cry and turned to face him.

'Meehan,' Fallon said. 'Is he up there?'

Bonati was shaking like a leaf in a storm, frightened out of his wits. He tried to speak, but could only manage to nod his head vigorously.

'All right.' Fallon smiled and Bonati saw that face again, a face to frighten the Devil. 'Go home and change your ways.'

Bonati needed no second bidding and ran up the aisle clutching his wrist. The door banged behind him, the candles fluttered. It was quiet again. Fallon moved into the cage and pressed the button to ascend.

On the catwalk, Meehan, Anna and Father da Costa waited, the rain falling in silver strands through the yellow light. The cage jerked to a halt, the door swung open. It was dark in there.

Meehan raised his Browning slightly. 'Bonati?'

Fallon drifted out of the darkness, a pale ghost. 'Hello, you bastard,' he said.

Meehan started to take aim and Father da Costa ducked low in spite of his bound hands and shouldered him to the rail, tripping him deftly so that Meehan fell heavily. The Browning skidded along the catwalk and Fallon kicked it into space.

He leaned against the rail for support, suddenly strangely tired, his arm really hurting now, and gestured with the Ceska.

'All right, untie him.'

Meehan did as he was told reluctantly and the moment he was free, Father da Costa untied Anna. He turned to Fallon, concern in his voice. 'Are you all right?'

Fallon kept all his attention on Meehan. 'The bomb? Have you set the fuse?'

'Get stuffed,' Meehan told him.

'Bomb?' Father da Costa demanded.

'Yes,' Fallon said. 'Did he have a bag with him?'

'Over there,' Father da Costa pointed to where the canvas holdall stood in the shadows.

'All right,' Fallon said. 'You'd better get Anna out of here fast and I mean out. If that thing goes off it will bring the whole church down like a house of cards.'

Father da Costa didn't even hesitate. He grabbed Anna by the arm and guided her towards the hoist, but she pulled free and turned towards Fallon. 'Martin!' she cried and caught at his trenchcoat. 'We can't go without you.'

'The cage only takes two at a time,' he said. 'Be sensible.'

There was blood on her hand from his sleeve and she held it close to her face as if trying to see it. 'Oh my God,' she whispered.

Father da Costa put an arm around her shoulders and said to Fallon, 'You're hurt.'

'You're running out of time,' Fallon said patiently.

Father da Costa pushed Anna inside the cage and followed her in. As he pressed the button to descend he called through the bars, 'I'll be back, Martin. Wait for me.'

His voice was swallowed up by darkness and Fallon turned to Meehan and smiled, 'You and me, Jack at the final end of things. Isn't that something? We can go to hell together.'

'You're mad,' Meehan said. 'I'm not waiting here to die. I'm going to get rid of this thing.'

He moved towards the holdall and Fallon raised the Ceska threateningly. 'I've had experience, remember? At this stage it'll go up at the slightest touch.' He chuckled. 'I'll tell you what we'll do. We'll leave it to God. If the cage gets back in time, we leave. If not . . .'

'You raving bloody lunatic.' Meehan was shouting now.

Fallon said calmly, 'By the way, I've just remembered I've got something for you.' He produced a crumpled white card with a black border and held it out.

Meehan said, 'What in hell is that supposed to be?'

'A Rest-in-Peace card, isn't that what you call them? It's for Billy. Plot number five hundred and eighty-two at Pine Trees.'

Meehan seemed stunned. 'You're lying.'

Fallon shook his head. 'I killed him last night because he tried to rape Anna da Costa. I took him up to the crematorium and put him through the whole process, just like you showed me. Last I saw of your brother, he was five pounds of grey ash scattered across damp grass.'

Meehan seemed to break into a thousand pieces. 'Billy!' he screamed and went for Fallon, head down.

Fallon pulled the trigger of the Ceska. There was a dull click and then Meehan was on him, smashing him back against the guard rail. It splintered, sagged, then gave way and Fallon went over the edge into space. He hit the canvas tarpaulin stretched over the hole in the roof and went straight through.

Meehan turned and reached for the holdall. As he picked it up and turned to throw it out into the darkness, it exploded.

As Father da Costa and Anna went out of the door into the street, two police cars arrived at speed. Miller scrambled out of the first one and hurried towards them. As he put foot on the first step leading up to the porch, the bomb exploded.

The effect was extraordinary, for the whole church started to fall in, almost in slow motion, first the tower, the steel scaffolding crumpling around it, and then the roof.

Miller grabbed Anna's other arm and he and Father da Costa ran her down into the safety of the street between them. As they reached the cars, a scaffolding pole rebounded from the wall of the warehouse above their heads and everyone ducked.

Father da Costa was first on his feet and stood, fists clenched, gazing up at the church. As the dust cleared, he saw that most of the walls and the rear entrance porch were still standing.

A young constable came forward from one of the police cars holding a spot lamp and Father da Costa simply took it from him and turned to Miller. 'I'm going back in.'

He started forward and Miller grabbed him by the arm. 'You must be crazy.'

'Fallon was in there,' Father da Costa said. 'He saved us, don't you understand? He might still be alive. I must know.'

'Fallon?' Miller said in astonishment. 'My God, so it was Fallon all the time.'

Father da Costa hurried up the steps to the porch and pushed open the door. The scene inside was incredible. Holy Name was finished; at the end of things at last, but the worst damage was by the tower or what was left of it.

Father da Costa went up the central aisle, flashing the spot before him. The area in front of the altar where the tower and roof had come down together was a mountain of bricks and mortar.

The spot picked out something inside. It could have been a face, he wasn't sure. There seemed to be a tunnel of sorts. He got down on his hands and knees and started to crawl through, holding the spot before him.

He found Fallon at the end of the tunnel, only his head and shoulders exposed. The figure of Christ on the cross, the large one which had stood by the altar, had fallen across him protectingly, at least for the moment.

Father da Costa crouched beside him and the great cross sagged under the weight it was holding and dust descended on his head.

'Martin?' he said. 'Can you hear me?'

There was a scraping sound behind him as Miller arrived. 'For God's sake, Father,' he said, 'We must get out of here. The whole damn lot might come down at any moment.'

Father da Costa ignored him. 'Martin?'

Fallon opened his eyes. 'Did you get Anna out?'

'I did, Martin.'

'That's all right, then. I'm sorry. Sorry for everything.'

The cross sagged a little more, stones and rubble cascaded over Father da Costa's back and he leaned across Fallon to protect him.

'Martin,' he said. 'Can you hear me?' Fallon opened his eyes. 'I want you to make an act of contrition. Say after me: O my God, who art infinitely good in Thyself . . .'

'O my God,' Martin Fallon said and died.

There was a long silence. Even that mass of rubble and debris seemed to have stopped moving. For some strange reason Miller suddenly felt as if he didn't belong, as if he had no right to be there. He turned and started to crawl out.

Behind him, Father Michael da Costa got down on his knees, head bowed beneath that frail roof, and started to pray for the soul of the man who had called himself Martin Fallon.

Day of Judgement

Freedom has many difficulties and democracy is not perfect, but we never had to put up a wall to keep our people in.

President John F. Kennedy
June 26th, 1963

For Mike Green, with thanks

Berlin 1963

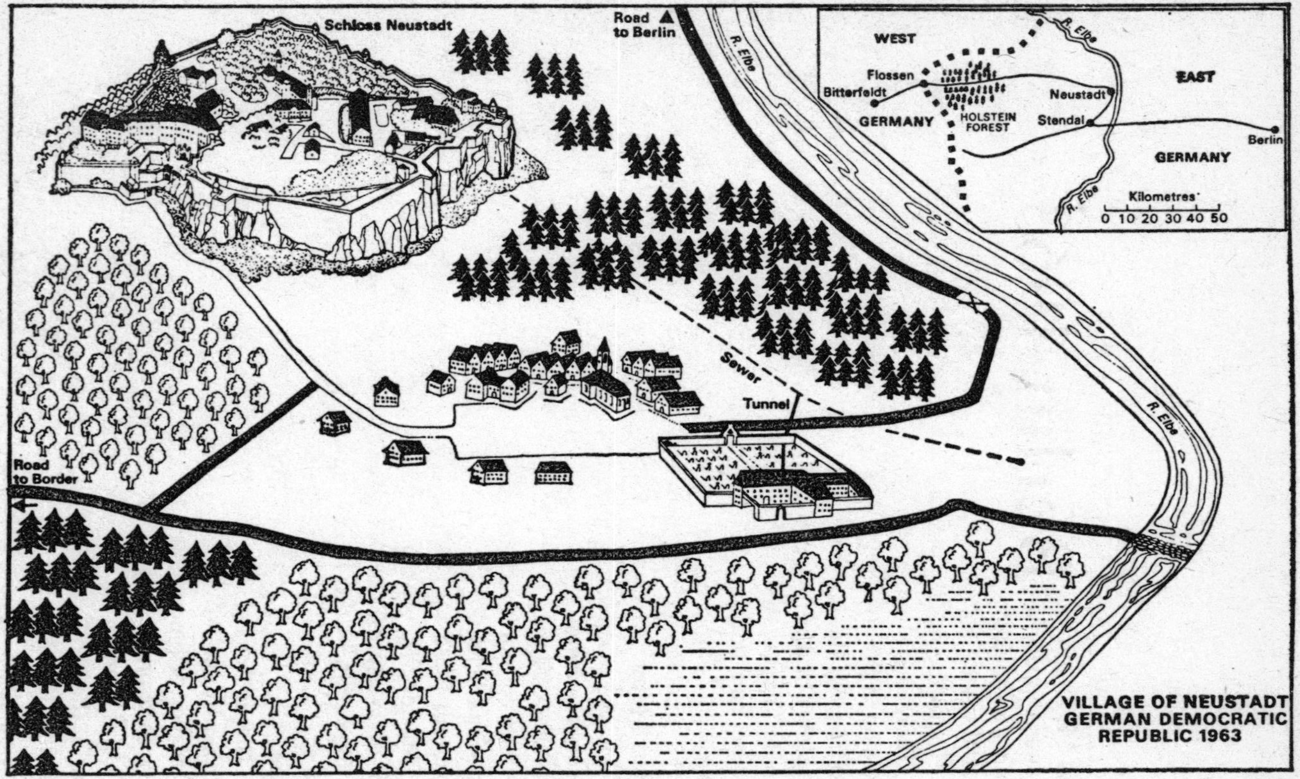

Schloss Neustadt
Road to Berlin
R. Elbe
WEST
EAST
Flossen
Bitterfeldt
Neustadt
GERMANY
HOLSTEIN FOREST
Stendal
Berlin
GERMANY
R. Elbe
Kilometres
0 10 20 30 40 50
Sewer
Tunnel
R. Elbe
Road to Border
VILLAGE OF NEUSTADT
GERMAN DEMOCRATIC
REPUBLIC 1963

1

As Meyer turned the corner in the old hearse he reduced speed, his hands slippery with sweat as they gripped the wheel, his stomach tightening as he drove towards the checkpoint, clear in the night under the harsh white light of the arc lamps.

'I must be mad,' he said softly. 'Crazy. The last time, I swear it.'

There were two Vopos at the red and white barrier wearing old-fashioned Wehrmacht raincoats, rifles slung. An officer lounged in the doorway of the hut smoking a cigarette.

Meyer braked to a halt and got out as one of the sentries opened the door. The street ran to the wall itself through an area in which every house had been demolished. Beyond, in a patch of light, was the Western Zone checkpoint.

He fumbled for his papers and the officer came forward. 'You again, Herr Meyer. And what have we this time? More corpses?'

Meyer passed his documents across. 'Only one, Herr Leutenant.' He peered anxiously at the officer through steel-rimmed spectacles. With his shock of untidy grey hair, the fraying collar, the shabby overcoat, he looked more like an unsuccessful musician than anything else.

'Anna Schultz,' the lieutenant said. 'Age nineteen. A trifle young, even for these hard times.'

'Suicide,' Meyer explained. 'Her only relatives are an uncle and aunt in the Western Zone. They've claimed her body.'

One of the Vopos had the back of the hearse open and was starting on the brass screws of the ornate coffin lid. Meyer hastily grabbed his arm.

The lieutenant said, 'So, you don't want us to look into the coffin? Now why should that be, I wonder?'

Meyer, wiping sweat from his face with a handkerchief, seemed at a loss for words.

At that moment a small truck pulled in behind. The driver leaned out of the window holding his documents. The lieutenant glanced over his shoulder impatiently and said, 'Get rid of him.'

One of the Vopos ran to the truck and examined the driver's papers quickly. 'What's this?'

'Diesel engine for repair at the Greifswalder Works.'

The engine was plain to see, roped into position on the truck's flat back. The Vopo returned the documents. 'All right – on your way.'

He raised the red and white pole, the truck-driver pulled out from behind the hearse and started towards the gap in the wall.

The lieutenant nodded to his men. 'Open it.'

'You don't understand,' Meyer pleaded. 'She was in the Spree for a fortnight.'

'We shall see, shall we?'

The Vopos got the lid off. The stench was immediate and all-pervading so that one of them vomited at the side of the hearse. The other flashed his torch for the lieutenant to peer inside. He moved back hurriedly.

'Put the lid on, for God's sake.' He turned to Meyer. 'And you, get that thing out of here.'

The truck passed through the barriers on the other side and pulled in at the checkpoint hut. The driver got out, a tall man in a black leather jacket and flat cap. He produced a crumpled packet of cigarettes, stuck one in his mouth and leaned forward to accept a light from the West German Police sergeant who had moved to join him. The match, flaring in the sergeant's hands, illuminated a strong face with high cheekbones, fair hair, grey eyes.

'Don't you English have a saying, Major Vaughan?' the sergeant said in German. 'Something about taking the pitcher to the well too often.'

'How do things look back there?' Vaughan asked.

The sergeant turned casually. 'There appears to be a little confusion. Ah yes, the hearse is coming now.'

Vaughan smiled. 'Tell Julius I'll see him at the shop.'

He climbed into the cab and drove away. After a while he kicked one heel against the front of the bench seat. 'Okay in there?' There was a muffled knock in reply and he grinned. 'That's all right then.'

The area of the city into which he drove was one of mean streets of old-fashioned warehouses and office blocks, alternating with acres of rubble, relic of the wartime bombing campaign. Some fifteen minutes after leaving the checkpoint, he turned into Rehdenstrasse, a dark street of decaying warehouses beside the River Spree.

Half way along, a sign lit by a single bulb read *Julius Meyer and Company, Undertakers*. Vaughan got out, unlocked the large gates, opened them and switched on a light. Then he got into the truck and drove inside.

The place had once been used by a tea merchant. The walls were of whitewashed brick and rickety wooden steps led up to a glass-walled office. Empty coffins were stacked on end in one corner.

He paused to light a cigarette and the hearse drove in. Vaughan moved past it quickly and closed the doors. Meyer switched off the engine and got out. He was extremely agitated and ceaselessly mopped sweat from his face with the grimy handkerchief.

'Never again, Simon, I swear it. Not if Schmidt doubles the price. I thought the bastard was on to me tonight.'

Vaughan said cheerfully, 'You worry too much.' He leaned into the cab of the truck, fumbled for a hidden catch so that the front of the bench seat fell forward. 'All right, you can get out now,' he said in German.

'This is a life, this life we lead?' Meyer said. 'Why do we have to live this way? What are we doing this for?'

'Two thousand marks a head,' Vaughan said. 'Paid in advance by Heini Schmidt, who's got so many of the poor bastards lined up over there that we can do it every night if we want to.'

'There's got to be an easier way,' Meyer told him. 'I know one thing. I need a drink.' He started up the steps to the office.

The first passenger, a young man in a leather overcoat, crawled out of the hidden compartment and stood blinking in the light, clutching a bundle. He was followed by a middle-aged man in a shabby brown suit whose suitcase was held together by rope.

Last of all came a girl in her mid-twenties with a pale face and dark sunken eyes. She wore a man's trench-coat and a scarf tied peasant-fashion round the head. Vaughan had never seen any of them before. As usual, the truck had been loaded in advance for him.

He said, 'You're in West Berlin now and free to go anywhere you please. At the end of the street outside you'll find a bridge across the Spree. Follow your nose from there and you'll come to an underground station. Good night and good luck.'

He went upstairs to the office. Meyer was sitting at the desk, a bottle of Scotch in one hand, a glass in the other which he emptied in one quick swallow.

He refilled it and Vaughan took it from him. 'Why do you always look as if you expect the Gestapo to descend at any moment?'

'Because in my youth there were too many occasions when that was a distinct possibility.'

There was a tapping at the door. As they both turned the girl entered the office hesitantly. 'Major Vaughan, could I have a word with you?'

Her English was almost too perfect, no trace of any accent. Vaughan said, 'How did you know my name?'

'Herr Schmidt told me when I first met him to arrange the crossing.'

'And where was that?'

'In the restaurant of the old Hotel Adlon. Herr Schmidt's name was given to me by a friend as a reliable man to arrange these matters.'

'You see?' Meyer said. 'Every minute it gets worse. Now this idiot hands your name out to strangers.'

'I need help,' the girl said. 'Special help. He thought you might be able to advise me.'

'Your English is really very good,' Vaughan told her.

'It should be. I was born in Cheltenham. My name is Margaret Campbell. My father is Gregory Campbell, the physicist. You've heard of him?'

Vaughan nodded. 'Between them, he and Klaus Fuchs handed the Russians just about every atomic secret we had back in nineteen-fifty. Fuchs ended up in the dock at the Old Bailey.'

'While my father and his twelve-year-old daughter found sanctuary in East Germany.'

'I thought you were supposed to live happily ever after,' Vaughan said. 'Socialist paradise and all that. Last I heard, your father was Professor of Nuclear Physics at Dresden University.'

'He has cancer of the lung,' she said simply. 'A terminal case. A year at the most, Major Vaughan. He wants out.'

'I see. And where would he be now?'

'They gave us a place in the country. A cottage at a village called Neustadt. It's near Stendhal. About fifty miles from the border.'

'Why not try British Intelligence? They might think it worth their while to get him back.'

'I have,' she said. 'Through another contact at the University. They're not interested – not any longer. In my father's field, you're very quickly yesterday's news and he's been a sick man for a long time now.'

'And Schmidt? Couldn't he help?'

'He said the risk involved was too great.'

'He's right. A little border-hopping here in Berlin is one thing, but your father – that's Indian territory out there.'

Whatever it was that had kept her going went out of her then. Her shoulders slumped, there was only despair in the dark eyes.

She seemed very young and vulnerable in a way that was curiously touching.

'Thank you, gentlemen.' She turned wearily, then paused. 'Perhaps you can tell me how to get in touch with Father Sean Conlin.'

'Conlin?' Vaughan said.

'The League of the Resurrection. The Christian Underground movement. I understood they specialized in helping people who can't help themselves.'

He sat staring at her. There was silence for a long moment. Meyer said, 'So what's the harm in it?' Vaughan still didn't speak and it was Meyer who turned to her. 'Like Simon said earlier, cross the bridge at the end of the street and straight on, maybe a quarter of a mile, to the underground station. Just before it, there's a Catholic church – the Immaculate Heart. He'll be hearing confessions round about now.'

'At four o'clock in the morning?'

'Night workers, whores, people like that. It makes them feel better before going to bed,' Vaughan said. 'He's that kind of man, you see, Miss Campbell. What some people would term a holy fool.'

She stood there, hands in pockets, a slight frown on her face, then turned and went out without a word.

Meyer said, 'A nice girl like that. What she must have gone through. A miracle she got this far.'

'Exactly,' Vaughan said. 'And I gave up believing in those long ago.'

'My God,' Meyer said. 'Have you always got to look for something under every stone you see? Don't you trust anybody?'

'Not even me,' Vaughan said amiably.

The judas gate banged. Meyer said, 'So you're just going to stand there and let a young girl walk all that way on her own and in a district like this?'

Vaughan sighed, picked up his cap and went out. Meyer listened to the echo of his footsteps below. The door banged again.

'Holy fool.' He chuckled to himself and poured another glass of Scotch.

Vaughan could see Margaret Campbell pass through the light of a street lamp thirty or forty yards in front of him. As she crossed the road to the bridge and started across, a man in slouch hat and dark overcoat moved out of the shadows on the far side and barred her way.

The girl paused uncertainly and he spoke to her and put a hand on her arm. Vaughan took a .38 Smith & Wesson from his inside pocket, cocked it and held it against his right thigh.

'No way to treat a lady,' he called in German as he mounted the half-dozen steps leading to the bridge.

The man was already turning very fast, his hand coming up holding a Walther. Vaughan shot him in the right forearm, driving him back against the rail, the Walther jumping into the dark waters below.

He made no sound, simply gripped his arm tightly, blood oozing between his fingers, lips compressed, a young man with a hard, tough face and high Slavic cheekbones. Vaughan turned him around, rammed him against the handrail and searched him quickly.

'What did he say to you?' he asked Margaret Campbell.

Her voice shook a little as she replied. 'He wanted to see my papers. He said he was a policeman.'

Vaughan had the man's wallet open now and produced a green identity card. 'Which, in a manner of speaking he is. SSD. East German State Security Service. Name of Röder, if you're interested.'

She seemed genuinely bewildered. 'But he couldn't have followed me. Nobody could. I don't understand.'

'Neither do I. Maybe our little friend here can help us.'

'Go to hell,' Röder said.

Vaughan hit him across the face with the barrel of the Smith & Wesson, splitting flesh, and Margaret Campbell cried out and grabbed him by the arm.

'Stop it!'

She was surprisingly strong and during the brief struggle, Röder ran to the end of the bridge and stumbled down the steps into the darkness. Vaughan finally managed to throw her off and turned in time to see Röder pass under a lamp at the end of the street, still running, and turn the corner.

'Congratulations,' he said. 'I mean, that really does help a lot, doesn't it?'

Her voice was the merest whisper. 'You'd have killed him, wouldn't you?'

'Probably.'

'I couldn't stand by and do nothing.'

'I know. Very humanitarian of you and a great help to your father, I'm sure.' She flinched at that, her eyes wide, and he slipped the Smith & Wesson into his inside pocket. 'I'll take you to see Father Conlin now. Another one big on the noble gesture. You and he should do rather well together.'

He took her arm and together they started across the bridge.

Father Sean Conlin had, with Pastor Niemoller, survived the hell of both Sachsenhausen and Dachau. Afterwards, five years in Poland had made him realize that nothing had really changed. That he was still fighting the enemy under a different name.

But a tendency to do things in his own way and a total disregard for any kind of authority had made him a thorn in the side of the Vatican for years, on one famous occasion censured by the Pope himself, which perhaps accounted for the fact that a man who was a legend in his own lifetime should still be a humble priest at the age of sixty-three.

He sat in the confessional box, a frail, white-haired man in steel-rimmed spectacles, dressed in alb, a violet stole about his neck, tired and cold for there had been more than usual that morning.

What he very much hoped was his last client, a local streetwalker, departed. He waited for a while, then started to get up.

There was a movement on the other side of the screen and a familiar voice said, 'You know, I've been thinking. Maybe people decide to give themselves to God when the Devil wants nothing more to do with them.'

'Simon, is that you?' the old man replied.

'Together with a true penitent. A young woman whose confession runs something like this. Forgive me, Father, for I have sinned. I am Gregory Campbell's daughter.'

Conlin said quietly, 'I think you'd better bring her into the sacristy and we'll have a cup of tea and see what she's got to say for herself.'

The sacristy was almost as cold as the church itself. Conlin sat at the small deal table with a cup of tea, smoking a cigarette while the girl told him about herself. She was, it seemed, a doctor by profession; had only taken her finals at Dresden the previous year.

'And your father? Where is he now?'

'Near Stendhal, in the country. A village called Neustadt. A very small village.'

'I know it,' he told her. 'There's a Franciscan monastery there.'

'I wouldn't know about that, but then I don't know the place well at all. There is an old castle by the river.'

'That will be Schloss Neustadt. It was presented to the Franciscans by some baron or other at the beginning of the century. They're Lutherans, by the way, not Catholic.'

'I see.'

He said to Vaughan, 'And what do you have to say?'

'I'd give this one a miss.'

'Why?'

'The SSD man at the bridge. What was he doing there?'

'It could be that they are on to you and Julius. Bound to happen after a while.'

'Excuse me, but is Major Vaughan's opinion relevant?' Margaret Campbell asked.

The old man smiled. 'You could have a point there.'

Vaughan got up. 'I think I'll take a little walk, just to see how things stand.'

'You think there could be others?' she asked.

'It's been known.'

He went out. She said to Conlin, 'He scares me, that one.'

Conlin nodded. 'A very efficient and deadly weapon, our Simon. You see, Miss Campbell, in the kind of game he plays he has a very real advantage over his opponents.'

'What is that?'

'That it is a matter of supreme indifference to him whether he lives or dies.'

'But why?' she demanded. 'I don't understand.'

So he told her.

When Vaughan went back into the sacristy they were talking quietly, heads together. The old priest glanced up and smiled. 'I'd like you to see Miss Campbell safely back into East Berlin later today. You'll do that for me, won't you, boy?'

Vaughan hesitated. 'All right,' he said, 'but that's as far as I go.'

'No need for more.' Conlin turned to Margaret Campbell. 'Once back on their side, return to Neustadt and wait for me. I'll be there the day after tomorrow.'

'Yourself?'

'But of course.' He smiled almost mischievously. 'Why should others have all the fun?' He stood up and put a hand on her shoulder. 'Never fear, my love. The League of the Resurrection has something of a reputation in this line of work. We won't let you down.'

She turned and went out. The old man sighed and shook his head. Vaughan said, 'What are you thinking about?'

'A child of twelve who, with only her father's hand to hold on to, was suddenly spirited away by night from everything warm and secure and recognizable, to a strange and rather frightening country with an alien people whose language she didn't even understand. I think now that in some ways she is still that lost and frightened little girl.'

'Very touching,' Vaughan said. 'But I still think you're wrong.'

'O, ye of little faith.'

'Exactly.'

Margaret Campbell was at the church gate when Vaughan caught up with her.

The street was deserted, grim and forbidding in the grey morning light. As they started along the pavement she said, 'Why do you live like this, a man like you? Is it because of what happened out there in Borneo?'

'Conlin and you *have* been improving the shining hour,' he said calmly.

'Do you mind?'

'I seldom mind anything.'

'Yes, that was the impression I got.'

He paused in a doorway to light a cigarette and she leaned against the wall and watched him.

Vaughan said, 'The old man was very taken.'

He very carefully tucked a wet strand of hair under her headscarf. She closed her eyes and took a hesitant step forward. His arm slipped around her waist and she rested her head against his shoulder.

'I'm so tired. I wish everything would stand up and walk away and leave me alone to sleep for a year and a day.'

'I know the feeling,' he said. 'But when you open those eyes of yours, you'll find nothing's changed. It never does.'

She looked up at him blankly. 'Not even for you, Vaughan? But I thought from what Father Conlin said you were the kind of man for whom the impossible only takes a little longer?'

'Even the Devil has his off-days, didn't he tell you that as well?'

He kissed her gently on the mouth. She was suddenly filled with a kind of panic and pulled away from him, turned and continued along the pavement. He fell in beside her, whistling cheerfully.

There was an all-night café by the bridge. As they neared it, it started to rain. He reached for her hand and they ran, arriving in the entrance slightly breathless and very wet.

The café was a small, sad place, half a dozen wooden tables and chairs, no more. A man in a dark blue overcoat was fast asleep in a corner. He was the only customer. The barman sat at the zinc-topped counter reading a newspaper.

She waited at a table by a window overlooking the river. Behind her, she could hear Vaughan ordering coffee and cognac.

As he sat down she said, 'You speak excellent German.'

'My grandmother came from Hamburg. She grew up by the Elbe, I was raised on the Thames. She lived with us when I was a boy. Raised me after my mother died. Made me speak German with her all the time. Said it made her feel at home.'

'And where was this?'

'Isle of Dogs near the West India Docks. My old man was captain of a sailing barge on the Thames for years. I used to go with him when I was a kid. Down to Gravesend and back. Even went as far as Yarmouth once.'

He lit a cigarette, the eyes dark, as if looking back across an unbridgeable gulf. She said, 'Where is he now?'

'Dead,' he said. 'A long time ago.'

'And your grandmother?'

'Flying bomb, November 'forty-four. There's irony for you.'

The barman appeared with a tray, placed a cup of coffee and a glass of cognac in front of each of them and withdrew. Vaughan took his cognac in one easy swallow.

'A little early in the day, I should have thought,' she commented.

'Or too late, depending on your point of view.'

He reached for her glass, she put a hand on his. 'Please?'

There was something close to surprise in his eyes and then he laughed softly. 'Definitely too late, Maggie. You don't mind if I call you that, do you? In fact, very definitely far too far gone. You know that poem of Eliot's where he says that the end of our exploring is to arrive where we started and recognize the place for the first time?'

'Yes.'

'He was wrong. The end of our exploring is to recognize the whole exercise for what it's been all along. One hell of a waste of time.'

He reached for the glass again and she knocked it over and sat staring at him, her face very white.

'And what's that supposed to prove?'

'Nothing,' she said. 'Just take it as sound medical advice.'

He sighed. 'All right. If you're ready, we'll move on. I'm sure you can't wait to get back on your side of the fence anyway.'

As they started towards the bridge she said, 'You still don't trust me, do you?'

'Not really.'

'Why?'

'No particular reason. Instinct, if you like. A lifetime of bad habits.'

'Yet you'll take me back across the wall because Father Conlin asked you to. I don't understand.'

'I know. Confusing, isn't it?'

He took her arm and they started across the bridge, footsteps hollow on the boards.

2

It was ten o'clock on Tuesday evening when the old army truck loaded with turnips pulled up the hill out of the village of Neustadt. About a quarter of a mile further on it turned in to the side of the road under pine trees.

Father Conlin wore a corduroy jacket and peaked cap, a grimy blue scarf knotted around his neck. His companion, the driver of the truck, wore an old army tunic and badly needed a shave.

'This is it, Karl, you are certain?' Conlin asked in German.

'The cottage is a couple of hundred yards from here at the end of the farm track through the woods, Father. You can't miss it, it's the only one,' Karl told him.

Conlin said, 'I'll take a look. You wait here. If everything's all right I'll be back for you in a few minutes.'

He moved away. Karl took the stub of a cigar from behind his ear and lit it. He sat there smoking for a while, then opened the door, got down and stood at the side of the truck to relieve himself. There was no sound at all, so that the blow that was delivered to the back of his head came as a total surprise. He went down with a slight groan and lay still.

There was a light at one of the cottage windows for the curtains were partially drawn. When Father Conlin approached cautiously and peered inside he saw Margaret Campbell, dressed in sweater and slacks, sitting in front of a blazing log fire reading a book.

He tapped on the pane. She glanced up, then crossed to the window and peered out at him. He smiled, but she did not smile in return. Simply went to the door and opened it.

Conlin moved into the warmth of the room, shaking rain from his cap. 'A good night for it.'

'You came,' she said in a choked voice.

'Didn't you think I would?' He was warming himself at the fire and smiled at her. 'Your father – how is he?'

'I wouldn't know,' she said tonelessly. 'I haven't seen him for weeks now. They wouldn't allow me.'

He saw it then of course, saw all of it, now that it was too late. 'Oh, my poor child,' he said and there was only concern for her in his voice, compassion in the faded blue eyes. 'What have they made you do?'

The kitchen door creaked open behind, a draught of air touched his neck coldly and he turned. A man was standing there, tall, rather distinguished-looking, dark hair turning to silver, a strong face – a soldier's face. He wore a heavy overcoat with a fur collar and smoked a thin cheroot.

'Good evening, Father Conlin,' he said in German. 'You know who I am?'

'Yes,' Conlin said. 'Helmut Klein. I believe you once enjoyed the dubious distinction of being the youngest full colonel in the Waffen SS.'

'Quite right,' Klein said.

Two men in raincoats emerged from the kitchen to stand beside him. At the same moment, the outside door opened and a couple of Vopos entered armed with machine-pistols, followed by a sergeant.

'We got the truck-driver, sir.'

'What, no comrade?' Father Conlin said. 'Not very socialistic of you, Colonel.' He turned to Margaret Campbell. 'Colonel Klein and I are old adversaries, at a distance. He is Director of Section Five, Department Two of the State Security Service which is charged with the task of combating the work of refugee organizations in Western Europe by any means possible. But then, you'd know that.'

Her eyes were burning, her face very pale. She turned to Klein. 'I've done what you asked. Now can I see my father?'

'Not possible, I'm afraid,' Klein said calmly. 'He died last month.'

The room was very quiet now and when she spoke it was in a whisper. 'But that can't be. It was only three weeks ago that you first sent for me. First suggested that I . . .' She gazed at him, total horror on her face. 'Oh, my God. He was dead. He was already dead when you spoke to me.'

Father Conlin reached out for her, but she pulled away and launched herself on Klein. He struck her once, knocking her back into the corner by the door. She lay there dazed. As Conlin tried to move towards her, the two men in raincoats grabbed him and the Vopos advanced.

'Now what?' the old priest asked.

'What do you except, whips and clubs, Father?' Klein asked. 'Nothing like that. We have accommodation reserved for you at Schloss Neustadt.

Comfortable – or otherwise – the choice is yours. A change of heart is what I seek. As publicly as possible, naturally.'

'Then you're wasting your time entirely,' the old man said.

Behind them, the door banged as Margaret Campbell slipped out into the night.

She had no idea where she was going, her brain unable to focus properly after the stunning shock she had received. Klein had lied to her. Used her love for her father to betray a remarkable man.

Her mind rejected the idea totally so that she ran as if from the consequences of her action, blundering through the trees in the darkness, aware of the cries of her pursuers behind. And before her was only the river, its waters, swollen by heavy rain, flooding across the weir.

One of the Vopos loosed off a burst from his machine-pistol and she cried out in fear, running even faster, one arm raised against the flailing branches, tripped over a log and rolled down the steep bank into the river.

The Vopos arrived a moment later and the sergeant flashed his torch in time to see her out there in the flood, an arm raised despairingly, and then she went under.

It was just after eight o'clock on the following evening when the black Mercedes saloon drew up to the entrance of the Ministry of State Security at 22 Normannenstrasse in East Berlin. Helmut Klein got out of the rear and hurried up the steps to the main entrance for he had an appointment to keep – probably the most important appointment of his entire career – and he was already late.

Section Five was located on the third floor. When he went into the outer office, his secretary, Frau Apel, rose from her desk considerably agitated.

'He arrived ten minutes ago,' she whispered, glancing anxiously at the three men in dark overcoats who stood by the inner door. Hard, implacable faces, ready for anything and capable of most things, from the look of them.

There was a fourth man, lounging in the window-seat reading a magazine. Small, with good shoulders, dark hair and grey eyes that had a transparent look to them. The left-hand corner of the mouth was lifted into a slight ironic half-smile that contained no humour, only a kind of contempt directed at the world in general. He wore a dark trench-coat.

Klein gave his coat to Frau Apel and moved towards him, hand outstretched. He spoke in English. 'Well, we got him, Harry. It worked, just like you said. The girl did exactly as she was told.'

'I thought she might.' The voice was soft and pleasant. Good Boston-American. 'Where is she now?'

'Dead.' Klein explained briefly what had happened.

'What a pity,' the small man said. 'She was rather pretty. You've got the man himself in there, by the way. I almost got to touch the hem of his garment as he swept by.'

Klein glanced quickly at the security men by the door and dropped his voice. 'Exactly the kind of remark we can do without. When I call you in, try and behave yourself.'

He opened the door to his office and entered. The man in the trench-coat stuck a cigarette in the corner of his mouth, but didn't bother to light it. He smiled down at Frau Apel and for some reason she was aware of a slight flutter of excitement.

'Big night, eh?' he said in German.

'A great honour.' She hesitated. 'They may be a while. Perhaps I could get you a cup of coffee, Herr Professor?'

He smiled. 'No, thanks. I'll just go back to the window-seat and wait. I get an excellent view of your legs from there under the desk. You really are a very disturbing person, did anyone ever tell you that?'

He returned to the window. She sat there, her throat dry, unable to think of a thing to say and he stared at her with those grey, dead eyes that gave nothing away, the perpetual smile as if he was laughing at her. She reached for a sheet of typing paper quickly. As she put it into the machine, her hands were shaking.

When Klein entered his office, the man behind the desk glanced up sharply. His suit was neat, conservative, the beard carefully trimmed, the eyes behind the thick lenses of the glasses apparently benign. Yet this was the most powerful man in East Germany – Walter Ulbricht, chairman of the Council of State.

'You're late,' he said.

'A fact which I sincerely regret, Comrade Chairman,' Klein told him. 'Several main roads leading into the city from the west are flooded. We were obliged to make a detour.'

'Never mind the excuses,' Ulbricht said impatiently. 'You got him?'

'Yes, Comrade.'

Ulbricht showed no particular emotion. 'I fly to Moscow in the morning and as I shall be away for a week at least I want to make sure this thing is fully under way. The man you have chosen to accomplish the task, the American, Van Buren. He is here?'

'Waiting outside.'

'And you believe he can do it?'

Klein opened his briefcase, took out a folder which he placed on the desk before Ulbricht. 'His personal file. If you would be kind enough to have a look at it before seeing him, Comrade. I think it speaks for itself.'

'Very well.' Ulbricht adjusted his glasses, opened the file and began to read.

In the early months of 1950 Senator Joseph McCarthy charged that he had evidence that a number of employees of the American State Department were Communists. Arthur Van Buren, a Professor in Moral Philosophy at Columbia University, was injudicious enough to write a series of letters to the *New York Times* in which he suggested that in this new development the seeds of a fascist state were being sown in America.

Like others, he was called to Washington to stand before a Senate sub-committee in the greatest witch-hunt the nation had ever seen. He emerged from it totally discredited, branded a Communist in the eyes of the world, his career in ruins. In March 1950 he shot himself.

Harry Van Buren was his only son, at that time twenty-four years of age. He had majored in psychology at Columbia, researched in experimental psychiatry at Guy's Hospital in London, taking his doctorate at London University in February 1950.

He arrived home in time to stand beside his father's grave when they buried him. He didn't really know what to make of it all. His mother had died when he was five.

His father's brother was in the machine-tool business and almost a millionaire; his Aunt Mary was married to a man who owned forty-seven hotels. They seemed more concerned with the possibility that the senator from Wisconsin had been right. That his father was indeed a Red. It was up to Harry to restore the family honour, which he did by joining the Marine Corps the moment the Korean war started.

Nonsensical behaviour, of course. As a professional psychologist he could see that. Could even understand the reasons for it and yet he went ahead, lying on his enlistment papers about his education, a need, he told himself, to purge some kind of guilt.

He pulled mess duty, swabbed out the heads, endured the close proximity of companions he found both brutal and coarse and kept himself to himself. He took everything they handed out to him and developed a kind of contempt for his fellows that he would not have thought possible.

And then came Korea itself. A nightmare of stupidity. A winter so cold that if the M1 was oiled too much it froze. Where grenades did not explode, where the jackets of the water-cooled heavy machine-guns had to be filled with anti-freeze.

In November of 1950 he found himself part of the First Marine Division facing northwards to Koto-Ri to end the war at one bold stroke as General Douglas MacArthur intended. Except that the Chinese Army had other ideas and the Marines walked into a trap that was sprung at the Choisin Reservoir and led to one of the greatest fighting retreats in the history of war.

For a while he played his part with the others who fought and died around him. He killed Chinese with bullet and bayonet, urinated on the bolt mechanism of his carbine when it froze, and staggered on with frostbite in his left foot and a bullet in the right shoulder. And when a boot in the side stirred him into waking one misty morning, it was something like a relief to look up into a Chinese face.

It was at the camp in Manchuria that he'd decided he'd had enough after the first month in the coal mine. The indoctrination sessions had given him his opportunity. The chief instructor was crude in the extreme. Easy enough not to contradict, but to reinforce the points he was making. A few days of that and Van Buren was sent for special interrogation during which he made a full and frank confession of his background.

He was used at first to work as a missionary amongst his fellow prisoners until he came to the attention of the famous Chinese psychologist, Ping Chow, of Peking University, who at that time was making a special study of the behaviour patterns of American prisoners of war. Chow was a Pavlovian by training and his work on the conditioning of human behaviour was already world-famous at an academic level.

In Van Buren he found a mind totally in tune with his own. The American moved to Peking to research in the psychology department of the university there. There was no question in his own mind now of any return to America.

Soon enough both the Pentagon and the State Department became uncomfortably aware of his existence, but kept quiet about it for obvious reasons so that he remained on that list of those missing, presumed dead, in Korea.

By 1959 he was an expert in thought reform and by special arrangement moved to Moscow to lecture at the university there. By 1960 his reputation in the field of what the Press popularly termed 'brainwashing' was already legendary. There was not a security department in any Iron Curtain country which had not called upon his services.

And then, in April 1963, while lecturing at the University of Dresden in the German Democratic Republic, he had received a visit from Helmut Klein, Head of Section Five in the State Security Service.

Walter Ulbricht closed the file and looked up. 'There is one flaw in all this.'

'Which is, Comrade Chairman?'

'Professor Van Buren is not, and never has been, a Communist.'

'I agree entirely,' Klein said. 'But for our purposes he is, if I may say so, something far more important – a dedicated scientist. He is a man obsessed by his work to an astonishing degree. I have every faith in his ability to accomplish the task we set him.'

'Very well,' Ulbricht said. 'Show him in.'

Klein opened the door and called. 'Harry – in here.'

Van Buren entered, hands in the pockets of his coat. He stood in front of the desk, that slight, mocking smile set firmly in place.

'You find something amusing?' Ulbricht enquired.

'My deep regrets, Comrade Chairman,' Van Buren said. 'But the smile is beyond my control. A Chinese bayonet in the face at Koto-Ri in Korea in the winter of nineteen-fifty when I was serving with the American Marines. Eight stitches, very badly administered by a medical orderly who didn't really know much better. He left me looking on the bright side permanently.'

'This Conlin affair,' Ulbricht said impatiently. 'You understand the implications?'

'They've been explained to me.'

'Then allow me to refresh your memory. Conlin, as you know, stood beside Niemoller in opposition to the Nazis. Went to Dachau for it.'

'And survived,' Van Buren said. 'Which means he must be quite a man. I've been looking him up. At his trial in nineteen-thirty-eight the Nazis were able to prove that his organization had helped more than six thousand Jews to escape from Germany over a two-year period. The Israelis gave him honorary citizenship two years ago.'

'None of which is material to the present issue,' Ulbricht said. 'We have a situation in which thousands of misguided comrades persist in attempting to cross over to West Germany. In the main, they have to rely on the help of organizations based on the other side who operate purely for financial gain.'

'Or try Conlin?'

'Exactly. This League of the Resurrection of his asks for nothing.'

'Very charitable of them.'

'Which unfortunately makes for excellent publicity,' Klein said. 'It has made Conlin a celebrity again. He was featured on the front of *Life* magazine in America only four months ago. Last year he was recommended for a Nobel peace prize and had to turn it down because the Church didn't approve.'

'I should imagine that must have been the first time in years he took any notice of the Vatican,' Van Buren commented.

Ulbricht said, 'You know that President Kennedy visits Berlin next month?'

'I had heard.'

Ulbricht was angry now, removed his glasses and polished them vigorously. A dedicated Communist of the old school, he had managed to prevent, in East Germany at any rate, the de-Stalinization movement which had swept Eastern Europe after the death of the Russian dictator. There was no one he hated more than the present American president, especially since his triumph in the Cuban crisis.

'If it could be proved in a public trial that Father Conlin's actions were motivated not so much by Christian ideals as by political ones; if he could be made to admit to the world his involvement with the American CIA and their espionage activities directed against our Republic; this would have the most damaging effect on Kennedy's visit to Berlin. It would, in fact, make it totally worthless as a diplomatic gesture.'

'I understand.'

'For God's sake, man.' Ulbricht was almost angry now. 'Rats in cages, dogs oozing saliva at the sound of a bell. I know as much of this Pavlovian psychology as anyone, but can you really change a man? Make him act like a different person? Because that's what we need.

Conlin to stand up in court before the cameras of the world and freely admit to having been a political agent acting for the Western powers.'

'Comrade,' Harry Van Buren said crisply, 'I could make the Devil himself think he was Christ walking on the water, given enough time.'

'Which is exactly what we don't have,' Klein said. 'The problem of the Campbell girl and her knowledge of the affair has solved itself, but there will be others. Conlin's associates in this League of Resurrection will be aware, within a matter of days, that something has gone badly wrong.' He hesitated, then said carefully to Ulbricht, 'And then, of course, Comrade, there are certain traitors in our own ranks still . . .'

'I know that, man, I'm not a fool,' Ulbricht said impatiently. 'What you are saying is that there are those in the West who will discover what's happened and attempt to do something about it?' He shook his head. 'Not officially, believe me. The Americans are heavily concerned to improve relations with Russia at the moment and Pope John's attempts to come to terms with the Eastern bloc speak for themselves. And what can they say? Conlin has simply ceased to exist. After all, he shouldn't have been here in the first place, should he?'

He actually permitted himself a smile.

'Of course, Comrade,' Klein said.

'I have every confidence in your ability to deal with any such attempts with your usual efficiency, Colonel.'

There was a slight silence. Ulbricht adjusted his glasses and said to Van Buren, 'You have a month. One month, that's all, before Kennedy's visit. You have those papers, Colonel Klein?' Klein produced a sheaf of documents instantly and laid them before Ulbricht, who took out his pen and signed them, one after the other.

'These give you full authority, civil and military, in the district of Neustadt where Conlin is being held at the Schloss. Power of life and death, total and complete, Comrade. See that you use it wisely.'

Var Buren took them from him without a word and Klein came forward with the Chairman's coat as Ulbricht stood up. He helped him into it, then escorted him to the door.

Ulbricht turned, looking from one to the other. 'When I was a boy, my mother was very fond of reading the Bible to me. "Well done, thou good and faithful servant." I remember that phrase particularly. The Council of State feels exactly like that, Comrades, towards those who succeed, but for the failures . . .'

He put on his hat and went out, closing the door behind him.

Klein turned to Van Buren. 'So, my friend, it begins,' he said.

3

For Margaret Campbell re-birth was a nightmare. Of suffocation, of freezing cold and then a long darkness from which she finally surfaced to find a middle-aged, grey-haired man at her side. He wore a brown habit, with a knotted cord at his waist from which a large crucifix was suspended.

Her mouth was dry so that she found it impossible to speak and he got an arm around her shoulders and put a glass to her lips.

'Easy now,' he said in German.

She coughed a little and said hoarsely, 'Who are you?'

'Brother Konrad, of the Franciscan order of Jesus and Mary. This is our house at Neustadt.'

'How did I come here?'

'One of my brothers found you this morning, caught on the weir, draped across the trunk of a tree. The Elbe is in flood because of the heavy rains.'

She tried to move and was aware of an excruciating pain in her left leg. Her hand, moving instinctively to the spot, encountered heavy bandages. 'Is it broken?'

'I think not. Very badly sprained. A torn thigh muscle.'

'You seem very sure.'

'I'm not without experience in these matters, Fräulein. During the war I served as a volunteer with the medical corps, mainly on the Russian front. Unfortunately the nearest doctor is at Stendhal, but if you think it necessary . . .'

'No,' she said. 'The nearest doctor is here.'

'I see.' He nodded calmly. 'On the other hand, although our Lord said, "Physician, heal thyself", this is not the easiest of precepts to follow.'

'I am in your hands, it would seem.'

'Exactly.' He gave her two white tablets and a glass of water. 'Take these, they will help with the pain.' He arranged the pillow behind her head to make her more comfortable. 'Sleep now. We will talk again later, Fräulein . . . ?'

'Campbell,' she said. 'Margaret Campbell.'
'Is there someone I can notify of your safety?'
'No.' She leaned back, staring up at the ceiling. 'There is no one.'

It was towards evening and she was wide awake when he came in, her head turned to one side, trying to look over the sill out of the window.

He put a hand to her forehead. 'Better,' he said. 'The fever has gone down. A miracle when one thinks how long you were out there in the water.'

His face was full of strength, firm, ascetic and touched with a tranquillity that she found completely reassuring.

'The Society of Jesus and Mary?' she said, and remembered her first meeting with Conlin. 'You're Lutherans, isn't that so?'

'That's right,' he told her. 'Our movement started in England in the closing years of the last century. There was a great interest at that time in the work of St Francis and a desire, by some people, to continue his mission within the framework of the Church of England.'

'And how did you end up in Neustadt?'

'A lady called Marchant married the Graf von Falkenberg, the greatest landowner in these parts. On the death of her husband, she offered Schloss Neustadt to the order. They came here in nineteen hundred and five, led by Brother Andrew, a Scot. There were twelve friars then, just like the disciples, and eight nuns.'

'Nuns,' she said blankly. 'There are nuns here?'

'Not any more.'

'But this is not Schloss Neustadt,' she said. 'It can't be.'

He smiled. 'We were moved out of the castle in nineteen-thirty-eight. The Army used it as a local area headquarters for a time. Towards the end of the war it served to house prominent prisoners.'

'And since then?'

'The State has failed to find any particular use for it, but on the other hand has never shown any great desire to return it. This house, in which we have lived for some years now, is called Home Farm. If I raise you against the pillows you can see the river and the Schloss on the hill above.'

He sat beside her, an arm about her shoulders, and now she could see a pleasant garden surrounded by a high wall. On the other side there was a cemetery. To the right, the River Elbe raced between trees, a brown, swollen flood. Beyond, on the hill above the village, stood

Schloss Neustadt behind its massive walls, pointed towers floating up there in the light mist, the approach road zig-zagging up the face of the hill towards the great gate of the entrance tunnel.

The door opened and another middle-aged man entered carrying a tray. 'And this,' Konrad said, 'is Brother Florian who fished you out of the river.'

Florian placed the tray across her knees. There was soup in a wooden bowl, black bread, milk. She put a hand on his sleeve. 'What can I say?'

He smiled again and went out without a word. 'He cannot speak,' Konrad told her. 'He is under vow of silence for a month.'

She tried a little of the soup and found it excellent. 'The nuns,' she said. 'What happened to them?'

His face was grave now, something close to pain in his eyes. 'They left,' he said. 'The last of them about two years ago. There are only six of us here now, including myself. A year from now I should imagine we'll all be gone if the State has its way.'

'But I don't understand,' she said. 'It states quite clearly in the constitution that no individual shall be prevented from practising whatever religion he chooses.'

'True, The youngest among us, Franz, joined our order only six months ago in spite of every obstacle that officialdom tried to put in his way. Are you a Christian, Fräulein Campbell?'

'No,' she said. 'When it comes right down to it, I don't suppose I'm anything.'

'The State is rather more equivocal. The rights to religious free expression, as you have said, are enshrined in the constitution. At the same time Walter Ulbricht himself has told the country in more than one speech that church membership is not compatible with being a good Party member.'

'But the constitution remains. What can they do?'

'Provide State services as substitutes for Christian ones. Marriage, baptism, funeral – all taken care of. To go to church is to deny the State, which explains why there hasn't been a Catholic priest here for five years and why, in what has always been a mainly Catholic area, the church door remains barred.'

Her mind was full of disturbing emotions. Religion had never interested her. There had been no place for it in her home background, for her father had been an atheist for most of his adult life. Her education had followed the path set for the children of all important officials in the Socialist Democratic Republic. Privileged schooling and an open door to university. A private, enclosed world in which all was perfection. What Brother Konrad was saying was new to her and difficult to take in.

'Why did the nuns go?' she said.

'There was an article in *Neues Deutschland* implying that orders such as ours were immoral. Old wives' tales, common for centuries. That in pools near convents, the bodies of new-born infants had been discovered. That sort of nonsense. Then the State medical authorities started monthly inspections for venereal disease.' He smiled sadly. 'It takes great strength of will to stand up to such ceaseless pressure. The nuns of our order, one by one, gave in and returned to life outside, as did most of our brothers.'

'But you hang on,' she said. 'A small handful, in spite of everything. Why?'

He sighed. 'So difficult to explain.' And then he smiled. 'But perhaps I could show you.'

He brought an old wheelchair, a robe to put about her shoulders, and took her out and along the stone-flagged corridor into the courtyard, pausing only to push open the gnarled oaken door on the far side.

It was like plunging into cool water, a tiny, simple chapel with no seating at all. Whitewashed walls, a wooden statue of St Francis, the plainest of altars with an iron crucifix, a small rose-coloured window through which the evening light sprayed colour into the room.

'For me,' Konrad said, 'there is joy in simply being here, for in this place I am aware of all my faults and weaknesses with utmost clarity. Here it is that I see myself as I truly am and here also that I am most aware of God's infinite compassion and love. And that, Fräulein, gives me joy in life.'

She sat, staring up at that rosy window and made her decision. 'Have you ever heard of the League of the Resurrection?'

'Why do you ask?'

'Have you and your friends ever assisted with its work?'

'We are an enclosed order,' he said gravely. 'The contemplative life is what we seek.'

'But you know of the work of Father Sean Conlin?'

'I do.'

'And approve?'

'Yes.'

She swung to face him. 'He's up there now in Schloss Neustadt. Dachau all over again and it's all my fault.'

It was cold with the bedroom window open, but her face was hot, burning as from a fever again, and the evening breeze eased it a little. She stirred restlessly in the chair and the door opened and Konrad entered with a glass.

'Cognac,' he said. 'Drink it down. It will make you feel better.' He pulled a chair forward. 'Now tell me more about this American professor, Van Buren.'

'I first met him in Dresden about eighteen months ago. I was just finishing my medical studies and he was lecturing on parapsychology, a fringe interest of his. He made a point of visiting my father. Said he'd always admired his work. They became good friends. He even obtained a medical appointment for me in his own department at the Institute of Psychological Research. A wonderful opportunity – or so I thought at the time.'

'You didn't like working there?'

'Not really. Harry Van Buren is a remarkable man – certainly the most brilliant intellect I've ever been exposed to. But it seems to me he has one fatal flaw. He's obsessed with his subject to such a degree that human beings become of secondary importance. At the Institute I saw him turn people around, change them completely. Oh yes, there were the psychotics where it was a good thing – a miracle, if you like. But the others . . .'

Konrad said gently, 'So – he betrayed you?'

'My father was ill – terminal cancer of the lung. They took him into hospital several weeks ago – I'm not certain of the exact date. They told me that the medical superintendent wanted to see me. When they took me to his office, I found Harry and a Colonel Klein from State Security.'

'What happened then?'

'Colonel Klein told me that the radio-therapy treatment needed to keep my father alive was costly and the equipment needed elsewhere. It was usual medical policy to allow such cases to run their own course. If I did as I was told, they might be able to make an exception.'

'Which was to entice Conlin over the border for them?'

She nodded. 'Harry explained why it was necessary in the finest detail. It was as if he was trying to persuade me. How Father Conlin could be made to stand up before the world and say exactly what he had been told. Harry said it was necessary because Conlin was an enemy of the State. That he and his organization had been engaged in espionage.'

'And you believed him?'

'My only thought was for my father.'

'Honestly put.'

She carried on. 'Harry calls his technique thought reform. And it works. He'll have Father Conlin denying everything he's ever believed in before he's through.'

There was a long pause, then Konrad said, 'And what is it you would have me do, Fräulein?'

'When they sent me across, they used a man called Schmidt in East Berlin who specializes in such matters. Klein said they allowed him to operate because it suited their purposes. Sometimes they put agents across to the other side in the guise of refugees. That sort of thing.'

'Which makes sense. And they had you followed?'

'Oh yes. An SSD operative, not that he lasted very long. The man who handled the actual crossing was an Englishman – a Major Vaughan. He and his partner have an undertaker's establishment in Rehdenstrasse in the West Zone. Julius Meyer & Co.'

'You think he can help?'

'Perhaps. He was the only one who could see I was lying. Isn't that a strange thing?'

She broke down then, harsh sobs racking her body. Konrad rested a hand on her shoulder briefly, turned and went out. He paused for a moment, a slight frown on his face, then went to the far end of the corridor and opened a door which gave access to the farmyard at the rear of the main building. There was a monotonous jangle of cowbells as the small dairy herd was shepherded in from the water-meadow by Brother Urban, a frail old man with white hair who wore a sack across his shoulders.

Brother Konrad opened the main door to the cow byres for him. 'Tell me,' he said, 'what time does Franz deliver the milk to the inn in the morning?'

'Seven-thirty is the usual time, I believe, Brother,' the old man replied.

'And Berg, from the Schloss? What time does he collect his milk? Do you know?'

'He's usually waiting at the inn when Franz gets there.'

'Good.' Brother Konrad nodded. 'When you see Franz, tell him that in the morning I will take the milk.'

Strange how cheerful he felt. He slapped the rear cow on its bony rump and they all tried to squeeze through the entrance into the byre together, bells clanking.

In the bedroom, Margaret Campbell stood at the open window awkwardly, all her weight on one leg as she leaned across the sill to cool her burning face. It was almost dark and yet it was still possible to discern the darker mass of Schloss Neustadt against the evening sky.

There was a light up there, gleaming faintly from one window after another as if someone was moving along a corridor. It was suddenly extinguished. She thought of Conlin alone up there in the darkness and was afraid.

The car which Klein had placed at Van Buren's disposal was a Mercedes staff car of the war years. It was in excellent condition, a pleasure to handle, and he enjoyed the hour and a half's run from Berlin in spite of the poor visibility towards evening.

It gave him time to think about the task ahead, and in any case he liked being alone like this. But then, he always had. An onlooker instead of a participant. In that way one could see things more clearly. Sum up the strength of the opposition, which, in this case, meant Conlin.

It was almost completely dark when he reached Neustadt. There were lights at the windows in the village, but the Schloss was in complete darkness. He drove up the narrow approach road, negotiating the sharp bends with care as it climbed the hill. There was a sentry standing in the mouth of the entrance tunnel out of the rain.

Van Buren held his identity card out of the window. 'Captain Süssmann is expecting me.'

The Vopo examined the card by torchlight and nodded. 'Straight on to the main courtyard. I'll telephone through and tell them you're on your way.'

Van Buren drove on, along the dark tunnel. There was a barrier at the far end, another sentry who examined his identity card again before raising the pole and allowing him through. Security was thorough enough, or so it seemed.

He drove across the inner courtyard and braked to a halt at the foot of a row of wide stone steps rising to a massive wooden door which stood open. A small group of Vopos waited to greet him. Two privates holding lanterns, a sergeant and a young man whose uniform carried a captain's tabs.

The captain saluted as Van Buren got out of the car. 'A pleasure to meet you, Herr Professor. Hans Süssmann.' He nodded to the sergeant, a large, brutal-looking man. 'Becker.'

Van Buren looked up at the dark bulk of the Schloss. 'What's going on here?'

'The place has its own power plant from the days when it was an army group headquarters. The dynamo is giving trouble. Nothing serious. There are a couple of electricians working on it now.'

Van Buren took out a leather case and selected a cigarette. Süssmann offered him a light. The American said, 'You've had your orders from Colonel Klein? You understand the situation here?'

'Perfectly.'

'How many men have you got?'

'Twenty. All hand picked.'

'Good. Let's go in.'

The entrance hall was impressive, a marble staircase lifting into the darkness above. A silver candelabrum stood on the table in the centre with half a dozen lighted candles in it. A short, stocky man stood there. His dark beard was flecked with grey, his hair tangled, and the elbows of his old tweed jacket were crudely patched.

'This is Berg,' Süssmann said. 'The caretaker. The place hasn't been occupied for any official purpose since the war.'

Van Buren said to Berg, 'We spoke on the telephone earlier. You've done as I said?'

'Yes, Herr Professor.'

'Good – I'll see Conlin now.'

Süssmann nodded to Berg, who picked up the candelabrum and led the way up the marble stairs. As they followed, Van Buren said, 'What's the situation in the village?'

'Population, one hundred and fifty-three – agricultural workers in the main. The local innkeeper is the mayor – Georg Ehrlich. He's Berg's brother-in-law. There has never been any trouble here – not from anyone. Oh, there are a handful of monks in the old farm at the bottom of the hill by the river.'

'Good God!' Van Buren said, genuinely astonished.

'Franciscans. Berg says they supply the village with milk.'

They were passing along an upper corridor now, the light from the candelabrum in Berg's hand throwing shadows on the walls.

At the far end, two guards stood outside a door. Süssmann unlocked it. Van Buren said, 'I'll see him alone first.'

'As you wish, Herr Professor.'

Süssmann opened the door for him. Van Buren took the candelabrum from Berg and moved inside.

It was a fairly ornate bedroom with a painted ceiling. Conlin was crouched at the end of the bed, his wrists handcuffed to one of the legs. He glanced up, blinking in the sudden light. Van Buren stood there, the candelabrum held high, looking down at him. He placed it carefully on the floor and squatted, taking out a cigarette and lighting it.

'I understand you smoke rather heavily?'

'It's been said.'

Van Buren placed the cigarette between the old priest's lips. 'Enjoy it while you can. The last for a long time. My name is Harry Van Buren. Does that mean anything to you?'

'Oh yes,' the old man said calmly. 'I think you could say that. Thought reform – an interesting concept.'

'You know what to expect, then.'

'You're wasting your time, boy.' Conlin smiled. 'I've been worked on by experts.'

'Not really,' Van Buren said. 'You only think you have.' He took the cigarette from Conlin's mouth, turned to the door and opened it. He handed the candelabrum to Berg and said to Süssmann, 'We'll take him below now.'

At the rear of the main staircase in the great hall an oak door gave access to the lower reaches of the Schloss.

As he unlocked it, Berg said, 'There are three levels, as I explained to you on the telephone, Herr Professor, dating back to the fourteenth century.'

They descended a long flight of stone steps and then a tunnel which sloped into darkness before them. Berg led the way, holding a lantern, and Van Buren and Süssmann followed, Becker bringing up the rear with Conlin between two Vopos.

Berg had to unlock two gates to reach the lowest level. It was very cold now and damp. He paused finally at an iron-bound door and unlocked it. The passageway stretched onwards into darkness.

Van Buren said, 'Where does that go?'

'More tunnels, Herr Professor. Dungeons, storage cellars. The place is a rabbit-warren.'

Berg opened the door. Van Buren followed him in and the caretaker held up his lantern. The cell was very old, stone walls smoothed by time, shining with damp. There was no window. The floor was stone-flagged and the only furnishing was an enamel bucket in one corner and an iron cot with no mattress. The door had a small flap at the bottom for food to be passed through.

'Is this what the Herr Professor wanted?'

'Exactly.' Van Buren turned to Süssmann. 'Let's have him inside. No shoes – shirt and pants only and leave the handcuffs on.'

He moved out, ignoring Conlin as Becker and the two guards hustled him in. 'Nothing to say, Professor?' the old man called.

'Why yes, if you like.' Van Buren turned to face him through the open doorway. 'Frances Mary. Will that do?'

Conlin's face sagged, he turned white. Becker and the two guards came out, the sergeant closed the door and locked it.

'I'll take the key.' Van Buren held out his hand for it. 'And I want a sentry here at all times – understood?'

'Yes,' Süssmann said.

'He stays in here for a week. Total darkness and no communication in any way. One meal a day. Bread and cheese, cold water, passed through the flap at the bottom of the door. Above all, no noise. Better make your sentries wear socks over their boots or something like that.'

'I'll see what can be done.'

'Good. I'm returning to Berlin tonight. If anything comes up, contact Colonel Klein.'

'And we shall see you again?'

'Exactly seven days from now. Then we really start to get down to it.'

They moved away along the passage, leaving Becker with one of the guards. The sergeant gave him his instructions, then followed.

Inside the cell, Conlin stood listening, aware only of the muffled sounds of their going. *Frances Mary*. So long since he had thought of her. And if Van Buren knew about her, what else did he know? His heart raced and the anguish at that moment was physical in its intensity.

He took a deep breath and shuffled cautiously through the darkness until he found the cot, then lay down on it carefully, the springs digging into his back. It was very quiet. *Phase One*, he thought. *Sensory deprivation leading to complete alienation of the subject.*

The darkness seemed to move in and complete panic seized him as he remembered Dachau. To be alone, so alone, of course, was the worst thing of all – and then it occurred to him, as it had many times before, that he was not. He closed his eyes, folded his hands, awkwardly because of the handcuffs, and started to pray.

It was just before seven-thirty on the following morning when Brother Konrad and Franz pulled their hand-cart, loaded with milk churns, into the courtyard of the local inn. Berg's old truck stood beside the front door and the caretaker leaned against it, smoking a pipe and talking to his brother-in-law.

Georg Ehrlich was a small dark man with an expression of settled gravity on his face that never altered. A widower, he left the running of the inn mainly to his daughter, for not only was he mayor, but chairman of the farm co-operative and local Party secretary.

He managed a smile for the Franciscan. 'Konrad – we don't often see you.'

'I wanted a word,' Konrad said. 'Official business, and besides – I thought the boy here might like a little help for a change.'

Franz, who at nineteen was the youngest member of the order and built like a young bull, grinned and swung a full milk churn to the ground with ease.

Berg said, 'I'm going to need at least one of those a day from now on. Put it on the truck for me, Franz, there's a good lad.'

'A full churn?' Konrad said in surprise. 'What on earth for?'

'Vopos up at the Schloss. Twenty of the bastards.'

'Come on in,' Ehrlich said. 'Sigrid's just made fresh coffee.'

They moved along a whitewashed corridor and entered an oak-beamed kitchen. Ehrlich's daughter Sigrid, a pretty, fair-haired girl of seventeen in a blue dress and white apron, fed logs into the stove. She glanced up and Ehrlich said, 'Coffee and perhaps a brandy to go with it? A cold morning.'

'That's kind of you,' Konrad said, 'but a little early in the day for me.' He turned to Berg. 'What's all this about Vopos up at the Schloss? I don't understand. What are they doing?'

'Guarding a prisoner they brought in the night before last. Twenty of them plus a sergeant and captain for one man. I ask you.'

Konrad accepted the cup of coffee Sigrid passed him with a smile of thanks. 'Someone important, obviously.'

'That's not for me to say, is it?' Berg said. 'I only follow orders like we all have to these days.' He leaned forward, the hoarse whisper of his voice dropping even lower. 'I'll tell you one thing you'll never believe. You know where they're holding him? In a cell on the third level. Solitary confinement to start with. A full seven days before we even open the door on him again. That's what the man from Berlin said and off he went with the key in his pocket. Van Buren, his name is. Professor Van Buren.'

Konrad frowned. 'Merciful heaven! I would have thought that even the rats might have difficulty surviving down there.'

'Exactly.' Berg emptied his glass. 'I'd better be getting back with that milk now. They'll be wanting their breakfasts up there.'

He went out. Ehrlich took down his pipe and started to fill it. Konrad said, 'Some political prisoner or other, I imagine.'

'I don't know and I don't care,' Ehrlich said. 'In times like these it pays to mind your own business. He talks too much, that one.'

'He always did.'

The innkeeper applied a match to his pipe. 'What was it you wanted to see me about?'

'Ah yes,' Konrad said. 'I'd like a travel permit, to go to Berlin to see my sister. I think I mentioned when we last spoke that she'd had a heart attack.'

'Yes, I was sorry to hear that,' Ehrlich said. 'When do you want to go?'

'This morning, if possible. I'd like to stay a week. I'll remember, of course –' here he smiled – 'to wear civilian clothes.'

Ehrlich said, 'I'll make you a permit out now.' He reached for the bottle. 'But first, that brandy I mentioned, just to start the day right.'

'If you insist,' Konrad relented. 'But just a small one.' When he raised the glass to his lips, he was smiling.

Margaret Campbell had spent a restless night. Her leg ached and she had fallen into a sleep of total exhaustion just before dawn. She was awakened at eight-fifteen by a knock at her door and Konrad entered with a breakfast tray. She had a splitting headache and her mouth was dry.

He took her temperature and shook his head. 'Up again. How do you feel?'

'Terrible. It's the leg mainly. The pain makes it difficult to sleep. The pills you gave me last night didn't do much good.'

He nodded. 'I've something stronger in the dispensary, I think. I'll leave them out for Urban to give you while I'm away.'

He placed the tray across her knees. She looked up in surprise. 'You're going somewhere?'

'But of course,' he said. 'West Berlin, to see this Major Vaughan of yours. Isn't that what you wanted me to do?'

There was an expression of utter astonishment on her face. 'But that's impossible.'

'Not at all. The co-operative produce truck leaves the square at nine for Stendhal, from which there are regular buses to Berlin. I'll be there by noon.'

'But how will you get across?'

'The League will help me.'

'The League of the Resurrection? But when I asked if you and your friends had ever assisted with its work, you said . . .'

'That we are an enclosed order. That the contemplative life is our aim.'

She laughed suddenly and for the first time since he had known her, so that for the moment it was as if she had become a different person. 'You are a devious man, Brother Konrad. I can see that now.'

'So I've been told,' he said, smiling, and poured her coffee.

In West Berlin, Bruno Teusen stood at the open window leading to the terrace of his apartment in one of the new blocks over-looking the Tiergarten and sipped black coffee. He was at that time fifty, a tall, handsome man with a pleasant, rather diffident manner, that concealed an iron will and a razor-sharp mind.

A lieutenant-colonel of ski troops on the Russian Front at twenty-five, a serious leg wound had earned him a transfer to Abwehr headquarters at Tirpitz Ufer in Berlin, where he had worked for the great Canaris himself.

His wife and infant son had been killed in an air raid in nineteen-forty-four and he had never remarried. In nineteen-fifty when the Office for the Protection of the Constitution, popularly known as the BfV, was formed, he was one of the first recruits.

The function of the BfV was primarily to deal with any attempted undermining of the constitutional order, which, in practice, came down to a constant and daily battle of wits with the thousands of Communist agents operating in West Germany. Teusen was Director of the Berlin office, a difficult task in a city whose inhabitants still tended to equate any kind of secret service with the Gestapo or SD.

It had been a hard day and he was considering the merits of dining on his own and having an early night or phoning a young lady of his acquaintance when his bell rang. He cursed softly, went to the door, and peered through the security bullseye.

Simon Vaughan was standing there, Brother Konrad behind him, wearing corduroy trousers, a reefer jacket and tweed cap.

Teusen opened the door.

'Hello, Bruno.'

'Simon.' Teusen looked Konrad over briefly. 'Business?'

'I'm afraid so.'

'You'd better come in, then.'

He closed the door and turned to face them. Konrad took off his cap. Vaughan said, 'This is Colonel Bruno Teusen. Bruno, Brother Konrad of the Franciscan Order of Jesus and Mary at Neustadt on the other side. I think you'll want to hear what he has to say.'

He walked across to the drinks cabinet, poured himself a Scotch and went out on the terrace. It was really very pretty, the lights of the city down there, but for some reason all he could think of was Margaret Campbell, trapped at Neustadt with her injured leg and probably frightened to death.

'Poor stupid little bitch,' he said softly. 'You shouldn't have joined, should you?'

It was perhaps fifteen minutes later that Teusen and Konrad came out on the terrace.

'Not so good,' the Colonel said.

'Can you do anything?'

'For Conlin?' Teusen shrugged. 'I don't hold out much hope. I'll get in touch with the Federal Intelligence Service in Munich, but I don't see what they can do, other than inform interested parties.'

'And who might they be?'

'The Vatican, for one. He is a priest, after all. Where was he born – Ireland?'

'Yes, but he's an American citizen.'

'They might be interested then, but I wouldn't count on it. And we haven't any proof that Conlin's over there. If anyone approaches the East German Government officially, they'll simply deny any knowledge of him. In any case, from the sound of it, getting him out of Schloss Neustadt would take a company of paratroopers dropping in at dawn, and Skorzenys are thin on the ground these days.'

Brother Konrad said, 'And the girl?'

'We might be able to do something for her.' Teusen turned to Vaughan. 'Would you be willing to help there?'

For a moment Vaughan saw again her pale face, the dark weary eyes in the early morning light on the bridge over the Spree. He smiled. 'Julius won't like it.'

'I know. Something for nothing again.' Teusen glanced at Konrad. 'When do you have to be back?'

'My permit allows me a seven-day stay in East Berlin.'

'And where are you staying now?'

Konrad turned uncertainly to Vaughan, who said, 'At our place in Rehdenstrasse. You might have to sleep in a coffin, but it's home.'

Teusen said, 'I'll be in touch. Possibly tomorrow – certainly by the day after. We should have the responses of all the interested parties by then.'

He closed the door behind them and poured himself a cognac. Then he went to the telephone, dialled a Munich number and asked to speak to General Reinhardt Gehlen, Director of BND, the Federal Intelligence Service. Strange that he no longer felt tired.

4

In Rome, on the following morning, in an upper room of the Vatican, His Holiness Pope John XXIII, close to death due to the effects of the stomach tumour from which he had been suffering for a year, held audience propped up by pillows in his bed.

A young monsignor sat by his side, reading from one letter after another in a low voice. His Holiness listened with closed eyes, opening them occasionally to sign a document when requested and again when his physician entered to administer a pain-killing injection.

The phone at the side of the bed buzzed and the monsignor answered it. He said, 'Father Pacelli is here.'

The Pope nodded. 'Admit him.'

'This is not good,' the doctor said. 'Your Holiness knows . . .'

'That he has very little time, and a great deal to do.'

The doctor turned away, closing his bag, and the monsignor opened the door to admit a tall, gaunt old man with white hair and deepset eyes, a strangely mediaeval figure in the plainest of black habits.

'You look more like a bird of prey than usual this morning,' the Pope said.

Father Pacelli smiled slightly, for this was an old game between them. He was almost seventy years of age, a Jesuit, second only in that illustrious order to the Father General himself, Director of Historical Research at the Collegio di San Roberto Bellarmino on the Via del Seminario, from where he had been responsible for more than twenty-five years for the organization of the closest thing the Vatican had to a Secret Service department.

The Pope looked up from the document he was reading. 'You Jesuits, Pacelli. The plain black habit, the lack of pomp. A kind of humility in reverse, don't you think?'

'I remind myself of the fact in my prayers each day, Holiness.'

'Soldiers of Christ.' The Pope waved the document at him. 'Like Father Conlin. He reminds me strongly of a certain colonel of infantry I knew when I served as a military chaplain during the First World War.

Whenever he went over the top to lead an attack he never ordered his men to follow him. Simply took it for granted that they would.'

'And did they, Holiness?'

'Invariably. There's a moral arrogance to that sort of action that I've never been too sure about. Still . . .' He handed the document to the young monsignor. 'You're certain as to the accuracy of this information?'

'It comes from my valued contact in the West German Intelligence Service.'

'And the Americans – have they been informed?'

'Naturally, Holiness. Father Conlin is an American citizen.'

'For whom they can do nothing.'

Pacelli nodded. 'If the facts are as stated, the East Germans would certainly deny his presence.'

'Even to us,' the Pope pointed out.

There was a moment's silence. Pacelli said, 'There would, of course, be the inevitable moment when they produce him for this show trial.'

'Like Cardinal Mindszenty, saying all the right things? That the Church with the aid of the CIA is engaged in some kind of underground struggle aimed at the destruction of the German Democratic Republic and everything Ulbricht and his friends stand for?'

'A suggestion not entirely without merit,' Pacelli said. 'But in my opinion, Holiness, it seems to me that on this occasion it is not so much the Church that is the target as the Americans. It would certainly cause President Kennedy considerable embarrassment if they succeeded in stage-managing the affair to coincide with his trip to Germany.'

'Exactly, and the Berlin visit is of primary importance. When he stands at the Wall, Pacelli, he places himself in the forward trench. He shows the Communist bloc that America is firm with the other Western powers.'

The Pope closed his eyes, one hand gripping the edge of the damask coverlet of his bed. There was sweat on his face and the doctor leaned over him and sponged it away.

Pacelli said, 'So, Holiness, we do nothing?'

'To do anything official is not possible,' Pope John said. 'On the other hand, Father Conlin is a member of the Society of Jesus, which has always, or so it seems to me, proved singularly apt at looking after its own.' He opened his eyes, a touch of the old humour there again in spite of the pain. 'You will, I trust, find time to keep me informed, Pacelli.'

'Holiness.' Pacelli leaned down to kiss the ring on the extended hand and went out quickly.

The black limousine bearing the licence plates of the Pope which had brought Pacelli to his audience returned him to the Collegio di San Roberto Bellarmino within twenty minutes of leaving the Vatican City, in spite of the heavy traffic.

When he entered the small library which served as his office on the first floor overlooking the courtyard at the rear of the building, Father Macleod, the young Scot who had been his secretary for two years now, rose to greet him.

'Neustadt,' Pacelli said. 'Have you come up with anything of interest?'

'I'm afraid not,' Macleod told him. 'An agricultural village, typical of the region. These Franciscan Lutherans are the only remarkable thing about the place.'

'And we have no church there?'

'Yes, Father. Holy Name. Founded in twelve hundred and three. It's been closed for five years.'

'Why?'

'Officially, because there's no congregation.'

'The old story. You can't be a good Party member and go to church as well.'

'I suppose so, Father. Is there anything further you would like me to do in this matter?'

'Contact Father Hartmann, at the Secretariat in East Berlin. Get a message to him by the usual means. I wish to see him in West Berlin at the Catholic Information Centre the day after tomorrow. Get me a seat for the morning flight on that day. Inform him of Father Conlin's predicament and tell him I will expect the fullest possible information.'

'Very well, Father. The file on the American, Van Buren, is on your desk.'

'Good.' Pacelli picked it up. 'Get me the Apostolic Delegate in Washington on the telephone. I'll be with the Father General.'

The young Scot looked bewildered. 'But Father, it's three o'clock in the morning in Washington. Archbishop Vagnozzi will be in bed.'

'Then wake him,' Pacelli said simply, and walked out.

The Father General of the Jesuits, leader of the most influential order in the Catholic Church, wore a habit as plain as Pacelli's. He removed his glasses and closed the file on Van Buren.

'The Devil and all his works.'

'A genius in his own way,' Pacelli said.

'And how will Father Conlin fare at his hands, would you say?'

'He survived Sachsenhausen and Dachau.'

'A remarkable man.' The Father General nodded. 'We all know that, but times have changed. New techniques of interrogation. The use of drugs, for example.'

'I have known Sean Conlin for forty years,' Pacelli said. 'His is a faith so complete that in his presence I feel humble.'

'And you think this will be enough to sustain his present situation?'

'With God's help.'

The phone rang. The Father General lifted the receiver, listened, then handed it to Pacelli with a slight, ironic smile. 'For you. Archbishop Vagnozzi – and he doesn't sound too pleased.'

It was a surprisingly chilly evening in Washington for the last day in May, and in the White House the Secretary of State, Dean Rusk, stood at a window in the Oval Office. The room was dark, the only light the table lamp on the massive desk, the array of service flags behind it. The door clicked open and as he turned the President entered.

John Fitzgerald Kennedy had celebrated his forty-sixth birthday only three days before and looked ten years younger. He wore dinner jacket and black tie, white shirt-front gleaming.

He smiled as he moved behind the desk. 'We were just going in to dinner and I've got the Russian Ambassador down there. Is it important?'

'The Apostolic Delegate came to see me this evening, Mr President. It occurred to me that it might be advisable for you to have a word with him.'

'The Conlin affair?'

Rusk nodded. 'You've read the file I prepared for you?'

'I've got it right here.' The President sat down at his desk and opened a folder. 'Tell me – did this come in through the German desk of the State Department?'

'No. A coded message to me personally from Gehlen himself.' There was a pause while the President leafed through the file. Rusk said, 'So what do we do?'

The President glanced up. 'I'm not certain. It's one hell of a mess, that's for sure. Let's see what the Vatican has to say.'

The Apostolic Delegate, the Most Reverend Egidio Vagnozzi, wore a scarlet zapata on his head and the red cassock of an archbishop. He smiled warmly as he entered the room and the Secretary of State brought a chair forward for him.

'It's good of you to see me on such short notice, Mr President.'

'A bad business,' the President said.

'And one which could be a considerable personal embarrassment to you if Father Conlin is brought to trial, as is suggested. I refer, of course, to your Berlin visit.'

'Does the Vatican intend to make any kind of official representation to the East German Government?' Dean Rusk asked.

'What would be the point? At this stage in the game they would certainly deny having him in their hands, and there are other considerations. The position of Roman Catholics, indeed of all declared Christians, is a difficult one in East Germany these days. We must tread very carefully.'

'In other words, you'll do nothing,' the President said.

'Nothing official,' Vagnozzi said. 'On the other hand, Father Pacelli of the Society of Jesus is going to Berlin as soon as possible to assess the situation.'

The President smiled. 'Pacelli himself, eh? So you're letting him off the leash? Now that is interesting.'

'His Holiness, in spite of his unfortunate illness, is taking a personal interest in this matter. He would like to know, in view of the fact that Father Conlin is an American citizen, what your own views are.'

The President stared down at the folder, a slight frown on his face, and it was the Secretary of State who answered. 'There are various aspects which are far from pleasant. This man, Van Buren, for example, has been a considerable embarrassment to us for years. Naturally, we've kept a very low profile on him, and so far that's worked.'

'And then there's Conlin's own position,' the President said. 'They'll try to brainwash him into saying his Christian Underground has been a tool of the CIA for years. The point of the exercise: a total smear to ruin every good thing I'm hoping to achieve by the German trip. The improvement in relations between ourselves and Moscow since Cuba has been considerable. Together with the British, we're to resume three-power talks in Moscow aimed at a nuclear test-ban treaty. In a few days' time I'm making a speech here in Washington at the American University in which I intend to make clear our recognition of the post-war status quo in Eastern Europe.'

'A move of profound significance,' Vagnozzi said.

The President continued. 'As far as East Germany is concerned, Ulbricht is a Stalinist. He hates Krushchev, so my visit to Berlin is of great importance in the general scheme of things because it shows Ulbricht that we mean business.'

'Which helps Krushchev to handle him.'

'But more than that – it shows the Russians where we stand also. That trying to be reasonable doesn't mean we've gone soft. We stand by West Berlin.'

Vagnozzi said, 'So there is nothing we can do about Conlin?'

The President shook his head and the steel that was always there just beneath the surface showed coldly in the eyes for a moment. 'I didn't say that. What I'd like you to do is give me a little more time, that's all.'

Vagnozzi stood up. 'Very well, Mr President. I will delay making my official reply until I hear from you.'

'Before morning,' the President assured him. 'I think I can promise you that.'

The archbishop went out. Dean Rusk said, 'With the greatest respect, Mr President, I must point out that to attempt an official move at this time – to involve the CIA, for example – would be madness. If anything went wrong, it could only add substance to the kind of charges they intend to bring against Conlin anyway.'

'Exactly,' the President said. 'Which is why anything that is done will have to be on a completely unofficial basis.' He reached for a copy of the *Washington Post*. 'Did you know Charles Pascoe was in town?'

'No.'

'There's an article here on page three. He's giving the Vanderbilt Memorial Lecture at the Smithsonian tonight.'

'I thought he'd given up the academic life,' the Secretary of State said. 'I heard his brother died last year and left him a fortune.'

'No, he's still Professor of Modern English Literature at Balliol.' The President folded the newspaper, stood up and eased his back. 'I'd like to see him – when he's finished his lecture, of course.'

'As you say, Mr President.'

The Secretary of State started for the door and President Kennedy called softly, 'And – Dean?'

'Yes, Mr President?'

'Let's make it the west basement entrance when you bring him in. No Press on this one – by request.'

Professor Charles Pascoe was bored, for the subject of his lecture at the Smithsonian, Aspects of the Modern Novel, was one he found increasingly unrewarding, as he did the company of the academics who surrounded him at the reception afterwards. The arrival of the polite young man from the State Department with a request that he visit the White House that very night had come as a happy release.

Charles Browning Pascoe was at that time sixty-six. The second son of a Birmingham cutler, he had chosen to go to the University of Heidelberg in nineteen-fourteen, an error of judgement which had cost him three years of internment. He had finally escaped to England by way of Holland and spent the last year of the war in Military Intelligence.

Afterwards came a brilliant academic career which had included eight years as Professor of Modern Literature at Harvard before a return to Oxford to his old college, Balliol. And then came Hitler's war, during which he was called back to Intelligence, first working with Masterman at MI5, helping to smash the German spy network in England, then transferring to Special Operations Executive where, more than anyone else, he had been responsible for the successful organization of the British and American Intelligence network in occupied France.

His wife had died in nineteen-forty-three. There were no children. After the war he had returned to Oxford, to the academic life that was his first love. And then, in the summer of nineteen-sixty-two, his elder brother Robert, who had created one of the major electronics firms in England, died, leaving him a fortune which even after heavy death duties was considerably in excess of one million pounds, a circumstance which had occasioned him little excitement. Certainly nothing like as much as he felt now, leaning back against the seat as the car moved along Constitution Avenue.

The limousine delivered him to the west basement entrance at the White House. The polite young man in the blue raincoat who had escorted him from the Smithsonian led the way past the Secret Service agents in the corridor and straight through to the Oval Office where the Secretary of State was waiting.

He smiled and held out his hand. 'Professor Pascoe. We have met, I think? A reception at the Ambassador's house in London three years ago.'

Pascoe was slightly built, with stooped shoulders, a shock of iron-grey hair falling across his forehead. He wore a dark evening coat over his dinner jacket, an old-fashioned wing collar and black tie.

'And just exactly what is all this about?'

The Secretary of State indicated the manilla folder on the desk. 'If you'd be kind enough to read that, I think it covers the situation more than adequatetly.'

'And then?'

'The President himself will explain what comes after. I'll leave you now.'

The door closed behind him. Pascoe sat down without removing his overcoat, took a pair of half-moon reading glasses from his breast pocket, put them on and opened the file.

Twenty minutes later the door opened and President Kennedy entered, followed by the Secretary of State. Pascoe glanced up.

'I couldn't resist trying the seat of power, if only for a time.'

Kennedy grinned and turned to the Secretary of State. 'You know, when *While England Slept* was published, this man wrote me a letter twenty-two pages long, taking it apart word by word.'

'A necessary stage in your education, Mr President.' Pascoe smiled mildly, and closed the file.

'Interesting?' Kennedy asked.

'Yes – I think you could say that. I've admired Conlin's work for many years. He's a remarkable man. I'm sorry to see him in such a plight.' Pascoe removed his glasses. 'A strange coincidence here, by the way. Colonel Teusen, the West German Intelligence Officer who passed on the news from Berlin, is an old adversary.'

The President frowned and the Secretary of State said, 'Teusen served under Canaris at Abwehr Headquarters in Berlin during the war.'

'Another remarkable man, the Admiral.' Pascoe stood up. 'However . . .'

The President moved to the window, looked out and said, 'You spoke about the seat of power. You know what power is? Real power? It's not being able to do a damned thing because you're President and you've got to think of the country or the UN or what the Russians will do – or not do.'

Pascoe said, 'Yes, I can see how hard it must be to have to stand back and watch a good man go down the drain like this.'

'Oh no.' The President shook his head gently. 'I'm not prepared to do that, and in any event I can't afford to. The Berlin trip is too crucial.'

'The point is, we can't do anything official – not at this stage,' Rusk said.

'So where do I come in?' Pascoe asked.

'Donovan once expressed the opinion that you were the greatest mind at work in Intelligence operations on either side during the war,' the President told him.

'As Mark Twain said, I can live for two months on a good compliment.'

'One is all you've got. My European schedule has me visiting West Berlin on June twenty-sixth.'

Pascoe said, 'You're serious? You really want me to try and do something about Conlin?'

'How many times did you handle similar operations during the war?'

'True.' Pascoe nodded. 'But that was eighteen years ago.'

'No official help, of course. Not from anyone. The West German Government can't afford any kind of involvement at this stage.'

'And the Vatican?'

'Pacelli arrives in Berlin tomorrow,' the Secretaty of State said. 'Again, entirely unofficially. Do you know him?'

'Worked with him at a distance during the war, but we never met.'

There was a pause. The President said, 'There would be the question of the necessary funds.'

'Hardly a problem,' Pascoe told him. 'My situation in that respect has changed considerably of late. I'm more concerned with my tutorials. My students are expecting me back next week. But I suppose something could be arranged.'

The Secretary of State said, 'If I might suggest, Mr President. Archbishop Vagnozzi . . .'

'The Apostolic Delegate,' the President said to Pascoe. 'He's fully informed on the whole affair. It might be a good idea if you had words with him before leaving. He could arrange a meeting with Pacelli when you arrive in Berlin.'

'And when exactly did you plan that to be, Mr President?' Charles Pascoe enquired.

'I had a word with my appointments secretary while you were reading the file. There's a BOAC flight that leaves for London just before midnight, which would give you time to speak with Vagnozzi. You'd be in Berlin tomorrow afternoon.'

'Presumably they have space available?'

'Already booked,' the President said.

Pascoe nodded. 'Very well. I have only one stipulation.'

'Yes?'

'A meeting with Teusen and a request that he has ready, on my arrival, all possible information known to the West German Intelligence Service on the situation at Neustadt.'

The President glanced at the Secretary of State, who nodded. 'I don't think there will be any difficulty there.'

'Good.' Pascoe picked up the file. 'I'm in your hands, it would seem. We don't have too much time if I'm to catch that plane.'

They started towards the door. The President said, 'I'd like to thank you, Professor.'

Pascoe smiled. 'Did I really have any choice? It is rather in the nature of a royal command, after all.' He turned and followed the Secretary of State out.

5

Father Erich Hartmann, SJ of the Catholic Secretariat in East Berlin, was an extraordinarily handsome man, yet he seldom smiled and there was a faintly chilling quality in the blue eyes that made most people who dealt with him proceed with considerable caution.

This included the Vopos at Checkpoint Charlie who had grown used to the young priest in the battered little Volkswagen in which he regularly passed through to the West Zone on Vatican business. After six months he was a familiar sight, as was the man in the black leather raincoat who followed him at a discreet distance on a light motor-cycle.

Erich Hartmann was thirty-three, born in Dresden in 1930, the son of a butcher who was not only a Communist, but also local Party secretary. He had continued his activities after the rise to power of the National Socialists and on February 3rd, 1934, his wife had found him hanging from a meat hook in his cold store. The official verdict was suicide.

Frau Hartmann sold the business and sent her son to her brother in New York. She herself stayed on, working actively against the Nazis with the Communist underground until she was arrested in October of 1944 and sent to Dachau, where she was executed by firing squad just before Christmas of that year.

Her brother and his wife were devout Catholics, who raised the boy in the faith and spoke nothing but German in the home against the day when he could be re-united with his mother.

The news of her death, not confirmed until 1946, affected him deeply. He had always been something of an introvert. Now, he withdrew completely into himself, even during his period at Notre Dame where he was not only a brilliant scholar, but an All-American quarterback two years running.

No one had been particularly surprised when he declared his vocation for the priesthood. In the Society of Jesus he found an order of discipline and intellect that was perfectly in tune with his own rigid attitude to the world about him.

Except for a brief curacy in Naples he had been employed mainly in the administrative section of the order, where Pacelli had discovered him and the curious fact that he was still officially a citizen of the German Democratic Republic.

His transfer to the Catholic Secretariat in East Berlin had been immediate, to duties ostensibly of an administrative nature, but in reality to be his superior's eyes and ears in the capital.

It was just after two-thirty when Hartmann pulled in to the kerb in front of the Catholic Information Centre in Budapesterstrasse. As he got out of the Volkswagen, the man in the black leather coat parked his motor-cycle by a tree on the opposite side of the road and dismounted. He started to light a cigarette and Hartmann crossed over.

'If you get bored, there's the Zoological Gardens behind you, Horst. I might be quite some time.'

The man smiled genially. He had high cheekbones and a slightly flattened nose that gave him the look of an ex-prize-fighter.

'On the other hand, Father, you could be on your way again before I know where I am and that would never do.'

Hartmann shrugged, turned and hurried across the street. He ran up the steps of the old building and moved straight through the reception hall, nodding briefly to the young woman behind the desk as he went up the stairs. He passed along an uncarpeted corridor, opened a door marked 'Private' without knocking and went in.

It was a small untidy room, furnished as an office and cluttered with filing cabinets. Pacelli sat behind a desk by the window, reading a typed report. He glanced up and smiled.

'You're looking well, Erich.'

'I can't complain, Father.'

Hartmann moved to the window and looked out across the road at the man in the leather coat sheltering under a tree. Pacelli joined him.

'SSD?'

'His name is Horst Schaefer. A Section Six man. Surveillance of all important Church leaders is their speciality.'

'You should be flattered.' Pacelli sat down, watching as Hartmann took off his coat. The old man smiled. 'But then, you couldn't allow such an unworthy emotion.'

'If you say so.'

'You have the look, Erich, of some fanatical Roundhead in the England of Cromwell's time. The kind of man who could cry out on the

Lord with fervour and in the same breath cheerfully burn young girls as witches.'

'You sent for me, Father.'

'Yes, you're quite right. I did.'

He explained the situation quickly. When he was finished, Hartmann said, 'I heard Van Buren lecture at the University of Dresden only three months ago.'

Pacelli got up and walked to the window. 'How regularly have you been making the crossing?'

'Twice a week – sometimes three times. I've even stayed the night on occasion.'

'What about our friend with the motor-cycle when you stay over? Don't tell me he stands out there all night? Or does someone else take over?'

'No,' Hartmann said. 'One agent per priest. That's bureaucracy for you. I usually warn him. A ridiculous situation, but no more than the world we live in. There's a small hotel with a bar just along the street. The sort of place streetwalkers use. He stays there. I always give him the keys of the car. It reassures him. He's a simple man.'

'So?' Pacelli went back to the desk. He opened a black leather brief-case, took out a large envelope and pushed it across.

'As at the moment your movements are restricted to East and West Berlin only, here's a present from the Vatican, signed by the Cardinal Secretary of State himself in the name of the Holy Father. A formal request that you be allowed to visit Neustadt without delay to consider the possibility of re-opening the church there.'

Hartmann opened the envelope and took out the letter. It was an imposing-looking document, stamped with a red seal. 'This must be submitted to the Ministry of State Security, as you well know, Father, which means the information will automatically pass to Klein at Section Five.'

'Who will be expecting something – some move or other from some-one – or I miss my guess. You are correct. Father Conlin's presence at Neustadt and our official request for your visit is beyond coincidence, but my own feeling is that they will grant you leave to go. Under surveil-lance, of course.'

'Why should they?'

'Why not? We have the right, under the constitution and under the Secret Treaty of Accord signed with the Vatican only last July.' He smiled slightly. 'And they can hardly use Conlin's presence as a reason for saying no, can they?'

'But what is the purpose of all this?' Hartmann demanded. 'What do we gain?'

'Submit your request to the Ministry of State Security immediately on your return this afternoon,' Pacelli told him. 'You should have a decision one way or the other, tomorrow. I'll expect to see you back here the day after – and be prepared to stay overnight. It may be necessary.'

Hartmann said, 'Do I understand you to mean by all this that you contemplate an attempt to . . .' he hesitated. 'To retrieve Father Conlin?'

'I'm not sure what I intend at this stage. I've a meeting with Colonel Teusen of West German Intelligence later today. He's expecting Charles Pascoe to arrive from America this afternoon, which could prove interesting.'

'Pascoe?'

'Before your time. One of the great minds behind the British Intelligence system during the Second World War.'

'So – you think something could be done?'

Pacelli said, 'I'd formed the opinion that you did not approve of Father Conlin?'

'Of his work – no. I've always doubted the usefulness of this League of the Resurrection of his.'

'A little too dramatic for your taste?'

'Something like that. But the man himself . . .'

'I know exactly what you mean. Infuriating, isn't it? The people's saint, *Life* magazine called him. Vulgar, but apt.' Pacelli got up and went to the window and peered down at Schaefer. 'He's still there, waiting for you. Better be off.'

Hartmann picked up his raincoat and moved to join him. 'He isn't such a bad sort.'

'As a Communist or as a man?'

'Three daughters and his wife is pregnant again.'

He buttoned his coat. Pacelli looked out of the window and sighed. 'You know, Erich, I was just thinking how nice it would be to be a child again when life is full of innocent surprise.'

'Interesting, Father, but hardly practical.'

Hartmann went out. Pacelli stayed at the window, saw him emerge on the pavement below and get into the Volkswagen. As it moved away, Schaefer mounted his motor-cycle and went after it.

It was evening again when Charles Pascoe moved on to the terrace of Teusen's apartment and looked out across the lights of the city. He should have been tired after his long journey, but instead felt a sense of exhilaration. There was a footstep behind him and the German emerged, a glass in each hand.

'You may find this difficult to believe,' Pascoe said, 'but this is my first visit and yet, twenty years ago, there wasn't a day in my life that wasn't focused completely on Berlin and Section Three of Abwehr Headquarters on the Tirpitz Ufer where a certain Oberstleutnant Bruno Teusen gave me considerable trouble.'

'Who, in his turn, concentrated his attentions on SOE Headquarters at St Michael's House, Eighty-two Baker Street. It used to take you twenty minutes to walk there from your flat in Ardmore Court each morning – when you didn't stay overnight. Do you still like to ruin excellent Courvoisier with three large cubes of ice?'

Pascoe took the glass with a smile. 'Do you still prefer those appalling Russian cigarettes you picked up a taste for in the Winter War?'

'You know, Pascoe, I learned so much about you, the most intimate of details, that in the end I actually grew to like you. Isn't that strange?'

'We could have met in June of 'forty-five,' Pascoe told him. 'I was offered the chance to handle your interrogation. I refused.'

'May I ask why?'

'It would, I think, by then have been too personal. Like turning over one's own stone. Still . . . to business. You've had certain orders about this Conlin affair, I believe?'

'Not orders – just a phone call from General Gehlen.'

'You know who I'm acting for?'

'Yes.'

'Again, quite unofficially.'

'Just like Pacelli from the Vatican, who's also here unofficially. I'm expecting him within the hour. They're all rather fond of that word, aren't they – as if we really had choice? Afterwards, of course, win, lose or draw, they'll say it never happened.'

Pascoe said, 'Can I count on your full co-operation as regards use of resources?'

'That's what I take my instructions to mean. There could be limits, of course. We'll just have to take each item on its merits. There is another factor of some importance also – Conlin himself.'

'You know him?'

'A marvellous man.'

'Good.' Pascoe emptied his glass and placed it down carefully. 'I'd like to get started, then.'

In the study there were several files on the desk, and on the wall a map of the general area from the border to Neustadt. There was also a large-scale plan of Schloss Neustadt, with several photographs pinned beside it.

'Thorough as ever, I see?' Pascoe put on his half-moon reading glasses and peered at the plan. 'Where did you get it?'

'In the files,' Teusen said. 'No difficulty at all. It was an army group headquarters for most of the war, then a prison for *prominenti*.'

Pascoe examined the photos. 'It certainly looks formidable.'

'During the First War it was used as a prison for French officers. There was not one single recorded instance of escape.'

Pascoe nodded. 'That I can believe.'

'You'll find other maps and various drawings on the desk. Army engineers' stuff. New roads at various times during the war – drains. That sort of thing.'

Pascoe turned to the desk. 'And the rest?'

'Information on the various people involved. The Franciscans, for example, although I'll take you to meet this Brother Konrad later. The caretaker at Schloss Neustadt, Heinrich Berg, who served in entirely the wrong branch of the SS. And there's as much information there as we have on Van Buren, which is considerable.'

'The Secretary of State provided me with a very comprehensive file on that gentleman before I left, courtesy of the CIA. No – I think this man Vaughan you were telling me about is the man I'm interested in at this stage.'

'Then this is the one you need.' Teusen pushed a manilla folder across the desk. 'Something of a cosmopolitan, our Simon, German grandmother, Irish mother.'

'What was his father?'

'Captain of one of those sailing barges on the Thames for many years. He died just before the war.'

'And what happened to Vaughan?'

'It seems that in nineteen-seventeen, when serving on the Western Front, the father carried in his colonel under fire. He was severely wounded during this exploit and awarded the Distinguished Conduct Medal. On hearing of his death, his old colonel insisted on making himself responsible for the boy's education. Sent him to Winchester, which I have always understood to be one of your most important public schools.'

'My God,' Pascoe said.

'Exactly.' Teusen tapped the manilla folder. 'I think you'll find it makes interesting reading.'

It was an hour later when Teusen came back to the study. Pascoe had turned the swivel chair behind the desk and sat, arms folded, looking up at the plan of Schloss Neustadt.

'You think there's a way?' Teusen said.

'Oh yes.' Pascoe removed his glasses and ran a hand over his face. 'There's always a way, if only one looks close enough. You were right about Vaughan. A fascinating story. I've had a look at the rest of the stuff, only briefly. I'll work through it more thoroughly later.'

'Father Pacelli is here.'

'Excellent.' Pascoe swung round in his chair. 'Let's have him in.'

Pacelli was wearing a collar and tie, and a rather nondescript tweed suit under an old raincoat. Pascoe went round the desk to meet him.

'A real pleasure. How many years is it since we were last in touch?'

Pacelli took his hand. 'Almost twenty. Nineteen-forty-three when you warned us of the Führer's ridiculous scheme to kidnap the Pope.'

'Don't look at me, either of you,' Teusen said. 'Even Skorzeny nearly had a heart attack over that one. Your coat, Father?'

'No need. I only have a few minutes, so I'd like to get down to business right away.'

'Certainly.' Pascoe waved him to a chair and sat down himself.

Pacelli said, 'I had a call from Archbishop Vagnozzi in Washington who explained to me that you would be acting in this affair, Professor.'

'If I can see any way to act,' Pascoe said mildly. 'May I enquire your intentions?'

When Pacelli was finished, Pascoe said, 'He sounds an interesting man, your Father Hartmann. How did you get the East German authorities to accept his appointment to your secretariat over there? I'm thinking particularly of his American background now.'

'He's a citizen of the German Democratic Republic by birth. Even more important, both his father and mother were Communists who died for the cause. We can staff the secretariat as we choose. In their eyes, he would perhaps seem a better choice than most.'

'If they have to have your people there at all?'

'Exactly. The position of the Church, of all Christians over there, is an ambiguous one. Guaranteed by the constitution. The existence of these Franciscans at Neustadt, for example, is proof of this.'

'But subject to continual harassment?'

'Exactly.'

Pascoe nodded. 'So what do you think you gain, by sending Hartmann to Neustadt?'

'I haven't the slightest idea. We have the right to ask that he be given permission to inspect the situation of the church there. A right which I happen to think, for rather delicate political reasons vis-à-vis the Vatican, they will not deny.'

'Under surveillance?'

'Naturally.'

'And you accept that the request will indicate to Klein that you know they have Conlin there?'

'Of course.'

Pascoe glanced up at Teusen. 'An interesting situation.'

'Which is putting it mildly,' the German commented.

Pacelli said carefully, 'Are your own plans in any way advanced in this matter?'

'Hardly,' Pascoe said. 'Why do you ask?'

'It occurs to me that Father Hartmann's presence in Neustadt could be useful.'

'True,' Pascoe said. 'But in a way that might not prove acceptable to you.'

'As a kind of tethered goat, you mean, to draw the tiger?'

'No, more of a Trojan horse.'

'You have something in mind?'

'The glimmering of an idea only. Not far enough advanced to discuss at this point. It would mean Father Hartmann becoming the focus of their attentions.'

'While something quite different was going on behind their backs?'

'That would be the point of the operation.'

There was a long pause. The old Jesuit nodded calmly. 'That would be perfectly acceptable.'

'And Father Hartmann?' Teusen asked.

'Will comply with whatever is required of him.' Pascoe started to speak and Pacelli raised a hand. 'Let me make something quite clear. I have known Sean Conlin for the best part of forty years. He is a stubborn and rebellious old Irishman, who loves his fellow creatures so much that he has proved totally incapable of following anything but the dictates of his own conscience all his life. He has been on many occasions a considerable source of embarrassment both to the Church and the order he serves. In so doing, he has become a living symbol of faith in action to thousands of people. We, of the Society of Jesus, are not prepared to see him go under. Do I make myself plain?'

'I think so,' Pascoe said.

'Good.' Pacelli got up and buttoned his raincoat. 'When may I hear from you?'

'You expect Father Hartmann to return the day after tomorrow?'

'Yes.'

Pascoe glanced up at Teusen. 'Perhaps you'll arrange a meeting then?'

Pacelli didn't offer to shake hands. 'Let's hope, in the meantime, that you come up with something substantial.'

He went out, followed by Teusen. When the German returned Pascoe had swivelled in the chair again and was looking up at the plan of Schloss Neustadt. Teusen took out a cigarette and lit it.

Pascoe removed his glasses and ran a hand over his face as if weary. Teusen said, 'You could do with some sleep.'

Pascoe looked up at him. 'Good God, no! At my age, my dear Bruno, there's time enough for that when you're dead.' He got to his feet. 'No, I think, if you'd be so good enough to take me, it's time I made the acquaintance of Major Vaughan.'

The Mercedes turned into Rehdenstrasse and pulled up in front of the sign *Julius Meyer and Company, Undertakers*.

'Is this wholly a front or do they really offer a service?' Pascoe asked as they got out.

Teusen smiled. 'Oh yes. They're quite prepared to bury you, if that's what you want.'

He opened the judas gate and led the way through. The garage was in darkness, but there was a light in the glass-walled office.

The door opened and Meyer looked out. 'Who's there?'

There was a certain alarm in his voice. Teusen paused at the bottom of the rickety wooden steps. 'It's me – Bruno. I've got a friend with me. Is Brother Konrad there?'

'Yes – come on up.'

Pascoe followed Teusen up the stairs. There was a chessboard on the desk and Konrad, who was sitting on the other side, got to his feet.

Meyer switched off the cassette-player. 'Where's Simon?' Teusen asked.

'He went to the bar at the end of the street for cigarettes. Who's this?'

'My name is Pascoe,' the Professor told him. 'Charles Pascoe.'

Meyer ignored him and addressed himself to Teusen again. 'What's he want?'

'To offer you a great deal of money,' Pascoe said. 'In return for your help in retrieving Father Sean Conlin from his present predicament.'

Meyer gazed at him in total astonishment. 'What is this? Some kind of joke?'

'Ten thousand pounds, Mr Meyer. Perhaps more,' Pascoe said calmly.

Brother Konrad said carefully in halting English, 'Is this true? You really intend to do something about Father Conlin?'

'That would depend,' Pascoe said. 'On many things. On you yourself, for example, and your friends at Neustadt.'

The judas gate banged and Vaughan appeared from the shadows below. He paused at the bottom of the steps and it was Pascoe who moved out on the small landing first and looked down at him.

'Good evening, Major Vaughan.'

Vaughan glanced up and went very still.

'You know who I am?' Pascoe asked.

'You're on the syllabus at Sandhurst, didn't they ever tell you that?'

Pascoe started down the steps and Vaughan sat on a coffin, unzipped his jacket and took out a cigarette. Teusen and Brother Konrad stayed on the landing.

Meyer came down the steps. 'Money can't buy a life, Simon. Tell him that.'

'Money,' said Pascoe, 'always helps. One of the sadder facts of this grey little world, or so I've always found.'

Vaughan lit his cigarette. 'You've come for Conlin?'

'That is correct. Naturally, I'd like your assistance.'

'Not interested.'

'Ten thousand pounds.' Pascoe glanced at Meyer. 'Each.'

'Money –' Vaughan shrugged – 'at the best of times is only a medium of exchange.'

Meyer turned and went up the steps. He said to Teusen, 'You want a drink, because I need one. Maybe even two. When he starts talking to himself, that Devil down there, I know I'm in trouble again.'

He vanished into the office. Pascoe said, 'Do it for Conlin, then. I understand you like him?'

'He's been walking bare-footed towards some kind of stake since the day he was born.'

'All right,' Pascoe said patiently. 'Do it for yourself. Because there isn't really anything else left for you to do.'

'Isn't there?'

'Let's look at the facts. Simon Vaughan, born July twenty-seventh, nineteen-twenty-six, not a stone's throw from the West India Docks.'

'I'm a Sun-Leo,' Vaughan said. 'Most fortunate week of the zodiac. Did you know that?'

'A hell of a leap from the Isle of Dogs to Winchester. Did you make it?'

'Not really.' Vaughan smiled without humour. 'It's in the voice mainly. They got to me too late to make me word perfect.'

'So you joined up in nineteen-forty-four, a year under age and served with the twenty-first Independent Parachute Squadron at Arnhem. Military Medal there. Afterwards, when someone discovered you spoke surprisingly good German, thanks to that grandmother of yours, they commissioned you into the Intelligence Corps. After the war, they kept you on. Even sent you to Sandhurst.'

'See what a Labour government can do for you,' Vaughan said.

'Captain with Field Intelligence in Korea, captured on the Hook, spent nearly two years in a Chinese prison camp. Afterwards, back to Military Intelligence where you specialized in handling subversives, revolutionary movements generally and so on. The Communists in Malaya, six months chasing Mau-Mau in Kenya, then Cyprus and EOKA. The DSO for that little lot and a bullet in the back that nearly put paid to things.'

'I wonder how I managed to fit it all in.'

'And then Borneo and the confrontation with the Indonesians. You commanded a company of native irregulars. The area around Kota Baru was rotten with terrorists. You were told to go in and clear them out.'

'No one can say I failed to do that.'

'You were certainly thorough. How many prisoners did you have shot? How many captives interrogated and tortured in custody? The newspapers made a lot out of that at the time. What did they call you? The Beast of Selangar. I suppose it was your medals that saved you. And the time in prison camp must have been useful. At least you weren't cashiered.'

'Previous gallant conduct,' Vaughan said. 'Must do what we can. Pity the Military Academy couldn't make a gentleman out of him.'

'To sum up,' Pascoe said. 'You were told to clear the last terrorist out of Kota Baru and you did just that. A little ruthlessly, perhaps, but you did it. Your superiors heaved a sigh of relief and threw you to the wolves.'

'Leaving me with the satisfaction of having done my duty.' Vaughan stuck another cigarette in the corner of his mouth. 'Water under the bridge, Professor. Meyer knows Berlin. I speak fluent German. It isn't much but it's a living.'

There was a long pause. Pascoe said, 'Well?'

'All right,' Vaughan said. 'I'll call your bluff. Twenty thousand – each,' he added.

'You know, somehow, I thought you might prove reasonable – in the end.'

Teusen woke just after three o'clock in the morning with a bad headache. He found an aspirin and went to the kitchen to get a glass of water. To his astonishment, there was a light under the study door. He opened it, to find Pascoe seated at the desk, working his way through the files.

'Good God,' Teusen said. 'Haven't you been to bed?'

'Couldn't sleep.' Pascoe removed his glasses. 'Actually, I'm glad you're here. You can fill in a blank for me.' He swivelled to the map. 'Here, along the border, there must be dozens of crossing points, especially on the country back roads. Are there any where your intelligence people have a special arrangement to come and go when it suits them?'

'If you mean, are there border guards on the other side who are bribable, yes,' Teusen said. 'But it's getting tighter all the time.'

'What about here, west of Neustadt? The direct route out?'

'Yes.' Teusen moved closer, then found what he was looking for.

'There's a crossing at Flossen. A hell of an area. Holstein Heath. I used to go shooting there when I was a youth. Wild boar.'

'So – it could be arranged?'

'Yes, I think so. It would be difficult. Also expensive. If you want me to, I'll get in touch with my man in the area in the morning.'

'It's morning now,' Pascoe pointed out.

He put on his half-moon spectacles and returned to his files. Teusen stood looking down at him for a moment, feeling strangely helpless, then he turned and went out, closing the door behind him. He went back into his bedroom and sat on the edge of the bed.

'Now I know how we lost the war,' he said to himself wearily, and reached for the telephone.

6

Pascoe, as a rule, did not enjoy flying in small aircraft. They were noisy, uncomfortable and lacking in the more obvious amenities, but he could certainly find no fault with the plane Teusen had arranged to fly them from Tempelhof to East Germany at eleven o'clock that morning. It was a Hawker-Siddeley 125 and not long from the factory, a twin jet executive aircraft of some luxury in which it was actually possible to conduct a conversation without shouting.

'We land here,' Teusen ringed a spot on the map with pencil. 'Bitterfeld. A Luftwaffe night fighter base during the war. Not been used for years, but very convenient for the border. The field agent for the area will pick us up there.'

'And how far to this crossing you mentioned at Flossen?'

'Seven or eight miles.'

Pascoe examined the map in silence for a while, then opened his briefcase, took out a file and started to make notes.

Teusen said, 'When are you going to tell me what you have in mind?'

'When I know myself.'

The German produced a case and extracted one of his Russian cigarettes. 'But Vaughan provides an essential ingredient, I think?'

'Oh yes.' Pascoe closed the file and replaced it in his brief-case. 'Perfect for our purposes. A highly trained professional soldier. He speaks German as well as he does English – rather better, in fact. Also excellent Russian and passable Chinese. A legacy of nearly two years in that prison camp in Manchuria.'

'A killer by trade and by instinct.'

'But with brains. A combination not always to be found.'

Teusen shook his head. 'A great tragedy, what happened to Vaughan. A brilliant career in ruins – and for what?'

'He did his duty as he saw it.'

'You sympathize with him, I think?'

'Men like Vaughan are like the hangman,' Pascoe said. 'They carry the guilt for the rest of us. It takes a rather special brand of courage to do that.'

'You think he was right to do what he did?'

'Not necessarily, but he did and that's what's important.'

'So did the SS.'

Pascoe smiled slightly. 'Point taken, but in this present situation, it's a purely academic one. Whether he was right or wrong to do what he did out there doesn't concern me. I need him now. That's all that matters.'

They landed at Bitterfeld twenty minutes later. There were four hangars and the watchtower was still intact, but the grass between the runways was waist-high and there was an air of desolation to everything.

A black Mercedes was parked in front of the old operations building and a small, heavily-built man in a hunting jacket and forester's hat got out quickly as the Hawker-Siddeley taxied towards him.

Teusen was first out and shook hands. 'This is Werner Böhmler, the field agent for the area.'

'Herr Professor – a pleasure.'

Pascoe had turned and was looking out across the runway. 'This place is entirely unused, you say?'

'That's right.'

'Good.' Pascoe opened the rear door and got into the Mercedes. 'Can we get started, then?'

Father Conlin opened his eyes. Not that it mattered for it was still dark. For a little while he lay there, his body so numb that he couldn't even feel the springs of the iron cot digging into his back and then something clicked in his brain and he was filled with a sense of dreadful unease. Of some horror beyond understanding, crouched there on the far side of the cell.

He got to his feet, took a hesitant step forward and blundered into a stone wall. He took two paces back, hand outstretched and touched the other side. Three cautious paces brought him to the rear wall. From there to the door was four more. He was in a stone womb. Unbelievably cold. There was no beginning, no end. Only the fact of it.

I am a man. I exist, he thought. I will not give in. He lay down carefully on the bed and started to pray.

When Klein went to Van Buren's office at the University Medical Centre in East Berlin, there was only a young medical secretary available, a pretty, dark-haired girl in a white hospital coat.

'Colonel Klein,' he said.

She jumped at once. 'Oh yes, Comrade. Professor Van Buren is expecting you. If you'd follow me, please.'

She led the way along the corridor, knocked at a door at the far end, opened it and motioned him through into a small room, neatly carpeted and furnished only with several easy chairs. Van Buren was sitting in one of them by what appeared to be a window looking into the next room. It was in semi-darkness but as Klein approached, he saw that there was a man in there, strapped into what looked like a dentist's chair.

'What is this?' he demanded.

'General observation. I like to see how my patients are going on,' Van Buren told him. 'He can't see us, by the way.'

In the other room, a picture appeared on a screen. A girl – very young and extremely pretty. Suddenly the shadowy figure in the chair bucked, straining against the straps, and from the sound-box above the window there issued a cry of agony. Van Buren reached up and turned it off and slid a panel across the window.

'What was that?' Klein demanded.

'One of the techniques we try here. The subject has a long history of rape and he prefers them young. We show him suitable pictures, which naturally arouse him, then administer severe electric shock. If he's a bad boy, he gets hurt you see. Childish, but extremely effective. The trouble is, it takes rather a long time.'

'My God,' Klein said.

'There are also several drugs which can be used in place of the electric shock to induce severe vomiting, but that becomes rather unpleasant for everyone. What did you want to see me about?'

'We're having trouble with the Vatican.'

'To do with Neustadt?'

'Yes. It's still in the hands of the Ministry for State Security so I can't give you full details yet. I'll see you this evening. Seven o'clock at my office.'

'All right.' Van Buren lit a cigarette. 'I'm glad you looked in. I wanted a word with you about Conlin.'

Klein sat down. 'Nothing wrong, is there?'

'No, but I think there's something we should get straight. There isn't enough time for a thought reform programme.'

Klein paused in the act of lighting one of his cheroots. 'But you told Ulbricht . . .'

'What he wanted to hear.'

There was something close to horror on Klein's face. 'Then what are you going to do?'

'To Conlin?' Van Buren said calmly. 'Oh, break him, I think. It's all there's time for. Reduce him to a state where he'll simply do as he's told.'

'You think you can do that?'

'I've done it before. In my early days in Peking I saw Ping Chow break a Catholic priest very effectively by putting him in a cell with ten other prisoners. Ordinary criminals. They had to take turns at keeping him awake, otherwise they didn't get fed. Within a couple of weeks, he was so disorientated that he was agreeing to anything his interrogators told him.'

'Then why aren't you down there at Neustadt now? Why are you here?'

'I've left Conlin to rot for a week in his own filth in total darkness,' Van Buren said. 'He comes out on the seventh day, then we start.'

Klein stood up, walked nervously to the door, then turned. 'I hope you know what you're doing, Harry, because if you don't . . .'

'Then both our heads will roll. I'll see you later.'

Van Buren turned, slid back the screen and peered into the other room and Klein opened the door and left hurriedly.

Peter Bulow was a large, pleasant-looking man, in spite of the bad shrapnel wound on his right cheek. He was a sergeant in the people's police in command of the border post at Flossen, not because he was a good Communist, but because the small farm on which his parents had raised him had found itself a quarter of a mile on the wrong side of the line at the end of the war.

Flossen itself was half a mile into Western Germany. Bulow had attended the village school as a boy. Half his relatives still lived there, which explained his frequent visits. And there was the village store, of course, where he could obtain delicacies not so readily to hand on his own side.

But that morning he had a special mission for it was his daughter

Lotte's birthday. He had ordered a dress for her a month previously. Something very special from Hamburg to surprise her with at her party that evening.

He hurried up the single street past the inn and crossed to the store. He went inside and unbuttoned his jacket.

Muller, the storekeeper, looked up and smiled. 'Ah, there you are, Peter. I was beginning to think you'd forgotten.'

They were second cousins and Bulow grinned as he shook hands across the counter. 'Has it come?'

'Of course – I'll get it for you.'

He went into the back. Bulow walked to the window and peered out into the street, taking out his pipe. He put a match to it and turning, found Böhmler and Bruno Teusen standing behind the counter.

'Hello, Peter,' Teusen said.

'Herr Oberst.' Bulow was no longer smiling.

'I'd like a word with you.'

'No.' Bulow put a hand out as if to ward him off. 'No more. You promised.'

'I know, Peter, but this is special,' Teusen said.

'How special?'

It was Pascoe who answered him, pushing back the curtain at the rear entrance to join them. 'Fifty thousand marks.'

Bulow gazed at him in astonishment, then turned back to Teusen, who said, 'Plus asylum for you and your family in West Germany, a good job and housing guaranteed.'

'Or the same in the USA if you prefer it,' Pascoe added.

There was a moment's silence. Böhmler said, 'You would do well to listen to the Herr Professor, Peter.'

'No, thanks. For that kind of offer this has to be big – too big for me.'

'Not at all,' Böhmler said. 'All you have to do is let a little traffic through on a few selected occasions during the next three or four weeks. For the next month you and young Hornstein will be on the night shift. I know that. Six p.m. till six in the morning. Is he still sneaking over twice a week to visit the mayor's daughter?'

'The same terms for him,' Pascoe said.

Bulow shook his head violently. 'I won't do it. We nearly got caught passing that agent of yours through in March and there's Sergeant Hofer to consider. He's got a mind like a steel trap. A solid Party member, too.'

'He'll be on the day shift,' Böhmler pointed out. 'What he doesn't know won't hurt him.'

'No,' Bulow said.

Teusen sighed. 'I could get very unpleasant, Peter. I could point out that a word in the ear of the right person in Berlin about your activities on our behalf in the past would have the SSD on your back before you knew it.'

'You wouldn't,' Bulow said.

'No – because there isn't any need. Tell him, Werner.'

Böhmler said, 'The good times are coming to an end, Peter. We know of a secret meeting at highest government level last week in which Ulbricht ordered a crash programme aimed at strengthening the border in rural areas, with the specific intention of keeping you lot firmly on your own side.'

'No more visits to the store,' Teusen said.

'It's also been decided as a matter of policy to transfer people like you, men with local connections, to duties in the east. By autumn, all men on frontier guard duty will be from other parts of the Republic.'

'You're lying,' Bulow said, but there was no conviction in his voice.

'Don't be stupid,' Böhmler told him. 'You've been expecting something like this for a year now.'

'And now it's come and here we are throwing you a lifeline,' Teusen told him. 'You should be grateful. Hornstein will be interested, would you say?'

Bulow sighed wearily and sat down in a chair by the counter, shoulders slumped. 'Yes – I've been expecting him to defect for months now. He's crazy about the Conrad girl. He'll jump at a chance like this.'

'Excellent.'

'My wife – my daughter?'

'It will all be taken care of. When you come over for the last time, so do they – and Hornstein, of course.'

'All right – what do you want me to do?'

'For the moment, nothing,' Teusen said. 'Werner will be in touch with you again during the next few days.'

'Very well.' Bulow got to his feet. He seemed to have aged ten years since entering the shop and looked very tired. 'Can I go now?'

Muller moved forward from the back of the store hesitatingly, holding a large package which he placed on the counter. His face was grave.

'The dress. And there's a ham and a bottle of wine with my compliments.'

Bulow gazed at him blankly and then something clicked. 'Of course – how stupid of me. Thank you.'

'I'm sorry, Peter,' Muller said.

'For what?' Bulow replied bitterly. 'Russia was worse, but only just.'

He went out. Teusen moved to the window and watched him go. 'We use people,' he said. 'Even when we think we're in the right, we use people as if they were paper coffee cups to serve our purpose and be tossed on one side.'

'Yes,' Pascoe said calmly. 'War *is* hell and make no mistake, my dear Bruno. That's exactly what we're engaged in.' He glanced at his watch. 'And now I think we'd better be getting back to Berlin. I've seen what I want to see here.'

In East Berlin towards evening storm clouds moved in across the city, and in Klein's office, Harry Van Buren, seated behind the massive desk, worked his way through Erich Hartmann's file. Klein was standing at the window, peering out morosely and drinking coffee.

'My God,' he said. 'What weather. I've never known such a June.' He turned. 'What do you think?'

Van Buren held Hartmann's photo under the light. 'Interesting face. He and Ulbricht would have a lot in common.'

Klein frowned. 'I don't understand?'

'Religious obsession on the one hand – political on the other. Two sides of the same coin.'

Klein, who had been raised a Catholic, was aware of a faint anger stirring somewhere deep inside. Strange how one could never quite erase the imprint of those early years.

'You would dismiss religion so lightly?'

'I don't see why not. Fear of the dark – a rage against dying. People have to have something and if there's nothing there, they invent it. When was this application made?'

'Late yesterday, to the appropriate department. They passed it straight to me.'

'I like the phraseology,' Van Buren picked up the typed letter. 'Father Erich Hartmann, appointed Vatican Inspector General to report on the state of the church at Neustadt to the Holy Father.' He helped himself to a cigarette from the box on the desk. 'Presumably you're going to tell them where to put their application?'

'No.' Klein shook his head. 'Not possible.'

Van Buren glanced up sharply, a look of genuine astonishment on his face. 'But this is nonsense. That church in Neustadt has been closed down tight for five years now and they haven't done a thing about it. This application isn't just coincidence. It means they know we've got Conlin.'

'Exactly.'

'And Hartmann. Good God, you know what he is? A Vatican spy. It's here in your own file.'

'Of course I know,' Klein said calmly. 'And Hartmann's superiors know that I do.'

'Oh, I see,' Van Buren said. 'It has a certain ring to it, I must admit. A kind of lunatic logic.'

'Politics, Harry,' Klein said. 'Let me explain. Last year, we signed the Secret Treaty of Accord with the Vatican. A kind of blueprint for future relations.'

'Which doesn't mean a thing. You're still screwing the Catholic Church into the ground at every chance you get.'

'But we have to continue some sort of dialogue at governmental level. A political decision on the part of the Council of Ministers.'

'Under the inspired leadership of our esteemed Comrade Chairman.'

Klein ignored the remark. 'Relations with the Vatican have altered considerably. Unavoidable with a man like Pope John at the helm. His Peace on Earth encyclical in April was warmly received, I must remind you, not only in the West but as far east as Moscow.'

'Beautiful,' Van Buren said. 'I hope you're all having a fine time. But underneath all that garbage, I presume what you're really trying to tell me is that Hartmann comes to Neustadt whether I like it or not. Do you actually expect some sort of rescue attempt?'

'Not really. I think he's going there to sniff out what he can, that's all. I'll hold him off for ten days.'

'That's very kind of you.'

'Naturally he'll have a Section Six operative tugging at the skirt of his cassock. A man called Schaefer. He'll have orders to report to you.'

'That's it then.' Van Buren got up, belting his coat and crossed to the door.

Klein sat down behind the desk. 'Cheer up, Harry. After all, what can Hartmann hope to accomplish? I would have thought you might find the situation quite amusing.'

'Just what I'm looking for, something to lighten the more depressive periods of my daily round.'

He opened the door. Klein said, 'I must say I'd like to be there at that first meeting. What will you say to him, Harry?'

'Oh, that's an easy one.' Van Buren smiled. 'Bless me, Father, for I have sinned.'

When Vaughan opened the judas gate and went into the warehouse, everyone seemed to be there. Meyer, Teusen, Brother Konrad, and at the top of the steps in the glass-walled office he could see Charles Pascoe with Father Pacelli and a grey-haired man.

Meyer, who was pacing up and down, hurried forward. 'You got my message.'

'I'm here, aren't I?' Vaughan unzipped his jacket. 'What is this, a board meeting?'

'Something like that,' Teusen said, without getting up from the coffin on which he was sitting with Konrad.

Vaughan nodded to the Franciscan. 'Still here?'

Konrad smiled. 'So it would seem.'

'Who are the new arrivals?' Vaughan looked up to the office.

Teusen said, 'The grey-haired one is Kurt Norden, professor of forensic pathology at the university.'

'Forensic pathology?' Vaughan said in astonishment. 'Now what in the hell does he need him for?'

Teusen shrugged. 'I presume that in his own good time he'll tell us.'

Meyer smiled tightly. 'More corpses.'

'It comes to us all, Julius,' Vaughan told him cheerfully. 'And the other one?' he asked. 'Who's he?'

'Later, Simon,' Teusen said.

Vaughan shrugged, lit a cigarette and leaned against the side of the truck. There was silence and then the office door opened and Pascoe appeared with Norden.

'My thanks,' he said in English. 'I look forward to receiving your report, Herr Professor.'

Norden shook hands, then came down the steps, a tall, thin man with stooped shoulders in a tweed overcoat. He paused at the bottom, a slightly bemused look on his face, then pulled on a tweed hat that matched his overcoat, hurried to the gate, opened it and disappeared into the night.

Pascoe looked down at them calmly. 'Ah, there you are, Major.

Good. We can get started, then. If you'd kindly come up.' And he turned and went back into the office.

On the wall were pinned a map of that section of the border stretching from Flossen to Neustadt and one of the large-scale military plans of the Schloss and the village which Teusen had provided.

Pascoe said, 'I'll take things step by step, gentlemen, and if you bear with me, I think you will see how several apparently disparate items join together to make a whole in the end.'

No one said anything and he carried on. 'To start with, here just outside Flossen at Bitterfeld is a disused Luftwaffe fighter station which will serve as our base. The border post at Flossen itself is in our pocket. The Vopo sergeant and private who will form the night shift for the next twenty-eight days have agreed to come over. That gives us unrestricted access to the other side, within limits.'

'And when you get there what have you got?' Vaughan put in. 'Around fifty miles to Neustadt and most of that is Holstein Heath, one of the most sparsely populated areas in the country. A few woodcutters, a handful of farmers and very little else.'

Pascoe nodded. 'I should imagine the traffic, such as there is, would tend to be Vopo military vehicles and prowler guards.'

'Prowler guards?' Meyer said.

'Vopo motor-cyclists with no set routine. Their brief is to roam the area at will, so that no one can ever be certain where they will be next.'

Vaughan said, 'In other words, anyone else passing through, even in an old potato truck, is going to stick out like a sore thumb.'

'Oh, I don't know.' It was Teusen who spoke. 'We have a saying in the Harz mountains. If you want to hide in a forest, you must pretend to be a tree.'

'Exactly,' Pascoe said. 'I presume you are capable of riding a motorcycle, Major Vaughan?'

'I always did look better in uniform.' Vaughan turned to Pascoe. 'Nice one, Professor. Yes, I think I could manage that. What kind of machine? Cossack?'

'Yes,' Teusen told him.

'Good.' Pascoe said. 'In principle, what I am saying is that any transport we use between Flossen and Neustadt will be of a military nature. Colonel Teusen assures me he can supply any kind of Vopo vehicle we need.'

'No problem,' Teusen said. 'And the real thing, too. So many of them have come over to our side during the last couple of years.'

'The map, of course, will have to be studied in detail and the roads committed to memory, so that the chosen route and at least two alternatives to allow for unforeseen contingencies can be tackled by night at reasonable speed. Under most conditions, I see no reason why the trip from Neustadt to the border should ever take longer than an hour and a half.'

There was another of those pauses while everyone seemed to wait and Vaughan said patiently, 'All right, so now we're at Neustadt, where Conlin is being held . . .'

'By only twenty men.'

'. . . in a fortress so impregnable that when it was used as a prison for officers, there wasn't a single recorded instance of escape, am I right, Bruno?' Teusen looked uncomfortable and Vaughan carried on, 'Look at it. That zig-zag approach road, walls like cliffs, tunnel entrance, one guarded gate, then another. A Panzer column would have difficulty getting in.'

'But not a plumber or an electrician if they were needed,' Pascoe said. 'It isn't getting in that's the problem. It's doing it in such a way that you can come out with Conlin.'

'All right, surprise me.'

Pascoe indicated the plan of Schloss Neustadt again. 'Three levels – and our information is that Conlin is kept on the lowest, which makes sense because conditions will be extremely bad down there. Now, look at this.' He unrolled another plan. 'During the war, when the Schloss was an army group headquarters, there were considerable improvements made to the sewage system. Here, in the third level, not far from the cells, an inspection chamber gives access to a sewer pipe, concrete lined and eight feet in diameter, dropping through several levels to the Elbe, which it never reached, by the way. According to the engineer's working report, work stopped a hundred and fifty yards from the river.'

'Why?'

Teusen shrugged. 'It was nineteen-forty-five and the Russians were coming. No one needed army group headquarters any more.'

Vaughan looked down at the plan, a slight smile on his lips, for there was a certain black humour to the whole thing which rather appealed to him; the thought of those wretched army engineers labouring away down there in the darkness while their whole world collapsed above them.

'Which hardly helps Conlin.'

'It does if you notice the interesting fact that the tunnel passes close by the Home Farm, which is the headquarters of the Franciscan Order of Jesus and Mary at Neustadt,' Pascoe pointed out. 'There is a large barn, as you can see, directly on the boundary line. From there, sixty-five feet in a straight line to break into the main sewer.'

'Through a cemetery,' Vaughan said to Meyer. 'Now you see why the forensic pathologist was called in. I wonder just how many terminal diseases can be caught digging through that kind of compost heap?'

'Nothing that can't be handled with proper precautions and the right drugs,' Pascoe said. 'And as Miss Campbell is at Neustadt it does give us the advantage of having a doctor on site.'

'And who does the digging?' Vaughan turned to Konrad. 'Your people, is that the idea? All six of you? And just how long do you expect it would take?'

'A week,' Pascoe said. 'Ten feet down and easy soil, so Brother Konrad informs me.'

'Then what? So Conlin comes out through this – this rabbit hole. How long before the bloodhounds find their way to the farm?'

'By then the cupboard will be bare. Brother Konrad and his friends come over too.'

Konrad smiled almost apologetically. 'We were nearing the end of things in any event. I do not think we could survive another year with the kind of political pressure mounted against us.'

Vaughan nodded towards Pacelli. 'Who's this?'

'My name is Pacelli,' the old man said. 'I represent the Society of Jesus in this affair. Of which Father Conlin is a member.'

'What's he talking about?' Meyer looked bewildered.

'Jesuits, Julius,' Vaughan told him. 'Soldiers of Christ. They had such a fun time playing devious games with Elizabeth the First that they've never been able to stop since. And where does your little lot fit in, Father?'

'We will arrange for one of our representatives in East Berlin, Father Hartmann, to visit Neustadt to report on the state of the church there which has been closed for five years.'

'And what do you hope to gain from that?'

'Nothing,' Pacelli said serenely.

'East German Intelligence would be justified in expecting someone,' Pascoe said.

'So you give them Hartmann?'

'To keep them occupied.'

'And he's happy about that?'

'Perfectly,' Pacelli interjected.

'Good for him.' Vaughan shrugged. 'That's it then. What happens now?'

'Brother Konrad returns tomorrow, the same way he came. You follow in two, perhaps three days, but we can discuss that later. There is one other point. It occurs to me that Conlin's state of health is likely to be such that, once out, it might be advisable to get him to the West as fast as possible. I see here on the map, a quarter of a mile south of the farm, a meadow beside the river.'

'Water Horse Meadow,' Konrad said. 'I don't know where it got the name. It is good firm ground. Three hundred yards of open space between trees.'

'I understand it's not unknown for light aircraft to fly in by night on occasion under their radar screen to bring people out,' Pascoe said. 'Would you know anyone that foolhardy, Bruno?'

Teusen shook his head. 'No, but they would.'

Pascoe waited and Vaughan sighed and looked at Meyer. 'Any idea what Max is doing these days?'

'Max,' Pascoe said, 'is good, I presume.'

'The Luftwaffe thought so.'

'A long time ago.'

'He did shoot down seventy-two Lancasters by night and some things you never forget.'

'Can you find him for me?'

'I can try.'

'Good. As soon as possible, please.'

Pacelli stood up. 'If there is nothing else, I'd like to get back. I've work to do.'

'Of course,' Pascoe said. 'Major Vaughan, perhaps you could drive Father Pacelli back to the Catholic Information Centre?'

The old man shook his head. 'Not necessary. Just point me in the direction of the nearest underground station, Major. I need the exercise.'

'I wanted a chance to talk to you, Major Vaughan,' Pacelli said as they walked along the canal towards the bridge.

'So?' Vaughan said.

'You were a prisoner of war in Korea, I understand. The Chinese had you for two years so you're something of an expert on Pavlovian and similar techniques. What will happen to Conlin?'

'I can only guess,' Vaughan said. 'Because this isn't a normal case.'

'Explain.'

'Our friend Van Buren doesn't have much time. And time is what you need for really good long-term results with thought reform. He's got to go for quick answers, possibly helping things along with drugs. But a lot can be done in two or three weeks if you can find the right soft spots.'

'And Father Conlin is an old man and in failing health.'

'That could be in his favour. They don't want him dead, remember. Another thing – they'll have to go easy on the physical side of things and not just because the bruises would show. I wouldn't have thought his heart would take too much at his age.'

'So – how will Van Buren begin?'

'Sensory deprivation, I'd say. A week or so in a dark room cut off from human contact. Can lead to a feeling of alienation so terrible that some subjects will grab the first hand that reaches out.'

'This was done to you?'

'Several times.'

'And you survived?'

'Let's say the cracks don't show.' Vaughan smiled. 'I've a vivid imagination, Father. The Irish bit of me. I used to make up stories to pass the time.'

Pacelli smiled. 'Father Conlin will survive.'

'For a while. On the other hand, I don't know what his soft spots are. If Van Buren finds them, then he could be in trouble.'

'And you think Father Conlin has these weaknesses? These soft spots you speak of?'

'He's a man, isn't he? What is it the Bible says? Conceived in wickedness? We're all touched by original sin, I thought that was what you lot preached.' They had reached the bridge and went up the steps. 'Follow your nose on the other side and you'll find an underground station about a quarter of a mile along the road.'

Pacelli turned to face him. 'So you will see this thing through, Major Vaughan, but not for the money, I think.'

Vaughan stopped smiling. 'What then?'

'Nor the young lady. Oh, in part perhaps, but that would be too easy an answer. No, Major, you can be a hard man, your record proves it, but this is only surface stuff. The protecting shell. Underneath is the boy who crewed his father's barge that long, long summer on the Thames and never wanted it to end. The boy who found life more corrupt than he had hoped.'

'You go to hell,' Vaughan said harshly and he turned and went back down the steps.

7

In Rome on the following day, His Holiness Pope John XXIII died at the age of eighty-one. In his bedchamber at the Vatican Palace the circle of kneeling cardinals chorused the *De profundis*, first of the millions who, throughout the world, would mourn the best-loved Pope of modern times.

In his office at the Collegio di San Roberto Bellarmino, the Father General of the Jesuits was standing at the window when there was a light tap at the door and Father Macleod entered.

'You wanted me, Father?'

'Yes – Father Pacelli. Contact him in Berlin. He is to return with all possible speed.'

'And Father Hartmann?'

'Is Father Pacelli's concern,' the Father General replied, without looking round.

The door closed softly and he dropped to his knees and began to pray for the repose of the soul of the man who had started life as Angelo Giuseppe Roncalli.

Pacelli was standing impatiently at the window of his office at the Catholic Information Centre in West Berlin when the battered little Volkswagen turned into Budapesterstrasse and pulled in at the kerb below. The old priest gave an exclamation of relief and Vaughan, who had been sitting in a chair in the corner reading a newspaper, got to his feet and joined him at the window.

'So that's him,' he said as Hartmann got out and crossed the road to Schaefer, who was pulling his motor-cycle up on its stand.

'And that's Schaefer, his Section Six man.'

'They seem pretty chummy.'

'You're sure you can handle him?'

Vaughan nodded. 'I should think so.'

'Good. I would offer you my blessing, but somehow I do not think it would be well received.' The old priest smiled and held out his hand. 'I can only wish you luck, then, Major Vaughan.'

'Which always helps,' Vaughan said and went out.

After a while there was a tap, the door opened again and Hartmann entered.

'Ah, there you are, Erich.'

'Father.'

He was carrying a leather briefcase which he placed on the desk. Pacelli said, 'You've heard the news?'

Hartmann stared at him blankly. 'News, Father?'

'The chair of Peter is vacant, Erich. The Pope is dead. I received word only an hour ago.'

Hartmann was visibly shocked and crossed himself automatically. Pacelli sat down behind the desk. 'You were successful?'

'Yes, Father.' Hartmann opened the briefcase, produced a large official-looking envelope and passed it across.

Pacelli opened it and unfolded the document it contained. 'Excellent,' he said. 'And countersigned by the minister himself.'

'You will notice that I am not permitted to proceed to Neustadt for several days.'

Pacelli shrugged. 'So they delay things as long as possible. It was to be expected.'

'And I am also to consider myself at the orders of the military governor for the district.'

'Who will probably be Van Buren.' Pacelli nodded, folded the permit and handed it back. 'I had hoped to stay to see you through this thing, Erich, but now I must return to Rome. You understand?'

'Yes, Father.' Hartmann hesitated, then said carefully, 'The new situation in Rome. Does it change things?'

'Will the new Pope approve, do you mean?' Pacelli smiled coldly. 'I think not, if the candidate who immediately springs to mind succeeds. He was once heard to say that he had little time for the Mafia, whether it was in or outside the Church.'

'And that is how he sees our order?'

'The Society of Jesus has always had its enemies, Erich, you know that. Those who object to our power, our influence.'

'So your orders in this matter could be countermanded?'

'Not if we move fast. There are eighty-two members of the Sacred College who should be present at the conclave in the Sistine Chapel when the new Pope is elected. Cardinal Mindszenty can't come, he's still trapped in the US legation in Budapest and the Primate of Ecuador is too old to travel, but the rest will come, from every corner of the globe, and that will take time.'

'How long?'

'A fortnight at the earliest, probably closer to three weeks before we see a pope in Rome again.'

'And the general plan concerning Father Conlin is well advanced now?'

Pacelli nodded. 'At our last meeting I mentioned an Englishman to you – Professor Charles Pascoe.'

'I remember.'

'He is now in complete charge – of everything.' Pacelli emphasized the phrase. 'From now on you will take your orders from him. A meeting is arranged for you this afternoon when the entire operation will be explained in detail. I think you'll find that Pascoe has an aptitude for this sort of thing.'

'And Schaefer?' Hartmann walked to the window. 'What about him?'

Pacelli joined him. 'No problem. When you leave here, go down to the basement garage. You'll find an old truck there with Meyer & Company painted on the side. Just climb in the back and you'll be taken to meet Pascoe.' He smiled and placed a hand on the younger man's shoulder. 'Are you frightened, Erich, at the prospect of Neustadt?'

'No, Father.'

Pacelli sighed. 'No, I didn't really think you would be, and in some ways that's a pity.'

'Father!' Hartmann hesitated and Pacelli knew that he was debating whether to ask for a blessing.

Pacelli said gently, 'You'd better go now, Erich. Professor Pascoe will be waiting.'

Hartmann went out. Pacelli crossed to the window. Schaefer was pacing up and down under the trees, collar turned up, looking thoroughly miserable. Pacelli felt sorry for him, but that would never do. He went back to his desk and started to pack his small case.

The basement garage was surprisingly large. It contained half a dozen cars and the truck, as Pacelli had indicated. Hartmann approached the rear and started to climb over the tailboard as ordered. He hesitated, then walked round to the front and peered into the cab.

Vaughan leaned back in the driver's seat, cap over his eyes. He pushed it up and sighed. 'In the back, the man said. Rule number one in this game, always do as you're told.'

Without a word Hartmann turned, went round to the rear and climbed over the tailboard. He sat down on the floor, his back against the cab, well out of view, and a moment later the truck moved away.

In Teusen's study, Hartmann sat at the desk and worked his way through the last of the files Pascoe had given him – the one concerning Simon Vaughan. He closed it and leaned back with a sigh, running his hands over his eyes.

The door opened and Pascoe entered. 'Finished?

'So – now you know as much as I do, Father. Our intentions in the matter. The background details of those you will be working with.'

'Yes – most interesting. This Major Vaughan, for instance.'

'You don't approve?'

'His motives worry me.'

'I'm not interested in whether a man is a thief, Father. Only in whether he's a reliable thief. Vaughan works for wages. That makes him very reliable indeed.'

There was a knock at the door and Teusen looked in. 'Konrad is here, Charles. He's ready to go.'

'Good. Show him in.'

Konrad entered. In his corduroy trousers, reefer coat and tweed cap, he looked more like a workman than ever.

'Father Hartmann, this is Brother Konrad of the Franciscan Order of Jesus and Mary at Neustadt.'

The two men shook hands. 'You return to Neustadt today?' Hartmann enquired.

'No, only to East Berlin. I shall spend the night at my sister's house. Go on to Neustadt tomorrow.'

'What situation will I find there?' Hartmann asked. 'There are still good Catholics in the village, I presume?'

'Plenty, but it's the old story. You can't be a good Party member and go to church at the same time. You know what happened at Holy Name, do you?'

'Yes – it was closed five years ago. Lack of support was the official excuse.'

'The last priest was Father Honecker. A marvellous man and much loved. He was eighty and very frail and the district commander was displeased because his congregation was so large. Honecker welcomed everyone, you see. It didn't matter to him if you were a Party member or not.'

'What happened?'

'There was a famous cross at Holy Name – mediaeval, I think – called the Cross of St Michael. It was oak with a marvellous carving of Our Saviour on it. It stood in a stone socket by the altar. One night the district commander had it removed and taken down to the bottom of the hill and planted in a grove of trees by the Elbe. Honecker went to see him. He was told that the church stayed shut until the Cross of St Michael was restored to its rightful place. The only stipulation was that Father Honecker had to carry it himself, which as the thing weighed around a couple of hundredweight was hardly likely.'

'He tried, of course.'

'And died of a heart attack.'

There was a silence and beyond Konrad, Hartmann was aware of Vaughan in the doorway.

Pascoe said, 'Yes, well, we mustn't detain you, Konrad.' He picked up an envelope from the desk and handed it to the Franciscan. 'That's for Doctor Campbell, Professor Norden's report.'

'Good.' Konrad slipped it into his breast pocket and turned to Vaughan. 'So – I will expect you when? The day after tomorrow?'

'I don't see why not,' Vaughan said.

Konrad turned to face them all and bowed in a strangely old-fashioned way. 'Gentlemen.'

He went out. Pascoe said to Hartmann, 'Right, Major Vaughan will take you back to the Catholic Information Centre now and this is what I want you to do.'

Schaefer was out of cigarettes, cold and thoroughly miserable when Hartmann came out of the Catholic Information Centre and crossed the road to join him.

Schaefer managed a smile. 'There you are, Father. Can we go home now?'

'Sorry, Horst,' Hartmann said. 'I'm afraid I'm going to have to stay the night. I hope it won't inconvenience you too much.'

'It won't have to, will it?'

Schaefer tried to sound injured, but women were his one great weakness and his pulse had already quickened at the prospect of the streetwalkers who patronized the Astoria Hotel. He could see the entrance now, a hundred yards down on the other side of the road.

'I'll have to have your car keys, Father.'

'Of course.' Hartmann gave them to him. 'There's one other thing I wanted to mention. Next Sunday . . .'

'You go down to Neustadt, some village or other that God forgot on the edge of Holstein Heath. Yes, I had heard, Father. The office does like to keep me informed about little things like that.'

'How very efficient of them. I could be there for a couple of weeks, I'm afraid.'

'The country air will be good for me. I smoke too much.'

'And your wife?'

'She'll be fine. The baby isn't due for another three months and besides, she has her mother living with us now. Another good reason to get away for a while. I'll see you in the morning, Father.'

He kicked his BMW down off the stand and pushed it along the pavement towards the Astoria and Hartmann hurried back across the road. When he went into the office on the first floor, Vaughan and Meyer were standing by the window.

'He took it quite well,' Hartmann told them.

'Is that a fact?' Vaughan said. 'Julius, take Father Hartmann to Bruno's place. Come back for me in an hour.'

Hartmann looked puzzled. 'You're staying here?'

'That's right.'

Vaughan ignored him, intent on Schaefer down there, almost at the hotel. Hartmann hesitated, then followed Meyer out. Schaefer was at the Astoria now. He parked the BMW outside, locked the rear wheel with a chain and padlock and went in. Vaughan brought a chair to the window, lit a cigarette and settled himself down to wait.

When Schaefer went into the Astoria's tiny bar he saw, to his disappointment, that it was quite empty except for the hotel's proprietor, Willi Scheel, a grossly fat man who was never seen anywhere else except perched on a stool behind the zinc cash register reading the sports papers.

He looked up. 'Herr Schaefer. Nice to see you. You're staying, I hope?'

He reached for a bottle of cognac, opened it and poured some into a glass which he pushed across.

'Just for tonight, Willi.' Schaefer took the cognac down in one swallow. 'I'll have a packet of cigarettes. Trade a little slack?'

'Early yet,' Scheel told him. 'They'll be packed in here like sardines in another couple of hours with the weather like it is.' He touched the lapel of Schaefer's coat with one podgy hand and shuddered. 'You're wet through. What you need is a hot bath.'

'Sounds good,' Schaefer said.

Scheel raised his voice. 'Jutta? Where are you? Get in here.' He poured Schaefer another cognac.

'Jutta?' Schaefer asked. 'New, is she?'

Scheel nodded. 'God knows, it's difficult enough to get decent help these days, but this one is the limit. An absolute slut. Around anything in trousers she's like a bitch in heat.'

Schaefer drank a little of his cognac. 'Is that so?'

'You'll have to watch yourself with this one.' Scheel smiled amicably.

'Yes, what do you want?'

The voice was hoarse, petulant. Schaefer turned and found a young woman standing in the entrance to the bar. She was small with high cheekbones and almond-shaped eyes and had the face of a corrupt child. Her black dress was far too short, crumpled and soiled. The one incongruity was the shoes which were black patent leather with immensely high heels.

Schaefer almost choked on the rest of the cognac as Scheel said, 'Take Herr Schaefer up to number nine and run him a bath. You can take your break then.' He pushed the bottle of cognac across the bar to Schaefer. 'Better take this, do you good. Bring on a sweat when you're in the bath, eh?'

He started to laugh and Schaefer took the bottle, throat dry, and hurried after the girl. She was already half way up the stairs, the skirt straining at the seams across her buttocks; there were ladders in her black stockings. He stood close behind her as she fumbled with the key in the door and she pushed back against him and he felt the same old excitement surging inside him that never failed.

She turned to look at him calmly. 'Better get that coat off quick. You'll catch your death. I'll turn the bed down for you.'

Schaefer put down the bottle and unbuttoned his coat and she leaned across the bed to turn back the coverlet, the skirt sliding back to expose bare flesh at the top of the dark stockings. It was more than he could stand and he seized her from behind, his hands sliding over her breasts.

'Naughty,' she said as he pushed against her. 'You'll catch your death, I warned you. What you need is a good stiff drink to warm you up.'

'And then?' he demanded.

'We'll see.'

She went into the bathroom and came back with a glass which she filled almost to the brim. He was already down to shirt and trousers.

She held out the glass. 'There we are, sweetheart. A nice big one, just to slow you up. I mean, you'd like that, wouldn't you?'

He almost choked getting it down, and then he dropped the glass and pulled her to the bed, sprawling across her thighs, his hands at the buttons of her dress. His fingers felt thick and clumsy and the buttons refused to obey. She was talking to him, but he couldn't hear what she was saying and then she just wasn't there at all.

The girl adjusted her dress, then went to the window, opened it and leaned out. She came back to the bed, searched in the pocket of Schaefer's jacket, found his cigarettes and lit one. Then she lay on the bed beside him, propped against a pillow and waited.

After a while the door opened and Vaughan entered. 'Oh, very nice,' he said in German. 'The Blue Angel, slightly rundown version, if that's possible.'

The girl smiled and her voice when she spoke, was now crisp and very upper-class. 'I don't know what you put in the bottle, but it's certainly knocked him cold. Only just in time, too. The original randy bull, that one.'

Vaughan lifted one of Schaefer's eyelids. 'Good for ten or twelve hours, I'd say. Good stuff, but you need a strong heart to stand it. Hope he qualifies.'

'You bastard,' she said.

He went through Schaefer's jacket and found the wallet. It contained a few hundred marks, a photo of Margarete and the children, army discharge papers in the rank of sergeant, Schaefer's SSD identity card and various social security papers.

He replaced them in the wallet. 'I'll have this back to you in two hours. Put it back in his jacket, then you can go.'

'Thanks very much.'

'Are you working at the moment?'

'I've got a television play next week and an audition in Munich the week after for a war picture.'

'All go, isn't it?'

Vaughan went out, closing the door gently behind him. She lit another cigarette and leaned back, staring at the ceiling. Beside her Schaefer started to snore gently.

Teusen examined the identity papers in the light of his desk lamp and nodded in satisfaction.

'I told Jutta she could have the wallet back within a couple of hours,' Vaughan said.

'No problem. I'll have one of my men deliver it.'

'Good – I think she'd like to get out of there. She's a good actress, but playing the whore on a television stage is one thing – the reality is something else again.'

'You haven't said anything to Hartmann about this?'

'Didn't think he'd like it.'

Teusen nodded. 'Yes, he could be a problem, that one.'

'Where's Pascoe?'

'At the American Embassy. They had a call booked for him on the scrambler to the Secretary of State. What are you going to do now?'

'Is Pascoe still keen on the idea of using a light plane to bring Conlin out?'

'Yes.'

'Then I'd better find Max Kubel and quick.'

'Do you anticipate any problems there?'

'Not really. You know how Max moves around, but Julius has put a few feelers out. Maybe he's come up with something.'

They went into the other room. Hartmann was standing on the terrace looking out across the city. Meyer was on the telephone. He replaced it and turned to Vaughan.

'That was Ziggy. He doesn't know where Max is playing this week, but it seems he's been using Madame Rosa as post-office.'

'Playing?' Teusen looked puzzled.

'Piano,' Meyer said. 'He makes his rent money playing jazz in some of the clubs.'

Vaughan said, 'We'll call on Rosa and drop you off on the way, Father.'

Hartmann said, 'Perhaps I could accompany you? It sounds as if it could be interesting.'

'Possibly even rough. Too rough for that collar.'

Teusen went into his bedroom and returned with a black silk evening scarf which he handed to Father Hartmann. 'Whose side are you on?' Vaughan demanded.

Hartmann adjusted the scarf to conceal his clerical collar. 'Satisfied, Major?'

'Why not?' Vaughan said. 'It could be an interesting evening,' and he led the way out.

Vaughan drove, the three of them crammed into the cab of the truck. Over the Kurfürstendamm, West Berlin's smartest street, towered the floodlit Kaiser Wilhelm Memorial Church.

'Berlin,' Meyer said. 'What a place. Would you believe it, Father, but a third of it is green. There are more than a hundred working farms within the city limits, twenty theatres, the Berlin Philharmonic . . .'

'And a considerable variety on more fleshly levels of entertainment for those inclined,' Vaughan added drily.

'Still the finest city in the world to eat in.'

'You wouldn't think the Gestapo chased him out of the place in 'thirty-nine,' Vaughan said.

But Meyer ignored him. 'It's a terrible thing for an old Jew to confess, Father, but I adore Berlin food and it's anything but kosher, believe me.'

Vaughan turned into a street of old-fashioned apartment houses, pulled in at the kerb and got out. He went up the steps and checked the cards.

Hartmann said. 'You've been together some time?'

'Not really,' Meyer said. 'Simon was in the army, then he had a little trouble in the Far East.'

'Yes, I know about that.'

'He was chief of police in a little Arab state in the Gulf when I met him. He saved my skin.'

'You think a lot of him.'

'He's a good boy.'

Vaughan called, 'This is it.'

He pressed the bell-push, then spoke into the wall mike. As they arrived, the door clicked open and he led the way inside. It was decent enough, the walls painted in cream and carpet on the narrow stairs. The apartment was on the first floor and the brass plate on the door said: Rosa – Chinese Astrologer.

'My God,' Meyer said. 'The people we deal with.'
'You don't approve?' Hartmann asked.
'Astrology, Chinese or otherwise, is a nonsense.'
The door opened. The woman who stood there was very old. She wore a long black dress, gold ear-rings, and white hair was drawn back tightly from the parchment face. The eyes were darkly luminous.
'When were you born?' she said to Meyer in a voice that was little more than a whisper. 'December twenty-eight or nine?'
He was genuinely shocked. 'Twenty-seventh.'
'Typical Capricorn,' she said. 'If he was dying and they brought him a doctor he'd ask to see his diploma.'
Vaughan grinned. 'I'd say that was a pretty accurate reading, wouldn't you, Julius? I'm looking for Max, by the way. Max Kubel. Ziggy Schmidt thought you might be able to help.'
'Max?' she said. 'You're friends of his?'
'Definitely.'
'All right, come in.'
The sitting-room was warm, a good fire in the stove, two white cats sleeping in front of it. Untidy but comfortable, and there were books everywhere.
She sat down at a circular mahogany table and motioned them to join her. 'I thought you might have come for a reading.'
It was Hartmann who answered. 'And why not? A little something for your time. How much?'
'Any gift is welcome.' She was looking at him intently and he took out his wallet and produced a hundred-mark note. 'Which year were you born? With the Chinese it is the year which is important.'
'Nineteen-thirty.'
'Year of the Horse.' She nodded. 'Late April, I think.'
'That's right.'
'Horse Taurus, then. You serve a hard master. The hardest in the world to follow, I think.' She reached forward and pulled the scarf to one side. 'See, I am right.'
'So it would appear.'
'Driven by fire and by fire consumed. You must take care.'
'Thank you, I will,' he replied gravely.
She turned to Meyer who held his hands in front of his face. 'No – not a word. I don't want to listen to such nonsense.'
'Don't waste your time,' Vaughan said. 'Try me. July twenty-seventh, nineteen-twenty-six.'

'The Tiger and the Lion,' she said. 'Both beasts of prey and all men fear the tiger by night. You walk on corpses, Major.' She stood up. 'I'm tired. You'll find Max at a club called Tabu in Josephstrasse.'

She walked out. Hartmann said softly, 'Madame Sosostris, the wisest woman in Europe. You are familiar with the quotation, Major?'

'Particularly the line which comes later,' Vaughan replied. 'I do not find the Hanged Man. I've a feeling she just did. Eliot knew what he was talking about.'

'Eliot?' Meyer demanded. 'Eliot who?'

'Never mind, Julius.'

'This club – the Tabu. You know it?' Hartmann asked.

'The Berliner, Father, likes to boast that he can offer you anything from the most elegant nightclubs in the world to seedy bars that can't supply much more than an odour of urine and petty crime.'

'And the Tabu?'

'It could be worse, but not much. Maybe we'd better drop you off on the way.'

'Nonsense,' Erich Hartmann said. 'A necessary stage in my education, wouldn't you say, Major?'

8

During the Second World War there was an almost incredible superiority of German fighter pilots in terms of confirmed victories. The Luftwaffe's leading ace was credited with almost nine times as many victories as his British and American adversaries and no less than thirty-five Germans had scores in excess of one hundred and fifty, which charmed circle did not include Max Kubel, who had ended the war with a score of one hundred and forty-nine.

He was only twenty years old when he first saw combat flying with the Condor Legion in Spain. In Poland he was shot down and parachuted to safety, the first of eight such occasions.

The heady summer of the Battle of Britain when victory had seemed so near had been followed by the Eastern Front. Shot down near Kiev on June 12th, 1943, and taken prisoner by the Russians, Kubel had escaped, seized a Yak fighter and flown back to German-held territory.

This exploit earned him the Oak Leaves to his Knight's Cross and made him something of a hero to the German people for some considerable time after. Forbidden to fly in combat, he had endured a desk job with the Luftwaffe inspectorate for almost a year before securing an active posting with a night fighter unit in the spring of 1944.

In September 1944 he had joined a test unit operating the Messerschmitt 262, at that time the most advanced jet fighter plane in the world. On the morning of October 2nd that year, he crashed in flames near Hamburg and on Goering's personal instructions, was flown to a hospital at Weissach in Bavaria, which had developed special techniques in the treatment of half-cooked human flesh. It was March of 1946 before he had been judged fit enough to emerge into the outside world again.

Seated at the piano in the Tabu, he seemed considerably younger than his forty-five years with his fair hair and the insolent blue eyes that women found so appealing.

He looked rather dashing in the old black leather Luftwaffe flying jacket and he was surrounded by girls on the stand above the small dance floor. As Vaughan, Hartmann and Meyer leaned over the balcony rail, he moved into a solid, driving arrangement of *St Louis Blues*.

'He's good,' Hartmann said.

'He'd agree with you. Max is a great one for self-advertisement. He'd wear his Knight's Cross if he thought he could get away with it.'

Meyer sat down at the table, called over a waiter. 'You want something to eat, you two?'

Vaughan glanced at Hartmann and shook his head. 'Bottle of wine, maybe. Niersteiner. Something like that.'

Kubel glanced up and caught sight of them and waved. Hartmann said, 'Such a flight by night would require great courage.'

'At Innsbruck they have one of the oldest ski jumps in the world. When you take off you can see one of the city's cemeteries by the church at the bottom. If you're genius standard you may just land in one piece three hundred and sixteen metres below.' Vaughan lit a cigarette. 'Max still does that kind of thing for fun. He was wounded so many times during the war I think they must have taken his nerves out while they were at it.'

Max Kubel stopped playing and an accordionist took over. The club was crowded, mostly middle-aged men or older, and the girls were on the whole past their prime.

'Love for sale,' Vaughan said.

'A strange phenomenon,' Hartmann observed. 'We always assume we can give it, but we usually mean on our own terms. And why should you assume that sin should shock me, Major? The average priest listens to more evil and wickedness in the confessional in a week than the average man experiences in a lifetime.'

Kubel appeared at the head of the stairs at that moment. He paused to light a cigarette, then pulled a chair forward and joined them at the table.

'Simon – Julius.' He examined Hartmann coolly and then his eyes widened. He reached out and pulled the scarf to one side. 'Good God.'

'Don't worry, he isn't after your soul.'

'Not this time, at any rate.' The priest smiled and held out his hand. 'Erich Hartmann.'

The waiter was unloading his tray and Kubel reached for the bottle of wine. Vaughan said casually, 'Are you still flying the Black Bitch?'

'Wouldn't part with her.'

'Where do you keep her?'

'Private club field near Celle.' Kubel's voice was lazy, but there was an alert wariness in the eyes.

'Black Bitch?' Hartmann asked.

'An old Fieseler Storch spotter plane that Max owns. Painted black for camouflage on certain night flights he's in the habit of making.'

'Not any more,' Kubel said. 'They're getting too good over there these days. One of their MiGs intercepted Heini Braun in his Henschel in April and blew him out of the skies.'

'A load of Russian rubbish,' Vaughan said. 'You could handle that, an old-timer like you.'

Kubel smiled beautifully. 'I've decided to settle for the simple things in my old age, Simon. A good piano, a glass of wine, an accommodating lady . . .'

'Nothing more?' Hartmann said. 'Is there nothing more than this that you would like in the whole world?'

Kubel turned to him. 'Not really, Father. All is vanity. Isn't that what the Bible says?'

Vaughan leaned forward. 'One flight, Max, some time during the next two weeks. Neustadt on the Elbe, fifty miles inside the line. Twenty minutes in – twenty out. Two passengers.'

'I told you, you're wasting your time.'

'One hundred thousand marks, or any other currency you prefer.'

'My God, who do you want to bring out, Walter Ulbricht?'

'Not quite.'

Kubel's fingers tapped restlessly on the table as he thought about it. 'Who would I be working for?'

'I can take you to meet him now.'

A buxom woman of forty or so had been hovering anxiously for some time. Her make-up had been applied a little too carefully and the blonde hair was piled up in several layers in a style that would have suited a younger girl, but she did have a certain undeniable appeal.

Kubel smiled. 'Good. Then we go to see this friend of yours, but later, Simon.' He reached for the woman's hand. 'First I must dance with Frau Ziegler because she is the owner of this disgusting establishment and one must always keep the boss happy.'

Hartmann and Vaughan leaned on the rail and watched Kubel and the woman move on to the crowded dance floor.

'I thought he'd bite,' Vaughan said.

'You consider yourself a man of sound judgment, Major?'

'I understand men like Max,' Vaughan said calmly. 'They're a breed on their own.'

'Why?'

'His is a world of the senses. You think about it – he just does it.'

'And what exactly do you mean by it?'

'Politics or conversation. Philosophy or sex.' Vaughan glanced down to the centre of the dance floor where Kubel was massaging Frau Ziegler's buttocks with some feeling. 'See what I mean?'

'And you, Major Vaughan?'

'When I was fifteen, my old grandma told me there were three things to avoid like the plague. Drink, cards and loose women.'

'Have you followed her advice?'

'Well, I don't play poker, Father, because I've nothing to lose.'

'On the contrary,' Hartmann told him, 'I would have said everything.'

Vaughan laughed out loud and turned to Meyer who had just finished eating. 'Hear that, Julius? There's hope for me yet. For God's sake, let's pick up Max and get out before our friend here starts preaching from the balcony.'

Outside, rain poured down relentlessly. The street was badly congested because one side of it had been excavated so that the old sewer pipe could be renewed. There was some sort of commotion going on at the far end. A small crowd had gathered, made up of workmen and passers by. A police car drew up and then another.

'Where did you park?' Kubel asked, looking up at the rain with distaste.

'In the next street,' Vaughan said. 'I couldn't get any closer.'

As they neared the crowd, he caught at the arm of one of the workmen hurrying past. 'What's going on? Car accident?'

'One of the pipe-layers is trapped in the storm drain and the water level's rising by the minute with this rain.'

He pulled himself free and Hartmann strode forward. The ease with which he forced his way through the crowd was immediately apparent and for the first time Vaughan was aware of the size of the man, the breadth of his shoulders.

'What's he playing at?' Meyer demanded as Hartmann paused to speak to a police sergeant.

In the sewer excavation below, water swirled three feet deep in a chaos of mud and broken planking.

A figure emerged from the dark mouth of the pipe, followed by three others. They reached wearily and willing hands pulled them up.

'I've ordered everyone out,' the first man said. 'Had to. There's only a couple of feet of headroom left between the waterline and the roof and the level's rising all the time.'

Hartmann said, 'Is he still alive, the man in there?'

'Not for long. There was nothing we could do. A half-ton block on his legs.'

'What's his name?'

'Günther Braun.'

'Good.' Hartmann handed his raincoat to Vaughan. 'Hold this, please, Major.'

He leapt down into the excavation, ducked inside the dark mouth of the tunnel and disappeared.

'Is he mad?' Meyer cried.

Vaughan didn't bother to answer, simply shoved the priest's coat into Meyer's hands, grabbed a handlamp from an astonished policeman, jumped into the pit and went after Hartmann.

The pipe was perhaps five feet in diameter and the level of the water was now closer to four than three. He found Hartmann at once, the beam from the lamp picking him out of the darkness and the white desperate face of Günther Braun, the waters of the storm drain running with such force that they were already washing across his head.

As the light revealed Hartmann's clerical collar, Braun cried, 'That's all I need, a priest. Come to hear my confession, Father?'

'Not at all, my friend.' Hartmann leaned over him, feeling under the water.

Vaughan crouched beside them. 'You're wasting your time. That block weighs half a ton. You heard what the foreman said.'

'Just hold his head,' Hartmann said calmly. 'And pull him clear when he tells you to.'

'Mad!' Braun cried. 'Crazy!'

The Jesuit took a deep breath and plunged his head under the surface. The mighty shoulders heaved and then, incredibly, his face came up out of the water, carved in stone, every muscle taut.

Braun screamed and Vaughan lurched backwards, dropping the lamp, plunging them into darkness, aware of the man's body floating free. A moment later he emerged into the excavation crater to the astonishment of the crowd. There were excited cries and men dropped in to help.

Max Kubel reached down to pull him up. Vaughan said, 'Half a ton, Max. The bastard lifted half a ton with his hands under water.'

Hartmann had appeared beside them, soaked to the skin, his face streaked with mud. Meyer helped him into his raincoat, an expression of awe on his face.

For the moment, the attention of the crowd was concentrated on Braun as he was lifted into a waiting ambulance. Hartmann said, 'I think we'd better go now, gentlemen, while the going's good.'

'He's right,' Meyer said. 'The last thing he needs is his picture on the front page of the *Berliner Zeitung*.'

Hartmann moved away quickly and they followed. Kubel said, 'A remarkable man, this priest of yours.'

'I know,' Vaughan said. 'Just what I needed. Another holy fool.'

9

Emerging from the Berlin air corridor into Western Germany, Max Kubel banked south and took the Storch down to a thousand feet.

Pascoe, sitting next to him, said, 'I don't fly myself, but it seems a beautiful plane to handle. Wasn't it one of these Skorzeny used to airlift Mussolini off Gran Sasso in 'forty-three?'

'That's right, and during the last week of the war Hannah Reitsch landed one under Russian artillery shells on the east-west axis in the heart of Berlin.'

Bitterfeld was below them now and as Kubel turned into the wind and dropped the Storch down in a landing that was pure perfection, the black Mercedes drove to meet them, Werner Böhmler at the wheel. Kubel switched off the engine and they sat there in the silence.

'You've never used this place, not even in the war?' Pascoe asked.

Kubel shook his head. 'No. You say the landing lights still work?'

'So I'm informed. Also the radio communication system in the watch-tower is regularly serviced by the Luftwaffe in case of need.'

'What for?' Kubel said. 'Do those bastards at HQ think we might get lucky third time around?' He looked angry. 'I always did hate their guts. Big men behind desks.'

'Like me?' Pascoe said.

'Exactly like you, Professor. Different uniform.'

'Of course,' Pascoe said. 'But to the business in hand. Could you make the kind of flight I require to Neustadt under the conditions described?'

'No problem.'

'And those MiG interceptors the East Germans are flying in the area – they don't worry you?'

'Of course they do,' Kubel said. 'On the other hand, their radar can't reliably discriminate between low altitude targets and ground clutter, which means that if I take this old bitch in under six hundred feet all the way, they won't even know I'm there. And those kids they have flying those things – all they have is flight training. No combat experience at all.'

'So you'll do it?'

'I suppose so,' he said morosely. 'Deserted airfields always did bring out the worst in me. This is a bad place. Good men died here. Not that it matters. The same for all of us in the end.' He shivered and opened the door. 'Come on. You'd better introduce me to this man of yours.'

In Washington, it was still very early in the morning and President Kennedy, unable to sleep because of the pain in his back, sat at his desk in the Oval Office and worked on one of his speeches for the coming visit to Germany.

There was a light tap on the door and Dean Rusk looked in. 'I heard you were up.'

The President put down his pen. 'Anything important?'

'The Conlin affair. I've heard from Pascoe.'

'Fine. Help yourself to coffee and bring me up to date.'

Dean Rusk did so. When he was finished the President said, 'I suppose Pascoe knows what he's doing. God help them, that's all I can say.'

Rusk stood up. 'Oh, and General Gehlen has briefed Chancellor Adenauer on this one, as you requested. I think that just about covers everything for the moment.'

'Good,' the President said. 'Keep me informed.'

Rusk went out and the President moved to the window, pulled a curtain and peered outside. It was still dark – no sign of light at all and for some unaccountable reason, he felt depressed. But that, as always, was something to be fought against. He went back to his desk, picked up his pen and started to write again – *for unless liberty flourishes in all lands, it cannot flourish in one.*

It was just before three o'clock in the afternoon when the co-operative produce truck pulled up in front of the inn at Neustadt and Konrad climbed down. Georg Ehrlich and Berg were standing in the porch talking and the mayor smiled and waved.

'So you're back, Konrad.'

A Mercedes staff car crossed the square and drove past. Harry Van Buren was at the wheel and a young woman in Volkspolizei uniform sat beside him.

'My God,' Berg said. 'That's him – the new boss. Back a day early. I'd better get up there.' He jumped into his pick-up truck and drove away at once.

'Poor Heinrich,' the mayor said. 'For him, life is just one damn thing after another. How was Berlin?'

'As Berlin always is.'

'And your sister?'

'About the same, thank you. How about here? Have the changes up at the Schloss made any difference to things?'

'Not really. Some of the Vopos come in for a drink. The commander is a Captain Süssmann and there's a sergeant called Becker who's the original bastard. Still, it takes all sorts. Have you time for a coffee?'

'Not just now, thank you. Later perhaps. I'd like to see how things have been getting on at the farm,' Konrad told him, and went back down the steps.

Margaret Campbell was sitting by the window in her wheelchair reading when he entered her room. She glanced up and her delight was immediate.

'Brother Konrad. How marvellous to see you.' She dropped her book to the floor and held out her hands.

Konrad said, 'You're looking well. Are you walking yet?'

'A little. But never mind that. What happened?'

He walked to the window and looked up at Schloss Neustadt. 'He's back.'

'Who is?'

'Van Buren. He just drove through the village in his car. He had a Vopo lieutenant with him. A woman.' He turned to face her. 'I saw him, this Major Vaughan of yours.'

'My Major Vaughan?' She was blushing now.

'Oh yes, I think so. A remarkable man.'

'But can he *do* anything?'

'You could ask him yourself. If everything goes according to plan, he should be here tomorrow night.'

She went very pale and held out her hands again. 'Tell me – tell me everything.'

The room which Berg had shown Van Buren into was at the top of the main stairway leading up from the hall. It was comfortable enough, furnished as an office with a large, empty, stone fireplace.

'Yes, this should do very well,' Van Buren said. 'Especially when you get a fire in here.'

'This was always the general officer commanding's office both for our own people and the Russians when they were here.'

Van Buren had been going through the desk drawers and smiled, holding up a Russian pineapple grenade. 'Evidently. There's at least a dozen of these things in here. The last man in charge must have been the kind of paranoid who expected the paratroopers to drop in at dawn.'

'Another advantage . . .' The caretaker moved to a door in the corner and opened it.

Van Buren joined him and peered down a dark stone spiral stairway. 'Where does that go?'

'The rear courtyard. It makes a convenient private entrance in case of need.'

He glanced nervously at the lieutenant standing by the window, a military overcoat with fur collar slung from her shoulders.

'Lieutenant Leber will require a room,' Van Buren said coldly.

'Certainly, Herr Professor.'

Süssmann hurried in, buttoning his tunic. 'My apologies, Comrade. I was only just informed of your arrival.'

'Lieutenant Ruth Leber. She'll be with us for a while.'

'Comrade.'

Van Buren said, 'All right, Berg. See that she gets the best.'

Berg picked up her suitcase and she followed him and Süssmann watched her go, frank admiration in his eyes.

Van Buren said, 'Let me make one thing clear. She isn't here to supply comforts for the troops. She's important to my plans for Conlin.'

'As you say, Comrade.'

'How is he?'

'I have no idea. As you ordered, he has been left in total isolation.'

'Take me to him now.'

On the third level it was cold and very damp and the sentry outside the cell wore a winter greatcoat and woollen scarf.

'Anything to report?' Süssmann demanded.

'No, Comrade. Not a sound.'

'Open the trap,' Van Buren ordered.

The sentry did so and the American crouched. The stench from inside the cell was immediately apparent.

'Perhaps he's dead,' Süssmann suggested.

'No, he's fine.' Van Buren kicked the trap shut. 'I have an instinct for these things. He's just as I want him and tomorrow, we get to work.'

Margaret Campbell sat by the window in her wheelchair reading Professor Norden's report. It was succinct and to the point and quite fascinating.

She read it once, sat thinking about it for a while, then worked her way through it again.

Working in a cemetery in the manner indicated should not pose too many difficulties. The area, being close to the river, must be fairly damp. Most of the occupants will be poor to middle class in simple wooden coffins rather than lead.

If the working party were to come across a recent body, that is, one buried within say twelve months, things could be very nasty.

The coffin will have dropped to pieces owing to gas pressure. The body will have distended, cavities will have ruptured and copious putrid gas and fluid will be permeating the soil.

There will be streptococci present of a virulent kind. If any of the working party were to cut themselves, the result would be disastrous with the possibility of the infection leading to gas gangrene very quickly.

Most of the bodies will have been there for some time. They will have become partly converted to adipocuere, a fatty substance with an all-pervading stench. This is not dangerous, but the stench is appalling. There is a remote chance of infection by anthrax and TB but so remote as to be hardly worth considering.

Although the usually accepted depth for a grave is 6 feet, this is not always so. In this part of East Germany, 9 feet is common and in any case, changes in subsoil and compacting means that human remains may be found up to 12 feet deep.

The sewer could be the dangerous place, depending on how it has been used. There are often pockets of CO_2 and methane – choke damp and fire damp. The first will suffocate. The second will not only suffocate, but will explode from a spark if conditions are right. The immediate risk is to fall in the effluent. Nausea, vomiting and rapid death within hours can occur due to a gutful of human pathogenes.

There is also the possibility of viral hepatitis. No obvious scratch is needed for this. It may be transmitted orally and manually. There is a 10% morbidity rate.

It cannot be stressed too strongly that any kind of scratch or abrasion contracted during any phase of this operation MUST receive immediate drug therapy. If this procedure is not followed, septicæmia will be contracted within 12 hours, if not something worse.

So there it was. She sat there with the notes on her lap, thinking about it. After a while, the door opened and Konrad came in.

'Ready?' he asked.

'As I ever will be.'

He wheeled her out.

They were all seated round the wooden dining table in the kitchen when Konrad wheeled her in.

God, but they are all so old, she thought as she looked from one serene face to another. It just isn't possible.

There was Franz, of course, who was only nineteen and built like a young bull, but Florian, Gregor and Augustin were all in late middle age and Brother Urban was just a frail old man with not long to go under any circumstances.

They were waiting. She said, 'Brother Konrad has told me of your decision and I think it's marvellous, but do you really think it's possible?'

'Oh yes,' Konrad said. 'Gregor was an officer of engineers during the war. He considers it entirely practical.'

'The soil in question is extremely light,' Gregor said. 'Easy enough to work. We have plenty of wood for props and a considerable amount of corrugated iron sheeting in the barn which we can utilize as lining.'

'Won't there be a problem with air supply?' Margaret asked.

'No – not at that depth. And the length of the tunnel will be quite short, remember. Naturally one will need to see how work progresses for the first day or two, but I think it could be managed in a fortnight at the outside, possibly sooner.'

'All right,' she said. 'Fine, but there is one unusual aspect here. The fact that we'll be digging through a cemetery. This will involve certain grave health risks. Brother Konrad has brought me a detailed report from a very eminent Berlin pathologist on what to expect. I'd like to go through it with you now.'

The trap at the bottom of Conlin's door was pushed open. Light gleamed as a plate was pushed through. The trap was closed again. He waited, listening, and heard the rustle in the darkness of the solitary rat which had taken to appearing each day exactly at mealtime.

The fear left him then, as quickly as it had come, and he chuckled and said softly, 'Conditioned reflex, my friend. Pavlov would have approved of you.'

Then he lay down on the cot again, folded his hands and started to say his office from memory.

At Flossen, as darkness was descending, the heavy farm truck passed through the guard post on the West German side, through the neutral zone, and paused at the barrier pole where Private Gerald Hornstein stood waiting, rifle slung from his shoulder. The door of the guard hut opened, Peter Bulow emerged and approached the truck.

Werner Böhmler was at the wheel. He wore an old army fieldcap, filthy overalls and badly needed a shave. He held out his papers without a word. Bulow inspected them, then handed them back. He nodded to Hornstein, who raised the barrier and Böhmler drove through.

Ten minutes later he rolled to a halt at the side of the narrow road in thick forest, went round to the rear of the truck and unfastened the high tailgate, lowering it so that it formed a sloping ramp to the road.

There was the roar of an engine firing inside and Vaughan ran a Cossack motor-cycle and sidecar down the ramp and braked to a halt. He wore full Vopo uniform: heavy dispatch-rider's raincoat, ankle-length, helmet and heavy goggles which just now were pulled up. Across his chest was suspended on a sling a Russian AK assault rifle with folding stock, a thirty-round magazine in place, ready for instant action.

'Well, you look the part anyway,' Böhmler said.

Vaughan grinned. 'Let's hope the opposition thinks so. See you tomorrow night. Eleven-thirty as arranged. I'll try not to keep you hanging about.'

Böhmler listened until the sound of the Cossack had faded into the distance, then he got into the truck and drove back towards Flossen.

Vaughan rode on, the yellow beam of his headlight cutting through the darkness, pine trees crowding in on either side. He had burned the map into his brain, reducing the journey to a kind of formula beforehand. Right at the first crossing. Then left. Right at the crossroads. Then came the first village. Ploden. Half a dozen houses and an inn.

There was a Vopo fieldcar parked outside, a uniformed driver lounging beside it as if waiting for somebody. He raised a hand in salute as the Cossack went by. Vaughan waved back. It was as easy as that.

Filled with a sudden fierce exhilaration, he opened the throttle wide and roared on into the night.

Margaret Campbell was sitting in her wheelchair in the chapel. Ever since that first occasion on which Konrad had taken her there, the place had held a peculiar fascination. It was not that in any sense she had experienced a religious conversion, she was honest enough to admit that, but there was peace here of a kind she had never known before, with the wooden statue of St Francis smiling down at her in the candlelight. She didn't know what it meant yet, but that didn't matter.

The door creaked open behind and Konrad peered in. 'Ah, there you are,' he said. 'I was looking for you. Someone to see you.'

He stood back and a Vopo in ankle-length raincoat, helmet and goggles, a submachine-gun across his chest, moved into the room. She felt a moment of complete panic and then he pushed up the goggles.

Brother Konrad left them. Vaughan put a canvas pack he was holding in her lap.

'Present for you from Professor Norden.'

She found difficulty in speaking, so great was her emotion. 'What is it?'

'Medical supplies. Various drugs he thought you might find useful.'

She gazed up at him, eyes burning. 'You were right, weren't you? You saw through me like clear glass. The only one.'

He took off his helmet and put it down. 'You've had a hard time. It shows.'

'I'm so glad to see you. So glad.'

He smiled, lit a cigarette and sat down beside her. 'That's all right then.'

It was just after ten when Heinrich Berg stumbled out of the inn and made his way to his truck. He wasn't exactly drunk, but he did have a weakness for apricot brandy and that last glass had definitely been one too many.

He clambered up behind the wheel and fumbled for the key and the barrel of a pistol nudged his right ear. A cold voice said softly, 'Up the road towards the Schloss, there's a disused barn on the left hand side on the edge of the wood.'

'What is this?' Berg said. 'What do you want?'

'Do it!'

The pistol barrel screwed into his ear painfully and he hurriedly switched on the lights, aware that the other man was a Vopo, no more than that. The pistol nudged him again.

'Come on! Move it! I haven't got all night.'

In total panic now, Berg pressed the starter button and drove away rapidly.

It was cold and damp in the barn, but quiet as Berg moved uncertainly round into the light of the headlamps where Vaughan stood.

'Look, what is this?' Berg tried to sound firm. 'What do you want?'

'It's really quite simple,' Vaughan said. 'You've got a man called Conlin up there in the Schloss in a cell on what you call the third level. Am I right?'

Berg moistened dry lips. 'But that is a state security matter. The SSD are in charge.'

'Exactly,' Vaughan said cheerfully. 'But some friends of mine would like to get him out and we thought you might give us a hand.'

Berg gazed at him in total horror. 'You must be insane. Why should I do such a thing?'

'Because you've been a naughty boy, old chum. Staff-Sergeant Heinrich Berg, or should I say Hauptscharführer. Isn't that what they called the rank in the SS?'

Berg tried hard. 'This is nonsense. I don't know what you're talking about. I was an army man. Infantry for the whole of my service.'

'SS,' Vaughan said softly and took a bundle of papers from his pocket and laid them on the bonnet of the truck. 'Not Waffen SS. At least they were fighting men. You were Einsatzgruppen. Extermination squads, recruited from the gaols of Germany. You never faced a soldier in battle in your life. All you did was execute people. Lots of people. Anyone they told you to.'

'It's a lie!'

'See for yourself. Those are photostats of your military career, although as an ex-professional soldier myself, I must say it sticks in my throat having to use a phrase like that in connection with you.'

'If I was SS I would have my blood group tattooed under my left armpit,' Berg whispered.

'Normally, but in your case, you didn't finish training at Dachau until the autumn of 'forty-four and by then your superiors knew the game was up. The tattooing was stopped. I mean, they didn't want to make it too difficult for you after the war. It's all there, read it.'

With trembling hands, Berg opened the papers and Vaughan carried on relentlessly, 'Amazing how detailed these SS records are. They certainly had a mania for putting things on paper.'

'Go to hell!' Berg launched himself forward and Vaughan kicked him casually under the right kneecap, dodging out of the way as Berg fell to the ground.

'Which method did you favour? The gas chamber, a phenol injection or just a bullet in the back of the neck?'

On his knees now, Berg crumpled the papers in his hands. 'I'll tell. I'll confess. Why shouldn't I? There are SS at every level of government. The police, the SSD, are full of them.' He was momentarily beside himself, almost unaware of what he was saying. 'And when I tell them about you, they'll be grateful.'

'You'll still lose your head one way or the other,' Vaughan said. 'Here, let me show you. See here on the last sheet. Mauthausen, April 8th, 1945. You executed a man called Willi Stein, a man who'd been operating with the Communist underground against the Nazis right through the war.'

'I don't recall.'

'You should do. It's right here in the records. You hung him on a meat hook.'

And Berg remembered. It showed in his face. 'So?'

'I don't know how hot you are on political history, but back in nineteen-thirty-three when the Nazis came to power, one of the first things they did was to crush the old KPD, the German Communist Party, of whom a prominent member was Walter Ulbricht. Present Chairman of the Council of State. You have heard of him?'

'Yes,' Berg whispered, waiting for the axe to fall.

'Ulbricht escaped arrest because one of his closest friends in the movement risked everything to get him out. And you know who that man was?'

'God, no!' Berg cried.

Vaughan said, 'I wonder what Walter Ulbricht would do to the man who butchered Willi Stein?'

Berg crouched beside the truck, head in hands. Vaughan went to the door and peered out. As he turned, Berg stood up.

'What alternative do you offer?'

'Much as we object to helping a pig like you, asylum in the West with a guarantee of no criminal proceedings. You'll be transported out of here with everyone else involved at the appropriate time. No problems.'

'All right. What do you want me to do?'

'Van Buren came back today, didn't he?'

'Yes.'

'What's he like?'

'What can I tell you?' Berg shrugged. 'He's a cold fish.'

'Why do you say that?'

'Well, he's taken over the suite of rooms that's always been used by the commandant. It has a private entrance. A spiral staircase going down to a door in the rear courtyard. I thought I was doing him a favour when I mentioned it to him, especially with this woman he's brought with him. The Vopo lieutenant.'

'But he didn't think you were?'

'No.'

'Maybe he just doesn't like women.' Berg stirred uncomfortably and Vaughan lit a cigarette. 'All right, now you tell me about the set-up at the Schloss – everything. And then I'll tell you what you're going to do.'

10

'I will bless the Lord who gives me counsel, who even at night directs my heart. I keep the Lord ever in my sight. Since he is at my right hand I shall stand firm.'

The words, whispered aloud, comforted Conlin and it was necessary to hear a voice occasionally, even if it was only his own. It was an old story, this. He had experienced solitary confinement before at both Sachsenhausen and Dachau concentration camps under the Nazis, in company with that great and good man, Pastor Niemoller.

Niemoller had taught him how to fight using every resource of brain and intellect. To be especially strong at those darkest moments that sometimes struck on waking when the fear was for some nameless horror that would end all things.

The technique was a simple one. There was the missal to remember page by page, the correct order of services and so on. Then poetry which could be recited out loud. It was amazing how much came back, particularly the Irish of his youth which he'd not used for so long. *The Midnight Court*, for instance. As a boy, he had been able to recite the whole of it. Had received his own leather-bound Bible from his grandfather for doing so.

> *Ba ghanth me ag siubhail le chiumhais na na habhann,*
> *Ar bhainseach ur's an drucht go trom . . .*
> I used to walk the morning stream,
> The meadows fresh with the dew's wet gleam.

And then there were the books. *David Copperfield* for one. He'd read that many times anyway. It had all the reassurance of an old friendship.

He was re-living again the death of Steerforth in that terrible storm off Yarmouth when the door opened with total unexpectedness and light poured in.

Harry Van Buren was standing there, Süssmann and Becker behind him. The cell stank like a sewer and Süssmann stepped back hurriedly.

Van Buren held a handkerchief to his face. 'How are you, Father? Fighting fit?'

The rat streaked from under the bed and disappeared into the darkness of the far corner and Van Buren's eyes followed it.

'You really are being rather stupid if you do intend me to make my appearance in court, whole and unblemished,' Conlin said. 'As an old concentration-camp hand, I can assure you that six to twelve days after a rat bite in conditions like these, with human excrement present, it's usual for the victim to develop Weil's disease.'

'Is that so?' Van Buren said.

'Death follows due to liver failure in up to thirty per cent of cases.'

Van Buren turned to Süssmann. 'Bring him up, then have this place cleaned out.'

He turned and walked away along the passage and Süssmann and Becker followed, holding Conlin gingerly between them.

When Vaughan pushed Margaret Campbell into the old barn at the Home Farm, they found Konrad and Franz already waistdeep into a large hole over in the far corner. Brother Gregor pushed an empty wheelbarrow in through the open doorway to the next room. He started to fill it again from the growing pile of loose soil.

'How's it going?' Vaughan asked.

Konrad climbed up out of the excavation, wiping sweat from his brow with the back of one hand. 'So far so good.'

'How are you getting rid of your soil?'

'The least of our problems. Come, I'll show you.'

Brother Gregor had just filled his barrow again and Konrad took it into the next room and Vaughan followed, pushing the girl in front of him. The room had a stone floor and there was a jumble of rusting agricultural machinery. There was a well in the far corner, its wooden cover pulled back, into which Konrad tipped the contents of the barrow. It seemed a long time before they heard a splash.

'Seventeenth-century,' he explained. 'We haven't used it in years. I should think it will accommodate our tunnel refuse adequately.'

They moved back to the other room. Margaret said, 'Where are the rest?'

Konrad picked up his shovel. 'There is work to be done, Fräulein. The farm to run, milk and eggs for the villagers. We must keep up appearances. Brother Urban is too old for such work as this. He sees to the cows and chickens. Florian handles our milking and deliveries in place of Franz, and Augustin sees to the cooking and other household chores.'

'I could do that,' she said. 'It's time I got up on this leg more and I can operate from the wheelchair when I feel tired.' He looked uncertain and she pulled at Vaughan's arm. 'Tell him, Simon! Make him see! The courtyard gate is always barred. To gain admittance outsiders have to ring the bell. That means I can't be caught out.'

'She's right,' Vaughan said. 'Which would free Augustin to do what he can here. And while we're at it, if you can give me something to wear instead of the pretty uniform, I've got the rest of the day to kill.'

The bath was very old with brass taps and the water, when it came, spouted from the mouth of a cherub. None of which mattered, for the only important thing was that when Süssmann and Becker lowered him into it, it was blissfully warm. Conlin sighed and closed his eyes.

Van Buren nodded to the two Vopos who went out. Lieutenant Leber came in. She wore a white overall and carried towels over her arm.

'Wash him thoroughly and disinfect the water.'

'Have I got you worried then?' The old priest smiled and opened his eyes. And then he saw the woman. His smile faded, his hands moved down to cover himself defensively.

'You're ashamed to be seen naked by a trained nurse?' Van Buren said. 'Now there's an unhealthy attitude. There's nothing obscene in the human form, or did they teach you differently at the seminary when you were a boy? I've often wondered about those places. Celibate priests and adolescent boys.'

'I find it even stranger that a man of your training should find the notion of celibacy so difficult to take.' She was soaping his body now and Conlin winced. 'What is this supposed to be? A study in conscious humiliation?'

'You know, I really do find it interesting,' Van Buren said, 'that you should find the situation so disturbing. So shameful?'

For the first time, the old man lost his temper. 'God forgive me for saying it, but why don't you go to hell?'

'Ah, but I see now,' Van Buren said, as if suddenly gaining insight. 'Not shameful, but frightening. You're afraid in such a situation. That is interesting.' He turned to the woman and said in German, 'Have him out now and dress him. I'll see him when he's eaten.'

He left and Ruth Leber helped Conlin out of the bath and towelled his body without a word, handling him gently as if he were a child. Then she brought clean underwear, corduroy pants, a shirt and warm sweater, socks, slippers and waited for him to dress, still without speaking.

When he was ready, she opened the door and led the way into the next room. Van Buren was not at his desk, but a great fire of logs blazed on the stone hearth and a meal was waiting on a small card table in front of it.

She held the chair for him to sit, then walked to the door. As she opened it, he said in German, 'Thank you, my child.'

She didn't even pause, but kept right on going, closing the door softly behind her. Conlin sighed, reached for his fork and raised a piece of beef to his mouth. It was really excellent and the wine was Chablis, his favourite, and beautifully chilled. He was under no illusions as to the purpose of all this, none at all, but his body needed all the strength it could get to sustain it in the days to come.

When Berg went down to the third level, he found the Vopo sentry swilling out Conlin's cell with buckets of water carried from a tap in the passageway.

'He's still up above then?' Berg asked.

'That's right. What have you got there?'

Berg carried a spotlamp in one hand, a bucket in the other, and he lifted it up. 'Rat poison. Like some?'

The boy shuddered. 'No, thanks. Will you lay it in here?'

'No. Lower down. That's where the bastards breed,' Berg said. 'I'll see you later.'

He moved along the passageway and turned the corner, his spotlamp cutting into the total darkness ahead. A hundred yards, descending all the way and he entered a vaulted chamber. What he was seeking was in the centre, a heavy metal plate, bolted and padlocked. He knelt down, took a bunch of keys from his pocket and got to work.

He had never had occasion to open the plate before and had to try six keys before he found the right one. The plate was heavy and took both hands and all his strength to lift.

He probed the darkness below. There was an iron ladder perhaps ten feet deep and he descended it quickly. The tunnel stretched before him, ten feet in diameter, sloping downwards and perfectly dry.

It was twenty minutes later when he emerged. He snapped the padlock back into place, then reached for the bucket and laid down some of the rat poison, thinking of Vaughan as he did so. He'd like to have had him back at Mauthausen in the old days. By God, he'd have made him dance. But the bastard did have the whiphand. The prospect of what would happen to him if Ulbricht ever got a sight of his SS service record was too terrible to contemplate.

On the other hand, there were certain advantages to this situation. It meant he could go to the West and in safety, relieved at last of the nagging fear which had plagued him for years that his past would catch up with him. As he retraced his steps along the passageway, he began to whistle softly.

Conlin rationed himself to one glass of wine and was just finishing the last of the food when Van Buren came in.

'You look like a different article.' He settled himself into the wing-back chair on the other side of the fire and lit a cigarette.

'What now?' Conlin asked.

'What do you think?'

'First you were nasty, then you offer me comfort. Nothing very extraordinary in that. The Gestapo were just the same when I first found myself in the cellars at Prinz Albrechtstrasse. There was the brute who beat me half to death with a whip, then the clean-cut boy who begged me to confess to save myself.'

'And in the end he turned out to be worse than the other guy. Right?'

'What is it you want of me?'

'Not me,' Van Buren said. 'I only work here. Klein wants the Christian Underground. Names, places. The works. Plus details of your connection with the CIA. That's the general idea.'

'But there isn't one.'

'Does it matter? What's truth? What's reality? It's all a question of perspective. It's a chain reaction in a way. Klein wants to please Ulbricht by giving him what *he* wants and I want to please Klein.' He smiled beautifully. 'And that means, old buddy, that you've got to please me.'

'I'm afraid I'd find that very difficult.'

'I thought you might.'

'So what happens now?'

'You tell me.'

'Phase two, the object of which will be to drive me to the edge of insanity. To take me to pieces, then put me together again in your image. Good Marxian psychology which believes that each man has his thesis, his positive side, and his antithesis, the dark side of his being. If you can find out what that is and encourage its growth, then the guilt will be too much for me to bear. Isn't that what you would tell your students?'

'Very good,' Van Buren said. 'And where would you say I should probe for your antithesis? In the sexual area? You certainly did seem a little disturbed over that slight incident in the bathroom with Lieutenant Leber.'

'Why is it you people find the notion of celibacy so bewildering?' Conlin asked. 'You really should pull yourself together, boy. Read a different class of book.'

Van Buren wasn't in the slightest put out. He pressed a button on the desk and Süssmann came in. 'Take him back now.'

Conlin stood up. 'Is that all?'

'Should there be any more?' Van Buren selected another cigarette. 'Good night, Father. Sleep well.'

Süssmann didn't say a word on the way back to the third level until they reached the cell where the sentry stood guard.

Conlin paused at the door and Süssmann said, 'No, the next one, if you please.'

The cell was exactly the same as the other except that it was clean and fresh. There was a chemical toilet, a mattress on the bed, blankets.

'You will be more comfortable here, I think, Father. Good night to you.' The door closed, the key turned in the lock.

A moment later, the light was switched off. Conlin unfolded the blankets. At least he had a breathing space. Why, he didn't know, but he at once relaxed, tension draining out of him and knelt down beside the bed to say his prayers.

The cell was filled with a hideous, frightening clamour. He scrambled to his feet and saw that a large bell was fixed just above the door that rang continually while a red light flickered on and off rapidly.

What a fool he'd been. The key rattled in the lock, the door was flung open and Süssmann and Becker appeared to drag him away along the passageway between them.

Vaughan climbed up out of the excavation wearily and young Franz dropped in beside Gregor to take his place. They were about seven feet down and the going was harder now.

Florian came in from the other room pushing the empty barrow. 'Had enough?'

'Just about. Not used to hard labour.' Vaughan glanced at his watch. 'In any case, I'm going to have to get moving.'

Margaret Campbell swung in through the door on a pair of old wooden crutches, followed by Konrad carrying a jug of coffee and several mugs on a tray.

'What's all this?' Vaughan demanded.

'Konrad found them for me,' she laughed. 'It makes me feel half way like a human being again.'

The gate bell rang. In the pit Franz paused, his pick raised above his head to swing. Everyone waited. Konrad said, 'I'll get it,' and went out.

Vaughan peered through the crack of the half-open door out through the rain. Margaret Campbell moved beside him and whispered, 'What do you think?'

Konrad had the gatelight on and was unbarring the postern. He opened it and Heinrich Berg stepped through. He muttered something to Konrad and peered around the courtyard nervously. Konrad shut the gate and came back to the barn.

'He wants you, Major.'

Berg paused inside the door, cap in hand, his dark, watchful eyes taking in everything. The excavation in the corner – the girl. Everyone waited. He managed an ingratiating smile. 'Major? I didn't realize.'

'Did you find it?' Vaughan asked impatiently.

'Oh yes, Herr Major, just like you said. A heavy manhole cover in the lower chamber. Padlocked and bolted.'

'And you went in?'

'Yes.'

'Tell me.'

'There was a ladder – a steel ladder, maybe twelve or fifteen feet down. The tunnel was around ten feet in diameter and sloped down all the way. At other stages there were two further ladders to descend. Ten foot each – no more.'

'You went all the way?'

'Yes. It's all concreted except for the last thirty or forty feet. That's still rough. You can see where they were digging when they finished and there's a certain amount of rubble.'

'And you were able to breathe – no foul air?'

'Fresh and clean. There was some water – perhaps a foot deep in places. Not sewage – spring water, I think.'

Konrad said, 'If the air is fresh, it means the tunnel must be vented to ground level and in more than one place.'

'Exactly.' Vaughan said to Berg, 'You've done well. I won't be seeing you for a while. A week at least.'

'Is there anything else you want me to do in the meantime?'

'Find out as much as you can about the day-to-day treatment of Father Conlin. Keep Brother Konrad informed – say every two days.'

'As you say.'

'All right, you can go now.'

Konrad saw him out and bolted the postern again. When he came back he said, 'You think we can trust him?'

'He doesn't have any other choice. He'd sell us out if he could, but he can't. For people like Berg life is just a series of accommodations.' He glanced at his watch. 'I'd better get changed. I don't want to keep my friend hanging around at the border.'

When he stepped out into the porch, he was once more in the heavy dispatch-rider's coat and helmet, the AK assault rifle across his chest.

Margaret Campbell said, 'I don't like you in that.'

'You're not meant to.' Behind her, Konrad pushed the Cossack and sidecar out of a shed into the courtyard, then went to open the gate.

Vaughan touched her cheek briefly with the back of a gloved hand. 'You look too good to leave standing there in the lamp-light, Maggie my love, and nicely helpless on those crutches.'

'And what would you do with me?'

'I'll think of something.' He mounted the Cossack. 'See you at the weekend.'

He drove out through the gate. Konrad closed it. The girl stood there, listening to the sound of the engine fade into the night, then she turned and went back inside.

In the old operations room at Bitterfeld, Pascoe sat at the controllers' desk, examining the plan of Schloss Neustadt in the light of a reading lamp. Bruno Teusen was asleep in a chair in the far corner. It was very quiet – almost midnight – and Pascoe wondered what had happened.

What had gone wrong. And then there was a knock on the door and Vaughan stepped into the room, followed by Böhmler.

Pascoe leaned back in his chair and smiled. 'You know, for a while there I was beginning to worry. I must be getting old. Everything went all right at the border?'

Vaughan removed his helmet. 'Like a charm. I didn't see a soul between Neustadt and Flossen, until I made contact with Böhmler here.'

'That was just after eleven,' Böhmler said. 'We put the bike in the back of the truck and proceeded to Flossen where Bulow passed us straight through – no fuss.'

'Excellent,' Pascoe said. 'Now, tell me what happened out there. Everything.'

Böhmler and Vaughan crossed the airstrip at Bitterfeld to what had been the officers' mess in the old days.

'It's not bad,' Böhmler said. 'Army cots, I'm afraid, but there are plenty of blankets and the caretaker got the boiler working again today. There should be plenty of hot water by tomorrow.'

One of the hangar doors stood partially open, light seeped through and there was the sound of an electric drill. 'What's going on?' Vaughan asked.

'That crazy friend of yours, Kubel. He seems to work on that plane of his every hour of the day or night.'

'I'll catch up with you,' Vaughan told him.

When he went into the hangar, he found the Storch standing all alone in the immensity of it. Max Kubel was working on one of the wings with an electric drill, whistling cheerfully. He wore a pair of black mechanics' overalls that had certainly seen better days.

He switched off the drill and grinned. 'So, return of the hero. What was it like?'

'Interesting. I see you still love planes more than women.'

'Much more reliable. Tell me, my friend, the girl you mentioned. You found her well?'

'About the only thing I'm sure of any more is that I did find her.' Vaughan paced restlessly to the partly opened door.

'And how do you feel?'

'Uneasy.'

'For whom? Yourself or this young woman of yours?' He laughed out loud. 'My poor Simon.'

'You go to hell,' Vaughan said and made for the door.

'Undoubtedly,' Max Kubel shouted cheerfully, and he picked up his electric drill and switched it on again.

Father Conlin crouched in the corner of a cell on the first level. It was painted white, contained no furniture at all and seemed filled with a hard, white light that hurt his eyes.

He was aware of a dull, solid, slapping sound, a continuous rhythm that never ceased. It seemed to be very near and yet far away. It made no sense.

The door opened and Van Buren appeared with a young Vopo guard. 'Bring him,' the American ordered.

When the Vopo got Conlin into the corridor, the old priest found Van Buren standing at the next cell, peering in through a barred window. The slapping sounds continued and when the guard hustled Conlin close enough, he saw, inside the cell, a man in tattered shirt and pants spread-eagled across a bench. Süssmann and Becker, stripped to the waist, were systematically beating him with rubber hoses.

The man on the bench moaned, turning his head, and Conlin saw to his horror that it was Karl, the driver who had delivered him by truck to Margaret Campbell's cottage that first night.

'What does this prove?' he asked Van Buren. 'He knows nothing about the Underground. He can't tell you a thing – that's the way I organized the system.'

'Oh, I believe you,' Van Buren said. 'But without a penitent, reform is not possible, isn't that what your church teaches? Shouldn't we take an interest in his soul? And pain is a purgative. I mean, take the Cross. What a way to go. Squalid, filthy and degrading, and yet three days later . . .'

11

It was just after eight o'clock on Saturday when Bulow waved the truck through at Flossen. About a mile up the road Böhmler forked left into a forest track, and a couple of hundred yards later emerged into a clearing in which stood the ruins of an old saw-mill beside a fast-flowing stream. The wheel which had once provided its source of power had not turned in years and the doors at the front of the building sagged on their hinges.

He drove inside, took a hand lamp, went round to the rear and dropped the tailboard. The Cossack and sidecar were inside, together with various other items and Vaughan, once more a Vopo. He passed down a foot pump with a long hose attached and a couple of plastic buckets. Böhmler took them without a word and went and filled them at a tap in the corner.

Rain started to drum against the roof and he grinned. 'Twenty minutes earlier and it would have saved us some work.'

'And exposed us to the chance that some nosey-parker might have seen a piece of Volkspolizei hardware entering East Germany from the West and wondered what was going on?' Vaughan pointed out.

He put the end of the foot pump in one of the buckets and started to operate it vigorously as Böhmler sprayed the truck. Very quickly, the dirty-grey water paint with which it had been painted dissolved away and the truck now stood revealed for what it was, a Volkspolizei field truck painted in the dark green and brown camouflage colours of the forest sector and bearing divisional and group signs.

Ten minutes was all it took and Böhmler went and threw the pump and buckets into the mill race. He came back, wiping his hands on a rag. 'All yours, Major.'

Vaughan clambered up behind the wheel. 'One hour after midnight. Okay?'

The engine roared into life and he drove out across the clearing. Böhmler went after him and by the time he reached the main road, the sound of the field truck had faded into the night. He turned and started to jog back towards the border post.

Vaughan should have known that it was too good to last. No matter how good your organization, it was always the unexpected that fouled things up. The stupid little things you hadn't planned for.

The first ten or fifteen miles passed uneventfully enough. Nothing but trees and darkness and then, as he passed through Ploden, he noticed a Cossack and sidecar that was twin to his own parked outside the inn. Obviously a regular stopping-off point for Vopo patrols. On the other hand, it was probably the only pub for miles.

The truck slewed violently as one of the rear tyres burst. He fought to control the wheel, stamping hard on the brake and managed to come to a halt in one piece in the grass verge.

Cursing softly, he got out, took the jack from the tool box and unbolted one of the two spare wheels. It was dark – too dark to see what he was doing so he got the hand lamp from the cab, placed it on the ground and started to unfasten the wheel bolts. They were apparently immovable and it struck him suddenly that they had probably been tightened automatically in the garage. It took all his strength, concentrating fiercely. It was perhaps because of that that he was unaware of the sound of the approaching engine until it was too late to do anything about it.

The Cossack pulled on to the verge and the Vopo came forward and stood over him. In other circumstances it might have been funny, for he could have been Vaughan's twin; helmet, goggles, coat, even the AK across the chest.

'Trouble, Comrade?'

'What do you think?' Vaughan demanded sourly. His hand slid into his right pocket, found the butt of the Walther he carried there and he slipped off the safety-catch.

'I'll give you a hand.'

The Vopo started to pump up the jack vigorously. 'Where are you heading?'

'Stendhal,' Vaughan told him. 'Divisional machine stores.'

An establishment which existed, he knew that. His new-found friend wrestled the old wheel off. 'What, on a Saturday night?'

Vaughan rolled the spare forward. 'An emergency. One of our recovery trucks ran off the road near Flossen and broke an axle. It's needed for Monday, so that means getting the part tonight and working through tomorrow.' He started to tighten the wheel bolts. 'There goes my weekend.'

He released the jack and air hissed. The Vopo chuckled. 'Had something good lined up, did you? Not Dirty Gerty at the inn at Ploden. Is that who you mean? I heard she was a certain turn.'

Vaughan slung the jack into the tool locker. 'Beggars can't be choosers, not in a dump like this.' He scrambled up behind the wheel. 'Anyway, thanks, Comrade. Got to get moving.'

The Vopo said, 'Hang on, you've forgotten the wheel you took off. I'll sling it in the back for you.'

Vaughan heard the footsteps go round to the rear and didn't wait for the reaction, simply stamped on the accelerator, and drove away.

He didn't stand a chance, not in any kind of a race with a machine as powerful as the Cossack. In his mirror he was aware of its headlight coming up fast and he swerved across the road as it tried to overtake him.

This manœuvre served him well for a while, but then he ran out of forest and emerged on to the dyke road above the Holstein Marshes, a causeway three miles long that ran across the wilderness of mudflats and great pale barriers of reeds higher than a man's head. An alien world inhabited only by birds.

And here it was no longer possible to weave because the slightest miscalculation would have the field truck over the causeway and into the marsh. Very sad for Sean Conlin and Margaret Campbell, not to mention Simon Vaughan.

Perhaps if he kept in close, inviting the Vopo to overtake, there would be a chance to crowd the Cossack over the edge into the marsh. Vaughan tried it, but the Vopo showed no intention of accepting the invitation, staying right on his tail.

There was a shot, then another as he fired his AK one-handed and Vaughan, doing the only possible thing, braked hard, skidding to a halt. He left his engine ticking over, slid across the passenger seat, went under the far door and crouched beneath the field truck.

The Cossack had stopped and footsteps approached. The boots, the tail of the coat, passed close to his face. The driving door was wrenched open.

There was silence and Vaughan came up from beneath the field truck behind the Vopo. His knee went into the small of the back, the left arm around the throat, bending the body back in an agonizing bow. The right hand jerked the helmet back hard against the nape of the neck. It broke cleanly as the Vopo gave one frantic choked cry and died.

Vaughan held him in his arms for a few moments, breathing heavily, then dragged him back to the motor-cycle and eased him into the side-car, which wasn't easy because he was a large man. Then he mounted the machine. When the engine was ticking over nicely, he jumped off and twisted the accelerator. The Cossack surged forward under its own power, over the edge of the causeway, into the marsh.

He got the hand lamp from the field truck. The Vopo had been pitched forward, the machine falling on top of him. It didn't take long to disappear, but Vaughan waited anyway, not satisfied until the surface mud was calm again.

So – one Vopo missing from patrol plus his machine, which with luck would indicate to security that he had defected to the West. And even if the marsh did decide to reveal its secret, there was nothing to indicate anything more than an unfortunate accident.

He got behind the wheel and lit a cigarette. It tasted foul. He threw it out of the window and drove away, gripping the wheel too tightly.

Vaughan walked down the sloping ramp of planks into the excavation with Brother Gregor and peered along the length of the tunnel.

'How far?' he asked.

'About twenty feet. It's really gone very well.'

It was well lit with electric light bulbs strung from a long flex at regular intervals. The roof and sides were lined with rusting corrugated iron sheets and propped up with baulks of timber.

'You can't exactly swing a pick in there,' Vaughan observed.

'No – admittedly only one man can actually work at the face itself with a labourer at his shoulder to help fill the cart. Four feet wide, three foot six high.'

'Couldn't you advance faster if two men could actually work on the face at the same time?'

'By widening the tunnel? Not really because the volume of soil to be brought out would increase dramatically. I spent some considerable time on the mathematics of it.' Gregor smiled apologetically. 'The engineer in me still comes out occasionally.'

'You're in charge,' Vaughan said. 'After all, as long as that tunnel is wide enough for a man to get through, that's all that's needed.'

'Exactly. I had the same problem during the final days in Stalingrad with trench communication.'

'I can imagine.'

There were three sharp raps from up ahead and Gregor looked up at Konrad and the others standing above. 'Haul away.'

Someone pulled on a rope and as Vaughan watched, a wooden cart mounted on a set of old pram wheels appeared, loaded with earth. It came straight out on crude rails and continued on up the ramp, where Konrad started to shovel the earth into a wheelbarrow.

Vaughan ducked into the tunnel and crawled along the centrepiece of wooden planks until he came to Franz, crouched at the soil face, hacking away with an old trenching shovel, Florian crouched at his shoulder. They were both stripped to the waist, their bodies streaked with sweat and dirt.

Franz grinned. 'Back again, Major. Do you want a shovel?'

'No, thanks,' Vaughan said. 'You seem to be enjoying yourself.'

'A nice, safe, enclosed feeling. Like being back in the womb. And interesting souvenirs.' He searched in the loose soil with his hand and came up with a finger bone. 'There you are. A present from Neustadt.'

Vaughan crawled back, out into the pit and went up the ramp. 'Nothing unpleasant so far?'

Gregor shook his head. 'Only old bones. I've inspected the cemetery and this side is mainly seventeenth and eighteenth century.'

'And what comes after?'

Konrad paused, leaning on his shovel. 'Considerably later, I'm afraid. Some graves as recent as last year.'

There was a nasty silence. No one seemed to know what to say and then the barn door opened and Margaret Campbell limped in, no crutches now. Just a heavy walking stick to lean on.

'Supper everyone,' she said, and when she smiled at Vaughan, it was as if a lamp had turned on inside.

It was towards the end of the meal that the gate bell sounded.

'That should be Berg,' Konrad said. 'I was expecting him tonight.'

He went out and came back presently with the caretaker. Berg was obviously surprised to see Vaughan and stood just inside the room, nervously twisting his cap in his hands.

'You're back, Major.'

'So it would appear. What's happening up there?'

'They don't exactly take me into their confidence. I only get to see some things.'

'Get on with it, man,' Vaughan told him.

'Well, Conlin is in good condition. I mean he can walk under his own power. I saw him leaving Van Buren's office this afternoon under guard.'

'Is he still on the third level?'

'Yes.' Berg hesitated. 'They've been concentrating on another man.'

'Who?'

'I overheard Captain Süssmann talking to Becker. It seems this man drove the truck Father Conlin was in when he first came here.'

'And what have they done to him?'

'Everything,' Berg said simply. 'They had him in the yard for hours tied to a pole. I'd say he hasn't got long myself.'

Margaret Campbell's distress was apparent to everyone. Vaughan took her hand under the table and held it tight.

'The Vopo officer – the woman he brought with him? What's her story?'

'Lieutenant Leber. A nurse from the medical corps.' He shrugged. 'Frankly, I hardly ever see her. She's up there with Van Buren most of the time.'

There was a pause while Vaughan thought about it, then he nodded. 'All right, you'd better stay and hear what I have to say as you'll be a part of it.' He stood up. 'Tonight I drove here in a Vopo field truck, a troop carrier. It's in one of the sheds in the courtyard.'

'And that's our way out when the time comes?' Konrad asked.

'Exactly. There are Vopo uniforms and rifles in the back for everyone, including you, Berg. Even if the whole countryside is roused, in such a vehicle, you'd never be questioned.'

Berg cleared his throat. 'But surely all border posts would be notified by phone to allow no traffic through.'

'Exactly,' Vaughan said. 'By happy chance, the one we shall use is in the hands of friends.'

'And what about a timetable?' Margaret Campbell asked. 'How can you possibly arrange that?'

'No need for one.' He went to the sideboard and picked up a leather army knapsack. He brought it back to the table, opened it and took out a small black wireless transmitter.

'You intend radio communications?' Konrad said. 'But such a thing is madness. The security forces have dozens of units whose sole task is to monitor all radio frequencies. They would track you down in a matter of hours.'

'Exactly,' Vaughan said. 'But bear with me and you'll understand. At Bitterfeld, from next Wednesday on, my friends will be on constant standby. A Storch spotter plane is waiting with a pilot who has made this sort of flight many times. The day I decide to go in for Conlin, this transmitter is switched on. It sends out an ultra-high-frequency signal, specially coded, and switches itself off automatically after two minutes. That alerts them at Bitterfeld. That procedure will be repeated the moment I bring Conlin out, and when that signal is received at Bitterfeld, the Storch will take off.'

'And how long will the flight take?' Margaret asked.

'Twenty minutes at the outside. The pilot will land at a spot called Water Horse Meadow by the Elbe about half a mile from here.'

'But can he land in such a place at night?'

'This pilot can and I have all the help he needs right here in this knapsack. Konrad will deliver me to the landing site with Conlin. The old man and I will return to Bitterfeld in the Storch.'

'And the rest of us?' Berg demanded.

'Konrad drives back here to pick you all up, in uniform, of course.' He smiled at the girl. 'There's even one for you.'

'I didn't know they made them that small.'

'Neither did I. You'll have to pull your cap down over your eyes. There's a map in the truck with the fastest route to Flossen clearly marked. You'd better find time to memorize that, Konrad.'

'Of course.'

'And one more thing and burn this into your brains. On the night in question, whenever it is, it's absolutely essential that everyone does what they have to exactly on time. If anyone is missing at the final stage, then they're on their own.' He turned to Konrad. 'You don't hang about for anyone.'

Berg shook his head. 'Crazy,' he said. 'Absolutely crazy.'

'No, it isn't,' Konrad told him. 'It's really very simple, if you think about it. One part fitting neatly into another like a good Swiss watch.'

'And you know what happens to those when something goes wrong with one of the parts,' Berg said morosely. He pulled on his cap. 'Anyway, I'd better be off. I'll see you again the day after tomorrow.'

Konrad took him out and the others got up. 'Back to the salt mines,' Franz said cheerfully and they all went out.

The girl turned to Vaughan and there was concern in her eyes. 'You look tired.'

For a moment he almost told her of the incident on the causeway. That he had recently killed a man. But it was better left unsaid. She was not someone who would ever be able to accept such things lightly, however good the cause.

'I must be getting old,' he said, and smiled.

Konrad came back in. 'What time do you leave?'

Vaughan glanced at his watch. 'In about an hour. My contact man expects me at one o'clock on the dot.'

The girl put a hand on his arm. 'You're going back tonight?'

'Yes, it's necessary. I've got things to do. But I'll be back next Wednesday. You know about that.'

Konrad said, 'You think it will work, this scheme of yours?'

'I don't see why not.'

'And Father Hartmann? You haven't told him?'

'I'd rather present him with the situation as a fact. He might argue about it.'

'You know best.' Konrad hesitated, glancing from one to the other. 'I'll leave you for a while, if I may, and see how things are progressing in the barn.'

He went out. Vaughan lit a cigarette. Margaret Campbell folded her arms and leaned back in her chair, watching him.

'How long have I known you? A year? A hundred?'

'It never pays to be specific.'

'Have you any idea how I felt on the bridge that morning? How much I wanted to tell you everything?'

He leaned across and touched her face. 'More water under the bridge.'

'And you believe in all this?' she said. 'Believe in what you're doing? You must do. You couldn't go to such lengths otherwise.'

'If you mean do I dislike what goes on over here, then you'd be right,' he said. 'There are thirty thousand troops guarding the wall, did you know that? Any soldier who prevents the escape of a fellow guard gets promotion two ranks, the Merit Badge of the National People's Army, five hundred marks and a vacation in Moscow for two. I don't suppose they told you that at University.'

'No, they didn't.'

'Not that it's doing the bastards much good. More than two thousand guards have defected already. You see, they'd rather experience the fleshpots of Western capitalism than the purity of Marxist ideology.'

'You're angry,' she said.

'Am I?'

'Tell me about Borneo.'

'Why?'

'I'd like to know, from your point of view. Please.'

She laid a hand on his arm very lightly.

'Last year, in Borneo, there was an area around Kota Baru that was absolutely controlled by terrorists and most of them weren't Indonesians. They were Chinese Communist infiltrators. They burned villages wholesale, coerced the Dyaks into helping them by butchering every second man or woman in some of the villages they took, just to encourage the others.'

'And they put you in to do something about it?'

'I was supposed to be an expert in that sort of thing so they gave me command of a company of irregulars, Dyak scouts, and told me to clean things up. I didn't have much luck until they burned the mission at Kota Baru, raped and murdered four nuns and eighteen girls. That was it as far as I was concerned.'

'What did you do?'

'An informer tipped me off that a Chinese merchant in Selangar named Hui Lui was a Communist agent. I arrested him and when he refused to talk, handed him over to the Dyaks.'

'To torture him?'

'He only lasted a couple of hours, then he told me where the group I'd been chasing were holed up.'

'And did you get them?'

'Eventually. They split into two groups which didn't help, but we managed it.'

'They said you shot your prisoners.'

'Only during the final pursuit when I was hard on the heels of the second group. Prisoners would have delayed me.'

'I see. And Mr Hui Lui?'

'Shot trying to escape. Absolutely true and that's the most ironic part of it. I was quite prepared to take him down to the coast and let him stand trial, but he tried to make a break for it the night before we left.'

'And do you regret any of this now?'

'What I did to him he'd have done to me. The purpose of terrorism is to terrorize. Lenin said it first and it's on page one of every Communist handbook on revolutionary warfare. You can only fight that kind of fire with fire. I did what had to be done. Malaya, Kenya, Cyprus, Aden. I'd seen it all and I was tired of people justifying the murder of the innocent by pleading it was all in the name of the cause. When I finished, there was no more terror by night in Kota Baru. No more butchering of little girls. That should count for something, God knows.'

Her face was very calm, the eyes hooded, brooding, arms folded beneath her breasts as she leaned on the table. 'So you ruined yourself. Career, reputation – everything.'

'I'd better go now.'

He got up, took his long dispatch-rider's raincoat from behind the door and buttoned it up. He slung the AK assault rifle across his chest and put on his helmet, adjusting the strap.

'Will I do?'

'I should think so.'

He had the door open when she said softly, 'I see now what it was I saw in you from that first moment – sensed and never understood. There is always in your heart, I think, a sense of justice outraged.'

There was silence between them. The door closed softly and he was gone.

It was just after two a.m. and Meyer was lying in one of the narrow military cots of Bitterfeld, blankets piled thickly about him for he felt the cold easily. He was reading one of Vaughan's books, a critical appreciation of the philosophy of Heidegger.

The door opened and Vaughan came in. 'Simon, you're back!' Meyer said.

'You sound surprised.' Vaughan stripped off his helmet and raincoat, sat wearily on the edge of the bed and lit a cigarette.

'Everything go all right?'

'I had to kill a Vopo prowler guard who tried to stop me on the road.'

'My God!'

'Don't worry. I dumped him and his motor-cycle in a place called the Holstein Marsh. With any luck, his superiors will think he's defected.'

'There are times when all you can do is close the windows and wait for darkness to pass,' Meyer said gravely.

'A century or so ago when I was seventeen, I used to go dancing,

Julius, at the old Trocadero. Your kind of music. You'd have loved it.'

'So what's the point?'

'That seventeen is an age of infinite promise. Seventeen is walking girls home five miles from a dance in the rain for not much more than a kiss. Seventeen is being filled with a restless excitement, the knowledge that something is waiting just around the next corner. Seventeen is standing under a street lamp with a girl in your arms and rain drifting down like silver spray.'

Meyer said, 'That was then, this is now, Simon. You're thirty-seven years of age and you've been a professional soldier for twenty of them. Let's face it, business is business and killing is your trade. You can't stop. Malaya, Kenya, Cyprus – all those little wars you served in. Now this. For you, there'll always be another little war because you can't stop it, this game you play. In the end it has you by the balls, my friend, and one day, no matter how good you are, how smart, a sniper is waiting on a rooftop somewhere to put a bullet in your back. No honour there.'

'I spent two years in a Chinese prison camp,' Vaughan said wearily. 'That's honour enough for one lifetime.'

'You're damaged goods, Simon. Let her go, there's a good boy. Get her out safe for a mitzvah, a good deed, then let her go. She's entitled to a life.'

Vaughan got undressed and climbed into the other bed. Meyer said, 'Do you mind if I keep on reading? Does the light bother you?'

'No.'

'Interesting fellow, this Heidegger. He says that for authentic living what is necessary is the resolute confrontation of death. Do you agree?'

Vaughan's voice was muffled when he replied, 'A good man in his day, Heidegger. Just like me.'

Walter Ulbricht's office was furnished with spartan simplicity. A framed photograph of Stalin with a dedication occupied a prominent position on one wall and the generally chilly atmosphere was not solely the product of the Comrade Chairman's well-known dislike of central heating.

Early morning sunlight streamed into the room through one of the narrow windows, but did little to lighten the sombre atmosphere as he sat there at the desk, methodically working his way through a pile of papers presented to him by a male secretary, signing the occasional letter where requested.

There was a tap at the door and Helmut Klein entered. He made a distinguished enough looking figure in the heavy overcoat with the fur collar, and yet in the presence of the older man he seemed to shrink. Ulbricht ignored him for a while, continuing to sign letters. Finally he paused, removed his glasses and ran a hand over his eyes.

'Leave us,' he said softly, and the secretary went to the door at once, opened it and left without a word.

Ulbricht looked up at the other man for a full minute before speaking. 'Well, Klein, I'm waiting. I've been back from Moscow two days and no word from you.'

'Comrade Chairman,' Klein began, 'these things take time.'

'You told me that this American, Van Buren, was the best. I wasn't happy about his lack of political commitment, but you assured me that didn't matter. You promised me results. In fact, it wouldn't be exaggerating the position to say that you actually guaranteed me results.'

Klein's mouth was bone dry. He moistened his lips and managed to whisper, 'Yes, Comrade Chairman.'

'Good. Failure in this affair will not be tolerated. I hold you personally responsible. I look forward to hearing from you soon with favourable news.'

He picked up his pen and returned to his documents and Klein got out as fast as he could.

He had his driver take him to the Ministry of State Security at Normannenstrasse at once. When he entered the outer office of Section Five, Frau Apel rose to greet him. 'Good morning, Colonel. The Leipzig office has been on the line.'

'Never mind that now,' Klein told her. 'Get me Captain Süssmann at Schloss Neustadt.'

He went into his office and sat behind his desk without taking off his coat. He saw now that he stood on the brink of a precipice. He had placed his life, his career, entirely in Harry Van Buren's hands.

The phone rang, and when he picked it up the voice said 'Süssmann here.'

'What's happening there, Süssmann? Is he getting anywhere? The truth, now.'

'Not in my opinion. Too much conversation. Now if Sergeant Becker and I could have a free hand . . .'

'No,' Klein said. 'Another week and then we review the situation.

Naturally, I expect you to report to me on Van Buren's activities in minutest detail.'

'Of course, Comrade.'

'This affair could mean considerable advancement for you, Süssmann, if we can reach a successful conclusion.'

'I'll do my best.'

'Another thing. This priest, Hartmann, will be turning up the day after tomorrow. I want to know what he gets up to as well. Telephone me at any hour. You have the private number where you can reach me at night if I'm not at the office. Now transfer me to Van Buren.'

Van Buren was alone in his office with Ruth Leber, going over his notes on the last session with Conlin when the phone rang.

He picked it up and Klein said cheerfully, 'Hello, Harry. I haven't heard from you for a few days so I thought I'd see how things were going.'

'Fine,' Van Buren said. 'I'm making real progress.'

'Good. It's just that I had to see Chairman Ulbricht on other matters this morning and he did mention the Conlin affair. He told me he expects to see some really positive result quite soon now. If Conlin's trial is to coincide with Kennedy's visit, then preparations must be put in hand as soon as possible.'

'I see.'

'Would it help if I came down?'

'No, that wouldn't do at all,' Van Buren said hastily. 'The whole technique of this thing depends on the closeness of my personal contact with him. The fact that no one else is allowed to enter the private area of our relationship.'

'A week, Harry, that's all I can give you.'

'But that's ridiculous.'

'No it isn't. It's Ulbricht.'

The line went dead. Van Buren replaced his receiver and sat there frowning.

'Trouble?' Ruth Leber asked.

'No, I don't think so. We're just going to have to move a little faster, that's all.' He stood up. 'I think I'll have another word with Conlin.'

When he opened the cell door, Conlin was sitting on the bed staring at the wall. He looked very frail, the flesh on his face reduced so that every bone showed clearly.

'You don't look too good,' Van Buren said.

'I'm getting old, that's all.'

Van Buren lit a cigarette and the smoke was pungent on the cold air. Conlin smiled drily. 'A waste of time. I've gone through my nicotine withdrawal symptoms. I haven't breathed so well in years. You've done me a favour there, Harry.'

It was totally unexpected, the use of his name and Van Buren was aware of a spurt of anger – or was he trying to rationalize a fear syndrome? Perhaps deep inside he felt the old man's familiarity as a personal threat.

He said to Becker, 'Bring him along,' went out and along the passage and unbolted the door to another cell.

The truck-driver, Karl, lay in the corner. Blood oozed from his nostrils, the corner of his mouth, his eyes were fixed as if on some spot in the middle distance.

'We pride ourselves on a sense of logic and order,' Van Buren said, 'but inside, we are savages. A predisposition to violence is man's most enduring attribute.'

Conlin got down on his knees painfully and leaned over the broken body. There was a flicker of recognition, the lips moved. Karl said, 'Save me, Father. Help me.'

He tried to clutch at the old man's shirt front, but he hadn't the strength, and slumped back again. 'For pity's sake, Harry,' Conlin said, 'get him a doctor.'

'Too late,' Van Buren told him. 'But I've done the next best thing. I've brought him a priest.'

He went out, the door closed, the bolts rammed home. Conlin put an arm around Karl and leaned the broken head against his shoulder.

'Karl,' he whispered, 'I want you to make an act of contrition. Say after me, O my God, who art infinitely good in thyself . . .'

12

L'Osservatore Romano is one of the world's oldest newspapers, but its distribution is not confined to the Vatican alone and there are special weekly versions in English, French, Spanish and Portuguese.

Although the editorial staff pride themselves on their coverage of general world news, there is little doubt that anything of significance to the position of the Roman Catholic Church has special importance for them. The report from one of their German correspondents was received on Wednesday morning and a reporter took it straight into Manzini, the Managing Editor.

'Where did this come from?' he asked.

'West Berlin. You think there could be any truth in it?'

'I don't know. If there is, it could be a hot one. Leave it with me and I don't want it discussed. Not with anyone.'

The reporter went out. Manzini sat there thinking about it for a while, then reached for his phone and told his secretary to get him the Father General of the Jesuits at the Collegio di San Roberto Bellarmino.

Over six hundred thousand people, the greatest number ever assembled to honour a Roman pontiff, had filed past the embalmed body of Pope John as it lay in state for three days in St Peter's Basilica. In addition to the Italian President and his entire Cabinet, diplomatic representatives of fifty-five countries had been among the mourners. And finally, he was buried in the Crypt of St Peter in private, in accordance with his dying wish.

For Pacelli, it had been a busy time. So many Church dignitaries arriving in Rome from all over the world; conferences to attend with various departments of the Italian security services; new policies to be hammered out.

When he knocked on the door and went in, the Father General was standing by the window. He turned. 'Ah, there you are. I've just had Manzini on the phone, from *L'Osservatore Romano*. They've got wind of the Conlin affair.'

'To what extent?'

'A minor report from one of their Berlin correspondents, totally unconfirmed, that Conlin has disappeared and that the East Germans have him.'

'What did you tell Manzini?'

'I asked him not to use the story, naturally. I told him that matters of the gravest security were concerned. He agreed at once. He is a man of the utmost dependability. He did point out that if the rumour exists, then sooner or later it must come to the attention of other news agencies, and there is nothing we can do about that.'

'An unfortunate situation,' Pacelli said. 'It's amazing how minor leaks of this nature can take place, no matter how strict one's security system. I'll see about the other news agencies. We do have a certain influence in these areas.'

'Do what you can.'

'May I remind you that it is today that Father Hartmann proceeds to Neustadt?'

The Father General, who had sat down behind his desk, looked up. 'Then we must pray for him.'

'Indeed we must,' Pacelli said, 'for he will need all our prayers, I think.'

In the basement garage of the Catholic Secretariat in East Berlin, Erich Hartmann was loading his suitcase into the back of the Volkswagen. The garage was dimly lit. There were only two other cars to be seen and a State Medical Service ambulance. He wondered what it was doing there and then there was the rattle of a motor-cycle engine and Schaefer came down the ramp in his BMW.

He wore his trench-coat, a cap and goggles, and there was a canvas suitcase strapped to the luggage carrier of the BMW. He pulled the machine up on its stand and walked across, pushing up his goggles.

'Why couldn't we have gone down this afternoon, Father, in daylight? I hate biking after dark.'

'I had a considerable amount of paperwork to clear up this afternoon,' Hartmann said, which was not strictly true. He had left his departure until eight o'clock at night because Pascoe had asked him to, although there had been no explanation why.

'All right, Father, we might as well get started.'

'This is nonsense,' Hartmann said. 'Why can't you drive down with me in comfort?'

'Regulations,' Schaefer replied. 'Where you go, I follow.'

'Which seems to me to be stretching bureaucracy to the limits.'

'That's democratic socialism for you, Father.'

Hartmann smiled. 'How's your wife?'

'Glad to get rid of me for a week,' Schaefer grinned. 'I'll tell you what, Father. Half way there on the far side of Rathenow there's a roadside café called the Astor. Pull up there and I'll let you buy me a coffee.'

'Done,' Hartmann said, and he got into the Volkswagen and drove out of the garage.

Schaefer paused to pull on his gloves and a voice called softly from behind, 'Excuse me.'

He turned and found a tall man advancing towards him, hands in pockets. There was something strange about him, something Schaefer couldn't put his finger on, and then he realized what it was. The other man was wearing a trench-coat that was twin to his own, tweed cap, navy blue polo-neck sweater, grey tweed trousers. All the same.

'Horst Schaefer?'

Schaefer, sensing that something was very badly wrong here, reached for the holstered Walther under his left armpit. Too late; for already he found himself staring down the muzzle of its twin.

'So am I,' Vaughan smiled.

The ambulance rolled forward and braked to a halt and two men in white uniforms got out. One of them jerked Schaefer's arms behind and handcuffed him and Vaughan removed his wallet. He took out the identity papers only and slipped them into one of Schaefer's pockets. He kept the more personal items, a letter from Schaefer's father, a couple of snaps of his wife and children.

He produced identical identity papers which he slipped into the wallet, then put it in his own inside breast pocket. He removed Schaefer's goggles and put them on.

'What is this?' Schaefer was frightened now. 'Who are you?'

'I'm Horst Schaefer,' Vaughan told him amicably. 'These two gentlemen are members of what you would call an illegal organization – the Christian Underground. I wouldn't advise you to give them any trouble. They're not too good at turning the other cheek.'

One of them led Schaefer to the rear of the ambulance, the other opened the door and they pushed him inside and down on one of the bunks. Before he knew what was happening, a hypodermic appeared and the needle was jammed into his arm, right through the leather sleeve.

On the opposite bunk there was a body totally covered by a red blanket. Vaughan pulled it back to disclose the waxen features of a young girl, eyes closed in death.

'We always try to make it a young girl. It makes the Vopos feel bad at the checkpoint.'

'I don't understand.' Schaefer could hardly keep his eyes open now and his limbs felt as heavy as lead.

'Into the Western Zone. All quite legitimate. These gentlemen have got the papers.'

A concealed trap was lifted in the floor, a space revealed about the size of a coffin. Schaefer was lowered into it, his senses already slipping away from him as the lid was lowered.

It was a quiet night at the Astor café. There were only four people in the place, the girl behind the counter, two truck-drivers having their evening meal and Erich Hartmann who sat with a cup of coffee in front of him at a corner table.

He made a conspicuous enough figure in his broad-brimmed shovel hat and black cassock and the others watched him curiously. He wondered what could be keeping Schaefer, for traffic on the road had been light. He became aware of the sound of a motor-cycle engine outside and looked out and saw the BMW turn into the car park and pull up beside the Volkswagen.

'Fräulein?' he called to the girl. 'Another coffee, if you please.'

A moment later, the door opened. He turned with a smile and then the smile faded as, to his total astonishment, Simon Vaughan entered the café.

Vaughan spooned sugar into his coffee. Hartmann waited for the girl to go back behind the counter before whispering, 'What on earth is going on here?'

Vaughan took out his wallet, extracted his card and passed it over. 'Horst Schaefer, your friendly local SSD man.'

The card was a perfect facsimile of Schaefer's own, except that the thumbprint, the physical characteristics, where appropriate, and the photo, were Vaughan's.

Hartmann passed the card back. 'Where's Schaefer? What have you done to him?'

'Should be in West Berlin right about now,' Vaughan told him. 'Sleeping soundly and when he wakes up, he'll find Bruno Teusen at his bedside.'

Hartmann's face was calm, but there was anger in the eyes and his right fist had clenched. 'Why wasn't this discussed with me?'

'Because it was felt you might argue about it. Now you can't.'

'Damn you, Vaughan.'

'Strong words for a man of the cloth, Father,' Vaughan said. 'And while we're on the subject, why the fancy dress? Conspicuous consumption by any standards, I should have thought.'

'I want them to know who I am when I get to Neustadt. I thought that was the idea. To pull all attention on to me.'

'Something like that,' Vaughan said. 'Well, is it war or peace between us?'

Hartmann smiled ruefully. 'Do I have a choice?'

He got up and moved out and Vaughan followed him.

It was shortly after ten when Hartmann pulled up in front of the inn at Neustadt. A Vopo fieldcar was parked a few yards away. Hartmann sat there for a while, then reached for his suitcase and got out. He went up the steps to the entrance, paused, then opened the door.

Georg Ehrlich was behind the bar with Sigrid. Heinrich Berg and half a dozen of the village men sat in a circle together drinking beer, Süssmann and Becker were at a table by the fire, plates of stew before them.

It was Sigrid who saw Hartmann first and sucked in her breath sharply. And then the whole room went silent. Hartmann put down his suitcase and moved to the bar.

'Are you Herr Ehrlich, the mayor here?'

'That's right.'

'My name is Hartmann. I believe you've been warned to expect me. I'm here to consider the question of the church.'

Ehrlich's eyes flickered nervously to the two Vopos by the fire. 'Yes,' he said slowly. 'I received word from the Ministry of State Security some days ago. You're wasting your time here, Father, you must know that.'

The door opened and Vaughan entered carrying his canvas holdall. He dropped it beside Hartmann's suitcase and came forward. 'So you made it, Father?' Heinrich Berg stared at him, his mouth gaping in astonishment, a kind of horror in his eyes, and Vaughan nodded cheerfully.

Süssmann got up, wiping his mouth on a napkin and walked across the room. He stood for a moment, looking them both over. 'Papers,' he said curtly.

Hartmann handed him his Ministry of State Security permit.

Süssmann examined it, handed it back to him without a word, then turned to Vaughan.

'And you?'

'Schaefer – Section Six.'

Vaughan proferred his SSD card and Süssmann checked it. 'So where he goes, you follow?'

'Something like that.'

He returned Vaughan's card and Hartmann said, 'Would you be the military commander of this area?'

'No,' Süssmann said. 'Why do you ask?'

'I was told to report my presence to him on arrival.'

Süssmann hesitated. 'The person you seek is busy tonight. You must try tomorrow. In the morning at Schloss Neustadt.'

He walked back to the table and sat down, saying something to Becker who laughed coarsely. Hartmann said, 'Have you room for us to stay, Herr Ehrlich?'

Ehrlich shook his head. 'That is not possible.'

'I see,' Hartmann said calmly. 'Is there a priest's house still?'

'Yes,' Ehrlich said reluctantly. 'But it has not been used for some time. I have the key.'

'Perhaps if you could spare a few blankets,' Hartmann said, 'I'm sure Herr Schaefer and I could manage, unless, of course, you can find him room here.'

Ehrlich looked hunted and Vaughan said cheerfully, 'Can't let you out of my sight, now can I, Father? I think we'd better stick together.'

'All right,' Ehrlich said. 'I'll find you some blankets and get the key.'

'And the church?' Hartmann said. 'Have you the key to the church?'

'The church stays locked.' It was Süssmann who had spoken.

Hartmann turned to look at him and Ehrlich said hurriedly, 'I'll get the blankets,' and fled.

The villagers were discussing the situation among themselves in low tones and Hartmann and Vaughan sat down at a table to wait. Sigrid brought two beers without a word. She was a pretty girl in traditional costume, her flaxen hair plaited about her head. She gazed at Hartmann in fascination, unable to take her eyes off him.

He toasted her, 'Thank you, that's very kind.'

Becker got up and swaggered forward, a stein of beer in his left hand. He emptied it, put it down on the table and stood over Hartmann, looking down at him contemptuously.

'Skirts on men. What next?' He made a kissing sound with his lips and patted Hartmann's cheek.

Hartmann's hand fastened around the wrist and the smile was wiped from Becker's face. He staggered, then fell to one knee, forced down by the relentless pressure of all that enormous strength. Hartmann released him suddenly so that Becker lost his balance and fell back. His rage was terrible to see and he pulled at the flap of his pistol-holster.

'Becker!' Süssmann called. 'Enough!'

The sergeant got to his feet, his hand on the butt of his Walther now. This time, when Süssmann spoke there was iron in his voice. 'Becker! For the last time!'

The sergeant went back to the table and Ehrlich returned with the blankets and an oil lamp. 'All right, gentlemen, if you'll follow me.'

The house was next to the church, a small, two-storeyed building with wooden shutters which were closed.

'I'm surprised you haven't let someone move in,' Hartmann said.

'There is no shortage of housing in this village, Father. Agriculture is declining in these parts and most young people move to Berlin if they can to get work in the factories there. I'm afraid the electricity is not connected, which is why I've brought the oil lamp, but there's water on tap and a lavatory. You should be all right.'

The front door opened on to a stone-flagged passage. There was a wooden staircase going up to the second floor and he led the way along to the kitchen. There was a wooden table, chairs and an old iron stove.

'Plenty of wood out at the back if you want to light a fire. Two bedrooms upstairs. I don't know what condition the mattresses will be in.'

'We'll manage,' Hartmann said. 'You've been very kind.'

'That's all right, Father,' Ehrlich told him gruffly. For a moment it seemed as if he might say something more; then he thought better of it and went out.

'Now what?' Hartmann said.

'Make a fire. Fill in a little time. Then I'd like to see how the Franciscans have been getting on.'

'May I come with you?'

'If you like. One thing is definite. We stay as far away from that place as possible during the day. Not even a hint of a connection.'

'As you say.'

Vaughan lit a cigarette. 'I like what you did to that big ox back at the inn. I didn't know your lot went in for things like that.'

'Soldiers of Christ, Major Vaughan. Didn't you know?' Hartmann picked up the lamp. 'And now, I'll see if I can find some wood in the yard.'

The gate bell made a lonely sound, rather eerie, and there was no response for some considerable time, then footsteps. The shutter was opened and frail old Brother Urban peered out. The bolt was withdrawn, he opened the gate.

'Major,' he said in his dry old voice. 'They're in the barn.'

'How are things?'

'Not good.'

It was the smell which was most noticeable the moment Vaughan opened the door. Konrad and Florian were loading on the edge of the excavation and both of them were wearing bandages wrapped about their faces to cover mouth and nose. The half-light of the barn enhanced the effect, strange and disturbing.

When Konrad paused to speak, leaning wearily on his shovel, his voice was thick, muffled. 'Good, you made it. Did everything go all right?'

'Perfectly. This is Father Hartmann.'

'I won't shake hands,' Konrad said. 'For obvious reasons.'

Hartmann moved to the edge of the excavation, his face pale. 'Is it bad in there?'

'I'm afraid so. We've made excellent progress, but we've started to hit more recent graves and it isn't nice.'

'That smell is terrible.'

There was a movement down below and someone emerged on hands and knees. When he stood, Vaughan saw that it was Gregor, in spite of the fact that the head was swathed in bandages as well as the mouth and nose. He carried a piece of sacking in both hands, holding it out in front of him, and from the bulge it was obvious that it contained something.

'An arm, or what's left of one,' he said to Konrad. 'It's not going to be pleasant getting the rest out.'

He went through to the other room. 'The well?' Vaughan asked.

Konrad nodded. 'Then lime and more soil. Nothing else we can do.'

'Where's Doctor Campbell?'

'In the house attending to Franz. He cut himself and she's most insistent that every injury, even the slightest scratch, is treated at once.'

'We'll have a word with her.'

They found her in the kitchen with Franz who was stripped to the waist. There was a large zinc bath of heavily disinfected water on the table and an assortment of drugs. She was giving him an injection as they went in and Vaughan saw the dressing at once on the boy's left arm, fastened into place by surgical tape.

'Simon.' She smiled, but her cheeks were sunken.

'How goes it?'

'Fine. Have you seen Konrad?'

'Yes, we took a look. Nasty.'

Franz said, 'I'll get back now.'

'And don't forget,' she told him. 'The slightest thing – any kind of ache or pain or headache – come and see me at once.'

'Fräulein.' He grinned. 'I ache all over already.'

He went out and she said, 'So this is Father Hartmann.'

Hartmann took her hand and smiled warmly. 'A pleasure, Fräulein. I've heard a great deal about you.'

'Can I get you coffee?'

He hesitated, glancing at Vaughan. 'No, thanks. I think I'd like to go back to the barn. There may be something I could do.'

'Tea and sympathy,' Vaughan said with brutal directness. 'No more than that. They've got their job to do – you have yours. I don't want you getting your cassock dirty. Spend too much time in there and the villagers will smell you coming as you cross the square.'

'All right,' Hartmann said angrily, 'I take your point.'

When he'd gone, Vaughan turned to the girl. She was putting the kettle on the stove and turned to face him, looking tired and somehow past everything that ever was and totally vulnerable.

'You've no idea how glad I am to see you,' she said and came into his arms.

Every resolve he had made faded away. He held her close. 'Bad, is it?'

When she looked up at him, her eyes were filled with a deep disgust. 'Horrible, Simon. Like something out of a nightmare and the trouble is, I think it's going to get worse.'

It was cold in the early dawn and still dark when the two Vopos dragged Conlin into the courtyard. He stood between them, shivering, wondering what was to come. The headlamps of a fieldcar parked close by were switched on and their twin shafts picked Karl out of the darkness, strapped to a post in the centre of the courtyard.

Süssmann and Becker appeared and the captain said, 'Bring him,' and went forward with the sergeant, the two Vopos dragging Conlin behind.

Karl hung in the straps, his head lolling to one side. Becker peered closely at him. 'I think he's dead,' he announced.

'Make sure,' Süssmann said coldly.

Becker took out his Walther, cocked it and fired into the skull at point blank range. Pieces of bone and blood sprayed, the body sagged. Conlin cried out sharply. Süssmann and Becker walked away, the two Vopos released their grip and Conlin sank to the ground at Karl's feet, all strength going out of him.

Footsteps approached, the damp air was scented with cigarette smoke. Harry Van Buren squatted beside him.

'You could have prevented this if you'd been sensible. He'd have still been alive if it hadn't been for that incredible self-righteousness of yours. The insistence that you must be right in all things, even when it kills people.'

'Go away,' Father Conlin said in a low voice.

'Like poor Karl here,' Van Buren told him. 'Or your sister.'

He stood up and walked away quite quickly, his footsteps echoing on the cobbles. Conlin crouched there, his head against Karl's knee.

'Oh dear God, Frances Mary,' he said. 'I never wanted it, you know that.'

For the first time in years he started to cry.

Vaughan and Hartmann sat on two chairs on the landing outside Van Buren's office and waited. After a while, Vaughan got up, went to the balustrade and looked down at the imposing sweep of the great staircase, the hall below.

'Perfect for a remake of *The Prisoner of Zenda*, but not exactly comfortable,' Hartmann remarked.

The door opened and Süssmann looked out. 'He'll see you now – together.'

Hartmann led the way into the room, Vaughan at his heels and Süssmann closed the door behind them and stood against it. Van Buren waited, seated at his desk. Hartmann produced his permit.

Van Buren ignored it and looked him over, an amused, slightly contemptuous smile on his face. 'Are you going to a costume ball?'

'I think you know why I am here,' Hartmann said carefully. 'I was ordered to report to the area commander on arrival and I have now done so. Am I permitted to leave?'

'Very good,' Van Buren clapped his hands solemnly. 'Nothing like a religious education for teaching a man how to behave.'

'I heard you lecture at Dresden three months ago. The Psychological Basis of Religious Persuasion. You were very eloquent.'

'But failed to make my case?'

Hartmann said, 'I happen to believe that in every human being there is something profound and mysterious that can never answer to your more rational explanation.'

Van Buren held up a hand to cut him off. 'No, thanks, I'm not interested in philosophical argument, not at this time of day. Let's stick to the facts. Just what do you intend to do while you're here?'

'Examine the state of the church. Meet the people. Discuss their religious needs.'

'With a view to re-opening the church itself?'

'If that is what people want. The right of each and every citizen to follow the religion of his choice is part of the constitution.'

'So is censorship of the papers. And the fact that trade unions are forbidden the right to strike. Which is right, which is wrong!'

'I thought you said you'd no time for philosophical discussion at the moment?'

Van Buren smiled. 'Your point, Father.' He lit a cigarette and leaned back. 'All right. Play your little games if you must, but don't get underfoot. Any incident of the most minor nature and I'll have you back to Berlin within the hour.'

'As you say. There is one thing. I understand you have the key of the church?'

Van Buren sat staring up at him for a while, then opened a drawer, took out three large keys on a ring and threw them across the desk. 'There you are, but no public services.'

'Which means you think I'd actually get a congregation. Thank you. That's most encouraging. And thank you for your time.'

Hartmann moved to the door. As Süssmann opened it for him, Van Buren said in English, 'They tell me you were at Notre Dame. All-American quarterback two years running.'

'That's right.'

Van Buren laughed. 'A jock,' he said. 'In a black frock. That I should live to see the day.'

Hartmann refused to be drawn and went out without a word. Van Buren laughed, got up and moved to the fire, not a bit put out. He threw on another log and turned to Vaughan. 'So you're Schaefer?' he said in German.

'That's right, Comrade.'

'I hear you've moved into the priest's house with him.'

'There was little choice. The mayor said he couldn't accommodate us at the inn and besides, I like to stick close to him. That's my job.'

'And that's exactly what you will do,' Van Buren said. 'Stick like glue. Anything he does that's the slightest bit out of the ordinary, I want to know about it.'

'You're in charge, Comrade.'

Van Buren nodded. 'All right. On your way and stay in touch.'

Vaughan went out and Süssmann closed the door.

'Are you going to let him get away with it, this priest?'

'His permit is signed by the Minister for State Security himself. All a question of politics, Süssmann. Tell Lieutenant Leber I want her, will you?'

The Captain went out and Van Buren sat down at his desk and, opening a drawer in search of blank paper, discovered the Russian grenades again. He took one out and saw that it was very similar in design to the American version. A ring pin to pull with finger or teeth, the safety-lever to hold until the final second before throwing.

He was handling one when Süssmann came back. 'Nasty little item,' Van Buren said.

'A fragmentation grenade.'

'Yes, we used babies like this in Korea and they suffer from the defects of their kind. If you ever want to throw one, make sure you're under cover. They can scatter fragments for a two hundred metre radius.'

Süssmann, who had never seen action and secretly envied Van Buren his war experience, nodded. 'I'll remember that, Comrade. Lieutenant Leber will be along in a moment.'

'Good.'

'Is there anything else, Comrade?'

'Yes, you'd better bring Conlin up here again and we'll see how he's getting on.'

13

The church was cold and smelt of damp, which was only to be expected. It was rather dark, the glass of its narrow windows stained in sombre hues that were not particularly pleasing.

'Nineteenth-century,' Hartmann said. 'But these pillars are mediaeval.'

It took Vaughan straight back to his boyhood and the forced attendance at church each Sunday evening with his grandmother. There had been a church smell then, there was a church smell now. Nothing changed.

There was a row of oak pews on either side of the aisle, a small dark chapel to the left with an image of the Virgin floating there in the half-light. Hartmann walked along the aisle and genuflected in front of the altar.

Vaughan followed him and Hartmann said, 'See, here beside the altar rail.'

There was a square hole set into the floor and lined with brass.

'What is it?' Vaughan asked.

'The socket for St Michael's Cross, I should imagine.' He stared across the church, a slight frown on his face. 'There's something unusual here. Have you noticed how clean everything is?' He ran a finger along the altar rail. 'Not only is there no dust, but it smells of polish.'

He crossed to the sacristy and opened the door. There wasn't much in there. A table, chairs, a cupboard which, when he opened it, contained the church registers and also a plentiful supply of candles.

It was Vaughan who made the most interesting discovery of all, for when he tried the side door, it proved to be unlocked and opened to his touch.

'Now, what do you make of that?' he asked. 'At least we now know how the cleaning staff get in.'

'I wonder if our friend the mayor knows about this?' Hartmann tried the light switch which proved to work. 'See,' he said. 'Even the electricity is still connected, which is more than you can say for the house. I wonder why?'

Vaughan lit a cigarette. 'Probably there are hordes of lovable peasants out there just aching to come back to the arms of Mother Church.'

'Perhaps,' Hartmann said. 'Tell me, do you think it at all possible that Brother Konrad and his friends might manage what he was talking about last night?'

'What, break through within the next three days? I don't see why not. Is it important?' And then Vaughan saw the way things were going. 'You'd like more time here, is that it? You'd like to really get your teeth into the situation. Well, forget it, Father. We're not here to save souls. We're here to save Conlin.'

Hartmann didn't reply, but got up and went back into the church. Vaughan sat there finishing his cigarette, and suddenly, to his complete astonishment, heard organ music.

When he went in, he couldn't see Hartmann at first, then discovered him seated at the organ masked by a curtain above the choir stalls. As Vaughan went up the steps to join him, Hartmann was experimenting, pulling out one stop after another, his hands running over the keys.

'Something else you managed to pick up in the football squad at Notre Dame?'

'Not good,' Hartmann said. 'But not bad. One could hardly expect an outstanding instrument in a village like this and the reed stops have suffered in all this damp.'

He moved into the opening of the Bach Prelude and Fugue in D Major and he was good. Vaughan sat down in one of the choir stalls, hands in pockets, head back, and simply listened, and one didn't have to be a music lover to enjoy it. The music filled the church, echoing into the rafters as Hartmann played on, lost in some private world of his own.

Finally he stopped. Vaughan said quietly, 'You should have made All-American for that, too.'

Hartmann turned on the seat, smiling hugely for the first time since Vaughan had known him, obviously genuinely pleased, and then he paused, looking out over Vaughan's shoulder.

When Vaughan turned, he found Sigrid Ehrlich sitting in the front pew.

A scarf was bound round her head and her tweed coat was simply slung from her shoulders as if put on in a hurry. She sat there, clutching it about her, her eyes never leaving Hartmann, a kind of awe in them.

He came down the steps from the choir stalls, smiling. 'Fräulein Ehrlich, isn't it? It's good to see you here.'

'Father.' Her voice was almost a whisper.

'And what brings you?' He sat down in the pew beside her.

'I could hear the organ.'

'In the inn?'

'Yes.'

'You must forgive me. I was obviously forgetting myself.'

She leaned forward eagerly. 'No – not at all. It was wonderful. It's a long time since I heard anything like it. Father Honecker used to play, but I was only a child then and didn't really appreciate such things.'

'You knew Father Honecker?'

'Oh yes.'

'I see,' Hartmann said carefully. 'Tell me, are you a Catholic, Fräulein?'

She flushed. 'I – I am baptized, Father, but there has been no priest here since Father Honecker's death.'

'Yes, I know that.' There was a slight pause. She stared down at her hands, folded now in her lap. Hartmann said gently, 'The church is obviously well looked after. Clean, sweet. Do you do that?' She glanced at Vaughan, her face troubled. 'Come on, you can speak freely. Herr Schaefer won't tell.'

'All right. Several of the older women come in regularly each week.'

'I see.' He was not smiling, but there was a light in his eyes that somehow illuminated his entire face. 'I will pray for you, my child. All of you.'

He started to get up and she caught hold of his sleeve, her face strained and anxious. 'Father, hear my confession.' He seemed transfixed, staring down at her, his face pale.

And suddenly she was on her knees, clutching at his hand, tears running uncontrollably down her cheeks. 'Oh, Father, it's been so long.'

'Of course, my child.' He raised her up and sat her down. 'Stay there.'

He went out into the sacristy and Vaughan followed, but when he got there, there was no sign of Hartmann. He opened the side door and saw the priest going into the house.

Vaughan sat on the table and lit a cigarette. 'Oh my God,' he whispered, 'that's all I need. A truly good man.'

A few moments later, the door opened and Hartmann entered holding a black velvet bag. 'Don't tell me,' Vaughan said. 'Let me guess. Your vestments and other assorted goodies.'

Hartmann opened the bag and started to take things out. 'You surely didn't think I came unprepared, Major.' He put on his alb and threw a violet stole over his shoulder.

'Would it be too much to ask you to remember why we're here?'

Hartmann paused, a hand on the door. 'Major Vaughan, there is one thing I have that I share with the Pope himself. Whatever else I am, whatever my background, however high I rise, I am still priest, first and foremost. That is something I can never escape. It is my reason for being.'

'So we're back in the drainpipe again?'

'If you like.'

Hartmann went into the church and Vaughan followed him to the door, watched him speak to Sigrid Ehrlich. She stood up and they walked together to the confessional box and entered their separate compartments.

There was a murmur of voices and then the sound of passionate weeping from the girl. Vaughan shivered as if suddenly aware that he had no right to be there. He closed the door softly, let himself out into the garden and walked up and down aimlessly under the plane trees, smoking.

It was a good half-hour before Hartmann and the girl appeared. He had taken off his alb and stole and was once more attired in black cassock and dark hat. The girl gazed up at him intently as he talked to her.

As they approached, Hartmann said cheerfully, 'Ah, there you are, Horst. Kind of you to wait.' He smiled down at Sigrid. 'Herr Schaefer is in some respects my keeper.' She glanced up at Vaughan, a certain alarm in her eyes and Hartmann laughed. 'Don't worry. He won't bite. We have what you might call a working relationship.'

He was in excellent spirits, more animated than at any time since Vaughan had known him. 'You've finished in there, I presume?'

'For the moment, yes. Sigrid's going to show us the Cross of St Michael, down by the river.'

'That should be nice,' Vaughan said.

The irony in his voice seemed totally lost on Hartmann. 'How far did you say it was, Sigrid? A mile? Then we'll walk, I think.'

It was a nonsense, of course, the whole affair, but in a sense Vaughan was trapped, a fact of which, he decided, Hartmann was only too well aware. He trailed along behind the priest and the girl, across the square and along the main street, attracting curious glances from the few villagers that they passed. Beyond the last house, the road sloped down to the Elbe between a double row of pine trees and the view was rather beautiful.

At one point, the girl laughed and he heard Hartmann say, 'But there is no law forbidding priests to visit you. Surely one or two must have come here during the past five years, from neighbouring villages perhaps?'

'With Party cards in their pockets,' she said contemptuously. 'They only seem like priests.'

The road turned to the right to follow the course of the river. To the left, a rough track led to a grove of trees and the cross stood there, plain to see, black heavy oak as was the figure of Christ nailed to it. It was obviously the work of a peasant hand and had no great artistic merit, but it possessed a certain dignity for all that. It had been set into the earth and grass grew thickly about the base.

Hartmann stood looking up at the figure of Christ intently. 'And Father Honecker tried to lift this on his own?'

'He must have been mad,' Vaughan said.

'No. Desperate, I think.'

'He died here,' Sigrid said. 'Died trying, here on this very spot.'

Hartmann bowed his head in prayer.

Vaughan took the girl by the elbow and led her some little distance away.

The Elbe rushed by, brown and swollen, and he took out his cigarettes. 'Do you use these things?'

'No,' she said.

'Good for you.' He put one in his mouth and lit it.

'My father says you're a policeman.'

'You could put it that way.'

'Why are you always with Father Hartmann?'

'Oh, he needs looking after, wouldn't you say?'

'He's a good man,' she said. 'A wonderful man.' And turned to where Hartmann stood at the foot of the cross.

His voice was blown to them by the wind, strong and firm. '*Requiem æternam dona eis, Domine, et lux perpetua luceat eis*.'

He was saying the Mass for the Dead.

On the way back, Vaughan expressed interest in the Catholic cemetery and the girl took them in. It was surprisingly well looked after, the grass cut, some of the newer graves decorated with flowers. The tunnel line stretched from the wall of the barn to the north-east corner of the cemetery, Vaughan knew that, but above ground things looked perfectly normal. A fall down there, of course, and that would be something else again. The consequences would be disastrous.

He turned away and followed Hartmann and the girl out of the entrance and across the street to the church. The mayor was standing in the porch of the inn and came down the steps and moved a few paces towards them.

'Sigrid, go in at once, you're needed.'

She glanced uncertainly at Hartmann. He nodded gently and she hurried past her father and went inside.

'Don't be angry with your daughter, Herr Ehrlich,' Hartmann said. 'She was kind enough to show me one or two places I wanted to see.'

Ehrlich moved close and his voice was low and full of passion. 'She was in the church, do you think I don't know this? I don't want her in there again. I don't want her mixed up in this sort of thing, you understand? In the world we live in today, Father, it's too dangerous.'

'It's always been dangerous, my friend,' Hartmann said. 'But surely as mayor and local Party secretary, you'd be the last person to deny the constitution under which each individual has the right to exercise free will in the matter of religion?'

'Oh, go to the Devil!' Ehrlich turned and hurried back towards the inn.

'What are you after?' Vaughan demanded as they went up the steps to the entrance of the church. 'What are you trying to prove?'

'I'm supposed to provide a diversion, am I not? I should have thought I was succeeding admirably.' Hartmann opened the door and moved inside, and then he stopped with an intake of breath.

There were flowers everywhere or so it seemed. In the Lady Chapel and on the altar. And more. There was a ruby glow to the sanctuary lamp. Hartmann walked slowly down the aisle and stood at the bottom of the steps. There were even fresh candles, neatly stacked beside the offertory box.

'So, Sigrid is not alone, it would seem.' He picked up a candle and placed it in one of the holders and said to Vaughan, 'Light it, please.'

Vaughan struck a match and touched it to the wick. As the candle flared Hartmann turned to him and smiled. 'To St Jude, patron saint of the impossible.'

Conlin was tired and listless, eyes sore from lack of sleep. When he closed them, all he could see was the back of Karl's skull dissolving as the bullet fragmented bone endlessly and, occasionally, he seemed to hear the voice in his ear, begging him to confess.

Which was all perfectly understandable, of course. Such hallucinations were common under conditions of extreme stress and his physical state was not good now. Experience and logic told him as much, but it didn't help him sleep. It didn't enable him to close his burning eyes.

He vomited into the bucket and the guard looked in to see what was happening. Conlin sat on the bed feeling very ill indeed. Finally he heard steps approaching, the door was opened and Van Buren appeared. Lieutenant Leber was with him in her white coat, carrying her medical bag. It occurred to Conlin, and for no particular reason, that he had never heard her talk.

Van Buren said, 'Are you ill?'

'It's nothing,' Conlin told him wearily. 'I was sick a couple of times, that's all, and I can't sleep.'

'We can do something about that at any rate,' Van Buren said solicitously and turned to the woman. 'Give him a shot.'

Conlin didn't argue. There would have been no point. She produced a hypodermic and gave him an injection in his right arm. It hurt rather a lot because there wasn't too much flesh on his bones now, but he was really past caring. When she rubbed it afterwards, her fingers were particularly light and soothing.

Van Buren said, 'We'll leave you. Try and get a good night's sleep. I need you fresh for the morning.'

'What was it she gave me?' Conlin asked, already aware of the languour that seeped through his veins.

'Something good, I promise you.' The door clanged shut. The echo seemed to go on for a very long time and then there was silence.

He was lying on a bed and it was not dark and there was a pale, diffused light to things which he found rather pleasant. It was warm, which was an improvement for he seemed to have been cold for so long now.

He was aware of a slight movement and turned his head and saw

Lieutenant Leber standing on the other side of the room. She was wearing her Vopo uniform – tunic, skirt and leather boots. Her face was very calm as she started to unbutton the tunic.

Underneath, she wore a white cotton blouse and when she moulded her hands to her waist the blouse tightened, a nipple blossoming at the tip of each breast.

She came across to the bed, leaned down and put a hand on him. He tried to push her away, but there was no strength in him at all, his arms moving in a kind of slow motion.

She spoke in a distorted and remote voice, 'There's nothing to fear. Nothing to be ashamed of.'

She unfastened the zip at the side of her skirt and slipped out of it. And then she sat on the edge of the bed and unfastened the blouse. Her breasts were round and full and very beautiful and then, as she leaned over and put a hand on him, he started to laugh uncontrollably, his entire body shaking with helpless mirth, eyes tightly shut.

And after a while, when he opened them again, she had gone.

Van Buren was standing staring down into the heart of the fire, a glass of cognac in one hand, when there was a knock on the door and Ruth Leber entered. She was in full uniform, including her greatcoat which was unbuttoned at the front. The one incongruous feature was the small vanity case she carried in one hand.

'I left one or two things in the bathroom,' she said. 'Can I get them?'

'Help yourself.'

He lit a cigarette and she returned and stood looking at him, as if waiting for something. 'Are you sure you want me to go?'

'Nothing for you to stay for, is there?'

'I don't suppose there is.'

'You can take the Mercedes.'

She paused, a hand on the door. 'Is there any way you can get out of this thing, Harry?'

He turned to look at her, surprise on his face. 'Why should I want to?'

'How many times have I worked with you? How many cases? Fifteen – twenty?'

'So?'

'He's different, this old man. He isn't like the others.'

'Why? Because he's got God on his side?'

'Perhaps.'

He smiled coldly. 'Careful, angel. If Klein heard you talking like that . . .'

'Goodbye, Harry.'

The door closed softly behind her.

He sat, slightly dazed, in front of Van Buren's desk, a blanket around his shoulders. His mouth was dry, obviously the after-effect of the drug, and he sipped eagerly at the coffee provided. After a while the door opened and Van Buren came in. He sat down on the other side of the desk.

'How do you feel?'

'Terrible. Sorry about that drug of yours, whatever it was.'

'We'll have to go back to the lab and try again.'

'That poor girl.' Conlin shook his head. 'What was she supposed to do? Prove I'm a sinner like anyone else? I already know that. Arouse my dormant sexuality? Induce an erection?' He shook his head. 'There are times, Harry, when I despair of you. Didn't it ever occur to you that the Almighty might consider that a perfectly reasonable chemical reaction?'

Van Buren smiled in spite of himself. 'You could have a point there.'

'I could indeed. Man is a creature of instinct as well as reason. Even that old fraud Sigmund Freud admitted that sometimes a cigar is only a cigar.'

'You'll have to be careful,' Van Buren said. 'Much more of this and you'll leave me only one choice.'

'The same as you gave Karl? But I'm not afraid to die, Harry. Maybe that's the difference between you and me. One loses consciousness – sleeps. The corruption of the body afterwards is something else. One isn't involved. We die from the day we're born.'

'Only some of us go rather sooner than others,' Van Buren said. 'Frances Mary, for instance.'

It was just after eight when Vaughan went across the square to the inn. When he went in, Van Buren was sitting at the best table, the one beside the fire, with Süssmann. They were deep in conversation. Becker sat at a smaller table on his own, obviously excluded and not liking it. He scowled at Vaughan, who ignored him and went to the bar.

Ehrlich nodded formally. 'What can I get you?'

'A bottle of hock would be fine and what about something to eat?'

'Potato soup, cold sausage, sauerkraut. I can do nothing more.'

'That would be fine.'

Ehrlich withdrew, and Van Buren called, 'And where's the Holy Father tonight?'

If he'd expected to draw a laugh from the locals, it failed miserably and the silence which followed was one of disapproval.

Vaughan moved across. 'Seeking out the faithful. He's like a travelling salesman, going round knocking on doors, hoping someone will buy.'

Süssmann said, 'Shouldn't you be with him?'

Schaefer's position in the SSD gave him the equivalent rank of a lieutenant in the Volkspolizei, so Vaughan didn't see any pressing need to be polite to Süssmann. He said, 'My official brief is to keep him under observation and know where he is at all times. As far as I'm concerned, I do.'

He nodded to Van Buren, walked across to another table and sat down. Becker was scowling at him harder than ever. Sigrid came in from the kitchen with a tray. There was soup and black bread, a bottle of Hock with the cork already drawn.

'Where's your father?' Vaughan asked.

'In the kitchen. He thinks he's a better cook than I am.'

She was really very pretty in her peasant skirt.

As she went back to the bar, Becker grabbed her hand and pulled her on to his knee. He acted as if two-thirds drunk, but Vaughan suspected otherwise. There was too much of the brute to Becker for his liking. A suggestion of the animal.

As the girl struggled, Becker laughed, one hand fondling her left breast, the other sliding up under the skirt. She writhed, tears of humiliation in her eyes, and he laughed again coarsely.

'You like that, eh?'

Vaughan glanced across at the villagers. No one made a move. *They're frightened to death*, he thought and turned to Van Buren and Süssmann. The Vopo captain seemed totally unconcerned and Van Buren poured a glass of wine and threw another log on the fire. But now it was beyond enduring. There was only lust on Becker's face and the girl moaned in pain. Vaughan said, 'Let her go!'

Becker turned his head sharply. 'What was that?'

'I said, let her go. I mean, she doesn't know where you've been, does she?'

Van Buren was interested now, his eyes watchful over the rim of his glass as Becker pushed Sigrid to one side and got up. He crossed the room with exaggerated slowness and leaned on the table with both hands.

'You know what I'm going to do with you?'

Vaughan was in the act of pouring a glass of Hock. In an almost casual gesture, he reversed his grip and smashed the bottle across the side of the Vopo's head. As Sigrid cried out, Becker staggered and fell to one knee.

Vaughan picked up a chair and brought it down across the great shoulders. Becker grunted and started to heel over and Vaughan smashed the broken chair down again. He threw the pieces to one side and backed away.

Slowly, painfully, Becker reached for the edge of the table and pulled himself up. He hung there for a moment, then turned to Vaughan, wiping blood from his face casually.

And then, incredibly, he charged, head down, hands reaching out to destroy. Vaughan judged his moment exactly, swerved to one side and punched him in the kidneys. Becker cried out and fell to the floor. He tried to get up again, but there was nothing left and he rolled on to his back, moaning.

Sigrid's face was very white and she was trembling. Her father, who had appeared from the kitchen, drew her behind the bar. Süssmann came forward, his face angry and knelt down beside Becker.

He looked up at Vaughan. 'This is a serious matter.'

Van Buren pulled on his coat, smiling cheerfully. 'Nonsense. He asked for it – he got it. You'd better see if you can wire him together again while I have words with our good comrade here.'

Vaughan followed him outside. Van Buren paused at the top of the steps to light a cigarette. 'Very good for a Section Six man. I didn't think your training took you quite that far.'

'We do our best,' Vaughan said warily.

'And Father Hartmann? Has he been behaving himself? He's not trying to pack them in there or anything, is he?'

'Not as far as I know.'

Van Buren was already on his way across the square and Vaughan followed. The American pushed upon the main door and they went in. Candles flickered in many places now and half a dozen women and three men sat in a row beside the confessional box, waiting their turn.

'Now what do you make of that?' Van Buren said. 'Very naughty indeed, I'd call it.'

'I know,' Vaughan said. 'Karl Marx was right. Opiate of the people. Just like cigarettes. One taste and you're hooked again.'

'That's good. I'll remember that one.' Van Buren pulled up his collar. 'So far and no farther. Tell him that from me.' He turned and went out.

Vaughan waited for a while, but it was obvious that Hartmann was going to be some little while yet and it was time he checked on how things were going at the farm. He went out, hurried across the square and disappeared into the darkness of the side street opposite.

His pull on the gate bell was answered by old Brother Urban, and as he crossed the yard Konrad opened the barn door and peered out.

'Oh, it's you. What about Hartmann?'

'About God's holy work,' Vaughan said. 'I think he's decided Neustadt needs him.'

'He could be right, Major. Stranger things have happened.'

There was mild reproof in Konrad's voice, no more than that and they went into the barn. Gregor was doing some measurements on a plan opened out on a small table. Margaret Campbell stood beside him pouring coffee into several mugs, and Berg was there also, peering over Gregor's shoulder, a cigarette in his mouth.

Augustin, stripped to the waist, came in from the other room pushing a barrow. He wore no bandaging about his face and Vaughan suddenly realized that the dreadful all-pervading smell had gone.

'Considerably fresher than when I was last in here.'

Konrad nodded. 'In that respect, things have improved tremendously. We have made real progress. Far, far better than any of us could have hoped.'

'Where are the others?'

'Franz and Florian are working at the coal face, which is what we call it now.'

As he talked, Vaughan was watching the girl. She had not looked at him directly. She had a scarf tied around her hair and seemed absurdly young, with great sunken eyes.

He pulled himself together and turned to Berg. 'Well, how are things up at the Schloss?'

'Not so good. The truck-driver, Karl. You remember?'

'What about him?'

'They executed him. Tied him to a pole in the courtyard and shot him. I saw it all from an upstairs window.'

'When was this?'

'Very early this morning – dawn. It was still pretty dark, you understand, but I managed to see enough.'

'And Father Conlin?'

'He was there too. They made him watch. When I left earlier this evening, he was back on the third level.'

'Anything else to report?'

'I don't think so. Oh, yes. The woman – the Vopo lieutenant.'

'What about her?'

'She's gone – drove back to Berlin this evening.'

Gregor said, 'Fifty feet by my reckoning. We're almost at the cemetery boundary and the sewer pipe is approximately six feet on the other side.'

'We could reach it by tomorrow afternoon,' Konrad said.

'Easily. Perhaps sooner.'

'You're sure of this?' Vaughan demanded.

'I don't see why not. There's the question of breaking into the sewer pipe but that shouldn't present any kind of difficulties,' Gregor told him.

'Which means we could try to bring him out tomorrow night,' Konrad said. 'Unless you think that too soon for any reason.'

'Good God, no.' Vaughan shook his head. 'The sooner the better. We can't be sure from one day to the next what Van Buren might try with Conlin. The wrong kind of drugs, for instance.' He turned to Berg. 'You go down there again tomorrow with your rat poison and get the padlock off that manhole cover.'

'I understand,' Berg said. 'But at what time will things really start to happen? When do we leave?'

'It must be after dark for obvious reasons. I'd say nine o'clock would be as good a time to strike as any.'

'Call in with some milk churns at six,' Konrad said. 'I'll give you the final details then.'

Berg nodded. 'Fine. I'll go now.'

He went out. Konrad turned to examine the plan again with Gregor and Margaret Campbell handed Vaughan a mug of coffee without a word. They walked to the door, which was partly open. Rain drifted through the courtyard light outside. It was as if they were alone.

'You look tired,' he said.

'Everyone is tired. So much must be done at night and there's the appearance of things. The milk and eggs to be delivered round the village each day. The cows to be taken to pasture and so on. These things must be seen to be done, otherwise someone might wonder what's happening.'

'How's your leg?'

'I manage very well.' Her shoulder touched his, she leaned against him wearily. 'Not long now, Simon.'

'Not long.'

'And then what?'

'You'll be able to go home.'

'And where would that be?' There was a bitterness, an anger in her voice that he had never heard before. 'If you find out, let me know, Major. I've never been too sure myself.'

And suddenly, he was desperately anxious to say the right thing, for her, not himself. 'You've got to start fresh, Maggie. Unstamped metal. All right, you've had one hell of a life so far, but the kind of knowledge you get from bitter experience has a limited value. It sets your thinking in a pattern built on that experience and that's no good.'

'So what do I do?'

'Practise your trade, I suppose. You're a doctor, aren't you? Pascoe should be able to get you a choice of England or America if you want. Or you could stay in West Germany.'

'And you?' The eyes were darkly watchful as if someone was inside looking out at him.

He remembered what Meyer had said about the sniper on the roof and tried hard. 'God knows. Something will turn up. It always does for people like me.'

'And what kind of person are you? How do you see yourself?'

'Old Chinese saying,' he said. 'There's always an official executioner. If you try to take his place, it's like trying to be a master carpenter and cutting wood. You'll only hurt your hand.'

'And what is that supposed to mean?'

'It means, give it up, Maggie. Let me go.'

'No,' she said simply. 'Which doesn't mean that I approve of you or how you live, or what you've done in the past. It simply means I love you.'

Her hand was on his arm, her eyes serene, calm. He gazed down at her, suddenly desperate. From behind them in the tunnel came the most dreadful cry he had ever heard.

Franz had turned to take the sheet of corrugated iron from Florian when it happened. There was a trickle of soil on his head. He glanced up.

Florian scrambled back. 'Careful, I think the roof goes.'

The soil bulged, a rotting coffin appeared. The end broke away and two decaying feet poked through, minus the toes. The stench was immediate and appalling. Franz cried out in horror and tried to scramble back. As he moved the entire coffin descended, the rotting wood breaking to reveal what was left of the corpse inside.

Vaughan and Gregor slipped through the darkness of the cemetery and crouched by the wall.

'This should be the place,' Gregor whispered.

Vaughan switched on his torch. There was a grave – a comparatively recent one. An old man who had died ten months previously. It was more ornate than some, a marble slab on the ground surrounded by railings.

'Is this the one?'

Gregor nodded. 'It has to be. Thank God for that slab. Without it there might have been one hell of a hole to explain.'

They returned to the farm quickly. There was that smell in the barn again only worse now, and Konrad and Augustin had the bandaging wrapped around their faces. Margaret Campbell had the medical chest open on the table and was filling a hypodermic.

'I'm going to give everyone a shot. Just as a precaution and that includes you, Major. The possibilities of infection are appalling.'

'Where are Franz and Florian?' Vaughan asked. 'Not still in there surely?'

'But of course,' Konrad said. 'It must be brought out, that thing, before we can break through the final few feet.'

There was a movement below and Florian appeared, pulling a long, sacking-enshrouded bundle. Franz appeared at the other end. Konrad jumped down to help them and they struggled up the ramp.

In spite of the sacking, the smell was terrible and he said, 'Keep back, the rest of you.'

They went into the other room and Vaughan followed in time to see them drop the body into the well. Konrad poured a sack of lime after it, Florian followed this with a barrowful of soil.

When they returned, Margaret Campbell was waiting to give them their injections. Franz was breathing hard, his eyes wild, and the stench on him was terrible.

Konrad said, 'Better go and have a bath, Franz. We'll carry on here.'

'A bath?' Franz glared at him. 'You think I can wash that thing in there off me with soap and water? It will be with me till the day I die.'

He rushed out. In the silence, Konrad picked up a shovel and said calmly, 'Last lap, my friends, so let's get to it,' and he went down the ramp and crawled into the tunnel.

Hartmann was sitting in the sacristy at the table reading *The City of God* by St Augustine. It was very quiet. There was the lightest of taps at the outside door. It opened and Sigrid looked in.

'May we come in, Father?'

To his astonishment, he saw that her father was with her. Georg Ehrlich looked embarrassed and thoroughly uncomfortable.

'What is it?' Hartmann asked. 'What can I do for you?'

'Go on, Father,' the girl urged.

'It's my aunt,' the mayor said. 'She's an old woman. Eighty-two.'

'Well?'

'She's dying, Father,' Sigrid told him simply. 'And she hasn't seen a priest in a long time.'

'I'll come at once,' Hartmann said. 'Is it far?'

'The edge of the village.'

He opened his vestment bag and rummaged in it quickly. There was a ciborium from which he took a Host and hung it in a silver pyx around his neck, a small silver jar containing holy oil to anoint the dying woman's ears, nose, mouth, hands and feet.

He threw a stole over his shoulder and picked up his missal. 'I'm ready.'

The door opened and Vaughan entered. The mayor was obviously considerably put out. Vaughan said, 'What's going on?'

'Herr Ehrlich's aunt is dying, Horst. She needs me. You can come if you want, but we haven't got time to argue.'

He took Sigrid's arm and went out like a strong wind. Vaughan said to Ehrlich, 'I'm supposed to follow him everywhere, did you know that? Not only the day but half the bloody night as well. I'll be glad when they transfer me to another assignment.'

He went out, the mayor hurrying at his side. 'She's an old woman, my aunt, and old people, you have to humour them. On the other hand, it could be very embarrassing for me in the Party if this got out, Comrade. You know what I mean.'

Vaughan turned up his collar against the rain, 'Yes,' he said sourly, 'I know exactly what you mean.'

The bedroom was on the ground floor, the door half-open. Vaughan could see the old woman clearly, propped up against pillows. Hartmann was celebrating Mass and she followed every move, hands clasped together. After he gave her communion she started to cry and he held her hands at the end.

'*Ite, missa est.*'

'*Deo gratias*,' she said through her tears.

And Sigrid, too, was crying, as she hurried from the room.

As they walked back towards the church, Vaughan explained in detail what had taken place at the Home Farm.

Curiously enough, Hartmann didn't refer to the incident of the body in the tunnel, but simply said, 'So you could be ready for Father Conlin tomorrow night? That's much sooner than I'd imagined.'

'Or any of us did,' Vaughan said. 'You almost sound sorry.'

'There's work to be done here. A real need to be filled.' Hartmann smiled. 'Remember what I told you? One is always a priest before everything else. Still . . .'

They went up the steps to the church and he opened the door. A man and a woman were sitting in one of the rear pews with three young children. They stood up at once and the woman pushed the children forward. The eldest looked no more than seven.

'Please, Father,' she said. 'I'd like them baptized.'

Her husband stood at her side, cap in hand, his face anxious. Beyond them Vaughan saw another half-dozen people at the confessional box.

'But it's two o'clock in the morning.'

Erich Hartmann smiled. 'You see, my friend?' he said. 'You see now what I mean?'

14

The Franciscans worked on relentlessly through the night and it was just before five o'clock in the morning when Franz's shovel sliced through soft earth and rattled against something harder.

'I think we're there,' he said to Gregor who was acting as labourer. He renewed his attack with vigour, pulled the soil away and the curved side of the great concrete pipe started to take shape.

'I'll be back,' Gregor said excitedly and crawled away.

Franz kept on working, shovelling the soil back into the cart, until the pipe wall was completely clear. Gregor returned with Konrad. They carried a sledgehammer and a couple of steel crowbars.

'Give it to me and keep back,' Franz said.

He took the sledge and when they had pulled the cart out of range swung it with all his strength against the pipe. There was a hollow booming sound, but he had made no visible impression on the concrete. He tried again, slightly awkwardly, for because of the confined space it was only possible to swing sideways.

Gregor crawled forward. 'Try it this way,' he said.

There was a join where one length of pipe had been cemented to another. He got the sharp end of the crowbar into it and lay flat, keeping his head down.

Franz swung again, connecting squarely with the head of the crowbar which sank in immediately. He grunted with effort, swinging again with all his strength and a crack appeared in the concrete and then another.

'I hoped that might happen,' Gregor said. 'It's pre-stressed.'

Franz swung against the concrete this time and a large piece fell inwards. There was an immediate blast of cold air, a draught sweeping the length of the tunnel. He swung the hammer again and again, Gregor working beneath him with the crowbar, and within a few minutes had made an entrance large enough to pass through.

From the kitchen window of the priest's house, Vaughan could see Berg standing beside his truck outside the inn talking to Ehrlich. The milk cart appeared from the direction of the Home Farm. To his surprise, he saw that Brother Konrad was pushing it.

Hartmann was at the stove frying eggs. Vaughan said, 'That's interesting. Konrad's doing the milk round himself this morning. I think I'll see what's going on.'

He found a jug and went out. As he approached the inn, Konrad was helping Berg lift a couple of churns on to the back of the truck. Ehrlich was standing watching.

Vaughan said, 'Good morning, Comrade.'

The mayor mumbled a reply and went inside. Vaughan held out his jug for Konrad to fill. 'We broke through at five o'clock,' he said.

'And how are things?'

'Fine. Gregor, Franz and I went the whole length of the sewer as far as the exit. The manhole cover is, of course, closed.'

'You get down there as soon as you can and get that padlock off,' Vaughan said to Berg. 'I want you at the farm tonight as late as possible with any news at all on the state of the game up there. Say seven o'clock.'

'All right.' Berg climbed into his truck and drove away.

'Anything else you want me to do?' Konrad asked as he picked up the shafts of the cart.

'Activate the transmitter as soon as you get back,' Vaughan said. 'That will alert them at Bitterfeld to expect something tonight.'

The Franciscan moved away and Vaughan went back into the house. 'Anything I should know?' Hartmann asked, passing him a plate with two fried eggs and a slice of black bread on it.

'They've broken through.'

'So – tonight it is.'

Vaughan found that the eggs were really quite reasonable. 'You should be at the farm no later than nine, by the way.'

'Why?'

'To get yourself ready to move out with the others.'

'We made no such arrangement.'

'Good God, you can't stay here, man. You can't stay anywhere in East Germany. Within five minutes of finding Conlin gone, they'll put two and two together and make it five where you're concerned. You've no choice. You've got to leave with the others while you can.'

'Yes, I suppose you're right,' Hartmann said. 'It hadn't really occurred to me before.'

Strange how he had suddenly lost his appetite. He pushed the plate away from him.

Berg removed the padlock from the manhole cover, slipped it into his pocket, then picked up his lamp and went to check his poison bait. There were several dead rats and he collected half a dozen and went back up the passage, holding them in one hand by their tails.

As he came to the Vopo outside Conlin's cell he held them up. 'Six at one blow, just like the tailor in the fairy tale.'

The young Vopo shuddered. 'Stinking things. I can't stand them.'

Berg laughed and moved on up the passage to where the next guard stood at the door to the steps leading to the second level.

In his cell, Conlin slept fitfully. He couldn't get the fact of Karl's death out of his mind and the knowledge, as Van Buren had said, that he could have saved him, just as he could have saved Frances Mary. At the thought of her, all the pain, all the distress welled up in him again as it had not done for years.

She was his only sister, nine years his junior and they had always been close, especially since the death of their parents. She had lived with an old aunt during the years of his training, was so delighted when a parish appointment took him back to Dublin.

And then she'd fallen in love with Michael, a young assistant lecturer in History at Trinity College, a Protestant, but a lovely boy for all that. And then there was the child coming.

He could hardly breathe, remembering, his hands clutching at the blanket. That December night, just before Christmas. The car skidded, overturned, killing Michael instantly. And Frances Mary, seriously injured, had gone into labour.

It was two o'clock in the morning when he'd got there and the doctor in charge of the case had faced him with a terrible decision. She needed immediate surgery; under the circumstances, there was no question that she could be allowed to continue in labour and in the condition she was in, a Caesarian was impossible.

What they wanted was simple: Conlin's permission for them to destroy the child; and that was something he could not give for such a thing ran contrary to everything he had believed all his life.

'All right,' the doctor had said. 'If we wait until after the birth, there's a strong possibility your sister will die. The choice is yours.'

But as a good Catholic, he had no choice. And he sat and waited until four in the morning when the doctor had returned to tell him they were both dead, Frances Mary and the daughter who had barely lived.

It was snowing when he left the hospital and bitterly cold – almost as cold as it was now. What was it Donne said?

Under the rod of God's Wrath having been.
He hath broke my bones, worn out by flesh and skin.

Oh God, help me, he thought. I killed Karl, just as I killed my own sister out of my own selfish stubborn pride. The iron conviction that I alone know what is right and true.

In that moment he was in total despair, at the bottom of a pit so dark there seemed no way out. He had never felt so totally alone in his life.

'God forgive me,' he said. And wept.

A hand reached out to take his and a fierce aching excitement filled his heart. It was as if it was the third day and he was waiting for the stone to roll aside.

At Bitterfeld, Pascoe went into the hangar and found Kubel working on the Storch, Meyer sitting on a box watching him. The plane had had a fresh coat of dull black paint and looked remarkably sinister.

'How goes it?' Pascoe asked.

Meyer chuckled. 'If he touches that engine once more it'll complain to the union.'

'Half the airmen who bought it during the war weren't shot down by the enemy. They died through engine failure of one sort or another,' Kubel said. 'That's why I made sure I knew more about them than the mechanics.'

There was the sound of running steps and Teusen appeared in the hangar entrance, so much out of breath that he could hardly speak.

'What is it?' Pascoe demanded.

'It's come – the preliminary signal. We've just picked it up.'

There was silence. Max Kubel walked across to the hangar door and looked out. Grey clouds hung heavily over the airfield and a curtain of rain swept towards the hangar.

'Ah well,' he said softly to himself. 'At least it should prove interesting.'

Süssmann and Becker took Conlin into the room between them and sat him down in the chair opposite Van Buren.

'Wait outside,' he said.

They withdrew. Conlin straightened himself wearily. 'Well?'

'You look tired.'

'Yes, I'll admit to that.'

'Which isn't surprising. The unfortunate business with Karl. My reminding you of Frances Mary.' Van Buren shrugged. 'There's a limit to how many stones we can turn over.'

'It's no good, Harry.' Conlin smiled gently. 'You're wasting your time. I didn't kill Karl – you did. And I didn't kill Frances Mary either. It was the circumstance of life that killed her – something I was unable to prevent because of my religious belief. I have no right to judge myself. God will do that for me.'

'You still find time for belief?'

'Oh yes, I think you could say that. In the depths of total despair, I reached out and he was there like a cold wind on the face in the morning. Excitement, Harry – the indescribable hollow, frightening excitement of knowing totally. I discovered then that nothing could ever touch me again.'

'And that's your final word?'

The old man smiled gently. 'Harry, your father was a fine man. What happened to him was a terrible thing, but that doesn't excuse you making war on the whole world. Rats aren't people, Harry. A rat in a cage does what you teach him to do, but a man in a cage always has free choice.'

Van Buren had gone very pale, his fingers interlocked tightly together. He said slowly, 'I have a new drug with me which is used as a muscle relaxant in certain surgical operations, but the crucial point about it is that the patient has to be unconscious. You see, the effect on a conscious person is so horrifying that where accidents have occurred, the standard procedure is to inject scopolamine to erase the incident from the patient's memory.'

'You learn something new every day,' Father Conlin said.

Van Buren opened a drawer, took out a bottle and a hypodermic syringe and started to fill it. 'Succinyl choline causes convulsive muscular spasms, then leaves the subject totally paralysed, unable to breathe, in agonizing pain – but conscious. You'll feel yourself dying of lack of oxygen. The effect only lasts for two minutes, but the experience is so terrible that few people can stand the threat of a repeat performance.'

And Conlin knew fear then as he had never known it in his life before. His mouth went dry and his hands started to shake so much that he could only still them by clasping them tightly behind him.

And in the end, can the human spirit be broken so easily? Did you really intend such a thing, Lord? No, I can't believe it. I stand by my faith, now and always.

He took a deep breath and managed the bravest smile of his life. 'Come on, boy. Surely you can do better than that? If the measure of a man is to be decided by which drug you pump into him, then where does that leave you, Harry?'

Van Buren stared at him fixedly, then pressed the buzzer on his desk, the door opened and Sussmann and Becker entered.

'Hold him,' he said.

It was just before seven when Vaughan went up the steel ladder and gently raised the manhole cover. The chamber above was in total darkness. He listened for a few moments, then lowered the cover again and went back down the ladder. Ten minutes later he was crawling along the cemetery tunnel back into the barn.

They were all waiting and Berg had arrived while he'd been exploring the tunnel.

'Satisfied?' Konrad asked.

Vaughan nodded. 'Ten minute at the outside to get there, five to get Conlin, ten – maybe fifteen – to get back.'

'You'll have to carry him,' Berg said. 'I saw him leaving Van Buren's office an hour ago over Becker's shoulder, and he didn't look good.'

'Had he been beaten?'

'Not that I could see.'

Vaughan reached for his leather trench-coat and pulled it on. 'Probably drugs. There are some pretty nasty ones in use for Van Buren's kind of purpose these days. You get back up to the Schloss. Stay there till about eight-forty-five and keep your eyes open. Anything happens before then, get down here with the news as fast as you can.'

Berg nodded and went out. Konrad said, 'What now?'

'We wait. I'll go and see Hartmann. Fill him in on what's happening, if I can tear him away long enough from his endless confessions and baptisms. The only thing he hasn't done is hold a public service.'

As he moved to the door, Margaret Campbell joined him. They crossed the courtyard together, his arm about her shoulder.

He said, 'Once things start hotting up I may be too busy to notice what you're doing, so promise me to do as Konrad tells you and get into that truck at the right time like a good girl.'

'We could have breakfast together at Bitterfeld,' she said.

'I don't see why not.'

'And that café on the end of the bridge in Berlin. You'll take me there again if I ask you?'

'We'll see.' He touched her cheek lightly with the back of his hand. 'Look after yourself.' He stepped out through the gate and hurried away.

It was just after eight o'clock when Hartmann opened the side door and went into the sacristy and found Vaughan waiting for him.

'Where in the hell have you been?' Vaughan demanded.

'Visiting the sick. House calls,' Hartmann said. 'I told you there was a need here. Why?'

'Because at approximately nine I go in,' Vaughan said. 'At nine-twenty I come out again with Conlin, at nine-forty Kubel will pick us up at Water Horse Meadow, and shortly after that you'll all be on your way to the border in the field truck. So – get together what you want of your things and you can come back to the farm with me now.'

'No,' Hartmann said. 'I've been thinking about that and I think I have a rather better idea. My only real purpose in this whole affair was to act as a decoy to a certain degree. It seems to me I'd be most useful doing that right now.'

'What in hell are you talking about?' Vaughan demanded.

So Hartman told him.

Van Buren was going over his notes when there was a knock on the door and Süssmann entered with Becker.

'Trouble?' Van Buren said.

'In a manner of speaking. I've just had a phone call from the village. An anonymous well-wisher who was in the inn a short while ago when the priest came in and spoke to the mayor.'

'And?'

'It seems he told him he intended to bring the Cross of St Michael back to the church.'

'I don't understand.'

Süssmann explained briefly. When he had finished, he added, 'An act of direct defiance, or so it seems to me. You did warn him.'

Van Buren said. 'Where is this cross?'

'I know,' Becker said. 'By the Elbe about half a mile outside the village. I've seen it. I was told the story by Berg, the caretaker, when I first got here.' He laughed contemptuously. 'Hartmann must be crazy. There's no way he could carry that thing over such a distance.'

'If he did, of course, and claimed the right to open the church again for public worship . . .' Süssmann said.

Van Buren nodded. 'No, we can't have that.' He smiled. 'An interesting situation, though. Let's go and see how he's getting on.'

At that precise moment, Erich Hartmann was attacking the ground at the base of the cross vigorously with a spade. Twenty or so villagers, women as well as men, some with lanterns stood in a half circle some little distance away and watched.

Sigrid and her father were closest. The mayor said, 'Father, this is madness. When the news reaches the castle, the military will come.'

Hartmann said, 'You see, Sigrid, we make progress. He worries for me.'

'They'll arrest you, Father,' Ehrlich said.

Hartmann kept on digging. 'Did you phone them up there to tell them what I intended to do? After all, you are the local Party secretary.'

'No,' Ehrlich said. 'I did not.'

'Then they will arrest you too, my friend. That's the kind of people they are. The kind of society you have.' He turned to address the crowd now. 'And you use the word democratic to describe it.'

The cross swayed and started to fall. He threw the spade aside and caught it, easing it down. The evidence of his enormous strength drew an audible gasp from the crowd.

Sigrid ran forward and put a hand on his arm. 'Please, Father, don't do it.' Her face was strained, pleading. 'You'll kill yourself.'

'But I must, my child,' he said gently. 'You see, it occurs to me now that this is very likely what it's all about, my life up to now, I mean. What I do now is what gives it purpose.'

He looked at the hill, black in the rain, rising up towards the village. 'Dear God, give me strength,' he murmured.

He hoisted the cross on his left shoulder, braced himself to the weight and started forward.

Brother Konrad, in the uniform of a Vopo lieutenant, was standing at the table in the barn with Margaret Campbell, examining the sewer plans, when Vaughan came in. He wore dark pants and sweater, and a black balaclava helmet covered most of his face, giving him a sinister and deadly appearance.

Margaret Campbell's eyes widened. 'You look . . .' She hesitated.

He scooped up dirt from the floor with his hands and rubbed it over the exposed part of his face. 'Look like what?' he demanded.

'Different – another person.'

He was filled with a fierce energy that seemed to crackle around him like static electricity.

'The real me,' he said. 'The man I've always been. Rising to the occasion because this is what I'm good at.'

There was something close to hurt in her eyes. He turned from it and said to Konrad, 'Is Franz in the tunnel?'

'Yes.'

Vaughan took a Mauser from his belt, the pre-war model with the bulbous silencer, specially manufactured for the Gestapo and still the best silenced handgun in his experience. He checked the clip, then pushed the Mauser back into his waistband.

'I wonder which Station of the Cross Hartmann's reached now?'

There was anger in Margaret Campbell's voice when she said, 'He's doing what he thinks is right. It's not proper for you to make fun of him.'

'A holy fool,' Vaughan said. 'Just like Sean Conlin, which is why we're all here if you think about it. God, the trouble the good of this world cause the rest of us.' He glanced at his watch and saw that it was a quarter to nine. 'To hell with it,' he said. 'I'm not going to wait any longer.'

'And this?' Konrad touched the transmitter which stood on the table. 'What about this?'

'Press that button at ten past nine,' Vaughan said. 'That should be about right.'

'But what if something should go wrong?' Margaret Campbell said in a sudden panic. 'The timing is the critical point, you said so yourself.'

'Not any more,' he said. 'From now on, things just happen. You see, we don't control the game any longer – it controls us.'

He ducked into the tunnel and was gone.

At Bitterfeld, Teusen had switched on the outside lights. Heavy mist blanketed the airfield. The Storch was ready on the apron and Max Kubel, Pascoe and Meyer stood in the shelter of the hangar.

Meyer said, 'Look at the weather. It's times like these I wonder if there's a God. What a thing to happen.'

Kubel wore his old flying jacket, a white scarf wrapped around his neck. He was smoking a cigar and looked enormously cheerful. 'Taking off in filth like this is nothing, Julius. It's landing that's the difficulty.'

'And if it's like this at Neustadt?' Pascoe asked him.

'Then we have a problem,' Kubel said simply.

Never had Hartmann carried such a weight on his shoulders and as he came up to the crest of the hill, he paused. His entire body was one great ache, his left shoulder was rubbed raw and the right, to which he had shifted position, was no better.

The crowd had swelled considerably and people were still arriving. The strange thing was their silence. Only the occasional murmur of a voice, here and there.

He started forward again, giving an involuntary groan of pain as the weight settled on his shoulder. He lost his balance almost at once and went down heavily and lay there, under the cross.

There was a rush of feet as people surged forward to help. 'No!' he shouted. 'No!'

They paused. He stayed there, on his hands and knees for a while. And then Sigrid started to recite the creed in a firm, clear voice. 'I believe in one God, the father, the almighty, maker of heaven and earth, and of all things, seen and unseen.'

Another voice joined in, hesitantly at first and then another and another.

Hartmann had never known such joy. 'I am not worthy of this burden,' he murmured. 'I accept it as a cross.'

And then he was on his feet again and going forward over the brow of the hill.

Franz waited at the bottom of the steel ladder with the lamp while Vaughan went up and cautiously raised the manhole cover. It was dark in the chamber, but a certain amount of diffused light indicated the entrance to the passageway. He lifted the manhole cover back carefully, then climbed out, taking the Mauser from his belt and cocking it.

When he peered round the corner, he saw the Vopo guard at once, leaning against the wall negligently, an AK slung from one shoulder. Fifty or sixty feet away and the corridor was well lit, but there was no choice. Vaughan started forward, keeping to the wall, holding the Mauser against his right thigh. It was all a question of how close he could get before his presence was noted.

At that moment, another Vopo emerged from the gloom at the far end of the passage, rifle slung and carrying a jug in one hand. He saw Vaughan at once and cried out in alarm. He dropped the jug and started to unsling his rifle. Vaughan fired twice, both bullets ripping into the heart, killing the man instantly.

Even as the Vopo went down, the Mauser was already arcing towards the other guard, whose AK was just coming up. Vaughan shot him in the right shoulder, the heavy bullet turning him around in a circle. The next shattered his spine, slamming him against the cell door. His greatcoat started to smoulder at the point of entry and there was a tiny flicker of flame as he slid to the floor.

The silenced pistol had made virtually no sound at all, but there was the question of the first Vopo's cry. Vaughan ran along the passage lightly and paused at the door at the bottom of the steps, listening. There was no sound and, satisfied, he came back.

He pulled back the bolts on the cell door and went in. Father Conlin lay on the bed, fully clothed, breathing heavily, apparently sleeping, but when Vaughan shook him, there was no response.

Vaughan pushed the Mauser back into his belt, lifted the priest into a sitting position, leaned down and took him across his shoulder. He went out and hurried back to the chamber.

Franz was peering over the edge of the manhole as he arrived. 'Trouble, Major?'

'Nothing I couldn't handle,' Vaughan said. 'He's unconscious. Drugged, I think. I'll pass him down to you.'

Franz stood at the bottom of the ladder and gently took the old man's weight, cradling him in his arms like a child. Vaughan followed, pulling the manhole cover back into place.

He glanced at his watch. It was just coming up to ten past nine. 'Okay, let's get moving.'

They started forward and a moment later Brother Konrad in the barn pressed the button on the transmitter that sent that final vital signal to the West.

At Bitterfeld, Max Kubel boosted power and let the Storch go, the Argus engine responding magnificently. The landing lights had been switched on, but he could only see the first few – not that it mattered.

As the fog swallowed him up, Meyer, standing by the hangar entrance with Pascoe and Teusen, said, 'Right, so he made it. What happens now?'

'The worst part, as it always is,' Pascoe said. 'The waiting.'

Even before they got to the square, Van Buren could hear the singing. Becker was driving the fieldcar, Süssmann beside him in the front seat, and when they turned into the square most of the village seemed to be there. Heinrich Berg, standing at the back of the crowd, saw them at once, and he moved back into the shadows.

'We would appear to have a religious revival on our hands,' Van Buren observed.

Süssmann stood up, holding on to the top of the windshield. 'I can see him now.'

Hartmann entered the square on the far side, moving steadily, the crowd surging around him. He kept on coming doggedly and people started to clap and cheer. As he neared the bottom of the broad steps leading up to the church door, Van Buren got out of the fieldcar and moved to cut him off.

'Father Hartmann!' he called.

Hartmann paused. The singing died away, there was silence. It started to rain, heavily in a great rush as they confronted each other.

'I told you that if you gave me any trouble, I'd pack you back to Berlin.'

Süssmann stood up in the fieldcar to address the crowd. 'Go home – all of you. That's an order.'

No one moved. Hartmann said, 'I'm taking the cross into the church. It is my right.'

He started up the steps. Van Buren said to Becker, 'I've had enough of this charade. Stop him.'

Becker went up the steps quickly and grabbed at one end of the cross, pulling Hartmann off balance, putting him down on one knee. Becker kicked out, sending him toppling.

'You're under arrest,' he said.

Hartmann ignored him completely, got on one knee again and picked up the cross. Becker took out his Walther and cocked it.

'No!' he said as Hartmann rose to his full height.

The priest stood there swaying, obviously very tired, and when he moved, he almost lost his balance, one arm of the cross catching Becker a painful blow, sending him back against the church doors. Becker, in a kind of reflex action, fired twice. Hartmann fell back across the steps, the cross on top of him.

There was an immediate uproar. The crowd surged forward and Sigrid was the first to reach Hartmann, falling on her knees beside him. Süssmann drew his own pistol and fired it into the air.

'Go home!' he shouted. 'I order you to disperse – all of you.'

Van Buren leaned over Hartmann. The Jesuit's eyes were open, there was a touch of blood at one corner of his mouth. Becker came down the steps.

'You fool,' Van Buren told him. 'There was no need for this.'

'Murderer!' Sigrid cried.

'Oh no,' Van Buren said. 'He's still with us, but not if you leave him lying out here.'

Behind him, another fieldcar appeared in a hurry, scattering the crowd. The Vopo driver jumped out and hurried forward. It was bad news, Van Buren could tell by his face, before he even got close enough to start pouring out his story.

When Berg pulled on the bell at Home Farm, it was Brother Florian who let him in.

'Where's the Major?' Berg demanded.

'Left five minutes ago in the field truck,' Florian said. 'It all worked perfectly. He and Franz brought Conlin out between them and now Konrad's taken them to meet the plane.'

Margaret Campbell appeared in the entrance to the barn. 'There seems to be quite a disturbance in the village. What's been going on? Where's Father Hartmann?'

'Dead or dying from what I saw,' Berg said, and explained what had happened.

She went into the barn without a word and returned with her medical bag.

'Take me to him.'

'Don't be crazy,' he said. 'Konrad will be back here very soon now and we've all got to be ready to leave with him.' He added desperately, 'Look. he was shot twice at close quarters. He must be dead by now.'

'Take me to him,' she said.

Brother Florian opened the gate. 'Hurry. I'll tell Konrad when he returns. We'll wait for you.'

Van Buren came out of Conlin's cell and stood looking down at the dead guard by the door.

'Impossible,' Süssmann said. 'It doesn't make sense.'

'Of course it does,' Van Buren told him. 'There must be another way out of this rat trap somewhere down there in the darkness. If you search, you'll probably find it.'

He started to walk away and Süssmann called, 'And you, Professor? Where are you going?'

'To visit the priest. It seems to me a remarkable coincidence that he should be putting on such a conspicuous display at the same time this little lot was going on.'

He stepped over the other body and hurried away along the passage.

The field truck was parked at the northern edge of Water Horse Meadow. Brother Konrad was looking after Conlin while Vaughan, after checking the wind direction, took half a dozen cheap cycle lamps from his knapsack, switched them on and laid them out in a row. Then he ran to the other end of the meadow, following the direction of the wind, and laid two more. Simple but effective, and Kubel, coming in fast at six hundred feet a few minutes later, saw the pattern at once. He'd had an excellent flight on the whole, except for that earlier part where things had been so dirty he had been compelled to go up rather higher than he would have liked. Still . . .

As the Storch dropped in for a perfect landing, Vaughan put Conlin across his shoulder and said to Konrad, 'Off you go, then. See you at Bitterfeld at about eleven o'clock.'

Konrad got in the truck and drove away as Vaughan ran across to the Storch where Kubel waited for him, the door open. He leaned out to catch Conlin under the armpits to pull him in and Vaughan scrambled up to join them, slamming the door.

The Storch was already turning into the wind for take-off. Max grinned. 'See, my friend, nothing to it.'

He boosted the engine, the Storch surged forward and lifted into the night.

Hartmann was quite dead, Margaret Campbell knew that from the moment she entered the crowded bedroom at the priest's house, but she went through the motions of searching for a pulse and listening for a heartbeat. He looked very calm, very peaceful, and she started to put her stethoscope away.

Georg Ehrlich said, 'He is dead, then?'

'I'm afraid so.'

Sigrid, on her knees at the bedside, started to weep and there was a general murmuring among those who crowded into the room.

Ehrlich said, 'We haven't met. Are you new to the district, Doctor?'

'Passing through.'

She closed her bag, stood up and found Harry Van Buren standing in the doorway.

'Hello, Margaret,' he said. 'This *is* a surprise.'

15

Max Kubel, pushing the Storch towards the border at one hundred and sixty miles an hour, had been in trouble for some considerable time. On his run in, he had climbed to a height of just over one thousand feet because of bad visibility. He had been able to go down again within minutes, but during the intervening period, his presence had been noted on the radar screens at Allersberg.

Such a brief appearance could indicate a ghost image or ground clutter due to wave reflection. On the other hand, it could be an intruder and the chief controller at Allersberg was not one to take chances.

The rain had reduced visibility considerably and Kubel decided to go up. It was only six or seven minutes to the border now anyway. He pulled back the control column and the Storch started to climb, emerging into clean air at just over a thousand feet.

There was a quarter moon, pale, rainwashed, but it touched the low clouds with a kind of luminosity. He turned and shouted to Vaughan across the head of the unconscious Conlin. 'Not long now.'

There was a roaring that filled the night, the Storch bucked like a wild horse in the turbulence so that it took everything Kubel had to hold her as a dark shadow banked overhead and took up station to starboard.

'What is it?' Vaughan demanded.

'MiG fighter. We've got trouble, my friend.'

The MiG waggled its wings. 'He's signalling,' Vaughan said.

'I know that.' Kubel switched on the radio. Reception was very clear. The voice said, 'Adopt course three-four-zero for Allersberg airbase. I will follow you down.'

Kubel switched off the radio. 'This doesn't look too good. Those cannon of his could blow us to pieces.'

'Is there anything you can do?'

'In this kind of contest a jet's speed can be a disadvantage. I'm really too slow for him to handle. I'll go down low and see if I can make him do something stupid.'

He banked to port and went down fast and the MiG banked too in a sweeping curve that would bring him in on the Storch's tail. He started to fire his cannon, too soon, his speed so excessive that he had to bank to starboard to avoid collision.

Kubel was at six hundred when the MiG came in again, and this time the Storch staggered under the impact as cannon shells punched holes in the wings.

The MiG turned away in a great curve, then came in again, and once more the Storch shuddered under the impact of cannon shell. The windscreen disintegrated and Kubel cried out sharply.

Vaughan said, 'Are you all right?'

Kubel's flying jacket was ripped just under the left shoulder. When Vaughan reached over to touch it, he found blood.

'Never mind that, I'll live,' Kubel said. 'Just hang on tight because this time, I'll show the bastard how to fly.'

They were now down to five hundred feet, the countryside clear below them, the border very close. The MiG came in for the kill, sliding in on their tail perfectly. Pieces flew off the wings as the cannon shells struck home and Kubel dropped his flaps.

The Storch seemed to stand still in mid-air and the pilot of the MiG, totally unprepared, banked steeply to starboard to avoid a collision. Too steeply and the MiG, with no space to work in, ploughed straight into the forest below.

There was a mushroom of flame, spectacular in the night, and then it was behind them, already fading as they pushed on to the border.

The engine seemed to miss a beat and Kubel worked at the controls frantically. 'Come on, you bitch. Don't let me down now.'

Vaughan checked Conlin. The old man was still unconscious, but his breathing seemed regular enough.

'Is he okay?' Kubel shouted.

Vaughan nodded. 'Are you?'

'So I've taken a little steel in the back. I've had worse and this time it was worth it.' He laughed out loud. 'Don't you see, Simon? I've got my one hundred and fiftieth.'

A moment later, they coasted across the border and he banked to starboard and commenced his descent for Bitterfeld.

Franz closed the barn doors and barred them with a baulk of timber. Like the others, he was dressed in the uniform of the Volkspolizei.

They stood by the field truck in the rain, each man with an AK rifle slung across his chest in approved fashion.

Konrad peered out through the side gate anxiously. 'Come on,' he whispered. 'Where are you, Margaret?'

Gregor moved to join him. 'It's no good, we must go. It is only a matter of time before our tunnel is discovered. We can't afford to stay here any longer.'

There was the sound of running footsteps and Berg appeared from the darkness, face distraught, totally panic-stricken. Konrad brought him to a halt and held him at arm's length.

'What is it? Where's the girl!'

Berg, struggling to catch his breath, had difficulty in speaking. 'He's got her. Van Buren's got her.'

Konrad shook him. 'What are you talking about?'

'She went to see the priest to see if there was anything she could do, but he was dead. Then Van Buren turned up.'

'And?'

'They took her away in a Vopo fieldcar. To Schloss Neustadt.'

Konrad gazed at him in horror, still holding on to the front of Berg's coat. Berg said urgently, 'We must go, don't you see? It's only a matter of time and they'll be here.'

'He's right,' Gregor said gently to Konrad. 'Remember Major Vaughan's orders? We were to wait for no one.'

'But we can't leave her,' Konrad said. 'We must do something.'

'She's at Schloss Neustadt by now,' Gregor said. 'We can do nothing.' He prised Konrad's fingers away from Berg's jacket. 'You get in the back of the truck.' He turned to the others. 'All of you – mount up.'

Konrad said in a dead voice, 'What a thing to happen after all this. As if she hasn't suffered enough.' He turned and his voice was savage now. 'You know something, Gregor. This God I've been serving all these years – I'm beginning to wonder whether he's at home any more.'

He climbed up behind the wheel and Gregor got in beside him. Konrad pressed the starter and drove out through the gates.

The sound of the engine faded into the night, the courtyard lay silent and deserted. It was a good twenty minutes before there were the first sounds of movement inside the barn and someone started banging on the door.

'The Resurrection was astonishing,' Van Buren said. 'If true, that is, which I've always doubted, but your case, Margaret – that's what I call a miracle. Old mother Elbe was supposed to take you to her bosom weeks ago.'

She sat there beside the desk, hands folded in her lap, very calm. 'I've nothing to say.'

'Nothing new in that,' he said. 'You always were an introverted little thing. Understandable, of course, after the kind of conditioning you went through.'

The door opened and Süssmann hurried in. 'A manhole cover on the lower level gives access to a sewer pipe from the war days that's never been used. We found a tunnel from it leading under the cemetery, emerging in the barn at the Home Farm.'

'The Home Farm?'

'The Franciscans.'

Van Buren laughed out loud, head thrown back. 'Oh, but that's beautiful. That really is a pearl. They're not there now, of course?'

'No. The place is deserted.'

Van Buren turned again to Margaret Campbell. 'So that's where you've been hiding out for the past few weeks?'

She made no reply. Süssmann said. 'Berg, the caretaker, appears to be missing, also Schaefer.'

'Schaefer?' Van Buren said sharply. 'But of course, that would fit very nicely. Schaefer and the priest. I always did wonder about him.'

'Another thing. There's been a report of a light aircraft landing and taking off again in the vicinity of the river some time during the past hour.'

'Is that so?' Van Buren appeared curiously indifferent.

'For God's sake,' Süssmann said. 'What are we going to do?'

'I don't know,' Van Buren told him amiably. 'Call out the guard. Alert the border. After all, you're the military genius around here.'

'But we must get Conlin back again,' Süssmann shouted, 'or we're all finished, and this bitch can tell us where he is.'

'You obviously weren't very good at mathematics when you were at school,' Van Buren said patiently. 'If a plane landed and took off again within the past hour, who the hell do you think was on it?'

Süssmann turned and strode angrily from the room, slamming the door behind him. He went down the staircase quickly and entered his office where he found Becker waiting.

'What happens now?' the sergeant asked.

'God knows, Rudi,' Süssmann said. 'We could all find our heads on the block for this one. Get on the phone to HQ. Send out a red alert to all Volkspolizei units between here and the border to pick up anyone they find on the roads who is in the slightest way suspicious.'

Becker went out. Süssmann lit a cigarette and paced up and down nervously.

'Schaefer,' Van Buren said. 'He has to be the key figure. I should have known after he knocked hell out of Becker so superbly. He won't get far.'

'The plane,' she said serenely.

'He was also on board, was he? So he's safe and that pleases you.' He leaned back, watching her closely. 'Are you in love with him?'

'Too late for games,' she said. 'You've lost. If I were you, I'd be packing my bags right now.'

'But where would I go?' He smiled gently. 'I've been everywhere, that's the problem. But to get back to Schaefer. If he was on the plane, that means he left you and that doesn't fit. He isn't the type.'

She was silent and he continued. 'You were supposed to leave with the others, weren't you? And then you heard about Hartmann and just had to play doctors. He isn't going to like that, Schaefer, or whatever his name is.'

'Vaughan.' There was pride in her voice. 'Major Simon Vaughan.'

'English? Now, there's a thing.' He nodded slowly. 'He'll come back for you.'

'Don't be absurd.' She was genuinely alarmed now.

'He'll come back for you, Margaret. That kind of man always comes back. It's my business to know these things,' he said cheerfully. 'I am, after all, one of the world's better psychologists.'

'No,' she said. 'No!' as if by repetition she could make it so.

He poured himself an enormous brandy. 'You've got a problem, I can help you.' His grimace was painful. 'The only trouble is, and this will make you fall about laughing, I could never understand my own. Problems, I mean.'

There was silence while he brooded. For no accountable reason she said, 'I'm sorry.'

'Well, that's handsome of you. Excuse me for a moment, will you?'

Instead of going out, he simply picked up the phone and dialled Klein's office number. Frau Apel answered at once.

'Working late, aren't you?' he said. 'Is he in?'

'I think so, Professor.'

A moment later Klein came on. 'Hello, Harry, I was just leaving. What's the news at your end?'

'All black,' Van Buren said. 'Conlin escaped.'

'What?' Klein said. 'That isn't possible.'

'My dear Helmut, anything is possible in this wicked old world of ours,' Van Buren told him. 'I'd have thought a man of your varied experience would have realized that by now. The details aren't important at the moment. The fact is that an assorted group which included that damn priest of yours, got Conlin out of Schloss Neustadt earlier this evening and flew him out by light plane. For some obscure reason, I wanted the pleasure of telling you all this myself.'

'You're sure of your facts?' Klein said. 'You're certain he's got clean away?'

'Goodbye, Helmut.' Van Buren put down the phone and poured another brandy.

'What happens now?' she asked.

'We wait,' he said. 'We wait to see if I'm right about this Major Vaughan of yours.'

Süssmann was just about to leave his office when the phone rang. When he picked it up, Klein was on the other end.

'I've just heard from Van Buren. I want your version of what's happened there tonight. Quickly now.'

Süssmann told him, leaving nothing out. When he was finished, there was silence. He said tentatively, 'Colonel, are you there?'

'Yes,' Klein said. 'I was thinking.'

'What do you want me to do, Colonel?'

'You're a promising officer, Süssmann. A pity to see you pulled down by your association with a man who is most certainly a traitor to the State. The only conceivable explanation for this whole sorry affair. I should be there in about a couple of hours to interrogate Van Buren personally. Naturally, if he attempts to leave before I arrive, you would be within your rights to prevent him by any means possible. Such action would redound to your credit. You understand me?'

'Perfectly, Colonel.'

'Good, I'll see you later.'

Süssmann put down the phone, then he took out his Walther and checked the clip.

After speaking to Süssmann, Klein turned to the rows of books which lined the wall behind him. He removed several to reveal a small wall-safe which he opened quickly. He took out a very ordinary-looking office file and a set of false identity papers which he had long had ready for such a day. The file contained a list of the identities of all agents of his department at that time operating in West Germany.

He slipped it into his briefcase and checked the false identity papers. A good thing that as a security chief, his face was not generally known to the military. He slipped the papers into his breast pocket, pulled on his coat and picked up his briefcase.

Frau Apel was still at her desk. She glanced up. 'You're going now, Colonel?'

'Yes. Good of you to stay so late, Clara. Get yourself home now and I'll see you in the morning.'

He went out, whistling cheerfully. Twenty minutes later he passed through a little used checkpoint near Koenigstrasse and presented himself to the policeman on duty on the other side with the astonishing request that he be put in touch at once with General Reinhardt Gehlen, Director of the Federal Intelligence Service.

It was still raining at Flossen where Bulow paced up and down outside the guard hut impatiently. At nine-thirty he had received the red alert signal from the HQ which meant no traffic of any description to be allowed through. His wife was already safe on the other side with their child and all he wanted now was to join them.

Hornstein, who had moved a little way up the road, turned excitedly. 'There's a vehicle coming.'

He moved to the sergeant's side. They waited anxiously and then a Volkspolizei field truck moved out of the night and braked to a halt.

Konrad leaned out of the window. 'I believe you've been waiting for us.'

Bulow didn't even bother to reply. Hornstein was already raising the barrier. They both scrambled over the tailgate, helped by willing hands as the field truck started to roll again, moving across to the West.

Pascoe was in the control room at Bitterfeld on his own when Böhmler came in to tell him that the truck had arrived safely. They went across to the hangars together and found a state of some confusion. The Franciscans were standing by the truck talking to Teusen and Meyer.

As Pascoe entered, Meyer said passionately, 'Madness, that's the only word for it. He goes to his death.'

'What's going on?' Pascoe demanded.

'I'm afraid we lost Doctor Campbell, Professor,' Konrad told him. 'She is now in Van Buren's hands at Schloss Neustadt.'

'Simon says he's going back for her,' Teusen said.

There was the sound of footsteps. They all turned and Vaughan entered the hangar once again in his Vopo uniform and dispatch-rider's raincoat. The AK was slung across his chest and he was fastening his helmet strap.

Pascoe said, 'There's no point to this.'

Vaughan ignored him and said to Konrad, 'Is there much activity over there?'

'Oh yes,' Konrad said. 'We passed several patrols, but no one bothered us. They assumed we were after the same game.'

'So why should they treat me any differently?' Vaughan mounted the Cossack and kicked the engine into life.

Teusen said, 'Don't be a fool, Simon.'

'You want to do something for me, keep that crossing point open for as long as you can.' Vaughan opened the throttle and roared away.

There was silence. Pascoe sighed and turned to Sergeant Bulow and young Hornstein. 'It would seem you gentlemen are going to have to return to duty for a while.'

'Oh no,' Bulow said. 'That wasn't in the contract.'

'But my dear man, you must see the necessity. If your HQ phones through and you're not there to answer, they'll come looking.'

'That may have happened already,' Bulow said.

'We'll just have to take our chances on that one.'

'No!'

There was an AK rifle on the driver's seat of the truck. Pascoe picked it up and cocked it. 'I'm not disposed to argue. You go back over there and I'll go with you.'

'Let me,' Teusen said.

Pascoe smiled wearily. 'No, Bruno, for once, this is my show. I was always good at sending other men out into the field, but not this time.' He turned back to Bulow. 'After you, Sergeant, if you please.'

Vaughan drove up the narrow approach road to Schloss Neustadt with care and when he went over the crest of the hill, he found a sentry standing in a box at the tunnel entrance out of the rain.

Vaughan brought the Cossack to a halt. 'Dispatch for Professor Van Buren from Berlin.'

The sentry waved him on without hesitation and Vaughan drove in through the dark tunnel. This time there was no sentry at the other end and he moved on across the cobbled square past the main entrance, following the narrow passage between high walls that brought him finally into the rear courtyard.

He switched off the engine and dismounted, remembering Berg's description of the private entrance to the commandant's quarters. It had to be here somewhere. He unslung his AK and moved forward.

Margaret Campbell lay on the bed in Van Buren's bedroom in the dark, her eyes open. She was thinking about Vaughan, wondering what had happened to him. But most of all, she was praying that he wouldn't act in the way Van Buren had predicted.

At that moment the door opened and the light was switched on. Van Buren stood looking at her, a glass in his hand. 'Come in here,' he said, and went back into the other room.

When she joined him, he was standing by the fire pouring another brandy. He seemed more than a little drunk. 'He disappoints me, this boy-friend of yours. Where is he?'

There was a slight creak, a sudden cold draught. They both turned as the narrow door in the far corner swung open and Vaughan stepped into the room, holding the AK at the ready.

Margaret Campbell ran to his side. 'Oh, you fool – you marvellous bloody fool. Wasn't once enough for you? Haven't I been enough trouble?'

He smiled. 'I decided to forgive you all that.' He put an arm around her.

Van Buren laughed delightedly. 'You see, I'm never wrong. The mind of man is an open book to the great Van Buren.'

Vaughan said, 'If you make a sound, I'll cut you in half with this thing.'

'And bring every man in the castle on the run? Don't be stupid, Schaefer or Vaughan or whatever your name is.'

'I'm taking her out of here.'

'Who's stopping you?'

Van Buren poured another brandy and turned away. Vaughan lowered the gun. 'What's going on here?'

Margaret Campbell put a hand on his arm. 'Don't argue, Simon. Just go.' She turned to Van Buren. 'I'm sorry, Harry. In spite of everything you did concerning my father, I'm still sorry for you.'

'So am I.' Van Buren raised his glass. 'L'Chayim. Now get out of here.'

Vaughan led the way quickly down the spiral stone staircase. At the bottom, he opened the door and peered out, but there was no one in evidence. He took her arm and hurried her across to the Cossack.

'You'll have to crouch down in the sidecar cockpit and I'll cover you with the rain tarpaulin.'

She climbed in and as she settled herself, said, 'What was it he said up there just before we left?'

'L'Chayim,' Vaughan told her. 'It's a Hebrew word. It means "to life".'

She didn't say anything to that, simply crouched down as he had instructed her. He stretched the rain cover across the cockpit, snapping the studs into place, then he swung a leg over the Cossack and started the engine. A few moments later, the sentry was waving them through the main entrance.

Van Buren stood in front of the fire, staring back into the past. 'Well, at least I was a pretty good corporal of Marines,' he said softly. 'Maybe that counts for something.'

He emptied his glass, put it down, then crossed to the door and opened it, intending to look for Süssmann. There was a murmur of voices from the hall below and when he peered over the balustrade he saw Süssmann and Becker standing down there.

'The sooner it's done, the better,' Süssmann was saying. 'When Klein gets here, he wants to find him dead. It's important for all of us, Rudi. He takes all the guilt.'

Becker took out his Walther and checked it and Van Buren stepped back into his office. A few moments later, he came out again and stood at the head of stairs as they started up.

'Ah, there you are, Süssmann. I wanted a word with you.'

The two men paused on the landing half way up the stairs and took out their Walthers. 'You're under arrest,' Süssmann said. 'For treason against the State. You will deliver the woman Campbell into my charge.'

'Not possible, I'm afraid,' Van Buren told him. 'I let her go ages ago.'

'You're lying.'

'No, my friend, with all my faults that's something I never did do. When does the shooting start?' Becker glanced uncertainly at Süssmann and Van Buren said, 'Shot while trying to escape. Isn't that how it goes?'

'If you say so.'

Süssmann fired three times. As Van Buren cried out, he opened both hands, dropping the two Russian pineapple grenades he was holding. They bounced down the stairs, one after the other. Becker uttered a cry of fear and, turning to run, collided with Süssmann. The grenades exploded a second later.

It was half past two when the Cossack emerged from the darkness and braked to a halt where Bulow and Hornstein stood waiting outside the guard hut at Flossen. Pascoe appeared in the doorway, the AK in his hands. Vaughan pushed up his goggles wearily.

'Were you successful, Major?'

Vaughan pulled back the canvas rain cover and Margaret Campbell sat up. 'Are we here?' she asked. 'Are we in the West?'

'No,' Vaughan said. 'But we soon will be.'

He drove on and Charles Pascoe, Bulow and Hornstein followed on foot. Behind them, the telephone started to ring in the guard hut. It rang for quite some time before it stopped. It was quiet then, only the door creaking a little as it swung to and fro in the slight wind.

16

On June 21st in Rome, Cardinal Giovanni Battista Montini was elected to the papal throne by the Sacred College, taking the name of Paul VI. In a room at the Collegio di San Roberto Bellarmino, Father Sean Conlin was in bed, propped up against pillows and reading a book when Pacelli entered to give him the news.

Conlin said, 'So – life goes on?'

'So it would appear.'

'But not for Erich Hartmann. Tell me, Father, what was he like? What was he really like?'

'Who knows? A mystery – like all men – known only to his maker.'

'A bit of a saint, would you say?'

'Certainly not. Erich was entirely lacking in the kind of humility needed for that office. What he did at Neustadt was magnificent nonsense – but thank God for it.'

'Ah, well,' Sean Conlin sighed. 'I'll remember him in my prayers for the rest of my life.'

'I, too.' Pacelli smiled. 'And now you must excuse me. I have a great deal to do. The work goes on.'

He went out. It was very quiet in the room as Father Conlin closed his eyes, folded his hands and prayed for the repose of the soul of Erich Hartmann.

On June 26th, President Kennedy paid an eight-hour visit to West Berlin. Landing at Tegel airfield in the French sector, he made a thirty-mile drive through the city, accompanied by Dr Adenauer and Willi Brandt, amid the frenzied cheering of one million, two hundred and fifty thousand people.

The party finally reached the West Berlin town hall in Schöneberg where the President was expected to make the most important speech of his tour.

The room on the first floor to which he was taken was crowded, and among those waiting there were Charles Pascoe and Simon Vaughan. The President moved through the crowd, stopping here and there.

When he got to Pascoe and Vaughan he shook hands, the smile easy and relaxed, no different from what it had been for the others. Only his words carried their own meaning.

'Gentlemen, we are glad, believe me, to see you here today.'

He moved out on the balcony to an enormous cheer from the crowd. He started to speak. Pascoe said, 'I know I'm getting old, but it's still better to travel hopefully. He could be what we all need, that man. At least he says the right things. The things that should be said.'

Kennedy's voice drifted in. 'Today in the world of freedom, the proudest boast is *Ich bin ein Berliner*.'

He was leaning over the balcony, touched by light, and then it was as if a shadow passed over the face of the sun, and the light on him died, but only for a moment.

For some unaccountable reason, Vaughan went cold. He said to Pascoe, 'Let's get out of here. You can read all about it in the papers.'

He turned and worked his way through the crowd, Pascoe following him. Margaret Campbell was standing against the wall at the head of the stair with Meyer.

She reached for his hand. 'What's wrong, Simon? What is it?'

'Nothing,' he said. 'Someone just walked over my grave, that's all.'

As they went down the stairs, the President's voice rang out across the crowd like a trumpet blast. 'Freedom has many difficulties and democracy is not perfect, but we never had to put up a wall to keep our people in.'

The Thousand Faces of Night

For my

MOTHER AND FATHER

1

They released Marlowe from Wandsworth shortly after eight o'clock on a wet September morning. When the gate was opened he hesitated for a moment before stepping outside and the man on duty gave him a push forward. 'See you again,' he observed, cynically.

'Like hell, you will,' Marlowe said over his shoulder.

He walked down towards the main road, a big, dangerous-looking man, massive shoulders swelling under the cheap raincoat they had given him. He stood on the corner watching the early morning traffic and a flurry of wind lifted cold rain into his face. On the opposite side of the road was a snack bar. For a moment he hesitated, fingering the money in his pocket, and then he took advantage of a break in the traffic and crossed over.

When he pushed open the door, a bell tinkled in the stillness. The place was deserted. He sat on one of the high stools at the counter and waited. After a few moments an old, white-haired man emerged from a door at the rear. He peered over the top of steel-rimmed spectacles and a slow smile appeared on his face. 'What would you like, son?' he said.

Marlowe's fingers tightened over the coins. For a moment he was unable to speak and then he managed to say, 'Give me twenty cigarettes.'

The old man was already reaching for them. For a brief second Marlowe looked at the packet and then he quickly opened it and took out a cigarette. A match flared in the old man's hands and Marlowe reached forward. He inhaled deeply and blew out the smoke with a great sigh. 'Christ, but I was waiting for that,' he said.

The old man chuckled sympathetically and poured strong coffee from a battered metal pot into a mug. He added milk and pushed it across. Marlowe reached for his money and the old man smiled and raised a hand. 'It's on the house.'

For a moment they looked at each other steadily and then Marlowe laughed. 'How can you tell?' he said.

The old man leaned on the counter and shrugged. 'I've kept this place for twenty years. Nearly every day during that time someone has walked down the street opposite and stood on that corner. Then they see this place and it's straight in for a packet of cigarettes.'

Marlowe grinned. 'You can't blame them can you?' He drank some of the coffee and sighed with pleasure. 'That tastes good. After five years of drinking swill I'd forgotten what good coffee was like.'

The old man nodded and said quietly. 'That's a long time. Things can change a lot in five years.'

Marlowe looked out of the window. 'You're damned right they can. I've been watching the cars. They all look different somehow. Even people's clothes look different.'

'They are different,' the old man said. 'And the people inside them are different too.'

Marlowe laughed bitterly and swallowed the rest of his coffee. 'Aren't we all?' he said. 'Everything changes. Everything.'

'More coffee?' the old man asked gently.

Marlowe shook his head and stood up. 'No, I've got to get moving.'

The old man produced a cloth and carefully wiped the counter. 'Where are you going, son? The Prisoners' Aid Society?'

Marlowe laughed briefly and a flash of genuine amusement showed in his cold grey eyes. 'Now I ask you. Do I look the sort of bloke that would apply to those people?'

The old man sighed and shook his head. 'No,' he said sadly. 'You look like a man who would never ask anybody for anything.'

Marlowe grinned and lit another cigarette. 'That's right, Dad. That way you never owe anybody anything.' He opened the door. 'Thanks for the cigarettes. I'll be seeing you.'

The old man shook his head. 'I hope not.'

Marlowe grinned again. 'Okay, Dad, I'll try to oblige.' He closed the door behind him and began to walk along the pavement.

The rain had increased in force and bounced from the pavement in long solid rods. It soaked through the cheap raincoat within a few seconds and he cursed and hurried towards a bus shelter. The traffic had slackened down to an occasional truck or car and the pavements were deserted. As he approached the shelter a large black saloon turned into the kerb slightly ahead of him.

As he moved alongside the car a voice said, 'Hallo, Hugh. We've been waiting for you. It's been a long time.'

Marlowe stood quite still. The skin had tightened over his prominent cheekbones, but otherwise he showed no emotion. He approached the car and looked in at the man who sat behind the wheel. 'Hallo, you bastard!' he said.

A rough voice snarled from the rear seat. 'Watch it, Marlowe! You can't talk to Mr Faulkner like that.'

The man who had spoken was thick set with the coarse, battered features of a prizefighter. Next to him sat a small wiry man whose cold beady eyes were like holes in his white face.

Marlowe's gaze flickered over them contemptuously, 'The old firm. It must smell pretty high in there when you have the windows closed.'

The large man made a convulsive movement and Faulkner cried warningly, 'Butcher!' He subsided, swearing violently under his breath, and Faulkner said, 'Yes, the old firm, Hugh, and don't forget you're still a partner.'

Marlowe shook his head. 'You dissolved our partnership a long time ago.'

Faulkner frowned. 'I think not, my friend. We still have some unfinished business to settle.'

Marlowe smiled coldly. 'Five years inside has made me greedy, Faulkner. I'm not declaring a dividend this year.' He laughed harshly. 'What kind of a mug do you think I am? Go on, get out of it. And keep away from me.'

As he straightened up, the rear door started to open and a hairy paw reached out towards him. He slammed the door shut with all his force, trapping the hand so that blood spurted from beneath the fingernails. Butcher gave a cry of agony, and Marlowe leaned in the window and said, 'That's for leaving me in the lurch the night we did the Birmingham job.' He spat in Butcher's face and turned away.

He ducked into a narrow alley and began to walk rapidly along the uneven pavement. Behind him cardoors slammed and there was a heavy pounding of footsteps. He threw a hasty glance over his shoulder as the small man rounded the corner, steel glinting in his hand. Behind him lumbered Butcher, cursing freely as he wrapped a handkerchief about his right fist.

At any other time he would have turned and faced them, but not now. He had other things to do. He started running along the alley, splashing in the rainfilled gutter, his feet slipping dangerously on the greasy cobbles.

The small man gave a cry of triumph and Marlowe ground his teeth together with rage. So they thought they had him on the run, did they?

They thought the years behind the high wall had made him soft. He resisted the impulse to stop running and increased his pace.

He rounded the corner at the end of the alley into a quiet street of terrace houses. For a brief moment he hesitated and then, as he started forward, he slipped and crashed to the pavement. As he scrambled to his feet a door opened and a woman stepped out with a shopping-basket on one arm. Marlowe lurched towards her and she stepped back quickly with a cry of alarm and slammed the door in his face. There came another shout from behind, and as he started to stumble painfully along the pavement a large black saloon turned into the road and came towards him.

A sudden burning anger rose inside and he clenched his fists as the car swerved into the kerb a few yards away. The rear door opened and a large, heavily built man in a brown raincoat and Homburg hat clambered out and stood, hands in pockets, waiting.

Marlowe came to a sudden halt. Behind him he could hear the sound of his pursuers' footsteps fading rapidly into the distance. The large man smiled and shook his head, white teeth gleaming beneath a clipped moustache. 'You haven't wasted any time, Marlowe.'

Marlowe grinned and walked towards him. 'I never thought the day would come when I'd be glad to see you, Masters,' he said.

'It's a day for surprises,' Masters retorted. 'I never thought I'd live to see you run from a couple of rats like Butcher and Harris.'

Marlowe scowled. 'I've got more important things to do. I can deal with those two any time.'

Masters nodded. 'I don't doubt it, but there's always Faulkner.' He took out a short pipe and began to fill it from a leather pouch. 'He saw us coming, by the way, and took off. I'm afraid Butcher and Harris are going to get very wet looking for him.' He frowned suddenly as if the idea had just occurred to him. 'Of course, you could always prefer charges.'

Marlowe grinned. 'What for? We were only having a little exercise.'

The rain increased in volume with a sudden rush, and Masters opened the rear door of the car and said, 'Let's continue this conversation in comfort at least.'

For a moment Marlowe hesitated and then he shrugged and climbed in. There was a tall young man in a fawn raincoat behind the wheel. He turned his head and said, 'Where to, Superintendent?'

Marlowe whistled. 'A super now, eh? They must be getting hard up.'

Masters ignored the thrust. 'Anywhere in particular you'd like to go?'

Marlowe raised one eyebrow and took out his cigarettes. Masters smiled faintly and said to the driver, 'Just take us towards town, Cameron. My friend and I have a lot to talk over.'

Marlowe blew smoke out and leaned back. 'I've got nothing to say to you, Masters.'

Masters held a match to his pipe. After a moment he leaned back with a sigh. 'I wouldn't say that. There's a little matter of twenty thousand quid I want from you.'

Marlowe threw back his head and laughed. 'You've got a hope.' He looked the policeman squarely in the eye. 'Listen, Masters. I was sent up for seven years. I've done five like a good little boy and now I'm out. Nobody can lay a finger on me. I'm clean as a whistle as far as the law is concerned.'

Masters shook his head. 'There's nothing very clean about you, Marlowe.'

Marlowe turned towards him, a fist raised, and the driver braked suddenly so that the car skidded a little. Masters smiled calmly. 'Keep going, Cameron. My friend isn't going to cause any trouble.'

Marlowe cursed and reached for the door handle. 'Okay, Masters. I've had enough. Stop the car and let me out.'

Masters shook his head. 'Oh, no, I haven't finished with you yet.' He puffed at his pipe reflectively for a moment. 'I've never been able to understand you, Marlowe. Not at your trial and not now. You had a normal enough background, a good education. You were even decorated in Korea, and then you came home and turned yourself into a lousy crook, a cheap hoodlum hanging round the big boys looking for easy pickings.'

Marlowe was calmer now. He said, 'I never waited around for anyone's pickings and you know it.'

'But you were driving for Faulkner and his bunch, weren't you?'

Marlowe shrugged. 'Why ask me? You seem to know all the answers.'

Masters shook his head. 'Not all of them, but I intend to.' He applied another match to his pipe and continued, 'It's just over five years since that Iron Amalgamated job was done in Birmingham. Whoever did it lifted over twenty thousand pounds, the wages for the following day. But they didn't cosh the nightwatchman hard enough. He raised the alarm and the car was chased through the city. It crashed in a side street, and when a patrol car got there you were behind the wheel, half conscious. They dragged you out of the wreck clutching a black case. You wouldn't let go of it. One of the constables went to the end of the street to guide the other cars in and when he returned, his partner was laid out and you'd disappeared – with the bag, of course.'

Marlowe raised his eyebrows and yawned deliberately. 'I'm beginning to get bored. This is like seeing a film round twice.'

Masters smiled pleasantly. 'Wait a minute. It gets more interesting. You were picked up in Paddington Station next day. How the hell you managed to get clear of Birmingham I'll never know, but the important thing was that the money was gone.' He held the stem of his pipe against the side of his nose and said,

'Now I wonder where it got to?'

Marlowe shrugged. 'I said all I had to say at the trial. They proved I was driving the car. They gave me seven years, and now I'm out. So what?'

Masters nodded. 'But there's still the question of the money. You never did get around to telling us what you did with it.'

'You know, you've got a point there.' Marlowe dropped his voice a tone. 'Promise you won't let this go any further, but I gave all the money to a charity that's very near to my heart. It's a society that takes care of destitute policemen.'

'Very funny,' Masters said. 'As it happens, I prefer my own version. Faulkner pulled that Birmingham job, though we've never been able to prove it because you kept your mouth shut.'

Marlowe shrugged. 'So where does that get you?'

'To this,' Masters said. 'Faulkner pulled the job, but he never got his hands on the cash.' Marlowe started to speak but the policeman went on, 'It's no use denying it. I've got my contacts and I know he's been keeping pretty close tabs on you while you've been inside. The way I see it this is what happened. When your car crashed that night, Faulkner, Butcher and Harris were with you. You were stunned. In a blind panic, they ran for it leaving you. Maybe they forgot the money in the heat of the moment or perhaps they left it deliberately, hoping the police would think it was a one-man job. By a miracle you got away, because I picked you up myself in Paddington Station next day, but the money had disappeared.'

Marlowe stared out of the window, a frown on his face. 'What if it's all true? What if it happened exactly as you say? It still won't get you anywhere.' He laughed contemptuously. 'If you caught me with the money in my pockets you couldn't touch me. I've served my time.'

Masters sighed deeply. 'You know. I thought you were smart, Marlowe. That's what used to make you stand out amongst the crowd of mugs that hung around Faulkner's club in the old days.' He shook his head. 'Do you think you'll ever get to spend that money? Will you hell. I'm after it because to me it's part of an unfinished case. Faulkner's after it, and Butcher and Harris and every other cheap crook that knows the story. You're branded clear to the bone.'

Marlowe swung round and gripped Masters by the right arm. His face had turned to stone and there was a terrible expression in his eyes. 'Listen to me, Masters,' he said, 'and listen good. If anybody gets in my way I'll stamp him into the ground, and that goes for you, too.' His fingers dug painfully into the policeman's arm and his voice trembled slightly. 'I spent three years in a Chinese prison camp, Masters. Did you know that? I worked in a coal mine in Manchuria for twelve hours a day up to my knees in water. Most of my friends died, but I came home. And do you know what? Nobody seemed to know a war had been going on.'

'Is that supposed to be an excuse?' Masters said.

Marlowe ignored him. 'I took a job as a driver with Faulkner. Good money and no questions asked. He tried to make a monkey out of me, but I ended up making him look pretty stupid.' He released the policeman's arm. 'I've spent eight years of my life in prison, Masters, and I'm only thirty.' He leaned back suddenly. 'Okay, I've got the money. I earned it and now I'm keeping it.'

Masters shook his head slowly, and there was something like pity in his voice. 'You'll never get away with it. If Faulkner doesn't catch up with you, I will.'

Marlowe shrugged. 'I wouldn't count on that if I were you.'

The car slowed as they approached a junction, and as the lights changed it started to pick up speed again. With a sudden movement, Marlowe jerked open the offside door, jumped out into the road, and slammed it behind him. He threaded his way quickly through heavy traffic and dodged down a side street.

Once away from people he started to run. He knew he had only a few minutes' start at the most. As he approached the end of the street he slowed and turned into another main road. A bus was pulling away from a stop in front of him, and he broke into a run and jumped on to the platform as it gathered speed.

As the bus moved away into the main traffic stream he slumped down into a corner seat. His chest was heaving and there was a slight film of sweat on his brow. He wiped it away with the back of his hand and smiled wryly. Things had moved fast, faster than he had anticipated, but he was still ahead of the game and that was all that counted.

He dropped off the bus at the next stop and went into a hardware store where he purchased a cheap screwdriver. Then he crossed the road and plunged into a maze of back-streets. He walked quickly, head lowered against the driving rain, and finally emerged into another main road where he caught a bus for the City.

A little more than an hour after giving Masters the slip he was in the vicinity of Paddington Station. It was raining harder than ever now and the streets were almost deserted. He crossed the road towards the station and turned into a narrow street that was lined on each side with tall, decaying Victorian houses.

About half-way along the street he paused and looked up at one of the houses. Above the door a grimy glass sign carried the legend 'Imperial Hotel' in faded letters. It was typical of a certain type of establishment to be found in the area. Places where a room was usually required for only an hour or two and never longer than a night. He mounted the steps slowly and passed inside.

He found himself in a narrow hall with several doors opening off it. Directly in front of him stairs that were covered with a threadbare carpet lifted to a gloomy landing. On his left a middle-aged woman was sitting in a cubicle reading a newspaper. She looked up and blinked red-rimmed watery eyes, and then carefully folded the paper. She spoke in a light, colourless voice. 'Yes, sir. What can I do for you?'

Marlowe's eyes moved quickly over the rows of keys that hung on the board behind her head. 'I'd like a room,' he said. 'Just for three or four hours.'

The woman's wet eyes flickered briefly over him. She produced a battered register and pen, and said, 'Sign here, please.'

Marlowe took the pen and hastily scrawled 'P. Simons – Bristol'. The woman examined the entry and said politely, 'Any luggage, sir?'

He shook his head. 'I've left it at the station. I'm catching a train for Scotland this afternoon. Thought I could do with some sleep while I'm waiting.'

She nodded. 'I see, sir. That will be fifteen shillings.'

He gave her a pound note and, when she turned to the board, said, 'I'll take number seven if it's vacant.' He laughed lightly. 'My lucky number.'

The woman handed him the key. 'It's facing you at the top of the stairs, sir,' she said. 'Would you like me to give you a call?'

He shook his head. 'No thanks. I'll be all right.'

He mounted the stairs quickly and stood on the landing listening. The hotel was wrapped in quiet. After a moment he unlocked the door of room seven and went in.

Light filtered palely through one dirty window, giving a touch of colour to the faded counterpane that covered the double bed. The only other furniture was an ancient mahogany wardrobe and a plain wooden chair which stood on the far side of the bed. There was a door marked 'Toilet' in one corner.

Marlowe wrinkled his nose in disgust. The room smelt musty and damp. Somehow there was an odour of corruption over everything. He went to the window and wrestled with the catch. After a moment it gave, and he lifted the sash as far as it would go and leaned out into the rain.

The hotel backed on to a maze of railway lines and he could see Paddington Station over to the left. Beneath the window a pile of coke reared against the wall, and there was an engine getting up steam not far away. He lit a cigarette and leaned out into the rain. There was a hint of fog in the air and already things were becoming misty and ill-defined. He shivered suddenly as a gust of wind lifted rain in his face, but he did not shake because of the cold. He was afraid. For one brief moment his courage deserted him and he allowed the thought to creep into his mind that perhaps the long years had been wasted. Perhaps what he had come for was no longer here.

With a sudden convulsive movement he tossed his cigarette far out into the rain and crossed to the toilet door. A small rounded oval plate had 'Toilet' printed on it in black letters, and was secured by two screws. Marlowe took out his screwdriver and started to unscrew the plate with hands that trembled slightly.

When he had taken one screw completely out, the plate swivelled and the thing which had been concealed behind it fell to the floor. He dropped to one knee and picked it up with trembling fingers. It was a small metal key. He held it in the palm of his hand, staring at it, and a sudden exultation lifted inside him. It was there. After all this time it was there.

He heard nothing and yet some instinct told him that he was not alone. He was conscious of a slight draught on one cheek and knew that the door was open. He turned slowly. Faulkner was standing just inside the door. He held up what was obviously a duplicate key to the room and twirled it gaily round one finger. 'I've got one too, old man, though nothing like as valuable as that one. What's it open, a safe-deposit box? Very clever of you.'

He came into the room followed by Butcher and Harris, who closed the door and leaned against it. Marlowe slipped the key into his pocket and said, 'How the hell did you manage to follow me?'

Faulkner sat down on the bed and fitted a cigarette into an elegant holder. 'We didn't need too, old man. You see, I knew something the police didn't. The day you were arrested I had a bit of luck. A pal of Butcher's happened to see you coming out of this place. I took the room for a couple of days, and we went over it with a fine tooth comb. Couldn't find a thing, but I always had a hunch about it. There had to be a connexion.'

Marlowe took out a cigarette and lit it carefully. 'I'm surprised at you, Faulkner,' he said. 'You must be slipping.' He looked quickly towards the two men at the door. Butcher was watching his every move, hate blazing out of his eyes. Harris had produced a flick-knife with which he was quietly cleaning his finger-nails.

Faulkner said, 'Actually it was a damned ingenious hiding place, Hugh. But then you always were a cut above the average.' He smiled and leaned forward. 'Now come clean like a good chap and tell me where I can find the lock that key fits.' His smile became even more charming. 'I wouldn't try anything silly if I were you. Butcher and Harris are praying for an excuse to cut you into pieces.'

A quick fierce anger surged in Marlowe, and he grabbed Faulkner by the tie and jerked him up from the bed. 'You lousy bastard,' he said coldly. 'Do you think I'm scared of you and your third-rate toughs?'

Faulkner's eyes started from his head as he began to choke, and then Marlowe was aware of a movement to his left. He released Faulkner and turned as Harris cut viciously at his face with the knife. He warded off the blow with his right arm and was conscious of pain as the knife ripped his sleeve. He caught the small man by his left wrist and with a sudden pull, jerked him across the room to crash against the wall.

As he turned, Butcher struck at him with a heavy rubber cosh, the blow catching him across the left shoulder and almost paralysing his arm. He chopped Butcher across the right forearm with the edge of his hand and the big man cried out in pain and dropped the cosh. Marlowe turned towards the door and Faulkner pushed out a foot and tripped him so that he fell heavily to the floor. Butcher moved in quickly, kicking at his ribs and face. Marlowe rolled away, avoiding most of the blows and scrambled up. Harris was back on his feet, shaking his head in a dazed fashion. He stumbled across the room and stood beside Butcher. For a moment there was a brief pause as the four men stood looking at each other and then Faulkner pulled an automatic out of his inside breast pocket.

Marlowe moved backwards until he faced them from the other side of the bed, the open window behind him. Faulkner appeared to be having difficulty with his voice. He choked several times before he managed to say, 'I'll take that key, Hugh, and you'll tell me where the money is. I don't want to use this, but I will if I have to.'

'I'll see you in hell first,' Marlowe said.

Faulkner shrugged and covered him carefully with the automatic. 'Go and get the key,' he told Butcher.

The big man started forward. Marlowe waited until he was almost on him and then he grabbed the wooden chair and tossed it straight at Faulkner. In the same moment he turned and vaulted through the open window.

He landed knee-deep in the pile of coke and lost his balance, rolling over and sliding to the bottom. He got to his feet and looked up. Butcher and Faulkner were at the window. For a moment they stared down at him and then they were pulled aside and Harris scrambled on to the windowsill. As he jumped, Marlowe turned and ran across the tracks towards some railway coaches which were standing in a nearby siding.

The fog was thickening rapidly now and visibility was poor. He stumbled across the tracks into the shelter of the coaches and paused for a moment to look back. Harris was running well and the blade of his knife gleamed dully in the rain. Marlowe started to run again. There was a terrible pain in his side where Butcher had kicked him and blood was dripping from his left arm.

As he emerged from the shelter of the coaches he saw a goods train moving slowly along a nearby track, gathering speed as it went. He lurched towards it and ran alongside, pulling at one of the sliding doors until it opened. He grabbed at the iron rail and hauled himself up.

As he leaned against the door Harris appeared, running strongly, his face white with effort. As he grabbed for the handrail, Marlowe summoned up his last reserve of strength and kicked him in the chest with all his force. The small man disappeared and then the train moved forward rapidly, clattering over the points as it travelled away from London towards the North.

For a moment longer Marlowe leaned in the opening and then he pushed the sliding door shut and slid gently down on to the straw-littered floor.

2

He lay face downwards in the straw for a long time, chest heaving as his tortured lungs fought for air. After a while he pushed himself up and sat with his back against a packing case.

The wagon was old and battered with many gaps in its slatted sides through which the light filtered. Gradually his breathing became easier and he stood up and removed his raincoat and jacket. The slash in his arm was less serious than he had imagined. A superficial cut, three or four inches long, where the tip of the knife had sliced through his sleeve. He took out his handkerchief and tied it around the wound, knotting it with his teeth.

He shivered and pulled on his jacket as wind whistled between the slats carrying a faint spray of cold rain. As he buttoned his raincoat he examined the packing cases that stood about him and was amused to find they were addressed to a firm in Birmingham. So the wheel had come full circle? He had escaped from Birmingham in a goods train five years before. Now he was on his way back again. Masters would have been amused.

He sat down with his back against a packing case by the door and wondered what Masters was doing now. Probably making sure that every copper in London had his description, Faulkner would be doing exactly the same thing, in his own way. Marlowe frowned and fumbled for a cigarette. London was out of the question for the moment. With every crook in town on the watch for him, he wouldn't last half an hour.

He thrust his hands deep into his pockets and considered the position. Perhaps things had worked out the best after all. A week or two in the Midlands or the North to let things cool off and then he could return quietly and collect what he had left in the safe deposit of the firm near Bond Street.

His fingers fastened over the key in his jacket pocket and he took it out and examined it. Twenty thousand pounds. He smiled suddenly. He had waited for five years. He could afford to wait for another week or two. He replaced the key in his pocket, pulled his cap down over his eyes, and went to sleep.

He came awake slowly and lay in the straw for a moment trying to decide where he was. After a while he remembered and struggled to his feet. He was cold and there was a dull, aching pain in his side where Butcher had kicked him. The train was moving fast, rocking slightly on the curves, and when he pulled the door open a gust of wind dished violently into his face.

A curtain of fog shrouded the fields cutting visibility down to thirty or forty yards. The cold air made him feel better and he sat down again, leaving the door open, and considered his next move.

Birmingham was out. There was always the chance that Faulkner might have discovered the train's destination. There could easily be a reception committee waiting. Faulkner had friends everywhere. It would be best to leave the train at some small town farther along the line. The sort of place that had a name no one had ever heard of.

He emptied his pockets and checked on his available assets. There was an insurance card, his driving licence which he had renewed each year he had been in prison, and fifteen shillings in silver. He still had ten cigarettes left in the packet he had bought in the snack bar. He smiled ruefully and decided it was a good job he had the licence. With luck he might be able to get some sort of a driving job. Something that would keep him going until he was ready to return to London.

The train began to slow down and he got up quickly and closed the door leaving a narrow gap through which he could stare out into the fog. A signal box loomed out of the gloom and a moment later, the train moved past a small station platform. Marlowe just had time to make out the name LITTON before the station was swallowed up by the fog.

He shrugged and a half-smile appeared on his face. This place sounded as good as any. He pushed open the door and as the train slowed even more, he dropped down into the ditch at the side of the track. Before him there was a thorn hedge. He moved along it for a few yards until he found a suitable gap through which he forced his way into a quiet road beyond. The rain was hammering down through the fog unmercifully and he pulled up his coat collar and began to walk briskly along the road.

When he came to the station he paused and examined the railway map that hung on the wall in a glass case. He had little difficulty in finding Litton. It was on the main line, about eighty miles from Birmingham. The nearest place of any size was a town called Barford, twelve or fifteen miles away.

The hands of the clock above the station entrance pointed to three and he frowned and started down the hill towards the village, dimly seen through the fog. He had obviously slept on the train for longer than he had imagined.

The main street seemed to be deserted and the fog was much thicker than it had been on the hill. He saw no one as he walked along the wet pavement. When he paused for a moment outside a draper's shop his reflection stared out at him from a mirror in the back of the window. With his cap pulled down over his eyes and his great shoulders straining out of the sodden raincoat, he presented a formidable and menacing figure.

He lifted his left hand to wipe away the rain from his face and cursed softly. Blood was trickling down his arm, soaking the sleeve of his raincoat. He thrust his hand deep into his pocket and hurried on. He had to find somewhere quiet where he could fix that slash before he ran into anyone.

The street seemed to be endless. He had been walking for a good ten minutes before he came to a low stone wall topped by spiked railings. A little farther along there was an open iron gate and a sign which read CHURCH OF THE IMMACULATE HEART, with the times of Mass and Confession in faded gold letters beneath it.

He walked along the flagged path and mounted the four or five steps that led to the porch. For a moment he hesitated and then he pulled off his cap and went inside.

It was warm in there and very quiet. For a little while he stood listening intently and then he slumped down in a pew at the back of the church. He looked down towards the winking candles and the altar and suddenly it seemed to grow darker and he leaned forward and rested his head against a stone pillar. He was more tired than he had been in a long time.

After a while he felt better and stood up to remove his raincoat and jacket. The handkerchief had slipped down his arm exposing the wound and blood oozed sluggishly through the torn sleeve of his shirt. As he started to fumble with the knotted handkerchief there was a slight movement at his side. A voice said quietly, 'Are you all right? Can I help you?'

He swung round with a stifled exclamation. A young woman was standing beside him. She was wearing a man's raincoat that was too big for her and a scarf covered her head. 'How the hell did you get there?' Marlowe demanded.

She smiled slightly and sat down beside him. 'I was sitting in the corner. You didn't notice me.'

'I didn't think anyone would be in church in the middle of the afternoon,' he said. 'I came in out of the rain to fix my arm. The bandage has slipped.'

She lifted his arm and said calmly, 'That looks pretty nasty. You need a doctor.'

He jerked away from her and started to untie the handkerchief with his right hand. 'It's only a bad cut,' he said. 'Doesn't even need stitching.'

She reached over and gently unfastened the knot. She folded the handkerchief into a strip and bound it tightly about the wound. As she tied it she said, 'This won't last for long. You need a proper bandage.'

'It'll be all right,' Marlowe said. He stood up and pulled on his coat. He wanted to get away before she started asking too many questions.

As he belted his raincoat she said, 'How did you do it?'

He shrugged. 'I've been hitch-hiking from London. Going to Birmingham to look for work. I ripped myself open on a steel spike when I was climbing down from a lorry.'

He started to walk away and she followed at his heels. At the door, she kneeled and crossed herself and then she followed him out into the porch.

'Well, I'd better be off,' Marlowe said.

She looked out into the driving rain and the fog and said, with a slight smile, 'You won't stand much chance of a lift in this.'

He nodded and said smoothly, 'If I can't, I'll catch a bus to Barford. I'll be all right.'

'But there isn't a bus until five,' she said. 'It's a limited service on this road.' She appeared to hesitate and then went on, 'You can come home with me if you like. I'll bandage that cut for you properly. You've plenty of time to spare before the bus goes.'

Marlowe shook his head and moved towards the top step. 'I wouldn't dream of it.'

Her mouth trembled and there was suppressed laughter in her voice as she replied, 'My father should be home by now. It will be all quite proper.'

An involuntary smile came to Marlowe's face and he turned towards her. For the first time he realized that she had a slight foreign intonation to her speech and an oddly old-fashioned turn of phrase. Suddenly and for some completely inexplicable reason, he felt completely at home with her. He grinned and took out his cigarettes. 'You're not English, are you?'

She smiled back at him, at the same time refusing a cigarette with a slight gesture of one hand. 'No, Portuguese. How did you know? I rather prided myself on my accent.'

He hastened to reassure her. 'It isn't so much your accent. For one thing, you don't look English.'

Her smile widened. 'I don't know how you intended that, but I shall take it as a compliment. My name is Maria Magellan.'

She held out her hand. He hesitated for a moment and then took it in his. 'Hugh Marlowe.'

'So! Now we know each other and it is all very respectable,' she said briskly. 'Shall we go?'

He paused for only a moment before following her down the steps. As she passed through the gate in front of him he noticed that she was small, with the ripe figure peculiar to southern women and hips that were too large by English standards.

They walked along the pavement, side-by-side, and he glanced covertly at her. Her face was smoothly rounded with a flawless cream complexion. The eye-brows and the hair that escaped from under the scarf, were coal black and her red lips had an extra fulness that suggested sensuality.

She turned her head unexpectedly at one point and caught him looking at her. She smiled. 'You're a pretty big man, Mr Marlowe. How tall are you?'

Marlowe shrugged. 'I'm not sure. Around six-three, I think.'

She nodded, her eyes travelling over his massive frame. 'What kind of work are you looking for?'

He shrugged. 'Anything I can get, but driving is what I do best.'

There was a gleam of interest in her eyes. 'What kind of driving?'

'Any kind,' he said. 'Anything on wheels. I've driven the lot, from light vans to tank-transporters.'

'So! You were in the Army?' she said and her interest seemed to become even more pronounced.

Marlowe flicked his cigarette into the rain-filled gutter. 'Yes, I think you could say I was in the Army,' he said and there was a deadness in his voice.

She seemed to sense the change of mood and lapsed into silence. Marlowe walked moodily along beside her trying to think of something to say, but it was not necessary. They turned into a narrow lane and came to a five-barred gate which was standing open. She paused and said, 'Here we are.'

A gravel drive disappeared into the fog in front of them and Marlowe could make out the dim shape of a house. 'It looks like a pretty big place,' he said.

She nodded. 'It used to be a farmhouse. Now there's just a few acres of land. We run it as a market garden and fruit farm.'

He looked up into the rain. 'This kind of weather won't be doing you much good.'

She laughed. 'We haven't done too badly. We got nearly all the apples in last week and most of our other produce is under glass.'

A gust of wind lifted across the farmyard, rolling the fog in front of it, and exposed the house. It was an old, grey stone building, firmly rooted into the ground and weathered by the years. On one side of the yard there were several outbuildings and on the other, a large, red-roofed barn.

The front door was protected by an old-fashioned glass porch and outside it a small yellow van was parked. INTER-ALLIED TRADING CORPORATION – BARFORD, was printed on its side in neat black letters. Maria Magellan paused abruptly and there was something like fear on her face. She darted forward and entered the house.

Marlowe followed more slowly. He ducked slightly under the low lintel of the door and found himself in a wide, stone-flagged hall. The girl was standing outside a door on the left through which angry voices could be heard. She flung the door open and entered the room and Marlowe waited in the hall, hands thrust deep into his pockets, and watched.

Inside the room two men faced each other across a table. One of them was old with grizzled hair and a white moustache that stood out clearly against swarthy skin that was the colour of tanned leather.

The other was a much younger man, powerfully built with good shoulders. His face was twisted menacingly as he said, 'Listen you old fool. Either you come in with us or you go out of business. That's Mr O'Connor's last word.'

The old man's eyes darted fire and he slammed a hand hard against the table. His English was good but with a heavy accent and his voice was trembling with rage. 'Listen, Kennedy. You tell O'Connor this from me. Before he puts me out of business I put a knife into him. On my life I promise it.'

Kennedy laughed contemptuously. 'You bloody old fool,' he said.

'Mr O'Connor can stamp you into the dirt any time he wants. You're small stuff, Magellan.'

The old man gave a roar of anger and moved fast around the table. He swung hard with his right fist, but the years were against him. Kennedy blocked the punch with ease. He grabbed the old man by the shirt and started to beat him across the face with the flat of his hand. The girl screamed and ran forward, tearing at Kennedy with her fingers. He pushed her away with such force that she staggered across the room and lost her balance.

A cold rage flared in Marlowe and he moved forward into the room. Kennedy raised his hand to strike the old man again and Marlowe grabbed him by the shoulder and swung him round so that they faced each other. 'How about trying me?' he said. 'I'm a bit nearer your size.'

Kennedy opened his mouth to speak and Marlowe smashed a fist into it. The tremendous force of the blow hurled Kennedy across the table. He gave a terrible groan and pulled himself up from the floor. Marlowe moved quickly around the table and grabbed him by the front of his jacket. 'You bastard!' he said. 'You dirty, lousy bastard.'

And then a mist came before his eyes and it wasn't Kennedy's face that he saw before him. It was another face. One that he hated with all his being and he began to beat Kennedy methodically, backwards and forwards across the face, with his right hand.

The girl screamed again, high and clear, 'No, Marlowe! No – you'll kill him!'

She was tugging at his arm, pleading frantically with him, and Marlowe stopped. He stood for a moment staring stupidly at Kennedy, fist raised, and then he gently pushed him back against the table.

He was trembling slightly and there was still that slight haze before his eyes, almost as if some of the fog had got into the room. He clenched his fists to try and steady the trembling and noticed that blood was trickling down his left sleeve again.

The girl released her hold on him. 'I'm sorry,' she said. 'I had to stop you. You would have killed him.'

Marlowe nodded slowly and passed a hand across his face. 'You did right. Sometimes I don't know when to stop and this rat isn't worth hanging for.'

He moved suddenly and grabbing Kennedy by the collar, propelled him roughly out of the room and into the hall. He pushed him through the porch and flung him against the van. 'If you've got any sense you'll get out of here while you've got a whole skin,' he said. 'I'll give you just five minutes to gather your wits.'

Kennedy was already fumbling for the handle of the van door as Marlowe turned and went back into the house.

3

When he went into the room there was no sign of Maria, but her father was busy at the sideboard with a bottle and a couple of glasses. His face split into a wide grin and he walked quickly across and handed Marlowe a glass. 'Brandy – the best in the house. I feel like a young man again.'

Marlowe swallowed the brandy gratefully and nodded towards the window as the engine of the van roared into life. 'That's the last you'll see of him.'

The old man shrugged and an ugly look came into his eyes. 'Who knows? Next time I'll be prepared. I'll stick a knife into his belly and argue afterwards.'

Maria came into the room, a basin of hot water in one hand and bandages and a towel in the other. She still looked white and shaken, but she managed a smile as she set the bowl down on the table. 'I'll have a look at that arm now,' she said.

Marlowe removed his raincoat and jacket and she gently sponged away congealed blood and pursed her lips. 'It doesn't look too good.' She shook her head and turned to her father. 'What do you think, Papa?'

Papa Magellan looked carefully at the wound and a sudden light flickered in his eyes. 'Pretty nasty. How did you say you got it, boy?'

Marlowe shrugged. 'Ripped it on a spike getting off a truck. I've been hitching my way from London.'

The old man nodded. 'A spike, eh?' A light smile touched his mouth. 'I don't think we need bother the doctor, Maria. Clean it up and bandage it well. It'll be fine inside a week.'

Maria still looked dubious and Marlowe said, 'He's right. You women make a fuss about every little scratch.' He laughed and fished for a cigarette with his right hand. 'I walked a hundred and fifty miles in Korea with a bullet in my thigh. I had too. There was no one available to take it out.'

She scowled and quick fury danced in her eyes. 'All right. We don't get the doctor. Have it your own way. I hope your arm poisons and falls off.'

He chuckled and she bent her head and went to work. Papa Magellan said, 'You were in Korea?' Marlowe nodded and the old man went over to the sideboard and came back with a framed photo. 'My son, Pedro,' he said.

The boy smiled stiffly out of the photo, proud and self-conscious of the new uniform. It was the sort of picture every recruit has taken during his first few weeks of basic training. 'He looks like a good boy,' Marlowe remarked in a non-committal voice.

Papa Magellan nodded vigorously. 'He was a fine boy. He was going to go to Agricultural College. Always wanted to be a farmer.' The old man sighed heavily. 'He was killed in a patrol action near the Imjin River in 1953.'

Marlowe examined the photo again and wondered if Pedro Magellan had been smiling like that when the bullets smashed into him. But it was no use thinking about that because men in war died in so many different ways. Sometimes quickly, sometimes slowly, but always scared, with fear biting into their faces.

He grunted and handed back the photograph. 'That was a little after my time. I was captured in the early days when the Chinese took a hand.'

Maria looked up quickly. 'How long were you a prisoner?'

'About three years,' Marlowe told her.

The old man whistled softly. 'Holy Mother, that's a long time. You must have had it rough. I hear those Chinese camps were pretty tough.'

Marlowe shrugged. 'I wouldn't know. I wasn't in a camp. They put me to work in a coal mine in Manchuria.'

Magellan's eyes narrowed and all humour left his face. 'I've heard a little about those places also.' There was a short silence and then he grinned and clapped Marlowe on the shoulder. 'Still, all this is in the past. Maybe it's a good thing for a man, like going through fire. A sort of purification.'

Marlowe laughed harshly. 'That sort of purification I can do without.'

As Maria pressed plaster over the loose ends of the bandage she said quietly, 'Papa has had a little of that kind of fire in his time. He was in the International Brigade in Spain. The Fascists held him in prison for two years.'

The old man shrugged expressively and raised a hand in protest. 'Why speak of these things? They are dead. Ancient history. We are living in the present. Life is often unpleasant and always unfair. A wise man puts it all down to experience and does the best he can.'

He stood, hands in pockets, smiling at them and Maria said, 'There, it is finished.'

Marlowe stood up and began to turn down the tattered remnants of his shirt sleeve. 'I'd better be going,' he said. 'What time did you say that bus left?'

A frown replaced the smile on Magellan's face. 'Going? Where are you going?'

'Birmingham,' Marlowe told him. 'I'm hoping to get a job there.'

'So you go to Birmingham tomorrow,' the old man said. 'Tonight you stay here. In such weather to refuse shelter to a dog would be a crime. What kind of a man do you think I am? You appear from the fog, save me from a beating, and then expect me to let you disappear just like that?' He snorted. 'Maria, run a hot bath for him and I will see if I can find a clean shirt.'

Marlowe hesitated. Every instinct told him to go. To leave now before he became further involved with these people and he looked at Maria. She smiled and shook her head. 'It's no use, Mr Marlowe. When Papa decides on something the only thing to do is agree. It saves time in the long run.'

He looked out of the window in the gloom outside and thought about that bath and a meal and made his decision. 'I give in,' he said. 'Unconditional surrender.'

She smiled and went out of the room. The old man produced a briar pipe and filled it from a worn leather pouch. 'Maria told me a little about you when you were outside with Kennedy,' he said. 'She tells me you're a truck driver.'

Marlowe shrugged. 'I have been.'

Magellan puffed patiently at his pipe until it was drawing properly. 'That slash on your arm,' he said. 'How did you say you got it?'

'From a broken hook in the tailboard of a truck,' Marlowe told him. 'Why?'

The old man shrugged. 'Oh, nothing,' he said carefully, 'except that I had a very active youth and I know a knife wound when I see one.'

Marlowe stiffened, anger moving inside him. He clenched a fist and took a step forward and the old man produced a battered silver cigarette case and flicked it open. 'Have a cigarette, son,' he said calmly. 'They soothe the nerves.'

Marlowe sighed deeply and unclenched his fist. 'Your eyes are too good, Papa. One of these days they're going to get you into trouble.'

The old man shrugged. 'I've been in trouble before.' He held out a match in cupped hands. 'How about you, son?'

Marlowe looked into the wise, humorous face and liked what he saw. 'Nothing I couldn't handle, Papa.'

The old man's eyes roved briefly over his massive frame. 'I can imagine. It would take a good man to put you down, but there's another kind of trouble that isn't so easy to handle.'

Marlowe raised an eyebrow. 'The law?' He smiled and shook his head. 'Don't worry, Papa. They won't come knocking at your door tonight.' He raised his arm. 'I can explain this. I was asleep in the back of a truck. Woke up to find some bloke going through my pockets. He pulled a knife and ripped my sleeve. I smacked his jaw and dropped off the truck. That's how I arrived here.'

Magellan threw back his head and laughed. 'Heh, I bet that fella doesn't wake up till the truck gets to Newcastle.'

Marlowe sat down in a chair and laughed with him. He felt easier now and safer. 'It's a good job we were near here,' he said. 'I didn't even know Litton was on the map.'

Magellan nodded. 'It's a quiet little place. Only seven or eight hundred people live around here.'

Marlowe grinned. 'Seems to me it's getting pretty lively for a quiet little place. What about the character I tossed out on his ear?'

The old man frowned. 'Kennedy? He was working for me until a few days ago as a driver. Now he's with Inter-Allied Trading.'

Marlowe nodded. 'I noticed the fancy yellow van when I came in. Who's this bloke O'Connor? The big boss?'

The old man snorted and fire glinted in his eyes. 'He likes to think he is, but I remember him when he was small. Very small. He had an old truck and did general haulage work. The war was the making of him. He wasn't too fussy about what he carried and always seemed to be able to get plenty of petrol when other people couldn't. Now he has twenty or thirty trucks.'

'And doesn't like competition,' Marlowe said. 'What's he trying to do? Put you out of business?'

'He offered to buy me out, but I told him I wasn't interested. The smallholding on its own isn't enough to give us a good living. I have three Bedford trucks as well. Once a month we deliver coal round the village and the outlying farms. The rest of the time we do general haulage work. I've formed a little co-operative between seven or eight market gardeners near here. They're all in a pretty small way. Together we can make it pay by using my trucks for transportation and selling in bulk.'

Marlowe was beginning to get interested. 'Even so, there can't be a fortune in that, Papa,' he said. 'What's O'Connor after?'

The old man hastened to explain. 'It isn't the haulage work he's interested in. It's the produce itself. You see about eighteen months ago he took over a large fruit-and-vegetable wholesalers in Barford Market. Since then he's bought out another and purchased a controlling interest in two more. Now he virtually controls prices. If you want to sell, you sell through him.'

Marlowe whistled softly. 'Very neat, and legal too. What's he got against you?'

The old man shrugged. 'He doesn't like my little co-operative. He prefers to deal with all the small men individually. That way he can get the stuff at rockbottom prices and re-sell in Birmingham and other large cities at an enormous profit.'

'Hasn't anybody tried to stand up to him?' Marlowe asked.

Magellan nodded. 'Naturally, but O'Connor is a powerful man and Barford is a very small town. He can exert influence in many ways. Besides his more subtle methods there are others. A gang of young hooligans started a fight the other day in the crowded market and a stall was wrecked in the process. Of course, O'Connor knew nothing about it, but the stallholder now toes the line.'

'What about Kennedy?' Marlowe said. 'Where does he fit in?'

The old man's face darkened. 'He worked for me for nearly six months. I never liked him, but good drivers are scarce in a place like this. One day last week he told me he was leaving. I offered him a little more money if he would stay, but he laughed in my face. Said he could double it working for O'Connor.' He sighed deeply. 'I think O'Connor is beginning to think he's God in these parts. It's difficult to know what to do.'

'I suppose it hasn't occurred to anybody to kick his bloody teeth in,' Marlowe said.

Papa Magellan smiled softly. 'Oh, yes, my friend. Even that has passed through my mind, but O'Connor's business has many ramifications these days. He has imported some peculiar individuals to work for him. Anything but country-bred.'

'Sounds interesting,' Marlowe said, 'but even that kind can be handled.' He stood up and stretched, and walked a few paces across the room. 'How are you going to fight him?'

Magellan smiled. 'I've already started. My other driver is a young fellow called Bill Johnson, who lives in the village. O'Connor offered him a good job at better money. Bill told him to go to hell. I've sent him into Barford today with a truck-load of fruit and vegetables. He's making the rounds of all the retail shops, offering to sell to them direct.'

'And you think that will work?'

Magellan shrugged. 'I don't see why not. Even O'Connor can't control everybody. He certainly can't intimidate every shopkeeper in Barford and district.'

Marlowe shook his head slowly. 'I don't know, Papa. It's a little too simple.'

The old man jumped up impatiently. 'It's got to work. He isn't God. He can't control everybody.'

'He can have a damn good try,' Marlowe said.

For a moment it seemed as if Magellan was going to explode with anger. He glared, eyes flashing, and then turned abruptly and went over to the fireplace. He stood looking down into the flames, shoulders heaving with suppressed passion, and Marlowe helped himself to another brandy.

After a while the old man spoke without turning round. 'It's a funny world. After the Spanish war when I returned home to Portugal, I found I was an embarrassment to the government. Franco was able to touch me even there. So I came to England. Now, after all these years, I find he can still touch me. Franco – O'Connor. There isn't any difference. It's the same pattern.'

'You're learning, Papa,' Marlowe said. 'It's the same problem, and the solution is always the same. You've got to fight. If he uses force, use more force. If he starts playing it dirty, then you've got to play it dirtier.'

'But that's horrible. We aren't living in a jungle.' Maria had come quietly back into the room and spoke from just inside the door.

Marlowe raised his glass to her and grinned cynically. 'It's life. You either survive or go under.'

Papa Magellan had turned to face them. For a moment he looked searchingly at Marlowe, and then he said, 'That job you're looking for. Why go to Birmingham? You can have one right here working in Kennedy's place.'

Marlowe swallowed the rest of his brandy and considered the idea.

It was just what he was looking for. A job in a quiet country town where nobody knew him. He could lie low for a few weeks, and then return to London to pick up the money when all the fuss had died down. After that, Ireland. There were ways and means if you know the right people.

The whole idea sounded very attractive, but there was the added complication of the trouble with O'Connor. If that got too messy the police would step in. Contact with the police was the last thing he wanted at the moment.

He put down his glass carefully. 'I don't know, Papa. I'd have to think it over.'

'What's the matter? Are you afraid?' Maria said bitingly.

Her father waved a hand at her impatiently. 'You could stay here, son. You could have Pedro's old room.'

For several moments there was a silence while they waited for him to answer. The old man was trembling with eagerness, but the girl seemed quiet and withdrawn. Marlowe looked at her steadily for several moments, but she gave no sign of what she hoped his decision would be. As he looked at her she blushed and frowned slightly, and he knew that she didn't like him.

He half smiled and turned back to the old man. 'Sorry, Papa. I'm all for a quiet life, and it sounds to me as if you're in for quite a party in the near future.'

Magellan's face crumpled in disappointment and his shouldlers sagged. All at once he was an old man again. A very old man. 'Sure, I understand, son,' he said. 'It's a lot to ask a man.'

Maria moved over beside him quickly and slipped a hand round his shoulders. 'Don't worry, Papa. We'll manage.' She smiled proudly at Marlowe. 'My father had no right to ask you, Mr Marlowe. This is our quarrel. We can look after ourselves.'

Marlowe forced a smile to hide the quick fury that moved inside him. He was seething with anger, and mostly it was against himself. For the first time in years he felt ashamed. 'We can look after ourselves,' she said. An old man a young girl. He wondered just how long they would last when O'Connor's tough boys moved in and really cracked down on them.

He reached for his coat and kept his face steady. Whatever happened he wasn't going to get involved. All he had to do was keep his nose clean and lie low for a couple of weeks and there was a fortune waiting for him. A man would be a fool to risk everything after five years of blood and sweat. And for what? For an old man and a girl he'd known for precisely an hour.

He buttoned his coat and said, 'Maybe I'd better be leaving after all.'

Before Magellan could reply there was the sound of a truck turning into the yard outside. It halted at the door and the engine died. 'It must be Bill,' Maria said, and there was excitement in her voice. 'I wonder if he's had any luck?'

The outside door rattled and steps dragged along the corridor. A figure appeared in the doorway and stood there, swaying slightly. He was a young man of medium size wearing a leather jacket and corduroy cap. His fleshy, good-natured face was drawn and white with pain. One of his eyes was disfigured by a livid bruise, and his mouth was badly swollen, with blood caking a nasty gash in one cheek.

'Bill!' Maria said in a horrified voice. 'What is it? What have they done to you?'

Johnson moved forward unsteadily and sank down into a chair while Papa Magellan quickly poured brandy into a glass and handed it to him. Marlowe stood in the background quietly watching.

'Who beat you up, boy?' Magellan demanded grimly. 'O'Connor's men?'

Johnson swallowed his brandy and gulped. He appeared to find difficulty in speaking. Finally he said, 'Yes, it was that big chap, Blackie Monaghan. I went round the shops like you told me, and it worked fine. I got rid of all the stuff for cash.' He pulled a bundle of banknotes out of his jacket pocket and tossed them on to the table. 'One or two people told me they weren't interested. I think someone must have tipped O'Connor off.'

He paused again and closed his eyes as if he was on the point of passing out. Marlowe had been watching him closely. A cynical grin curled the corners of his mouth. Johnson had been slapped around a little, but nothing like as badly as he was trying to make out. He was over-dramatizing the whole thing, and there had to be a reason.

'Go on, son,' Magellan said sympathetically. 'Tell us what happened then.'

'I was having a cup of tea in the transport café just this side of Barford on the Birmingham road. Monaghan came in with a couple of young toughs that hang around with him. They always turn up at the Plaza on Saturday nights after the pubs close, causing trouble. Monaghan followed me outside and picked a fight. Said I'd been messing around with his girl at the dance last Saturday night.'

'Is that true?' Magellan asked.

Johnson shook his head. 'I didn't even know what he was talking about. I tried to argue with him, but he knocked me down. One of his friends kicked me in the face, but Monaghan stopped him and said I'd had enough. He told me I'd stay out of Barford if I knew what was good for me.'

Magellan shook his head in bewilderment. 'Why this?' he said. 'I don't understand?'

Marlowe laughed shortly. 'It's the old tactics, Papa. Officially this has nothing to do with O'Connor's feud with you. It's just a coincidence that Johnson works for you.'

Maria's face was white with anger. 'We must go to the police,' she said. 'He can't get away with this.'

Marlowe shrugged. 'Why not? If Johnson went to the police what good would it do? I wouldn't touch O'Connor. Monaghan would be fined a couple of pounds for common assault and that would be that.'

'I don't want to go to the police,' Johnson interrupted, and there was alarm in his voice.

Papa Magellan frowned. 'Why not, son? You could have the satisfaction of seeing Monaghan in court, at least.'

Johnson got up. All at once he seemed capable of standing without swaying. His voice was a little shrill as he said, 'I don't want any more trouble. I don't want to get mixed up in this any further. I didn't know it was going to be like this.' His face was stained with fear, and there was a crack in his voice. 'I'm sorry, Mr Magellan. You've been pretty good to me, but I'll have to look for another job.' He stood there, twisting the cap between his hands. 'I won't be in tomorrow.'

There was a moment of shocked silence, and Maria turned away, stifling a sob. Magellan reached out blindly for support, his whole body sagging so that he looked on the point of collapse.

Marlowe found himself reaching for the old man, supporting him with his strong arms, easing him down into a chair. 'Don't worry, Papa,' he said. 'It's going to be all right. Everything's going to be fine.'

He straightened up and looked at Johnson. Shame was beginning to replace the look of fear on the other's face, and then that terrible, uncontrollable anger that he was powerless to control, lifted inside Marlowe. He surged forward and grabbed Johnson by the throat and shook him like a rat. 'You dirty, yellow little swine,' he raged. 'I'll give you something you really will remember.'

He flung Johnson out into the hall with all his force. The man lost his balance and fell to the floor. As Marlowe advanced towards him he scrambled to his feet gibbering with fear, and then Maria grabbed at Marlowe's hair, wrenching back his head. She slapped him across the face and screamed, 'Stop it! Hasn't there been enough of this for one day?'

As Marlowe raised an arm to brush her away, Papa Magellan ducked through the door, suddenly active, and clutching Johnson by the shoulder pushed him towards the outside door. 'Go on, get out of here for God's sake!' he said. Johnson threw one terrified look over his shoulder and scrambled through the door and out into the fog.

There was quiet except for Marlowe's heavy breathing. Maria was not crying this time. Her face was flushed and her eyes were flashing. 'What is wrong with you?' she demanded fiercely. 'Do you want to hang some day? Can't you control yourself? Is your answer to everything violence?'

Marlowe stirred and looked down at her. He swallowed hard and said, 'When I was a kid my father wanted me to be a doctor. He was a wages clerk, so I had to be a doctor. I didn't want to be one, but that didn't make any difference. He beat me all the way through school until one day, when I was seventeen, I discovered I was stronger than he was. I slammed him on the jaw and left home.'

He fumbled for a cigarette with shaking hands and continued. 'There was a Chinese officer in charge of the prisoners at that coal mine they sent me to in Manchuria. Li, they called him. A little name for a little man. He had a complex about his size, so he didn't like me because I was big. I used to work in a low level, up to my knees in freezing water, for twelve hours a day. Sometimes if he didn't think I'd worked hard enough, he used to leave me in there all night when the others were brought up. I still get dreams about that. He used to turn up in the middle of the night and call down the shaft to me, his voice echoing along the passage. Other times he'd have me strung up and he'd beat me with a pick handle.'

Maria was crying softly, her head shaking from side to side. 'No more. Please, no more.'

Marlowe ignored her and went on. 'And what have I learned from all this? I'll tell you. It's quite simple really.' He raised a clenched fist. 'This! This is what counts. The boot and the fist. I've been shoved around by someone or other all my life. My father, Captain Li, O'Connor, or Monaghan. They're all the same breed, and they can only be handled in one way.'

She turned away blindly, and Magellan moved forward and put a hand on Marlowe's arm. There was a great pity in his face. 'I know what it's like to have a devil on your shoulder, but he's the one you've got to fight. Not the rest of the world.'

Marlowe nodded wearily. 'I think I'll have that bath now, Papa. I could do with it.'

He moved forward and paused, one foot on the bottom stair. 'Another thing, Papa. That job you were talking about. If it's still open I'll take it. O'Connor is beginning to annoy me. He reminds me of someone I once knew.'

The old man smiled, his whole face coming alive, and he nodded. 'That's fine, son. You go and have that bath and we'll talk about it afterwards.'

Marlowe turned and started to climb the stairs. His whole body was full of an inexpressible weariness. Already he was beginning to regret his decision, but he was committed to it. Whatever happened now he would not go back on his given word. He felt as if some strong force had him in its grip and was bearing him swiftly along to an unknown destination.

He shrugged and a half-smile came to his mouth. What the hell. He wasn't scared of O'Connor or Monaghan or any of them. His smile changed into a wide grin as he went into the bathroom. He felt almost sorry for O'Connor. He was certainly in for a hell of a surprise.

4

The morning was cold with no rain, and a trace of mist hung over the fields behind the house as Marlowe crossed the yard towards the old barn. He could hear voices inside, and he paused for a moment on the threshold to light a cigarette before going in.

Cold, clammy air enveloped him like a shroud, and he shivered. The place was brightly illuminated by several bulbs strung from an electric cable, and Maria Magellan and an old man were busy loading boxes and sacks on to a Bedford three-ton truck which stood in the centre of the barn. Two more were parked in the shadows down at the far end.

As he moved forward the girl turned quickly. 'Good morning.' she said.

'It's like an ice-box in here,' Marlowe told her.

She shrugged. 'The walls are three feet thick. Just what we need to store fruit.' She moved towards a table that stood against the wall and lifted a metal pot from a small electric stove. 'Coffee?'

He nodded briefly. 'Where's your father this morning?'

'In bed.' She made a tiny grimace. 'Rheumatism, and he isn't very pleased about it. He gets an attack now and then when the weather turns damp. I'll probably have to lock his door to keep him inside.'

He drank some of the scalding black coffee and grunted with pleasure as its warmth moved through him. He nodded towards the truck and the old man, still busy loading boxes. 'You keep early hours.'

'You have to in this game if you want to make a living,' she said.

'You should have awakened me and I'd have given you a hand,' he told her.

'Oh, don't worry,' she said. 'I shall do another morning. Just breaking you in gently.'

The old man approached, his gnarled hand busy with a pipe and tobacco pouch. He was wearing a greasy corduroy cap and an ancient patched suit. He looked seventy at least. 'That's the lot, Miss Maria,' he said in a cracked voice. 'I'll go over to the greenhouse now.'

Maria smiled warmly. 'All right, Dobie. Breakfast at nine.' He turned to go and she added quickly. 'Oh, Dobie, this is Hugh Marlowe. He's going to drive for us.'

The old man looked at Marlowe with vacant, watery eyes and nodded. Then he turned away, lighting his pipe as he went, and disappeared into the grey morning.

'Is he much use?' Marlowe asked. 'He looked pretty old to be still doing a day's work.'

Maria poured herself a cup of coffee and shrugged. 'If he stopped working he'd die. He's that kind of man. Anyway, he knows more about market gardening than any man I know. We wouldn't be without him.'

Marlowe helped himself to more coffee. 'He's still too old to be humping sacks of potatoes on to trucks. Another morning wake me.'

Her eyes flashed angrily. 'Don't worry, Mr Marlowe. I'll see you earn your money.'

He grinned and lit another cigarette. 'I'll earn it all right.'

He moved towards the truck and lifted the tailboard into place. 'What do I do with this lot?'

'One of two things,' she told him. 'Either sell the stuff at the market or go round the shops like Bill Johnson did yesterday.'

'Is there any point in going to the market?' he said. 'I thought O'Connor had everything sewed up there.'

She nodded. 'Just about, but there's one independent wholesaler left. Old Sam Granby. He's been ill for a long time and his nephew Tom has been in charge. Tom's mixed up with O'Connor, but the old man isn't. We heard yesterday that he might be back today. It's worth a try.'

Marlowe nodded. 'I'd better get cracking then.'

She frowned and took a slip of paper from her pocket. 'I nearly forgot this,' she said. Marlowe examined the paper. It was a list of various kinds of fruits and vegetables with prices marked beside them. 'You mustn't go below those prices,' she explained, 'otherwise we shan't make a profit.'

Marlowe grinned. 'That wouldn't do at all,' he said. 'Don't worry. I'll get the price you want.'

She took an old fur-lined jeep coat from a cupboard and threw it across to him. 'You'd better put it on,' she said. 'It can get pretty cold in the cab of that truck.'

He pulled on the coat and climbed up behind the wheel. As he slammed the door she moved a little nearer and added, 'Don't forget, Marlowe. Stay out of trouble.'

He pulled the starter and the engine roared into life.

He grinned mockingly at her. 'Don't worry about me, angel. I hate trouble.'

Disbelief showed clearly on her face, and he released the handbrake and drove out into the yard before she could reply.

The journey into Barford took just under half an hour. For most of the way he drove with the side window down, the cool morning breeze fanning his cheek. He felt no particular anxiety about what might happen when he reached the market even though it was probable that Kennedy had already reported the happenings of the previous day to O'Connor.

The streets of Barford were quiet and deserted, but when he drove into the large cobbled square in the centre of the town he found thirty or forty trucks and vans parked. The place was a hive of activity and noise, with men passing rapidly between the vehicles pushing large handcarts loaded with produce.

Half-way along the south side of the square on the corner of a narrow street a large warehouse lifted into the sky. A yellow painted board stretched high across the face of the building carrying the legend: 'Inter-Allied Trading Corporation'. A few yards farther along on the same side of the square a faded wooden board indicated the premises of Sam Granby.

Marlowe parked the truck not far from O'Connor's place and threaded his way through the busy crowd of porters. There was a small loading ramp outside Sam Granby's warehouse, and as he walked towards it he saw Kennedy leaning against the large double door that led into the interior of the building, smoking a cigarette.

Kennedy's face was badly marked and his lips were bruised and swollen to several times their normal size. As Marlowe mounted the steps that led up on to the loading ramp Kennedy recognized him. For a moment he stared at Marlowe in astonishment and then an expression of fear came into his eyes. He turned and darted into the interior of the building. Marlowe paused long enough to light a cigarette and then followed him in.

Inside the warehouse several men worked busily packing apples into wooden boxes. There was a glassfronted office at the top of a flight of old-fashioned iron stairs in one corner and Kennedy was clearly visible as he talked excitedly to someone who was sitting down.

Marlowe mounted the stairs and opened the door of the office. There were two other men present besides Kennedy. The one who sat behind the desk was young and dark haired with sharp, crafty eyes. The other reclined in an old easy chair, the springs of which sagged dangerously. He was the fattest man Marlowe had ever seen with a great, fleshy face that carried an expression of perpetual good humour and candid blue eyes that sparkled merrily.

Kennedy turned quickly, an expression of alarm on his face and Marlowe smiled contemptuously. 'For Christ's sake, Kennedy, try not to look as though you're going to wet yourself each time you see me.'

An expression of rage appeared on Kennedy's face and he pushed past Marlowe, jerked open the door and disappeared down the stairs. The fat man chuckled explosively, his great frame shaking with mirth. 'Poor Kennedy,' he said in a peculiarly light voice. 'He can't take a joke. Never could.'

Marlowe ignored him and spoke to the man behind the desk. 'Where can I find Sam Granby?'

The young man sat back, a wary expression in his eyes. 'Across the square at the undertaker's,' he said. 'He died last night.' He showed his teeth in a mirthless grin. 'I'm his nephew – Tom Granby. I'm the owner now.'

Marlowe nodded slowly. So much for Maria Magellan's hopes. 'I've got a load of stuff outside,' he said. 'Are you interested?'

Granby picked up a pencil and examined it thoughtfully. 'That depends. Who are you from?'

Marlowe tried to control his rising anger. 'You know damned well who I'm from, sonny,' he said. 'Let's stop fooling around.'

The fat man exploded into laughter again. 'That's good,' he wheezed. 'That's really very funny.'

Marlowe said coldly over his shoulder, 'Who asked you to stick your nose in?'

The face still smiled but there was a different expression in the eyes. Another chuckle shook the huge frame. 'That's even funnier. You'd better tell him, Tom.'

Granby cleared his throat and said, with obvious pleasure. 'This is my new partner – Mr O'Connor.'

Marlowe turned towards the fat man and looked him over contemptuously. 'So you're the great O'Connor?' he said at last.

O'Connor wiped his eyes with a large white handkerchief. 'And you're the bloke that knocked hell out of Kennedy yesterday.' His eyes flicked over Marlowe's massive frame and he nodded. 'I'd like to have seen that. You're a big man, son. A very big man.'

'But not so big that he can't be cut down to size,' Granby said viciously.

Marlowe turned, his left hand darting out. He grabbed Tom Granby by the shirt front and half dragged him across the desk. For a moment he looked coldly into the frightened eyes. 'The next time you cross me I'll stamp you into the ground, you worm,' he said. He released his grip and Granby fell back into his chair.

O'Connor shook his head and clicked his tongue. 'Very silly, Tom. You really asked for that.' He switched his glance back to Marlowe. 'Old man Magellan's washed up. A week from now he won't be able to pay you wages.'

Marlowe didn't even bother to reply. He turned and walked towards the door. O'Connor moved surprisingly fast for a man of his bulk. He caught him by the arm and said, 'Let's be reasonable, son. I can always use a good man.'

Marlowe looked down at the podgy hand on his sleeve and said coldly, 'Take your paw off me.' O'Connor's hand dropped as if it had been stung and Marlowe looked straight into his face. 'I wouldn't cut you down if you were hanging, you fat pig.'

The tiny blue eyes filled with malevolence. For a moment they looked steadily at each other and then O'Connor smiled. 'All right, son,' he said. 'Have it your own way.'

As Marlowe opened the door he half turned. 'One more thing, O'Connor. Try to crowd me and you'll curse the day you were born. I promise you.' He closed the door quietly and descended the stairs.

Once outside he stood on the ramp for a moment, lighting a cigarette and considered the problem. Obviously he would have to do the round of the retail shops that Bill Johnson had done the previous day. Somehow he didn't think O'Connor would leave that loophole open for long, if he hadn't already closed it.

He walked slowly back towards the truck. As he passed the loading bay at the front of O'Connor's warehouse he noticed Kennedy standing in a doorway talking to a young girl. She wore tight denim jeans and a hip-length leather driving jacket. Her face was round and soft like a young child's and framed in hair that was almost pure white, like soft flax glinting palely in the morning sun.

Kennedy said something to her and she looked up quickly towards Marlowe. He gazed steadily at her for several seconds and then continued across the front of the building towards the truck. He looked back once and she was still staring after him.

A little way along the narrow street that ran down one side of O'Connor's warehouse, Marlowe noticed a café sign and market men passing in and out. He was suddenly aware that he was hungry and he turned into the street and walked towards the café.

There was a narrow alley at the rear of O'Connor's warehouse and as he drew abreast of it he saw a crowd standing on the corner and heard voices raised in anger. He crossed the street quickly and shouldered his way through the crowd.

There was another loading bay at the rear of the building and four men stood arguing furiously on its edge. One of them was a negro and on the ground at his feet stood a battered, fibre suitcase tied with string. The man who was doing most of the shouting was well over six feet tall with a chest like a barrel and a mane of black curly hair. He was swearing vilely with a pronounced Irish accent and he held up a clenched fist menacingly. 'We don't like spades round here,' he said. 'They make the place smell bad. Get back to bloody Jamaica where you came from.' He lifted his boot back and kicked the man's suitcase several feet through the air until it crashed against the far wall.

The Jamaican took a step forward and his fists clenched. For a moment Marlowe hoped he was going to strike the Irishman and then his chin dropped and he relaxed. He turned to step down from the ramp and one of the other men stuck out a foot and tripped him so that he fell heavily to the ground.

The big Irishman jumped down beside him, a huge grin on his face. 'That's where you belong, nigger. In the muck,' he said.

The Jamaican was on his feet like a cat. He moved forward in one beautiful fluid motion and slammed his fist hard against the Irishman's jaw. He went down as if he had been poleaxed.

He scrambled to his feet with a roar of rage and at the same moment his two friends jumped down from the loading bay and grabbed the negro's arms from behind. 'Go on, Blacky,' one of them cried. 'Knock hell out of him.'

The Irishman stood back for a moment, wiping blood from his mouth, and then he moved forward, a smile of pleasure on his face. Marlowe turned and said to the crowd contemptuously, 'What kind of men are you? Isn't anyone going to give the bloke a hand?'

An old man in battered corduroy cap and greasy raincoat turned to him. 'You must be new around here. It doesn't pay to interfere with Blacky Monaghan.'

There was a street cleaner's cart standing nearby with a brush and spade inside it. Marlowe picked up the spade and moved down the alley towards the four men.

As he approached, Monaghan turned towards him, surprise on his face. 'What the hell do you want?' he demanded truculently.

Marlowe ignored him. He hefted the spade in his right hand and spoke to the two men who were holding the Jamaican. They were looking at the spade, complete unbelief on their faces, and he said calmly, 'If you two don't get to hell out of here I'll break your arms.'

He swung the spade once through the air. The two thugs jumped back, horror on their faces. They released the Jamaican and scrambled up on to the loading bay.

The negro smiled, showing even white teeth.' 'Thank's a lot, friend,' he said in a soft, Jamaican voice. 'I'll remember that.'

Monaghan stood with his back against the wall, mouthing obscenities. 'I'll catch you without that spade, bucko, one of these dark nights,' he snarled. 'It'll be my turn then.'

Marlowe ignored him. He stood back against the loading bay, still gripping the spade, and smiled at the negro. 'It's your turn now, pal.'

A grin of unholy joy crossed the Jamaican's face and he moved towards Monaghan. The Irishman spat and doubled his fists and a quiet voice said, 'Now then, what are you trying to do? Turn Barford into a frontier town?'

Marlowe turned his head quickly. The crowd at the end of the alley had melted away and a quiet, middle-aged man was approaching them. He wore a brown gaberdine raincoat and an old blue felt hat. A greying, tobacco-stained moustache added the finishing touch to a sad, Spaniel face.

The Jamaican moved quickly to Marlowe's shoulder and whispered, 'Watch yourself. This one's a copper.'

Very carefully Marlowe slipped his right hand behind him and propped the spade up against the wall. He wasn't quite quick enough. The moustache twitched and a humorous expression appeared in the eyes. 'What are you going to do with that, son?' the policeman demanded. 'Plant your rose trees?'

Marlowe grinned amiably. 'How did you guess?'

The moustache twitched again and the policeman turned to Monaghan and said calmly, 'Get out of it you, before I run you in.'

Blackie glared and his mouth half opened as if he was about to speak and then he scrambled up on to the loading bay and disappeared into the warehouse.

The policeman turned to the Jamaican and said, 'Now then, Mac, what started it?'

The Jamaican shrugged. 'Oh, the usual thing, Mr Alpin. They just don't like having me around. I guess.'

Alpin nodded soberly and turned his eye speculatively on Marlowe. 'What's you name, son? Where do you fit into this?'

Marlowe shrugged. 'There were three of them working him over. I just stepped in to see fair play. I drive a truck for Mr Magellan, of Litton. Marlowe's my name.'

Alpin nodded towards the spade. 'You certainly believe in shock tactics, don't you.' He shook his head. 'That's the way to end up in the dock on a capital charge.'

The Jamaican picked up his suitcase and they all walked towards the end of the alley. Alpin said, 'What are you going to do now, Mac?'

The negro shook his head. 'I don't know, Mr Alpin. Maybe I'll try London again. It's hard enough for a white man to get a job in a rural area.'

Alpin nodded. 'Well, I hope you make out all right.' He produced a patent inhaler, inserted it in one nostril and sniffed deeply. 'That's better,' he observed. 'Damned hay fever again.' He blew his nose loudly into a khaki handkerchief and said, 'Well, I've got to be off. If I can do anything for you, Mac, don't hesitate to get in touch.' He nodded to Marlowe. 'Give my regards to Papa Magellan and tell him I was asking after him.' He started to move away and then he paused and added, 'And you keep out of Blacky Monaghan's way, especially on dark nights, and keep away from spades.' He turned without waiting for a reply and walked down towards the square, his raincoat flapping about his legs in the slight breeze.

The Jamaican said quietly, 'He's a good man. It's a pity there aren't more like him.' He sighed deeply and then turned with a smile and held out his hand. 'I haven't thanked you yet, friend. My name's Mackenzie – Henry Mackenzie. Most people just call me Mac.'

Marlowe grasped the proferred hand. 'Hugh Marlowe,' he said. He nodded towards the café. 'I was just going in for a coffee. How about joining me?'

Mac nodded and picked up his suitcase and they crossed the road and entered the café. The place was crowded, but they managed to find a small table by the window and Marlowe brought two coffees from the counter. He offered the Jamaican a cigarette. 'That was one hell of a smack on the jaw you gave Monaghan. You looked as if you knew how to use yourself.'

Mac grinned. 'I should do. I came over here as a professional boxer.'

'Do any good?' Marlowe asked.

The Jamaican shrugged. 'I was going great there for a year or two until the night I got in a clinch on the ropes with a guy and fell through. I fractured my foot.' He sighed. 'They managed to fix it, but when I started training again I found I was only good for one fast round before the pain started.'

'That's pretty rough luck,' Marlowe said.

The Jamaican grinned and sat back in his chair. 'Don't think I'm crying in my beer, man. Life's just a big wheel going round. Now I'm down, next time I go up.' He spread his hands. 'It's the law of nature.'

Marlowe grinned and nodded. 'Maybe you've got something there,' he said. 'What were you doing for O'Connor?'

Mac shrugged. 'Anything that came to hand, packing fruit, making up loads. He took me on as a truck driver.'

'What did you think of him?' Marlowe said.

The smile faded from the Jamaican's face. 'I didn't like him. They're a bad lot over there. If it hadn't been for Miss Jenny I'd have left long ago. She was the only one that treated me decent.'

'And who's Miss Jenny?' Marlowe asked him.

'O'Connor's niece,' Mac said. 'She's like a flower on a dung heap over there.' He laughed shortly and added, 'One good thing. There isn't a man in that crowd who'd dare to lay a finger on her. O'Connor would sure have his scalp.' He glanced across at a clock on the wall. 'I guess I'd better be moving. There's a train for London in twenty minutes.'

Marlowe reached across and pulled him back down into his seat. 'Why go to London?' he said. 'I can get you a job right here.'

Mac frowned. 'You mean that, friend? What kind of a job?'

Marlowe pushed his cigarettes across. 'Truck driving, but I warn you. It might get a little rough. I work for a man called Magellan, in Litton. O'Connor is trying to put him out of business.'

'O'Connor's put quite a few people out of business. How are you going to stop him doing the same thing to you?'

Marlowe held up a clenched fist. 'There are ways,' he said. 'There are ways.'

A slow smile appeared on the Jamaican's face. He held out his hand. 'Mr Marlowe, it'll be a pleasure working with you.'

'Right,' Marlowe said in satisfaction. 'Let's get out of here.'

They left the café and went down the street and back into the square. Men were still working busily on every side and when they reached the truck Marlowe said, 'Climb in. You do the driving. We'll go back to Litton and I'll introduce you to Papa Magellan.'

Suddenly he was aware of a hand on his arm. He turned and looked down into the blue eyes of the girl with the flaxen hair. They looked at each other without speaking for a brief moment and he was conscious of a sudden dryness in his throat and a crawling sensation in the pit of his stomach. 'Mr Marlowe?' she said.

He nodded and cleared his throat. 'That's me. What can I do for you?'

'I'm Jenny O'Connor,' she said, 'Mr O'Connor's niece.'

Mac leaned out of the cab and said, 'Hallo, Miss Jenny.'

She glanced up and there was pain on her face. 'I heard what happened. I'm really sorry, Mac. What are you going to do?'

He smiled. 'I'll make out, Miss Jenny. I'm going to work for Mr Magellan, at Litton.'

Her eyes clouded over and she turned to Marlowe and there was urgency in her voice, 'But that makes it even worse. Please, Mr Marlowe, you must go away. Believe me, I know my uncle. He can't bear to be crossed. He'll stop at nothing to put Mr Magellan out of business. Any outsider who gets involved will only end up by getting hurt.'

Marlowe shook his head. 'No man can play God for ever and expect to get away with it, Miss O'Connor.'

'But he'll break you,' she said desperately. 'I've seen him do it to other people.'

'I don't break easily,' Marlowe told her. For a moment it seemed as if she would speak again and then her shoulders drooped and she turned away. 'Thanks for the warning, anyway,' Marlowe said.

He stood watching her as she walked back to the warehouse and went inside. He climbed up into the cab beside Mac and said, 'Well, now we know where we stand. Let's go, boy.'

As they moved away. Marlowe turned his head and looked back towards the warehouse in time to see Kennedy, Monaghan and O'Connor emerge from the interior and stand on the ramp gazing after them. For a brief moment he had them in view and then Mac turned the truck into the main road and they roared out of the town, back towards Litton.

5

Marlowe was sitting on the end of Papa Magellan's bed. It was just after nine o'clock and the old man was finishing a hearty breakfast that Maria had brought to him on a tray. A light drift of rain pattered against the window and Magellan cursed and said, 'More rain, more rheumatism. It's a vicious circle and the whole damned winter still to come.'

Marlowe grinned sympathetically. 'Never mind, Papa,' he said. 'A couple of days in bed will do you a power of good.'

Magellan snorted. 'Nothing doing. That's what Maria thinks I need, but there's work to do and I'm the only one who can do it. This afternoon I've got to go round the market gardeners picking up produce and seeing how the land lies. Who knows what O'Connor is getting up to while I'm lying here in idleness.'

The door opened and Maria came in with a coffee pot and some cups on a tray. She filled two cups, gave one to her father and the other to Marlowe. 'How's Mac managing?' he asked her.

'Oh, fine,' she said. 'He helped me to put a spare bed in your room and I've left him unpacking.'

'What do you think of him?' Marlowe said.

'He's a good boy,' Papa Magellan cut in. 'I can always tell. He's got a good heart, that one.'

Maria nodded. 'I agree with papa. He's a fine man. I trust him. I felt it the moment I looked at him. He's not the kind who would ever let you down.'

For a moment a feeling that was suspiciously like jealousy moved in Marlowe. He gave her a twisted grin and said, 'Not like me at all.'

An expression of pain appeared on her face. 'Please, I didn't mean it to sound like that.'

He held up a hand. 'It doesn't matter. It doesn't matter at all.' When he turned to Papa Magellan he saw to his surprise, that the old man had a sly smile on his face. 'I'll take that load round the shops now, Papa,' Marlowe told him. 'Put Mac on the coal delivery run. As soon as I get back, I'll give him a hand.'

'Maybe I should get up and go round with the boy myself,' Papa Magellan said. 'He may find it a little strange at first.'

'You'll do nothing of the kind,' Maria said firmly. 'You can stay in bed and do as you're told for a change.'

'But Maria, there's work to be done,' the old man protested.

Marlowe shook his head and grinned. 'I'll leave you two to argue it out.' He grinned at the old man. 'Might as well give in, Papa. She can be pretty determined when she wants to be.' He closed the door quickly as the argument flared up again and went along to his bedroom.

Mac was unpacking his case and he looked up and smiled as Marlowe entered the room. 'Man, it was my lucky day today.'

Marlowe grinned. 'I thought you'd fit in here all right.' He lit a cigarette and went on, 'I'm going out with that load of stuff again. I'll try the retail shops and see what I can get rid of, but I don't feel too happy about it. O'Connor must know what's going on by now.'

Mac frowned and shook his head. 'He didn't exactly take me into his confidence. I hadn't even heard of Mr Magellan until I met you this morning.'

Marlowe nodded slowly. 'You're going to do the coal delivery run for the rest of the day. It shouldn't be too difficult. I'll be back by lunchtime and you can let me know how you're making out.'

Mac smiled and half saluted. 'Okay, boss,' he said. Marlowe grinned and left him to finish his unpacking.

As he drove back towards Barford it disturbed him to realize that in some inexorable way he seemed to be taking control of everything. He was beginning to get involved and he hadn't intended that to happen at all. For a little while he considered the point and then he pushed it firmly out of his mind and concentrated on the job in hand.

Maria had given him a list of the shops Bill Johnson had done business with on the previous day. The first one was on a new housing estate on the very edge of Barford and Marlowe made straight for it.

The shop was a greengrocer's a fine, red-brick, double-fronted building on the end of a large parade. When he went inside the place was deserted. He stood at the counter as the jangling of the door bell faded away and waited. After a moment or two, a man emerged from a rear door wiping his mouth with a napkin. He smiled cheerfully. 'Sorry to keep you. We have a late breakfast, you know. We're just finishing.'

Marlowe nodded. 'That's all right,' he said. 'I'm from Magellan's, of Litton. Our other man was round here yesterday. I thought you might be interested in some more stuff today.'

The grocer looked puzzled. 'I don't understand,' he said, 'your man's been round already this morning.'

Marlowe answered him automatically. 'I must have got the lists mixed up. He's working one part of the town and I'm supposed to be covering the other. We've probably got you down twice.'

The grocer smiled and said amiably, 'Never mind, young man. At the prices you're quoting this morning you won't have any difficulty in selling everything you've got.'

Marlowe forced a smile to his lips. 'I hope so. We need big sales to make it profitable.' He moved towards the door. 'Anyway, thanks a lot. I'll sort the mistake out with my friend when I see him.'

He got back into the cab of the truck and sat with his hands resting lightly on the wheel and stared out through the windscreen. He was seething with rage. When he looked down he saw that his hands were trembling and he gripped the wheel and swore violently. As the black, killing rage swept through him he hung on to the wheel and closed his eyes.

After a few minutes he felt a little better. He lit a cigarette and leaned back in the seat to consider the position. So Bill Johnson had played Judas? O'Connor must have discovered what was going on during the previous day. That was the real reason why Blacky Monaghan and his thugs had waylaid Johnson at the roadside café. They must have slapped him around a little until he had agreed to play things their way.

Marlowe leaned forward and pulled the starter. As the engine coughed into life he reflected that it wouldn't have taken a great deal of persuasion to make a rat like Johnson agree to do as he was told. All men had their price. That was the first great lesson and it was the knowing of it that made men like O'Connor so successful. The one thing that rankled above everything else was the fact that all this had been planned. O'Connor must have been laughing up his sleeve during their meeting in Tom Granby's office.

After making another half-dozen calls he turned the truck back towards Litton. Everywhere he went it was the same story. Johnson had already called and his prices were heavily reduced. For the moment O'Connor had beaten them.

As he passed the roadside café on the outskirts of Barford he glanced idly across to the car park and saw Bill Johnson come out and walk towards a truck painted in a familiar yellow. Marlowe pulled into the side of the road and jumped down to the ground.

Johnson was reaching up to open the door of his cab when Marlowe grabbed him by the shoulder and spun him round. Abject fear showed on his face and he opened his mouth to scream. Marlowe hit him with all his force in the pit of the stomach. 'You rat,' he said bitterly. 'You dirty little rat.'

Johnson doubled over and sank to the ground. Marlowe lifted his foot back to deliver a final blow when there was a shout from behind him. He swung round and saw Monaghan and his two friends emerging from the café.

For a moment he wanted to stay and then discretion moved him to turn and run back across the road to his truck. As the engine drowned the cries of rage in the background, he reflected grimly that there would be other times. As he moved into top gear a grin of satisfaction appeared on his face. One thing was certain. Bill Johnson wouldn't forget him in a hurry.

As he pulled up outside the farmhouse door Papa Magellan appeared and stood on the top step waiting for him. Marlowe jumped down from the cab and as he approached, shook his head. 'No good, Papa,' he said. 'O'Connor hasn't wasted any time.'

The old man nodded and said heavily, 'You'd better come inside and tell me all about it.'

As they went into the living-room Maria appeared from the kitchen, wiping her hands on an apron. There was hope on her face and it died rapidly as she looked at her father. 'What is it, Papa?' she asked. 'What happened.'

The old man waved her to silence. 'Go on, son,' he told Marlowe.

Marlowe told them everything that had occurred. When he had finished Maria exploded with rage. 'Wait till I see Bill Johnson again,' she cried. 'I'll give him something to remember me by.'

Papa Magellan looked puzzled and there was pain on his face. 'Bill Johnson was a good boy,' he said. 'I don't understand. What can have happened to him?'

Marlowe shook his head impatiently. He held up his hand and rubbed his thumb across his index finger 'Money, Papa. The only thing that really counts. With it, you're somebody. Without it, you're just nothing.'

'No!' Maria cried. 'I won't accept that. It isn't true.'

'For God's sake grow up,' Marlowe told her. 'Money means power. With it you can do anything. Money and fear. They have the greatest effect on men. Bill Johnson was weak and he was afraid. They threatened him and they offered him money. Of course he accepted.'

The old man sighed deeply and there was an air of hopelessness about him. 'What do we do now?' he asked. 'If we can't find a market we're finished.'

'You won't find one round here,' Marlowe told him forcibly. 'O'Connor only has to undercut your prices and he can afford to do that until you're broke.'

The old man managed a wry smile. 'And that won't take long, boy.'

There was a silence for a space before Maria said slowly, 'What about Birmingham? Why can't we take the stuff there?'

Marlowe shook his head, 'O'Connor has too many contacts. He could follow every move we made, undercut us at every turn.'

The old man nodded emphatically. 'Hugh is right, Maria. Birmingham is no good.'

Marlowe frowned as an idea suddenly came to him. 'What about London?' he said. 'Covent Garden. O'Connor is strictly a provincial. He can't throw much weight around there.'

Papa Magellan shook his head, 'It's too far.' Marlowe started to protest and the old man held up a hand. 'No, listen to me, son. Most of our produce is perishable. We're dealing in soft fruit a lot at the moment. It's got to be delivered first thing in the morning, so they can get it out to the shops fresh and in good condition.'

'Where's the problem?' Marlowe demanded. 'We drive to London through the night. It fits in beautifully. O'Connor won't even know what we're up to.'

Maria looked dubious. 'I don't know, Hugh, it's a long drive. Probably two hundred miles. You'd be taking on quite a job.'

Marlowe shrugged. 'What's two hundred miles. The roads will be empty. It'll be as easy as falling off a log.'

He looked from Maria to her father. The old man still looked uncertain and Marlowe said impatiently, 'For God's sake, Papa, this is your only chance. At least give it a try.'

The old man slapped a hand against his knee and stood up. 'By God, you're right,' he cried, eyes flashing. 'At least we'll go down fighting.' He took his jacket down from behind the door and pulled it on. 'We'll give that pig a run for his money yet.'

'Now where do you think you're going, Papa?' Maria demanded.

He held up his hand and his voice was stern. 'Maria, don't try to interfere. I'm going out in the other truck. I've got to make the rounds of the market gardeners to let them know we have things under control.

Another thing, we need more produce. If Hugh is going to drive all the way to London we must make it worth while.'

'But your meal is nearly ready, Papa,' she told him. 'You can't go now.'

'So I have the meal when I come back,' he replied. 'Is that such a hardship when our livelihood is at stake?'

He walked out of the room and the front door closed with a bang. Marlowe laughed. 'The old boy's still got plenty of starch left in him,' he observed.

Maria nodded. 'Papa can be pretty determined when he gets set on a thing. He's twice the man O'Connor will ever be.'

There was an awkward silence for a few moments and Maria played nervously with her apron. Rain had started to fall again and tapped on the window with ghostly fingers. She laughed self-consciously. 'It's rather a sad sound, isn't it?'

Marlowe remembered the many times he had lain on the cot in his cell listening to that same sound and longing to be free. 'It's just about the saddest sound in the world,' he said, with feeling.

For a brief moment they were very close. It was as if each had discovered in the other something they had not realized existed. A warm smile blossomed on Maria's face and she said, 'Come into the kitchen and I'll make you a cup of tea. You've had a hard morning.'

He followed her along the corridor and into the large, old-fashioned farm kitchen, warm with the smell of cooking. He sat on the edge of the table, swinging a leg and smoking a cigarette and felt at peace in a way that he hadn't experienced for a long time.

He watched her as she moved about the room, preparing the tea. Her limbs were softly rounded and as she bent down to pick up a cloth, her dress tightened showing the sweeping curve of her thigh and accentuating her large hips. Real child-bearing hips, he mused to himself.

His thoughts drifted idly to Jenny O'Connor with her boyish slimness and he tried to compare the two women. He decided it was impossible. Jenny had a tremendous surface attractiveness, something completely animal that gripped a man by the bowels like a fever, lighting a fire that could only be extinguished by full and complete possession.

With Maria he knew it would be something very different. A sensuality that smouldered deep inside, ready to burst into a flame which could never be extinguished. She was a woman who would demand much, but who would give greatly in return.

She turned from the stove and handed him his tea. Her smile was like a lamp switching on inside her, illuminating her whole face. 'I think I owe you an apology, Hugh,' she said.

It was the second time within half an hour that she had used his Christian name. He frowned slightly. 'What are you talking about?'

She coloured and nervously played with her hands. 'I've been pretty unpleasant. You see, somehow I got the impression that you weren't really interested in our problems. I thought you were just using us because you needed a job.'

'And what makes you think I'm not?' he demanded.

That wonderful deep smile turned on again. 'Now, I know you're doing everything you can to help Papa. You've proved it.'

Marlowe sipped his tea and schooled his face to steadiness. Why did she have to put her own interpretation on everything he did? Couldn't she see that everything he had done so far had been done because he didn't like being pushed around? He was bitterly angry and he stood up and walked quickly to the window. He had to clench his teeth to keep himself from making an angry reply and yet, in his heart, he knew that it wasn't Maria he was annoyed with. It was himself. In some queer way he was sorry that he was not the kind of man that she believed him to be.

She moved beside him and placed a hand on his arm. 'What is it, Hugh?' she said. 'What's the matter?'

Her faint, womanly odour filled his nostrils and he was acutely aware of her physically. He turned abruptly, his hands reaching out and grasping her arms, and an answering flame flared in her eyes. At that moment the front door opened and Mac shouted, 'Hugh, are you in, boy? We got trouble.'

Marlowe released her and turned to the door as the Jamaican entered. There was excitement on his face and he pushed his cap back and brushed sweat from his brow. 'Man, am I glad you're here.'

'What's happened?' Marlowe demanded. 'Don't tell me O'Connor's started up in the coal business?'

Mac nodded. 'That's it, boy. That guy Kennedy who used to work here. He's delivering coal in the village. I've made several calls on farms and they've all told me the same story. Kennedy called today and told them Papa Magellan had given up the coal delivery side and that he'd taken over.'

'But he can't do that,' Maria cried. Her eyes filled with tears and she sank down into a chair. 'It isn't fair, Hugh. It isn't fair. This will be the finish of Papa.'

Marlowe gave her shoulder a hurried squeeze. 'Don't worry, angel,' he told her. 'I'll fix that rat Kennedy once and for all. He won't show his face round here again in a hurry when I get through with him.'

She raised her head at once, an expression of fear on her face. 'No, Hugh, please. No trouble. I'm scared what might happen.' He smiled once reassuringly and hurried out of the house, Mac at his heels.

It was raining quite heavily as they drove down into the village. They cruised through several streets without any luck and after ten minutes Marlowe was cursing steadily. 'Where the hell is he?' he demanded.

Mac shrugged. 'We can't be sure, Hugh. He may be calling on some of the outlying farms.'

At that moment a yellow truck turned out of a side street and passed them going in the opposite direction. Marlowe turned into a side street and reversed quickly. As they drove back along the main street he said to Mac, 'Did he spot us?'

Mac shook his head. 'Didn't even notice us. Too busy watching where he was going.'

The yellow truck slowed down and turned into a side street and Marlowe followed. A few yards past a public house there was a piece of waste land and Kennedy drove on to it and parked the truck. As they drove past, he climbed down and walked back to the public house.

'Gone for his lunchtime pint,' Marlowe said.

Mac nodded. 'What are you going to do?'

Marlowe had been examining the yellow truck closely with a slight frown. A smile appeared on his face and he started to laugh. 'I've just had a flash of genius,' he said. 'You wait here for me.'

He jumped down from the cab and walked back to the yellow truck. He paused for a moment and looked carefully about him to make sure that he wasn't observed. He jerked open the door of the cab, reached inside and pulled on a certain lever, and closed the door again. He turned and hurried back to Mac.

As he approached the truck, the Jamaican was leaning out, a delighted expression on his face. 'Man oh man, but that should fix him good.'

Marlowe turned and looked back. O'Connor's first venture into the coal business had obviously been hastily planned because the truck Kennedy was using was an hydraulic tipper. As Marlowe watched, the back slowly lifted into the air and sacks of coal started to topple. Inexorably, the back continued to rise until the last bag of coal had fallen to the road. At the very moment that happened, there was a cry of dismay from the public house and Kennedy emerged from the doorway.

Marlowe climbed up behind the wheel and started the engine. He reversed the truck and drove back towards the scene of the disaster. As they approached he slowed down and leaned out of the window. 'Having trouble, Kennedy?' he inquired.

Kennedy turned and his expression of dismay changed to one of fury. 'You bastard,' he shouted. 'O'Connor will fix you for this.'

Marlowe ignored the threat. 'Just give him a message from me,' he said. 'Tell him he'd better not try this stunt again. I shan't play games next time.' He moved into gear and drove away before Kennedy could reply.

When the truck rolled to a halt inside the barn, Maria came running from the house, tremendous anxiety on her face. 'What happened?' she demanded. 'You didn't start any trouble, Hugh? Please say you didn't.'

Marlowe grinned. 'Everything went fine,' he said. 'I never even laid a finger on Kennedy. He had an accident as a matter of fact. All his coal got spilled on to the road. He was in a bit of a mess when we left.'

Relief showed on her face and something suspiciously like laughter sparkled in her eyes. 'You don't think he'll be back again?'

Marlowe shook his head gravely. 'No, somehow I don't think he will.'

She nodded. 'Thank goodness. Papa's back. I haven't told him anything yet. I didn't want to worry him.' She smiled brightly. 'Anyway, there's a meal ready. Hurry and get washed before it's spoiled.'

During the meal Mac told Papa Magellan and Maria in detail what had happened to Kennedy. He was a natural story-teller and had them both laughing heartily before he had finished. Afterwards, over coffee, they discussed the projected London trip. Mac was in full agreement with the idea. 'Seems to me it's the one way to putting one over on O'Connor,' he observed.

'I'm glad you agree,' Marlowe told him, 'because you're the one who'll have to make the trip.'

There was a momentary surprise in Mac's eyes that was immediately replaced by something like understanding. Maria said in puzzlement, 'But why shouldn't you go as well, Hugh? Wouldn't it be easier with two drivers?'

Papa Magellan cut in hastily. 'Hugh has his reasons, Maria. If he doesn't want to go to London that's his affair. Let it rest.'

Maria sat back in her chair, frowning and Marlowe said easily, 'What about the market gardeners, Papa? What have they got to say?'

The old man shrugged and looked grave. 'I was right about O'Connor. He's been round to most of the people I deal with, offering to buy direct and at much better prices.'

'How many have accepted?' Marlowe asked.

Magellan shrugged. 'Not as many as you would think. They're pretty shrewd, these men. Most of them are intelligent enough to realize that he won't pay them such fancy prices when he's squeezed me out of business. The majority have stuck with me, but I've had to guarantee them a price.'

'That means you've got to pay them whatever happens?' Maria said.

The old man nodded and Marlowe frowned. 'In other words, the only person who's risking anything is you?'

Papa Magellan smiled. 'I have enough ready cash to guarantee the first couple of loads. But if anything goes wrong . . .' he shrugged and left the sentence unfinished.

Mac sighed and got to his feet. 'I guess that means we can't afford any mistakes,' he observed.

At that moment there was the sound of a vehicle. As the engine was cut, Marlowe moved to the window and looked out. A green Jaguar was standing outside. The door opened and a slim, boyish figure slid gracefully out of the upholstered seat. 'Now I wonder what *she* wants?' Maria said softly at his shoulder.

It was Jenny O'Connor.

6

As the front door bell rang they looked at each other. After a moment or two, Marlowe said, 'It might be a good idea if someone let the girl in.'

'Maria!' Papa Magellan said in a tone that admitted no denial. 'Answer the door.'

Maria went without further argument. They heard the murmur of voices in the hall and then Jenny O'Connor stood hesitating in the doorway. Maria looked over her shoulder, a hostile expression on her face. 'She wants to speak to Hugh,' she said.

Jenny O'Connor smiled and shook her head quickly. 'No, please don't anyone leave. What I have to say concerns you all.'

She was wearing a tailored skirt and a brown suède jacket and her slim legs were encased in the sheerest of nylon stockings. Marlowe was conscious of the same crawling sensation in his stomach and the dryness in throat he had experienced during their first meeting. He swallowed hard and said. 'What did you want to see me about, Miss O'Connor?'

She coloured with embarrassment and dropped her eyes. For a moment she seemed at a loss for words and Papa Magellan with old-fashioned Latin courtliness took her by the arm and led her to a chair. 'Sit down, my dear,' he said. 'You have no enemies here.'

Maria snorted with anger and folded her arms. Her lips were pressed tightly together as if to bottle up her rage. Jenny O'Connor smiled at her. 'Please, Miss Magellan. Don't condemn me until you've heard what I have to say.'

There was silence as they waited for her to carry on. She seemed to experience even greater difficulty in speaking, but quite suddenly, the words poured from her like a torrent. 'I know Mr O'Connor is my uncle and my action in coming here must seem very strange, but I can't stand by and see all this trouble and violence going on without a stop.'

Maria made an impatient sound and Marlowe said gently, 'What do you suggest we do about it, Miss O'Connor?'

She looked up slowly and there was great trouble in her candid blue eyes. 'Mr Magellan must sell,' she said simply.

There was a brief moment of astonished silence and then Maria threw back her head and laughed. 'So this is why you have come to see us,' she said. 'What do you think we are, fools?'

Papa Magellan turned on her angrily. 'Maria, if you cannot keep quiet you must leave the room.' For a second her eyes challenged him and then she turned and rushed out into the corridor, slamming the door behind her. Magellan turned to Jenny and inclined his head. 'I am sorry, Miss O'Connor. You must forgive my daughter. She has worried a great deal about this matter.'

'Why should Mr Magellan sell out now?' Marlowe asked her, his eyes fixed on her face.

'Because if he doesn't my uncle will break him,' she replied. 'Kennedy returned an hour ago. When my uncle heard what you had done he was furious. Insane with rage. I've never seen him so angry.'

'Did he send you here?' Marlowe asked her.

She smiled sadly and shook her head. 'Mr Marlowe, my uncle has very firm ideas about a woman's place. He never allows me to meddle in his business affairs. I I love driving and he's humoured me to the extent of allowing me to take out one of the trucks now and then.'

Papa Magellan frowned slightly. 'May I inquire then, what has brought you here this morning?'

She stood up and walked over to the window and stood staring out at the rain. 'I hate to see useless violence,' she said quietly. 'There's been too much already. If this state of affairs goes on there will be more.' She turned quickly and said, 'I know my uncle is in the wrong in this matter, but he has money and power and a large organization. He can put you out of business by using methods which are quite legal.'

Marlowe smiled softly. 'And what if we don't intend to be put out of business?'

'But what else can you do?' There was real concern on her face. 'He has stopped you from dealing with the market. This morning he's blocked off your retail shops outlet by undercutting your prices. All quite legal.' She appeared to hesitate and then went on, 'I must sound like a complete traitor telling you this, but I know that he's started to approach the market gardeners you deal with, Mr Magellan. He can offer better prices than you can. How can you possibly stand up to pressure like this?'

Mac grinned and said impulsively, 'There are more ways of killing a cat than drowning, Miss Jenny. Maybe we've got a trick or two left that might surprise your uncle.'

Marlowe kicked him sharply on the ankle as Jenny O'Connor's face clouded with puzzlement. 'It was good of you to come here,' he said. 'But I'm afraid there's no prospect of us selling out. Your uncle started this affair. He'll have to stick it out to the bitter end now.'

Her shoulders drooped again as they had done when they had last met. She looked completely defeated. 'I seem to have wasted my time.' She raised her head and forced a smile. 'I'm glad to have met you, Mr Magellan. Believe me, if I have any influence on my uncle at all, I'll use it to try and bring this sorry business to an end.'

She nodded to Mac and moved out into the hall. Marlowe went with her. As he opened the door of the Jaguar and handed her in she said, 'I seem to have made rather a fool of myself.'

He shook his head and replied gently, 'You could never do that.'

She looked surprised and paused for a moment, her hands resting on the wheel. 'You seem to know a lot about me?'

He nodded and said calmly, 'I'd know a lot more if you'd let me see you tonight. Perhaps we could have a drink and a bite to eat somewhere?'

She stared steadily at him and a slow, grave smile appeared on her face. 'You're a strange man,' she said.

He grinned. 'I get even stranger the longer you know me. Shall I see you tonight?'

She hastily scribbled in a tiny leather diary and tore out the page. 'There's my address,' she said, handing it to him. 'Pick me up at about seven thirty.' She pressed the starter button and as the superb engine began to tick over, said, 'You'd better go in now. You're getting rather wet.'

He stood with the slip of paper between his fingers and watched the car disappear into the distance and then he turned and went back into the house.

'And what was all that about?' Maria demanded, eyes flashing, when he returned to the living-room.

He grinned and held up the slip of paper. 'The lady's address,' he said. 'I'm taking her out tonight.'

For a moment only there was an expression of complete dismay on her face, but it was quickly replaced by one of fury. 'What exactly do you think you're playing at?' she demanded.

He ignored her and went over to the sideboard and helped himself to brandy. He turned and silently toasted the three of them and tossed it down his throat in one quick gulp. As the warmth moved through him he grinned in satisfaction. 'Yes, I'm going to take the lady out tonight,' he said. 'We'll spend the evening in Barford where I'll be nice and conspicuous.'

Understanding came to Papa Magellan and Mac at the same time. 'You're going to act as a decoy,' the Jamaican said.

As Marlowe nodded, the old man shook his head vigorously. 'It's insane. Barford at night-time will be pretty unhealthy. Monaghan and his thugs must be waiting for a chance to get you in a dark alley.'

Marlowe grinned. 'That's the idea. The whole mob will be concentrating on me, wondering what the hell I'm doing in Barford in the first place. They'll probably spend so much time trying to find an answer, they won't get around to any rough stuff.'

'And is that the only reason you're going?' Maria asked, her eyes fixed on him.

'What other reason could there be?' he told her. For a moment their eyes were locked together and then he turned and said, 'Come on, Mac. We've got to get that truck checked and loaded for your big trip.' Together they left the room and Marlowe was conscious of the girl's eyes burning into him as he went.

She was perfectly right, of course. There was another reason for seeing Jenny O'Connor, and with her woman's intuition Maria had guessed it. As Marlowe alighted from the bus in the main square at Barford that evening he saw himself reflected in a mirror and he shook his head and decided that he would never understand women.

Maria had carefully brushed and pressed the tweed suit he had been given on his release from Wandsworth and his shirt was gleaming white and freshly ironed. The suit didn't look too bad at all, he decided. At least it had been made to measure and fitted in all the right places.

As he walked along the pavement a church clock struck the hour and he checked his watch. It was seven o'clock and Mac was starting for London at eight. It would be dark enough then, Marlowe decided, looking up at the sky.

He had no difficulty in finding her address. It was a gay mews flat in a small courtyard not far from the square. The window boxes were painted bright red and one or two flowers still bloomed in them. He pressed the bell push and glanced about him as he waited. There was no sign of her car and he listened to the silence from within with a slight frown, wondering whether he had made a mistake.

As he reached in his pocket for the slip of paper he heard a football and the door opened. She stood there smiling at him. She was wearing a long red housecoat of heavy silk and her hair gleamed like spun gold. She stood to one side. 'Come in, Mr Marlowe. You're a little early.'

She led the way across an oak-panelled hall and into a beautiful room. Rose carpeting completely covered the floor and cleverly concealed lights tinted the walls the same colour. A large fire flickered in a superb Adam fireplace and rich velvet curtains were drawn across the windows, somehow cutting the room off from the outside world. She motioned him into a large, wing-backed chair and went across to a cocktail cabinet and poured two drinks from a shaker. 'I had these ready mixed,' she said, as she handed him one of the glasses. 'Martinis. I hope you like them.'

Marlowe nodded. 'An old favourite of mine.' He sipped his drink and leaned back in the chair and watched her.

She curled up on a long, high-backed settee that matched his chair, and smiled. 'There isn't any great rush,' she said. 'I've booked dinner at a place I know a few miles out of Barford. Unfortunately, something's gone wrong with the car. The garage have taken it away. It's nothing serious. They promised to have it fixed in an hour.'

He nodded and offered her a cigarette. 'That's too bad.' As he sat back in his chair he smiled and added, 'However, I'm not complaining. This will do very nicely. It's a beautiful room.'

She nodded and got up to replenish his drink. 'I like beautiful things,' she said. 'They make me feel good. Life can be so drab.'

'The trouble is they all cost money,' he said as she came back with his drink.

She smiled. 'Oh, I don't know. Some things are still pretty inexpensive.' She flicked a switch by the fireplace and plunged the room into half darkness. 'Firelight for instance.' She settled back on the settee. 'It's one of the few things that haven't changed.'

Marlowe was puzzled. 'Changed?' he said.

'From the old days.' She pillowed her head on one arm like a little girl and turned towards the fire and her eyes glinted, amber and gold. 'When I was a little girl I can remember having tea with my father in his study at four o'clock on Autumn afternoons. It was a special treat, something to look forward to. It was a wonderful room, lined with books and there was always an immense fire. The maid used to bring in tea and hot muffins on a tray and my father would let me be hostess.' She chuckled. 'I loved handling the silver teapot and the beautiful china cups. There was a special intimacy about it with the dead leaves falling outside the long window and the shadows moving from the corners of the room.' She shivered and there was an utter desolation in her voice. Marlowe didn't speak and for a moment there was silence and then she said briskly, 'But that was a long time ago. Before the flood.'

Marlowe frowned. There was something he didn't understand here. 'What happened?' he said.

She shrugged. 'My father lost his money. He got mixed up in some financial swindle.' She hesitated and said briefly, 'He blew his brains out.'

'I'm sorry,' Marlowe told her. 'That was a rough break.'

She smiled and shrugged. 'The only trouble about being born into money is that you find it impossible to do without it. It means one has to look for a solution and sometimes it may be rather unpleasant.'

The picture was becoming a little clearer. 'And you found your solution?'

She smiled wistfully. 'Solutions are usually hard to come by. How old do you think I am, Mr Marlowe?'

He shrugged. 'It's hard to say. Eighteen – nineteen.'

She laughed. 'I'm twenty-eight next month. When I was seventeen I married a wealthy man because I wanted security. He gave me ten years of hell. He was unfaithful, a drunkard and when the mood was on him, he wasn't above knocking me around. I put up with him because I didn't have the courage to go out and face life on my own. When he died in a car crash last year I thought I was free. Unfortunately he left nothing but debts.'

'And that's when O'Connor stepped in?' Marlowe said.

She nodded. 'That's right. He was my father's half-brother. I knew very little about him. I believe there was some scandal when he was young and he had to leave home. He got in touch with me six months ago and offered to provide for me.'

'And you accepted,' Marlowe said.

She shrugged. 'Why not? I'm weak.' She indicated the room with a gesture of one hand. 'He's good to me. In some queer way of his own he's proud of me. He likes people to know that I'm his niece. I suppose he's looking for a veneer of respectability now that he's rich.'

'Are you happy?' Marlowe asked her.

She smiled sadly. 'Isn't it the Bible which tells us we must pay for our weaknesses, Mr Marlowe?' She laughed in a strange way and reached for a cigarette from a silver box on a small table beside her. 'I have everything I want. Everything. It's just that I get so lonely at times. So damned lonely.'

For a long moment they stared at each other and the terrible dryness clutched at Marlowe's throat again. As the firelight flared up, illuminating her face, he saw tears glisten in her eyes and then the cigarette fell from her fingers and her face crumpled up like a child's. 'So lonely,' she repeated. 'So damned lonely.'

Marlowe got to his feet, a terrible vital force rushing through him. There was a great roaring in his ears and as he stumbled forward, her arms reached out and pulled him down. Her mouth fastened hungrily on his and she moaned his name once. As his hands moved over her she gave a cry of ecstasy and her fingers clawed at him like a tigress as the fury swelled to envelop the both of them.

The room was almost in darkness and the few remaining embers glowed fitfully in the grate. She stirred and moved her head against his shoulder. 'We'll have to be going,' he told her. 'It's past eight. That dinner you ordered will be spoilt.'

She turned her softness into him and slipped an arm round his neck. 'There's no rush,' she said. 'The garage haven't phoned about the car yet.'

Marlowe reached for a cigarette and lit it from the silver table lighter that went with the box. As he blew smoke out in a long streamer to the dark ceiling she picked at his shirt with her fingers and said, 'Are you really going to go on defying my uncle?'

'I don't see why not,' he said.

'But you don't stand a chance,' she told him. She slipped an arm around his neck and kissed him. 'I don't want you to get hurt.'

He grinned, his teeth gleaming in the darkness. She struggled up beside him and said, 'What's so funny?'

'That last remark of yours,' he told her. 'You see, I think it's your uncle who's going to end up getting hurt.' He glanced at the luminous dial of his watch and said, 'Round about now Mac must be just leaving for London.'

She switched on a standard lamp and there was incredulity on her face. 'But why is he going to London?'

Marlowe shrugged. 'To sell a truckload of produce at the greatest market in the world, Covent Garden. Even your uncle doesn't cut much ice there.'

For a moment she looked dubious and then she smiled and hugged him. 'Oh, I think it's a wonderful idea. I hope it works for you.' She stood up and stretched and looked at herself in the mirror. She gave a little shriek. 'My goodness, what a sight I look. I must go and change.' She smiled and rumpled his hair. 'Straighten your tie like a good boy and have another drink while I'm getting ready.' As she walked to the door she added, 'I'll phone the garage and see what the delay is.'

Marlowe helped himself to another Martini and listened to the muffled sound of her voice as she used the telephone in the hall. A moment later she opened the door and said, 'They'll deliver it within fifteen minutes. I shan't be long.' She closed the door again and Marlowe picked up a magazine and idly browsed through it.

After a moment or two he tossed it to one side and considered the events of the evening. He didn't try to pretend to himself that he was in love with Jenny O'Connor. There was no need. It was a peculiar type of relationship he had experienced only once before in his life. A tremendous chemistry which gave rise to a physical craving that had to be satisfied.

He checked his watch again. It was almost nine o'clock. By now Mac should be fairly started. He leaned back and stared at the ceiling and tried to calculate the time the Jamaican would arrive in London. Probably about three in the morning. They should see him back by lunchtime easily. One thing was certain. The plan had to succeed. If it didn't it would put Magellan out of business. Of that there was no doubt.

The door clicked open and she entered the room. She was wearing a black, sleeveless knitted dress that was completely form fitting. She smiled and held out a fur coat and he draped it across her shoulders. 'I'm beginning to wonder if I can afford you,' he told her.

She smiled and led the way towards the front door. 'Don't worry about that. I've got plenty of money.'

For a moment some essential core of male pride caused him to feel resentful and then he smiled. After all, why not? It was O'Connor's money. A car horn sounded outside and when she opened the door they found a white-overalled mechanic standing beside the Jaguar. 'You shouldn't have any trouble with it now, Miss O'Connor,' he said cheerfully.

'Thanks, Jerry,' she told him. She turned to Marlowe. 'You can drive if you like.' He handed her in and then went round to the other side and climbed behind the wheel.

The big car handled like a dream when they reached the main road leading out of Barford, Marlowe accelerated until the needle lifted towards eighty. 'It's a lovely car,' he told her.

She smiled. 'The best. Haven't you ever wanted a car like this?'

For a brief moment he hovered on the brink of telling her about his past. About the days when he'd driven a car like this all the time. When he'd had money and clothes and women. Everything a man could ever want and yet he didn't tell her these things. He didn't tell her because he suddenly realized that things like that had lost their importance. A car was a car, it had an engine and four wheels and it got you from place to place. Was it really so important to have one that cost two thousand pounds?

He cursed silently. If he went on thinking things like that he was going to spoil the evening. Deliberately he pushed them back into some dark corner of his mind and turned into the car park of the road house which they had now reached. As they walked towards the entrance, he forced his mind to concentrate on enjoying the rest of the evening.

It was eleven o'clock when he turned the car into the courtyard outside Jenny O'Connor's flat and stopped the engine. For a moment they sat in silence and then she said, 'I really enjoyed myself. You dance exceptionally well for such a big man.'

He shrugged. 'Give the credit to those Martinis. I wasn't with you half the time.'

She chuckled. 'Coming in for a night-cap?' She placed a warm hand on his arm and something stirred inside him. After all, why not? He opened the door and started to get out.

A fist lifted into his face and some inexplicable reflex action caused him to duck so that the blow glanced off his cheek. He slammed the door outwards and it thudded against some solid body as he hurled himself forward, ice cold rage surging through him.

A foot tripped him and he hurtled to the cobbles, instinctively putting his hands to his face and rolling away to avoid the swinging kicks. A foot caught him in the side, another grazed his face and then he was on his feet again. Jenny O'Connor hadn't screamed once. For a moment, a terrible suspicion surged through him that perhaps she had played him false and then her front door opened. Light flooded in a golden shaft across the courtyard.

'Inside, Hugh! Inside!' she cried.

In the shaft of light, Blacky Monaghan and his two friends stood revealed. One of them was holding a length of iron railing in both hands and he suddenly darted forward and swung for Marlowe's head. Marlowe ducked and the bar rang against the stone wall behind him. He lifted his foot savagely into the man's crutch. The bar rattled against the cobbles and the man gave a terrible, choking cry and sank to the ground.

Monaghan stood back and wiped a hand across his brow. From the sound of him he'd been drinking. 'That won't do you much good, you bastard,' he snarled. He spoke to his remaining ally without taking his eyes off Marlowe, 'Go get him, Paddy. Slice him up good.'

Paddy took his hand out of his right pocket and slowly opened an old-fashioned bone-handled razor. He started towards Marlowe, his hand extended. Marlowe waited until he was only three or four feet away, then he dropped to one knee, picked up the iron bar his first assailant had dropped and smashed it across Paddy's right arm. The bone snapped like a dry twig. Paddy slipped to the cobbles in a dead faint, his face contorted into a mask of agony.

As Marlowe started to get up from his knee, Monaghan came in with a rush and kicked him in the side, lifting him over and backwards against the wall. The Irishman moved in fast, his foot raised to stamp down on the unprotected face. Marlowe grabbed the foot and twisted and Monaghan fell heavily across him. For several moments they rolled over and over across the cobbles tearing at each other's throats and then, as they crashed into the far wall, Marlowe pulled himself on top. He slammed his fist solidly against the Irishman's jaw, twice and Monaghan's head rolled to one side and he lay still.

Marlowe scrambled to his feet and leaned against the wall for a moment. After a while he turned and walked towards the door. Jenny was standing there looking at him, a strange expression in her eyes. 'My God, can't anyone get the better of you?' she said.

He ignored the remark and pushed her inside. 'You didn't phone the police did you?' She shook her head and he nodded. 'Good! Let me have a double brandy. When I've gone, phone your uncle and tell him what's happened. He'll have to come round to pick his boys up himself.'

She quickly poured brandy and handed him the glass. 'Are they all right?' she said, uncertainty in her voice.

He shrugged. 'That kind are always all right. If you mean have I killed any of them, the answer is no. Your uncle will have to get a doctor though, and the kind of doctor who handles cases like this doesn't come cheap.'

'Blacky Monaghan will kill you next time,' she said with conviction.

Marlowe shrugged and straightened his tie. 'A lot of people have tried to kill me,' he told her. 'I'm still here.'

'Your face is an awful mess,' she said, 'You'd better come into the bathroom and I'll fix it.'

He managed a grin. 'No thanks. O'Connor might have somebody waiting in there for me as well.' He leaned over and brushed her cheek. 'It's been nice, angel, but the party's over for now. I'd better get out of here. Give me five minutes and then phone him.'

As he passed through the courtyard, Paddy was beginning to moan and the third man sobbed steadily like a small child. Marlowe moved rapidly along the dark street. He was lucky. As he emerged into the square, a taxi crossed in front of him and he flagged it down.

He lay back against the upholstered seat and closed his eyes. He was tired, very tired and his body was a mass of bruises. Each time he breathed in, his chest hurt where Monaghan's boot had landed and he wondered if anything was broken. When he considered what had happened he realized that he had been expecting it all night. After all, Monaghan had given him fair warning. He and his friends must have planned the whole thing very carefully.

Marlowe twisted his face into a tired smile. At least he'd kept them busy for the evening while Mac was taking the stuff South. His plan had worked beautifully and he'd got to know Jenny O'Connor very well indeed. Taking it all in all, it had been a profitable evening, kicks and bruises notwithstanding.

He got out of the taxi at the gate and paid the man. For a moment he stood in the darkness listening to the sound of the engine dying away in the distance and then he turned and walked across the yard to the front door.

There was a light on in the kitchen, showing faintly through the crack under the door, and he groped his way towards it and turned the knob. Maria was sitting in an old rocking chair by the kitchen fire crying steadily. She raised a tear-stained face and gave a gasp of horror. 'Oh, Hugh, what have they done to you?'

In a moment she was across the room and in his arms. He held her close as sobs shook her small body and gently smoothed her hair. 'What is it, angel?' he said. 'There's nothing to worry about. They've only chipped the edges a little.'

She raised her face, swollen and puffed up with weeping and said brokenly, 'Mac telephoned through from a little place near Peterborough. He went into a roadside café for a cup of tea and when he came out someone had stolen the truck.' She shook her head helplessly from side to side. 'Don't you see what this means, Hugh? We're finished. There's nothing more we can do.'

As her body was shaken with fresh sobs Marlowe held her close and stared bitterly into space. He decided that if O'Connor had been in the room at that moment he would have killed him with his bare hands.

7

Mac returned in the late afternoon of the following day. Marlowe was working on one of the trucks when he heard the engine. He straightened up and started to wipe his hands on an old rag as Mac drove straight into the barn and came to a halt. He switched off and jumped to the ground.

'So you got the truck back?' Marlowe said as he approached.

The Jamaican shook his head. 'Yes, but the load was missing when the police found it. Man, I feel real bad about this.'

Marlowe offered him a cigarette. 'Don't start blaming yourself. The same thing would have happened to me.'

'How's the old man?' Mac asked.

Marlowe struck a match on the wall and held it out to him. 'Not so good. He's taken it pretty hard, and on top of that his rheumatism's got worse. He's in bed.'

'This is going to break him,' Mac said bitterly. 'The dirty bastards.'

'Never mind about them at the moment,' Marlowe said. 'Tell me what happened.'

Mac spread his hands in a gesture of bewilderment. 'That's the crazy thing. Nothing happened. I'd been driving for about three hours when I came to this transport café near Peterborough. I parked alongside about fifteen other trucks, and went in and had a cup of tea and a sandwich. When I came out fifteen minutes later, the truck had gone.'

'What did you do then?'

'Got straight on to the local police. The sergeant who handled the case was a nice guy.' Mac laughed shortly. 'He told me it happens every night somewhere along the road.'

Marlowe nodded. 'He's right, it does. That's where O'Connor has been so clever. No hold-up, no coshing, nothing so dramatic. To the police it's just a routine job, and he knows we won't tell them any different.'

Mac nodded and sighed. 'They found the truck at ten o'clock this morning. It was parked up a side road about ten miles from the café.'

Marlowe leaned against the wall, his brow knitted in thought. After a while he said, 'Tell me, Mac, what other interests has O'Connor got besides the fruit-and-vegetable game?'

Mac shrugged. 'He has his own sand quarry. That does pretty well, and there's his haulage contract with the Coal Board. Mainly he does general trucking, I'd say.'

Marlowe shook his head impatiently. 'I don't mean his legitimate interests. What does he do under cover of darkness? Papa Magellan told me he had a pretty bad reputation during the war.'

Mac shook his head. 'I wouldn't know about that. I was only there for five or six weeks.' He frowned and narrowed his eyes. 'I'm pretty sure there's plenty of crooked work going on there, but nobody ever took me into their confidence.'

Marlowe was disappointed. 'That's a pity,' he said. 'I was hoping you might have known something.'

Mac suddenly brightened. 'Heh, wait a minute. There's the garage on the Birmingham road.'

Marlowe was immediately interested. 'On the Birmingham road?' he said. 'That's on the other side of Barford. What goes on there?'

'That's just the trouble,' Mac told him. 'I don't know. But it's something might peculiar. Only Monaghan and the hard boys were ever allowed up there. Once or twice they sent me up with messages from O'Connor and they never even let me through the doors.'

Marlowe's eye narrowed and he said softly, 'So they wouldn't let you see inside, eh?' He grinned and clapped the Jamaican on the back. 'I think we'll pay them a little visit this evening, Mac. What do you say?'

Mac grinned. 'Anything to get a crack in at those bastards is okay with me, boy.'

Marlowe grinned. 'That's fine. You'd better come in and have something to eat now.' As they walked towards the house he added, 'Whatever you do, don't tell the old man or Maria where we're going tonight. Especially Maria. Leave any explaining to me.'

Mac looked surprised, but nodded his head. 'Okay, boy, have it any way you want.'

Maria was in the kitchen when they went in. She looked tired and pale, and gave Mac a wan smile. 'I'm sure sorry about what's happened,' Mac told her.

She managed a smile. 'Don't blame yourself. We know it wasn't your fault.'

'Can I see your father?' the Jamaican asked her.

She sighed. 'He's pretty sick at the moment. The doctor's been to give him a check up. He thinks he's got a touch of the flu. He's running a temperature, anyway.'

She led the way upstairs and cautiously opened the door of the old man's bedroom. He looked about ten years older, and his cheeks were hollow and sunken. From the sound of his heavy breathing he was asleep.

Maria gently closed the door and they went back downstairs. 'He sure doesn't look good,' Mac observed soberly.

'Everything's hit him at once,' Maria said. 'And he's facing ruin. It's a wonder he isn't dead.'

Marlowe felt desperately sorry for her. She gave a little sob and leaned on the table, her head down. He slipped an arm round her waist. 'Now then, angel. This isn't like you. Keep smiling. Mac and I are going to canvass the market gardeners this evening. We'll get another load together, perhaps even two. We'll try for London again tomorrow night.'

She smiled and wiped a tear from her cheek with the back of her hand. 'Yes, you're right, Hugh. I'm just being silly, and that won't help at all. 'She squeezed his hand. 'You're so good to me – both of you.' She smiled again. 'I'll get you your meal.'

They started for Barford in one of the trucks just after seven that evening as the sky was beginning to darken. Marlowe purposely avoided the square on their way through the town, and when Mac tapped him on the shoulder he swung the truck on to a piece of waste ground and killed the motor.

It was by now, quite dark and the street lamps were strung away through the darkness back towards Barford like yellow beads. The garage was three or four hundred yards farther along the road, and as they approached it a thin rain began to fall.

When they were about fifty yards away Marlowe stopped and said, 'We won't go any closer this way. You never know who's watching. Let's find a way to get round to the back.'

They tried a narrow alley that was lit with a single old-fashioned gas lamp, and stumbled along its uneven paving. It turned sharply to the right after thirty or forty yards, and continued along the rear of the garage. The brick wall was old and crumbling and about nine feet high. Mac looped his hands, and Marlowe used them as a step and scrambled up on to the wall. He reached down his right hand and heaved the Jamaican up beside him. For a little while they sat there, gaining their bearings, and then they dropped down into the yard inside.

There was an old iron fire-escape up to the second floor, and Marlowe cautiously led the way. They paused on the landing, and he tried the knob of the door. It was locked. For a moment he hesitated, and then Mac stretched out to a near-by window. A moment later he gave a grunt of satisfaction. 'It's open,' he said. There was a creak as the sash was raised, and then he climbed over the rail of the fire-escape and scrambled in through the window. Marlowe followed him.

They stood in the darkness listening, and Marlowe was conscious of a peculiar smell. He frowned and sniffed experimentally, and then his brow cleared and he pulled Mac close. 'It's whisky,' he said. 'The real stuff. Can you smell it?'

Mac nodded, and led the way cautiously along the corridor. There was a door at the far end with a broken panel in it through which light streamed. He opened it carefully, and the full aroma of the whisky filled their nostrils.

The room was crowded with crates of bottles, and at the far end there were a great many barrels. Marlowe tapped one of them experimentally. 'It's full,' he observed. He moved over to a near-by table and picked up a handful of labels. 'Look at these,' he said. 'All well-known branded names.'

'But what's going on here?' Mac asked in puzzlement.

'It's a racket as old as the hills,' Marlowe told him. 'Cut liquor. They buy whisky in bulk – it may even be quite good stuff – and dilute it with water. Then they bottle it, stick a well known quality label on, and make at least two hundred per cent profit on each bottle.'

Mac frowned. 'But any drinking man can tell if good liquor's been tampered with.'

Marlowe nodded. 'I know, but this stuff is mainly for the night-club trade, and I don't mean high-class establishments either. The sort of places in Soho where the floozies take the suckers and get a percentage.'

Mac looked about him in awe. 'Man, if we sicked the cops on to this lot friend O'Connor would find himself in real trouble.'

Marlowe nodded grimly. 'About five year's worth.' He went to a door in the corner and opened it quietly. After a moment he beckoned Mac over, motioning him to silence.

They were looking into the main part of the garage. It was empty except for one Bedford three-tonner. It looked like a war-surplus job and was still painted a dull shade of khaki green. There seemed to be no one around. Marlowe approached the truck and peered inside. The interior was full of neatly stacked boxes.

He clambered in and Mac followed him. They squatted down and Marlowe took out a pocket-knife and prised up a corner of the cover of one of the boxes. Inside he could just make out the top of a whisky bottle. He grinned and turned to Mac. 'This must be a load waiting to go out.'

Before Mac could reply there was the sound of a door opening and footsteps approaching the truck. Marlowe quickly motioned to him and they crouched down on the floor. They could hear the conversation quite clearly through the canvas canopy.

There were two people standing outside – O'Connor and Kennedy. O'Connor said, 'Here's the address. It's not far from Lime Street, down towards the docks. If you push this crate along you should be there not much after midnight.'

'Hell, Mr O'Connor, I'd have to sprout wings,' Kennedy protested. 'Liverpool's a hell of a long way off.'

O'Connor's voice was cold as ice-water. 'Listen, Kennedy. I'm paying you good money. I want to see some results for a change. You've made a habit of bungling things lately.' His tone became menacing. 'If you don't like working for me we can always make other arrangements.'

'Oh, no, I didn't mean anything like that, Mr O'Connor,' Kennedy hastened to reassure him, and there was fear in his voice.

O'Connor grunted contemptuously. 'Then see you do things right this time,' he said. 'Sid Brown will hand you a paper packet in exchange for this load. There'll be two thousand quid in it. That's a lot of cash. I want to see you and every penny of it back here for breakfast in the morning, and no excuses.'

The door banged, and the whole truck shook as the engine started. A moment later Marlowe heard the rattle of the sliding-doors being rolled back, and then the truck bumped out into the darkness and picked up speed along the main road.

Marlowe settled himself comfortably with his back against the wooden cases, and said to Mac, 'Where did he say we were going? Near Lime Street and not far from the docks?'

The Jamaican's teeth gleamed in the darkness. 'I've never been to Liverpool,' he said. 'I'm quite looking forward to it.'

Marlowe grinned, turned his coat collar up and pulled his cap down over his eyes. 'Better make yourself as comfortable as you can,' he told Mac. 'We're in for a long trip.'

Several times he fell asleep, but always he came awake again as the old truck bumped or swerved over some particularly bad piece of road.

Kennedy made quite good time, and on some of the stretches where traffic was light he pushed the Bedford up to sixty.

On the last occasion that he awakened, Marlowe found they were moving through the suburbs of Liverpool, and when he checked his watch he saw that it was just coming up to midnight. He gently nudged Mac, and the Jamaican came awake like a cat. 'We're nearly there.' Marlowe told him. 'Friend Kennedy's certainly pushed this old bus along.'

'What's our next move going to be?' Mac asked.

Marlowe shrugged. 'I don't know. We'll make it up as we go along.'

About fifteen minutes later, they turned into a quiet, dark street and halted. There was complete silence, and in the distance Marlowe could hear the eerie, mournful hooting of the ships out in the Mersey.

There was no immediate sign of activity, and then the door opened and Kennedy jumped down from the cab. They heard his footsteps along the side of the truck, and then he clambered up over the tailboard and shone a torch. Marlowe plucked it from his hand and directed the beam on to him. 'Hallo, Kennedy,' he said. 'Fancy meeting you here.'

There was an expression of ludicrous dismay on Kennedy's face, and he opened his mouth to cry out. Mac hit him with a beautiful short-arm jab in the stomach, and he collapsed across them, gasping for breath. Marlowe stuffed a handkerchief into his mouth and tied his hands with his own belt. Then they pulled several cases out from the back of the pile and pushed him into the space.

They had just dismounted from the truck when two vans appeared from the darkness and parked a few feet away. Four men came forward, and Marlowe leaned against the tailboard of the truck, fists clenched in the darkness in case of trouble.

A small bird-like man grinned and lit a cigarette. 'I'm Sid Brown,' he said. 'You boys from O'Connor?'

'That's right,' Marlowe told him. 'We've got the stuff inside and not a bottle broken.'

Sid Brown nodded. 'New aren't you? I ain't seen you before.'

Marlowe nodded. 'No, we've just started working for O'Connor.'

Sid leered and placed a finger against one side of his nose. 'A good boy, O'Connor,' he said. 'Very wide. You'll do well with him.'

His three assistants were transferring the contents into the two vans at a fantastic speed. 'Doesn't pay to hang around here for long,' Sid said. 'The coppers are too bloody keen for my liking.'

'What about the cash?' Marlowe said. 'If we have to move in a hurry I'd like to take it with me.'

Sid grinned. 'Oh, yes, the old lolly. I was forgetting.' He took a paper packet out of his raincoat and handed it over. 'All in fivers,' he said. 'And they aren't hot.'

Marlowe tore open the packet and examined the money in the light of Kennedy's torch. It was all there. 'You're a cautious one, I must say,' Sid Brown told him in an injured voice. 'You won't find me getting up to any of those tricks. I pay good money for good stuff. Always have done, always will do. It's the only way to get a reputation.'

As his men took the last of the cases out of the truck one of them said, 'Here, what the hell's this?'

Sid moved over to the tailboard and shone a powerful torch on the inanimate form of Kennedy. 'Here, what's going on?' he said. 'Who's that bloke?'

Marlowe grinned and slapped him on the back. 'Don't worry about him,' he said. 'That's my cousin Charlie. He likes to travel that way.'

At the first sign of an alarm Mac had quietly melted into the darkness, and now the truck engine roared into life. Marlowe turned quickly and jumped up into the cab. As he slammed the door he leaned out. 'Nice to have done business with you, Sid. See you again sometime.'

The truck moved forward into the darkness, leaving the astonished Sid and his vans behind.

Mac was laughing so much he could hardly keep the wheel steady. 'Man, is O'Connor going to be sick?'

'Two thousand pounds. All your troubles are over.'

'And he can't go to the police without exposing his whole racket,' Marlowe said. He leaned back and lit a cigarette. 'Yes, I'd call it a very satisfactory night's work.' He looked at his watch. It was almost one o'clock. 'We'll take turns driving,' he said. 'With luck we'll be back by six.'

It rained hard during the next few hours, and it was nearer seven when they turned the truck on to the waste ground near the garage and halted beside their own.

When Marlowe climbed into the back of the Bedford he found that Kennedy had managed to get rid of the bandage. As he bent down to untie him, Kennedy said, 'You'll never get away with this.'

Marlowe dragged him to his feet and half threw him over the tailboard. 'What are you going to do?' he jeered. 'Go to the police and tell them you had a cargo of cut whisky hi-jacked? I should imagine they'd be very interested.'

Kennedy was almost crying. 'For God's sake, Marlowe, what am I going to do? O'Connor will kill me if I go back to him now.'

He seemed near to breaking point. Marlowe stood looking at him, and something like pity moved inside him. 'If you've got any sense you won't go back to him,' he said. 'You'll get to hell out of here as fast as you can.' He took the packet of fivers from his pocket and extracted ten. 'There's fifty quid,' he said, handing the money to Kennedy. 'The London express leaves in an hour.'

He ignored the mumbled words of thanks and pulled himself up into the cab of their own truck beside Mac, who was sitting behind the wheel with the engine ticking over. 'That was a pretty decent thing to do, man,' the Jamaican said as they moved away.

Marlowe shrugged. 'Mugs like Kennedy shouldn't be allowed out on their own.' He rested his head in the corner and closed his eyes, effectively cutting off any further attempts at conversation.

When they rolled into the farmyard half an hour later, Maria was in the act of walking towards the barn. She ran forward as Marlowe jumped to the ground. 'Where have you been?' she demanded. 'I've been worried sick.'

He ignored her question. 'How's your father?' he said.

'Much better this morning,' she told him.' He's sitting up in bed asking for you. I didn't know what to tell him.'

She led the way indoors and they followed her up stairs to the old man's room. Papa Magellan was sitting up in bed with a woollen scarf around his neck. His half-finished breakfast was on a tray in front of him. His face lit up as Marlowe appeared in the doorway. 'Hugh, where have you been, boy? What have you been up to?' he demanded.

'They won't tell me anything,' Maria said.

Mac leaned against the door, and Marlowe unbottoned his coat and took out the packet of five-pound notes. 'Your troubles are over, Papa,' he said, and tossed the packet on to the bed. 'There's two thousand quid in there.'

Maria gasped and put a hand to her throat, and her face went bone white. 'Hugh, what have you done?' she said fearfully.

The old man's face was puzzled. 'Where did this money come from?'

Marlowe shrugged. 'From O'Connor. We found out he runs a racket in cut liquor. Last night we delivered one of his loads for him in Liverpool. All the customer was interested in was getting the whisky. He gave us the money without a murmur.' He grinned. 'So there you are, Papa. No more troubles.'

The old man's face was stern. He said to the girl, 'Maria, bring me one of the large manilla envelopes from the drawer over there.'

Maria did as she was told and handed him the envelope silently. 'Now give me a pen and some stamps,' he told her. Marlowe watched silently as the old man counted thirty notes out of the pile and put them on one side. 'I've taken a hundred and twenty pounds,' he said. 'That's what I reckon that load would have brought in London.'

Marlowe was amazed. 'You mean you're sending the rest of it back to O'Connor?' he cried. 'That's crazy.'

Papa Magellan shook his head. 'It's good sense. This is dirty money, wrongly come by. I've taken what I reckon O'Connor owes me. No more, no less.' He finished addressing the envelope and carefully stuck down the flap. When he had affixed the stamps he held the envelope out to Marlowe. 'I want you to post this.' For a moment Marlowe hesitated, and the old man said, 'Post it now.'

Marlowe sighed and took the envelope. 'All right, Papa. Have it your own way.'

He left the room without another word and went downstairs. The post box was several hundred yards down the road. It was an old-fashioned, rectangular box set in a rough stone wall with Queen Victoria's initials still engraved on it in wrought iron.

He stood in front of the box and hesitated for a moment, and then he slipped the letter into his inside breast pocket and retraced his steps to the house.

When he reached the gate Mac was leaning against the wall. There was a sombre expression on his face, and he said, 'You didn't post it, did you?'

Marlowe shook his head. 'No, it would have been a stupid thing to do.'

Mac sighed. 'I sure hope you know what you're doing, man,' he said, and followed Marlowe into the house.

Maria was in the kitchen cooking breakfast. When he entered the room she turned, an eager smile on her face, and said, 'You've posted it?'

Marlowe forced a smile to his lips. 'Yes, much against my better judgement.'

A radiant smile blossomed on her face. 'Oh, I'm so glad, Hugh. Papa was right, you know.'

She turned back to the stove and Marlowe sat down at the table, rage in his heart. He knew what he was doing all right. He wasn't going to throw good money away because of an old man's whim. He knew what he was doing, and yet he ground his nails into the palms of his hands in impotent rage because she believed him when he had lied to her.

8

Marlowe made the rounds of the market gardeners that afternoon and paid them off. When he drove back into the barn Maria was sitting on the table, swinging her legs and talking to Mac, who was working on the engine of one of the trucks. As Marlowe climbed down she poured coffee into a cup and offered it to him. 'You're just in time.'

He drank some of the coffee gratefully. 'That's good. It's turning pretty cold outside now.'

'How did you get on with the growers?' she asked.

He shrugged. 'No trouble there at the moment. They all got their money, so they were pretty satisfied.' He nodded towards the truck. 'I've got a hell of a load on this time. Apples and pears, some tomatoes, and quite a few plums.'

He gave her the list and she nodded in satisfaction. 'That's good. There's a steady demand for all these things in the main London markets. I checked in the morning paper.'

Marlowe turned to Mac with a grin. 'You should have no difficulty in getting rid of this lot when you get there.'

Before the Jamaican could reply Maria said quickly, 'But surely you'll go with him, Hugh? It will obviously be so much safer with two of you.'

Marlowe shook his head and clapped Mac on the shoulder. 'He doesn't need me.'

Mac grinned good naturedly. 'You'd only be in the way, man.'

'It's not fair, Hugh,' Maria stormed. 'Why should Mac have to do it on his own?' There was an expression of anger on her face. 'I think you should go with him.'

Marlowe choked back an angry retort and managed to keep his voice steady. 'Listen, angel, I don't give a damn what you think. I'm not going to London. I've got my reasons, and they aren't any of your business.'

Her face was white and two red spots flared in her cheeks. As she opened her mouth to reply he turned abruptly and walked out of the barn across the yard towards the house.

When he entered Papa Magellan's room the old man was sitting up reading a newspaper. He looked over the top of his reading-glasses and said, 'You look pretty mad, son. What's the trouble?'

Marlowe lit a cigarette and paced up and down the room. 'It's your damned daughter,' he said. 'She's getting all steamed up again because I'm sending Mac to London.'

The old man nodded. 'And being a woman she wants to know why you can't go?'

Marlowe sighed and sat down in a chair. 'Why the hell can't she take a hint, like you and Mac have done, and mind her own business?'

Magellan smiled. 'Open that cupboard, son. There's an album on the top shelf.' Marlowe did as he was asked and handed him the old-fashioned red-morocco photograph album. 'Have a look at this,' Magellan said, opening the album to a certain page.

Marlowe twisted the album round so that he could see properly. For a moment he thought he was looking at Maria. 'Is this her mother?' he asked.

Papa Magellan nodded. 'Yes, that was my Maria. As you can see they are like peas in a pod.' He smiled gently and closed the book. 'Not only in looks. I'm afraid that by nature my wife thirsted after knowledge, very much as Maria does.' He shrugged and handed the album back to Marlowe. 'It's a fault common to most women.'

Marlowe got up and put the album back on the shelf. As he was about to close the door he noticed a shotgun leaning in a corner of the cupboard, partially obscured by hanging clothes. He took it out and examined it closely. It was a double-barrelled twelve-bore, beautifully polished and engraved. He whistled softly. 'This must have cost you a pound or two.'

Papa Magellan smiled faintly. 'Yes, I like the feel of a good gun. There was a time when I was fond of an early morning tramp over the fields, and a try at a pigeon or two, but I'm past it now.' He leaned forward and tried to see into the cupboard. 'There should be a box of cartridges on that shelf somewhere.'

Marlowe found them with no difficulty. 'Yes, they're here.'

'Good!' Papa Magellan said. 'Then take the gun. You and Mac can have a little relaxation in the fields at the back.'

Marlowe grinned. 'We can always pretend we're blasting away at O'Connor.'

He examined the gun with real pleasure and there was a short silence that was broken by the old man. 'Maria is in love with you, isn't she?'

Marlowe looked up slowly. For a moment he hesitated and then he shrugged. 'Yes, I suppose she is.'

The old man nodded. 'From the beginning it was obvious to me.' He smiled gently and went on, 'Are you in love with her?'

Marlowe laughed harshly. 'Papa, I'm not in love with anyone. I've got other things to worry about.' He shook his head and got up. 'I don't want to be tied down. I can't afford it.'

The old man nodded, his eyes clouding over a little. 'Then it will be better if you go soon. Maria will suffer a great deal over this.'

Marlowe sighed and nodded. 'I'm sorry about that, Papa, but you needn't worry. I'll be moving on very soon anyway. Perhaps in another week. If things work out all right we should have O'Connor straightened out by then and when I leave you'll still have Mac. He's a good man.'

Magellan nodded and smiled faintly. 'So are you, son. Don't rate yourself too low.' He coughed several times and lay back against the pillow. 'This trouble you are in that keeps you from going to London? Is it bad trouble?'

Marlowe paused at the door, the shotgun under one arm and shook his head. 'A few old friends who want to see me and I don't want to see them,' he said. 'Nothing I can't handle.'

The old man nodded and smiled and his eyes half closed. 'Good,' he said. 'I am pleased. Now I think I will sleep.' Marlowe gently closed the door and went downstairs.

During the remainder of the afternoon Maria made a point of avoiding him. When he and the Jamaican were having their evening meal she addressed herself to Mac only and completely ignored Marlowe. At first he was faintly amused by her attitude, but after a while he was conscious of a slight feeling of resentment that increased as the evening wore on.

He and Mac spent several hours checking the engine of the truck that was to make the London trip and packed the boxes and skips containing the produce with infinite care. Marlowe left the Jamaican to make one or two last minute preparations and walked through the darkness towards the house.

Maria was sitting by the kitchen fire reading a magazine. 'Mac's almost ready to move,' he told her. 'I'll take the thermos flask and sandwiches to him if you like.'

'I can manage myself, thank you,' she replied frostily, getting up from her chair.

Marlowe shrugged and went back along the corridor to the front door.

He stood in the porch for a moment, breathing in the cold night air and suddenly there was a crash of glass as something hurtled out through the window of the barn.

Marlowe started to run and behind him he heard Maria call out in fear. As he approached the barn three figures ran out through the lighted doorway and disappeared into the dark. He paused for a moment and glanced hurriedly inside. Mac was sprawled out on the floor by the truck. Even as Marlowe hesitated, the sudden roar of a motor shattered the stillness nearby. A moment later it was dwindling into the distance.

He ran forward into the barn and knelt down by the Jamaican. There was a trickle of blood down one temple and when his fingers gently explored the scalp they encountered a fast rising bump.

Maria dropped on her knees beside him. 'Is he all right?' she demanded, anxiously. Marlowe nodded. 'Just a nasty knock on the head.' He lifted the Jamaican in his arms and walked out of the barn back towards the house. He kicked open the door of the living-room and placed his burden on the old-fashioned settee.

Maria dropped on her knees beside him with a damp cloth and gently washed away the blood. After a moment Mac groaned and opened his eyes. 'Hallo there, man,' he said to Marlowe. 'Somebody sure cracked down on my skull.'

Marlowe nodded. 'What happened?' he demanded.

Mac tried to sit up and Maria gently pushed him down. 'I was tightening a nut on the engine cowling when I heard a footfall behind me,' he said. 'As I turned round someone swung at me. I figured it was the trucks they were after so I hurled the spanner I was holding through the window.'

'That was a bright idea,' Marlowe told him. 'It frightened them off before they could do any damage.'

Mac tried to get up again. 'I'll have to be moving,' he said.

Marlowe pushed him down. 'Nothing doing. You couldn't drive five miles in your present state.'

He moved towards the door and Mac said, 'But what are we going to do?'

Marlowe grinned. 'I'll have to go for you.' As Mac started to protest, he added, 'It's the only possible thing. Don't worry. Nobody's going to stop me getting there.'

He crossed the yard to the barn and went inside. He opened one of the tool cupboards at the back of the work bench and took out the shotgun. He broke it and examined the barrels. They were in perfect condition. He tore open the box of cartridges and loaded the weapon, then he put a handful of cartridges into one of his pockets and replaced the box in the cupboard.

As he walked back to the truck, Maria came in carrying a thermos flask and a tin containing sandwiches. She paled at the sight of the gun. 'What are you going to do with that?' she demanded.

He opened the door of the cab and placed the shotgun along the rear of the bench seat. 'That's my ace-in-the-hole,' he said. 'If they try any funny business this trip they'll find they've made a big mistake.'

She shook her head. 'Guns are bad business,' she told him. 'When you start that sort of thing who knows where it will end?'

He took the coffee and sandwiches from her and stowed them under the seat. 'Don't worry,' he said gently. 'I'm not going to kill anybody. I won't need to. It's amazing how quickly the average thug deflates when he finds himself looking down the barrel of a gun.'

He smiled reassuringly and patted her cheek and then he climbed up behind the wheel and started the engine. As he eased off the handbrake she ran forward and said desperately, 'I'm sorry, Hugh. I'm sorry for the way I've treated you today.'

'That's all right, angel,' he said and pressed his foot on the accelerator. The roar of the engine filled the barn and he was unable to hear the next thing she said. Her mouth worked desperately and he nodded and smiled and took the truck forward out into the darkness.

As he dropped down the hill into Litton he wondered what she had been trying to say to him and he remembered Papa Magellan's words and sighed. Perhaps things were working out for the best after all. Perhaps it would be a good idea if he took advantage of this trip to London to wrap up his own business. Afterwards he could leave the Magellans and their problems far behind. He had done enough.

He reached inside his shirt and pulled out the length of string which hung around his neck. On the end of it was the key to the safe deposit box. He slipped the key back inside his shirt and a feeling of elation swept through him. Yes, everything was happening for the best after all. The safe deposit firm probably opened at nine or nine-thirty. He could be driving out of London again by ten o'clock. He lit a cigarette and leaned back comfortably in the seat.

After he had been driving for about an hour it began to rain. He cursed softly and switched on the windscreen wipers. He turned on all his headlights and settled back again into his seat. At that moment the truck lifted over a small hill and the powerful beam of his headlights picked out a green Jaguar parked about thirty or forty yards along the road. A figure stood at the side of the car flagging him down.

Marlowe grinned savagely and started to depress the accelerator and then he frowned and slammed his foot hard against the hydraulic brake. The truck skidded to a halt and he cut the engine and looked down into the pale, rain-soaked face of Jenny O'Connor.

'What on earth are you doing here?' he demanded.

She seemed to have difficulty in speaking and there was desperation in her eyes. There was complete silence except for the rain drumming hard against the canopy of the truck and Marlowe smiled and reached for the shotgun as the dark shadows rose from behind the Jaguar and moved forward.

Monaghan pulled the girl out of the way and reached for the door handle. 'Right, you bastard,' he said. 'This is where you get yours.'

Marlowe pushed the double barrels of the shotgun out through the window. An expression of complete fury appeared on Monaghan's face. 'You wouldn't dare,' he snarled.

'Wouldn't I?' Marlowe said gently and he thumbed back the hammers.

The other three men were strangers to him, but they bore the mark of hired bullies. One of them said savagely, 'Here, you didn't tell us it was going to be like this.'

Marlowe raised the gun very deliberately and pointed it at them. 'Maybe you haven't heard about a shotgun and what it can do. I'll tell you. It spreads. If I fire it now all three of you'll get it right in the face. If anyone's kicking after that I still have another barrel.'

The three men moved back hurriedly and Jenny clutched at the window and said desperately, 'They made me come, Hugh. They knew you would stop for me. It was my uncle who forced me to come.'

She started to cry bitterly, the tears coursing down her face and mingling with the rain and Marlowe said, 'Go round to the other door and get in. You told me you could drive a truck. Now you can show me how good you are.'

As Monaghan opened his mouth, she darted round to the far side of the cab, wrenched open the door, and scrambled up behind the wheel. In a moment the engine roared and she moved into gear as competently as any truck driver Marlowe had ever seen.

Monaghan gave a roar of rage and reached for the door handle. Marlowe rammed the barrel into the Irishman's stomach. As the truck moved away he looked back and saw Monaghan huddled over in the road, his three bravos standing around him.

As he stowed the shotgun behind the seat he said, 'How did they know I'd be going to London tonight?'

She spoke without turning her head, her eyes concentrating on the road ahead. 'My uncle sent someone round to buy produce from some of the market gardeners Mr Magellan deals with. He found out that you'd been round already today and guessed you'd be trying for London again.'

Marlowe grunted and lit a cigarette. 'Somebody paid us a call tonight and laid Mac out cold. Who was it? Monaghan and his pals?'

She nodded and glanced briefly across at him. 'I was outside in the lane in the car with my uncle. They meant to put your trucks out of commission, but you arrived on the scene too quickly.'

They seem to be using you quite a lot at the moment,' he said.

She turned the heavy truck into a difficult bend with the skill of a racing driver. 'My uncle doesn't trust me any more. He was furious about what happened the other night. Monaghan's two friends are still in bed. One of them has a broken arm.'

'Who were those characters he had with him tonight?' Marlowe asked.

'They arrived from Birmingham this afternoon.' She shuddered. 'Revolting men. My uncle forced me to go with them. They thought you would stop when you saw me and my car.'

He reached for the thermos and poured himself a cup of coffee. 'Well, their little scheme didn't work. Thanks to my ace-in-the-hole.' As he put the flask back under the seat he added, 'You can pull up now and I'll take over.'

When they had halted she sat silently at the wheel for a moment. After a while she turned and said, with something like horror in her voice, 'You wouldn't have used that gun, would you?'

Marlowe looked surprised. 'What the hell do you think I brought it for?' He laughed harshly. 'Don't start telling me it isn't proper behaviour. I suppose you'd have preferred to stand by and watch Monaghan and his pals use me as a football?'

She sighed. 'No, I suppose you're right in a way.'

She slid from behind the wheel. As he moved over and took her place he said, 'I'm damned sure I'm right. With a certain kind of man you have to use the first thing that comes to hand and Monaghan's that kind.'

He rested his hands on the wheel. 'Well, next stop London as far as

I'm concerned. You can come all the way or I'll drop you off at the first big town if you like.'

'I'll come all the way if you don't mind.' She leaned back into the darkness of the corner and as he reached for the starter said, 'Hugh, you don't love me, do you?'

He turned and looked straight at her. 'I don't love anyone.'

She nodded. 'Yes, I thought so.'

'Do you still want to go all the way?' he demanded.

He couldn't see her face in the darkness but she answered in a steady voice, 'Yes, I'll still go all the way with you.' He pulled the starter and a moment later they were moving again.

It was almost seven-thirty when they reached Covent Garden due to carburettor trouble on the way which had taken Marlowe over an hour to diagnose and put right. The main rush of the day was already over at the great market, but to his surprise, Marlowe found no difficulty in disposing of his entire load. The first wholesaler he tried came straight out, examined his load and gave him a cheque for one hundred and sixty pounds on the spot. What was even better, he asked for another load of the same quality to be delivered on the following day.

Jenny O'Connor looked surprisingly well considering the way in which she had spent the night. Her skirt was of such excellent material that it had creased little and she produced a ribbon from a pocket of her suède jacket and tied her flaxen hair in a pony tail.

'Even by London standards you look pretty good,' Marlowe assured her as he stopped the truck on Shaftesbury Avenue, not far from Piccadilly.

She smiled. 'I don't know about that, but it makes me feel better, anyway.'

He offered her a cigarette. 'What are you going to do? Come back with me?'

She shook her head and said slowly, 'No, I don't think so. I'll return by train. I want to take my time. I've got a lot to think over in view of what's happened.'

'Are you all right for money?' he said.

She smiled and laid a hand on his arm. 'Yes, I've got plenty. I may even decide to stay for a couple of days.'

At that moment Marlowe glanced casually through the windscreen at a black limousine which had pulled into the kerb a few yards in front of the truck. There was something vaguely familiar about it. The door opened and Faulkner, dapper and correct in an elegant grey flannel suit and Homburg hat, got out and turned to speak to someone who was still in the car.

Marlowe ducked rapidly, a hand to his face and Jenny said, 'What is it, Hugh? What's the matter?'

'That man standing by the limousine,' he told her. 'An old accquaintance I'd prefer not to meet.'

Faulkner straightened up and the limousine moved away from the kerb. He seemed to look directly at the truck and then he turned and crossing the pavement, entered a restaurant.

Jenny O'Connor squeezed Marlowe's arm. 'You can look up now. He's gone into that restaurant.' She opened the door, jumped down to the ground and said urgently, 'Go on, Hugh. Get moving.' She merged into the crowd and he moved into the main traffic stream. He looked back once and caught a glimpse of her flaxen hair and then she was gone.

His business at the safe deposit took him precisely ten minutes. They opened for business at nine-thirty and he was waiting on the doorstep, key in hand. As the clerk opened the small safe he said pleasantly, 'It's been a long time since you last called, sir.'

Marlowe smiled. 'Yes, I've been out of the country.'

Inwardly his stomach was churning and as the clerk talked, his words became a meaningless mumble. The safe door opened and he took out the shabby, old-fashioned Gladstone bag. He was still talking as they went upstairs, but Marlowe didn't hear a word.

Outside the pavement seemed to move beneath his feet and the bright, early morning sun dazzled him. The truck was parked in a side street and he almost ran towards it. He scrambled up into the cab and slammed the door. He placed the Gladstone bag on the seat beside him and lit a cigarette with trembling hands.

For a long time he just looked at the bag and he was conscious of sweat trickling down from his armpits and of a sudden dryness in the throat. With a muffled curse, he reached for the bag and wrenched it open.

The money was there, all in neat little bundles, most of it as crisp and clean as the day it had been drawn from the bank. For a moment or two he looked at it. Twenty thousand pounds, he thought, and it's all mine. I sweated for it and I earned it. Every penny of it.

He closed the bag and pushed it under the seat. A moment later the truck was moving northwards through the main traffic stream and he was grinning all over his face like a little boy.

9

The truck lurched across the cobbles of the farmyard and rolled to a halt inside the barn. Marlowe switched off the engine and checked the time. It was almost two o'clock.

He pulled the Gladstone bag from beneath the seat and jumped down to the ground. For several moments he stood, weighing the bag in one hand, his eyes searching the barn for a suitable hiding place. At the far end of the building a rickety ladder lifted to a loft and he walked towards it, eyeing it speculatively.

The ladder creaked and swayed as he mounted it. He paused at the top and surveyed the loft. It was crammed with the accumulated junk of years. A smile crossed his face and he put the Gladstone bag down beside several old suitcases and pulled the corner of a decaying cricket net half over it. The Gladstone bag looked perfectly at home and he climbed back down the ladder, satisfied.

He paused in the entrance of the barn to light a cigarette. The farm rested quietly in the damp warmth of the afternoon and he saw no sign of anyone as he approached the house.

There was a fire on in the kitchen and the table was laid for one. On the plate he found a hastily scribbled note from Maria telling him his dinner was in the oven and that she and Mac had gone to pick up another load of produce.

Marlowe grinned, screwed the note into a ball and flicked it into the fire. He left the kitchen and went up the back stairs. He opened the door to Papa Magellan's room cautiously and peered in. The old man was propped up against the pillows reading a book. He turned quickly, a smile of welcome on his face. 'Come in, son. Come and tell me what happened.'

Marlowe closed the door and sat on the end of the bed. He took the cheque he had received from the Covent Garden wholesaler and flipped it across to the old man. 'That's what happened,' he said.

The old man examined the cheque incredulously and pursed his lips in a soundless whistle. 'A hundred and sixty pounds. That's wonderful.'

'That's not all,' Marlowe told him. 'They want another load for tomorrow morning.'

Magellan started to laugh and then he broke into a paroxysm of coughing. When he finally managed to catch his breath, he wiped tears from his eyes and said weakly, 'I feel a hundred per cent better already. I'd like to have O'Connor in front of me right now so that I could wave this cheque in his fat face.'

There was the sound of a car entering the yard. Marlowe went to the window and peered out as a large black saloon pulled up. After a second or two the door opened and O'Connor clambered out.

'Who is it?' asked Papa Magellan.

Marlowe frowned. 'You're about to have your wish granted.'

The old man looked bewildered. 'O'Connor?' he said. 'But what on earth can he want here?'

Marlowe shrugged. 'Perhaps he wants to make a deal. I'd better go and find out anyway.'

When he opened the porch door O'Connor was standing with his back to him looking out across the farmyard to the green-houses and the fields beyond. He turned slowly and took a cigar from his mouth. 'It's a nice piece of property,' he said. 'Very nice indeed.'

'We think so,' Marlowe told him.

For a few moments they challenged each other and then the fat man's face creased into a smile. 'Aren't you going to ask me in?'

Marlowe shrugged and stood to one side. 'Why not?' he said. 'We can always disinfect the place afterwards.'

O'Connor's smile faded, but he forced it back into place. 'Where's the old man? He's the one I've come to see. Not the hired help.'

Marlowe took a single step forward and the fat man backed hurriedly away. 'I don't want any trouble,' he gabbled in a frightened voice. 'I just want to make a straight business proposition to the old man.'

Marlowe looked him over coldly. 'I don't like you, O'Connor,' he said. 'It wouldn't take much to make me break your fat neck. Remember that.'

He turned abruptly and led the way upstairs. When he opened the door to Magellan's room the old man was waiting impatiently, an extra pillow behind him, his back as straight and unyielding as an iron bar.

O'Connor came into the room breathing heavily and flopped down into the chair by the window. It creaked ominously and he took out a handkerchief and ran it over his face. He seemed to find difficulty in breathing and fanned himself vigorously with his hat. After several moments he said, 'My heart isn't what it used to be.' He gulped and ran the handkerchief over his face again. 'Those stairs are damned steep.'

Papa Magellan said in a voice of iron, 'You won't get any sympathy here. Say what you've come to say and get out.'

O'Connor's smile slipped. 'All right,' he said. 'I'll come straight to the point. You're in my way, Magellan. I want you out of here. I'll give you three thousand pounds for this place, trucks included, and I'll settle your mortgage as well. You wouldn't get half that price on the open market and you know it.'

Papa Magellan adjusted his spectacles and picked up his newspaper. 'I'm not interested.'

There was another moment of silence and then O'Connor exploded. 'You damned old fool, you've got to accept. You'll be ruined otherwise.'

The old man looked at Marlowe, an expression of distaste on his face. 'Get him out of here, Hugh,' he said. 'The place is beginning to smell bad.'

O'Connor lurched to his feet and moved forward. 'I'm warning you,' he said threateningly. 'This is your last chance. After this I'll run you off the roads and I won't be too particular how I do it.'

Marlowe gripped him firmly by the arm and propelled him towards the door. Papa Magellan put down his paper and removed his spectacles. 'Just a minute, Hugh.'

Marlowe stopped in the doorway, his hand still gripping O'Connor's arm and the old man said, 'I've known you a long time, O'Connor. We've stood each other more drinks than I can remember. I never approved of some of the ways you made your money, but that didn't mean I disliked you.'

O'Connor tried to pull away and Marlowe tightened his grip painfully. 'Keep still,' he said threateningly.

'I don't know what happened to you,' Papa Magellan continued, 'But during the past year you've turned into a wild beast. Anyone who gets in your way you destroy.' He shook his head and spoke very deliberately. 'Well, I give you fair warning. I've had enough. If you harm anyone or anything belonging to me from now on, I'll seek you out and destroy you for the mad dog that you are.'

He turned back to his newspaper, his hands trembling slightly, and Marlowe pushed O'Connor through the door and along the corridor.

O'Connor seemed to have difficulty in negotiating the stairs and when they reached the bottom he suddenly clutched at the wall, gasping for air, one hand tearing at his collar.

The attack was obviously genuine. Marlowe pushed him down into a chair and loosened his tie and collar. O'Connor's face had turned purple and his lips assumed a peculiar bluish tinge. Marlowe went quickly into the living-room and returned with a glass of brandy.

O'Connor gulped at it greedily and brandy trickled down his chin and soaked into his shirt front. After a few moments his breathing was easier. He smiled weakly up at Marlowe. 'One of these days I'll have one too many of these attacks.'

Marlowe nodded soberly. 'You're carrying too much weight around. It's a wonder your heart's lasted out this long.'

O'Connor struggled to his feet. 'When I was younger I was just like you, son. Big and strong as an ox. Then something went wrong with my glands.' He grinned and coughed several times into his handkerchief. When he looked up moisture streamed from his eyes. 'It's a vale of tears,' he wheezed. 'You never know what's going to happen next.'

Marlowe laughed coldly. 'My heart bleeds for you.'

He took O'Connor by the arm and helped him out to the car and the fat man leaned heavily on him, every step an effort.

When he was safely seated behind the wheel, Marlowe slammed the car door and said, 'I don't want to see your face round here again.'

O'Connor pressed the starter and leaned out of the window. 'You tell the old man to think it over,' he said. 'I'll give him until tonight. I'll be at the warehouse till nine. He can phone me there.'

Before Marlowe could reply the car moved rapidly away across the farmyard in a burst of speed, swerving dangerously as it went through the gate, narrowly avoiding a collision with the Bedford which was about to enter.

Mac halted the truck beside Marlowe and leaned out of the window. 'Heh there, man,' he said. 'It's good to see you. How did it go?'

Marlowe raised a thumb. 'Perfect. I'd no difficulty in getting rid of the stuff at all. In fact, I've promised another load for tomorrow.'

Maria had jumped down from the other side of the cab and she came round, a smile of welcome on her face. 'Was it really a success, Hugh?' she said excitedly.

Marlowe nodded. 'A hundred and sixty quid I got,' he told her. 'As long as we can make up a full load each time, there'll be no difficulty in making it pay.'

'Who was that crazy guy who just left in the saloon?' Mac demanded.

Marlowe grinned. 'No less a person than Mr O'Connor himself.'

An expression of alarm crossed Maria's face. 'What did he want, Hugh? Has there been any trouble?'

Marlowe shook his head. 'There's nothing to worry about. He was here on business. He offered to buy your father out again, but the old man wasn't interested.'

She looked puzzled. 'But what made him try again, I wonder? Papa told him very definitely last time that nothing would make him sell.'

'Yes, but things have changed some since then,' Mac put in. 'We've got him on the run now. And what's more, he knows it.'

The girl turned to Marlowe. 'Do you think that's it, Hugh?' she demanded.

Marlowe nodded reassuringly. 'That's about the size of it, angel. There's nothing to worry about. You go on up to your father and Mac and I will see to this load.'

She smiled in relief and went into the house. Marlowe went round to the other side of the truck and climbed up beside Mac and they drove down into the barn.

'Did you have any trouble on the way?' Mac asked when he had switched off the engine.

Marlowe lit a cigarette and nodded. 'Plenty,' he said and gave the Jamaican a quick summary of the events of the previous night.

When he had finished Mac whistled softly. 'Man, it was a good thing you took that shotgun along.'

Marlowe nodded. 'You're telling me.'

They climbed down from the cab and Mac said, 'Do you think they'll try anything tonight?'

'I don't know,' Marlowe frowned. 'I still can't quite understand why O'Connor turned up here today. It doesn't fit.' He grinned and slapped the Jamaican on the shoulder. 'Anyway, not to worry. You can take the shotgun along, just in case.' He shook his head. 'Somehow I don't think you'll need it.'

Mac nodded and said feelingly. 'I hope not.' As they walked round to the back of the truck he added, 'I'd sure like to know how Miss Jenny's getting on. I hate to think of her being mixed up with that mob.'

Marlowe frowned slightly. 'That's one thing I can't understand,' he said. 'O'Connor must be anxious to know what's happened to her and yet he never mentioned it to me.'

Mac considered the point for a moment. 'Perhaps she phoned through from London this morning and told him she wasn't coming back. I can't see her having anything more to do with him after the way she's been treated.'

'I wish I could be as sure,' Marlowe said and lowered the tailboard of the truck.

He yawned and closed his eyes momentarily as a tremendous wave of tiredness enveloped him. Mac put a hand gently on his shoulder. 'Why don't you go in and have a few hours' sleep. You sure could use some.' Marlowe started to protest and Mac gave him a push towards the door, 'Go on, boy, I can manage this lot on my own.'

He found it an effort to mount the stairs and when he passed along the corridor he could hear the murmur of voices from Papa Magellan's room as Maria talked to her father. For a moment he paused, undecided whether to go in or not, and then he went on to the far end of the corridor and opened the door of his own room.

He pulled off his jacket and sat wearily down on the edge of the bed and removed his shoes. He started to unbutton his shirt, but suddenly the effort seemed too great and he fell backwards. As his head struck the pillow he dived head first into darkness.

He came awake to find a hand on his shoulder. Mac was leaning over him, warmly dressed in a jeep coat with a woollen scarf round his neck and gloves on his hands. Marlowe sat up with a start and looked at his watch. It was almost seven-thirty and outside the sky was darkening rapidly.

'Why on earth didn't you wake me?' he said as he swung his legs to the floor.

Mac grinned. 'There wasn't any need, man. I managed to do most of the loading on my own and that old guy Dobie who works in the greenhouses, turned up to help me finish.' He smacked one gloved hand against another. 'Well, I'm raring to go. If anyone gets in my way tonight I'll roll straight over them.'

Marlowe pulled on his shoes and stood up. 'That's the style,' he said. 'Have you got the shotgun in the cab?' Mac nodded and Marlowe went on. 'Good, it gives you some kind of insurance, but don't stop for anything or anybody.'

Mac grinned and slapped him on the shoulder. 'Don't worry about me, man. Nothing's going to stop me this time.'

They went downstairs and out into the yard where the truck stood waiting. A chill breeze was blowing carrying a hint of rain with it and Marlowe shivered. 'It looks like being a murky night.'

Maria appeared from behind him, the thermos flask and a packet of sandwiches in her hand. 'Be careful,' she urged Mac as she handed them up to him.

He grinned down at them and revved up the engine. 'Don't you worry about me, Miss Maria. I feel really lucky tonight. Just like I used to feel before a big fight.'

He waved once and the truck lurched away across the yard, paused for a moment at the gate, and moved into the darkness, its red tail light growing smaller and smaller until it disappeared.

Maria sighed as she turned to go back into the house and Marlowe said, 'Don't worry, angel. He'll be all right this time.'

'I hope so,' she said. The telephone started to ring from the living-room and she went to answer it. After a few moments she returned, annoyance on her face. 'It's for you.'

Marlowe was surprised. 'Who is it?'

'Find out for yourself.' Maria tossed her head and disappeared into the kitchen, banging the door.

As Marlowe approached the telephone he could hear a voice calling anxiously. He picked up the receiver. 'Hugh Marlowe here. 'Who's speaking?'

'Hugh, is that you? Thank God you're still there.' It was Jenny O'Connor and she sounded frightened.

'So you decided to return after all,' Marlowe said. 'I hoped you'd have more sense.'

'Never mind that now.' She was almost sobbing. 'I must see you. Can you come to the flat?'

He frowned. 'I'm rather busy at the moment.'

'Please, Hugh, I'm in terrible trouble. You must help me.' There was desperation in her voice.

For a moment he hesitated and then he sighed. 'All right. Where are you.'

'At the flat,' she said. 'How soon can I expect you?'

He glanced at his watch. 'About eight-thirty.' She started to say something else and he cut her short. 'You can tell me when I get there,' he said and replaced the receiver.

He went up to the bedroom for his jacket and a scarf. When he came downstairs Maria was standing in the hall, drying her hands on her apron. 'Well, what did she want?' she demanded.

For a moment he was tempted to explain and then a feeling of annoyance took control and he said, 'What the hell has it got to do with you? If you must know, she wants me to go and see her.'

'And you'll go running to her,' Maria stormed jealously. 'She's got you just where she wants you. You're like a puppet on a string.'

He turned and walked out into the night before she could say any more. He took one of the two remaining trucks and drove into Barford, seething with anger. What right had she to say what he should, and should not, do? He cursed and swung the wheel savagely as he skidded on a dangerous bend. She'd appointed herself his conscience, judging everything he did and always finding him guilty. He lit a cigarette and began to calm down. After a while he was even smiling again. Now that he had the money he wouldn't have to put up with her much longer. A few more days at the most.

The truck skidded and lurched over the greasy cobbles of the square and he turned into the side street that led to Jenny O'Connor's flat and pulled into the pavement. He switched off the engine and walked the rest of the way.

He approached the flat cautiously and stood in the entrance of the court, his eyes carefully searching the shadows. After a moment or two he was satisfied and crossed to the door and rang the bell.

There was a short silence before footsteps approached and he heard her call, 'Who is it?'

'It's Marlowe,' he told her.

A bolt was withdrawn and a key clicked in the lock before the door opened to disclose her pale, frightened face. 'What's all the fuss about?' he demanded.

She pulled him inside and locked and bolted the door again before turning to him. 'Oh, Hugh, darling. You've no idea how glad I am to see you.' She threw her arms around his neck.

Marlowe held her for a little while and then gently pushed her away and frowned. 'What's been going on here?'

She led him into the lounge and pulled him down on to the settee beside her. 'I got back late this afternoon,' she said. 'I hadn't been in long when my uncle arrived.' She shuddered at the memory. 'He was almost insane with rage. He said I was a traitor and accused me of helping you. I told him I was leaving.'

'And what was his reaction to that?'

An expression of disgust crossed her face. 'He slapped me twice and knocked me down.' She pulled away the neck of her dress to disclose a livid bruise on her right shoulder. 'Look, that's what he did to me. He said I didn't have the guts to leave him. He took all my money and jewellery. Even my fur coat. He said I'd soon come to my senses.'

Marlowe leaned back, eyes narrowed. 'Frankly, it doesn't sound like a very healthy relationship to me. Did he ever make a pass at you?'

She shook her head. 'No, never. To tell you the truth, I used to wonder at first if he thought about me in that way, but until today he's always behaved perfectly.'

'Why did you lock the door?' Marlowe asked.

She smiled wanly. 'He sent Monaghan round to pick up my car. He tried to get into the house, and I had to slam the door in his face.' An expression of loathing appeared in her eyes. 'He called to me for ages through the letter-box.' She shuddered. 'The things he was saying were horrible.'

Marlowe scowled and clenched a fist. 'Don't worry about that, angel. Next time he crosses my path I intend to pay him back for a few things.'

She went to the cocktail cabinet and poured a whisky and soda. She smiled wryly as she handed it to him. 'What on earth am I going to do, Hugh? I've made such a mess of things.'

Marlowe put his drink down carefully. 'Why did you come back?'

'Because I'm weak,' she said candidly. 'Because the moment I was alone in London this morning, all my good intentions left me and I was afraid. Afraid of being on my own against the world. Afraid of not having any money.'

'Afraid of having to work for a living?' he asked, gently.

She made a face. 'Don't be cruel, Hugh. I know I'm weak. At least I'm honest about it. I came back because I thought I might be able to compromise, but instead I find that I've got to take sides.'

'And who's side are you on?'

An expression of hurt shadowed her eyes. 'Do I have to tell you?' she said. 'Do I really have to tell you?'

He stared into her beautiful, childlike face, and the old warmth moved inside him. He leaned towards her, and she slipped a hand behind his neck and fell backwards against the cushions, pulling him down. He felt the softness of her pressed against him, yielding to him, and he crushed his mouth against hers.

After a while, she pulled away slightly. 'I'm so glad I got through to you before you started for London.'

Marlowe kissed the warm hollow of her neck. 'I'm not going to London.'

'But why not?' she said in surprise. 'I thought it was essential for you to do another trip?'

'It is,' he told her. 'But Mac's gone tonight.'

'Oh, I see.' There was silence for a while and then she said, 'Hugh, what are we going to do?'

He grunted and kissed her shoulder. 'Hell, I don't know,' he said. 'I'll be moving on soon, I suppose.'

She stiffened and said sharply, 'I see.' There was another short silence. 'I believe my uncle called on you this afternoon?'

Marlowe pushed himself up and reached for a cigarette. 'That's right. He had a heart attack, as a matter of fact. I thought at first he was going to peg out on us.'

She played nervously with the collar of her dress. 'Yes, he's had several attacks.' She took a deep breath and went on, 'As a matter of fact I happen to know he's only got six months to live at the most.'

Marlowe paused, his glass half-way to his lips. 'That's interesting,' he said. 'It gives the Magellans some hope, anyway.'

She jumped up angrily. 'Oh, damn the Magellans. Can't you think of anything else?' She paced nervously across the floor and then swung round to face him. 'I'll put it in a nutshell for you. My uncle is going to die. Perhaps tonight or tomorrow, certainly within the next few months, and I'm his sole heir.'

Marlowe swallowed his whisky. 'So what?'

'Can't you see?' she said. 'If only you can persuade the Magellans to sell and we get everything back on an even keel, then it's only a matter of waiting.'

'Waiting for what?' Marlowe said softly.

She sighed impatiently. 'For my uncle to die. Then I'll get the business and you can run it for me. Don't you see, darling? We'll be secure for life.'

Marlowe carefully stubbed out his cigarette and stood up. 'You'll be secure for life, you mean.' He walked past her and went out into the hall.

She ran after him and grabbed at his shoulder as he started to unlock the front door. 'What's wrong?' she demanded. 'What are you doing?'

He pulled away from her and opened the door. 'I'm going,' he said. 'Why shouldn't I? You haven't any claim on me.'

There was an expression of complete shock on her face. She shook her head dumbly. 'I don't understand.'

'I could say it in four letter words,' Marlow told her, 'but even I have certain standards.' She still looked puzzled, and he sighed. 'Let's put it this way, angel. I've met all sorts, but you take the prize.' He shook his head. 'You don't even know what I'm talking about, do you? People like you never do.'

For a brief moment she continued to stare at him in that dumb, uncomprehending way, and then fury blazed in her eyes and she slashed her hand across his face. 'Get out!' she screamed. 'Go on! Get out!'

He gripped her wrists tightly and held her against him, fury moving inside him. She glared at him for a moment, and spat in his face. And then she called him a certain name.

He stared at her in amazement, and as he released her, he started to laugh. He was still laughing as he crossed the courtyard and went through the dark entry into the street.

He drove back to Litton with the window down, and somehow the cold wind seemed to have a cleansing effect. When he thought of Jenny O'Connor it was with pity. After all, she had to live with herself. That was probably the greatest punishment of all. He deliberately pushed all thoughts of her from his mind and concentrated on examining his own future.

His original idea about going to Ireland still seemed a good one. As he drove into the farmyard he decided to set things in motion at once.

He parked the truck at the front door and went inside. As he walked along the corridor he heard the sound of weeping from the sitting-room. When he looked in, Maria was huddled in a chair sobbing her heart out.

'What is it, angel?' he said, dropping to one knee beside her.

She raised her tear-stained face and said bitterly, 'Get away from me. I can still smell her perfume on you.'

He jumped up in anger. 'For God's sake tell me what all this is about?'

'It's Papa,' she said. 'He's gone out in the other truck.'

Marlowe frowned. 'He must be mad. He's a sick man.'

'I know,' she said. 'Mac phoned through over an hour ago. He'd had a breakdown and asked if you could drive the other truck through to him.'

Marlowe cursed savagely. 'And the old man insisted on going?'

She nodded. 'Yes, while you were having fun with Jenny O'Connor he had to drag himself out of bed and go out on a night like this.'

Before Marlowe could reply, the telephone rang. She rose quickly and answered it. 'Yes, who is it?' she said. There was a short silence as she listened, and then she swayed and clutched at the table. 'What did you say?' She started to shake her head dumbly from side to side, and then she dropped the receiver and turned her agonized face to Marlowe. 'Hugh!' she said. 'Hugh!' She slipped to the floor in a dead faint.

Marlowe dropped to one knee and picked up the receiver. 'Hello?' he said. 'Marlowe speaking. Who is that?'

'Hugh, is that you?' Mac's voice crackled over the line. 'I'm at a place called Bardon Bank about forty miles away. You'd better get here fast. The old man's dead.'

10

Marlowe arrived at Bardon Bank shortly after seven o'clock on the following morning. It wasn't difficult to locate the scene of the accident. Half-way down the hill a police car and a couple of breakdown wagons were parked at the roadside. He pulled in behind them and switched off the engine.

As he climbed down from the cab, a young police constable approached him with a frown. 'Now then, chum, we don't want any sightseers.'

'The man who crashed was my boss,' Marlowe told him. 'I got a phone call last night telling me to get here as soon as possible.'

An expression of sympathy appeared on the policeman's face. 'Oh yes, your other driver's been here. A Jamaican called Mackenzie. You'll find him at the transport café down at the bottom of the hill.'

Marlowe nodded. 'Thanks. I'd like to have a look before I go, if you don't mind.'

The policeman shrugged. 'Please yourself, but I'm warning you – it isn't very pretty.'

They walked a little way down the road and came to a gaping hole in the wall. The bank fell steeply on the other side through a plantation of firs to a stream fifty or sixty feet below.

The path of the truck was quite plain, and at the end of the lane it had cleared through the fir trees. Marlowe could see the blackened and twisted wreckage of the truck.

He cleared his throat. 'It looks pretty bad.'

The policeman nodded. 'I've been down there, and believe me it *is* bad. The whole damned thing went up in flames when it hit the bottom.'

'What about the old man?' Marlowe said slowly.

The policeman shook his head. 'He's still in there, or what's left of him. They're burning their way through the wreckage now to get him out.'

For a moment longer Marlowe looked down at the wreck, and then he turned away. 'Thanks,' he said. 'I'll probably see you later.' He climbed back into the truck and drove down to the transport café.

He found Mac sprawled half across a table in one corner, fast asleep. When Marlowe touched him the Jamaican came awake instantly. A slight smile came to his face. 'Hugh! I'd just about given you up.'

Marlowe explained. 'Maria passed out on me when she heard the news. I had to get the doctor in. He gave her a sedative and put her to bed. She was in such a state that I couldn't leave her.'

'How is she now?' Mac asked.

Marlowe shook his head. 'All frozen up inside, poor kid. She's taking it pretty hard. She had a lousy night until I made a cup of tea and slipped a couple of the pills in without telling her. She went out like a light.'

The Jamaican went to the counter and got two cups of coffee. When he returned he said, 'Man, this is a bad business. Mr Magellan shouldn't have turned out on a night like that.'

Marlowe nodded. 'That's what Maria thinks. She blames me. Jenny O'Connor phoned and said she wanted to see me urgently. Maria wasn't too pleased when I went. She thinks I should have been at the farm to take your phone call and come out with the spare truck.'

Mac shook his head. 'But that isn't fair, Hugh. You couldn't have known that I was going to have a breakdown.'

Marlowe smiled bitterly. 'Don't give me that crud, Mac. Under the circumstances I should have hung around the farm last night, just in case anything went wrong. I didn't and the old man's dead. Whichever way we look at it, I'm at least partially responsible.'

He pushed a cigarette into his mouth. 'I wonder what caused the accident?'

Mac was tracing patterns on the table with one finger in a pool of spilled tea. 'I was wondering,' he began hesitatingly. 'You don't suppose anything was wrong with the truck, do you?'

Marlowe looked at him inquiringly. 'O'Connor? I don't think so. When was that truck checked last?'

'Yesterday morning,' Mac said. 'I did it myself. It was in good order.'

'That's it then,' Marlowe said. 'There was someone around the place all the time. I can't see how anyone could have tampered with it.'

'What do you think happened?' Mac asked.

Marlowe stared into space and sighed deeply. 'I think Papa Magellan was just a sick, tired, old man who should have been in his bed. He probably passed out at the wheel or perhaps he fell asleep. Whatever happened, it only took a minute.' He stood up. 'Yes, he was just a sick old man who depended on me, and when he needed me most I wasn't around.' He turned and walked rapidly out of the café as the impotent fury surged into his throat in a strangled sob.

It was almost noon when they managed to get what was left of the old man out of the truck. They brought him up the hill wrapped in a blanket, and Marlowe and the Jamaican stood and watched silently as the body was put into the ambulance. As the man in charge of the breakdown team scrambled up, Marlowe walked across to him and said, 'Did you find anything that indicated why he'd run off the road?'

The man shook his head. 'We aren't likely to, either. Not in that heap of scrap.'

Marlowe turned away, sick at heart, and motioned to Mac. 'Come on, let's get out of here,' he said. 'It stinks like a charnel house.'

But all the way back to Litton he was unable to get the stench of burnt flesh out of his nostrils. It stayed with him even when he opened the side windows and filled the cab with air. He told himself it was all in the mind, and took even greater risks, driving into the curves at a dangerous speed, his hands gripping the wheel until his knuckles showed white.

Mac sat quietly beside him, saying nothing. When they finally turned into the farmyard and halted outside the door, he said to Marlowe, 'What you need is a good stiff drink, man. Come on in and I'll get you one.'

Marlowe shook his head. 'No, not for me.'

'What about Maria?' the Jamaican asked. 'She'll need you at a time like this.'

'Need me?' Marlowe said. 'Why should she need me?'

Mac shook his head. 'Man, you must be blind. That girl loves you.'

Marlowe laughed savagely. '*Did* love me, you mean. I'm the man who was responsible for her father's death, remember.' He turned abruptly and walked away across the yard to the barn.

He paused in the entrance to light a cigarette. It tasted like straw and he tossed it away with a curse. He walked forward into the barn, hands in pockets, head bowed down, and then he stiffened as his eyes lighted on something.

He dropped on one knee beside the pool of liquid and dipped a finger into it. He lifted the finger to his nostrils and sniffed deeply, and then he gently touched it to his lips. It was fluid from the hydraulic-braking system of the truck.

For a moment he stayed poised on one knee, paralysed and unable to fully comprehend the meaning of his discovery, and then he got to his feet, murder in his heart, and turned and walked out of the barn towards the truck.

It was all plain now. All very plain. The old man hadn't passed out at the wheel. He'd crashed through that wall because the truck had got out of control on the hill. It had got out of control because somebody had tampered with the brakes. It was as simple as that.

He scrambled behind the wheel of the truck and pulled the starter. The engine roared, drowning Mac's cry in the background, and Marlowe took the truck across the farmyard in a burst of speed and skidded out of the gate into the main road.

As he drove towards Barford he was conscious of one thing only. He was going to kill O'Connor. He was going to wrap his hands round that fat neck and squeeze all life out of the grotesque body. Anyone who got in his way would get stamped into the ground.

It started to rain and lightning forked across the sky. As he turned the truck into the square a clap of thunder tore the heavens apart and rain started to fall in a torrential sheet.

Marlowe braked to a halt in front of O'Connor's place and stepped from the cab on to the loading-platform. The rain buffeted him as he went towards the great sliding-doors. He pulled on them with all his strength, but they refused to yield. There was a small postern gate set slightly to one side, with a Yale lock. He tried the handle several times with no success. He pushed the rain away from his eyes and stood back a little. He took three quick paces forward and stamped his right foot hard against the little door. It burst open with a splintering crash as the lock yielded, and he stepped inside.

An eerie silence reigned except for the hard drumming of the rain against the windows. The warehouse was in half darkness, and he moved forward, senses alert for any sound. There was a slight click and the vast room was flooded with light. 'Who's there?' a voice called.

Marlowe raised his eyes. Blacky Monaghan was standing on the landing at the top of a long flight of wooden stairs. He had been sleeping, and he rubbed his eyes several times and blinked. After a while he seemed to get Marlowe into focus. 'What the hell do you want?' he shouted.

Marlowe approached the bottom of the stairs. 'I want O'Connor,' he said. 'I want O'Connor, and if you try to stop me getting to him I'll kill you.'

Something like fear flickered in the Irishman's eyes. 'You're wasting your time,' he said. 'He isn't here.'

Marlowe started to mount the stairs slowly, his eyes fastened unwinkingly on Monaghan. The Irishman licked his lips and stood back a little. 'I don't want any trouble with you, Marlowe,' he said. 'I've no quarrel with you.'

Marlowe smiled terribly. 'But I've got a quarrel with you, you bastard,' he said.

Stark terror showed in Monaghan's eyes, and his voice cracked like an old woman's. 'I tell you he isn't here,' he said. 'He's at the girl's place. It's the truth, I tell you.' He backed away along the landing as Marlowe neared the top of the stairs and screamed, 'Go on, get out of it. I've told you what you want to know.'

Marlowe shook his head and laughed tightly. 'I haven't finished with you yet,' he said. 'Not by a long way.'

An expression of utter desperation appeared on Monaghan's drink-sodden face. He looked around wildly. Hanging on the wall there was a fire extinguisher, a shovel, and a felling axe, all brightly painted in red. He grabbed at the axe and wrenched it from its fastenings on the wall. He turned to face Marlowe, gibbering with fear, the axe poised. 'Keep away from me,' he shrieked. 'I didn't kill the old man. It was the boss this time. You were supposed to go out in that truck.'

Marlowe stood rooted to the spot, staring at the Irishmen, and then a terrible surging fury rushed through him and he sprang forward.

Monaghan swung desperately with the axe. If he'd taken his time and judged the distance he could have split Marlowe's skull on the spot, but blind panic took possession of him. Marlowe ducked and the axe whistled over his head and rang against the wall. One terrible, rending hand gripped Monaghan by the throat and the other relentlessly twisted the axe from his grasp.

Monaghan's face turned purple. With a strength born of panic he kicked forward desperately and caught Marlowe on his right shin. Marlowe grunted in pain and his grip slackened. The Irishman staggered back against the wood railing. As Marlowe came forward he struck out at him desperately. Marlowe took the punch on one shoulder, slammed his left into Monaghan's belly and lifted his knee as the Irishman started to bend.

As the terrible blow in the face sent him backwards, Monaghan bounced against the wooden rail. There was a splintering crash as it gave way and he disappeared below with a single cry.

Marlowe moved forward to the edge of the landing and looked down. He gave a sudden roar of rage. Monaghan had fallen no more than ten or twelve feet on to a great mound of potato sacks. As Marlowe watched, the Irishman rolled to the bottom, lurched to his feet and staggered towards the splintered door through which Marlowe had entered the building. He paused once at the door to glance fearfully over his shoulder, and then he disappeared.

Marlowe jumped down on to the pile of potato sacks, lost his balance, and tumbled to the bottom. He picked himself up and ran across the floor to the door. As he emerged from the warehouse, an engine coughed into life and a small yellow van moved across the square and vanished up a side street.

He pulled himself up behind the wheel and turned the truck towards the street that led to Jenny O'Connor's flat. He was praying that Monaghan had not been lying and that he would find O'Connor there.

The quality of the fury which possessed him was such that he was conscious of only one burning thought. He was going to kill O'Connor.

Now he had the definite, final proof from Monaghan's own lips. O'Connor had planned his death, but the plan had misfired and Papa Magellan had died instead. It was fitting that O'Connor should make full and final reparation.

He parked the truck and ran through the rain into the little court. He leaned against the bell, pressing with all his force without stopping, so that the sound of it filled the entire house.

The door opened and Jenny stood before him. He brushed her aside and moved towards the lounge. As he came into the room, O'Connor rose from a seat by the fire, alarm on his face.

Jenny came hurriedly into the room behind him. 'For God's sake, what is it, Hugh?' she demanded. 'What's happened?'

Marlowe kept his eyes fixed on O'Connor. 'Papa Magellon's dead,' he said.

A curious expression appeared on O'Connor's face, and he took out a handkerchief and held it to his lips. Jenny gave a shocked gasp. 'Oh, no, Hugh! Not that poor old man. How did it happen?'

Marlowe nodded towards O'Connor. 'Ask him,' he said. 'He'll tell you. He knows all about it.'

'I don't know what you're talking about,' O'Connor said.

'You bloody swine,' Marlowe said deliberately. 'I've just dealt with Monaghan and he told me what happened. You got him to fix the brakes of one of the trucks. You expected me to go out in it, but unfortunately the old man took the truck out instead.' He laughed savagely. 'Would you be interested to know how he died? I'll tell you. He went through a wall, sixty feet down into a ravine. Then he fried. Have you ever smelt burning human flesh, O'Connor? I have. It's something you never forget.'

O'Connor seemed to be choking into his handkerchief. He took it away from his lips and gasped, 'I didn't have anything to do with it.'

Marlowe started to move towards him. 'I'm going to kill you, O'Connor,' he said. 'I'm going to kill you with my bare hands.'

The fat man dipped his left hand into his pocket. When it came out he was holding an automatic pistol. 'Keep away from me,' he said. He seemed to choke and his face was beginning to turn purple. 'You're going to listen to me, you damned fool.'

As Marlowe paused, O'Connor gurgled horribly and fell backwards into his chair, the pistol slipping from his nerveless hands. Marlowe moved forward and grabbed him by the shirt front. 'You bastard,' he said. 'You needn't think you can trick me this way.'

O'Connor's lips were blue and a line of foam appeared on his mouth. His eyes rolled and he managed to focus them on Marlowe with difficulty. A half-smile appeared on his face and he said faintly, 'You damned fool. You've got to . . .' His eyes swivelled upwards and his head fell limply to one side.

Jenny O'Connor pushed past him as Marlowe stood up, and dropped on her knees beside her uncle. She placed her ear to his chest and listened for several seconds. When she got up there was an expression that was almost triumph on her face. 'He's dead,' she said. 'I knew that heart of his wouldn't last much longer.'

All at once Marlowe felt completely deflated. He stumbled to the cocktail cabinet and splashed brandy into a glass. He poured it down his throat in one clean gulp, and coughed as the liquor burned its way into his stomach.

There was a mirror hanging on the wall and he looked at his reflection and felt apart from it as if it was someone he did not know – had never known. A hand slipped over his shoulder and a warm body was pressed against him. 'This is it, darling,' Jenny said. 'This is what I was talking about. You and me together. We could have everything we wanted.'

He turned, brushing her away as one might a fly, and looked at O'Connor lolling horribly in the chair. 'My God,' he croaked, 'you don't even bother to bury your dead, do you?'

She stared at him, frozen-faced, and he turned and lurched through the door, leaving her there with her dead uncle in her lovely room, surrounded by beautiful things.

It was an appalling drive back to Litton. The rain was falling so heavily that visibility was reduced to ten or fifteen yards and the windscreen-wipers were almost useless.

The cobbles in the farmyard were flooded with rain, and when he jumped down from the truck the water mounted over his shoes, chilling him to the bone. He stood in the hall and peeled off his wet jacket, and then he was conscious of the utter quiet. He stood quite still, his face lifted a little, nostrils moving slightly like some animal that scents danger.

'Mac!' he called. 'Where are you?' His voice echoed hollowly in the uncanny silence.

He mounted the stairs, two at a time, and turned along the landing. 'Mac!' he shouted, and threw open the door of their bedroom. He paused in the doorway, his jacket slipping from his fingers and gazed around him in bewilderment.

The room was a complete shambles. The bedding was scattered in every direction and the mattress had been slashed open exposing the horse-hair stuffing. Every drawer was pulled out and his personal belongings had been emptied on to the floor.

He turned quickly and went downstairs. The kitchen looked as it usually did, except that the fire was out in the old-fashioned grate. He stood in the doorway and his eyes moved slowly over everything.

A shudder ran through him and he moved forward and dropped on one knee beside the table. There was a pool of blood on the floor.

At that moment the telephone rang sharply, its harsh clamour shattering the silence. He ran along the corridor, fear gripping him by the vitals, and lurched into the sitting-room. He snatched up the receiver. 'Hello, Marlowe here. Who is that?'

The line crackled a little and a voice that was vaguely familiar said, 'Hallo, Hugh, old man. So glad you've got back. This is the fifth time I've phoned during the past hour.'

Marlowe swallowed hard and tried to keep his voice steady. 'Who is that?' he said.

A gay laugh drifted along the line. 'Don't you recognize me, old man? Now really, I'm quite hurt. This is Faulkner speaking.'

Marlowe closed his eyes for a moment and his hand tightened convulsively over the phone. 'How the hell did you find me?'

'Never mind that, old man,' Faulkner told him. 'The point is, we've already visited your present residence and found you out. However, we did find a young lady and a coloured gentleman, and suggested they might like to keep us company for an hour or two.'

Marlowe moistened his lips. 'Get to the point, Faulkner. What do you want?'

'Oh, come now, old man. Don't let's be naïve.'

'I found some blood on the kitchen floor,' Marlowe said. 'Who got hurt. It wasn't the girl, was it?'

Faulkner made an expression of distaste. 'No, it was your Jamaican pal. I'm afraid he didn't quite see eye to eye with us. Butcher had to persuade him a little. But don't worry. He's doing nicely.'

'And the girl?' Marlowe said.

'Oh, she's all right,' Faulkner assured him. 'At the moment, anyway. I'm given to understand you have quite an interest there, old man.'

'Who told you that?' Marlowe croaked.

'Never mind for the moment,' Faulkner said. 'For the young lady's sake I sincerely hope it's true. You'll find us at a place called Garvald Mill about four miles out of Litton. It's just off the Birmingham road. If you're not here within an hour with the twenty thousand, I'll turn the girl over to Harris. You know what he's like where young women are concerned.'

'Faulkner, wait a minute. Listen to me,' Marlowe shouted.

He was wasting his time. There was a slight click and the line went dead.

11

For several moments Marlowe stood holding the receiver to his ear and then he slowly replaced it in its cradle. He went out of the front door and ran across the farmyard, splashing through the heavy rain and not caring.

The ladder was still in position against the loft. For a moment he looked up at it and then he started to climb. The Gladstone bag was exactly where he had left it, and he pulled it from under the old cricket net and climbed quickly down to the ground.

He walked back to the house through the rain, the bag swinging in his right hand, and tried to work out his next move. When he went into the sitting-room he emptied the bag on the table and sat down in a chair and lit a cigarette.

The bundles of notes almost covered the table-top, and one or two had fallen down on to the floor. He stared at them, his heart thudding, and after a while an ironic laugh escaped from his lips. It was really very funny when you considered it. All the years, the long, hard years in the place with the high walls. The grey morning filtering in through the tiny window on to his face, the hopeless queues of men slopping out, the bad food, the squalor, the vice, the rottenness. All these things he had endured and one thing had kept him going. The knowledge that some day he would be free and with enough money to keep him comfortably for the rest of his life.

A man could live very well in a country like Ireland with twenty thousand pounds behind him. He sighed and laughed again. Yes, it was really rather ironic that in the end he should sacrifice all that for a young girl he'd known for a few days only.

He stood up and began to put the money back into the bag. He had tried to pretend to himself for a while that he had a choice, but deep inside he had known that there was only one choice for him. The veneer of toughness, the brutality he had raised like a fence around him during the years against life, could not help him now. He was faced with a simple human problem. It could be solved in one way only. By a sacrifice on his part.

He snapped the bag shut and pushed it on one side. He remembered having seen a map of the district in the sideboard, and he went and got it and spread it out on the table. As he pored over it he felt curiously light-hearted. It was a sensation he found impossible to analyse, even to himself.

Garvald Mill was clearly marked on a side road about a quarter of a mile off the main Birmingham road just outside Litton. He found an old stub of blue pencil in the table drawer, and he drew a circle around the mill and considered the situation.

It was situated on the bank of a stream and the area was heavily wooded. He frowned and went to the sideboard and poured himself a brandy. If it had been a simple matter of going and handing over the money it would have been all right, but Butcher and Harris were there as well. Faulkner was all right in his own twisted way. He did have some kind of code. Butcher and Harris were a different thing entirely. They were twisted in another way, and Marlowe had an uncomfortable feeling that this time they wouldn't be prepared to let him off so easily. Not Harris, certainly. The little man was a psychopath, and once he got started there was no knowing what he would do.

Marlowe remembered Faulkner's threat to turn the girl over to Harris, and he shuddered and went back to the map. The mill was near the edge of a wood, and the approach road turned sharply so that it was possible to move quite close without being seen.

He left the room and went into the kitchen. He opened the drawers until he found the one in which Maria kept her kitchen knives. She had a good selection. He finally chose a hollow-ground carver with a nine-inch blade. In another drawer he found a roll of insulating tape and he quickly cut several strips from it. He pulled up his left trouser-leg and carefully fixed the knife to the inside of his left shin with the strips of tape.

As he turned to leave the kitchen he heard the low rumble of thunder in the distance and the rain started to drum against the windows with increasing force. At that moment the doorbell rang sharply.

He stood still and listened. He could hear voices, and through the stained-glass panel at the side of the door a distorted image was visible. He moved forward slowly as the bell rang again, and opened the door. He looked straight into the kindly, spaniel-like face of Alpin, the Barford policeman. Alpin smiled and said, 'Now then, son, I've brought an old friend of yours along to see you. He's very anxious to have a few words with you.'

He stood slightly to one side and Superintendent Masters moved forward. 'Hello, Marlowe,' he said. 'Fancy seeing you here.'

Marlowe stared at him, completely off guard, and Alpin grinned. 'You don't mind if we come in, do you? It's rather wet out here.'

They brushed past him and entered the hall. As he closed the door, Alpin continued, 'We'll go in here, if it's all right with you. I think we ought to have a few words.' He led the way into the sitting-room and Masters followed.

Marlowe stood in the doorway and watched them carefully. Masters started to light his pipe and, as he did so, leaned over the table and examined the map. 'Hello, what's all this? Planning to make a trip?' he said. 'Bag packed and everything.'

He reached over and clicked the Gladstone bag open. There was a moment's silence as Alpin moved over and looked into the bag, and then Masters whistled. 'Funny looking stuff, isn't it?' He snapped the bag shut and shook his head. 'And to think what some men are prepared to do for it.'

'Aye, there's no accounting for taste,' Alpin observed, taking out his inhaler and sniffing deeply.

Marlowe made an exclamation of impatience. 'Let's cut out all the clever stuff and get down to essentials,' he said. 'How did you find me?'

It was Alpin who gave him his answer. 'My God, what do you think we do in the police force? Sit around on our backsides all day? The afternoon of the morning you had your first run-in with Monaghan and his two pals behind O'Connor's place, there was a full description of you going out over the wire.'

Masters smiled and puffed at his pipe. 'You see, Marlowe, even country policemen aren't quite as stupid as you tough boys seem to imagine. Do you really think a policeman doesn't give it any thought when a man like you arrives in a small country town and immediately takes on the three worst toughs in the place, single-handed?' He grinned. 'We've got files at Scotland Yard. There aren't many well-spoken young men of six feet four who favour the spade as a weapon. It took a day or two, but finally it reached me.'

Suddenly, Marlowe was filled with rage. He saw everything now. 'You lousy swine,' he snarled. 'You found out where I was and then sicked Faulkner and his mob on to me.'

Masters looked genuinely astonished. 'I don't know what you're talking about,' he said.

Marlowe was almost insane with rage. He took a quick step forward and swung a tremendous punch at the policeman's jaw. In his anger he miscalculated badly and the blow missed Masters by several inches. He grabbed Marlowe by the arm and twisted him round and Alpin moved in quickly and grabbed his other wrist.'

'Now use your bloody head,' Masters said forcefully. 'You've known me a long time, Marlowe. When did I ever play a trick like that on anyone?'

Marlowe relaxed completely. It was true. Masters was incapable of that sort of a trick. He had a reputation, even amongst the criminal fraternity, for being utterly fair and honest in his methods.

As they released him Marlowe turned and said, 'I'm sorry. I got things a bit twisted.'

'You've had things twisted for quite a while,' Masters told him. He patted the bag. 'It was all for nothing, Marlowe. If you'd had the sense to tell us where the money was at your trial you'd have got five years at the most. Instead, you were stubborn and the judge took that into account. You've served two extra years in prison and for nothing.'

Marlowe made an impatient movement. 'All right, so I was a mug, but there's something more important to discuss at the moment. You can't take that money now. I need it.' They stared at him in complete surprise and he went on, 'Faulkner's been here. That's why I was so mad. I thought you'd told him where I was. He's taken Maria Magellan with him. I had a telephone message a little while ago. He's given me an hour in which to hand over the money or else.' He glanced at the clock. 'I've only got thirty minutes left.'

Masters laughed coldly. 'Now really, Marlowe, you don't expect us to believe a story like that, do you? Let's face the facts. You were just getting ready to pull out of here.'

A feeling like panic moved in Marlowe. 'You've got to believe me. You can search the house. You won't find the girl here.'

Masters turned to Alpin and raised his eyebrows. 'What do you think?' he asked.

Alpin frowned and then moved over to the window. 'I know Maria Magellan and in the ordinary way of things she would be here.' He sighed. 'Unfortunately her father's just been killed in a road accident. She couldn't very well stay here on her own with Marlowe and Mackenzie.'

Masters nodded. 'That sounds reasonable.' He turned to Marlowe and shook his head. 'Sorry, chum, we aren't buying today.'

Marlowe was calm and completely sure of himself now. He took one step forward and this time he made no mistake. His left fist sank into Masters's stomach and the big policeman doubled over, the breath hissing out of his body.

Marlowe was out of the room and closing the door even as Alpin moved. He slammed the front door behind him and ran out into the rain. He scrambled up behind the wheel of the truck and switched on the engine. He was half-way across the yard and moving into second gear as the door opened and Alpin appeared in the porch.

The rain was slanting into the earth in solid sheets like glass and thunder rolled ominously in the distance. He wiped rain away from his eyes and concentrated on the road ahead. It was almost impossible to see through the windscreen and he couldn't afford accidents at this stage.

He glanced quickly at his watch. He still had twenty minutes in which to reach the mill, though what he was going to do when he got there was anybody's guess. The truck roared up the hill past the railway station, and a slight ironic smile twisted his lips as he passed the spot in the hedge through which he had squeezed on the fateful day he had arrived in Litton. He recalled everything that had happened. Perhaps he should never have got off the train? He shook his head. That was no answer. Life was a game and you never knew how the cards were going to fall from one minute to the next.

He braked, his foot hard against the pedal, and swung the truck into the narrow lane that led to Garvald Mill. He frowned and tried to recall the map in detail. The mill, he had calculated, was a quarter of a mile from the road, and it came into view rather unexpectedly round a bend. He slowed down and pulled the truck into the side of the road and halted.

He jumped down into the rain and went forward on foot. About fifty yards farther along the road was the bend, and when he reached it he cut into the woods and forced his way through a fir plantation towards the mill, dimly seen through the trees.

He crouched down under a bush and examined the place carefully. The bulk of the building consisted of a large, three-storeyed tower, roof gaping to the sky. Built on to the building was an extension in wood which looked rather like stables or a storehouse. It seemed to be in a slightly better state of repair than the rest of the building. At the far side there was an immense water-wheel, and it was moving round now with an unearthly creaking and groaning, forced by the rushing waters of the flooded stream.

Marlowe frowned for a moment as he considered his next move, and then he sighed and got to his feet. There was really nothing he could do except take a chance and hope that something would turn up. He stepped out into the open and walked towards the mill.

When he was a few yards away, the door of the wooden part of the building opened and Faulkner appeared. He smiled cheerfully and called, 'Good show, Hugh. I knew I could depend on you. I always did say you had slightly nobler basic instincts than the rest of us.'

He stood back slightly and Marlowe walked past him into the building. The place smelled of old hay and mice. There was a decrepit cart in one corner and a large loft ran round three sides of the building, with round, glassless windows letting in light.

In the centre of the room there was an old five-gallon oil-can with a fire burning in it. As Marlowe moved forward his eyes quickly passed over everything. He could hear the water-wheel splashing violently outside, and against the stone wall of the mill itself there was a pool of water, covered with green scum and surrounded with stones smoothed by the years.

Butcher and Harris were sitting by the fire on wooden boxes, and their eyes fastened on him malignantly, burning with hate. 'Hello, Marlowe,' Butcher said. 'I didn't think you'd come. I was wrong.'

'When were you ever right, you pig?' Marlowe said.

He turned away as Butcher half rose, and Faulkner quickly said, 'Now then, don't let's have any fuss, boys.'

Marlowe laughed harshly. 'They don't bother me,' he said. 'They don't even interest me. I want to see the girl and the Jamaican. Where are they?'

Faulkner smiled and walked over to the corner which was nearest the pool of water. There was a pile of old hay that smelled as if it had been mouldering there for years. He pulled some of it aside and disclosed the forms of Maria and the Jamaican. They were both bound and gagged.

'Take their gags out,' Marlowe ordered.

For a moment Faulkner hesitated, and then he shrugged. As he pulled away the Jamaican's gag, Mac smiled. 'Hello, boy. I knew you wouldn't let us down.'

'Are you okay?' Marlowe asked.

Mac grinned. 'That big dumb ox there cracked me on the head a little, but I'll survive.'

Maria gave a broken sob as her mouth was freed. 'Oh, Hugh, thank God you've come. What's this all about? What do these men want?'

Marlowe smiled reassuringly. 'Don't worry, angel. I'll have you out of here in a few minutes.'

He turned and walked back to the fire and Faulkner followed him. 'Well, are you satisfied?' he asked Marlowe.

Marlowe nodded. 'I'll get you the money now.'

The two men by the fire stood up quickly, and Faulkner frowned. 'You mean you haven't got it on you?'

Marlowe held up a hand. 'There's no need to panic,' he said. 'Did you think I was mug enough to walk in here without seeing what the situation was first?' He shrugged. 'I hid the bag containing the money under a bush a little way into the wood. I'll have to go and get it.'

Faulkner smiled. 'I should have known,' he said. 'You always were a little brighter than anyone else.' He motioned to Butcher. 'You go with him and watch him closely.' He took his hand out of his pocket and held up a Luger automatic pistol. 'No funny business, Marlowe. Remember the girl and your pal will still be in here with Harris and me.'

Marlowe opened the door without a word and walked across the clearing towards the wood. He plunged in without looking back and Butcher followed him. As they pushed their way forward, Butcher cursed and said, 'You would pick a place like this, Marlowe. I'm soaked to the skin already.'

Marlowe pushed a large branch to one side and started to speak. 'I'm not very interested in how you feel, Butcher.' He let the branch sweep backwards into Butcher's face.

He turned quickly, and as Butcher staggered back with a curse he flung himself forward and hit him across his throat with the edge of the hand. Butcher fell to the ground, choking and moaning faintly. Marlowe drew back his foot and kicked him savagely in the side of the head, and then, without stopping, he started back towards the mill, bearing slightly to the left.

He came out on to the bank of the stream about thirty or forty yards above the mill. The flood waters rushed past him, brown and foam-flecked, bearing all before them. For a brief moment he considered the position, and then he lifted his trouser-leg and pulled the knife from its hiding-place. He held it securely in his right hand and grasping the branches of a small bush that drooped into the stream, slid down the bank and lowered himself into the water.

For a moment he hung there, and then, as the current tugged at his body, he released his grip on the bush and was immediately carried away. At that point the stream was only three or four feet deep and as he was carried towards the mill, his feet scrabbled on the bottom as he tried to keep his balance.

And then the water deepened and he was swimming, kicking strongly with every ounce of strength that he possessed. Quite suddenly he was carried over a concrete apron and fell four or five feet into a deep pool. As he struggled to the surface the great, lumbering mill wheel thundered above his head, churning the water into white foam.

The current carried him relentlessly towards it and a terrible panic moved inside him. He thrashed his legs desperately and then a peculiar twist of the current came to his aid and swept him in behind the wheel against the moss-covered stone foundations of the mill.

For several moments he stayed there, hanging on to a ledge of stone with his left hand and coughing up the brown river water. He found, to his surprise, that he still held the knife in his right hand and he renewed his grip on it with white, numbed fingers. The water was icy and now that he was not moving he was conscious of the coldness of it seeping into him, chilling him to the bone.

He placed the knife carefully between his teeth, took a deep breath and sank down under the surface of the stream, his hands scrabbling at the rough stones of the foundations, pulling himself downwards. The great wheel revolved through the water alarmingly near to his body and panic moved again in him as an unexpected current pulled at his legs and one foot touched the wheel as it went round.

He surfaced once for air and then dived again. There had to be an outlet to that pool inside the mill and he dragged himself along the stones, his eyes straining through the brown, cloudy water. And then he found what he was looking for. It was the entrance to a low, arched tunnel some three feet high and half-way down the wall.

He decided to take a chance and pulled himself into it without surfacing for air. To his surprise he discovered that no more than the thickness of the mill wall separated the pool from the stream itself. He kicked forward and carefully surfaced through the green scum.

He kept well in to the side and raised only his eyes and nose above the surface of the water. Harris and Faulkner were standing over by the half-open door, peering outside.

'I don't like it,' Harris was saying. 'I never did trust Marlowe. He was always a tricky bastard.'

'For God's sake shut up,' Faulkner said impatiently. 'They've only been gone a short time.'

Very carefully Marlowe pulled himself over the edge of the pool and crawled towards the corner where Maria and the Jamaican were lying. As he approached, Mac turned his head and his face lit up. At the same moment Maria noticed him and she opened her mouth in an involuntary gasp.

Marlowe burrowed into the hay and froze for several moments, but the two men at the door didn't notice and after a while he moved beside the Jamaican and quickly sliced through his bonds. 'Whatever happens don't make a sound,' he mouthed.

As he crawled to Maria and started to free her, Mac said in a low voice, 'What do we do now?'

Marlowe didn't get a chance to reply. At that moment Harris turned and idly glanced across to the corner. His mouth dropped and for a moment he was speechless. He found his voice and grabbed at Faulkner's arm. 'He's in here,' he screamed. 'The bastard's tricked us.'

Faulkner swung round, the Luger in his right hand, and Marlowe turned and ran crouching for the pool. As the first shot thundered at him he flung himself head first into the pool and dived for the outlet. His hands clawed fiercely at the stones and then he was outside and surfacing.

There wasn't a moment to be lost and he released his grip on the wall and let himself drift out from under the wheel. The current swung in towards the bank, carrying him before it, and he clutched fiercely at a trailing branch from a tree and pulled himself out of the water.

Beside him a stone outbuilding leaned against the great bulk of the mill, and a few feet above it the lower windows gaped like sightless eyes. He jumped for the flat roof of the outbuilding, his fingers gripping the edge securely, and pulled himself up.

The sill of the first window was only three feet above the roof of the outbuilding and its glass was long since shattered. In a moment he was standing inside. He found himself in an empty, decaying room and he crossed quickly to a door and opened it. Outside there was a narrow corridor and another door hung crazily on one hinge in front of him. He could hear voices quite clearly and he tiptoed cautiously across the room towards the round window. He found himself looking down into the loft of the building he had just left so hurriedly.

Faulkner was standing near the fire, the Luger pointed threateningly at Maria and the Jamaican. Harris was cursing at the top of his voice. 'He's tricked us,' he raved. 'He'd no intention of bringing the money.'

'Shut your trap,' Faulkner said. 'And let me think this out.'

Harris turned and his eyes lighted on Maria. He pulled his flick-knife from his pocket and started towards her. 'I'll make the bastard sorry,' he said viciously. 'He won't recognize his girl-friend when I've finished with her.'

Mac jumped up and stood in front of Maria. 'You lay a finger on her and I'll kick your face in if it's the last thing I do on earth.'

Faulkner turned the gun menacingly towards Harris and said, 'Don't be stupid, you little fool. That won't get us anywhere now.'

Marlowe clambered through the round window and lowered himself gently on to the loft. The boards creaked a little and he crouched down and worked his way over to the edge on his hands and knees.

Harris and Faulkner were arguing furiously and then, as Marlowe looked desperately about him for a possible weapon, there was the sound of vehicles drawing up outside.

Faulkner ran quickly to the door and looked out. After a moment he turned, his face pale, and said tightly, 'It's the police. Superintendent Masters of all people.'

Masters's voice was raised outside, 'Marlowe, are you in there?'

Mac shouted at the top of his voice. 'Watch yourselves. There's a guy with a gun in here.'

There was a short silence and then Alpin's voice was heard. 'If you've got any sense you'll throw that gun down and come out.'

Faulkner started to laugh. He took out an elegant case and selected a cigarette and then lit it with a gold lighter. 'It's rather funny, really,' he said.

Harris cursed. 'You're off your rocker. We've got to get out of here.'

Faulkner shook his head gently. 'That's the trouble with your kind, Harris. You never know when it pays to give up. I do.'

Harris stared at him in amazement and said furiously, 'What do you mean, give up? There's no need. We've got the gun and the girl as a hostage. We can walk out of here with no trouble.'

Faulkner shook his head pityingly. 'It doesn't even work when they do it in the films,' he said.

He turned and started to walk towards the door. Harris took a hurried step after him, the blade clicked open in his knife and he plunged it into Faulkner's back.

As Faulkner crumpled to the floor several things happened at once. Maria screamed loud and long and the door began to shake as the police started to break it down.

Harris snatched up the Luger, which had fallen from Faulkner's hand,

and loosed a shot at the door. There was a line of white foam on his lips and he giggled horribly and fired two more shots through the door.

The banging ceased abruptly and Harris drew a hand across his eyes and turned. His eyes fastened on Maria and the Jamaican and a terrible expression appeared on his face. As he started to raise the weapon, Marlowe shouted, 'I'm here, Harris!' And vaulted to the floor.

The shock jarred his whole body and he bent at the knees and rolled over in a somersault. Harris turned and fired wildly. 'I've got you, you bastard,' he shrieked. 'I've got you.'

As he fired again, Marlowe rolled over desperately and reached for the oil drum containing the fire. A bullet scoured a furrow along one shoulder and then his hands fastened on the oil drum and he turned, lifted it aloft and dashed it straight into the madman's face.

Harris gave a ghastly scream and staggered back, the gun falling from his hand. He got to his feet and ran towards the door, his clothes ablaze, beating at the flames with his bare hands. He pulled the locking bar from its socket, wrenched open the door and disappeared outside into the rain, still screaming.

Maria ran forward and threw herself into Marlowe's arms. 'Oh, thank God, Hugh. Thank God,' she cried and broke into passionate sobs.

Marlowe winced as he gently touched her with his hands. Great blisters were beginning to show on his palms and some of the skin was blackened and raw. He handed the weeping girl over to Mac and turned to Faulkner.

Faulkner's breathing sounded bad and as Marlowe dropped on one knee beside him, a trickle of blood oozed from one corner of his mouth. He grinned faintly and said, 'You clever bastard, Marlowe. I always did say you were a little brighter than the rest of us.'

Faulkner closed his eyes, a spasm of pain moving through his body and Marlowe shook him gently. 'Faulkner, who told you I was hiding out in Litton? Was it Masters?'

Faulkner opened his eyes and a ghost of a smile appeared on his lips. 'Good God, no,' he said. 'It was an acquaintance of yours. A white-haired girl called O'Connor. I was having breakfast in a restaurant in Shaftesbury Avenue the other morning when she came up to me as bold as brass and asked me if I knew you.'

Marlowe was conscious of movement beside him and he looked up into Masters's face. He shook his head. 'He's had it,' he said.

As he turned back Faulkner shook his head several times and smiled faintly. 'Poor Hugh. I told you never to trust women, but you always were tender-hearted underneath that surface toughness.' He started to laugh. 'It's damned funny, really.' He choked suddenly and blood rushed from his mouth in a bright stream as his head lolled to one side.

Marlowe got to his feet slowly, his mind seething with conflicting emotions. He felt a hand on his shoulder and turned to gaze into Mac's troubled eyes. 'He was lying, Hugh,' Mac said. 'He must have been. Miss Jenny wouldn't do a thing like that.'

Marlowe shook his head. 'He wasn't lying, Mac. A man doesn't lie when he's dying. Nobody's that sure of where he's going.'

He slipped a hand round Maria's shoulders and helped her towards the door and Masters walked beside them. 'I'm sorry about this, Marlowe,' he said. 'It's a case of cry wolf, I suppose. We just didn't believe you until you took off without the money. Then Alpin looked at the map and found the circle you'd drawn around Garvald Mill. He called in a few reinforcements and we thought we'd take a look.'

'What about Harris?' Marlowe said.

Masters shrugged. 'He's in a bad way. They've taken him away in a car.' He shook his head. 'Those burns looked pretty bad.'

Marlowe shrugged. 'I'm not sorry. He stabbed Faulkner in the back and he was going to finish off Mackenzie and the girl. I had to do something pretty drastic.'

Masters sighed. 'Yes, I suppose you did. You always do seem to end up doing something drastic to somebody, don't you?'

They reached the two police cars that were parked on the edge of the clearing and Alpin came up, a lugubrious expression on his face. 'Well, you've given us a little action for once.' His eyes fastened on Marlowe's wounded shoulder and he clicked his tongue. 'We'd better have something done to that. I want you to survive till you've answered all my questions.'

Maria and the Jamaican got into the back of one of the cars and Marlowe stood against the door, the rain beating into him, while a young constable fastened a pad of cotton wool over the groove in his shoulder with surgical tape from a first-aid box.

As the constable dabbed iodine on Marlowe's hands, pain ran through him in great waves, but he was hardly conscious of it. His mind could only concentrate with a terrible burning force on one thing only. That Jenny O'Connor had played him false. That she had tricked him all along the line. That she was responsible for the death of Papa Magellan and he knew, with a terrible sureness, that he was going to kill her.

12

Marlowe stood in the porch and watched the last of the police cars turn out of the gate into the main road. The sound of its engine dwindled into the distance and he lit a cigarette awkwardly, because of his heavily bandaged hands, and stepped out into the driving rain.

As he walked down to the barn, he heard his name called from the house and Mac came out of the porch and ran towards him, splashing through the many pools. Marlowe kept on walking and was entering the barn as the Jamaican caught up with him. Mac pulled at his arm, 'Hey, man, where are you going?'

Marlowe jerked away from him and went over to the work bench. He pulled open various drawers and searched through them. After a moment or two he grunted with satisfaction and took out a pair of heavy leather driving mitts. 'I can just about get these on.'

Mac frowned. 'What is this, Hugh? You've been acting kind of strange since we got back.'

Marlowe shrugged impatiently. 'I'm all right,' he said. 'Don't worry about me. How's Maria?'

The Jamaican smiled. 'She's in the kitchen making a meal. Man, she's really come out of all this well. Most girls would have been flat on their backs after what she's been through.' He nodded his head. 'There's a lot of good stuff in that girl.'

Marlowe stared into the middle distance and eased the gloves over his bandaged hands. 'Yes, she's a good kid,' he said. 'She'll make some bloke a fine wife.' He shook his head as if he was dazed and continued, 'Listen, Mac, have you any idea where Monaghan lives?'

Mac nodded. 'Sure, he hangs out in a pub called the Grey Goose. It's in Dover Street not far from the main square.' He frowned. 'What do you want to know for?'

Marlowe bared his teeth and clapped him on the shoulder. 'Nothing important,' he said. 'I just want a word with him.'

He turned to the truck and Mac grabbed him by the arm. 'Is he the only one you're going to have a word with? You sure you're not going after Jenny O'Connor?'

Marlowe swung on him savagely. 'You listen to me,' he said, 'and listen good. Papa Magellan didn't fall asleep at the wheel like we thought. His brakes were fixed. As far as I'm concerned that means he was murdered. O'Connor may have been running things, but she was working with him all along, making a sucker out of me. She must have known what O'Connor intended to do. That makes her just as guilty.'

He pulled himself up behind the wheel and slammed the door. As he started the engine, Mac clambered up on the footboard and said desperately, 'If that's true, it's a police job. You should have told those coppers.' He shook his head. 'You can't go taking any private vengeance, man. They'll hang you just as high as they will her.'

Marlowe pushed him in the chest, sending him staggering back against the wall. 'Sorry, Mac,' he said. 'This is my affair and I'll handle it in my own way. Look after Maria.' He gunned the motor and roared out of the barn before the Jamaican could argue any more.

It was growing dark as he entered the outskirts of Barford and the heavy rain made visibility even poorer. He found Dover Street without difficulty and an illuminated glass sign swinging over the pavement in the rain, indicated the Grey Goose.

As he approached he saw a familiar yellow van parked outside and Monaghan in the act of getting in. The van moved quickly away from the kerb and Marlowe increased speed and followed it.

He wondered where Monaghan was going. Perhaps to meet Jenny O'Connor, but somehow he didn't think so. It was more likely the Irishman was deserting the sinking ship while the going was good.

The van turned into another square and halted in front of the railway station. As Monaghan was getting out of the cab Marlowe parked behind him and jumped down from the cab. 'Going somewhere, Monaghan?' he said.

The Irishman was taking a suitcase out of the cab of the van. He turned and looked at Marlowe in alarm and his jaw dropped. 'What do you want?' he said.

'I want a few more facts from you, Monaghan.' Marlowe spoke softly. 'Mainly about Jenny O'Connor.'

The Irishman threw the suitcase at Marlowe's head and turned and ran for the station steps.

Marlowe ducked and went after him. Monaghan disappeared into the entrance and when Marlowe followed him in, he found that the booking hall was quite crowded. He glanced about him hastily. There was no sign of the Irishman.

He walked over to the ticket barrier and saw, from a notice chalked on a blackboard, that the next train was the London Express leaving in five minutes. He quickly bought a platform ticket and passed through the barrier.

The train was standing at a platform on the far side of the track and as he passed over the footbridge, he caught a glimpse of Monaghan getting into a compartment about half-way along the train. He quickly descended the steps leading to the platform and hurried along, peering in through the windows of the compartments. As he reached the end of that particular coach, he saw Monaghan settling in a corner seat.

Their eyes met. A look of rage mingled with fear passed over the Irishman's face. He got up quickly and disappeared into the corridor. Marlowe moved to the nearest door, pushed an indignant passenger out of the way and entered the carriage.

As he turned into the corridor, he saw Monaghan disappear round the corner at the far end. Marlowe went after him, pushing his way along the crowded corridor, using his great size ruthlessly to force a passage. People were calling out angrily, somewhere behind him a woman screamed and then he pushed through the last door in the passenger section of the train and found himself in the guard's van.

As he entered, Monaghan was going out of the loading door on to the platform, pushing his way through the porters who were loading the van. Marlowe tripped over a suitcase as he followed and went sprawling on his face, hands outstretched to break his fall. He half-screamed in agony as pain coursed through his tortured hands and then he was on his feet and following Monaghan, who was running like a hare for the far end of the platform.

Slowly Marlowe overhauled him. The Irishman paused at the end of the platform and glanced back and then he turned and jumped down on to the track. There were several goods trains parked a few hundred yards away across a welter of tracks and he made towards them.

As Marlowe followed he heard the sound of an approaching train. He turned his head and saw a fast passenger train entering the station at the other end. Monaghan saw it also and redoubled his efforts to pass across the track, obviously hoping that the train would cut him off from his pursuer. Marlowe gritted his teeth and increased his speed.

There was a dreadful pain in his side and a red mist before his eyes. Somewhere near at hand he could hear the sound of the train. His stride increased and he flung himself forward and fell head first across the rails. The noise of the train was deafening and then, as he scrambled to his feet, he discovered that it was behind him.

Monaghan had disappeared behind the trucks of a near-by goods train. When Marlowe approached, he saw a steep bank on the far side of the train that lifted to a five-foot wire fence and the road beyond. Monaghan was half-way up the bank.

As Marlowe staggered forward the Irishman gave a despairing cry, his foot slipped and he fell backwards, sliding and slipping until he landed in a heap on the track.

Marlowe lifted him up in his great, glove-covered hands and Monaghan babbled in fear, 'For God's sake, Marlowe. Leave me alone. I'll tell you anything you want, only leave me alone.'

Marlowe slapped him back-handed, rocking his head to one side. 'Tell me about Jenny O'Connor and tell me fast. Did she know you were going to tamper with the brakes on my truck?' He shook the Irishman like a rat. 'Tell me!' he said savagely. 'I've got to know.'

Monaghan coughed and tried to pull the hands away from his throat. 'Of course she knew, you fool,' he gasped. 'She was the boss. She arranged everything.'

For a moment Marlowe's hands relaxed as his mind tried to grasp the full meaning of what the Irishman had said and Monaghan fell back against the bank. 'She was pumping you for information all the time,' he went on. 'It was because of what you told her that we knew you were going to truck stuff down to London.'

Marlowe still couldn't believe it. 'But why?' he demanded. 'What about O'Connor?'

Monaghan shrugged and felt his throat tenderly. 'They were married,' he said. 'She was a chorus girl in a cheap strip show. She was appearing in Birmingham when O'Connor saw her. They were married within a week. She made him promise to keep it a secret. He was crazy about her. He would have crawled on his belly from here to London if she'd told him to. He was always small time before. She was the one with all the ideas. She made him start the wholesaling racket and a few other things as well.'

Marlowe's mind was numb, but in some curious fashion his brain was as cold as ice. 'What happened the night you fixed the brakes on my truck?'

Monaghan shrugged. 'She thought you'd be going to London that night. She wanted to get you out of the way so that I could have a chance to work on the truck.'

Marlowe reached forward and grabbed the Irishman with his left hand. 'That's all I wanted to know, you dirty swine.' His right fist thudded again and again into Monaghan's face.

Somewhere a police whistle sounded, high and shrill through the rain. Marlowe released his grip on the unconscious body of the Irishman and scrambled hastily up the bank to the fence at the top. As he clambered over it he looked back and saw three policemen running across the tracks towards the goods train.

It was almost completely dark now. He ran along the pavement and turned into the first side street and kept on running. The police could have him afterwards if they wanted, but not now. He had work to do. He had to settle with Jenny O'Connor.

He ran on past the yellow street lamps, through the streets deserted in the heavy rain and after several minutes, came out into the main square. For a moment he hesitated and then he made his decision and turned into the side street that led to her flat.

The little courtyard was quiet and deserted and no light shone from the windows. He leaned against the door and pressed the bell push, but no one answered to its insistent demand.

He turned with a curse and went back the way he had come, back into the rainswept square and started to run towards the warehouse. A great fear had taken possession of him, a fear that she might have left. That he was perhaps too late.

The front of the warehouse was in darkness and when he climbed up on to the loading bay he found the small postern still smashed and hanging crazily on its hinges, as he had left it earlier that afternoon.

He moved through it and stood in the soundless dark. A line of light showed beneath a door in the far corner and he moved quietly towards it and stood for a moment listening. There was no sound. He opened the door and stepped through.

He was in the garage at the rear of the building. Before him, great double doors stood open to the night and a concrete ramp sloped steeply to a loading platform in the basement. As he stood there looking about him, there was the sudden roar of an engine and a truck turned in through the doors and rolled to a halt beside him. Jenny O'Connor looked at him in surprise for a moment or two and then she switched off the engine, applied the handbrake and jumped down from the cab.

She was wearing the black leather driving jacket and tight jeans. Her hair gleamed in the harsh white light of the lamp. She looked altogether lovely and desirable. A peculiar smile appeared on her face. 'Well, Hugh, what is it this time?'

'You lousy rotten bitch,' Marlowe said, in a dead voice.

Something flickered in her eyes. 'So you know?' She laughed harshly. 'Poor Hugh, you were so sure of yourself. So sure of your strength in every way. But I made a fool of you, didn't I?'

He shook his head slowly from side to side. 'All that stuff about your father,' he said. 'All lies. And the tales you told me about O'Connor.' He made an exclamation of disgust. 'And to think you were sleeping with that fat slug.' He shook his head again. 'What kind of a woman are you?'

Anger flared in her eyes. 'I was born in a tenement in Poplar,' she said. 'Maybe that doesn't mean anything to you, but it did to me. Five in a bed, filth and squalor and poverty.' She shook her head. 'That wasn't for me. All my life I've struggled to get on and when I met O'Connor, I seized my chance with both hands. Marrying him meant everything. Comfort, luxury and security.'

'And no price was too high to pay,' Marlowe said. 'Even to killing a poor old man who never harmed you.'

She shrugged. 'The old fool got in the way and, anyway, you were supposed to be in that truck.' She laughed in a curious brittle fashion. 'You know I liked you, Hugh Marlowe. I really liked you more than any man I've ever known. I gave you your chance and you wouldn't take it.' Her voice hardened and she said contemptuously. 'The trouble with you is that you're soft underneath. Really soft.' She shook her head. 'You'll never amount to anything.'

Marlowe was having difficulty in contracting his burnt fingers. He wondered in a detached way how he was going to kill her. 'Your little scheme to sick my old pals from London on to me came unstuck,' he said. 'Faulkner's dead and the other two are in the hands of the police.'

A frown appeared on her brow that was quickly erased. 'That's their hard luck,' she said.

Marlowe was beginning to feel a little faint. He passed a hand over his brow. 'Papa Magellan's death was murder. Doesn't that worry you?'

For a moment she was surprised and then an expression of amusement appeared on her face. 'Don't make me laugh,' she said. 'Even if they can prove anything, they can't put a finger on me. My late lamented husband was the boss here as far as anyone knew. He'll take any blame that's going and he's dead.'

She gazed around her at the building and the trucks parked on either side and said with satisfaction, 'Yes, he's dead and all this is mine now.' She smiled at Marlowe pityingly. 'And you could have shared it.' She took a deep breath and said harshly, 'Go on, get out of here, you stupid fool. You're on my property.'

She turned and walked away down the ramp towards the loading bay at the bottom. When she reached it, she took down a vehicle schedule and stood against the loading platform with her back to Marlowe and examined it.

Marlowe looked through the open door into the cab of the truck. In her hurry she had omitted to put the truck into reverse gear and it was held on the steep slope only by the handbrake.

Marlowe looked at the heavy truck, at the steep slope and Jenny O'Connor standing against the platform at the bottom and knew what he must do.

He moved forward and stretched out his hand to the handbrake. There was a gentle cough from behind and a voice said, 'Now that would be a very silly thing to do, son.'

Alpin moved out of the darkness and came forward, shaking rain from his hat, a uniformed sergeant and constable at his shoulder. 'It's you,' Marlowe said stupidly.

Alpin put a hand on his arm and said gently. 'The police handle this sort of thing much better, you know. It's about time you found that out, isn't it?'

Marlowe shook his head. 'But you haven't any proof?'

Alpin smiled and replaced his hat on his head. 'Monaghan's at the station now,' he said. 'He was unconscious when they brought him in, but he recovered enough to give me a few very interesting facts.' He gave Marlowe a gentle shove. 'Go on, get out of here. You're pal's waiting for you outside.'

He turned and went down the ramp towards Jenny O'Connor, the men in uniform walking with him. She turned to face them and as Marlowe watched, Alpin began to speak to her. For a moment she faced him boldly and then her shoulders dropped and she became an old woman.

As Marlowe turned and walked away he remembered the long years, the grey years in the tiny cells, with a little sunlight filtering in through small windows and he wondered how she would look after ten years of that. Would her loveliness last or would it wither away and wrinkle like an apple stored in a dark cupboard for too long?

A truck was standing at the kerbside, its engine gently ticking over and Mac called quietly, 'Over here, Hugh.'

Marlowe climbed up into the passenger seat and the Jamaican drove away. After a while he said, 'I had to tell the police, Hugh. I couldn't stand by and see you ruin yourself. She just isn't worth it.'

Marlowe nodded. 'That's all right, Mac,' he said and then, as an afterthought. 'The other truck's still parked outside the station.'

Mac shrugged. 'We'll pick it up tomorrow.'

Tomorrow, Marlowe thought. So there's going to be a tomorrow, is there? He suddenly realized that he was soaked to the skin and a tremendous wave of tiredness ran through him. 'How's Maria?'

Mac grinned. 'Plenty worried about you, man, but that's all.'

The rain had stopped and Marlowe let down the side window and breathed the cold night air deeply into his lungs. In some inexplicable way he was beginning to feel good about things. He turned to the Jamaican and said, 'What are you going to do now, Mac?'

Mac shrugged. 'That depends.'

'Depends on what?' Marlowe demanded.

'On how good an offer I get,' Mac retorted.

Marlowe smiled and shook his head. 'Don't run away with ideas like that,' he said. 'It's Maria's business now. She may have other notions.'

Mac shook his head and said definitely, 'That girl's got only one idea where you're concerned.'

Marlowe put a hand into his inside pocket and took out a sodden envelope that dripped water. He looked at it seriously and said, 'There's nearly two thousand quid in there, Mac. The way I look at it, Maria's entitled to a little compensation. A clever man could develop the business over the years and use this money without her ever realizing it.'

Mac grinned. 'Especially if he had the right kind of assistance.'

Marlowe clapped him on the shoulder. The truck swung into the farmyard, and as it moved forward the front door opened, flooding the porch with light.

She stood looking out from the step, her face in darkness. Marlowe wearily clambered down from the cab and turned towards her. He still couldn't see her face and as he took a hesitant step forward, she cried his name brokenly and ran towards him.

As he pulled her close in the prison of his arms, Marlowe was finally at peace. For the first time in his life he felt completely sure of himself and knew where he was going.

She turned and pulled him gently out of the darkness into the warm light of the house.